LATER SHORT STORIES
1888-1903

ANTON CHEKHOV

LATER SHORT STORIES

1888-1903

EDITED BY SHELBY FOOTE

TRANSLATED BY CONSTANCE GARNETT

THE MODERN LIBRARY

NEW YORK

1999 Modern Library Edition

LIBRARY OF CONGRESS CATALOGING-IN-PUBLICATION DATA
Chekhov, Anton Pavlovich, 1860–1904.
[Short stories. English. Selections]
Anton Chekhov: later short stories, 1888–1903/edited by Shelby Foote.
p. cm.
ISBN 0-679-60316-6
1. Chekhov, Anton Pavlovich, 1860–1904—Translations into English.
I. Foote, Shelby. II. Title.
PG3456.A15F66 1998
891.73'3—dc21 98-20048

Modern Library website address: www.modernlibrary.com

Printed in the United States of America on acid-free paper

4 6 8 9 7 5 3

ANTON CHEKHOV

Anton Pavlovich Chekhov was born on January 17, 1860, in Taganrog, a small provincial port in southern Russia located on the Sea of Azov. His grandfather had been a serf who for 3,500 rubles had purchased the family's freedom. Chekhov's domineering father was a lower-middle-class bigot: a petty merchant who kept a grocery store, bullied his wife, and beat his six children. Although Anton Pavlovich's early life was monotonous and oppressive ("In my childhood there was no childhood," the writer recalled), he found his own strange way of compensating for the dismal atmosphere. Possessing a natural gift for clowning and mimicry, the boy delighted schoolmates with hilarious imitations of virtually everyone in the village. (Much as in his later stories, things for him were funny and sad at the same time, but you would not see their sadness if you did not see their fun, because both were linked up.)

Chekhov was sixteen when the family business failed and his father escaped debtors' prison by fleeing to Moscow. The young man's mother and siblings soon followed, but Anton Pavlovich remained behind to complete his education at the Taganrog Secondary School; three years later, in 1879, he joined them in Moscow and entered the medical faculty of Moscow University. During his university years

Chekhov became the family's chief breadwinner: He supported them by writing stories, sketches, and parodies for humor magazines. All his early works were signed with pseudonyms, most frequently "Antosha Chekhonte." He completed medical school in 1884 and practiced medicine intermittently for several years while continuing to write. "Medicine is my lawful wife," Chekhov wrote to a friend, "and literature is my mistress. When I get fed up with one, I spend the night with the other. Though it is irregular, it is less boring this way, and besides, neither of them loses anything through my infidelity."

All the while, Chekhov's fiction continued to grow in depth and range. He published his first volume of stories, *Motley Stories,* in 1886; a year later he brought out his second collection, *In the Twilight,* for which he was awarded the Pushkin Prize for distinguished literary achievement by the Russian Academy. Fellow countryman Vladimir Nabokov perfectly explained Chekhov's appeal: "What really attracted the Russian reader was that in Chekhov's heroes he recognized the Russian idealist . . . a man who combined the deepest human decency of which man is capable with an almost ridiculous inability to put his ideals and principles into action; a man devoted to moral beauty, the welfare of his people, the welfare of the universe, but unable in his private life to do anything useful; frittering away his provincial existence in a haze of utopian dreams; knowing exactly what is good, what is worth while living for, but at the same time sinking lower and lower in the mud of a humdrum existence, unhappy in love, hopelessly inefficient in everything—a good man who cannot make good. This is the character that passes—in the guise of a doctor, a student, a village teacher, many other professional people—all through Chekhov's stories."

Despite the success of his literary career, Chekhov felt guilty about neglecting medicine. Moreover, he still owed a dissertation to obtain a full M.D. Partly to discharge this debt, partly for the sake of adventure, Chekhov in 1890 undertook an exhausting—and at times dangerous—six-thousand-mile journey (prerailroad) across Siberia to Sakhalin Island. There he made a thorough study of social, economic, and medical conditions, both of the Russian settlers (mostly convicts) and of native populations. Upon his return (by sea, via the Suez Canal) from this "descent into hell," circumstances quickly forced him back into medicine and public health service—first the terrible famine of 1891 and then the cholera epidemic that followed. In 1892 Chekhov bought a six-hundred-acre country estate near the village of Melihovo, where for the next five years he served as doctor to the local peasants and even helped build schools, while his literary output continued unabated.

The turn of the century witnessed a dramatic new phase in Chekhov's career. Between 1896 and 1903 he wrote the plays that established his reputation as one of the great dramatists of modern times: *The Sea Gull* (1896), *Uncle Vanya* (1897), *Three Sisters* (1901), and *The Cherry Orchard* (1904). However, in 1897 a massive pulmonary hemorrhage forced him finally to acknowledge that he was stricken with tuberculosis, an illness he had long concealed. For the remainder of his life, Chekhov was virtually a semi-invalid; he lived mostly in a villa at Yalta, his "warm Siberia" where he met Tolstoy and Gorky. In 1901 Chekhov married Olga Knipper, an actress with the Moscow Art Theater who had played the role of Irina in *The Sea Gull.*

Chekhov's last public appearance took place at the Moscow premiere of *The Cherry Orchard* on January 17, 1904, the playwright's forty-fourth birthday. Shaken with coughing, he was hardly able to stand and acknowledge a thunderous ovation. In June Chekhov was rushed to a health resort at Badenweiler in the Black Forest, where he died of consumption on July 2. His body was transported back to Moscow in a refrigerating car used for the transportation of oysters—a quirk of fate that no doubt he would have been amused to jot down in his notebook.

Contents

Introduction by Shelby Foote

Anton Chekhov had a writing life of just under twenty-five years—from 1880, when he turned twenty as a medical student in Moscow, to 1904, when he died of tuberculosis in a Black Forest sanitorium. Within this span, in addition to four plays admired worldwide as modern classics, he wrote perhaps five hundred "stories," long and short—ranging from newspaper squibs and fillers to near-*Gatsby*-length novellas—which set the pattern for the short story in the century whose beginning was all he saw before his forty-four years were up.

On its eve, in 1899, under pressure from his publisher and the unrelenting need for money to sustain his generosity, he began selecting from his so-far six books of stories—together with a clutch of fugitive pieces that had appeared in various periodicals all the way back to his youth—a *Collected Works* whose ten volumes were released in the course of the next two years. They contained 240 stories in all, and another 196 were added in ten supplementary volumes after his death. Of these 436 stories, Constance Garnett* translated 188, and I have

* I agree with V. S. Pritchett, who called her work "remarkable." Although he noted that "inaccuracies have been pounced on," he preferred her translations mainly, as he said, because "her voice is close to Chekhov's period." Moreover, it was she who passed his work on to Virginia Woolf, E. M. Forster, D. H. Lawrence, and H. E. Bates, as well as to practically every American short-story writer who, at one time or another, sat at his and her feet during the past eight decades.

chosen 123 for inclusion in these three Modern Library volumes: volume I, seventy "early" stories, from 1883 to 1888, his breakthrough year when he received the Pushkin Prize; volume II, forty-two "later" stories, 1888 to 1902, containing most of his best-known work; and finally volume III, eleven "Longer Stories of the Last Decade," which I believe calls attention to a broader and deeper talent than has generally been recognized, either by critics or the reading public, down the years. Aside from his one full-length novel, an early experimental detective story of limited literary worth, nearly all the omitted stories are quite brief ones out of his journalistic youth. By way of summation, then, these three volumes include barely one fourth of his fiction titles, but they do contain, by page count, about three fourths of his output in that category—including all fifty-five of the great stories of his final fifteen years. All are printed here in the order in which they were written.

Few major writers have had fewer detractors regarding either their person or their work. A rare detractive exception is Ernest Hemingway, who enjoyed turning bumptious in his spare time; and in one such, in his middle twenties, referred to Chekhov as "an amateur writer" who "wrote about six good stories." Six is rather a large figure in the category of goodness, but I would put the number closer to one hundred, and so would many grateful practitioners of the art of the short story. Raymond Carver, for example: "Chekhov's stories are as wonderful (and necessary) now as when they first appeared. They present, in an extraordinarily precise manner, an unparalleled account of human activity and behavior in his time; and so they are valid for all time. Anyone who reads literature, anyone who believes, as one must, in the transcendent power of art, sooner or later has to read Chekhov." Or Elizabeth Hardwick: "The short stories of Chekhov are an inexhaustible treasury of humanity and wisdom. The naturalness of their form and the luminous simplicity of their turning away from the forced conclusion defined a large part of the modern tradition in short fiction." Or Cynthia Ozick: "Each story, no matter how allusive or broken-off, is nevertheless exhaustive—like the curve of a shard that implies not simply the form of the pitcher entire, but also the thirsts of its shattered civilization." Or John Barth: "Dr. Chekhov is a superb anatomist of the human heart and an utter master of his literary means. The details of scene and behavior, the emotions registered—seldom bravura, typically muted and complex, often as surprising to the characters themselves as to the reader, but always right—move, astonish, and delight us, line after line, story after story, volume after volume." Or William Maxwell: "It seems to be part of the human condition that a wall of glass separates one life from another. For Chekhov it did not exist. . . . The greatest of his stories are, no matter how many times reread, always an experience that strikes deep into the soul and produces an alteration there."

Little or none of this was the case at the start. "Oh, with what trash I began; my God, with what trash!" Chekhov declared later, looking back with amused dismay. Parodies, jokes, boutades, all limited to a thousand words by close-fisted editors, earned him the roubles needed to pay for his education and that of his two younger brothers and his sister, along with the support of two older brothers and his mother and bankrupt father. After half a dozen years of this, having received his license to practice medicine, he confessed to an established older novelist, who urged him to take his work seriously, that he had never spent more than a day on a story, and moreover had written them "the way reporters write notices of fires: mechanically, half-consciously, without caring a pin either about the reader or myself." Coincidentally, around this time, he combined a baleful definition with a hopeful prophecy: "The word newspaper-writer means, at the very least, a scoundrel. I am one of them; I work with them; I shake hands with them; I'm even told that I've begun to look like one. But I shan't die as one."

He didn't, of course, though in the process of transition that followed close on the heels of his confession, he underrated what he had gained from those half-dozen years of comic-writer apprenticeship. For one thing, the elderly novelist had noted his "feeling for the plastic," and, for another, the stipulated compression had encouraged him to develop what William Trevor later called "the art of the glimpse," a start-to-finish major component of his style. Moreover, there were, among those various humoristic bits and pieces, such things as "A Daughter of Albion," "The Fish," and "The Huntsman," which had drawn the elderly novelist's attention and admiration. And now there followed, with the help of Maupassant's Norman and Parisian tales and Turgenev's *Sportsman's Sketches,* such things as "Anyuta," "Agafya," "The Chorus Girl," and "Vanka." Those came out in 1886. By then he had moved on to the so-called "thick journals," which paid better and, above all, gave him room to stretch his talent. The following year he produced a solid fifty stories, and "The Steppe"—at forty thousand words, the longest of his stories, called by Pritchett "a superb and sustained prose poem"—appeared in early 1888, followed by "Lights," which also broke new ground. By way of an upshot, he won the Pushkin Prize that year, along with the admiration of his fellow Russian writers, who two years before had mostly seen him, as he himself did, as a bits-and-pieces hack. He was clearly on his way.

That "way" has been marveled and wondered at by critics ever since, perhaps most successfully by his compatriot Vladimir Nabokov, who contrived to lift him to the skies by bringing him down to earth: "Chekhov managed to convey an impression of artistic beauty far surpassing that of writers who thought they knew what rich, beautiful prose was. He did it by keeping all his words in the same dim light of the same exact tint of gray, a tint between the color of an old fence and that of a low cloud. The variety of his moods, the flicker of his charming wit, the deeply artistic economy of characterization, the vivid detail, and the fade-out of human life—all peculiar Chekhovian features—are enhanced by being suffused and surrounded by a faintly iridescent verbal haziness." In simpler words Nabokov also defined a specific many Chekhov readers felt the force of down the years: "Things for him were funny and sad at the same time, but you would not see their sadness if you did not see their fun, because both were linked up." Chekhov himself pointed out something along this line, carried over from his early days, in advice to a fellow writer: "When you want to touch a reader's heart, try to be colder. It gives their grief, as it were, a background against which it stands out in greater relief." In much the same vein, he declared at another time: "Patients in a fever do not want food, but they do want something, and that vague craving they express as 'longing for something sour.' I want something sour."

For the most part, though, he kept his opinions and judgments to himself—especially in his fiction, where, as he said, he aimed not at solutions to problems but rather at their correct presentation. Walker Percy, a fellow physician-writer, called him a diagnostician, and in his choice of subjects for delineation he was guided by what Susan Sontag defined as "perfect moral pitch." As a result, there were those who, in the absence of didactic comments and summations in his work, accused him of having no philosophy of life. His friend Maxim Gorky found the charge absurd and such readers deaf and blind. "Often our ears can catch in his stories the melancholy but severe and deserved reproach that men do not know how to live. But at the same time, his sympathy with all men glows even brighter." Chekhov himself met the charge head-on, along with others by critics who fine-tooth-combed his work in search of "convictions," whether political or religious: "I am afraid of those who look for a tendency between the lines and insist on seeing me as necessarily a liberal or a conservative. I am not a liberal, not a conservative, not a gradualist, not a monk, not an indifferentist. I should like to be a free artist and nothing more, and I regret that God has not given me the power to be one. . . . I regard trademarks and labels as prejudicial. My holy of holies is the human body, health, intelligence, talent, inspiration, love, and absolute freedom—freedom from force and falsehood."

His overriding subject was the Russia of his time and the failure of men of goodwill to find contentment, or even peace, from having exercised that goodwill all their lives. "We Russians of the educated class have a partiality for questions that remain unanswered," he observed. He later added: "To an educated Russian his past is always beautiful, his present a state of calamity." He seemed always to have to ponder things, turning them over and over in his mind, as if in search not of an answer but of a new phrasing of the question. Once while abroad he was asked to write "an international story" set in the region, and he replied that he couldn't do it until he got back home, if at all. "I can write only from memory," he explained; "I never write directly from life. The subject must pass through the sieve of my memory, so that only what is important or typical remains, as on a filter."

He had a habit of expressing himself obliquely, as when he said of his portrait by an artist whose work he did not admire, "It smells of horseradish." And though he could be insightful—forty-odd years before the Holocaust, in the wake of the Dreyfus affair, he wrote to a friend a definition of anti-Semitism as "a fuel that reeks of the slaughterhouse"—he still could not abide the strained delivery of a "message" in a story or a novel. After reading *Uncle Tom's Cabin,* for example, he experienced "an unpleasant sensation which mortals feel after eating too many raisins or currants." He liked to be precise in a general way, as when he described "the genial expression of a man who has just said goodbye to his relatives and has had a good drink at parting." It is important in this depiction that the people are relatives and that the drink was a good one.

Similarly in a late story, "In the Ravine," a young woman loses her infant son to a sudden and painful death by scalding, and is comforted at the funeral dinner by a priest who, "lifting his fork on which there was a salted mushroom, said to her: 'Grieve not for the babe, for of such is the Kingdom of Heaven.' " The forked mushroom is very Chekhovian, and even more so are the words spoken earlier, in a quite different tone, by an old man who gave her a lift in his wagon while she was returning from the hospital, walking along the road at night with her dead baby wrapped in a quilt in her arms. "Never mind," he told her. "Yours is not the worst of sorrows. Life is long, there will be good and bad to come, there will be everything. Great is Mother Russia." Chekhov dealt in powerful iotas, such as a sidelong glance in his last story, "Betrothed," in which a young man "took off his hat, and his hair floated in the wind."

Consequential or inconsequential, such wonderments abound in the nearly two thousand pages of these three volumes. Moreover, like most good writers, his work is even better on rereading, since then you can better appreciate how he goes about getting where he's going. Often, after a stretch of such rereading, I wax enthusiastic beyond all bounds. (Like Hemingway, I sometimes play the fool, but in the opposite direction.) Walker Percy and I shared this reaction, and once, in the course of a discussion, I asked him if he had read "In the Ravine." He said he hadn't, and I said: "I'd rather have written 'In the Ravine' than *Moby Dick.*" His eyebrows rose at this, as well they might, but he went home and read that great last long story—in which all the author's talents seem to be gathered together as naturally as a hand closing into a fist—and wound up in a state of exaltation similar to my own. Echoing Nabokov on Chekhov's near-miraculous combination of the funny and the sad, he shook his head in wonder. "I don't know how it can be so pitiful and funny," he wrote me later. "I have to laugh out loud."

We saw clearly enough what this Russian master had done, but *how* he did it we could never really figure out—until finally we happened on the answer provided by Buffon in his mid-eighteenth-century *Discourse on Style*, which pronounces that "style is the man himself." We settled for that: Chekhov did it by being Chekhov. That was as close as we could come to a solution.

LATER SHORT STORIES
1888-1903

Sleepy

Night. Varka, the little nurse, a girl of thirteen, is rocking the cradle in which the baby is lying, and humming hardly audibly:

"Hush-a-bye, my baby wee,
While I sing a song for thee."

A little green lamp is burning before the ikon; there is a string stretched from one end of the room to the other, on which baby-clothes and a pair of big black trousers are hanging. There is a big patch of green on the ceiling from the ikon lamp, and the baby-clothes and the trousers throw long shadows on the stove, on the cradle, and on Varka.... When the lamp begins to flicker, the green patch and the shadows come to life, and are set in motion, as though by the wind. It is stuffy. There is a smell of cabbage soup, and of the inside of a boot-shop.

The baby is crying. For a long while he has been hoarse and exhausted with crying; but he still goes on screaming, and there is no knowing when he will stop. And Varka is sleepy. Her eyes are glued together, her head droops, her neck aches. She cannot move her eyelids or her lips, and she feels as though her face is dried and wooden, as though her head has become as small as the head of a pin.

"Hush-a-bye, my baby wee," she hums, "while I cook the groats for thee. . . ."

A cricket is churring in the stove. Through the door in the next room the master and the apprentice Afanasy are snoring. . . . The cradle creaks plaintively, Varka murmurs—and it all blends into that soothing music of the night to which it is so sweet to listen, when one is lying in bed. Now that music is merely irritating and oppressive, because it goads her to sleep, and she must not sleep; if Varka—God forbid!—should fall asleep, her master and mistress would beat her.

The lamp flickers. The patch of green and the shadows are set in motion, forcing themselves on Varka's fixed, half-open eyes, and in her half slumbering brain are fashioned into misty visions. She sees dark clouds chasing one another over the sky, and screaming like the baby. But then the wind blows, the clouds are gone, and Varka sees a broad high road covered with liquid mud; along the high road stretch files of wagons, while people with wallets on their backs are trudging along and shadows flit backwards and forwards; on both sides she can see forests through the cold harsh mist. All at once the people with their wallets and their shadows fall on the ground in the liquid mud. "What is that for?" Varka asks. "To sleep, to sleep!" they answer her. And they fall sound asleep, and sleep sweetly, while crows and magpies sit on the telegraph wires, scream like the baby, and try to wake them.

"Hush-a-bye, my baby wee, and I will sing a song to thee," murmurs Varka, and now she sees herself in a dark stuffy hut.

Her dead father, Yefim Stepanov, is tossing from side to side on the floor. She does not see him, but she hears him moaning and rolling on the floor from pain. "His guts have burst," as he says; the pain is so violent that he cannot utter a single word, and can only draw in his breath and clack his teeth like the rattling of a drum:

"Boo—boo—boo—boo. . . ."

Her mother, Pelageya, has run to the master's house to say that Yefim is dying. She has been gone a long time, and ought to be back. Varka lies awake on the stove, and hears her father's "boo—boo—boo." And then she hears someone has driven up to the hut. It is a young doctor from the town, who has been sent from the big house where he is staying on a visit. The doctor comes into the hut; he cannot be seen in the darkness, but he can be heard coughing and rattling the door.

"Light a candle," he says.

"Boo—boo—boo," answers Yefim.

Pelageya rushes to the stove and begins looking for the broken pot with the matches. A minute passes in silence. The doctor, feeling in his pocket, lights a match.

"In a minute, sir, in a minute," says Pelageya. She rushes out of the hut, and soon afterwards comes back with a bit of candle.

Yefim's cheeks are rosy and his eyes are shining, and there is a peculiar keenness in his glance, as though he were seeing right through the hut and the doctor.

"Come, what is it? What are you thinking about?" says the doctor, bending down to him. "Aha! have you had this long?"

"What? Dying, your honour, my hour has come.... I am not to stay among the living...."

"Don't talk nonsense! We will cure you!"

"That's as you please, your honour, we humbly thank you, only we understand.... Since death has come, there it is."

The doctor spends a quarter of an hour over Yefim, then he gets up and says:

"I can do nothing. You must go into the hospital, there they will operate on you. Go at once.... You must go! It's rather late, they will all be asleep in the hospital, but that doesn't matter, I will give you a note. Do you hear?"

"Kind sir, but what can he go in?" says Pelageya. "We have no horse."

"Never mind. I'll ask your master, he'll let you have a horse."

The doctor goes away, the candle goes out, and again there is the sound of "boo—boo—boo." Half an hour later someone drives up to the hut. A cart has been sent to take Yefim to the hospital. He gets ready and goes....

But now it is a clear bright morning. Pelageya is not at home; she has gone to the hospital to find what is being done to Yefim. Somewhere there is a baby crying, and Varka hears someone singing with her own voice:

"Hush-a-bye, my baby wee, I will sing a song to thee."

Pelageya comes back; she crosses herself and whispers:

"They put him to rights in the night, but towards morning he gave up his soul to God. . . . The Kingdom of Heaven be his and peace everlasting. . . . They say he was taken too late. . . . He ought to have gone sooner. . . ."

Varka goes out into the road and cries there, but all at once someone hits her on the back of her head so hard that her forehead knocks against a birch tree. She raises her eyes, and sees facing her, her master, the shoemaker.

"What are you about, you scabby slut?" he says. "The child is crying, and you are asleep!"

He gives her a sharp slap behind the ear, and she shakes her head, rocks the cradle, and murmurs her song. The green patch and the shadows from the trousers and the baby-clothes move up and down, nod to her, and soon take possession of her brain again. Again she sees the high road covered with liquid mud. The people with wallets on their backs and the shadows have lain down and are fast asleep. Looking at them, Varka has a passionate longing for sleep; she would lie down with enjoyment, but her mother Pelageya is walking beside her, hurrying her on. They are hastening together to the town to find situations.

"Give alms, for Christ's sake!" her mother begs of the people they meet. "Show us the Divine Mercy, kind-hearted gentlefolk!"

"Give the baby here!" a familiar voice answers. "Give the baby here!" the same voice repeats, this time harshly and angrily. "Are you asleep, you wretched girl?"

Varka jumps up, and looking round grasps what is the matter: there is no high road, no Pelageya, no people meeting them, there is only her mistress, who has come to feed the baby, and is standing in the middle of the room. While the stout, broad-shouldered woman nurses the child and soothes it, Varka stands looking at her and waiting till she has done. And outside the windows the air is already turning blue, the shadows and the green patch on the ceiling are visibly growing pale, it will soon be morning.

"Take him," says her mistress, buttoning up her chemise over her bosom; "he is crying. He must be bewitched."

Varka takes the baby, puts him in the cradle, and begins rocking it again. The green patch and the shadows gradually disappear, and now there is nothing to force itself on her eyes and cloud her brain. But she is as sleepy as before, fearfully sleepy! Varka lays her head on the edge of the cradle, and rocks her whole body to overcome her sleepiness, but yet her eyes are glued together, and her head is heavy.

"Varka, heat the stove!" she hears the master's voice through the door.

So it is time to get up and set to work. Varka leaves the cradle, and runs to the shed for firewood. She is glad. When one moves and runs about, one is not so sleepy as when one is sitting down. She brings the wood, heats the stove, and feels that her wooden face is getting supple again, and that her thoughts are growing clearer.

"Varka, set the samovar!" shouts her mistress.

Varka splits a piece of wood, but has scarcely time to light the splinters and put them in the samovar, when she hears a fresh order:

"Varka, clean the master's goloshes!"

She sits down on the floor, cleans the goloshes, and thinks how nice it would be to put her head into a big deep golosh, and have a little nap in it. . . . And all at once the golosh grows, swells, fills up the whole room. Varka drops the brush, but at once shakes her head, opens her eyes wide, and tries to look at things so that they may not grow big and move before her eyes.

"Varka, wash the steps outside; I am ashamed for the customers to see them!"

Varka washes the steps, sweeps and dusts the rooms, then heats another stove and runs to the shop. There is a great deal of work: she hasn't one minute free.

But nothing is so hard as standing in the same place at the kitchen table peeling potatoes. Her head droops over the table, the potatoes dance before her eyes, the knife tumbles out of her hand while her fat, angry mistress is moving about near her with her sleeves tucked up, talking so loud that it makes a ringing in Varka's ears. It is agonising, too, to wait at dinner, to wash, to sew, there are minutes when she longs to flop on to the floor regardless of everything, and to sleep.

The day passes. Seeing the windows getting dark, Varka presses her temples that feel as though they were made of wood, and smiles, though she does not know why. The dusk of evening caresses her eyes that will hardly keep open, and promises her sound sleep soon. In the evening visitors come.

"Varka, set the samovar!" shouts her mistress.

The samovar is a little one, and before the visitors have drunk all the tea they want, she has to heat it five times. After tea Varka stands for a whole hour on the same spot, looking at the visitors, and waiting for orders.

"Varka, run and buy three bottles of beer!"

She starts off, and tries to run as quickly as she can, to drive away sleep.

"Varka, fetch some vodka! Varka, where's the corkscrew? Varka, clean a herring!"

But now, at last, the visitors have gone; the lights are put out, the master and mistress go to bed.

"Varka, rock the baby!" she hears the last order.

The cricket churrs in the stove; the green patch on the ceiling and the shadows from the trousers and the baby-clothes force themselves on Varka's half-opened eyes again, wink at her and cloud her mind.

"Hush-a-bye, my baby wee," she murmurs, "and I will sing a song to thee."

And the baby screams, and is worn out with screaming. Again Varka sees the muddy high road, the people with wallets, her mother Pelageya, her father Yefim. She understands everything, she recognises everyone, but through her half sleep she cannot understand the force which binds her, hand and foot, weighs upon her, and prevents her from living. She looks round, searches for that force that she may escape from it, but she cannot find it. At last, tired to death, she does her very utmost, strains her eyes, looks up at the flickering green patch, and listening to the screaming, finds the foe who will not let her live.

That foe is the baby.

She laughs. It seems strange to her that she has failed to grasp such a simple thing before. The green patch, the shadows, and the cricket seem to laugh and wonder too.

The hallucination takes possession of Varka. She gets up from her stool, and with a broad smile on her face and wide unblinking eyes, she walks up and down the room. She feels pleased and tickled at the thought that she will be rid directly of the baby that binds her hand and foot. . . . Kill the baby and then sleep, sleep, sleep. . . .

Laughing and winking and shaking her fingers at the green patch, Varka steals up to the cradle and bends over the baby. When she has strangled him, she quickly lies down on the floor, laughs with delight that she can sleep, and in a minute is sleeping as sound as the dead.

The Beauties

I

I remember, when I was a high-school boy in the fifth or sixth class, I was driving with my grandfather from the village of Bolshoe Kryepkoe in the Don region to Rostov-on-the-Don. It was a sultry, languidly dreary day of August. Our eyes were glued together, and our mouths were parched from the heat and the dry burning wind which drove clouds of dust to meet us; one did not want to look or speak or think, and when our drowsy driver, a Little Russian called Karpo, swung his whip at the horses and lashed me on my cap, I did not protest or utter a sound, but only, rousing myself from half-slumber, gazed mildly and dejectedly into the distance to see whether there was a village visible through the dust. We stopped to feed the horses in a big Armenian village at a rich Armenian's whom my grandfather knew. Never in my life have I seen a greater caricature than that Armenian. Imagine a little shaven head with thick overhanging eyebrows, a beak of a nose, long gray mustaches, and a wide mouth with a long cherry-wood chibouk sticking out of it. This little head was clumsily attached to a lean hunch-back carcass attired in a fantastic garb, a short red jacket, and full bright blue trousers. This figure walked straddling its legs and shuffling with its slippers, spoke without taking the chibouk out of its mouth, and behaved with truly Armenian dignity, not smiling, but staring with wide-open eyes and trying to take as little notice as possible of its guests.

There was neither wind nor dust in the Armenian's rooms, but it was just as unpleasant, stifling, and dreary as in the steppe and on the road. I remember, dusty and exhausted by the heat, I sat in the corner on a green box. The unpainted wooden walls, the furniture, and the floors colored with yellow ocher, smelt of dry wood baked by the sun. Wherever I looked there were flies and flies and flies. . . . Grandfather and the Armenian were talking about grazing, about manure, and about oats. . . . I knew that they would be a good hour getting the samovar; that grandfather would be not less than an hour drinking his tea, and then would lie down to sleep for two or three hours; that I should waste a quarter of the day waiting, after which there would be again the heat, the dust, the jolting cart. I heard the muttering of the two voices, and it began to seem to me that I had been seeing the Armenian, the cupboard with the crockery, the flies, the windows with the burning sun beating on them, for ages and ages, and should only cease to see them in the far-off future, and I was seized with hatred for the steppe, the sun, the flies. . . .

A Little Russian peasant woman in a kerchief brought in a tray of tea-things, then the samovar. The Armenian went slowly out into the passage and shouted: "Mashya, come and pour out tea! Where are you, Mashya?"

Hurried footsteps were heard, and there came into the room a girl of sixteen in a simple cotton dress and a white kerchief. As she washed the crockery and poured out the tea, she was standing with her back to me, and all I could see was that she was of a slender figure, bare-footed, and that her little bare heels were covered by long trousers.

The Armenian invited me to have tea. Sitting down to the table, I glanced at the girl, who was handing me a glass of tea, and felt all at once as though a wind were blowing over my soul and blowing away all the impressions of the day with their dust and dreariness. I saw the bewitching features of the most beautiful face I have ever met in real life or in my dreams. Before me stood a beauty, and I recognized that at the first glance as I should have recognized lightning.

I am ready to swear that Masha—or, as her father called her, Mashya—was a real beauty, but I don't know how to prove it. It sometimes happens that clouds are huddled together in disorder on the horizon, and the sun hiding behind them colors them and the sky with tints of every possible shade—crimson, orange, gold, lilac, muddy pink; one cloud is like a monk, another like a fish, a third like a Turk in a turban. The glow of sunset enveloping a third of the sky gleams on the cross on the church, flashes on the windows of the manor house, is reflected in the river and the puddles, quivers on the trees; far, far away against the background of the sunset, a flock of wild ducks is flying homewards. . . . And the boy herding the cows, and the surveyor driving in his chaise over the dam, and the gentleman out for a walk, all gaze at the sunset, and every one of them thinks it terribly beautiful, but no one knows or can say in what its beauty lies.

I was not the only one to think the Armenian girl beautiful. My grandfather, an old man of seventy, gruff and indifferent to women and the beauties of nature, looked caressingly at Masha for a full minute, and asked:

"Is that your daughter, Avert Nazaritch?"

"Yes, she is my daughter," answered the Armenian.

"A fine young lady," said my grandfather approvingly.

An artist would have called the Armenian girl's beauty classical and severe, it was just that beauty, the contemplation of which—God knows why!—inspires in one the conviction that one is seeing correct features; that hair, eyes, nose, mouth, neck, bosom, and every movement of the young body all go together in one complete harmonious accord in which nature has not blundered over the smallest line. You fancy for some reason that the ideally beautiful woman must have such a nose as Masha's, straight and slightly aquiline, just such great dark eyes, such long lashes, such a languid glance; you fancy that her black curly hair and eyebrows go with the soft white tint of her brow and cheeks as the green reeds go with the quiet stream. Masha's white neck and her youthful bosom were not fully developed, but you fancy the sculptor would need a great creative genius to mold them. You gaze, and little by little the desire comes over you to say to Masha something extraordinarily pleasant, sincere, beautiful, as beautiful as she herself was.

At first I felt hurt and abashed that Masha took no notice of me, but was all the time looking down; it seemed to me as though a peculiar atmosphere, proud and happy, separated her from me and jealously screened her from my eyes.

"That's because I am covered with dust," I thought, "am sunburnt, and am still a boy."

But little by little I forgot myself, and gave myself up entirely to the consciousness of beauty. I thought no more now of the dreary steppe, of the dust, no longer heard the buzzing of the flies, no longer tasted the tea, and felt nothing except that a beautiful girl was standing only the other side of the table.

I felt this beauty rather strangely. It was not desire, nor ecstacy, nor enjoyment that Masha excited in me, but a painful though pleasant sadness. It was a sadness vague and undefined as a dream. For some reason I felt sorry for myself, for my grandfather and for the Armenian, even for the girl herself, and I had a feeling as though we all four had lost something important and essential to life which we should never find again. My grandfather, too, grew melancholy; he talked no more about manure or about oats, but sat silent, looking pensively at Masha.

After tea my grandfather lay down for a nap while I went out of the house into the porch. The house, like all the houses in the Armenian village, stood in the full sun; there was not a tree, not an awning, no shade. The Armenian's great courtyard, overgrown with goosefoot and wild mallows, was lively and full of gaiety in spite of the great heat. Threshing was going on behind one of the low hurdles which intersected the big yard here and there. Round a post stuck into the middle of the threshing-floor ran a dozen horses harnessed side by side, so that they formed one long radius. A Little Russian in a long waistcoat and full trousers was walking beside them, cracking a whip and shouting in a tone that sounded as though he were jeering at the horses and showing off his power over them.

"A—a—a, you damned brutes! . . . A—a—a, plague take you! Are you frightened?"

The horses, sorrel, white, and piebald, not understanding why they were made to run round in one place and to crush the wheat straw, ran unwillingly, as though with effort, swinging their tails with an offended air. The wind raised up perfect clouds of golden chaff from under their hoofs and carried it away far beyond the hurdle. Near the tall fresh stacks peasant women were swarming with rakes, and carts were moving, and beyond the stacks in another yard another dozen similar horses were running round a post, and a similar Little Russian was cracking his whip and jeering at the horses.

The steps on which I was sitting were hot; on the thin rails and here and there on the window-frames sap was oozing out of the wood from the heat; red ladybirds were huddling together in the streaks of shadow under the steps and under the shutters. The sun was baking me on my head, on my chest, and on my back, but I did not notice it, and was conscious only of the thud of bare feet on the uneven floor in the passage and in the rooms behind me. After clearing away the tea-things, Masha ran down the steps, fluttering the air as she passed, and like a bird flew into a little grimy outhouse—I suppose the kitchen—from which came the smell of roast mutton and the sound of angry talk in Armenian. She vanished into the dark doorway, and in her place there appeared on the threshold an old bent, red-faced Armenian woman wearing green trousers. The old woman was angry and was scolding someone. Soon afterwards Masha appeared in the doorway, flushed with the heat of the kitchen and carrying a big black loaf on her shoulder; swaying gracefully under the weight of the bread, she ran across the yard to the threshing-floor, darted over the hurdle, and, wrapt in a cloud of golden chaff, vanished behind the carts. The Little Russian who was driving the horses lowered his whip, sank into silence, and gazed for a minute in the direction of the carts. Then when the Armenian girl darted again by the horses and leaped over the hurdle, he followed her with his eyes, and shouted to the horses in a tone as though he were greatly disappointed:

"Plague take you, unclean devils!"

And all the while I was unceasingly hearing her bare feet, and seeing how she walked across the yard with a grave, preoccupied face. She ran now down the steps, swishing the air about me, now into the kitchen, now to the threshing-floor, now through the gate, and I could hardly turn my head quickly enough to watch her.

And the oftener she fluttered by me with her beauty, the more acute became my sadness. I felt sorry both for her and for myself and for the Little Russian, who mournfully watched her every time she ran through the cloud of chaff to the carts. Whether it was envy of her beauty, or that I was regretting that the girl was not mine, and never would be, or that I was a stranger to her; or whether I vaguely felt that her rare beauty was accidental, unnecessary, and, like everything on earth, of short duration; or whether, perhaps, my sadness was that peculiar feeling which is excited in man by the contemplation of real beauty, God only knows.

The three hours of waiting passed unnoticed. It seemed to me that I had not had time to look properly at Masha when Karpo drove up to the river, bathed the horse, and began to put it in the shafts. The wet horse snorted with pleasure and kicked his hoofs against the shafts. Karpo shouted to it: "Ba—ack!" My grandfather woke up. Masha opened the creaking gates for us, we got into the chaise and drove out of the yard. We drove in silence as though we were angry with one another.

When, two or three hours later, Rostov and Nahitchevan appeared in the distance, Karpo, who had been silent the whole time, looked round quickly, and said:

"A fine wench, that at the Armenian's."

And he lashed his horses.

II

Another time, after I had become a student, I was traveling by rail to the south. It was May. At one of the stations, I believe it was between Byelgorod and Harkov, I got out of the train to walk about the platform.

The shades of evening were already lying on the station garden, on the platform, and on the fields; the station screened off the sunset, but on the top-most clouds of smoke from the engine, which were tinged with rosy light, one could see the sun had not yet quite vanished.

As I walked up and down the platform I noticed that the greater number of the passengers were standing or walking near a second-class compartment, and that they looked as though some celebrated person were in that compartment. Among the curious whom I met near this compartment I saw, however, an artillery officer who had been my fellow-traveler, an intelligent, cordial, and sympathetic fellow—as people mostly are whom we meet on our travels by chance and with whom we are not long acquainted.

"What are you looking at there?" I asked.

He made no answer, but only indicated with his eyes a feminine figure. It was a young girl of seventeen or eighteen, wearing a Russian dress, with her head bare and a little shawl flung carelessly on one shoulder; not a passenger, but I suppose a sister or daughter of the station-master. She was standing near the carriage window, talking to an elderly woman who was in the train. Before I had time to realize what I was seeing, I was suddenly overwhelmed by the feeling I had once experienced in the Armenian village.

The girl was remarkably beautiful, and that was unmistakable to me and to those who were looking at her as I was.

If one is to describe her appearance feature by feature, as the practice is, the only really lovely thing was her thick wavy fair hair, which hung loose with a black ribbon tied round her head; all the other features were either irregular or very ordinary. Either from a peculiar form of coquettishness, or from short-sightedness, her eyes were screwed up, her nose had an undecided tilt, her mouth was small, her profile was feebly and insipidly drawn, her shoulders were narrow and undeveloped for her age—and yet the girl made the impression of being really beautiful, and looking at her, I was able to feel convinced that the Russian face does not need strict regularity in order to be lovely; what is more, that if instead of her turn-up nose the girl had been given a different one, correct and plastically irreproachable like the Armenian girl's, I fancy her face would have lost all its charm from the change.

Standing at the window talking, the girl, shrugging at the evening damp, continually looking round at us, at one moment put her arms akimbo, at the next raised her hands to her head to straighten her hair, talked, laughed, while her face at one moment wore an expression of wonder, the next of horror, and I don't remember a moment when her face and body were at rest. The whole secret and magic of her beauty lay just in these tiny, infinitely elegant movements, in her smile, in the play of her face, in her rapid glances at us, in the combination of the subtle grace of her movements with her youth, her freshness, the purity of her soul that sounded in her laugh and voice, and with the weakness we love so much in children, in birds, in fawns, and in young trees.

It was that butterfly's beauty so in keeping with waltzing, darting about the garden, laughter and gaiety, and incongruous with serious thought, grief, and repose; and it seemed as though a gust of wind blowing over the platform, or a fall of rain, would be enough to wither the fragile body and scatter the capricious beauty like the pollen of a flower.

"So—o! . . ." the officer muttered with a sigh when, after the second bell, we went back to our compartment.

And what that "So—o" meant I will not undertake to decide.

Perhaps he was sad, and did not want to go away from the beauty and the spring evening into the stuffy train; or perhaps he, like me, was unaccountably sorry for the beauty, for himself, and for me, and for all the passengers, who were listlessly and reluctantly sauntering back to their compartments. As we passed the station window, at which a pale, red-haired telegraphist with upstanding curls and a faded, broad-cheeked face was sitting beside his apparatus, the officer heaved a sigh and said:

"I bet that telegraphist is in love with that pretty girl. To live out in the wilds under one roof with that ethereal creature and not fall in love is beyond the power of man. And what a calamity, my friend! what an ironical fate, to be stooping, unkempt, gray, a decent fellow and not a fool, and to be in love with that pretty, stupid little girl who would never take a scrap of notice of you! Or worse still: imagine that telegraphist is in love, and at the same time married, and that his wife is as stooping, as unkempt, and as decent a person as himself."

On the platform between our carriage and the next the guard was standing with his elbows on the railing, looking in the direction of the beautiful girl, and his battered, wrinkled, unpleasantly beefy face, exhausted by sleepless nights and the jolting of the train, wore a look of tenderness and of the deepest sadness, as though in that girl he saw happiness, his own youth, soberness, purity, wife, children; as though he were repenting and feeling in his whole being that that girl was not his, and that for him, with his premature old age, his uncouthness, and his beefy face, the ordinary happiness of a man and a passenger was as far away as heaven....

The third bell rang, the whistles sounded, and the train slowly moved off. First the guard, the station-master, then the garden, the beautiful girl with her exquisitely sly smile, passed before our windows....

Putting my head out and looking back, I saw how, looking after the train, she walked along the platform by the window where the telegraph clerk was sitting, smoothed her hair, and ran into the garden. The station no longer screened off the sunset, the plain lay open before us, but the sun had already set and the smoke lay in black clouds over the green, velvety young corn. It was melancholy in the spring air, and in the darkening sky, and in the railway carriage.

The familiar figure of the guard came into the carriage, and he began lighting the candles.

The Party

I

After the festive dinner with its eight courses and its endless conversation, Olga Mihalovna, whose husband's name-day was being celebrated, went out into the garden. The duty of smiling and talking incessantly, the clatter of the crockery, the stupidity of the servants, the long intervals between the courses, and the stays she had put on to conceal her condition from the visitors, wearied her to exhaustion. She longed to get away from the house, to sit in the shade and rest her heart with thoughts of the baby which was to be born to her in another two months. She was used to these thoughts coming to her as she turned to the left out of the big avenue into the narrow path. Here in the thick shade of the plums and cherry-trees the dry branches used to scratch her neck and shoulders; a spider's web would settle on her face, and there would rise up in her mind the image of a little creature of undetermined sex and undefined features, and it began to seem as though it were not the spider's web that tickled her face and neck caressingly, but that little creature. When, at the end of the path, a thin wicker hurdle came into sight, and behind it podgy beehives with tiled roofs; when in the motionless, stagnant air there came a smell of hay and honey, and a soft buzzing of bees was audible, then the little creature would take complete possession of Olga Mihalovna. She used to sit down on a bench near the shanty woven of branches, and fall to thinking.

This time, too, she went on as far as the seat, sat down, and began thinking; but instead of the little creature there rose up in her imagination the figures of the grown-up people whom she had just left. She felt dreadfully uneasy that she, the hostess, had deserted her guests, and she remembered how her husband, Pyotr Dmitritch, and her uncle, Nikolay Nikolaitch, had argued at dinner about trial by jury, about the press, and about the higher education of women. Her husband, as usual, argued in order to show off his Conservative ideas before his visitors—and still more in order to disagree with her uncle, whom he disliked. Her uncle contradicted him and wrangled over every word he uttered, so as to show the company that he, Uncle Nikolay Nikolaitch, still retained his youthful freshness of spirit and free-thinking in spite of his fifty-nine years. And towards the end of dinner even Olga Mihalovna herself could not resist taking part and unskilfully attempting to defend university education for women—not that that education stood in need of her defence, but simply because she wanted to annoy her husband, who to her mind was unfair. The guests were wearied by this discussion, but they all thought it necessary to take part in it, and talked a great deal, although none of them took any interest in trial by jury or the higher education of women. . . .

Olga Mihalovna was sitting on the nearest side of the hurdle near the shanty. The sun was hidden behind the clouds. The trees and the air were overcast as before rain, but in spite of that it was hot and stifling. The hay cut under the trees on the previous day was lying ungathered, looking melancholy, with here and there a patch of colour from the faded flowers, and from it came a heavy, sickly scent. It was still. The other side of the hurdle there was a monotonous hum of bees. . . .

Suddenly she heard footsteps and voices; some one was coming along the path towards the beehouse.

"How stifling it is!" said a feminine voice. "What do you think—is it going to rain, or not?"

"It is going to rain, my charmer, but not before night," a very familiar male voice answered languidly. "There will be a good rain."

Olga Mihalovna calculated that if she made haste to hide in the shanty they would pass by without seeing her, and she would not have to talk and to force herself to smile. She picked up her skirts, bent down and crept into the shanty. At once she felt upon her face, her neck, her arms, the hot air as heavy as steam. If it had not been for the stuffiness and the close smell of rye bread, fennel, and brushwood, which prevented her from breathing freely, it would have been delightful to hide from her visitors here under the thatched roof in the dusk, and to think about the little creature. It was cosy and quiet.

"What a pretty spot!" said a feminine voice. "Let us sit here, Pyotr Dmitritch."

Olga Mihalovna began peeping through a crack between two branches. She saw her husband, Pyotr Dmitritch, and Lubotchka Sheller, a girl of seventeen who had not long left boarding-school. Pyotr Dmitritch, with his hat on the back of his head, languid and indolent from having drunk so much at dinner, slouched by the hurdle and raked the hay into a heap with his foot; Lubotchka, pink with the heat and pretty as ever, stood with her hands behind her, watching the lazy movements of his big handsome person.

Olga Mihalovna knew that her husband was attractive to women, and did not like to see him with them. There was nothing out of the way in Pyotr Dmitritch's lazily raking together the hay in order to sit down on it with Lubotchka and chatter to her of trivialities; there was nothing out of the way, either, in pretty Lubotchka's looking at him with her soft eyes; but yet Olga Mihalovna felt vexed with her husband and frightened and pleased that she could listen to them.

"Sit down, enchantress," said Pyotr Dmitritch, sinking down on the hay and stretching. "That's right. Come, tell me something."

"What next! If I begin telling you anything you will go to sleep."

"Me go to sleep? Allah forbid! Can I go to sleep while eyes like yours are watching me?"

In her husband's words, and in the fact that he was lolling with his hat on the back of his head in the presence of a lady, there was nothing out of the way either. He was spoilt by women, knew that they found him attractive, and had adopted with them a special tone which every one said suited him. With Lubotchka he behaved as with all women. But, all the same, Olga Mihalovna was jealous.

"Tell me, please," said Lubotchka, after a brief silence—"is it true that you are to be tried for something?"

"I? Yes, I am . . . numbered among the transgressors, my charmer."

"But what for?"

"For nothing, but just . . . it's chiefly a question of politics," yawned Pyotr Dmitritch—"the antagonisms of Left and Right. I, an obscurantist and reactionary, ventured in an official paper to make use of an expression offensive in the eyes of such immaculate Gladstones as Vladimir Pavlovitch Vladimirov and our local justice of the peace—Kuzma Grigoritch Vostryakov."

Pytor Dmitritch yawned again and went on:

"And it is the way with us that you may express disapproval of the sun or the moon, or anything you like, but God preserve you from touching the Liberals! Heaven forbid! A Liberal is like the poisonous dry fungus which covers you with a cloud of dust if you accidentally touch it with your finger."

"What happened to you?"

"Nothing particular. The whole flare-up started from the merest trifle. A teacher, a detestable person of clerical associations, hands to Vostryakov a petition against a tavern-keeper, charging him with insulting language and behaviour in a public place. Everything showed that both the teacher and the tavern-keeper were drunk as cobblers, and that they behaved equally badly. If there had been insulting behaviour, the insult had anyway been mutual. Vostryakov ought to have fined them both for a breach of the peace and have turned them out of the court—that is all. But that's not our way of doing things. With us what stands first is not the person—not the fact itself, but the trademark and label. However great a rascal a teacher may be, he is always in the right because he is a teacher; a tavern-keeper is always in the wrong because he is a tavern-keeper and a money-grubber. Vostryakov placed the tavern-keeper under arrest. The man appealed to the Circuit Court; the Circuit Court triumphantly upheld Vostryakov's decision. Well, I stuck to my own opinion. . . . Got a little hot. . . . That was all."

Pyotr Dmitritch spoke calmly with careless irony. In reality the trial that was hanging over him worried him extremely. Olga Mihalovna remembered how on his return from the unfortunate session he had tried to conceal from his household how troubled he was, and how dissatisfied with himself. As an intelligent man he could not help feeling that he had gone too far in expressing his disagreement; and how much lying had been needful to conceal that feeling from himself and from others! How many unnecessary conversations there had been! How much grumbling and insincere laughter at what was not laughable! When he learned that he was to be brought up before the Court, he seemed at once harassed and depressed; he began to sleep badly, stood oftener than ever at the windows, drumming on the panes with his fingers. And he was ashamed to let his wife see that he was worried, and it vexed her.

"They say you have been in the province of Poltava?" Lubotchka questioned him.

"Yes," answered Pyotr Dmitritch. "I came back the day before yesterday."

"I expect it is very nice there."

"Yes, it is very nice, very nice indeed; in fact, I arrived just in time for the haymaking, I must tell you, and in the Ukraine the haymaking is the most poetical moment of the year. Here we have a big house, a big garden, a lot of servants, and a lot going on, so that you don't see the haymaking; here it all passes unnoticed. There, at the farm, I have a meadow of forty-five acres as flat as my hand. You can see the men mowing from any window you stand at. They are mowing in the meadow, they are mowing in the garden. There are no visitors, no fuss nor hurry either, so that you can't help seeing, feeling, hearing nothing but the haymaking. There is a smell of hay indoors and outdoors. There's the sound of the scythes from sunrise to sunset. Altogether Little Russia is a charming country. Would you believe it, when I was drinking water from the rustic wells and filthy vodka in some Jew's tavern, when on quiet evenings the strains of the Little Russian fiddle and the tambourines reached me, I was tempted by a fascinating idea—to settle down on my place and live there as long as I chose, far away from Circuit Courts, intellectual conversations, philosophizing women, long dinners. . . ."

Pyotr Dmitritch was not lying. He was unhappy and really longed to rest. And he had visited his Poltava property simply to avoid seeing his study, his servants, his acquaintances, and everything that could remind him of his wounded vanity and his mistakes.

Lubotchka suddenly jumped up and waved her hands about in horror.

"Oh! A bee, a bee!" she shrieked. "It will sting!"

"Nonsense; it won't sting," said Pyotr Dmitritch. "What a coward you are!"

"No, no, no," cried Lubotchka; and looking round at the bees, she walked rapidly back.

Pyotr Dmitritch walked away after her, looking at her with a softened and melancholy face. He was probably thinking, as he looked at her, of his farm, of solitude, and—who knows?—perhaps he was even thinking how snug and cosy life would be at the farm if his wife had been this girl—young, pure, fresh, not corrupted by higher education, not with child. . . .

When the sound of their footsteps had died away, Olga Mihalovna came out of the shanty and turned towards the house. She wanted to cry. She was by now acutely jealous. She could understand that her husband was worried, dissatisfied with himself and ashamed, and when people are ashamed they hold aloof, above all from those nearest to them, and are unreserved wtih strangers; she could understand, also, that she had nothing to fear from Lubotchka or from those women who were now drinking coffee indoors. But everything in general was terrible, incomprehensible, and it already seemed to Olga Mihalovna that Pyotr Dmitritch only half belonged to her. . . .

"He has no right to do it!" she muttered, trying to formulate her jealousy and her vexation with her husband. "He has no right at all. I will tell him so plainly!"

She made up her mind to find her husband at once and tell him all about it: it was disgusting, absolutely disgusting, that he was attractive to other women and sought their admiration as though it were some heavenly manna; it was unjust and dishonourable that he should give to others what belonged by right to his wife, that he should hide his soul and his conscience from his wife to reveal them to the first pretty face he came across. What harm had his wife done him? How was she to blame? Long ago she had been sickened by his lying: he was for ever posing, flirting, saying what he did not think, and trying to seem different from what he was and what he ought to be. Why this falsity? Was it seemly in a decent man? If he lied he was demeaning himself and those to whom he lied, and slighting what he lied about. Could he not understand that if he swaggered and posed at the judicial table, or held forth at dinner on the prerogatives of Government, that he, simply to provoke her uncle, was showing thereby that he had not a ha'p'orth of respect for the Court, or himself, or any of the people who were listening and looking at him?

Coming out into the big avenue, Olga Mihalovna assumed an expression of face as though she had just gone away to look after some domestic matter. In the verandah the gentlemen were drinking liqueur and eating strawberries: one of them, the Examining Magistrate—a stout elderly man, *blagueur* and wit—must have been telling some rather free anecdote, for, seeing their hostess, he suddenly clapped his hands over his fat lips, rolled his eyes, and sat down. Olga Mihalovna did not like the local officials. She did not care for their clumsy, ceremonious wives, their scandal-mongering, their frequent visits, their flattery of her husband, whom they all hated. Now, when they were drinking, were replete with food and showed no signs of going away, she felt their presence an agonizing weariness; but not to appear impolite, she smiled cordially to the Magistrate, and shook her finger at him. She walked across the dining-room and drawing-room smiling, and looking as though she had gone to give some order and make some arrangement. "God grant no one stops me," she thought, but she forced herself to stop in the drawing-room to listen from politeness to a young man who was sitting at the piano playing: after standing for a minute, she cried, "Bravo, bravo, M. Georges!" and clapping her hands twice, she went on.

She found her husband in his study. He was sitting at the table, thinking of something. His face looked stern, thoughtful, and guilty. This was not the same Pyotr Dmitritch who had been arguing at dinner and whom his guests knew, but a different man—wearied, feeling guilty and dissatisfied with himself, whom nobody knew but his wife. He must have come to the study to get cigarettes. Before him lay an open cigarette-case full of cigarettes, and one of his hands was in the table drawer; he had paused and sunk into thought as he was taking the cigarettes.

Olga Mihalovna felt sorry for him. It was as clear as day that this man was harassed, could find no rest, and was perhaps struggling with himself. Olga Mihalovna went up to the table in silence: wanting to show that she had forgotten the argument at dinner and was not cross, she shut the cigarette-case and put it in her husband's coat pocket.

"What should I say to him?" she wondered; "I shall say that lying is like a forest—the further one goes into it the more difficult it is to get out of it. I will say to him, 'You have been carried away by the false part you are playing; you have insulted people who were attached to you and have done you no harm. Go and apologize to them, laugh at yourself, and you will feel better. And if you want peace and solitude, let us go away together.' "

Meeting his wife's gaze, Pyotr Dmitritch's face immediately assumed the expression it had worn at dinner and in the garden—indifferent and slightly ironical. He yawned and got up.

"It's past five," he said, looking at his watch. "If our visitors are merciful and leave us at eleven, even then we have another six hours of it. It's a cheerful prospect, there's no denying!"

And whistling something, he walked slowly out of the study with his usual dignified gait. She could hear him with dignified firmness cross the dining-room, then the drawing-room, laugh with dignified assurance, and say to the young man who was playing, "Bravo! Bravo!" Soon his footsteps died away: he must have gone out into the garden. And now not jealousy, not vexation, but real hatred of his footsteps, his insincere laugh and voice, took possession of Olga Mihalovna. She went to the window and looked out into the garden. Pyotr Dmitritch was already walking along the avenue. Putting one hand in his pocket and snapping the fingers of the other, he walked with confident swinging steps, throwing his head back a little, and looking as though he were very well satisfied with himself, with his dinner, with his digestion, and with nature. . . .

Two little schoolboys, the children of Madame Tchizhevsky, who had only just arrived, made their appearance in the avenue, accompanied by their tutor, a student wearing a white tunic and very narrow trousers. When they reached Pyotr Dmitritch, the boys and the student stopped, and probably congratulated him on his name-day. With a graceful swing of his shoulders, he patted the children on their cheeks, and carelessly offered the student his hand without looking at him. The student must have praised the weather and compared it with the climate of Petersburg, for Pyotr Dmitritch said in a loud voice, in a tone as though he were not speaking to a guest, but to an usher of the court or a witness:

"What! It's cold in Petersburg? And here, my good sir, we have a salubrious atmosphere and the fruits of the earth in abundance. Eh? What?"

And thrusting one hand in his pocket and snapping the fingers of the other, he walked on. Till he had disappeared behind the nut bushes, Olga Mihalovna watched the back of his head in perplexity. How had this man of thirty-four come by the dignified deportment of a general? How had he come by that impressive, elegant manner? Where had he got that vibration of authority in his voice? Where had he got these "what's," "to be sure's," and "my good sir's"?

Olga Mihalovna remembered how in the first months of her marriage she had felt dreary at home alone and had driven into the town to the Circuit Court, at which Pyotr Dmitritch had sometimes presided in place of her godfather, Count Alexey Petrovitch. In the presidential chair, wearing his uniform and a chain on his breast, he was completely changed. Stately gestures, a voice of thunder, "what," "to be sure," careless tones. . . . Everything, all that was ordinary and human, all that was individual and personal to himself that Olga Mihalovna was accustomed to seeing in him at home, vanished in grandeur, and in the presidential chair there sat not Pyotr Dmitritch, but another man whom every one called Mr. President. This consciousness of power prevented him from sitting still in his place, and he seized every opportunity to ring his bell, to glance sternly at the public, to shout. . . . Where had he got his short-sight and his deafness when he suddenly began to see and hear with difficulty, and, frowning majestically, insisted on people speaking louder and coming closer to the table? From the height of his grandeur he could hardly distinguish faces or sounds, so that it seemed that if Olga Mihalovna herself had gone up to him he would have shouted even to her, "Your name?" Peasant witnesses he addressed familiarly, he shouted at the public so that his voice could be heard even in the street, and behaved incredibly with the lawyers. If a lawyer had to speak to him, Pyotr Dmitritch, turning a little away from him, looked with half-closed eyes at the ceiling, meaning to signify thereby that the lawyer was utterly superfluous and that he was neither recognizing him nor listening to him; if a badly-dressed lawyer spoke, Pyotr Dmitritch pricked up his ears and looked the man up and down with a sarcastic, annihilating stare as though to say: "Queer sort of lawyers nowadays!"

"What do you mean by that?" he would interrupt.

If a would-be eloquent lawyer mispronounced a foreign word, saying, for instance, "factitious" instead of "fictitious," Pyotr Dmitritch brightened up at once and asked, "What? How? Factitious? What does that mean?" and then observed impressively: "Don't make use of words you do not understand." And the lawyer, finishing his speech, would walk away from the table, red and perspiring, while Pyotr Dmitritch, with a self-satisfied smile, would lean back in his chair triumphant. In his manner with the lawyers he imitated Count Alexey Petrovitch a little, but when the latter said, for instance, "Counsel for the defence, you keep quiet for a little!" it sounded paternally good-natured and natural, while the same words in Pyotr Dmitritch's mouth were rude and artificial.

II

There were sounds of applause. The young man had finished playing. Olga Mihalovna remembered her guests and hurried into the drawing-room.

"I have so enjoyed your playing," she said, going up to the piano. "I have so enjoyed it. You have a wonderful talent! But don't you think our piano's out of tune?"

At that moment the two schoolboys walked into the room, accompanied by the student.

"My goodness! Mitya and Kolya," Olga Mihalovna drawled joyfully, going to meet them: "How big they have grown! One would not know you! But where is your mamma?"

"I congratulate you on the name-day," the student began in a free-and-easy tone, "and I wish you all happiness. Ekaterina Andreyevna sends her congratulations and begs you to excuse her. She is not very well."

"How unkind of her! I have been expecting her all day. Is it long since you left Petersburg?" Olga Mihalovna asked the student. "What kind of weather have you there now?" And without waiting for an answer, she looked cordially at the schoolboys and repeated:

"How tall they have grown! It is not long since they used to come with their nurse, and they are at school already! The old grow older while the young grow up. . . . Have you had dinner?"

"Oh, please don't trouble!" said the student.

"Why, you have not had dinner?"

"For goodness' sake, don't trouble!"

"But I suppose you are hungry?" Olga Mihalovna said it in a harsh, rude voice, with impatience and vexation—it escaped her unawares, but at once she coughed, smiled, and flushed crimson. "How tall they have grown!" she said softly.

"Please don't trouble!" the student said once more.

The student begged her not to trouble; the boys said nothing; obviously all three of them were hungry. Olga Mihalovna took them into the dining-room and told Vassily to lay the table.

"How unkind of your mamma!" she said as she made them sit down. "She has quite forgotten me. Unkind, unkind, unkind . . . you must tell her so. What are you studying?" she asked the student.

"Medicine."

"Well, I have a weakness for doctors, only fancy. I am very sorry my husband is not a doctor. What courage any one must have to perform an operation or dissect a corpse, for instance! Horrible! Aren't you frightened? I believe I should die of terror! Of course, you drink vodka?"

"Please don't trouble."

"After your journey you must have something to drink. Though I am a woman, even I drink sometimes. And Mitya and Kolya will drink Malaga. It's not a strong wine; you need not be afraid of it. What fine fellows they are, really! They'll be thinking of getting married next."

Olga Mihalovna talked without ceasing; she knew by experience that when she had guests to entertain it was far easier and more comfortable to talk than to listen. When you talk there is no need to strain your attention to think of answers to questions, and to change your expression of face. But unawares she asked the student a serious question; the student began a lengthy speech and she was forced to listen. The student knew that she had once been at the University, and so tried to seem a serious person as he talked to her.

"What subject are you studying?" she asked, forgetting that she had already put that question to him.

"Medicine."

Olga Mihalovna now remembered that she had been away from the ladies for a long while.

"Yes? Then I suppose you are going to be a doctor?" she said, getting up. "That's splendid. I am sorry I did not go in for medicine myself. So you will finish your dinner here, gentlemen, and then come into the garden. I will introduce you to the young ladies."

She went out and glanced at her watch: it was five minutes to six. And she wondered that the time had gone so slowly, and thought with horror that there were six more hours before midnight, when the party would break up. How could she get through those six hours? What phrases could she utter? How should she behave to her husband?

There was not a soul in the drawing-room or on the verandah. All the guests were sauntering about the garden.

"I shall have to suggest a walk in the birchwood before tea, or else a row in the boats," thought Olga Mihalovna, hurrying to the croquet ground, from which came the sounds of voices and laughter.

"And sit the old people down to *vint*. . . ." She met Grigory the footman coming from the croquet ground with empty bottles.

"Where are the ladies?" she asked.

"Among the raspberry-bushes. The master's there, too."

"Oh, good heavens!" some one on the croquet lawn shouted with exasperation. "I have told you a thousand times over! To know the Bulgarians you must see them! You can't judge from the papers!"

Either because of the outburst or for some other reason, Olga Mihalovna was suddenly aware of a terrible weakness all over, especially in her legs and in her shoulders. She felt she could not bear to speak, to listen, or to move.

"Grigory," she said faintly and with an effort, "when you have to serve tea or anything, please don't appeal to me, don't ask me anything, don't speak of anything. . . . Do it all yourself, and . . . and don't make a noise with your feet, I entreat you. . . . I can't, because . . ."

Without finishing, she walked on towards the croquet lawn, but on the way she thought of the ladies, and turned towards the raspberry-bushes. The sky, the air, and the trees looked gloomy again and threatened rain; it was hot and stifling. An immense flock of crows, foreseeing a storm, flew cawing over the garden. The paths were more overgrown, darker, and narrower as they got nearer the kitchen garden. In one of them, buried in a thick tangle of wild pear, crab-apple, sorrel, young oaks, and hopbine, clouds of tiny black flies swarmed round Olga Mihalovna. She covered her face with her hands and began forcing herself to think of the little creature. . . . There floated through her imagination the figures of Grigory, Mitya, Kolya, the faces of the peasants who had come in the morning to present their congratulations. . . .

She heard footsteps, and she opened her eyes. Uncle Nikolay Nikolaitch was coming rapidly towards her.

"It's you, dear? I am very glad . . ." he began, breathless. "A couple of words. . . ." He mopped with his handkerchief his red shaven chin, then suddenly stepped back a pace, flung up his hands and opened his eyes wide. "My dear girl, how long is this going on?" he said rapidly, spluttering. "I ask you: is there no limit to it? I say nothing of the demoralizing effect of his martinet views on all around him, of the way he insults all that is sacred and best in me and in every honest thinking man—I will say nothing about that, but he might at least behave decently! Why, he shouts, he bellows, gives himself airs, poses as a sort of

Bonaparte, does not let one say a word. . . . I don't know what the devil's the matter with him! These lordly gestures, this condescending tone; and laughing like a general! Who is he, allow me to ask you? I ask you, who is he? The husband of his wife, with a few paltry acres and the rank of a titular who has had the luck to marry an heiress! An upstart and a *junker,* like so many others! A type out of Shtchedrin! Upon my word, it's either that he's suffering from megalomania, or that old rat in his dotage, Count Alexey Petrovitch, is right when he says that children and young people are a long time growing up nowadays, and go on playing they are cabmen and generals till they are forty!"

"That's true, that's true," Olga Mihalovna assented. "Let me pass."

"Now just consider: what is it leading to?" her uncle went on, barring her way. "How will this playing at being a general and a Conservative end? Already he has got into trouble! Yes, to stand his trial! I am very glad of it! That's what his noise and shouting has brought him to—to stand in the prisoner's dock. And it's not as though it were the Circuit Court or something: it's the Central Court! Nothing worse could be imagined, I think! And then he has quarrelled with every one! He is celebrating his name-day, and look, Vostryakov's not here, nor Yahontov, nor Vladimirov, nor Shevud, nor the Count. . . . There is no one, I imagine, more Conservative than Count Alexey Petrovitch, yet even he has not come. And he never will come again. He won't come, you will see!"

"My God! but what has it to do with me?" asked Olga Mihalovna.

"What has it to do with you? Why, you are his wife! You are clever, you have had a university education, and it was in your power to make him an honest worker!"

"At the lectures I went to they did not teach us how to influence tiresome people. It seems as though I should have to apologize to all of you for having been at the University," said Olga Mihalovna sharply. "Listen, uncle. If people played the same scales over and over again the whole day long in your hearing, you wouldn't be able to sit still and listen, but would run away. I hear the same thing over again for days together all the year round. You must have pity on me at last."

Her uncle pulled a very long face, then looked at her searchingly and twisted his lips into a mocking smile.

"So that's how it is," he piped in a voice like an old woman's. "I beg your pardon!" he said, and made a ceremonious bow. "If you have fallen under his influence yourself, and have abandoned your convictions, you should have said so before. I beg your pardon!"

"Yes, I have abandoned my convictions," she cried. "There; make the most of it!"

"I beg your pardon!"

Her uncle for the last time made her a ceremonious bow, a little on one side, and, shrinking into himself, made a scrape with his foot and walked back.

"Idiot!" thought Olga Mihalovna. "I hope he will go home."

She found the ladies and the young people among the raspberries in the kitchen garden. Some were eating raspberries; others, tired of eating raspberries, were strolling about the strawberry beds or foraging among the sugar-peas. A little on one side of the raspberry bed, near a branching apple-tree propped up by posts which had been pulled out of an old fence, Pyotr Dmitritch was mowing the grass. His hair was falling over his forehead, his cravat was untied. His watch-chain was hanging loose. Every step and every swing of the scythe showed skill and the possession of immense physical strength. Near him were standing Lubotchka and the daughters of a neighbour, Colonel Bukryeev—two anaemic and unhealthily stout fair girls, Natalya and Valentina, or, as they were always called, Nata and Vata, both wearing white frocks and strikingly like each other. Pyotr Dmitritch was teaching them to mow.

"It's very simple," he said. "You have only to know how to hold the scythe and not to get too hot over it—that is, not to use more force than is necessary! Like this. . . . Wouldn't you like to try?" he said, offering the scythe to Lubotchka. "Come!"

Lubotchka took the scythe clumsily, blushed crimson, and laughed.

"Don't be afraid, Lubov Alexandrovna!" cried Olga Mihalovna, loud enough for all the ladies to hear that she was with them. "Don't be afraid! You must learn! If you marry a Tolstoyan he will make you mow."

Lubotchka raised the scythe, but began laughing again, and, helpless with laughter, let go of it at once. She was ashamed and pleased at being talked to as though grown up. Nata, with a cold, serious face, with no trace of smiling or shyness, took the scythe, swung it and caught it in the grass; Vata, also without a smile, as cold and serious as her sister, took the scythe, and silently thrust it into the earth. Having done this, the two sisters linked arms and walked in silence to the raspberries.

Pyotr Dmitritch laughed and played about like a boy, and this childish, frolicsome mood in which he became exceedingly good-natured suited him far better than any other. Olga Mihalovna loved him when he was like that. But his boyishness did not usually last long. It did not this time; after playing with the scythe, he for some reason thought it necessary to take a serious tone about it.

"When I am mowing, I feel, do you know, healthier and more normal," he said. "If I were forced to confine myself to an intellectual life I believe I should go out of my mind. I feel that I was not born to be a man of culture! I ought to mow, plough, sow, drive out the horses."

And Pyotr Dmitritch began a conversation with the ladies about the advantages of physical labour, about culture, and then about the pernicious effects of money, of property. Listening to her husband, Olga Mihalovna, for some reason, thought of her dowry.

"And the time will come, I suppose," she thought, "when he will not forgive me for being richer than he. He is proud and vain. Maybe he will hate me because he owes so much to me."

She stopped near Colonel Bukryeev, who was eating raspberries and also taking part in the conversation.

"Come," he said, making room for Olga Mihalovna and Pyotr Dmitritch. "The ripest are here. . . . And so, according to Proudhon," he went on, raising his voice, "property is robbery. But I must confess I don't believe in Proudhon, and don't consider him a philosopher. The French are not authorities, to my thinking—God bless them!"

"Well, as for Proudhons and Buckles and the rest of them, I am weak in that department," said Pyotr Dmitritch. "For philosophy you must apply to my wife. She has been at University lectures and knows all your Schopenhauers and Proudhons by heart. . . ."

Olga Mihalovna felt bored again. She walked again along a little path by apple and pear trees, and looked again as though she was on some very important errand. She reached the gardener's cottage. In the doorway the gardener's wife, Varvara, was sitting together with her four little children with big shaven heads. Varvara, too, was with child and expecting to be confined on Elijah's Day. After greeting her, Olga Mihalovna looked at her and the children in silence and asked:

"Well, how do you feel?"

"Oh, all right. . . ."

A silence followed. The two women seemed to understand each other without words.

"It's dreadful having one's first baby," said Olga Mihalovna after a moment's thought. "I keep feeling as though I shall not get through it, as though I shall die."

"I fancied that, too, but here I am alive. . . . One has all sorts of fancies."

Varvara, who was just going to have her fifth, looked down a little on her mistress from the height of her experience and spoke in a rather didactic tone, and Olga Mihalovna could not help feeling her authority; she would have liked to have talked of her fears, of the child, of her sensations, but she was afraid it might strike Varvara as naïve and trivial. And she waited in silence for Varvara to say something herself.

"Olya, we are going indoors," Pyotr Dmitritch called from the raspberries.

Olga Mihalovna liked being silent, waiting and watching Varvara. She would have been ready to stay like that till night without speaking or having any duty to perform. But she had to go. She had hardly left the cottage when Lubotchka, Nata, and Vata came running to meet her. The sisters stopped short abruptly a couple of yards away; Lubotchka ran right up to her and flung herself on her neck.

"You dear, darling, precious," she said, kissing her face and her neck. "Let us go and have tea on the island!"

"On the island, on the island!" said the precisely similar Nata and Vata, both at once, without a smile.

"But it's going to rain, my dears."

"It's not, it's not," cried Lubotchka with a woebegone face. "They've all agreed to go. Dear! darling!"

"They are all getting ready to have tea on the island," said Pyotr Dmitritch, coming up. "See to arranging things. . . . We will all go in the boats, and the samovars and all the rest of it must be sent in the carriage with the servants."

He walked beside his wife and gave her his arm. Olga Mihalovna had a desire to say something disagreeable to her husband, something biting, even about her dowry perhaps—the crueller the better, she felt. She thought a little, and said:

"Why is it Count Alexey Petrovitch hasn't come? What a pity!"

"I am very glad he hasn't come," said Pyotr Dmitritch, lying. "I'm sick to death of that old lunatic."

"But yet before dinner you were expecting him so eagerly!"

III

Half an hour later all the guests were crowding on the bank near the pile to which the boats were fastened. They were all talking and laughing, and were in such excitement and commotion that they could hardly get into the boats. Three boats were crammed with passengers, while two stood empty. The keys for unfastening these two boats had been somehow mislaid, and messengers were continually running from the river to the house to look for them. Some said Grigory had the keys, others that the bailiff had them, while others suggested sending for a blacksmith and breaking the padlocks. And all talked at once, interrupting and shouting one another down. Pyotr Dmitritch paced impatiently to and fro on the bank, shouting:

"What the devil's the meaning of it! The keys ought always to be lying in the hall window! Who has dared to take them away? The bailiff can get a boat of his own if he wants one!"

At last the keys were found. Then it appeared that two oars were missing. Again there was a great hullabaloo. Pyotr Dmitritch, who was weary of pacing about the bank, jumped into a long, narrow boat hollowed out of the trunk of a poplar, and, lurching from side to side and almost falling into the water, pushed off from the bank. The other boats followed him one after another, amid loud laughter and the shrieks of the young ladies.

The white cloudy sky, the trees on the riverside, the boats with the people in them, and the oars, were reflected in the water as in a mirror; under the boats, far away below in the bottomless depths, was a second sky with the birds flying across it. The bank on which the house and gardens stood was high, steep, and covered with trees; on the other, which was sloping, stretched broad green water-meadows with sheets of water glistening in them. The boats had floated a hundred yards when, behind the mournfully drooping willows on the sloping banks, huts and a herd of cows came into sight; they began to hear songs, drunken shouts, and the strains of a concertina.

Here and there on the river fishing-boats were scattered about, setting their nets for the night. In one of these boats was the festive party, playing on home-made violins and violoncellos.

Olga Mihalovna was sitting at the rudder; she was smiling affably and talking a great deal to entertain her visitors, while she glanced stealthily at her husband. He was ahead of them all, standing up punting with one oar. The light sharp-nosed canoe, which all the guests called the "death-trap"—while Pyotr Dmitritch, for some reason, called it *Penderaklia*—flew along quickly; it had a brisk, crafty expression, as though it hated its heavy occupant and was looking out for a favourable moment to glide away from under his feet. Olga Mihalovna kept looking at her husband, and she loathed his good looks which attracted every one, the back of his head, his attitude, his familiar manner with women; she hated all the women sitting in the boat with her, was jealous, and at the same time was trembling every minute in terror that the frail craft would upset and cause an accident.

"Take care, Pyotr!" she cried, while her heart fluttered with terror. "Sit down! We believe in your courage without all that!"

She was worried, too, by the people who were in the boat with her. They were all ordinary good sort of people like thousands of others, but now each one of them struck her as exceptional and evil. In each one of them she saw nothing but falsity. "That young man," she thought, "rowing, in gold-rimmed spectacles, with chestnut hair and a nice-looking beard: he is a mamma's darling, rich, and well-fed, and always fortunate, and every one considers him an honourable, free-thinking, advanced man. It's not a year since he left the University and came to live in the district, but he already talks of himself as 'we active members of the Zemstvo.' But in another year he will be bored like so many others and go off to Petersburg, and to justify running away, will tell every one that the Zemstvos are good-for-nothing, and that he has been deceived in them. While from the other boat his young wife keeps her eyes fixed on him, and believes that he is 'an active member of the Zemstvo,' just as in a year she will believe that the Zemstvo is good-for-nothing. And that stout, carefully shaven gentleman in the straw hat with the broad ribbon, with an expensive cigar in his mouth: he is fond of saying, 'It is time to put away dreams and set to work!' He has Yorkshire pigs, Butler's hives, rape-seed, pine-apples, a dairy, a cheese factory, Italian bookkeeping by double entry; but every summer he sells his timber and mortgages part of his land to spend the autumn with his mistress in the Crimea. And there's Uncle Nikolay Nikolaitch, who has quarrelled with Pyotr Dmitritch, and yet for some reason does not go home."

Olga Mihalovna looked at the other boats, and there, too, she saw only uninteresting, queer creatures, affected or stupid people. She thought of all the people she knew in the district, and could not remember one person of whom one could say or think anything good. They all seemed to her mediocre, insipid, unintelligent, narrow, false, heartless; they all said what they did not think, and did what they did not want to. Dreariness and despair were stifling her; she longed to leave off smiling, to leap up and cry out, "I am sick of you," and then jump out and swim to the bank.

"I say, let's take Pyotr Dmitritch in tow!" some one shouted.

"In tow, in tow!" the others chimed in. "Olga Mihalovna, take your husband in tow."

To take him in tow, Olga Mihalovna, who was steering, had to seize the right moment and to catch hold of his boat by the chain at the beak. When she bent over to the chain Pyotr Dmitritch frowned and looked at her in alarm.

"I hope you won't catch cold," he said.

"If you are uneasy about me and the child, why do you torment me?" thought Olga Mihalovna.

Pyotr Dmitritch acknowledged himself vanquished, and, not caring to be towed, jumped from the *Penderaklia* into the boat which was overful already, and jumped so carelessly that the boat lurched violently, and every one cried out in terror.

"He did that to please the ladies," thought Olga Mihalovna; "he knows it's charming." Her hands and feet began trembling, as she supposed, from boredom, vexation from the strain of smiling and the discomfort she felt all over her body. And to conceal this trembling from her guests, she tried to talk more loudly, to laugh, to move.

"If I suddenly begin to cry," she thought, "I shall say I have toothache. . . ."

But at last the boats reached the "Island of Good Hope," as they called the peninsula formed by a bend in the river at an acute angle, covered with a copse of old birch-trees, oaks, willows, and poplars. The tables were already laid under the trees; the samovars were smoking, and Vassily and Grigory, in their swallow-tails and white knitted gloves, were already busy with the tea-things. On the other bank, opposite the "Island of Good Hope," there stood the carriages which had come with the provisions. The baskets and parcels of provisions were carried across to the island in a little boat like the *Penderaklia.* The footmen, the coachmen, and even the peasant who was sitting in the boat, had the solemn expression befitting a name-day such as one only sees in children and servants.

While Olga Mihalovna was making the tea and pouring out the first glasses, the visitors were busy with the liqueurs and sweet things. Then there was the general commotion usual at picnics over drinking tea, very wearisome and exhausting for the hostess. Grigory and Vassily had hardly had time to take the glasses round before hands were being stretched out to Olga Mihalovna with empty glasses. One asked for no sugar, another wanted it stronger, another weak, a fourth declined another glass. And all this Olga Mihalovna had to remember, and then to call, "Ivan Petrovitch, is it without sugar for you?" or, "Gentlemen, which of you wanted it weak?" But the guest who had asked for weak tea, or no sugar, had by now forgotten it, and, absorbed in agreeable conversation, took the first glass that came. Depressed-looking figures wandered like shadows at a little distance from the table, pretending to look for mushrooms in the grass, or reading the labels on the boxes—these were those for whom there were not glasses enough. "Have you had tea?" Olga Mihalovna kept asking, and the guest so addressed begged her not to trouble, and said, "I will wait," though it would have suited her better for the visitors not to wait but to make haste.

Some, absorbed in conversation, drank their tea slowly, keeping their glasses for half an hour; others, especially some who had drunk a good deal at dinner, would not leave the table, and kept on drinking glass after glass, so that Olga Mihalovna scarcely had time to fill them. One jocular young man sipped his tea through a lump of sugar, and kept saying, "Sinful man that I am, I love to indulge myself with the Chinese herb." He kept asking with a heavy sigh: "Another tiny dish of tea more, if you please." He drank a great deal, nibbled his sugar, and thought it all very amusing and original, and imagined that he was doing a clever imitation of a Russian merchant. None of them understood that these trifles were agonizing to their hostess, and, indeed, it was hard to understand it, as Olga Mihalovna went on all the time smiling affably and talking nonsense.

But she felt ill. . . . She was irritated by the crowd of people, the laughter, the questions, the jocular young man, the footmen harassed and run off their legs, the children who hung round the table; she was irritated at Vata's being like Nata, at Kolya's being like Mitya, so that one could not tell which of them had had tea and which of them had not. She felt that her smile of forced affability was passing into an expression of anger, and she felt every minute as though she would burst into tears.

"Rain, my friends," cried some one.

Every one looked at the sky.

"Yes, it really is rain . . ." Pyotr Dmitritch assented, and wiped his cheek.

Only a few drops were falling from the sky—the real rain had not begun yet; but the company abandoned their tea and made haste to get off. At first they all wanted to drive home in the carriages, but changed their minds and made for the boats. On the pretext that she had to hasten home to give directions about the supper, Olga Mihalovna asked to be excused for leaving the others, and went home in the carriage.

When she got into the carriage, she first of all let her face rest from smiling. With an angry face she drove through the village, and with an angry face acknowledged the bows of the peasants she met. When she got home, she went to the bedroom by the back way and lay down on her husband's bed.

"Merciful God!" she whispered. "What is all this hard labour for? Why do all these people hustle each other here and pretend that they are enjoying themselves? Why do I smile and lie? I don't understand it."

She heard steps and voices. The visitors had come back.

"Let them come," thought Olga Mihalovna; "I shall lie a little longer."

But a maid-servant came and said:

"Marya Grigoryevna is going, madam."

Olga Mihalovna jumped up, tidied her hair and hurried out of the room.

"Marya Grigoryevna, what is the meaning of this?" she began in an injured voice, going to meet Marya Grigoryevna. "Why are you in such a hurry?"

"I can't help it, darling! I've stayed too long as it is; my children are expecting me home."

"It's too bad of you! Why didn't you bring your children with you?"

"If you will let me, dear, I will bring them on some ordinary day, but to-day . . ."

"Oh, please do," Olga Mihalovna interrupted; "I shall be delighted! Your children are so sweet! Kiss them all for me. . . . But, really, I am offended with you! I don't understand why you are in such a hurry!"

"I really must, I really must. . . . Good-bye, dear. Take care of yourself. In your condition, you know . . ."

And the ladies kissed each other. After seeing the departing guest to her carriage, Olga Mihalovna went in to the ladies in the drawing-room. There the lamps were already lighted and the gentlemen were sitting down to cards.

IV

The party broke up after supper about a quarter past twelve. Seeing her visitors off, Olga Mihalovna stood at the door and said:

"You really ought to take a shawl! It's turning a little chilly. Please God, you don't catch cold!"

"Don't trouble, Olga Mihalovna," the ladies answered as they got into the carriage. "Well, good-bye. Mind now, we are expecting you; don't play us false!"

"Wo-o-o!" the coachman checked the horses.

"Ready, Denis! Good-bye, Olga Mihalovna!"

"Kiss the children for me!"

The carriage started and immediately disappeared into the darkness. In the red circle of light cast by the lamp in the road, a fresh pair or trio of impatient horses, and the silhouette of a coachman with his hands held out stiffly before him, would come into view. Again there began kisses, reproaches, and entreaties to come again or to take a shawl. Pyotr Dmitritch kept running out and helping the ladies into their carriages.

"You go now by Efremovshtchina," he directed the coachman; "it's nearer through Mankino, but the road is worse that way. You might have an upset. . . . Good-bye, my charmer. *Mille compliments* to your artist!"

"Good-bye, Olga Mihalovna, darling! Go indoors, or you will catch cold! It's damp!"

"Wo-o-o! you rascal!"

"What horses have you got here?" Pyotr Dmitritch asked.

"They were bought from Haidorov, in Lent," answered the coachman.

"Capital horses. . . ."

And Pyotr Dmitritch patted the trace horse on the haunch.

"Well, you can start! God give you good luck!"

The last visitor was gone at last; the red circle on the road quivered, moved aside, contracted and went out, as Vassily carried away the lamp from the entrance. On previous occasions when they had seen off their visitors, Pyotr Dmitritch and Olga Mihalovna had begun dancing about the drawing-room, facing each other, clapping their hands and singing: "They've gone! They've gone!" But now Olga Mihalovna was not equal to that. She went to her bedroom, undressed, and got into bed.

She fancied she would fall asleep at once and sleep soundly. Her legs and her shoulders ached painfully, her head was heavy from the strain of talking, and she was conscious, as before, of discomfort all over her body. Covering her head over, she lay still for three or four minutes, then peeped out from under the bed-clothes at the lamp before the ikon, listened to the silence, and smiled.

"It's nice, it's nice," she whispered, curling up her legs, which felt as if they had grown longer from so much walking. "Sleep, sleep. . . ."

Her legs would not get into a comfortable position; she felt uneasy all over, and she turned on the other side. A big fly blew buzzing about the bedroom and thumped against the ceiling. She could hear, too, Grigory and Vassily stepping cautiously about the drawing-room, putting the chairs back in their places; it seemed to Olga Mihalovna that she could not go to sleep, nor be comfortable till those sounds were hushed. And again she turned over on the other side impatiently.

She heard her husband's voice in the drawing-room. Some one must be staying the night, as Pyotr Dmitritch was addressing some one and speaking loudly:

"I don't say that Count Alexey Petrovitch is an impostor. But he can't help seeming to be one, because all of you gentlemen attempt to see in him something different from what he really is. His craziness is looked upon as originality, his familiar manners as good-nature, and his complete absence of opinions as Conservatism. Even granted that he is a Conservative of the stamp of '84, what after all is Conservatism?"

Pyotr Dmitritch, angry with Count Alexey Petrovitch, his visitors, and himself, was relieving his heart. He abused both the Count and his visitors, and in his vexation with himself was ready to speak out and to hold forth upon anything. After seeing his guest to his room, he walked up and down the drawing-room, walked through the dining-room, down the corridor, then into his study, then again went into the drawing-room, and came into the bedroom. Olga Mihalovna was lying on her back, with the bed-clothes only to her waist (by now she felt hot), and with an angry face, watched the fly that was thumping against the ceiling.

"Is some one staying the night?" she asked.

"Yegorov."

Pyotr Dmitritch undressed and got into his bed. Without speaking, he lighted a cigarette, and he, too, fell to watching the fly. There was an uneasy and forbidding look in his eyes. Olga Mihalovna looked at his handsome profile for five minutes in silence. It seemed to her for some reason that if her husband were suddenly to turn facing her, and to say, "Olga, I am unhappy," she would cry or laugh, and she would be at ease. She fancied that her legs were aching and her body was uncomfortable all over because of the strain on her feelings.

"Pyotr, what are you thinking of?" she said.

"Oh, nothing . . ." her husband answered.

"You have taken to having secrets from me of late: that's not right."

"Why is it not right?" answered Pyotr Dmitritch drily and not at once. "We all have our personal life, every one of us, and we are bound to have our secrets."

"Personal life, our secrets . . . that's all words! Understand you are wounding me!" said Olga Mihalovna, sitting up in bed. "If you have a load on your heart, why do you hide it from me? And why do you find it more suitable to open your heart to women who are nothing to you, instead of to your wife? I overheard your outpourings to Lubotchka by the bee-house to-day."

"Well, I congratulate you. I am glad you did overhear it."

This meant "Leave me alone and let me think." Olga Mihalovna was indignant. Vexation, hatred, and wrath, which had been accumulating within her during the whole day, suddenly boiled over; she wanted at once to speak out, to hurt her husband without putting it off till to-morrow, to wound him, to punish him. . . . Making an effort to control herself and not to scream, she said:

"Let me tell you, then, that it's all loathsome, loathsome, loathsome! I've been hating you all day; you see what you've done."

Pyotr Dmitritch, too, got up and sat on the bed.

"It's loathsome, loathsome, loathsome," Olga Mihalovna went on, beginning to tremble all over. "There's no need to congratulate me; you had better congratulate yourself! It's a shame, a disgrace. You have wrapped yourself in lies till you are ashamed to be alone in the room with your wife! You are a deceitful man! I see through you and understand every step you take!"

"Olya, I wish you would please warn me when you are out of humour. Then I will sleep in the study."

Saying this, Pyotr Dmitritch picked up his pillow and walked out of the bedroom. Olga Mihalovna had not foreseen this. For some minutes she remained silent with her mouth open, trembling all over and looking at the door by which her husband had gone out, and trying to understand what it meant. Was this one of the devices to which deceitful people have recourse when they are in the wrong, or was it a deliberate insult aimed at her pride? How was she to take it? Olga Mihalovna remembered her cousin, a lively young officer, who often used to tell her, laughing, that when "his spouse nagged at him" at night, he usually picked up his pillow and went whistling to spend the night in his study, leaving his wife in a foolish and ridiculous position. This officer was married to a rich, capricious, and foolish woman whom he did not respect but simply put up with.

Olga Mihalovna jumped out of bed. To her mind there was only one thing left for her to do now; to dress with all possible haste and to leave the house forever. The house was her own, but so much the worse for Pyotr Dmitritch. Without pausing to consider whether this was necessary or not, she went quickly to the study to inform her husband of her intention ("Feminine logic!" flashed through her mind), and to say something wounding and sarcastic at parting. . . .

Pyotr Dmitritch was lying on the sofa and pretending to read a newspaper. There was a candle burning on a chair near him. His face could not be seen behind the newspaper.

"Be so kind as to tell me what this means? I am asking you."

"Be so kind . . ." Pyotr Dmitritch mimicked her, not showing his face. "It's sickening, Olga! Upon my honour, I am exhausted and not up to it. . . . Let us do our quarrelling to-morrow."

"No, I understand you perfectly!" Olga Mihalovna went on. "You hate me! Yes, yes! You hate me because I am richer than you! You will never forgive me for that, and will always be lying to me!" ("Feminine logic!" flashed through her mind again.) "You are laughing at me now.... I am convinced, in fact, that you only married me in order to have property qualifications and those wretched horses.... Oh, I am miserable!"

Pyotr Dmitritch dropped the newspaper and got up. The unexpected insult overwhelmed him. With a childishly helpless smile he looked desperately at his wife, and holding out his hands to her as though to ward off blows, he said imploringly:

"Olya!"

And expecting her to say something else awful, he leaned back in his chair, and his huge figure seemed as helplessly childish as his smile.

"Olya, how could you say it?" he whispered.

Olga Mihalovna came to herself. She was suddenly aware of her passionate love for this man, remembered that he was her husband, Pyotr Dmitritch, without whom she could not live for a day, and who loved her passionately, too. She burst into loud sobs that sounded strange and unlike her, and ran back to her bedroom.

She fell on the bed, and short hysterical sobs, choking her and making her arms and legs twitch, filled the bedroom. Remembering there was a visitor sleeping three or four rooms away, she buried her head under the pillow to stifle her sobs, but the pillow rolled on to the floor, and she almost fell on the floor herself when she stooped to pick it up. She pulled the quilt up to her face, but her hands would not obey her, but tore convulsively at everything she clutched.

She thought that everything was lost, that the falsehood she had told to wound her husband had shattered her life into fragments. Her husband would not forgive her. The insult she had hurled at him was not one that could be effaced by any caresses, by any vows.... How could she convince her husband that she did not believe what she had said?

"It's all over, it's all over!" she cried, not noticing that the pillow had slipped on to the floor again. "For God's sake, for God's sake!"

Probably roused by her cries, the guest and the servants were now awake; next day all the neighbourhood would know that she had been in hysterics and would blame Pyotr Dmitritch. She made an effort to restrain herself, but her sobs grew louder and louder every minute.

"For God's sake," she cried in a voice not like her own, and not knowing why she cried it. "For God's sake!"

She felt as though the bed were heaving under her and her feet were entangled in the bed-clothes. Pyotr Dmitritch, in his dressing-gown, with a candle in his hand, came into the bedroom.

"Olya, hush!" he said.

She raised herself, and kneeling up in bed, screwing up her eyes at the light, articulated through her sobs:

"Understand . . . understand! . . ."

She wanted to tell him that she was tired to death by the party, by his falsity, by her own falsity, that it had all worked together, but she could only articulate:

"Understand . . . understand!"

"Come, drink!" he said, handing her some water.

She took the glass obediently and began drinking, but the water splashed over and was spilt on her arms, her throat and knees.

"I must look horribly unseemly," she thought.

Pyotr Dmitritch put her back in bed without a word, and covered her with the quilt, then he took the candle and went out.

"For God's sake!" Olga Mihalovna cried again. "Pyotr, understand, understand!"

Suddenly something gripped her in the lower part of her body and back with such violence that her wailing was cut short, and she bit the pillow from the pain. But the pain let her go again at once, and she began sobbing again.

The maid came in, and arranging the quilt over her, asked in alarm:

"Mistress, darling, what is the matter?"

"Go out of the room," said Pyotr Dmitritch sternly, going up to the bed.

"Understand . . . understand! . . ." Olga Mihalovna began.

"Olya, I entreat you, calm yourself," he said. "I did not mean to hurt you. I would not have gone out of the room if I had known it would have hurt you so much; I simply felt depressed. I tell you, on my honour . . ."

"Understand! . . . You were lying, I was lying. . . ."

"I understand. . . . Come, come, that's enough! I understand," said

Pyotr Dmitritch tenderly, sitting down on her bed. "You said that in anger; I quite understand. I swear to God I love you beyond anything on earth, and when I married you I never once thought of your being rich. I loved you immensely, and that's all . . . I assure you. I have never been in want of money or felt the value of it, and so I cannot feel the difference between your fortune and mine. It always seemed to me we were equally well off. And that I have been deceitful in little things, that . . . of course, is true. My life has hitherto been arranged in such a frivolous way that it has somehow been impossible to get on without paltry lying. It weighs on me, too, now. . . . Let us leave off talking about it, for goodness' sake!"

Olga Mihalovna again felt in acute pain, and clutched her husband by the sleeve.

"I am in pain, in pain, in pain . . ." she said rapidly. "Oh, what pain!"

"Damnation take those visitors!" muttered Pyotr Dmitritch, getting up. "You ought not to have gone to the island to-day!" he cried. "What an idiot I was not to prevent you! Oh, my God!"

He scratched his head in vexation, and, with a wave of his hand, walked out of the room.

Then he came into the room several times, sat down on the bed beside her, and talked a great deal, sometimes tenderly, sometimes angrily, but she hardly heard him. Her sobs were continually interrupted by fearful attacks of pain, and each time the pain was more acute and prolonged. At first she held her breath and bit the pillow during the pain, but then she began screaming on an unseemly piercing note. Once seeing her husband near her, she remembered that she had insulted him, and without pausing to think whether it were really Pyotr Dmitritch or whether she were in delirium, clutched his hand in both hers and began kissing it.

"You were lying, I was lying . . ." she began justifying herself. "Understand, understand. . . . They have exhausted me, driven me out of all patience."

"Olya, we are not alone," said Pyotr Dmitritch.

Olga Mihalovna raised her head and saw Varvara, who was kneeling by the chest of drawers and pulling out the bottom drawer. The top drawers were already open. Then Varvara got up, red from the strained position, and with a cold, solemn face began trying to unlock a box.

"Marya, I can't unlock it!" she said in a whisper. "You unlock it, won't you?"

Marya, the maid, was digging a candle end out of the candlestick with a pair of scissors, so as to put in a new candle; she went up to Varvara and helped her to unlock the box.

"There should be nothing locked . . ." whispered Varvara. "Unlock this basket, too, my good girl. Master," she said, "you should send to Father Mihail to unlock the holy gates! You must!"

"Do what you like," said Pyotr Dmitritch, breathing hard, "only, for God's sake, make haste and fetch the doctor or the midwife! Has Vassily gone? Send some one else. Send your husband!"

"It's the birth," Olga Mihalovna thought. "Varvara," she moaned, "but he won't be born alive!"

"It's all right, it's all right, mistress," whispered Varvara. "Please God, he will be alive! he will be alive!"

When Olga Mihalovna came to herself again after a pain she was no longer sobbing nor tossing from side to side, but moaning. She could not refrain from moaning even in the intervals between the pains. The candles were still burning, but the morning light was coming through the blinds. It was probably about five o'clock in the morning. At the round table there was sitting some unknown woman with a very discreet air, wearing a white apron. From her whole appearance it was evident she had been sitting there a long time. Olga Mihalovna guessed that she was the midwife.

"Will it soon be over?" she asked, and in her voice she heard a peculiar and unfamiliar note which had never been there before. "I must be dying in childbirth," she thought.

Pyotr Dmitritch came cautiously into the bedroom, dressed for the day, and stood at the window with his back to his wife. He lifted the blind and looked out of window.

"What rain!" he said.

"What time is it?" asked Olga Mihalovna, in order to hear the unfamiliar note in her voice again.

"A quarter to six," answered the midwife.

"And what if I really am dying?" thought Olga Mihalovna, looking at her husband's head and the window-panes on which the rain was beating. "How will he live without me? With whom will he have tea and dinner, talk in the evenings, sleep?"

And he seemed to her like a forlorn child; she felt sorry for him and wanted to say something nice, caressing and consolatory. She remembered how in the spring he had meant to buy himself some harriers, and she, thinking it a cruel and dangerous sport, had prevented him from doing it.

"Pyotr, buy yourself harriers," she moaned.

He dropped the blind and went up to the bed, and would have said something; but at that moment the pain came back, and Olga Mihalovna uttered an unseemly, piercing scream.

The pain and the constant screaming and moaning stupefied her. She heard, saw, and sometimes spoke, but hardly understood anything, and was only conscious that she was in pain or was just going to be in pain. It seemed to her that the name-day party had been long, long ago—not yesterday, but a year ago perhaps; and that her new life of agony had lasted longer than her childhood, her school-days, her time at the University, and her marriage, and would go on for a long, long time, endlessly. She saw them bring tea to the midwife, and summon her at midday to lunch and afterwards to dinner; she saw Pyotr Dmitritch grow used to coming in, standing for long intervals by the window, and going out again; saw strange men, the maid, Varvara, come in as though they were at home.... Varvara said nothing but, "He will, he will," and was angry when any one closed the drawers and the chest. Olga Mihalovna saw the light change in the room and in the windows: at one time it was twilight, then thick like fog, then bright daylight as it had been at dinner-time the day before, then again twilight... and each of these changes lasted as long as her childhood, her school-days, her life at the University....

In the evening two doctors—one bony, bald, with a big red beard; the other with a swarthy Jewish face and cheap spectacles—performed some sort of operation on Olga Mihalovna. To these unknown men touching her body she felt utterly indifferent. By now she had no feeling of shame, no will, and any one might do what he would with her. If any one had rushed at her with a knife, or had insulted Pyotr Dmitritch, or had robbed her of her right to the little creature, she would not have said a word.

They gave her chloroform during the operation. When she came to again, the pain was still there and insufferable. It was night. And Olga Mihalovna remembered that there had been just such a night with the stillness, the lamp, with the midwife sitting motionless by the bed, with the drawers of the chest pulled out, with Pyotr Dmitritch standing by the window, but some time very, very long ago. . . .

V

"I am not dead . . ." thought Olga Mihalovna when she began to understand her surroundings again, and when the pain was over.

A bright summer day looked in at the widely open windows; in the garden below the windows, the sparrows and the magpies never ceased chattering for one instant.

The drawers were shut now, her husband's bed had been made. There was no sign of the midwife or of the maid, or of Varvara in the room, only Pyotr Dmitritch was standing, as before, motionless by the window looking into the garden. There was no sound of a child's crying, no one was congratulating her or rejoicing, it was evident that the little creature had not been born alive.

"Pyotr!"

Olga Mihalovna called to her husband.

Pyotr Dmitritch looked round. It seemed as though a long time must have passed since the last guest had departed and Olga Mihalovna had insulted her husband, for Pyotr Dmitritch was perceptibly thinner and hollow-eyed.

"What is it?" he asked, coming up to the bed.

He looked away, moved his lips and smiled with childlike helplessness.

"Is it all over?" asked Olga Mihalovna.

Pyotr Dmitritch tried to make some answer, but his lips quivered and his mouth worked like a toothless old man's, like Uncle Nikolay Nikolaitch's.

"Olya," he said, wringing his hands; big tears suddenly dropping from his eyes. "Olya, I don't care about your property qualification, nor the Circuit Courts . . ." (he gave a sob) "nor particular views, nor those visitors, nor your fortune. . . . I don't care about anything! Why didn't we take care of our child? Oh, it's no good talking!"

With a despairing gesture he went out of the bedroom.

But nothing mattered to Olga Mihalovna now, there was a mistiness in her brain from the chloroform, an emptiness in her soul. . . . The dull indifference to life which had overcome her when the two doctors were performing the operation still had possession of her.

The Shoemaker and the Devil

It was Christmas Eve. Marya had long been snoring on the stove; all the paraffin in the little lamp had burnt out, but Fyodor Nilov still sat at work. He would long ago have flung aside his work and gone out into the street, but a customer from Kolokolny Lane, who had a fortnight before ordered some boots, had been in the previous day, had abused him roundly, and had ordered him to finish the boots at once before the morning service.

"It's a convict's life!" Fyodor grumbled as he worked. "Some people have been asleep long ago, others are enjoying themselves, while you sit here like some Cain and sew for the devil knows whom. . . ."

To save himself from accidentally falling asleep, he kept taking a bottle from under the table and drinking out of it, and after every pull at it he twisted his head and said aloud:

"What is the reason, kindly tell me, that customers enjoy themselves while I am forced to sit and work for them? Because they have money and I am a beggar?"

He hated all his customers, especially the one who lived in Kolokolny Lane. He was a gentleman of gloomy appearance, with long hair, a yellow face, blue spectacles, and a husky voice. He had a German name which one could not pronounce. It was impossible to tell what was his calling and what he did. When, a fortnight before, Fyodor had gone to take his measure, he, the customer, was sitting on the floor pounding something in a mortar. Before Fyodor had time to say good-morning the contents of the mortar suddenly flared up and burned with a bright red flame; there was a stink of sulphur and burnt feathers, and the room was filled with a thick pink smoke, so that Fyodor sneezed five times; and as he returned home afterwards, he thought: "Anyone who feared God would not have anything to do with things like that."

When there was nothing left in the bottle Fyodor put the boots on the table and sank into thought. He leaned his heavy head on his fist and began thinking of his poverty, of his hard life with no glimmer of light in it. Then he thought of the rich, of their big houses and their carriages, of their hundred-rouble notes. . . . How nice it would be if the houses of these rich men—the devil flay them!—were smashed, if their horses died, if their fur coats and sable caps got shabby! How splendid it would be if the rich, little by little, changed into beggars having nothing, and he, a poor shoemaker, were to become rich, and were to lord it over some other poor shoemaker on Christmas Eve.

Dreaming like this, Fyodor suddenly thought of his work, and opened his eyes.

"Here's a go," he thought, looking at the boots. "The job has been finished ever so long ago, and I go on sitting here. I must take the boots to the gentleman."

He wrapped up the work in a red handkerchief, put on his things, and went out into the street. A fine hard snow was falling, pricking the face as though with needles. It was cold, slippery, dark, the gas-lamps burned dimly, and for some reason there was a smell of paraffin in the street, so that Fyodor coughed and cleared his throat. Rich men were driving to and fro on the road, and every rich man had a ham and a bottle of vodka in his hands. Rich young ladies peeped at Fyodor out of the carriages and sledges, put out their tongues and shouted, laughing:

"Beggar! Beggar!"

Students, officers, and merchants walked behind Fyodor, jeering at him and crying:

"Drunkard! Drunkard! Infidel cobbler! Soul of a boot-leg! Beggar!"

All this was insulting, but Fyodor held his tongue and only spat in disgust. But when Kuzma Lebyodkin from Warsaw, a master-bootmaker, met him and said: "I've married a rich woman and I have men working under me, while you are a beggar and have nothing to eat," Fyodor could not refrain from running after him. He pursued him till he found himself in Kolokolny Lane. His customer lived in the fourth house from the corner on the very top floor. To reach him one had to go through a long, dark courtyard, and then to climb up a very high slippery stair-case which tottered under one's feet. When Fyodor went in to him he was sitting on the floor pounding something in a mortar, just as he had been the fortnight before.

"Your honor, I have brought your boots," said Fyodor sullenly.

The customer got up and began trying on the boots in silence. Desiring to help him, Fyodor went down on one knee and pulled off his old boot, but at once jumped up and staggered towards the door in horror. The customer had not a foot, but a hoof like a horse's.

"Aha!" thought Fyodor; "here's a go!"

The first thing should have been to cross himself, then to leave everything and run downstairs; but he immediately reflected that he was meeting a devil for the first and probably the last time, and not to take advantage of his services would be foolish. He controlled himself and determined to try his luck. Clasping his hands behind him to avoid making the sign of the cross, he coughed respectfully and began:

"They say that there is nothing on earth more evil and impure than the devil, but I am of the opinion, your honor, that the devil is highly educated. He has—excuse my saying it—hoofs and a tail behind, but he has more brains than many a student."

"I like you for what you say," said the devil, flattered. "Thank you, shoemaker! What do you want?"

And without loss of time the shoemaker began complaining of his lot. He began by saying that from his childhood up he had envied the rich. He had always resented it that all people did not live alike in big houses and drive with good horses. Why, he asked, was he poor? How was he worse than Kuzma Lebyodkin from Warsaw, who had his own house, and whose wife wore a hat? He had the same sort of nose, the same hands, feet, head, and back, as the rich, and so why was he forced to work when others were enjoying themselves? Why was he married to Marya and not to a lady smelling of scent? He had often seen beautiful young ladies in the houses of rich customers, but they either took no notice of him whatever, or else sometimes laughed and whispered to each other: "What a red nose that shoemaker has!" It was true that Marya was a good, kind, hard-working woman, but she was not educated; her hand was heavy and hit hard, and if one had occasion to speak of politics or anything intellectual before her, she would put her spoke in and talk the most awful nonsense.

"What do you want, then?" his customer interrupted him.

"I beg you, your honor Satan Ivanitch, to be graciously pleased to make me a rich man."

"Certainly. Only for that you must give me up your soul! Before the cocks crow, go and sign on this paper here that you give me up your soul."

"Your honor," said Fyodor politely, "when you ordered a pair of boots from me I did not ask for the money in advance. One has first to carry out the order and then ask for payment."

"Oh, very well!" the customer assented.

A bright flame suddenly flared up in the mortar, a pink thick smoke came puffing out, and there was a smell of burnt feathers and sulphur. When the smoke had subsided, Fyodor rubbed his eyes and saw that he was no longer Fyodor, no longer a shoemaker, but quite a different man, wearing a waistcoat and a watch-chain, in a new pair of trousers, and that he was sitting in an armchair at a big table. Two footmen were handing him dishes, bowing low and saying:

"Kindly eat, your honor, and may it do you good!"

What wealth! The footmen handed him a big piece of roast mutton and a dish of cucumbers, and then brought in a frying-pan a roast goose, and a little afterwards boiled pork with horse-radish cream. And how dignified, how genteel it all was! Fyodor ate, and before each dish drank a big glass of excellent vodka, like some general or some count. After the pork he was handed some boiled grain moistened with goose fat, then an omelette with bacon fat, then fried liver, and he went on eating and was delighted. What more? They served, too, a pie with onion and steamed turnip with kvass.

"How is it the gentry don't burst with such meals?" he thought.

In conclusion they handed him a big pot of honey. After dinner the devil appeared in blue spectacles and asked with a low bow:

"Are you satisfied with your dinner, Fyodor Pantelyeitch?"

But Fyodor could not answer one word, he was so stuffed after his dinner. The feeling of repletion was unpleasant, oppressive, and to distract his thoughts he looked at the boot on his left foot.

"For a boot like that I used not to take less than seven and a half roubles. What shoemaker made it?" he asked.

"Kuzma Lebyodkin," answered the footman.

"Send for him, the fool!"

Kuzma Lebyodkin from Warsaw soon made his appearance. He stopped in a respectful attitude at the door and asked:

"What are your orders, your honor?"

"Hold your tongue!" cried Fyodor, and stamped his foot. "Don't dare to argue; remember your place as a cobbler! Blockhead! You don't know how to make boots! I'll beat your ugly phiz to a jelly! Why have you come?"

"For money."

"What money? Be off! Come on Saturday! Boy, give him a cuff!"

But he at once recalled what a life the customers used to lead him, too, and he felt heavy at heart, and to distract his attention he took a fat pocketbook out of his pocket and began counting his money. There was a great deal of money, but Fyodor wanted more still. The devil in the blue spectacles brought him another notebook fatter still, but he wanted even more; and the more he counted it, the more discontented he became.

In the evening the evil one brought him a full-bosomed lady in a red dress, and said that this was his new wife. He spent the whole evening kissing her and eating gingerbreads, and at night he went to bed on a soft, downy feather-bed, turned from side to side, and could not go to sleep. He felt uncanny.

"We have a great deal of money," he said to his wife; "we must look out or thieves will be breaking in. You had better go and look with a candle."

He did not sleep all night, and kept getting up to see if his box was all right. In the morning he had to go to church to matins. In church the same honor is done to rich and poor alike. When Fyodor was poor he used to pray in church like this: "God, forgive me, a sinner!" He said the same thing now though he had become rich. What difference was there? And after death Fyodor rich would not be buried in gold, not in diamonds, but in the same black earth as the poorest beggar. Fyodor would burn in the same fire as cobblers. Fyodor resented all this, and, too, he felt weighed down all over by his dinner, and instead of prayer he had all sorts of thoughts in his head about his box of money, about thieves, about his bartered, ruined soul.

He came out of church in a bad temper. To drive away his unpleasant thoughts as he had often done before, he struck up a song at the top of his voice. But as soon as he began a policeman ran up and said, with his fingers to the peak of his cap:

"Your honor, gentlefolk must not sing in the street! You are not a shoemaker!"

Fyodor leaned his back against a fence and fell to thinking: what could he do to amuse himself?

"Your honor," a porter shouted to him, "don't lean against the fence, you will spoil your fur coat!"

Fyodor went into a shop and bought himself the very best concertina, then went out into the street playing it. Everybody pointed at him and laughed.

"And a gentleman, too," the cabmen jeered at him; "like some cobbler. . . ."

"Is it the proper thing for gentlefolk to be disorderly in the street?" a policeman said to him. "You had better go into a tavern!"

"Your honor, give us a trifle, for Christ's sake," the beggars wailed, surrounding Fyodor on all sides.

In earlier days when he was a shoemaker the beggars took no notice of him, now they wouldn't let him pass.

And at home his new wife, the lady, was waiting for him, dressed in a green blouse and a red skirt. He meant to be attentive to her, and had just lifted his arm to give her a good clout on the back, but she said angrily:

"Peasant! Ignorant lout! You don't know how to behave with ladies! If you love me you will kiss my hand; I don't allow you to beat me."

"This is a blasted existence!" thought Fyodor. "People do lead a life! You mustn't sing, you mustn't play the concertina, you mustn't have a lark with a lady. . . . Pfoo!"

He had no sooner sat down to tea with the lady when the evil spirit in the blue spectacles appeared and said:

"Come, Fyodor Pantelyeitch, I have performed my part of the bargain. Now sign your paper and come along with me!"

And he dragged Fyodor to hell, straight to the furnace, and devils flew up from all directions and shouted:

"Fool! Blockhead! Ass!"

There was a fearful smell of paraffin in hell, enough to suffocate one.

And suddenly it all vanished. Fyodor opened his eyes and saw his table, the boots, and the tin lamp. The lamp-glass was black, and from the faint light on the wick came clouds of stinking smoke as from a chimney. Near the table stood the customer in the blue spectacles, shouting angrily:

"Fool! Blockhead! Ass! I'll give you a lesson, you scoundrel! You took the order a fortnight ago and the boots aren't ready yet! Do you suppose I want to come traipsing round here half a dozen times a day for my boots? You wretch! you brute!"

Fyodor shook his head and set to work on the boots. The customer went on swearing and threatening him for a long time. At last when he subsided, Fyodor asked sullenly:

"And what is your occupation, sir?"

"I make Bengal lights and fireworks. I am a pyrotechnician."

They began ringing for matins. Fyodor gave the customer the boots, took the money for them, and went to church.

Carriages and sledges with bearskin rugs were dashing to and fro in the street; merchants, ladies, officers were walking along the pavement together with the humbler folk. . . . But Fyodor did not envy them nor repine at his lot. It seemed to him now that rich and poor were equally badly off. Some were able to drive in a carriage, and others to sing songs at the top of their voice and to play the concertina, but one and the same thing, the same grave, was awaiting all alike, and there was nothing in life for which one would give the devil even a tiny scrap of one's soul.

The Bet

I

It was a dark autumn night. The old banker was walking up and down his study and remembering how, fifteen years before, he had given a party one autumn evening. There had been many clever men there, and there had been interesting conversations. Among other things they had talked of capital punishment. The majority of the guests, among whom were many journalists and intellectual men, disapproved of the death penalty. They considered that form of punishment out of date, immoral, and unsuitable for Christian States. In the opinion of some of them the death penalty ought to be replaced everywhere by imprisonment for life.

"I don't agree with you," said their host the banker. "I have not tried either the death penalty or imprisonment for life, but if one may judge *à priori,* the death penalty is more moral and more humane than imprisonment for life. Capital punishment kills a man at once, but lifelong imprisonment kills him slowly. Which executioner is the more humane, he who kills you in a few minutes or he who drags the life out of you in the course of many years?"

"Both are equally immoral," observed one of the guests, "for they both have the same object—to take away life. The State is not God. It has not the right to take away what it cannot restore when it wants to."

Among the guests was a young lawyer, a young man of five-and-twenty. When he was asked his opinion, he said:

"The death sentence and the life sentence are equally immoral, but if I had to choose between the death penalty and imprisonment for life, I would certainly choose the second. To live anyhow is better than not at all."

A lively discussion arose. The banker, who was younger and more nervous in those days, was suddenly carried away by excitement; he struck the table with his fist and shouted at the young man:

"It's not true! I'll bet you two millions you wouldn't stay in solitary confinement for five years."

"If you mean that in earnest," said the young man, "I'll take the bet, but I would stay not five but fifteen years."

"Fifteen? Done!" cried the banker. "Gentlemen, I stake two millions!"

"Agreed! You stake your millions and I stake my freedom!" said the young man.

And this wild, senseless bet was carried out! The banker, spoilt and frivolous, with millions beyond his reckoning, was delighted at the bet. At supper he made fun of the young man, and said:

"Think better of it, young man, while there is still time. To me two millions are a trifle, but you are losing three or four of the best years of your life. I say three or four, because you won't stay longer. Don't forget either, you unhappy man, that voluntary confinement is a great deal harder to bear than compulsory. The thought that you have the right to step out in liberty at any moment will poison your whole existence in prison. I am sorry for you."

And now the banker, walking to and fro, remembered all this, and asked himself: "What was the object of that bet? What is the good of that man's losing fifteen years of his life and my throwing away two millions? Can it prove that the death penalty is better or worse than imprisonment for life? No, no. It was all nonsensical and meaningless. On my part it was the caprice of a pampered man, and on his part simple greed for money. . . ."

Then he remembered what followed that evening. It was decided that the young man should spend the years of his captivity under the strictest supervision in one of the lodges in the banker's garden. It was agreed that for fifteen years he should not be free to cross the threshold of the lodge, to see human beings, to hear the human voice, or to receive letters and newspapers. He was allowed to have a musical instrument and books, and was allowed to write letters, to drink wine, and to smoke. By the terms of the agreement, the only relations he could have with the outer world were by a little window made purposely for that object. He might have anything he wanted—books, music, wine, and so on—in any quantity he desired by writing an order, but could only receive them through the window. The agreement provided for every detail and every trifle that would make his imprisonment strictly solitary, and bound the young man to stay there *exactly* fifteen years, beginning from twelve o'clock of November 14, 1870, and ending at twelve o'clock of November 14, 1885. The slighest attempt on his part to break the conditions, if only two minutes before the end, released the banker from the obligation to pay him two millions.

For the first year of his confinement, as far as one could judge from his brief notes, the prisoner suffered severely from loneliness and depression. The sounds of the piano could be heard continually day and night from his lodge. He refused wine and tobacco. Wine, he wrote, excites the desires, and desires are the worst foes of the prisoner; and besides, nothing could be more dreary than drinking good wine and seeing no one. And tobacco spoilt the air of his room. In the first year the books he sent for were principally of a light character; novels with a complicated love plot, sensational and fantastic stories, and so on.

In the second year the piano was silent in the lodge, and the prisoner asked only for the classics. In the fifth year music was audible again, and the prisoner asked for wine. Those who watched him through the window said that all that year he spent doing nothing but eating and drinking and lying on his bed, frequently yawning and angrily talking to himself. He did not read books. Sometimes at night he would sit down to write; he would spend hours writing, and in the morning tear up all that he had written. More than once he could be heard crying.

In the second half of the sixth year the prisoner began zealously studying languages, philosophy, and history. He threw himself eagerly into these studies—so much so that the banker had enough to do to get him the books he ordered. In the course of four years some six hundred volumes were procured at his request. It was during this period that the banker received the following letter from his prisoner:

"My dear Jailer, I write you these lines in six languages. Show them to people who know the languages. Let them read them. If they find not one mistake I implore you to fire a shot in the garden. That shot will show me that my efforts have not been thrown away. The geniuses of all ages and of all lands speak different languages, but the same flame burns in them all. Oh, if you only knew what unearthly happiness my soul feels now from being able to understand them!" The prisoner's desire was fulfilled. The banker ordered two shots to be fired in the garden.

Then after the tenth year, the prisoner sat immovably at the table and read nothing but the Gospel. It seemed strange to the banker that a man who in four years had mastered six hundred learned volumes should waste nearly a year over one thin book easy of comprehension. Theology and histories of religion followed the Gospels.

In the last two years of his confinement the prisoner read an immense quantity of books quite indiscriminately. At one time he was busy with the natural sciences, then he would ask for Byron or Shakespeare. There were notes in which he demanded at the same time books on chemistry, and a manual of medicine, and a novel, and some treatise on philosophy or theology. His reading suggested a man swimming in the sea among the wreckage of his ship, and trying to save his life by greedily clutching first at one spar and then at another.

II

The old banker remembered all this, and thought:

"To-morrow at twelve o'clock he will regain his freedom. By our agreement I ought to pay him two millions. If I do pay him, it is all over with me: I shall be utterly ruined."

Fifteen years before, his millions had been beyond his reckoning;

now he was afraid to ask himself which were greater, his debts or his assets. Desperate gambling on the Stock Exchange, wild speculation, and the excitability which he could not get over even in advancing years, had by degrees led to the decline of his fortune, and the proud, fearless, self-confident millionaire had become a banker of middling rank, trembling at every rise and fall in his investments. "Cursed bet!" muttered the old man, clutching his head in despair. "Why didn't the man die? He is only forty now. He will take my last penny from me, he will marry, will enjoy life, will gamble on the Exchange; while I shall look at him with envy like a beggar, and hear from him every day the same sentence: 'I am indebted to you for the happiness of my life, let me help you!' No, it is too much! The one means of being saved from bankruptcy and disgrace is the death of that man!"

It struck three o'clock, the banker listened; everyone was asleep in the house, and nothing could be heard outside but the rustling of the chilled trees. Trying to make no noise, he took from a fireproof safe the key of the door which had not been opened for fifteen years, put on his overcoat, and went out of the house.

It was dark and cold in the garden. Rain was falling. A damp cutting wind was racing about the garden, howling and giving the trees no rest. The banker strained his eyes, but could see neither the earth nor the white statues, nor the lodge, nor the trees. Going to the spot where the lodge stood, he twice called the watchman. No answer followed. Evidently the watchman had sought shelter from the weather, and was now asleep somewhere either in the kitchen or in the greenhouse.

"If I had the pluck to carry out my intention," thought the old man, "suspicion would fall first upon the watchman."

He felt in the darkness for the steps and the door, and went into the entry of the lodge. Then he groped his way into a little passage and lighted a match. There was not a soul there. There was a bedstead with no bedding on it, and in the corner there was a dark cast-iron stove. The seals on the door leading to the prisoner's rooms were intact.

When the match went out the old man, trembling with emotion, peeped through the little window. A candle was burning dimly in the prisoner's room. He was sitting at the table. Nothing could be seen but his back, the hair on his head, and his hands. Open books were lying on the table, on the two easy-chairs, and on the carpet near the table.

Five minutes passed and the prisoner did not once stir. Fifteen years' imprisonment had taught him to sit still. The banker tapped at the window with his finger, and the prisoner made no movement whatever in response. Then the banker cautiously broke the seals off the door and put the key in the keyhole. The rusty lock gave a grating sound and the door creaked. The banker expected to hear at once footsteps and a cry of astonishment, but three minutes passed and it was as quiet as ever in the room. He made up his mind to go in.

At the table a man unlike ordinary people was sitting motionless. He was a skeleton with the skin drawn tight over his bones, with long curls like a woman's, and a shaggy beard. His face was yellow with an earthy tint in it, his cheeks were hollow, his back long and narrow, and the hand on which his shaggy head was propped was so thin and delicate that it was dreadful to look at it. His hair was already streaked with silver, and seeing his emaciated, aged-looking face, no one would have believed that he was only forty. He was asleep. . . . In front of his bowed head there lay on the table a sheet of paper on which there was something written in fine handwriting.

"Poor creature!" thought the banker, "he is asleep and most likely dreaming of the millions. And I have only to take this half-dead man, throw him on the bed, stifle him a little with the pillow, and the most conscientious expert would find no sign of a violent death. But let us first read what he has written here. . . ."

The banker took the page from the table and read as follows:

"To-morrow at twelve o'clock I regain my freedom and the right to associate with other men, but before I leave this room and see the sunshine, I think it necessary to say a few words to you. With a clear conscience I tell you, as before God, who beholds me, that I despise freedom and life and health, and all that in your books is called the good things of the world.

"For fifteen years I have been intently studying earthly life. It is true I have not seen the earth nor men, but in your books I have drunk fragrant wine, I have sung songs, I have hunted stags and wild boars in the forests, have loved women. . . . Beauties as ethereal as clouds, created by the magic of your poets and geniuses, have visited me at night, and have whispered in my ears wonderful tales that have set my brain in a whirl. In your books I have climbed to the peaks of Elburz and Mont Blanc, and from there I have seen the sun rise and have watched it at evening flood the sky, the ocean, and the mountain-tops with gold and crimson. I have watched from there the lightning flashing over my head and cleaving the storm-clouds. I have seen green forests, fields, rivers, lakes, towns. I have heard the singing of the sirens, and the strains of the shepherds' pipes; I have touched the wings of comely devils who flew down to converse with me of God. . . . In your books I have flung myself into the bottomless pit, performed miracles, slain, burned towns, preached new religions, conquered whole kingdoms. . . .

"Your books have given me wisdom. All that the unresting thought of man has created in the ages is compressed into a small compass in my brain. I know that I am wiser than all of you.

"And I despise your books, I despise wisdom and the blessings of this world. It is all worthless, fleeting, illusory, and deceptive, like a mirage. You may be proud, wise, and fine, but death will wipe you off the face of the earth as though you were no more than mice burrowing under the floor, and your posterity, your history, your immortal geniuses will burn or freeze together with the earthly globe.

"You have lost your reason and taken the wrong path. You have taken lies for truth, and hideousness for beauty. You would marvel if, owing to strange events of some sorts, frogs and lizards suddenly grew on apple and orange trees instead of fruit, or if roses began to smell like a sweating horse; so I marvel at you who exchange heaven for earth. I don't want to understand you.

"To prove to you in action how I despise all that you live by, I renounce the two millions of which I once dreamed as of paradise and which now I despise. To deprive myself of the right to the money I shall go out from here five hours before the time fixed, and so break the compact. . . ."

When the banker had read this he laid the page on the table, kissed the strange man on the head, and went out of the lodge, weeping. At no other time, even when he had lost heavily on the Stock Exchange, had he felt so great a contempt for himself. When he got home he lay on his bed, but his tears and emotion kept him for hours from sleeping.

Next morning the watchmen ran in with pale faces, and told him they had seen the man who lived in the lodge climb out of the window into the garden, go to the gate, and disappear. The banker went at once with the servants to the lodge and made sure of the flight of his prisoner. To avoid arousing unnecessary talk, he took from the table the writing in which the millions were renounced, and when he got home locked it up in the fireproof safe.

A Nervous Breakdown

I

A medical student called Mayer, and a pupil of the Moscow School of Painting, Sculpture, and Architecture called Rybnikov, went one evening to see their friend Vassilyev, a law student, and suggested that he should go with them to S. Street. For a long time Vassilyev would not consent to go, but in the end he put on his greatcoat and went with them.

He knew nothing of fallen women except by hearsay and from books, and he had never in his life been in the houses in which they live. He knew that there are immoral women who, under the pressure of fatal circumstances—environment, bad education, poverty, and so on—are forced to sell their honor for money. They know nothing of pure love, have no children, have no civil rights; their mothers and sisters weep over them as though they were dead, science treats of them as an evil, men address them with contemptuous familiarity. But in spite of all that, they do not lose the semblance and image of God. They all acknowledge their sin and hope for salvation. Of the means that lead to salvation they can avail themselves to the fullest extent. Society, it is true, will not forgive people their past, but in the sight of God St. Mary of Egypt is no lower than the other saints. When it had happened to Vassilyev in the street to recognize a fallen woman as such, by her dress or her manners, or to see a picture of one in a comic paper, he always remembered a story he had once read: a young man, pure and self-sacrificing, loves a fallen woman and urges her to become his wife; she, considering herself unworthy of such happiness, takes poison.

Vassilyev lived in one of the side streets turning out of Tverskoy Boulevard. When he came out of the house with his two friends it was about eleven o'clock. The first snow had not long fallen, and all nature was under the spell of the fresh snow. There was the smell of snow in the air, the snow crunched softly under the feet; the earth, the roofs, the trees, the seats on the boulevard, everything was soft, white, young, and this made the houses look quite different from the day before; the street lamps burned more brightly, the air was more transparent, the carriages rumbled with a deeper note, and with the fresh, light, frosty air a feeling stirred in the soul akin to the white, youthful, feathery snow. "Against my will an unknown force," hummed the medical student in his agreeable tenor, "has led me to these mournful shores."

"Behold the mill . . ." the artist seconded him, "in ruins now. . . ."

"Behold the mill . . . in ruins now," the medical student repeated, raising his eyebrows and shaking his head mournfully.

He paused, rubbed his forehead, trying to remember the words, and then sang aloud, so well that passers-by looked round:

> "Here in old days when I was free,
> Love, free, unfettered, greeted me."

The three of them went into a restaurant and, without taking off their greatcoats, drank a couple of glasses of vodka each. Before drinking the second glass, Vassilyev noticed a bit of cork in his vodka, raised the glass to his eyes, and gazed into it for a long time, screwing up his shortsighted eyes. The medical student did not understand his expression, and said:

"Come, why look at it? No philosophizing, please. Vodka is given us to be drunk, sturgeon to be eaten, women to be visited, snow to be walked upon. For one evening anyway live like a human being!"

"But I haven't said anything . . ." said Vassilyev, laughing. "Am I refusing to?"

There was a warmth inside him from the vodka. He looked with softened feelings at his friends, admired them and envied them. In these strong, healthy, cheerful people how wonderfully balanced everything is, how finished and smooth is everything in their minds and souls! They sing, and have a passion for the theatre, and draw, and talk a great deal, and drink, and they don't have headaches the day after; they are both poetical and debauched, both soft and hard; they can work, too, and be indignant, and laugh without reason, and talk nonsense; they are warm, honest, self-sacrificing, and as men are in no way inferior to himself, Vassilyev, who watched over every step he took and every word he uttered, who was fastidious and cautious, and ready to raise every trifle to the level of a problem. And he longed for one evening to live as his friends did, to open out, to let himself loose from his own control. If vodka had to be drunk, he would drink it, though his head would be splitting next morning. If he were taken to the women he would go. He would laugh, play the fool, gaily respond to the passing advances of strangers in the street. . . .

He went out of the restaurant laughing. He liked his friends—one in a crushed broad-brimmed hat, with an affectation of artistic untidiness; the other in a sealskin cap, a man not poor, though he affected to belong to the Bohemia of learning. He liked the snow, the pale street lamps, the sharp black tracks left in the first snow by the feet of the passersby. He liked the air, and especially that limpid, tender, naïve, as it were virginal tone, which can be seen in nature only twice in the year—when everything is covered with snow, and in spring on bright days and moonlight evenings when the ice breaks on the river.

"Against my will an unknown force,
Has led me to these mournful shores,"

he hummed in an undertone.

And the tune for some reason haunted him and his friends all the way, and all three of them hummed it mechanically, not in time with one another.

Vassilyev's imagination was picturing how, in another ten minutes, he and his friends would knock at a door; how by little dark passages and dark rooms they would steal in to the women; how, taking advantage of the darkness, he would strike a match, would light up and see the face of a martyr and a guilty smile. The unknown, fair or dark, would certainly have her hair down and be wearing a white dressing-jacket; she would be panic-stricken by the light, would be fearfully confused, and would say: "For God's sake, what are you doing! Put it out!" It would all be dreadful, but interesting and new.

II

The friends turned out of Trubnoy Square into Gratchevka, and soon reached the side street which Vassilyev only knew by reputation. Seeing two rows of houses with brightly lighted windows and wide-open doors, and hearing gay strains of pianos and violins, sounds which floated out from every door and mingled in a strange chaos, as though an unseen orchestra were tuning up in the darkness above the roofs, Vassilyev was surprised and said:

"What a lot of houses!"

"That's nothing," said the medical student. "In London there are ten times as many. There are about a hundred thousand such women there."

The cabmen were sitting on their boxes as calmly and indifferently as in any other side street; the same passers-by were walking along the pavement as in other streets. No one was hurrying, no one was hiding his face in his coat-collar, no one shook his head reproachfully.... And in this indifference to the noisy chaos of pianos and violins, to the bright windows and wide-open doors, there was a feeling of something very open, insolent, reckless, and devil-may-care. Probably it was as gay and noisy at the slave-markets in their day, and people's faces and movements showed the same indifference.

"Let us begin from the beginning," said the artist.

The friends went into a narrow passage lighted by a lamp with a reflector. When they opened the door a man in a black coat, with an unshaven face like a flunkey's, and sleepy-looking eyes, got up lazily from a yellow sofa in the hall. The place smelt like a laundry with an odor of vinegar in addition. A door from the hall led into a brightly lighted room. The medical student and the artist stopped at this door and, craning their necks, peeped into the room.

"Buona sera, signori, rigolleto—hugenotti—traviata!" began the artist, with a theatrical bow.

"Havanna—tarakano—pistoleto!" said the medical student, pressing his cap to his breast and bowing low.

Vassilyev was standing behind them. He would have liked to make a theatrical bow and say something silly, too, but he only smiled, felt an awkwardness that was like shame, and waited impatiently for what would happen next.

A little fair girl of seventeen or eighteen, with short hair, in a short light-blue frock with a bunch of white ribbon on her bosom, appeared in the doorway.

"Why do you stand at the door?" she said. "Take off your coats and come into the drawing-room."

The medical student and the artist, still talking Italian, went into the drawing-room. Vassilyev followed them irresolutely.

"Gentlemen, take off your coats!" the flunkey said sternly; "you can't go in like that."

In the drawing-room there was, besides the girl, another woman, very stout and tall, with a foreign face and bare arms. She was sitting near the piano, laying out a game of patience on her lap. She took no notice whatever of the visitors.

"Where are the other young ladies?" asked the medical student.

"They are having their tea," said the fair girl. "Stepan," she called, "go and tell the young ladies some students have come!"

A little later a third young lady came into the room. She was wearing a bright red dress with blue stripes. Her face was painted thickly and unskillfully, her brow was hidden under her hair, and there was an unblinking, frightened stare in her eyes. As she came in, she began at once singing some song in a coarse, powerful contralto. After her a fourth appeared, and after her a fifth. . . .

In all this Vassilyev saw nothing new or interesting. It seemed to him that that room, the piano, the looking-glass in its cheap gilt frame, the bunch of white ribbon, the dress with the blue stripes, and the blank indifferent faces, he had seen before and more than once. Of the darkness, the silence, the secrecy, the guilty smile, of all that he had expected to meet here and had dreaded, he saw no trace.

Everything was ordinary, prosaic, and uninteresting. Only one thing faintly stirred his curiosity—the terrible, as it were intentionally designed, bad taste which was visible in the cornices, in the absurd pictures, in the dresses, in the bunch of ribbons. There was something characteristic and peculiar in this bad taste.

"How poor and stupid it all is!" thought Vassilyev. "What is there in all this trumpery I see now that can tempt a normal man and excite him to commit the horrible sin of buying a human being for a rouble? I understand any sin for the sake of splendor, beauty, grace, passion, taste; but what is there here? What is there here worth sinning for? But . . . one mustn't think!"

"Beardy, treat me to some porter!" said the fair girl, addressing him.

Vassilyev was at once overcome with confusion.

"With pleasure," he said, bowing politely. "Only excuse me, madam, I . . . I won't drink with you. I don't drink."

Five minutes later the friends went off into another house.

"Why did you ask for porter?" said the medical student angrily. "What a millionaire! You have thrown away six roubles for no reason whatever—simply waste!"

"If she wants it, why not let her have the pleasure?" said Vassilyev, justifying himself.

"You did not give pleasure to her, but to the 'Madam.' They are told to ask the visitors to stand them treat because it is a profit to the keeper."

"Behold the mill . . ." hummed the artist, "in ruins now. . . ."

Going into the next house, the friends stopped in the hall and did not go into the drawing-room. Here, as in the first house, a figure in a black coat, with a sleepy face like a flunkey's, got up from a sofa in the hall. Looking at this flunkey, at his face and his shabby black coat, Vassilyev thought: "What must an ordinary simple Russian have gone through before fate flung him down as a flunkey here? Where had he been before and what had he done? What was awaiting him? Was he married? Where was his mother, and did she know that he was a servant here?" And Vassilyev could not help particularly noticing the flunkey in each house. In one of the houses—he thought it was the fourth—there was a little spare, frail-looking flunkey with a watch-chain on his waistcoat. He was reading a newspaper, and took no notice of them when they went in. Looking at his face Vassilyev, for some reason, thought that a man with such a face might steal, might murder, might bear false witness. But the face was really interesting: a big forehead, gray eyes, a little flattened nose, thin compressed lips, and a blankly stupid and at the same time insolent expression like that of a young harrier overtaking a hare. Vassilyev thought it would be nice to touch this man's hair, to see whether it was soft or coarse. It must be coarse like a dog's.

III

Having drunk two glasses of porter, the artist became suddenly tipsy and grew unnaturally lively.

"Let's go to another!" he said peremptorily, waving his hands. "I will take you to the best one."

When he had brought his friends to the house which in his opinion was the best, he declared his firm intention of dancing a quadrille. The medical student grumbled something about their having to pay the musicians a rouble, but agreed to be his *vis-à-vis*. They began dancing.

It was just as nasty in the best house as in the worst. Here there were just the same looking-glasses and pictures, the same styles of coiffure and dress. Looking round at the furnishing of the rooms and the costumes, Vassilyev realized that this was not lack of taste, but something that might be called the taste, and even the style, of S. Street, which could not be found elsewhere—something intentional in its ugliness, not accidental, but elaborated in the course of years. After he had been in eight houses he was no longer surprised at the color of the dresses, at the long trains, the gaudy ribbons, the sailor dresses, and the thick purplish rouge on the cheeks; he saw that it all had to be like this, that if a single one of the women had been dressed like a human being, or if there had been one decent engraving on the wall, the general tone of the whole street would have suffered.

"How unskillfully they sell themselves!" he thought. "How can they fail to understand that vice is only alluring when it is beautiful and hidden, when it wears the mask of virtue? Modest black dresses, pale faces, mournful smiles, and darkness would be far more effective than this clumsy tawdriness. Stupid things! If they don't understand it of themselves, their visitors might surely have taught them. . . ."

A young lady in a Polish dress edged with white fur came up to him and sat down beside him.

"You nice dark man, why aren't you dancing?" she asked. "Why are you so dull?"

"Because it is dull."

"Treat me to some Lafitte. Then it won't be dull."

Vassilyev made no answer. He was silent for a little, and then asked:

"What time do you get to sleep?"

"At six o'clock."

"And what time do you get up?"

"Sometimes at two and sometimes at three."

"And what do you do when you get up?"

"We have coffee, and at six o'clock we have dinner."

"And what do you have for dinner?"

"Usually soup, beefsteak, and dessert. Our madam keeps the girls well. But why do you ask all this?"

"Oh, just to talk. . . ."

Vassilyev longed to talk to the young lady about many things. He felt an intense desire to find out where she came from, whether her parents were living, and whether they knew that she was here; how she had come into this house; whether she were cheerful and satisfied, or sad and oppressed by gloomy thoughts; whether she hoped some day to get out of her present position. . . . But he could not think how to begin or in what shape to put his questions so as not to seem impertinent. He thought for a long time, and asked:

"How old are you?"

"Eighty," the young lady jested, looking with a laugh at the antics of the artist as he danced.

All at once she burst out laughing at something, and uttered a long cynical sentence loud enough to be heard by everyone. Vassilyev was aghast, and not knowing how to look, gave a constrained smile. He was the only one who smiled; all the others, his friends, the musicians, the women, did not even glance towards his neighbor, but seemed not to have heard her.

"Stand me some Lafitte," his neighbor said again.

Vassilyev felt a repulsion for her white fur and for her voice, and walked away from her. It seemed to him hot and stifling, and his heart began throbbing slowly but violently, like a hammer—one! two! three!

"Let us go away!" he said, pulling the artist by his sleeve.

"Wait a little; let me finish."

While the artist and the medical student were finishing the quadrille, to avoid looking at the women, Vassilyev scrutinized the musicians. A respectable-looking old man in spectacles, rather like Marshal Bazaine, was playing the piano; a young man with a fair beard, dressed in the latest fashion, was playing the violin. The young man had a face that did not look stupid nor exhausted, but intelligent, youthful, and fresh. He was dressed fancifully and with taste; he played with feeling. It was a mystery how he and the respectable-looking old man had come here. How was it they were not ashamed to sit here? What were they thinking about when they looked at the women?

If the violin and the piano had been played by men in rags, looking hungry, gloomy, drunken, with dissipated or stupid faces, then one could have understood their presence, perhaps. As it was, Vassilyev could not understand it at all. He recalled the story of the fallen woman he had once read, and he thought now that that human figure with the guilty smile had nothing in common with what he was seeing now. It seemed to him that he was seeing not fallen women, but some different world quite apart, alien to him and incomprehensible; if he had seen this world before on the stage, or read of it in a book, he would not have believed in it. . . .

The woman with the white fur burst out laughing again and uttered a loathsome sentence in a loud voice. A feeling of disgust took possession of him. He flushed crimson and went out of the room.

"Wait a minute, we are coming too!" the artist shouted to him.

IV

"While we were dancing," said the medical student, as they all three went out into the street, "I had a conversation with my partner. We talked about her first romance. He, the hero, was an accountant at Smolensk with a wife and five children. She was seventeen, and she lived with her papa and mamma, who sold soap and candles."

"How did he win her heart?" asked Vassilyev.

"By spending fifty roubles on underclothes for her. What next!"

"So he knew how to get his partner's story out of her," thought Vassilyev about the medical student. "But I don't know how to."

"I say, I am going home!" he said.

"What for?"

"Because I don't know how to behave here. Besides, I am bored, disgusted. What is there amusing in it? If they were human beings—but they are savages and animals. I am going; do as you like."

"Come, Grisha, Grigory, darling . . ." said the artist in a tearful voice, hugging Vassilyev, "come along! Let's go to one more together and damnation take them! . . . Please do, Grisha!"

They persuaded Vassilyev and led him up a staircase. In the carpet and the gilt banisters, in the porter who opened the door, and in the panels that decorated the hall, the same S. Street style was apparent, but carried to a greater perfection, more imposing.

"I really will go home!" said Vassilyev as he was taking off his coat.

"Come, come, dear boy," said the artist, and he kissed him on the neck. "Don't be tiresome. . . . Gri-gri, be a good comrade! We came together, we will go back together. What a beast you are, really!"

"I can wait for you in the street. I think it's loathsome, really!"

"Come, come, Grisha. . . . If it is loathsome, you can observe it! Do you understand? You can observe!"

"One must take an objective view of things," said the medical student gravely.

Vassilyev went into the drawing-room and sat down. There were a number of visitors in the room besides him and his friends: two infantry officers, a bald, gray-haired gentleman in spectacles, two beardless youths from the institute of land-surveying, and a very tipsy man who looked like an actor. All the young ladies were taken up with these visitors and paid no attention to Vassilyev.

Only one of them, dressed *à la Aïda,* glanced sideways at him, smiled, and said, yawning: "A dark one has come. . . ."

Vassilyev's heart was throbbing and his face burned. He felt ashamed before these visitors of his presence here, and he felt disgusted and miserable. He was tormented by the thought that he, a decent and loving man (such as he had hitherto considered himself), hated these women and felt nothing but repulsion towards them. He felt pity neither for the women nor the musicians nor the flunkeys.

"It is because I am not trying to understand them," he thought. "They are all more like animals than human beings, but of course they are human beings all the same, they have souls. One must understand them and then judge. . . ."

"Grisha, don't go, wait for us," the artist shouted to him and disappeared.

The medical student disappeared soon after.

"Yes, one must make an effort to understand, one mustn't be like this . . ." Vassilyev went on thinking.

And he began gazing at each of the women with strained attention, looking for a guilty smile. But either he did not know how to read their faces, or not one of these women felt herself to be guilty; he read on every face nothing but a blank expression of everyday vulgar boredom and complacency. Stupid faces, stupid smiles, harsh, stupid voices, insolent movements, and nothing else. Apparently each of them had in the past a romance with an accountant based on underclothes for fifty roubles, and looked for no other charm in the present but coffee, a dinner of three courses, wines, quadrilles, sleeping till two in the afternoon. . . .

Finding no guilty smile, Vassilyev began to look whether there was not one intelligent face. And his attention was caught by one pale, rather sleepy, exhausted-looking face. . . . It was a dark woman, not very young, wearing a dress covered with spangles; she was sitting in an easy-chair, looking at the floor lost in thought. Vassilyev walked from one corner of the room to the other, and, as though casually, sat down beside her.

"I must begin with something trivial," he thought, "and pass to what is serious. . . ."

"What a pretty dress you have," and with his finger he touched the gold fringe of her fichu.

"Oh, is it? . . ." said the dark woman listlessly.

"What province do you come from?"

"I? From a distance. . . . From Tchernigov."

"A fine province. It's nice there."

"Any place seems nice when one is not in it."

"It's a pity I cannot describe nature," thought Vassilyev. "I might touch her by a description of nature in Tchernigov. No doubt she loves the place if she has been born there."

"Are you dull here?" he asked.

"Of course I am dull."

"Why don't you go away from here if you are dull?"

"Where should I go to? Go begging or what?"

"Begging would be easier than living here."

"How do you know that? Have you begged?"

"Yes, when I hadn't the money to study. Even if I hadn't anyone could understand that. A beggar is anyway a free man, and you are a slave."

The dark woman stretched, and watched with sleepy eyes the footman who was bringing a trayful of glasses and seltzer water.

"Stand me a glass of porter," she said, and yawned again.

"Porter," thought Vassilyev. "And what if your brother or mother walked in at this moment? What would you say? And what would they say? There would be porter then, I imagine. . . ."

All at once there was the sound of weeping. From the adjoining room, from which the footman had brought the seltzer water, a fair man with a red face and angry eyes ran in quickly. He was followed by the tall, stout "madam," who was shouting in a shrill voice:

"Nobody has given you leave to slap girls on the cheeks! We have visitors better than you, and they don't fight! Impostor!"

A hubbub arose. Vassilyev was frightened and turned pale. In the next room there was the sound of bitter, genuine weeping, as though of someone insulted. And he realized that there were real people living here who, like people everywhere else, felt insulted, suffered, wept, and cried for help. The feeling of oppressive hate and disgust gave way to an acute feeling of pity and anger against the aggressor. He rushed into the room where there was weeping. Across rows of bottles on a marble-top table he distinguished a suffering face, wet with tears, stretched out his hands towards that face, took a step towards the table, but at once drew back in horror. The weeping girl was drunk.

As he made his way though the noisy crowd gathered about the fair man, his heart sank and he felt frightened like a child; and it seemed to him that in this alien, incomprehensible world people wanted to pursue him, to beat him, to pelt him with filthy words. . . . He tore down his coat from the hatstand and ran headlong downstairs.

V

Leaning against the fence, he stood near the house waiting for his friends to come out. The sounds of the pianos and violins, gay, reckless, insolent, and mournful, mingled in the air in a sort of chaos, and this tangle of sounds seemed again like an unseen orchestra tuning up on the roofs. If one looked upwards into the darkness, the black background was all spangled with white, moving spots: it was snow falling. As the snowflakes came into the light they floated round lazily in the air like down, and still more lazily fell to the ground. The snowflakes whirled thickly round Vassilyev and hung upon his beard, his eyelashes, his eyebrows. . . . The cabmen, the horses, and the passers-by were white.

"And how can the snow fall in this street!" thought Vassilyev. "Damnation take these houses!"

His legs seemed to be giving way from fatigue, simply from having run down the stairs; he gasped for breath as though he had been climbing uphill, his heart beat so loudly that he could hear it. He was consumed by a desire to get out of the street as quickly as possible and to go home, but even stronger was his desire to wait for his companions and vent upon them his oppressive feeling.

There was much he did not understand in these houses, the souls of ruined women were a mystery to him as before; but it was clear to him that the thing was far worse than could have been believed. If that sinful woman who had poisoned herself was called fallen, it was difficult to find a fitting name for all these who were dancing now to this tangle of sound and uttering long, loathsome sentences. They were not on the road to ruin, but ruined.

"There is vice," he thought, "but neither consciousness of sin nor hope of salvation. They are sold and bought, steeped in wine and abominations, while they, like sheep, are stupid, indifferent, and don't understand. My God! My God!"

It was clear to him, too, that everything that is called human dignity, personal rights, the Divine image and semblance, were defiled to their very foundations—"to the very marrow," as drunkards say—and that not only the street and the stupid women were responsible for it.

A group of students, white with snow, passed him, laughing and talking gaily; one, a tall thin fellow, stopped, glanced into Vassilyev's face, and said in a drunken voice:

"One of us! A bit on, old man? Aha-ha! Never mind, have a good time! Don't be down-hearted, old chap!"

He took Vassilyev by the shoulder and pressed his cold wet mustache against his cheek, then he slipped, staggered, and, waving both hands, cried:

"Hold on! Don't upset!"

And laughing, he ran to overtake his companions.

Through the noise came the sound of the artist's voice:

"Don't you dare to hit the women! I won't let you, damnation take you! You scoundrels!"

The medical student appeared in the doorway. He looked from side to side, and seeing Vassilyev, said in an agitated voice:

"You here! I tell you it's really impossible to go anywhere with Yegor! What a fellow he is! I don't understand him! He has got up a scene! Do you hear? Yegor!" he shouted at the door. "Yegor!"

"I won't allow you to hit women!" the artist's piercing voice sounded from above. Something heavy and lumbering rolled down the stairs. It was the artist falling headlong. Evidently he had been pushed downstairs.

He picked himself up from the ground, shook his hat, and, with an angry and indignant face, brandished his fist towards the top of the stairs and shouted:

"Scoundrels! Torturers! Bloodsuckers! I won't allow you to hit them! To hit a weak, drunken woman! Oh, you brutes! . . ."

"Yegor! . . . Come, Yegor! . . ." the medical student began imploring him. "I give you my word of honor I'll never come with you again. On my word of honor I won't!"

Little by little the artist was pacified and the friends went homewards.

"Against my will an unknown force," hummed the medical student, "has led me to these mournful shores."

"Behold the mill," the artist chimed in a little later, "in ruins now. What a lot of snow, Holy Mother! Grisha, why did you go? You are a funk, a regular old woman."

Vassilyev walked behind his companions, looked at their backs, and thought:

"One of two things: either we only fancy prostitution is an evil, and we exaggerate it; or, if prostitution really is as great an evil as is generally assumed, these dear friends of mine are as much slave-owners, violators, and murderers, as the inhabitants of Syria and Cairo, that are described in the 'Neva.' Now they are singing, laughing, talking sense, but haven't they just been exploiting hunger, ignorance, and stupidity? They have—I have been a witness of it. What is the use of their humanity, their medicine, their painting? The science, art, and lofty sentiments of these soul-destroyers remind me of the piece of bacon in the story. Two brigands murdered a beggar in a forest; they began sharing his clothes between them, and found in his wallet a piece of bacon. 'Well found,' said one of them; 'let us have a bit.' 'What do you mean? How can you?' cried the other in horror. 'Have you forgotten that to-day is Wednesday?' And they would not eat it. After murdering a man, they came out of the forest in the firm conviction that they were keeping the fast. In the same way these men, after buying women, go their way imagining that they are artists and men of science. . . ."

"Listen!" he said sharply and angrily. "Why do you come here? Is it possible—is it possible you don't understand how horrible it is? Your medical books tell you that every one of these women dies prematurely of consumption or something; art tells you that morally they are dead even earlier. Every one of them dies because she has in her time to entertain five hundred men on an average, let us say. Each one of them is killed by five hundred men. You are among those five hundred! If each of you in the course of your lives visits this place or others like it two hundred and fifty times, it follows that one woman is killed for every two of you! Can't you understand that? Isn't it horrible to murder, two of you, three of you, five of you, a foolish, hungry woman! Ah! isn't it awful, my God!"

"I knew it would end like that," the artist said frowning. "We ought not to have gone with this fool and ass! You imagine you have grand notions in your head now, ideas, don't you? No, it's the devil knows what, but not ideas. You are looking at me now with hatred and repulsion, but I tell you it's better you should set up twenty more houses like those than look like that. There's more vice in your expression than in the whole street! Come along, Volodya, let him go to the devil! He's a fool and an ass, and that's all. . . ."

"We human beings do murder each other," said the medical student. "It's immoral, of course, but philosophizing doesn't help it. Good-by!"

At Trubnoy Square the friends said good-by and parted. When he was left alone, Vassilyev strode rapidly along the boulevard. He felt frightened of the darkness, of the snow which was falling in heavy flakes on the ground, and seemed as though it would cover up the whole world; he felt frightened of the street lamps shining with pale light through the clouds of snow. His soul was possessed by an unaccountable, faint-hearted terror. Passers-by came towards him from time to time, but he timidly moved to one side; it seemed to him that women, none but women, were coming from all sides and staring at him. . . .

"It's beginning," he thought, "I am going to have a breakdown."

VI

At home he lay on his bed and said, shuddering all over: "They are alive! Alive! My God, those women are alive!"

He encouraged his imagination in all sorts of ways to picture himself the brother of a fallen woman, or her father; then a fallen woman herself, with her painted cheeks; and it all moved him to horror.

It seemed to him that he must settle the question at once at all costs, and that this question was not one that did not concern him, but was his own personal problem. He made an immense effort, repressed his despair, and, sitting on the bed, holding his head in his hands, began thinking how one could save all the women he had seen that day. The method for attacking problems of all kinds was, as he was an educated man, well known to him. And however excited he was, he strictly adhered to that method. He recalled the history of the problem and its literature, and for a quarter of an hour he paced from one end of the room to the other trying to remember all the methods practiced at the present time for saving women. He had very many good friends and acquaintances who lived in lodgings in Petersburg. . . . Among them were a good many honest and self-sacrificing men. Some of them had attempted to save women. . . .

"All these not very numerous attempts," thought Vassilyev, "can be divided into three groups. Some, after buying the woman out of the brothel, took a room for her, bought her a sewing-machine, and she became a sempstress. And whether he wanted to or not, after having bought her out he made her his mistress; then when he had taken his degree, he went away and handed her into the keeping of some other decent man as though she were a thing. And the fallen woman remained a fallen woman. Others, after buying her out, took a lodging apart for her, bought the inevitable sewing-machine, and tried teaching her to read, preaching at her and giving her books. The woman lived and sewed as long as it was interesting and a novelty to her, then getting bored, began receiving men on the sly, or ran away and went back where she could sleep till three o'clock, drink coffee, and have good dinners. The third class, the most ardent and self-sacrificing, had taken a bold, resolute step. They had married them. And when the insolent and spoilt, or stupid and crushed animal became a wife, the head of a household, and afterwards a mother, it turned her whole existence and attitude to life upside down, so that it was hard to recognize the fallen woman afterwards in the wife and the mother. Yes, marriage was the best and perhaps the only means."

"But it is impossible!" Vassilyev said aloud, and he sank upon his bed. "I, to begin with, could not marry one! To do that one must be a saint and be unable to feel hatred or repulsion. But supposing that I, the medical student, and the artist mastered ourselves and did marry them—suppose they were all married. What would be the result? The result would be that while here in Moscow they were being married, some Smolensk accountant would be debauching another lot, and that lot would be streaming here to fill the vacant places, together with others from Saratov, Nizhni-Novgorod, Warsaw. . . . And what is one to do with the hundred thousand in London? What's one to do with those in Hamburg?"

The lamp in which the oil had burnt down began to smoke. Vassilyev did not notice it. He began pacing to and fro again, still thinking. Now he put the question differently: what must be done that fallen women should not be needed? For that, it was essential that the men who buy them and do them to death should feel all the immorality of their share in enslaving them and should be horrified. One must save the men.

"One won't do anything by art and science, that is clear . . ." thought Vassilyev. "The only way out of it is missionary work."

And he began to dream how he would the next evening stand at the corner of the street and say to every passer-by: "Where are you going and what for? Have some fear of God!"

He would turn to the apathetic cabmen and say to them: "Why are you staying here? Why aren't you revolted? Why aren't you indignant? I suppose you believe in God and know that it is a sin, that people go to hell for it? Why don't you speak? It is true that they are strangers to you, but you know even they have fathers, brothers like yourselves. . . ."

One of Vassilyev's friends had once said of him that he was a talented man. There are all sorts of talents—talent for writing, talent for the stage, talent for art; but he had a peculiar talent—a talent for *hu-*

manity. He possessed an extraordinarily fine delicate scent for pain in general. As a good actor reflects in himself the movements and voice of others, so Vassilyev could reflect in his soul the sufferings of others. When he saw tears, he wept; beside a sick man, he felt sick himself and moaned; if he saw an act of violence, he felt as though he himself were the victim of it, he was frightened as a child, and in his fright ran to help. The pain of others worked on his nerves, excited him, roused him to a state of frenzy, and so on.

Whether this friend were right I don't know, but what Vassilyev experienced when he thought this question was settled was something like inspiration. He cried and laughed, spoke aloud the words that he should say next day, felt a fervent love for those who would listen to him and would stand beside him at the corner of the street to preach; he sat down to write letters, made vows to himself. . . .

All this was like inspiration also from the fact that it did not last long. Vassilyev was soon tired. The cases in London, in Hamburg, in Warsaw, weighed upon him by their mass as a mountain weighs upon the earth; he felt dispirited, bewildered, in the face of this mass; he remembered that he had not a gift for words, that he was cowardly and timid, that indifferent people would not be willing to listen and understand him, a law student in his third year, a timid and insignificant person; that genuine missionary work included not only teaching but deeds. . . .

When it was daylight and carriages were already beginning to rumble in the street, Vassilyev was lying motionless on the sofa, staring into space. He was no longer thinking of the women, nor of the men, nor of missionary work. His whole attention was turned upon the spiritual agony which was torturing him. It was a dull, vague, undefined anguish akin to misery, to an extreme form of terror, and to despair. He could point to the place where the pain was, in his breast under his heart; but he could not compare it with anything. In the past he had had acute toothache, he had had pleurisy and neuralgia, but all that was insignificant compared with this spiritual anguish. In the presence of that pain life seemed loathsome. The dissertation, the excellent work he had written already, the people he loved, the salvation of fallen women—everything that only the day before he had cared about or been indifferent to, now when he thought of them irritated him in the same way as the noise of the carriages, the scurrying footsteps of the waiters in the passage, the daylight. . . . If at that moment someone had performed a great deed of mercy or had committed a revolting outrage, he would have felt the same repulsion for both actions. Of all the thoughts that strayed through his mind only two did not irritate him: one was that at every moment he had the power to kill himself, the other that this agony would not last more than three days. This last he knew by experience.

After lying for a while he got up and, wringing his hands, walked about the room, not as usual from corner to corner, but round the room beside the walls. As he passed he glanced at himself in the looking-glass. His face looked pale and sunken, his temples looked hollow, his eyes were bigger, darker, more staring, as though they belonged to someone else, and they had an expression of insufferable mental agony.

At midday the artist knocked at the door.

"Grigory, are you at home?" he asked.

Getting no answer, he stood for a minute, pondered, and answered himself in Little Russian: "Nay. The confounded fellow has gone to the University."

And he went away. Vassilyev lay down on the bed and, thrusting his head under the pillow, began crying with agony, and the more freely his tears flowed the more terrible his mental anguish became. As it began to get dark, he thought of the agonizing night awaiting him, and was overcome by a horrible despair. He dressed quickly, ran out of his room, and, leaving his door wide open, for no object or reason went out into the street. Without asking himself where he should go, he walked quickly along Sadovoy Street.

Snow was falling as heavily as the day before; it was thawing. Thrusting his hands into his sleeves, shuddering and frightened at the noises, at the trambells, and at the passers-by, Vassilyev walked along Sadovoy Street as far as Suharev Tower; then to the Red Gate; from there he turned off to Basmannya Street. He went into a tavern and drank off a big glass of vodka, but that did not make him feel better.

When he reached Razgulya he turned to the right, and strode along side streets in which he had never been before in his life. He reached the old bridge by which the Yauza runs gurgling, and from which one can see long rows of lights in the windows of the Red Barracks. To distract his spiritual anguish by some new sensation or some other pain, Vassilyev, not knowing what to do, crying and shuddering, undid his greatcoat and jacket and exposed his bare chest to the wet snow and the wind. But that did not lessen his suffering either. Then he bent down over the rail of the bridge and looked down into the black, yeasty Yauza, and he longed to plunge down head-foremost; not from loathing for life, not for the sake of suicide, but in order to bruise himself at least, and by one pain to ease the other. But the black water, the darkness, the deserted banks covered with snow were terrifying. He shivered and walked on. He walked up and down by the Red Barracks, then turned back and went down to a copse, from the copse back to the bridge again.

"No, home, home!" he thought. "At home I believe it's better. . . ."

And he went back. When he reached home he pulled off his wet coat and cap, began pacing round the room, and went on pacing round and round without stopping till morning.

VII

When next morning the artist and the medical student went in to him, he was moving about the room with his shirt torn, biting his hands and moaning with pain.

"For God's sake!" he sobbed when he saw his friends, "take me where you please, do what you can; but for God's sake, save me quickly! I shall kill myself!"

The artist turned pale and was helpless. The medical student, too, almost shed tears, but considering that doctors ought to be cool and composed in every emergency, said coldly:

"It's a nervous breakdown. But it's nothing. Let us go at once to the doctor."

"Wherever you like, only for God's sake, make haste!"

"Don't excite yourself. You must try and control yourself."

The artist and the medical student with trembling hands put Vassilyev's coat and hat on and led him out into the street.

"Mihail Sergeyitch has been wanting to make your acquaintance for a long time," the medical student said on the way. "He is a very nice man and thoroughly good at his work. He took his degree in 1882, and he has an immense practice already. He treats students as though he were one himself."

"Make haste, make haste! . . ." Vassilyev urged.

Mihail Sergeyitch, a stout, fair-haired doctor, received the friends with politeness and frigid dignity, and smiled only on one side of his face.

"Rybnikov and Mayer have spoken to me of your illness already," he said. "Very glad to be of service to you. Well? Sit down, I beg. . . ."

He made Vassilyev sit down in a big armchair near the table, and moved a box of cigarettes towards him.

"Now then!" he began, stroking his knees. "Let us get to work. . . . How old are you?"

He asked questions and the medical student answered them. He asked whether Vassilyev's father had suffered from certain special diseases, whether he drank to excess, whether he were remarkable for cruelty or any peculiarities. He made similar inquiries about his grandfather, mother, sisters, and brothers. On learning that his mother had a beautiful voice and sometimes acted on the stage, he grew more animated at once, and asked:

"Excuse me, but don't you remember, perhaps, your mother had a passion for the stage?"

Twenty minutes passed. Vassilyev was annoyed by the way the doctor kept stroking his knees and talking of the same thing.

"So far as I understand your questions, doctor," he said, "you want to know whether my illness is hereditary or not. It is not."

The doctor proceeded to ask Vassilyev whether he had had any secret vices as a boy, or had received injuries to his head; whether he had had any aberrations, any peculiarities, or exceptional propensities. Half the questions usually asked by doctors of their patients can be left unanswered without the slightest ill effect on the health, but Mihail Sergeyitch, the medical student, and the artist all looked as though if Vassilyev failed to answer one question all would be lost. As he received answers, the doctor for some reason noted them down on a slip of paper. On learning that Vassilyev had taken his degree in natural science, and was now studying law, the doctor pondered.

"He wrote a first-rate piece of original work last year, . . ." said the medical student.

"I beg your pardon, but don't interrupt me; you prevent me from concentrating," said the doctor, and he smiled on one side of his face. "Though, of course, that does enter into the diagnosis. Intense intellectual work, nervous exhaustion. . . . Yes, yes. . . . And do you drink vodka?" he said, addressing Vassilyev.

"Very rarely."

Another twenty minutes passed. The medical student began telling the doctor in a low voice his opinion as to the immediate cause of the attack, and described how the day before yesterday the artist, Vassilyev, and he had visited S. Street.

The indifferent, reserved, and frigid tone in which his friends and the doctor spoke of the women and that miserable street struck Vassilyev as strange in the extreme. . . .

"Doctor, tell me one thing only," he said, controlling himself so as not to speak rudely. "Is prostitution an evil or not?"

"My dear fellow, who disputes it?" said the doctor, with an expression that suggested that he had settled all such questions for himself long ago. "Who disputes it?"

"You are a mental doctor, aren't you?" Vassilyev asked curtly.

"Yes, a mental doctor."

"Perhaps all of you are right!" said Vassilyev, getting up and beginning to walk from one end of the room to the other. "Perhaps! But it all seems marvelous to me! That I should have taken my degree in two faculties you look upon as a great achievement; because I have written a work which in three years will be thrown aside and forgotten, I am praised up to the skies; but because I cannot speak of fallen women as unconcernedly as of these chairs, I am being examined by a doctor, I am called mad, I am pitied!"

Vassilyev for some reason felt all at once unutterably sorry for himself, and his companions, and all the people he had seen two days before, and for the doctor; he burst into tears and sank into a chair.

His friends looked inquiringly at the doctor. The latter, with the air of completely comprehending the tears and the despair, of feeling himself a specialist in that line, went up to Vassilyev and, without a word, gave him some medicine to drink; and then, when he was calmer, undressed him and began to investigate the degree of sensibility of the skin, the reflex action of the knees, and so on.

And Vassilyev felt easier. When he came out from the doctor's he was beginning to feel ashamed; the rattle of the carriages no longer irritated him, and the load at his heart grew lighter and lighter as though it were melting away. He had two prescriptions in his hand: one was for bromide, one was for morphia. . . . He had taken all these remedies before!

In the street he stood still and, saying good-by to his friends, dragged himself languidly to the University.

The Princess

A carriage with four fine sleek horses drove in at the big so-called Red Gate of the N—— Monastery. While it was still at a distance, the priests and monks who were standing in a group round the part of the hostel allotted to the gentry, recognised by the coachman and horses that the lady in the carriage was Princess Vera Gavrilovna, whom they knew very well.

An old man in livery jumped off the box and helped the princess to get out of the carriage. She raised her dark veil and moved in a leisurely way up to the priests to receive their blessing; then she nodded pleasantly to the rest of the monks and went into the hostel.

"Well, have you missed your princess?" she said to the monk who brought in her things. "It's a whole month since I've been to see you. But here I am; behold your princess. And where is the Father Superior? My goodness, I am burning with impatience! Wonderful, wonderful old man! You must be proud of having such a Superior."

When the Father Superior came in, the princess uttered a shriek of delight, crossed her arms over her bosom, and went up to receive his blessing.

"No, no, let me kiss your hand," she said, snatching it and eagerly kissing it three times. "How glad I am to see you at last, holy Father!

I'm sure you've forgotten your princess, but my thoughts have been in your dear monastery every moment. How delightful it is here! This living for God far from the busy, giddy world has a special charm of its own, holy Father, which I feel with my whole soul although I cannot express it!"

The princess's cheeks glowed and tears came into her eyes. She talked incessantly, fervently, while the Father Superior, a grave, plain, shy old man of seventy, remained mute or uttered abruptly, like a soldier on duty, phrases such as:

"Certainly, Your Excellency. . . . Quite so. I understand."

"Has Your Excellency come for a long stay?" he inquired.

"I shall stay the night here, and to-morrow I'm going on to Klavdia Nikolaevna's—it's a long time since I've seen her—and the day after to-morrow I'll come back to you and stay three or four days. I want to rest my soul here among you, holy Father. . . ."

The princess liked being at the monastery at N——. For the last two years it had been a favourite resort of hers; she used to go there almost every month in the summer and stay two or three days, even sometimes a week. The shy novices, the stillness, the low ceilings, the smell of cypress, the modest fare, the cheap curtains on the windows—all this touched her, softened her, and disposed her to contemplation and good thoughts. It was enough for her to be half an hour in the hostel for her to feel that she, too, was timid and modest, and that she, too, smelt of cypress-wood. The past retreated into the background, lost its significance, and the princess began to imagine that in spite of her twenty-nine years she was very much like the old Father Superior, and that, like him, she was created not for wealth, not for earthly grandeur and love, but for a peaceful life secluded from the world, a life in twilight like the hostel.

It happens that a ray of light gleams in the dark cell of the anchorite absorbed in prayer, or a bird alights on the window and sings its song; the stern anchorite will smile in spite of himself, and a gentle, sinless joy will pierce through the load of grief over his sins, like water flowing from under a stone. The princess fancied she brought from the outside world just such comfort as the ray of light or the bird. Her gay, friendly smile, her gentle eyes, her voice, her jests, her whole personality in fact, her little graceful figure always dressed in simple black, must arouse in simple, austere people a feeling of tenderness and joy. Every one, looking at her, must think: "God has sent us an angel. . . ." And feeling that no one could help thinking this, she smiled still more cordially, and tried to look like a bird.

After drinking tea and resting, she went for a walk. The sun was already setting. From the monastery garden came a moist fragrance of freshly watered mignonette, and from the church floated the soft singing of men's voices, which seemed very pleasant and mournful in the distance. It was the evening service. In the dark windows where the little lamps glowed gently, in the shadows, in the figure of the old monk sitting at the church door with a collecting-box, there was such unruffled peace that the princess felt moved to tears.

Outside the gate, in the walk between the wall and the birch-trees where there were benches, it was quite evening. The air grew rapidly darker and darker. The princess went along the walk, sat on a seat, and sank into thought.

She thought how good it would be to settle down for her whole life in this monastery where life was as still and unruffled as a summer evening; how good it would be to forget the ungrateful, dissipated prince; to forget her immense estates, the creditors who worried her every day, her misfortunes, her maid Dasha, who had looked at her impertinently that morning. It would be nice to sit here on the bench all her life and watch through the trunks of the birch-trees the evening mist gathering in wreaths in the valley below; the rooks flying home in a black cloud like a veil far, far away above the forest; two novices, one astride a piebald horse, another on foot driving out the horses for the night and rejoicing in their freedom, playing pranks like little children; their youthful voices rang out musically in the still air, and she could distinguish every word. It is nice to sit and listen to the silence: at one moment the wind blows and stirs the tops of the birch-trees, then a frog rustles in last year's leaves, then the clock on the belfry strikes the quarter. . . . One might sit without moving, listen and think, and think. . . .

An old woman passed by with a wallet on her back. The princess thought that it would be nice to stop the old woman and to say something friendly and cordial to her, to help her. . . . But the old woman turned the corner without once looking round.

Not long afterwards a tall man with a grey beard and a straw hat came along the walk. When he came up to the princess, he took off his hat and bowed. From the bald patch on his head and his sharp, hooked nose the princess recognised him as the doctor, Mihail Ivanovitch, who had been in her service at Dubovki. She remembered that some one had told her that his wife had died the year before, and she wanted to sympathise with him, to console him.

"Doctor, I expect you don't recognise me?" she said with an affable smile.

"Yes, Princess, I recognised you," said the doctor, taking off his hat again.

"Oh, thank you; I was afraid that you, too, had forgotten your princess. People only remember their enemies, but they forget their friends. Have you, too, come to pray?"

"I am the doctor here, and I have to spend the night at the monastery every Saturday."

"Well, how are you?" said the princess, sighing. "I hear that you have lost your wife. What a calamity!"

"Yes, Princess, for me it is a great calamity."

"There's nothing for it! We must bear our troubles with resignation. Not one hair of a man's head is lost without the Divine Will."

"Yes, Princess."

To the princess's friendly, gentle smile and her sighs the doctor responded coldly and dryly: "Yes, Princess." And the expression of his face was cold and dry.

"What else can I say to him?" she wondered.

"How long it is since we met!" she said. "Five years! How much water has flowed under the bridge, how many changes in that time; it quite frightens one to think of it! You know, I am married. . . . I am not a countess now, but a princess. And by now I am separated from my husband too."

"Yes, I heard so."

"God has sent me many trials. No doubt you have heard, too, that I am almost ruined. My Dubovki, Sofyino, and Kiryakovo have all been sold for my unhappy husband's debts. And I have only Baranovo and Mihaltsevo left. It's terrible to look back: how many changes and misfortunes of all kinds, how many mistakes!"

"Yes, Princess, many mistakes."

The princess was a little disconcerted. She knew her mistakes; they were all of such a private character that no one but she could think or speak of them. She could not resist asking:

"What mistakes are you thinking about?"

"You referred to them, so you know them . . ." answered the doctor, and he smiled. "Why talk about them!"

"No; tell me, doctor. I shall be very grateful to you. And please don't stand on ceremony with me. I love to hear the truth."

"I am not your judge, Princess."

"Not my judge! What a tone you take! You must know something about me. Tell me!"

"If you really wish it, very well. Only I regret to say I'm not clever at talking, and people can't always understand me."

The doctor thought a moment and began:

"A lot of mistakes; but the most important of them, in my opinion, was the general spirit that prevailed on all your estates. You see, I don't know how to express myself. I mean chiefly the lack of love, the aversion for people that was felt in absolutely everything. Your whole system of life was built upon that aversion. Aversion for the human voice, for faces, for heads, steps . . . in fact, for everything that makes up a human being. At all the doors and on the stairs there stand sleek, rude, and lazy grooms in livery to prevent badly dressed persons from entering the house; in the hall there are chairs with high backs so that the footmen waiting there, during balls and receptions, may not soil the walls with their heads; in every room there are thick carpets that no human step may be heard; every one who comes in is infallibly warned to speak as softly and as little as possible, and to say nothing that might have a disagreeable effect on the nerves or the imagination. And in your room you don't shake hands with any one or ask him to sit down—just as you didn't shake hands with me or ask me to sit down. . . ."

"By all means, if you like," said the princess, smiling and holding out her hand. "Really, to be cross about such trifles. . . ."

"But I am not cross," laughed the doctor, but at once he flushed, took off his hat, and waving it about, began hotly: "To be candid, I've long wanted an opportunity to tell you all I think. . . . That is, I want to tell you that you look upon the mass of mankind from the Napoleonic standpoint as food for the cannon. But Napoleon had at least some idea; you have nothing except aversion."

"I have an aversion for people?" smiled the princess, shrugging her shoulders in astonishment. "I have!"

"Yes, you! You want facts? By all means. In Mihaltsevo three former cooks of yours, who have gone blind in your kitchens from the heat of the stove, are living upon charity. All the health and strength and good looks that is found on your hundreds of thousands of acres is taken by you and your parasites for your grooms, your footmen, and your coachmen. All these two-legged cattle are trained to be flunkeys, overeat themselves, grow coarse, lose the 'image and likeness,' in fact. . . . Young doctors, agricultural experts, teachers, intellectual workers generally—think of it!—are torn away from their honest work and forced for a crust of bread to take part in all sorts of mummeries which make every decent man feel ashamed! Some young men cannot be in your service for three years without becoming hypocrites, toadies, sneaks. . . . Is that a good thing? Your Polish superintendents, those abject spies, all those Kazimers and Kaetans, go hunting about on your hundreds of thousands of acres from morning to night, and to please you try to get three skins off one ox. Excuse me, I speak disconnectedly, but that doesn't matter. You don't look upon the simple people as human beings. And even the princes, counts, and bishops who used to come and see you, you looked upon simply as decorative figures, not as living beings. But the worst of all, the thing that most revolts me, is having a fortune of over a million and doing nothing for other people, nothing!"

The princess sat amazed, aghast, offended, not knowing what to say or how to behave. She had never before been spoken to in such a tone. The doctor's unpleasant, angry voice and his clumsy, faltering phrases made a harsh clattering noise in her ears and her head. Then she began to feel as though the gesticulating doctor was hitting her on the head with his hat.

"It's not true!" she articulated softly, in an imploring voice. "I've done a great deal of good for other people; you know it yourself!"

"Nonsense!" cried the doctor. "Can you possibly go on thinking of your philanthropic work as something genuine and useful, and not a mere mummery? It was a farce from beginning to end; it was playing at loving your neighbour, the most open farce which even children and stupid peasant women saw through! Take for instance your—what was it called?—house for homeless old women without relations, of which you made me something like a head doctor, and of which you were the patroness. Mercy on us! What a charming institution it was! A house was built with parquet floors and a weathercock on the roof; a dozen old women were collected from the villages and made to sleep under blankets and sheets of Dutch linen, and given toffee to eat."

The doctor gave a malignant chuckle into his hat, and went on speaking rapidly and stammering:

"It was a farce! The attendants kept the sheets and the blankets under lock and key, for fear the old women should soil them—'Let the old devil's pepper-pots sleep on the floor.' The old women did not dare to sit down on the beds, to put on their jackets, to walk over the polished floors. Everything was kept for show and hidden away from the old women as though they were thieves, and the old women were clothed and fed on the sly by other people's charity, and prayed to God night and day to be released from their prison and from the canting exhortations of the sleek rascals to whose care you committed them. And what did the managers do? It was simply charming! About twice a week there would be thirty-five thousand messages to say that the princess—that is, you—were coming to the home next day. That meant that next day I had to abandon my patients, dress up and be on parade. Very good; I arrive. The old women, in everything clean and new, are already drawn up in a row, waiting. Near them struts the old garrison rat—the superintendent with his mawkish, sneaking smile. The old women yawn and exchange glances, but are afraid to complain. We wait. The junior steward gallops up. Half an hour later the senior steward; then the superintendent of the accounts' office, then another, and then another of them . . . they keep arriving endlessly. They all have mysterious, solemn faces. We wait and wait, shift from one leg to another, look at the clock—all this in monumental silence because we all hate each other like poison. One hour passes, then a second, and then at last the carriage is seen in the distance, and . . . and . . ."

The doctor went off into a shrill laugh and brought out in a shrill voice:

"You get out of the carriage, and the old hags, at the word of command from the old garrison rat, begin chanting: 'The Glory of our Lord in Zion the tongue of man cannot express. . . .' A pretty scene, wasn't it?"

The doctor went off into a bass chuckle, and waved his hand as though to signify that he could not utter another word for laughing. He laughed heavily, harshly, with clenched teeth, as ill-natured people laugh; and from his voice, from his face, from his glittering, rather insolent eyes it could be seen that he had a profound contempt for the princess, for the home, and for the old women. There was nothing amusing or laughable in all that he described so clumsily and coarsely, but he laughed with satisfaction, even with delight.

"And the school?" he went on, panting from laughter. "Do you remember how you wanted to teach peasant children yourself? You must have taught them very well, for very soon the children all ran away, so that they had to be thrashed and bribed to come and be taught. And you remember how you wanted to feed with your own hands the infants whose mothers were working in the fields. You went about the village crying because the infants were not at your disposal, as the mothers would take them to the fields with them. Then the village foreman ordered the mothers by turns to leave their infants behind for your entertainment. A strange thing! They all ran away from your benevolence like mice from a cat! And why was it? It's very simple. Not because our people are ignorant and ungrateful, as you always explained it to yourself, but because in all your fads, if you'll excuse the word, there wasn't a ha'p'orth of love and kindness! There was nothing but the desire to amuse yourself with living puppets, nothing else. . . . A person who does not feel the difference between a human being and a lap-dog ought not to go in for philanthropy. I assure you, there's a great difference between human beings and lap-dogs!"

The princess's heart was beating dreadfully; there was a thudding in her ears, and she still felt as though the doctor were beating her on the head with his hat. The doctor talked quickly, excitedly, and uncouthly, stammering and gesticulating unnecessarily. All she grasped was that she was spoken to by a coarse, ill-bred, spiteful, and ungrateful man; but what he wanted of her and what he was talking about, she could not understand.

"Go away!" she said in a tearful voice, putting up her hands to protect her head from the doctor's hat; "go away!"

"And how you treat your servants!" the doctor went on, indignantly. "You treat them as the lowest scoundrels, and don't look upon them as human beings. For example, allow me to ask, why did you dismiss me? For ten years I worked for your father and afterwards for you, honestly, without vacations or holidays. I gained the love of all for more than seventy miles round, and suddenly one fine day I am informed that I am no longer wanted. What for? I've no idea to this day. I, a doctor of medicine, a gentleman by birth, a student of the Moscow University, father of a family—am such a petty, insignificant insect that you can kick me out without explaining the reason! Why stand on ceremony with me! I heard afterwards that my wife went without my knowledge three times to intercede with you for me—you wouldn't receive her. I am told she cried in your hall. And I shall never forgive her for it, never!"

The doctor paused and clenched his teeth, making an intense effort to think of something more to say, very unpleasant and vindictive. He thought of something, and his cold, frowning face suddenly brightened.

"Take your attitude to this monastery!" he said with avidity. "You've never spared any one, and the holier the place, the more chance of its suffering from your loving-kindness and angelic sweetness. Why do you come here? What do you want with the monks here, allow me to ask you? What is Hecuba to you or you to Hecuba? It's another farce, another amusement for you, another sacrilege against human dignity, and nothing more. Why, you don't believe in the monks' God; you've a God of your own in your heart, whom you've evolved for yourself at spiritualist séances. You look with condescension upon the ritual of the Church; you don't go to mass or vespers; you sleep till midday. . . . Why do you come here? . . . You come with a God of your own into a monastery you have nothing to do with, and you imagine that the monks look upon it as a very great honour. To be sure they do! You'd better ask, by the way, what your visits cost the monastery. You were graciously pleased to arrive here this evening, and a messenger from your estate arrived on horseback the day before yesterday to warn them of your coming. They were the whole day yesterday getting the rooms ready and expecting you. This morning your advance-guard arrived—an insolent maid, who keeps running across the courtyard, rustling her skirts, pestering them with questions, giving orders. . . . I can't endure it! The monks have been on the lookout all day, for if you were not met with due ceremony, there would be trouble! You'd complain to the bishop! 'The monks don't like me, your holiness; I don't know what I've done to displease them. It's true I'm a great sinner, but I'm so unhappy!' Already one monastery has been in hot water over you. The Father Superior is a busy, learned man; he hasn't a free moment, and you keep sending for him to come to your rooms. Not a trace of respect for age or for rank! If at least you were a bountiful giver to the monastery, one wouldn't resent it so much, but all this time the monks have not received a hundred roubles from you!"

Whenever people worried the princess, misunderstood her, or mortified her, and when she did not know what to say or do, she usually began to cry. And on this occasion, too, she ended by hiding her face in her hands and crying aloud in a thin treble like a child. The doctor suddenly stopped and looked at her. His face darkened and grew stern.

"Forgive me, Princess," he said in a hollow voice. "I've given way to a malicious feeling and forgotten myself. It was not right."

And coughing in an embarrassed way, he walked away quickly, without remembering to put his hat on.

Stars were already twinkling in the sky. The moon must have been rising on the further side of the monastery, for the sky was clear, soft, and transparent. Bats were flitting noiselessly along the white monastery wall.

The clock slowly struck three quarters, probably a quarter to nine. The princess got up and walked slowly to the gate. She felt wounded and was crying, and she felt that the trees and the stars and even the bats were pitying her, and that the clock struck musically only to express its sympathy with her. She cried and thought how nice it would be to go into a monastery for the rest of her life. On still summer evenings she would walk alone through the avenues, insulted, injured, misunderstood by people, and only God and the starry heavens would see the martyr's tears. The evening service was still going on in the church. The princess stopped and listened to the singing; how beautiful the singing sounded in the still darkness! How sweet to weep and suffer to the sound of that singing!

Going into her rooms, she looked at her tear-stained face in the glass and powdered it, then she sat down to supper. The monks knew that she liked pickled sturgeon, little mushrooms, Malaga and plain honey-cakes that left a taste of cypress in the mouth, and every time she came they gave her all these dishes. As she ate the mushrooms and drank the Malaga, the princess dreamed of how she would be finally ruined and deserted—how all her stewards, bailiffs, clerks, and maidservants for whom she had done so much, would be false to her, and begin to say rude things; how people all the world over would set upon her, speak ill of her, jeer at her. She would renounce her title, would renounce society and luxury, and would go into a convent without one word of reproach to any one; she would pray for her enemies—and then they would all understand her and come to beg her forgiveness, but by that time it would be too late. . . .

After supper she knelt down in the corner before the ikon and read two chapters of the Gospel. Then her maid made her bed and she got into it. Stretching herself under the white quilt, she heaved a sweet, deep sigh, as one sighs after crying, closed her eyes, and began to fall asleep.

In the morning she waked up and glanced at her watch. It was half-past nine. On the carpet near the bed was a bright, narrow streak of sunlight from a ray which came in at the window and dimly lighted up the room. Flies were buzzing behind the black curtain at the window. "It's early," thought the princess, and she closed her eyes.

Stretching and lying snug in her bed, she recalled her meeting yesterday with the doctor and all the thoughts with which she had gone to sleep the night before: she remembered she was unhappy. Then she thought of her husband living in Petersburg, her stewards, doctors, neighbours, the officials of her acquaintance . . . a long procession of familiar masculine faces passed before her imagination. She smiled and thought, if only these people could see into her heart and understand her, they would all be at her feet.

At a quarter past eleven she called her maid.

"Help me to dress, Dasha," she said languidly. "But go first and tell them to get out the horses. I must set off for Klavdia Nikolaevna's."

Going out to get into the carriage, she blinked at the glaring daylight and laughed with pleasure: it was a wonderfully fine day! As she scanned from her half-closed eyes the monks who had gathered round the steps to see her off, she nodded graciously and said:

"Good-bye, my friends! Till the day after tomorrow."

It was an agreeable surprise to her that the doctor was with the monks by the steps. His face was pale and severe.

"Princess," he said with a guilty smile, taking off his hat, "I've been waiting here a long time to see you. Forgive me, for God's sake. . . . I was carried away yesterday by an evil, vindictive feeling and I talked . . . nonsense. In short, I beg your pardon."

The princess smiled graciously, and held out her hand for him to kiss. He kissed it, turning red.

Trying to look like a bird, the princess fluttered into the carriage and nodded in all directions. There was a gay, warm, serene feeling in her heart, and she felt herself that her smile was particularly soft and friendly. As the carriage rolled towards the gates, and afterwards along the dusty road past huts and gardens, past long trains of waggons and strings of pilgrims on their way to the monastery, she still screwed up her eyes and smiled softly. She was thinking there was no higher bliss than to bring warmth, light, and joy wherever one went, to forgive injuries, to smile graciously on one's enemies. The peasants she passed bowed to her, the carriage rustled softly, clouds of dust rose from under the wheels and floated over the golden rye, and it seemed to the princess that her body was swaying not on carriage cushions but on clouds, and that she herself was like a light, transparent little cloud. . . .

"How happy I am!" she murmured, shutting her eyes. "How happy I am!"

The Horse-Stealers

A hospital assistant, called Yergunov, an empty-headed fellow, known throughout the district as a great braggart and drunkard, was returning one evening in Christmas week from the hamlet of Ryepino, where he had been to make some purchases for the hospital. That he might get home in good time and not be late, the doctor had lent him his very best horse.

At first it had been a still day, but at eight o'clock a violent snowstorm came on, and when he was only about four miles from home Yergunov completely lost his way.

He did not know how to drive, he did not know the road, and he drove on at random, hoping that the horse would find the way of itself. Two hours passed; the horse was exhausted, he himself was chilled, and already began to fancy that he was not going home, but back towards Ryepino. But at last above the uproar of the storm he heard the far-away barking of a dog, and a murky red blur came into sight ahead of him: little by little, the outlines of a high gate could be discerned, then a long fence on which there were nails with their points uppermost, and beyond the fence there stood the slanting crane of a well. The wind drove away the mist of snow from before the eyes, and where there had been a red blur, there sprang up a small, squat little house with a steep thatched roof. Of the three little windows one, covered on the inside with something red, was lighted up.

What sort of place was it? Yergunov remembered that to the right of the road, three and a half or four miles from the hospital, there was Andrey Tchirikov's tavern. He remembered, too, that this Tchirikov, who had been lately killed by some sledge-drivers, had left a wife and a daughter called Lyubka, who had come to the hospital two years before as a patient. The inn had a bad reputation, and to visit it late in the evening, and especially with someone else's horse, was not free from risk. But there was no help for it. Yergunov fumbled in his knapsack for his revolver, and, coughing sternly, tapped at the window-frame with his whip.

"Hey! who is within?" he cried. "Hey, granny! let me come in and get warm!"

With a hoarse bark a black dog rolled like a ball under the horse's feet, then another white one, then another black one—there must have been a dozen of them. Yergunov looked to see which was the biggest, swung his whip and lashed at it with all his might. A small, long-legged puppy turned its sharp muzzle upwards and set up a shrill, piercing howl.

Yergunov stood for a long while at the window, tapping. But at last the hoar-frost on the trees near the house glowed red, and a muffled female figure appeared with a lantern in her hands.

"Let me in to get warm, granny," said Yergunov. "I was driving to the hospital, and I have lost my way. It's such weather, God preserve us. Don't be afraid; we are your own people, granny."

"All my own people are at home, and we didn't invite strangers," said the figure grimly. "And what are you knocking for? The gate is not locked."

Yergunov drove into the yard and stopped at the steps.

"Bid your labourer take my horse out, granny," said he.

"I am not granny."

And indeed she was not a granny. While she was putting out the lantern the light fell on her face, and Yergunov saw black eyebrows, and recognized Lyubka.

"There are no labourers about now," she said as she went into the house. "Some are drunk and asleep, and some have been gone to Ryepino since the morning. It's a holiday. . . ."

As he fastened his horse up in the shed, Yergunov heard a neigh, and distinguished in the darkness another horse, and felt on it a Cossack saddle. So there must be someone else in the house besides the woman and her daughter. For greater security Yergunov unsaddled his horse, and when he went into the house, took with him both his purchases and his saddle.

The first room into which he went was large and very hot, and smelt of freshly washed floors. A short, lean peasant of about forty, with a small, fair beard, wearing a dark blue shirt, was sitting at the table under the holy images. It was Kalashnikov, an arrant scoundrel and horse-stealer, whose father and uncle kept a tavern in Bogalyovka, and disposed of the stolen horses where they could. He too had been to the hospital more than once, not for medical treatment, but to see the doctor about horses—to ask whether he had not one for sale, and whether his honour would not like to swop his bay mare for a dun-coloured gelding. Now his head was pomaded and a silver ear-ring glittered in his ear, and altogether he had a holiday air. Frowning and dropping his lower lip, he was looking intently at a big dog's-eared picture-book. Another peasant lay stretched on the floor near the stove; his head, his shoulders, and his chest were covered with a sheepskin—he was probably asleep; beside his new boots, with shining bits of metal on the heels, there were two dark pools of melted snow.

Seeing the hospital assistant, Kalashnikov greeted him.

"Yes, it is weather," said Yergunov, rubbing his chilled knees with his open hands. "The snow is up to one's neck; I am soaked to the skin, I can tell you. And I believe my revolver is, too. . . ."

He took out his revolver, looked it all over, and put it back in his knapsack. But the revolver made no impression at all; the peasant went on looking at the book.

"Yes, it is weather. . . . I lost my way, and if it had not been for the dogs here, I do believe it would have been my death. There would have been a nice to-do. And where are the women?"

"The old woman has gone to Ryepino, and the girl is getting supper ready . . ." answered Kalashnikov.

Silence followed. Yergunov, shivering and gasping, breathed on his hands, huddled up, and made a show of being very cold and exhausted. The still angry dogs could be heard howling outside. It was dreary.

"You come from Bogalyovka, don't you?" he asked the peasant sternly.

"Yes, from Bogalyovka."

And to while away the time Yergunov began to think about Bogalyovka. It was a big village and it lay in a deep ravine, so that when one drove along the highroad on a moonlight night, and looked down into the dark ravine and then up at the sky, it seemed as though the moon were hanging over a bottomless abyss and it were the end of the world. The path going down was steep, winding, and so narrow that when one drove down to Bogalyovka on account of some epidemic or to vaccinate the people, one had to shout at the top of one's voice, or whistle all the way, for if one met a cart coming up one could not pass. The peasants of Bogalyovka had the reputation of being good gardeners and horse-stealers. They had well-stocked gardens. In spring the whole village was buried in white cherry-blossom, and in the summer they sold cherries at three kopecks a pail. One could pay three kopecks and pick as one liked. Their women were handsome and looked well fed, they were fond of finery, and never did anything even on working-days, but spent all their time sitting on the ledge in front of their houses and searching in each other's heads.

But at last there was the sound of footsteps. Lyubka, a girl of twenty, with bare feet and a red dress, came into the room.... She looked sideways at Yergunov and walked twice from one end of the room to the other. She did not move simply, but with tiny steps, thrusting forward her bosom; evidently she enjoyed padding about with her bare feet on the freshly washed floor, and had taken off her shoes on purpose.

Kalashnikov laughed at something and beckoned her with his finger. She went up to the table, and he showed her a picture of the Prophet Elijah, who, driving three horses abreast, was dashing up to the sky. Lyubka put her elbow on the table; her plait fell across her shoulder—a long chestnut plait tied with red ribbon at the end—and it almost touched the floor. She, too, smiled.

"A splendid, wonderful picture," said Kalashnikov. "Wonderful," he repeated, and motioned with his hand as though he wanted to take the reins instead of Elijah.

The wind howled in the stove; something growled and squeaked as though a big dog had strangled a rat.

"Ugh! the unclean spirits are abroad!" said Lyubka.

"That's the wind," said Kalashnikov; and after a pause he raised his eyes to Yergunov and asked: "And what is your learned opinion, Osip Vassilyitch—are there devils in this world or not?"

"What's one to say, brother?" said Yergunov, and he shrugged one shoulder. "If one reasons from science, of course there are no devils, for it's a superstition; but if one looks at it simply, as you and I do now, there are devils, to put it shortly. . . . I have seen a great deal in my life. . . . When I finished my studies I served as medical assistant in the army in a regiment of the dragoons, and I have been in the war, of course. I have a medal and a decoration from the Red Cross, but after the treaty of San Stefano I returned to Russia and went into the service of the Zemstvo. And in consequence of my enormous circulation about the world, I may say I have seen more than many another has dreamed of. It has happened to me to see devils, too; that is, not devils with horns and a tail—that is all nonsense—but just, to speak precisely, something of the sort."

"Where?" asked Kalashnikov.

"In various places. There is no need to go far. Last year I met him here—speak of him not at night—near this very inn. I was driving, I remember, to Golyshino; I was going there to vaccinate. Of course, as usual, I had the racing droshky and a horse, and all the necessary paraphernalia, and, what's more, I had a watch and all the rest of it, so I was on my guard as I drove along, for fear of some mischance. There are lots of tramps of all sorts. I came up to the Zmeinoy Ravine—damnation take it—and was just going down it, when all at once somebody comes up to me—such a fellow! Black hair, black eyes, and his whole face looked smutted with soot. . . . He comes straight up to the horse and takes hold of the left rein: 'Stop!' He looked at the horse, then at me, then dropped the reins, and without saying a bad word, 'Where are you going?' says he. And he showed his teeth in a grin, and his eyes were spiteful-looking. . . . 'Ah,' thought I, 'you are a queer customer!' 'I am going to vaccinate for the smallpox,' said I. 'And what is that to you?' 'Well, if that's so,' says he, 'vaccinate me.' He bared his arm and thrust it under my nose. Of course, I did not bandy words with him; I just vaccinated him to get rid of him. Afterwards I looked at my lancet and it had gone rusty."

The peasant who was asleep near the stove suddenly turned over and flung off the sheepskin; to his great surprise, Yergunov recognized the stranger he had met that day at Zmeinoy Ravine. This peasant's hair, beard, and eyes were black as soot; his face was swarthy; and, to add to the effect, there was a black spot the size of a lentil on his right cheek. He looked mockingly at the hospital assistant and said:

"I did take hold of the left rein—that was so; but about the smallpox you are lying, sir. And there was not a word said about the smallpox between us."

Yergunov was disconcerted.

"I'm not talking about you," he said. "Lie down, since you are lying down."

The dark-skinned peasant had never been to the hospital, and Yergunov did not know who he was or where he came from; and now, looking at him, he made up his mind that the man must be a gypsy. The peasant got up and, stretching and yawning loudly, went up to Lyubka and Kalashnikov, and sat down beside them, and he, too, began looking at the book. His sleepy face softened and a look of envy came into it.

"Look, Merik," Lyubka said to him; "get me such horses and I will drive to heaven."

"Sinners can't drive to heaven," said Kalashnikov. "That's for holiness."

Then Lyubka laid the table and brought in a big piece of fat bacon, salted cucumbers, a wooden platter of boiled meat cut up into little pieces, then a frying-pan, in which there were sausages and cabbage spluttering. A cut-glass decanter of vodka, which diffused a smell of orange-peel all over the room when it was poured out, was put on the table also.

Yergunov was annoyed that Kalashnikov and the dark fellow Merik talked together and took no notice of him at all, behaving exactly as though he were not in the room. And he wanted to talk to them, to brag, to drink, to have a good meal, and if possible to have a little fun with Lyubka, who sat down near him half a dozen times while they were at supper, and, as though by accident, brushed against him with her handsome shoulders and passed her hands over her broad hips. She was a healthy, active girl, always laughing and never still: she would sit down, then get up, and when she was sitting down she would keep turning first her face and then her back to her neighbour, like a fidgety child, and never failed to brush against him with her elbows or her knees.

And he was displeased, too, that the peasants drank only a glass each and no more, and it was awkward for him to drink alone. But he could not refrain from taking a second glass, all the same, then a third, and he ate all the sausage. He brought himself to flatter the peasants, that they might accept him as one of the party instead of holding him at arm's length.

"You are a fine set of fellows in Bogalyovka!" he said, and wagged his head.

"In what way fine fellows?" enquired Kalashnikov.

"Why, about horses, for instance. Fine fellows at stealing!"

"H'm! fine fellows, you call them. Nothing but thieves and drunkards."

"They have had their day, but it is over," said Merik, after a pause. "But now they have only Filya left, and he is blind."

"Yes, there is no one but Filya," said Kalashnikov, with a sigh. "Reckon it up, he must be seventy; the German settlers knocked out one of his eyes, and he does not see well with the other. It is cataract. In old days the police officer would shout as soon as he saw him: 'Hey, you Shamil!' and all the peasants called him that—he was Shamil all over the place; and now his only name is One-eyed Filya. But he was a fine fellow! Lyuba's father, Andrey Grigoritch, and he stole one night into Rozhnovo—there were cavalry regiments stationed there—and carried off nine of the soldiers' horses, the very best of them. They weren't frightened of the sentry, and in the morning they sold all the horses for twenty roubles to the gypsy Afonka. Yes! But nowadays a man contrives to carry off a horse whose rider is drunk or asleep, and has no fear of God, but will take the very boots from a drunkard, and then slinks off and goes away a hundred and fifty miles with a horse, and haggles at the market, haggles like a Jew, till the policeman catches him, the fool. There is no fun in it; it is simply a disgrace! A paltry set of people, I must say."

"What about Merik?" asked Lyubka.

"Merik is not one of us," said Kalashnikov. "He is a Harkov man from Mizhiritch. But that he is a bold fellow, that's the truth; there's no gainsaying that he is a fine fellow."

Lyubka looked slily and gleefully at Merik, and said:

"It wasn't for nothing they dipped him in a hole in the ice."

"How was that?" asked Yergunov.

"It was like this . . ." said Merik, and he laughed. "Filya carried off three horses from the Samoylenka tenants, and they pitched upon me. There were ten of the tenants at Samoylenka, and with their labourers there were thirty altogether, and all of them Molokans. . . . So one of them says to me at the market: 'Come and have a look, Merik; we have brought some new horses from the fair.' I was interested, of course. I went up to them, and the whole lot of them, thirty men, tied my hands behind me and led me to the river. 'We'll show you fine horses,' they said. One hole in the ice was there already; they cut another beside it seven feet away. Then, to be sure, they took a cord and put a noose under my armpits, and tied a crooked stick to the other end, long enough to reach both holes. They thrust the stick in and dragged it through. I went plop into the ice-hole just as I was, in my fur coat and my high boots, while they stood and shoved me, one with his foot and one with his stick, then dragged me under the ice and pulled me out of the other hole."

Lyubka shuddered and shrugged.

"At first I was in a fever from the cold," Merik went on, "but when they pulled me out I was helpless, and lay in the snow, and the Molokans stood round and hit me with sticks on my knees and my elbows. It hurt fearfully. They beat me and they went away . . . and everything on me was frozen, my clothes were covered with ice. I got up, but I couldn't move. Thank God, a woman drove by and gave me a lift."

Meanwhile Yergunov had drunk five or six glasses of vodka; his heart felt lighter, and he longed to tell some extraordinary, wonderful story too, and to show that he, too, was a bold fellow and not afraid of anything.

"I'll tell you what happened to us in Penza Province . . ." he began.

Either because he had drunk a great deal and was a little tipsy, or perhaps because he had twice been detected in a lie, the peasants took not the slightest notice of him, and even left off answering his questions. What was worse, they permitted themselves a frankness in his presence that made him feel uncomfortable and cold all over, and that meant that they took no notice of him.

Kalashnikov had the dignified manners of a sedate and sensible man; he spoke weightily, and made the sign of the cross over his mouth every time he yawned, and no one could have supposed that this was a thief, a heartless thief who had stripped poor creatures, who had already been twice in prison, and who had been sentenced by the commune to exile in Siberia, and had been bought off by his father and uncle, who were as great thieves and rogues as he was. Merik gave himself the airs of a bravo. He saw that Lyubka and Kalashnikov were admiring him, and looked upon himself as a very fine fellow, and put his arms akimbo, squared his chest, or stretched so that the bench creaked under him. . . .

After supper Kalashnikov prayed to the holy image without getting up from his seat, and shook hands with Merik; the latter prayed too, and shook Kalashnikov's hand. Lyubka cleared away the supper, shook out on the table some peppermint biscuits, dried nuts, and pumpkin seeds, and placed two bottles of sweet wine.

"The kingdom of heaven and peace everlasting to Andrey Grigoritch," said Kalashnikov, clinking glasses with Merik. "When he was alive we used to gather together here or at his brother Martin's, and—my word! my word! what men, what talks! Remarkable conversations! Martin used to be here, and Filya, and Fyodor Stukotey. . . . It was all done in style, it was all in keeping. . . . And what fun we had! We did have fun, we did have fun!"

Lyubka went out and soon afterwards came back wearing a green kerchief and beads.

"Look, Merik, what Kalashnikov brought me to-day," she said.

She looked at herself in the looking-glass, and tossed her head several times to make the beads jingle. And then she opened a chest and began taking out, first, a cotton dress with red and blue flowers on it, and then a red one with flounces which rustled and crackled like paper, then a new kerchief, dark blue, shot with many colours—and all these things she showed and flung up her hands, laughing as though astonished that she had such treasures.

Kalashnikov tuned the balalaika and began playing it, but Yergunov could not make out what sort of song he was singing, and whether it was gay or melancholy, because at one moment it was so mournful he wanted to cry, and at the next it would be merry. Merik suddenly jumped up and began tapping with his heels on the same spot, then, brandishing his arms, he moved on his heels from the table to the stove, from the stove to the chest, then he bounded up as though he had been stung, clicked the heels of his boots together in the air, and began going round and round in a crouching position. Lyubka waved both her arms, uttered a desperate shriek, and followed him. At first she moved sideways, like a snake, as though she wanted to steal up to someone and strike him from behind. She tapped rapidly with her bare heels as Merik had done with the heels of his boots, then she turned round and round like a top and crouched down, and her red dress was blown out like a bell. Merik, looking angrily at her, and showing his teeth in a grin, flew towards her in the same crouching posture as though he wanted to crush her with his terrible legs, while she jumped up, flung back her head, and waving her arms as a big bird does its wings, floated across the room scarcely touching the floor. . . .

"What a flame of a girl!" thought Yergunov, sitting on the chest, and from there watching the dance. "What fire! Give up everything for her, and it would be too little. . . ."

And he regretted that he was a hospital assistant, and not a simple peasant, that he wore a reefer coat and a chain with a gilt key on it instead of a blue shirt with a cord tied round the waist. Then he could boldly have sung, danced, flung both arms round Lyubka as Merik did. . . .

The sharp tapping, shouts, and whoops set the crockery ringing in the cupboard and the flame of the candle dancing.

The thread broke and the beads were scattered all over the floor, the green kerchief slipped off, and Lyubka was transformed into a red cloud flitting by and flashing black eyes, and it seemed as though in another second Merik's arms and legs would drop off.

But finally Merik stamped for the last time, and stood still as though turned to stone. Exhausted and almost breathless, Lyubka sank on to his bosom and leaned against him as against a post, and he put his arms round her, and looking into her eyes, said tenderly and caressingly, as though in jest:

"I'll find out where your old mother's money is hidden, I'll murder her and cut your little throat for you, and after that I will set fire to the inn. . . . People will think you have perished in the fire, and with your money I shall go to Kuban. I'll keep droves of horses and flocks of sheep. . . ."

Lyubka made no answer, but only looked at him with a guilty air, and asked:

"And it is nice in Kuban, Merik?"

He said nothing, but went to the chest, sat down, and sank into thought; most likely he was dreaming of Kuban.

"It's time for me to be going," said Kalashnikov, getting up. "Filya must be waiting for me. Good-bye, Lyuba."

Yergunov went out into the yard to see that Kalashnikov did not go off with his horse. The snowstorm still persisted. White clouds were floating about the yard, their long tails clinging to the rough grass and the bushes, while on the other side of the fence in the open country huge giants in white robes with wide sleeves were whirling round and falling to the ground, and getting up again to wave their arms and fight. And the wind, the wind! The bare birches and cherry-trees, unable to endure its rude caresses, bowed low down to the ground and wailed: "God, for what sin hast Thou bound us to the earth and will not let us go free?"

"Wo!" said Kalashnikov sternly, and he got on his horse; one half of the gate was opened, and by it lay a high snowdrift. "Well, get on!" shouted Kalashnikov. His little short-legged nag set off, and sank up to its stomach in the drift at once. Kalashnikov was white all over with the snow, and soon vanished from sight with his horse.

When Yergunov went back into the room, Lyubka was creeping about the floor picking up her beads; Merik was not there.

"A splendid girl!" thought Yergunov, as he lay down on the bench and put his coat under his head. "Oh, if only Merik were not here." Lyubka excited him as she crept about the floor by the bench, and he thought that if Merik had not been there he would certainly have got up and embraced her, and then one would see what would happen. It was true she was only a girl, but not likely to be chaste; and even if she were—need one stand on ceremony in a den of thieves? Lyubka collected her beads and went out. The candle burnt down and the flame caught the paper in the candlestick. Yergunov laid his revolver and matches beside him, and put out the candle. The light before the holy images flickered so much that it hurt his eyes, and patches of light danced on the ceiling, on the floor, and on the cupboard, and among them he had visions of Lyubka, buxom, full-bosomed: now she was turning round like a top, now she was exhausted and breathless. . . .

"Oh, if the devils would carry off that Merik," he thought.

The little lamp gave a last flicker, spluttered, and went out. Someone, it must have been Merik, came into the room and sat down on the bench. He puffed at his pipe, and for an instant lighted up a dark cheek with a patch on it. Yergunov's throat was irritated by the horrible fumes of the tobacco smoke.

"What filthy tobacco you have got—damnation take it!" said Yergunov. "It makes me positively sick."

"I mix my tobacco with the flowers of the oats," answered Merik after a pause. "It is better for the chest."

He smoked, spat, and went out again. Half an hour passed, and all at once there was the gleam of a light in the passage. Merik appeared in a coat and cap, then Lyubka with a candle in her hand.

"Do stay, Merik," said Lyubka in an imploring voice.

"No, Lyuba, don't keep me."

"Listen, Merik," said Lyubka, and her voice grew soft and tender. "I know you will find mother's money, and will do for her and for me, and will go to Kuban and love other girls; but God be with you. I only ask you one thing, sweetheart: do stay!"

"No, I want some fun . . ." said Merik, fastening his belt.

"But you have nothing to go on.... You came on foot; what are you going on?"

Merik bent down to Lyubka and whispered something in her ear; she looked towards the door and laughed through her tears.

"He is asleep, the puffed-up devil ..." she said.

Merik embraced her, kissed her vigorously, and went out. Yergunov thrust his revolver into his pocket, jumped up, and ran after him.

"Get out of the way!" he said to Lyubka, who hurriedly bolted the door of the entry and stood across the threshold. "Let me pass! Why are you standing here?"

"What do you want to go out for?"

"To have a look at my horse."

Lyubka gazed up at him with a sly and caressing look.

"Why look at it? You had better look at me ..." she said, then she bent down and touched with her finger the gilt watch-key that hung on his chain.

"Let me pass, or he will go off on my horse," said Yergunov. "Let me go, you devil!" he shouted, and giving her an angry blow on the shoulder, he pressed his chest against her with all his might to push her away from the door, but she kept tight hold of the bolt, and was like iron.

"Let me go!" he shouted, exhausted; "he will go off with it, I tell you."

"Why should he? He won't." Breathing hard and rubbing her shoulder, which hurt, she looked up at him again, flushed a little and laughed. "Don't go away, dear heart," she said; "I am dull alone."

Yergunov looked into her eyes, hesitated, and put his arms round her; she did not resist.

"Come, no nonsense; let me go," he begged her. She did not speak.

"I heard you just now," he said, "telling Merik that you love him."

"I dare say.... My heart knows who it is I love."

She put her finger on the key again, and said softly: "Give me that."

Yergunov unfastened the key and gave it to her. She suddenly craned her neck and listened with a grave face, and her expression struck Yergunov as cold and cunning; he thought of his horse, and now easily pushed her aside and ran out into the yard. In the shed a sleepy pig was grunting with lazy regularity and a cow was knocking her horn. Yergunov lighted a match and saw the pig, and the cow, and the dogs, which rushed at him on all sides at seeing the light, but there was no trace of the horse. Shouting and waving his arms at the dogs, stumbling over the drifts and sticking in the snow, he ran out at the gate and fell to gazing into the darkness. He strained his eyes to the utmost, and saw only the snow flying and the snowflakes distinctly forming into all sorts of shapes; at one moment the white, laughing face of a corpse would peep out of the darkness, at the next a white horse would gallop by with an Amazon in a muslin dress upon it, at the next a string of white swans would fly overhead. . . . Shaking with anger and cold, and not knowing what to do, Yergunov fired his revolver at the dogs, and did not hit one of them; then he rushed back to the house.

When he went into the entry he distinctly heard someone scurry out of the room and bang the door. It was dark in the room. Yergunov pushed against the door; it was locked. Then, lighting match after match, he rushed back into the entry, from there into the kitchen, and from the kitchen into a little room where all the walls were hung with petticoats and dresses, where there was a smell of cornflowers and fennel, and a bedstead with a perfect mountain of pillows, standing in the corner by the stove; this must have been the old mother's room. From there he passed into another little room, and here he saw Lyubka. She was lying on a chest, covered with a gay-coloured patchwork cotton quilt, pretending to be asleep. A little ikon-lamp was burning in the corner above the pillow.

"Where is my horse?" Yergunov asked.

Lyubka did not stir.

"Where is my horse, I am asking you?" Yergunov repeated still more sternly, and he tore the quilt off her. "I am asking you, she-devil!" he shouted.

She jumped up on her knees, and with one hand holding her shift and with the other trying to clutch the quilt, huddled against the wall. . . . She looked at Yergunov with repulsion and terror in her eyes, and, like a wild beast in a trap, kept cunning watch on his faintest movement.

"Tell me where my horse is, or I'll knock the life out of you," shouted Yergunov.

"Get away, dirty brute!" she said in a hoarse voice.

Yergunov seized her by the shift near the neck and tore it. And then he could not restrain himself, and with all his might embraced the girl. But hissing with fury, she slipped out of his arms, and freeing one hand—the other was tangled in the torn shift—hit him a blow with her fist on the skull.

His head was dizzy with the pain, there was a ringing and rattling in his ears, he staggered back, and at that moment received another blow—this time on the temple. Reeling and clutching at the door-posts, that he might not fall, he made his way to the room where his things were, and lay down on the bench; then after lying for a little time, took the matchbox out of his pocket and began lighting match after match for no object: he lit it, blew it out, and threw it under the table, and went on till all the matches were gone.

Meanwhile the air began to turn blue outside, the cocks began to crow, but his head still ached, and there was an uproar in his ears as though he were sitting under a railway bridge and hearing the trains passing over his head. He got, somehow, into his coat and cap; the saddle and the bundle of his purchases he could not find, his knapsack was empty: it was not for nothing that someone had scurried out of the room when he came in from the yard.

He took a poker from the kitchen to keep off the dogs, and went out into the yard, leaving the door open. The snow-storm had subsided and it was calm outside. . . . When he went out at the gate, the white plain looked dead, and there was not a single bird in the morning sky. On both sides of the road and in the distance there were bluish patches of young copse.

Yergunov began thinking how he would be greeted at the hospital and what the doctor would say to him; it was absolutely necessary to think of that, and to prepare beforehand to answer questions he would be asked, but this thought grew blurred and slipped away. He walked along thinking of nothing but Lyubka, of the peasants with whom he had passed the night; he remembered how, after Lyubka struck him the second time, she had bent down to the floor for the quilt, and how her loose hair had fallen on the floor. His mind was in a maze, and he wondered why there were in the world doctors, hospital assistants, merchants, clerks, and peasants instead of simple free men? There are, to be sure, free birds, free beasts, a free Merik, and they are not afraid of anyone, and don't need anyone! And whose idea was it, who had decreed that one must get up in the morning, dine at midday, go to bed in the evening; that a doctor takes precedence of a hospital assistant; that one must live in rooms and love only one's wife? And why not the contrary—dine at night and sleep in the day? Ah, to jump on a horse without enquiring whose it is, to ride races with the wind like a devil, over fields and forests and ravines, to make love to girls, to mock at everyone. . . .

Yergunov thrust the poker into the snow, pressed his forehead to the cold white trunk of a birch-tree, and sank into thought; and his grey, monotonous life, his wages, his subordinate position, the dispensary, the everlasting to-do with the bottles and blisters, struck him as contemptible, sickening.

"Who says it's a sin to enjoy oneself?" he asked himself with vexation. "Those who say that have never lived in freedom like Merik and Kalashnikov, and have never loved Lyubka; they have been beggars all their lives, have lived without any pleasure, and have only loved their wives, who are like frogs."

And he thought about himself that he had not hitherto been a thief, a swindler, or even a brigand, simply because he could not, or had not yet met with a suitable opportunity.

—

A year and a half passed. In spring, after Easter, Yergunov, who had long before been dismissed from the hospital and was hanging about without a job, came out of the tavern in Ryepino and sauntered aimlessly along the street.

He went out into the open country. Here there was the scent of spring, and a warm caressing wind was blowing. The calm, starry night looked down from the sky on the earth. My God, how infinite the depth of the sky, and with what fathomless immensity it stretched over the world! The world is created well enough, only why and with what right do people, thought Yergunov, divide their fellows into the sober and the drunken, the employed and the dismissed, and so on. Why do the sober and well fed sleep comfortably in their homes while the drunken and the hungry must wander about the country without a refuge? Why was it that if anyone had not a job and did not get a salary he had to go hungry, without clothes and boots? Whose idea was it? Why was it the birds and the wild beasts in the woods did not have jobs and get salaries, but lived as they pleased?

Far away in the sky a beautiful crimson glow lay quivering, stretched wide over the horizon. Yergunov stopped, and for a long time he gazed at it, and kept wondering why was it that if he had carried off someone else's samovar the day before and sold it for drink in the taverns it would be a sin? Why was it?

Two carts drove by on the road; in one of them there was a woman asleep, in the other sat an old man without a cap on. . . .

"Grandfather, where is that fire?" asked Yergunov.

"Andrey Tchirikov's inn," answered the old man.

And Yergunov recalled what had happened to him eighteen months before in the winter, in that very inn, and how Merik had boasted; and he imagined the old woman and Lyubka, with their throats cut, burning, and he envied Merik. And when he walked back to the tavern, looking at the houses of the rich publicans, cattle-dealers, and blacksmiths, he reflected how nice it would be to steal by night into some rich man's house!

Gusev

I

It was getting dark; it would soon be night.

Gusev, a discharged soldier, sat up in his hammock and said in an undertone:

"I say, Pavel Ivanitch. A soldier at Sutchan told me: while they were sailing a big fish came into collision with their ship and stove a hole in it."

The nondescript individual whom he was addressing, and whom everyone in the ship's hospital called Pavel Ivanitch, was silent, as though he had not heard.

And again a stillness followed.... The wind frolicked with the rigging, the screw throbbed, the waves lashed, the hammocks creaked, but the ear had long ago become accustomed to these sounds, and it seemed that everything around was asleep and silent. It was dreary. The three invalids—two soldiers and a sailor—who had been playing cards all the day were asleep and talking in their dreams.

It seemed as though the ship were beginning to rock. The hammock slowly rose and fell under Gusev, as though it were heaving a sigh, and this was repeated once, twice, three times.... Something crashed on to the floor with a clang: it must have been a jug falling down.

"The wind has broken loose from its chain . . ." said Gusev, listening.

This time Pavel Ivanitch cleared his throat and answered irritably:

"One minute a vessel's running into a fish, the next, the wind's breaking loose from its chain. . . . Is the wind a beast that it can break loose from its chain?"

"That's how christened folk talk."

"They are as ignorant as you are then. . . . They say all sorts of things. One must keep a head on one's shoulders and use one's reason. You are a senseless creature."

Pavel Ivanitch was subject to sea-sickness. When the sea was rough he was usually ill-humoured, and the merest trifle would make him irritable. And in Gusev's opinion there was absolutely nothing to be vexed about. What was there strange or wonderful, for instance, in the fish or in the wind's breaking loose from its chain? Suppose the fish were as big as a mountain and its back were as hard as a sturgeon: and in the same way, supposing that away yonder at the end of the world there stood great stone walls and the fierce winds were chained up to the walls . . . if they had not broken loose, why did they tear about all over the sea like maniacs, and struggle to escape like dogs? If they were not chained up, what did become of them when it was calm?

Gusev pondered for a long time about fishes as big as a mountain and stout, rusty chains, then he began to feel dull and thought of his native place to which he was returning after five years' service in the East. He pictured an immense pond covered with snow. . . . On one side of the pond the red-brick building of the potteries with a tall chimney and clouds of black smoke; on the other side—a village. . . . His brother Alexey comes out in a sledge from the fifth yard from the end; behind him sits his little son Vanka in big felt over-boots, and his little girl Akulka, also in big felt boots. Alexey has been drinking, Vanka is laughing, Akulka's face he could not see, she had muffled herself up.

"You never know, he'll get the children frozen . . ." thought Gusev. "Lord send them sense and judgment that they may honour their father and mother and not be wiser than their parents."

"They want re-soleing," a delirious sailor says in a bass voice. "Yes, yes!"

Gusev's thoughts break off, and instead of a pond there suddenly appears apropos of nothing a huge bull's head without eyes, and the horse and sledge are not driving along, but are whirling round and round in a cloud of smoke. But still he was glad he had seen his own folks. He held his breath from delight, shudders ran all over him, and his fingers twitched.

"The Lord let us meet again," he muttered feverishly, but he at once opened his eyes and sought in the darkness for water.

He drank and lay back, and again the sledge was moving, then again the bull's head without eyes, smoke, clouds.... And so on till daybreak.

II

The first outline visible in the darkness was a blue circle—the little round window; then little by little Gusev could distinguish his neighbour in the next hammock, Pavel Ivanitch. The man slept sitting up, as he could not breathe lying down. His face was grey, his nose was long and sharp, his eyes looked huge from the terrible thinness of his face, his temples were sunken, his beard was skimpy, his hair was long.... Looking at him you could not make out of what class he was, whether he were a gentleman, a merchant, or a peasant. Judging from his expression and his long hair he might have been a hermit or a lay brother in a monastery—but if one listened to what he said it seemed that he could not be a monk. He was worn out by his cough and his illness and by the stifling heat, and breathed with difficulty, moving his parched lips. Noticing that Gusev was looking at him he turned his face towards him and said:

"I begin to guess.... Yes.... I understand it all perfectly now."

"What do you understand, Pavel Ivanitch?"

"I'll tell you.... It has always seemed to me strange that terribly ill as you are you should be here in a steamer where it is so hot and stifling and we are always being tossed up and down, where, in fact, everything threatens you with death; now it is all clear to me.... Yes.... Your doctors put you on the steamer to get rid of you. They get sick of looking after poor brutes like you.... You don't pay them anything, they have a bother with you, and you damage their records with your deaths—

so, of course, you are brutes! It's not difficult to get rid of you. . . . All that is necessary is, in the first place, to have no conscience or humanity, and, secondly, to deceive the steamer authorities. The first condition need hardly be considered, in that respect we are artists; and one can always succeed in the second with a little practice. In a crowd of four hundred healthy soldiers and sailors half a dozen sick ones are not conspicuous; well, they drove you all on to the steamer, mixed you with the healthy ones, hurriedly counted you over, and in the confusion nothing amiss was noticed, and when the steamer had started they saw that there were paralytics and consumptives in the last stage lying about on the deck. . . ."

Gusev did not understand Pavel Ivanitch; but supposing he was being blamed, he said in self-defence:

"I lay on the deck because I had not the strength to stand; when we were unloaded from the barge on to the ship I caught a fearful chill."

"It's revolting," Pavel Ivanitch went on. "The worst of it is they know perfectly well that you can't last out the long journey, and yet they put you here. Supposing you get as far as the Indian Ocean, what then? It's horrible to think of it. . . . And that's their gratitude for your faithful, irreproachable service!"

Pavel Ivanitch's eyes looked angry; he frowned contemptuously and said, gasping:

"Those are the people who ought to be plucked in the newspapers till the feathers fly in all directions."

The two sick soldiers and the sailor were awake and already playing cards. The sailor was half reclining in his hammock, the soldiers were sitting near him on the floor in the most uncomfortable attitudes. One of the soldiers had his right arm in a sling, and the hand was swathed up in a regular bundle so that he held his cards under his right arm or in the crook of his elbow while he played with the left. The ship was rolling heavily. They could not stand up, nor drink tea, nor take their medicines.

"Were you an officer's servant?" Pavel Ivanitch asked Gusev.

"Yes, an officer's servant."

"My God, my God!" said Pavel Ivanitch, and he shook his head mournfully. "To tear a man out of his home, drag him twelve thousand miles away, then to drive him into consumption and . . . and what is it all for, one wonders? To turn him into a servant for some Captain Kopeikin or midshipman Dirka! How logical!"

"It's not hard work, Pavel Ivanitch. You get up in the morning and clean the boots, get the samovar, sweep the rooms, and then you have nothing more to do. The lieutenant is all the day drawing plans, and if you like you can say your prayers, if you like you can read a book or go out into the street. God grant everyone such a life."

"Yes, very nice, the lieutenant draws plans all the day and you sit in the kitchen and pine for home. . . . Plans indeed! . . . It is not plans that matter, but a human life. Life is not given twice, it must be treated mercifully."

"Of course, Pavel Ivanitch, a bad man gets no mercy anywhere, neither at home nor in the army, but if you live as you ought and obey orders, who has any need to insult you? The officers are educated gentlemen, they understand. . . . In five years I was never once in prison, and I was never struck a blow, so help me God, but once."

"What for?"

"For fighting. I have a heavy hand, Pavel Ivanitch. Four Chinamen came into our yard; they were bringing firewood or something, I don't remember. Well, I was bored and I knocked them about a bit, one's nose began bleeding, damn the fellow. . . . The lieutenant saw it through the little window, he was angry and gave me a box on the ear."

"Foolish, pitiful man . . ." whispered Pavel Ivanitch. "You don't understand anything."

He was utterly exhausted by the tossing of the ship and closed his eyes; his head alternately fell back and dropped forward on his breast. Several times he tried to lie down but nothing came of it; his difficulty in breathing prevented it.

"And what did you hit the four Chinamen for?" he asked a little while afterwards.

"Oh, nothing. They came into the yard and I hit them."

And a stillness followed. . . . The card-players had been playing for two hours with enthusiasm and loud abuse of one another, but the motion of the ship overcame them, too; they threw aside the cards and lay down. Again Gusev saw the big pond, the brick building, the village.... Again the sledge was coming along, again Vanka was laughing and Akulka, silly little thing, threw open her fur coat and stuck her feet out, as much as to say: "Look, good people, my snowboots are not like Vanka's, they are new ones."

"Five years old, and she has no sense yet," Gusev muttered in delirium. "Instead of kicking your legs you had better come and get your soldier uncle a drink. I will give you something nice."

Then Andron with a flintlock gun on his shoulder was carrying a hare he had killed, and he was followed by the decrepit old Jew Isaitchik, who offers to barter the hare for a piece of soap; then the black calf in the shed, then Domna sewing at a shirt and crying about something, and then again the bull's head without eyes, black smoke....

Overhead someone gave a loud shout, several sailors ran by, they seemed to be dragging something bulky over the deck, something fell with a crash. Again they ran by.... Had something gone wrong? Gusev raised his head, listened, and saw that the two soldiers and the sailor were playing cards again; Pavel Ivanitch was sitting up moving his lips. It was stifling, one hadn't strength to breathe, one was thirsty, the water was warm, disgusting. The ship heaved as much as ever.

Suddenly something strange happened to one of the soldiers playing cards.... He called hearts diamonds, got muddled in his score, and dropped his cards, then with a frightened, foolish smile looked round at all of them.

"I shan't be a minute, mates, I'll . . ." he said, and lay down on the floor.

Everybody was amazed. They called to him, he did not answer.

"Stepan, maybe you are feeling bad, eh?" the soldier with his arm in a sling asked him. "Perhaps we had better bring the priest, eh?"

"Have a drink of water, Stepan . . ." said the sailor. "Here, lad, drink."

"Why are you knocking the jug against his teeth?" said Gusev angrily. "Don't you see, turnip head?"

"What?"

"What?" Gusev repeated, mimicking him. "There is no breath in him, he is dead! That's what! What nonsensical people, Lord have mercy on us . . . !"

III

The ship was not rocking and Pavel Ivanitch was more cheerful. He was no longer ill-humoured. His face had a boastful, defiant, mocking expression. He looked as though he wanted to say: "Yes, in a minute I will tell you something that will make you split your sides with laughing." The little round window was open and a soft breeze was blowing on Pavel Ivanitch. There was a sound of voices, of the plash of oars in the water. . . . Just under the little window someone began droning in a high, unpleasant voice: no doubt it was a Chinaman singing.

"Here we are in the harbour," said Pavel Ivanitch, smiling ironically. "Only another month and we shall be in Russia. Well, worthy gentlemen and warriors! I shall arrive at Odessa and from there go straight to Harkov. In Harkov I have a friend, a literary man. I shall go to him and say, 'Come, old man, put aside your horrid subjects, ladies' amours and the beauties of nature, and show up human depravity.' "

For a minute he pondered, then said:

"Gusev, do you know how I took them in?"

"Took in whom, Pavel Ivanitch?"

"Why, these fellows. . . . You know that on this steamer there is only a first-class and a third-class, and they only allow peasants—that is the riff-raff—to go in the third. If you have got on a reefer jacket and have the faintest resemblance to a gentleman or a bourgeois you must go first-class, if you please. You must fork out five hundred roubles if you die for it. Why, I ask, have you made such a rule? Do you want to raise the prestige of educated Russians thereby? Not a bit of it. We don't let you go third-class simply because a decent person can't go third-class; it is very horrible and disgusting. Yes, indeed. I am very grateful for such solicitude for decent people's welfare. But in any case, whether it is nasty there or nice, five hundred roubles I haven't got. I haven't pilfered government money. I haven't exploited the natives, I haven't trafficked in contraband, I have flogged no one to death, so judge whether I have the right to travel first-class and even less to reckon myself of the educated class? But you won't catch them with logic. . . . One has to resort to deception. I put on a workman's coat and high boots, I assumed a drunken, servile mug and went to the agents: 'Give us a little ticket, your honour,' said I. . . ."

"Why, what class do you belong to?" asked a sailor.

"Clerical. My father was an honest priest, he always told the great ones of the world the truth to their faces; and he had a great deal to put up with in consequence."

Pavel Ivanitch was exhausted with talking and gasped for breath, but still went on:

"Yes, I always tell people the truth to their faces. I am not afraid of anyone or anything. There is a vast difference between me and all of you in that respect. You are in darkness, you are blind, crushed; you see nothing and what you do see you don't understand. . . . You are told the wind breaks loose from its chain, that you are beasts, Petchenyegs, and you believe it; they punch you in the neck, you kiss their hands; some animal in a sable-lined coat robs you and then tips you fifteen kopecks and you: 'Let me kiss your hand, sir.' You are pariahs, pitiful people. . . . I am a different sort. My eyes are open, I see it all as clearly as a hawk or an eagle when it floats over the earth, and I understand it all. I am a living protest. I see irresponsible tyranny—I protest. I see cant and hypocrisy—I protest. I see swine triumphant—I protest. And I cannot be suppressed, no Spanish Inquisition can make me hold my tongue. No. . . . Cut out my tongue and I would protest in dumb show; shut me up in a cellar—I will shout from it to be heard half a mile away, or I will starve myself to death that they may have another weight on their black consciences. Kill me and I will haunt them with my ghost. All my acquaintances say to me: 'You are a most insufferable person, Pavel Ivanitch.' I am proud of such a reputation. I have served three years in the far East, and I shall be remembered there for a hundred years: I had rows with everyone. My friends write to me from Russia, 'Don't come back,' but here I am going back to spite them . . . yes. . . . That is life as I understand it. That is what one can call life."

Gusev was looking at the little window and was not listening. A boat was swaying on the transparent, soft, turquoise water all bathed in hot, dazzling sunshine. In it there were naked Chinamen holding up cages with canaries and calling out:

"It sings, it sings!"

Another boat knocked against the first; the steam cutter darted by. And then there came another boat with a fat Chinaman sitting in it, eating rice with little sticks.

Languidly the water heaved, languidly the white seagulls floated over it.

"I should like to give that fat fellow one in the neck," thought Gusev, gazing at the stout Chinaman, with a yawn.

He dozed off, and it seemed to him that all nature was dozing, too. Time flew swiftly by; imperceptibly the day passed, imperceptibly the darkness came on. . . . The steamer was no longer standing still, but moving on further.

IV

Two days passed, Pavel Ivanitch lay down instead of sitting up; his eyes were closed, his nose seemed to have grown sharper.

"Pavel Ivanitch," Gusev called to him. "Hey, Pavel Ivanitch."

Pavel Ivanitch opened his eyes and moved his lips.

"Are you feeling bad?"

"No . . . it's nothing . . ." answered Pavel Ivanitch, gasping. "Nothing; on the contrary . . . I am rather better. . . . You see I can lie down. . . . I am a little easier. . . ."

"Well, thank God for that, Pavel Ivanitch."

"When I compare myself with you I am sorry for you . . . poor fellow. My lungs are all right, it is only a stomach cough. . . . I can stand hell, let alone the Red Sea. Besides I take a critical attitude to my illness and to the medicines they give me for it. While you . . . you are in darkness. . . . It's hard for you, very, very hard!"

The ship was not rolling, it was calm, but as hot and stifling as a bath-house; it was not only hard to speak but even hard to listen.

Gusev hugged his knees, laid his head on them and thought of his home. Good heavens, what a relief it was to think of snow and cold in that stifling heat! You drive in a sledge, all at once the horses take fright at something and bolt. . . . Regardless of the road, the ditches, the ravines, they dash like mad things, right through the village, over the pond by the pottery works, out across the open fields. "Hold on," the pottery hands and the peasants shout, meeting them. "Hold on." But why? Let the keen, cold wind beat in one's face and bite one's hands; let the lumps of snow, kicked up by the horses' hoofs, fall on one's cap, on one's back, down one's collar, on one's chest; let the runners ring on the snow, and the traces and the sledge be smashed, deuce take them one and all! And how delightful when the sledge upsets and you go flying full tilt into a drift, face downwards in the snow, and then you get up white all over with icicles on your moustaches; no cap, no gloves, your belt undone. . . . People laugh, the dogs bark. . . .

Pavel Ivanitch half opened one eye, looked at Gusev with it, and asked softly:

"Gusev, did your commanding officer steal?"

"Who can tell, Pavel Ivanitch! We can't say, it didn't reach us."

And after that a long time passed in silence. Gusev brooded, muttered something in delirium, and kept drinking water; it was hard for him to talk and hard to listen, and he was afraid of being talked to. An hour passed, a second, a third; evening came on, then night, but he did not notice it. He still sat dreaming of the frost.

There was a sound as though someone came into the hospital, and voices were audible, but a few minutes passed and all was still again.

"The Kingdom of Heaven and eternal peace," said the soldier with his arm in a sling. "He was an uncomfortable man."

"What?" asked Gusev. "Who?"

"He is dead, they have just carried him up."

"Oh, well," muttered Gusev, yawning, "the Kingdom of Heaven be his."

"What do you think?" the soldier with his arm in a sling asked Gusev. "Will he be in the Kingdom of Heaven or not?"

"Who is it you are talking about?"

"Pavel Ivanitch."

"He will be . . . he suffered so long. And there is another thing, he belonged to the clergy, and the priests always have a lot of relations. Their prayers will save him."

The soldier with the sling sat down on a hammock near Gusev and said in an undertone:

"And you, Gusev, are not long for this world. You will never get to Russia."

"Did the doctor or his assistant say so?" asked Gusev.

"It isn't that they said so, but one can see it. . . . One can see directly when a man's going to die. You don't eat, you don't drink; it's dreadful to see how thin you've got. It's consumption, in fact. I say it, not to upset you, but because maybe you would like to have the sacrament and extreme unction. And if you have any money you had better give it to the senior officer."

"I haven't written home . . ." Gusev sighed. "I shall die and they won't know."

"They'll hear of it," the sick sailor brought out in a bass voice. "When you die they will put it down in the *Gazette,* at Odessa they will send in a report to the commanding officer there and he will send it to the parish or somewhere. . . ."

Gusev began to be uneasy after such a conversation and to feel a vague yearning. He drank water—it was not that; he dragged himself to the window and breathed the hot, moist air—it was not that; he tried to think of home, of the frost—it was not that. . . . At last it seemed to him one minute longer in the ward and he would certainly expire.

"It's stifling, mates . . ." he said. "I'll go on deck. Help me up, for Christ's sake."

"All right," assented the soldier with the sling. "I'll carry you, you can't walk, hold on to my neck."

Gusev put his arm round the soldier's neck, the latter put his unhurt arm round him and carried him up. On the deck sailors and time-expired soldiers were lying asleep side by side; there were so many of them it was difficult to pass.

"Stand down," the soldier with the sling said softly. "Follow me quietly, hold on to my shirt. . . ."

It was dark. There was no light on deck, nor on the masts, nor anywhere on the sea around. At the furthest end of the ship the man on watch was standing perfectly still like a statue, and it looked as though he were asleep. It seemed as though the steamer were abandoned to itself and were going at its own will.

"Now they will throw Pavel Ivanitch into the sea," said the soldier with the sling. "In a sack and then into the water."

"Yes, that's the rule."

"But it's better to lie at home in the earth. Anyway, your mother comes to the grave and weeps."

"Of course."

There was a smell of hay and of dung. There were oxen standing with drooping heads by the ship's rail. One, two, three; eight of them! And there was a little horse. Gusev put out his hand to stroke it, but it shook its head, showed its teeth, and tried to bite his sleeve.

"Damned brute . . ." said Gusev angrily.

The two of them, he and the soldier, threaded their way to the head of the ship, then stood at the rail and looked up and down. Overhead deep sky, bright stars, peace and stillness, exactly as at home in the village, below darkness and disorder. The tall waves were resounding, no one could tell why. Whichever wave you looked at each one was trying to rise higher than all the rest and to chase and crush the next one; after it a third as fierce and hideous flew noisily, with a glint of light on its white crest.

The sea has no sense and no pity. If the steamer had been smaller and not made of thick iron, the waves would have crushed it to pieces without the slightest compunction, and would have devoured all the people in it with no distinction of saints or sinners. The steamer had the same cruel and meaningless expression. This monster with its huge beak was dashing onwards, cutting millions of waves in its path; it had no fear of the darkness nor the wind, nor of space, nor of solitude, caring for nothing, and if the ocean had its people, this monster would have crushed them, too, without distinction of saints or sinners.

"Where are we now?" asked Gusev.

"I don't know. We must be in the ocean."

"There is no sight of land. . . ."

"No indeed! They say we shan't see it for seven days."

The two soldiers watched the white foam with the phosphorus light on it and were silent, thinking. Gusev was the first to break the silence.

"There is nothing to be afraid of," he said, "only one is full of dread as though one were sitting in a dark forest; but if, for instance, they let a boat down on to the water this minute and an officer ordered me to go a hundred miles over the sea to catch fish, I'd go. Or, let's say, if a Christian were to fall into the water this minute, I'd go in after him. A German or a Chinaman I wouldn't save, but I'd go in after a Christian."

"And are you afraid to die?"

"Yes. I am sorry for the folks at home. My brother at home, you know, isn't steady; he drinks, he beats his wife for nothing, he does not honour his parents. Everything will go to ruin without me, and father and my old mother will be begging their bread, I shouldn't wonder. But my legs won't bear me, brother, and it's hot here. Let's go to sleep."

V

Gusev went back to the ward and got into his hammock. He was again tormented by a vague craving, and he could not make out what he wanted. There was an oppression on his chest, a throbbing in his head, his mouth was so dry that it was difficult for him to move his tongue. He dozed, and murmured in his sleep, and, worn out with nightmares, his cough, and the stifling heat, towards morning he fell into a sound sleep. He dreamed that they were just taking the bread out of the oven in the barracks and he climbed into the stove and had a steam bath in it, lashing himself with a bunch of birch twigs. He slept for two days, and at midday on the third two sailors came down and carried him out.

He was sewn up in sailcloth and to make him heavier they put with him two iron weights. Sewn up in the sailcloth he looked like a carrot or a radish: broad at the head and narrow at the feet. . . . Before sunset they brought him up to the deck and put him on a plank; one end of the plank lay on the side of the ship, the other on a box, placed on a stool. Round him stood the soldiers and the officers with their caps off.

"Blessed be the Name of the Lord . . ." the priest began. "As it was in the beginning, is now, and ever shall be."

"Amen," chanted three sailors.

The soldiers and the officers crossed themselves and looked away at the waves. It was strange that a man should be sewn up in sailcloth and should soon be flying into the sea. Was it possible that such a thing might happen to anyone?

The priest strewed earth upon Gusev and bowed down. They sang "Eternal Memory."

The man on watch duty tilted up the end of the plank, Gusev slid off and flew head foremost, turned a somersault in the air and splashed into the sea. He was covered with foam and for a moment looked as though he were wrapped in lace, but the minute passed and he disappeared in the waves.

He went rapidly towards the bottom. Did he reach it? It was said to be three miles to the bottom. After sinking sixty or seventy feet, he began moving more and more slowly, swaying rhythmically, as though he were hesitating and, carried along by the current, moved more rapidly sideways than downwards.

Then he was met by a shoal of the fish called harbour pilots. Seeing the dark body the fish stopped as though petrified, and suddenly turned round and disappeared. In less than a minute they flew back swift as an arrow to Gusev, and began zig-zagging round him in the water.

After that another dark body appeared. It was a shark. It swam under Gusev with dignity and no show of interest, as though it did not notice him, and sank down upon its back, then it turned belly upwards, basking in the warm, transparent water and languidly opened its jaws with two rows of teeth. The harbour pilots are delighted, they stop to see what will come next. After playing a little with the body the shark nonchalantly puts its jaws under it, cautiously touches it with its teeth, and the sailcloth is rent its full length from head to foot; one of the weights falls out and frightens the harbour pilots, and striking the shark on the ribs goes rapidly to the bottom.

Overhead at this time the clouds are massed together on the side where the sun is setting; one cloud like a triumphal arch, another like a lion, a third like a pair of scissors.... From behind the clouds a broad, green shaft of light pierces through and stretches to the middle of the sky; a little later another, violet-coloured, lies beside it; next that, one of gold, then one rose-coloured.... The sky turns a soft lilac. Looking at this gorgeous, enchanted sky, at first the ocean scowls, but soon it, too, takes tender, joyous, passionate colours for which it is hard to find a name in human speech.

Peasant Wives

In the village of Reybuzh, just facing the church, stands a two-storeyed house with a stone foundation and an iron roof. In the lower storey the owner himself, Filip Ivanov Kashin, nicknamed Dyudya, lives with his family, and on the upper floor, where it is apt to be very hot in summer and very cold in winter, they put up government officials, merchants, or landowners, who chance to be travelling that way. Dyudya rents some bits of land, keeps a tavern on the highroad, does a trade in tar, honey, cattle, and jackdaws, and has already something like eight thousand roubles put by in the bank in the town.

His elder son, Fyodor, is head engineer in the factory, and, as the peasants say of him, he has risen so high in the world that he is quite out of reach now. Fyodor's wife, Sofya, a plain, ailing woman, lives at home at her father-in-law's. She is for ever crying, and every Sunday she goes over to the hospital for medicine. Dyudya's second son, the hunchback Alyoshka, is living at home at his father's. He has only lately been married to Varvara, whom they singled out for him from a poor family. She is a handsome young woman, smart and buxom. When officials or merchants put up at the house, they always insist on having Varvara to bring in the samovar and make their beds.

One June evening when the sun was setting and the air was full of the smell of hay, of steaming dung-heaps and new milk, a plain-looking cart drove into Dyudya's yard with three people in it: a man of about thirty in a canvas suit, beside him a little boy of seven or eight in a long black coat with big bone buttons, and on the driver's seat a young fellow in a red shirt.

The young fellow took out the horses and led them out into the street to walk them up and down a bit, while the traveller washed, said a prayer, turning towards the church, then spread a rug near the cart and sat down with the boy to supper. He ate without haste, sedately, and Dyudya, who had seen a good many travellers in his time, knew him from his manners for a businesslike man, serious and aware of his own value.

Dyudya was sitting on the step in his waistcoat without a cap on, waiting for the visitor to speak first. He was used to hearing all kinds of stories from the travellers in the evening, and he liked listening to them before going to bed. His old wife, Afanasyevna, and his daughter-in-law Sofya, were milking in the cowshed. The other daughter-in-law, Varvara, was sitting at the open window of the upper storey, eating sunflower seeds.

"The little chap will be your son, I'm thinking?" Dyudya asked the traveller.

"No; adopted. An orphan. I took him for my soul's salvation."

They got into conversation. The stranger seemed to be a man fond of talking and ready of speech, and Dyudya learned from him that he was from the town, was of the tradesman class, and had a house of his own, that his name was Matvey Savitch, that he was on his way now to look at some gardens that he was renting from some German colonists, and that the boy's name was Kuzka. The evening was hot and close, no one felt inclined for sleep. When it was getting dark and pale stars began to twinkle here and there in the sky, Matvey Savitch began to tell how he had come by Kuzka. Afanasyevna and Sofya stood a little way off, listening. Kuzka had gone to the gate.

"It's a complicated story, old man," began Matvey Savitch, "and if I were to tell you all just as it happened, it would take all night and more. Ten years ago in a little house in our street, next door to me, where now there's a tallow and oil factory, there was living an old widow,

Marfa Semyonovna Kapluntsev, and she had two sons: one was a guard on the railway, but the other, Vasya, who was just my own age, lived at home with his mother. Old Kapluntsev had kept five pair of horses and sent carriers all over the town; his widow had not given up the business, but managed the carriers as well as her husband had done, so that some days they would bring in as much as five roubles from their rounds.

"The young fellow, too, made a trifle on his own account. He used to breed fancy pigeons and sell them to fanciers; at times he would stand for hours on the roof, waving a broom in the air and whistling; his pigeons were right up in the clouds, but it wasn't enough for him, and he'd want them to go higher yet. Siskins and starlings, too, he used to catch, and he made cages for sale. All trifles, but, mind you, he'd pick up some ten roubles a month over such trifles. Well, as time went on, the old lady lost the use of her legs and took to her bed. In consequence of which event the house was left without a woman to look after it, and that's for all the world like a man without an eye. The old lady bestirred herself and made up her mind to marry Vasya. They called in a matchmaker at once, the women got to talking of one thing and another, and Vasya went off to have a look at the girls. He picked out Mashenka, a widow's daughter. They made up their minds without loss of time and in a week it was all settled. The girl was a little slip of a thing, seventeen, but fair-skinned and pretty-looking, and like a lady in all her ways; and a decent dowry with her, five hundred roubles, a cow, a bed.... Well, the old lady—it seemed as though she had known it was coming—three days after the wedding, departed to the Heavenly Jerusalem where is neither sickness nor sighing. The young people gave her a good funeral and began their life together. For just six months they got on splendidly, and then all of a sudden another misfortune. It never rains but it pours: Vasya was summoned to the recruiting office to draw lots for the service. He was taken, poor chap, for a soldier, and not even granted exemption. They shaved his head and packed him off to Poland. It was God's will; there was nothing to be done. When he said good-bye to his wife in the yard, he bore it all right; but as he glanced up at the hay-loft and his pigeons for the last time, he burst out crying. It was pitiful to see him.

"At first Mashenka got her mother to stay with her, that she mightn't be dull all alone; she stayed till the baby—this very Kuzka here—was born, and then she went off to Oboyan to another married daughter's and left Mashenka alone with the baby. There were five peasants—the carriers—a drunken saucy lot; horses, too, and dray-carts to see to, and then the fence would be broken or the soot afire in the chimney—jobs beyond a woman, and through our being neighbours, she got into the way of turning to me for every little thing. . . . Well, I'd go over, set things to rights, and give advice. . . . Naturally, not without going indoors, drinking a cup of tea and having a little chat with her. I was a young fellow, intellectual, and fond of talking on all sorts of subjects; she, too, was well-bred and educated. She was always neatly dressed, and in summer she walked out with a sunshade. Sometimes I would begin upon religion or politics with her, and she was flattered and would entertain me with tea and jam. . . . In a word, not to make a long story of it, I must tell you, old man, a year had not passed before the Evil One, the enemy of all mankind, confounded me. I began to notice that any day I didn't go to see her, I seemed out of sorts and dull. And I'd be continually making up something that I must see her about: 'It's high time,' I'd say to myself, 'to put the double windows in for the winter,' and the whole day I'd idle away over at her place putting in the windows and take good care to leave a couple of them over for the next day too.

" 'I ought to count over Vasya's pigeons, to see none of them have strayed,' and so on. I used always to be talking to her across the fence, and in the end I made a little gate in the fence so as not to have to go so far round. From womankind comes much evil into the world and every kind of abomination. Not we sinners only; even the saints themselves have been led astray by them. Mashenka did not try to keep me at a distance. Instead of thinking of her husband and being on her guard, she fell in love with me. I began to notice that she was dull without me, and was always walking to and fro by the fence looking into my yard through the cracks.

"My brains were going round in my head in a sort of frenzy. On Thursday in Holy Week I was going early in the morning—it was scarcely light—to market. I passed close by her gate, and the Evil One was by me—at my elbow. I looked—she had a gate with open trellis work at the top—and there she was, up already, standing in the middle of the yard, feeding the ducks. I could not restrain myself, and I called her name. She came up and looked at me through the trellis.... Her little face was white, her eyes soft and sleepy-looking.... I liked her looks immensely, and I began paying her compliments, as though we were not at the gate, but just as one does on namedays, while she blushed, and laughed, and kept looking straight into my eyes without winking.... I lost all sense and began to declare my love to her.... She opened the gate, and from that morning we began to live as man and wife...."

The hunchback Alyoshka came into the yard from the street and ran out of breath into the house, not looking at any one. A minute later he ran out of the house with a concertina. Jingling some coppers in his pocket, and cracking sunflower seeds as he ran, he went out at the gate.

"And who's that, pray?" asked Matvey Savitch.

"My son Alexey," answered Dyudya. "He's off on a spree, the rascal. God has afflicted him with a hump, so we are not very hard on him."

"And he's always drinking with the other fellows, always drinking," sighed Afanasyevna. "Before Carnival we married him, thinking he'd be steadier, but there! he's worse than ever."

"It's been no use. Simply keeping another man's daughter for nothing," said Dyudya.

Somewhere behind the church they began to sing a glorious, mournful song. The words they could not catch and only the voices could be heard—two tenors and a bass. All were listening; there was complete stillness in the yard.... Two voices suddenly broke off with a loud roar of laughter, but the third, a tenor, still sang on, and took so high a note that every one instinctively looked upwards, as though the voice had soared to heaven itself.

Varvara came out of the house, and screening her eyes with her hand, as though from the sun, she looked towards the church.

"It's the priest's sons with the schoolmaster," she said.

Again all the three voices began to sing together. Matvey Savitch sighed and went on:

"Well, that's how it was, old man. Two years later we got a letter from Vasya from Warsaw. He wrote that he was being sent home sick. He was ill. By that time I had put all that foolishness out of my head, and I had a fine match picked out all ready for me, only I didn't know how to break it off with my sweetheart. Every day I'd make up my mind to have it out with Mashenka, but I didn't know how to approach her so as not to have a woman's screeching about my ears. The letter freed my hands. I read it through with Mashenka; she turned white as a sheet, while I said to her: 'Thank God; now,' says I, 'you'll be a married woman again.' But says she: 'I'm not going to live with him.' 'Why, isn't he your husband?' said I. 'Is it an easy thing? . . . I never loved him and I married him not of my own free will. My mother made me.' 'Don't try to get out of it, silly,' said I, 'but tell me this: were you married to him in church or not?' 'I was married,' she said, 'but it's you that I love, and I will stay with you to the day of my death. Folks may jeer. I don't care. . . .' 'You're a Christian woman,' said I, 'and have read the Scriptures; what is written there?' "

"Once married, with her husband she must live," said Dyudya.

" 'Man and wife are one flesh. We have sinned,' I said, 'you and I, and it is enough; we must repent and fear God. We must confess it all to Vasya,' said I; 'he's a quiet fellow and soft—he won't kill you. And indeed,' said I, 'better to suffer torments in this world at the hands of your lawful master than to gnash your teeth at the dread Seat of Judgment.' The wench wouldn't listen; she stuck to her silly, 'It's you I love!' and nothing more could I get out of her.

"Vasya came back on the Saturday before Trinity, early in the morning. From my fence I could see everything; he ran into the house, and came back a minute later with Kuzka in his arms, and he was laughing and crying all at once; he was kissing Kuzka and looking up at the hay-loft, and hadn't the heart to put the child down, and yet he was longing to go to his pigeons. He was always a soft sort of chap—sentimental. That day passed off very well, all quiet and proper. They had begun ringing the church bells for the evening service, when the thought struck me: 'To-morrow's Trinity Sunday; how is it they are not decking the gates and the fence with green? Something's wrong,' I thought. I went over to them. I peeped in, and there he was, sitting on the floor in the middle of the room, his eyes staring like a drunken man's, the tears streaming down his cheeks and his hands shaking; he was pulling cracknels, necklaces, gingerbread nuts, and all sorts of little presents out of his bundle and flinging them on the floor. Kuzka—he was three years old—was crawling on the floor, munching the gingerbreads, while Mashenka stood by the stove, white and shivering all over, muttering: 'I'm not your wife; I can't live with you,' and all sorts of foolishness. I bowed down at Vasya's feet, and said: 'We have sinned against you, Vassily Maximitch; forgive us, for Christ's sake!' Then I got up and spoke to Mashenka: 'You, Marya Semyonovna, ought now to wash Vassily Maximitch's feet and drink the water. Do you be an obedient wife to him, and pray to God for me, that He in His mercy may forgive my transgression.' It came to me like an inspiration from an angel of Heaven; I gave her solemn counsel and spoke with such feeling that my own tears flowed too. And so two days later Vasya comes to me: 'Matyusha,' says he, 'I forgive you and my wife; God have mercy on you! She was a soldier's wife, a young thing all alone; it was hard for her to be on her guard. She's not the first, nor will she be the last. Only,' he says, 'I beg you to behave as though there had never been anything between you, and to make no sign, while I,' says he, 'will do my best to please her in every way, so that she may come to love me again.' He gave me his hand on it, drank a cup of tea, and went away more cheerful.

" 'Well,' thought I, 'thank God!' and I did feel glad that everything had gone off so well. But no sooner had Vasya gone out of the yard, when in came Mashenka. Ah! What I had to suffer! She hung on my neck, weeping and praying: 'For God's sake, don't cast me off; I can't live without you!' "

"The vile hussy!" sighed Dyudya.

"I swore at her, stamped my foot, and dragging her into the passage, I fastened the door with the hook. 'Go to your husband,' I cried. 'Don't shame me before folks. Fear God!' And every day there was a scene of that sort.

"One morning I was standing in my yard near the stable cleaning a bridle. All at once I saw her running through the little gate into my yard, with bare feet, in her petticoat, and straight towards me; she clutched at the bridle, getting all smeared with the pitch, and shaking and weeping, she cried: 'I can't stand him; I loathe him; I can't bear it! If you don't love me, better kill me!' I was angry, and I struck her twice with the bridle, but at that instant Vasya ran in at the gate, and in a despairing voice he shouted: 'Don't beat her! Don't beat her!' But he ran up himself, and waving his arms, as though he were mad, he let fly with his fists at her with all his might, then flung her on the ground and kicked her. I tried to defend her, but he snatched up the reins and thrashed her with them, and all the while, like a colt's whinny, he went: 'He—he—he!' "

"I'd take the reins and let you feel them," muttered Varvara, moving away; "murdering our sister, the damned brutes! . . ."

"Hold your tongue, you jade!" Dyudya shouted at her.

" 'He—he—he!' " Matvey Savitch went on. "A carrier ran out of his yard; I called to my workman, and the three of us got Mashenka away from him and carried her home in our arms. The disgrace of it! The same day I went over in the evening to see how things were. She was lying in bed, all wrapped up in bandages, nothing but her eyes and nose to be seen; she was looking at the ceiling. I said: 'Good-evening, Marya Semyonovna!' She did not speak. And Vasya was sitting in the next room, his head in his hands, crying and saying: 'Brute that I am! I've ruined my life! O God, let me die!' I sat for half an hour by Mashenka and gave her a good talking-to. I tried to frighten her a bit. 'The righteous,' said I, 'after this life go to Paradise, but you will go to a Gehenna of fire, like all adulteresses. Don't strive against your husband, go and lay yourself at his feet.' But never a word from her; she didn't so much as blink an eyelid, for all the world as though I were talking to a post. The next day Vasya fell ill with something like cholera, and in the evening I heard that he was dead. Well, so they buried him, and Mashenka did not go to the funeral; she didn't care to show her shameless face and her bruises. And soon there began to be talk all over the district that Vasya had not died a natural death, that Mashenka had made away with him. It got to the ears of the police;

they had Vasya dug up and cut open, and in his stomach they found arsenic. It was clear he had been poisoned; the police came and took Mashenka away, and with her the innocent Kuzka. They were put in prison. . . . The woman had gone too far—God punished her. . . . Eight months later they tried her. She sat, I remember, on a low stool, with a little white kerchief on her head, wearing a grey gown, and she was so thin, so pale, so sharp-eyed it made one sad to look at her. Behind her stood a soldier with a gun. She would not confess her guilt. Some in the court said she had poisoned her husband and others declared he had poisoned himself for grief. I was one of the witnesses. When they questioned me, I told the whole truth according to my oath. 'Hers,' said I, 'is the guilt. It's no good to conceal it; she did not love her husband, and she had a will of her own. . . .' The trial began in the morning and towards night they passed this sentence: to send her to hard labour in Siberia for thirteen years. After that sentence Mashenka remained three months longer in prison. I went to see her, and from Christian charity I took her a little tea and sugar. But as soon as she set eyes on me she began to shake all over, wringing her hands and muttering: 'Go away! go away!' And Kuzka she clasped to her as though she were afraid I would take him away. 'See,' said I, 'what you have come to! Ah, Masha, Masha! you would not listen to me when I gave you good advice, and now you must repent it. You are yourself to blame,' said I; 'blame yourself!' I was giving her good counsel, but she: 'Go away, go away!' huddling herself and Kuzka against the wall, and trembling all over.

"When they were taking her away to the chief town of our province, I walked by the escort as far as the station and slipped a rouble into her bundle for my soul's salvation. But she did not get as far as Siberia. . . . She fell sick of fever and died in prison."

"Live like a dog and you must die a dog's death," said Dyudya.

"Kuzka was sent back home. . . . I thought it over and took him to bring up. After all—though a convict's child—still he was a living soul, a Christian. . . . I was sorry for him. I shall make him my clerk, and if I have no children of my own, I'll make a merchant of him. Wherever I go now, I take him with me; let him learn his work."

All the while Matvey Savitch had been telling his story, Kuzka had sat on a little stone near the gate. His head propped in both hands, he gazed at the sky, and in the distance he looked in the dark like a stump of wood.

"Kuzka, come to bed," Matvey Savitch bawled to him.

"Yes, it's time," said Dyudya, getting up; he yawned loudly and added:

"Folks will go their own way, and that's what comes of it."

Over the yard the moon was floating now in the heavens; she was moving one way, while the clouds beneath moved the other way; the clouds were disappearing into the darkness, but still the moon could be seen high above the yard.

Matvey Savitch said a prayer, facing the church, and saying good-night, he lay down on the ground near his cart. Kuzka, too, said a prayer, lay down in the cart, and covered himself with his little over-coat; he made himself a little hole in the hay so as to be more comfortable, and curled up so that his elbows looked like knees. From the yard Dyudya could be seen lighting a candle in his room below, putting on his spectacles and standing in the corner with a book. He was a long while reading and crossing himself.

The travellers fell asleep. Afanasyevna and Sofya came up to the cart and began looking at Kuzka.

"The little orphan's asleep," said the old woman. "He's thin and frail, nothing but bones. No mother and no one to care for him properly."

"My Grishutka must be two years older," said Sofya. "Up at the factory he lives like a slave without his mother. The foreman beats him, I dare say. When I looked at this poor mite just now, I thought of my own Grishutka, and my heart went cold within me."

A minute passed in silence.

"Doesn't remember his mother, I suppose," said the old woman.

"How could he remember?"

And big tears began dropping from Sofya's eyes.

"He's curled himself up like a cat," she said, sobbing and laughing with tenderness and sorrow. . . . "Poor motherless mite!"

Kuzka started and opened his eyes. He saw before him an ugly, wrinkled, tear-stained face, and beside it another, aged and toothless, with a sharp chin and hooked nose, and high above them the infinite sky with the flying clouds and the moon. He cried out in fright, and Sofya, too, uttered a cry; both were answered by the echo, and a faint stir passed over the stifling air; a watchman tapped somewhere near, a dog barked. Matvey Savitch muttered something in his sleep and turned over on the other side.

Late at night when Dyudya and the old woman and the neighbouring watchman were all asleep, Sofya went out to the gate and sat down on the bench. She felt stifled and her head ached from weeping. The street was a wide and long one; it stretched for nearly two miles to the right and as far to the left, and the end of it was out of sight. The moon was now not over the yard, but behind the church. One side of the street was flooded with moonlight, while the other side lay in black shadow. The long shadows of the poplars and the starling-cotes stretched right across the street, while the church cast a broad shadow, black and terrible that enfolded Dyudya's gates and half his house. The street was still and deserted. From time to time the strains of music floated faintly from the end of the street—Alyoshka, most likely, playing his concertina.

Someone moved in the shadow near the church enclosure, and Sofya could not make out whether it were a man or a cow, or perhaps merely a big bird rustling in the trees. But then a figure stepped out of the shadow, halted, and said something in a man's voice, then vanished down the turning by the church. A little later, not three yards from the gate, another figure came into sight; it walked straight from the church to the gate and stopped short, seeing Sofya on the bench.

"Varvara, is that you?" said Sofya.

"And if it were?"

It was Varvara. She stood still a minute, then came up to the bench and sat down.

"Where have you been?" asked Sofya.

Varvara made no answer.

"You'd better mind you don't get into trouble with such goings-on, my girl," said Sofya. "Did you hear how Mashenka was kicked and lashed with the reins? You'd better look out, or they'll treat you the same."

"Well, let them!"

Varvara laughed into her kerchief and whispered:

"I have just been with the priest's son."

"Nonsense!"

"I have!"

"It's a sin!" whispered Sofya.

"Well, let it be. . . . What do I care? If it's a sin, then it is a sin, but better be struck dead by thunder than live like this. I'm young and strong, and I've a filthy crooked hunchback for a husband, worse than Dyudya himself, curse him! When I was a girl, I hadn't bread to eat, or a shoe to my foot, and to get away from that wretchedness I was tempted by Alyoshka's money, and got caught like a fish in a net, and I'd rather have a viper for my bedfellow than that scurvy Alyoshka. And what's your life? It makes me sick to look at it. Your Fyodor sent you packing from the factory and he's taken up with another woman. They have robbed you of your boy and made a slave of him. You work like a horse, and never hear a kind word. I'd rather pine all my days an old maid, I'd rather get half a rouble from the priest's son, I'd rather beg my bread, or throw myself into the well. . . ."

"It's a sin!" whispered Sofya again.

"Well, let it be."

Somewhere behind the church the same three voices, two tenors and a bass, began singing again a mournful song. And again the words could not be distinguished.

"They are not early to bed," Varvara said, laughing.

And she began telling in a whisper of her midnight walks with the priest's son, and of the stories he had told her, and of his comrades, and of the fun she had with the travellers who stayed in the house. The mournful song stirred a longing for life and freedom. Sofya began to laugh; she thought it sinful and terrible and sweet to hear about, and she felt envious and sorry that she, too, had not been a sinner when she was young and pretty.

In the churchyard they heard twelve strokes beaten on the watchman's board.

"It's time we were asleep," said Sofya, getting up, "or, maybe, we shall catch it from Dyudya."

They both went softly into the yard.

"I went away without hearing what he was telling about Mashenka," said Varvara, making herself a bed under the window.

"She died in prison, he said. She poisoned her husband."

Varvara lay down beside Sofya a while, and said softly:

"I'd make away with my Alyoshka and never regret it."

"You talk nonsense; God forgive you."

When Sofya was just dropping asleep, Varvara, coming close, whispered in her ear:

"Let us get rid of Dyudya and Alyoshka!"

Sofya started and said nothing. Then she opened her eyes and gazed a long while steadily at the sky.

"People would find out," she said.

"No, they wouldn't. Dyudya's an old man, it's time he did die; and they'd say Alyoshka died of drink."

"I'm afraid . . . God would chastise us."

"Well, let Him. . . ."

Both lay awake thinking in silence.

"It's cold," said Sofya, beginning to shiver all over. "It will soon be morning. . . . Are you asleep?"

"No. . . . Don't you mind what I say, dear," whispered Varvara; "I get so mad with the damned brutes, I don't know what I do say. Go to sleep, or it will be daylight directly. . . . Go to sleep."

Both were quiet and soon they fell asleep.

Earlier than all woke the old woman. She waked up Sofya and they went together into the cowshed to milk the cows. The hunchback Alyoshka came in hopelessly drunk without his concertina; his breast and knees had been in the dust and straw—he must have fallen down in the road. Staggering, he went into the cowshed, and without undressing he rolled into a sledge and began to snore at once. When first the crosses on the church and then the windows were flashing in the light of the rising sun, and shadows stretched across the yard over the dewy grass from the trees and the top of the well, Matvey Savitch jumped up and began hurrying about:

"Kuzka! get up!" he shouted. "It's time to put in the horses! Look sharp!"

The bustle of morning was beginning. A young Jewess in a brown gown with flounces led a horse into the yard to drink. The pulley of the well creaked plaintively, the bucket knocked as it went down. . . .

Kuzka, sleepy, tired, covered with dew, sat up in the cart, lazily putting on his little overcoat, and listening to the drip of the water from the bucket into the well as he shivered with the cold.

"Auntie!" shouted Matvey Savitch to Sofya, "tell my lad to hurry up and to harness the horses!"

And Dyudya at the same instant shouted from the window:

"Sofya, take a farthing from the Jewess for the horse's drink! They're always in here, the mangy creatures!"

In the street sheep were running up and down, baaing; the peasant women were shouting at the shepherd, while he played his pipes, cracked his whip, or answered them in a thick sleepy bass. Three sheep strayed into the yard, and not finding the gate again, pushed at the fence.

Varvara was waked by the noise, and bundling her bedding up in her arms, she went into the house.

"You might at least drive the sheep out!" the old woman bawled after her, "my lady!"

"I dare say! As if I were going to slave for you Herods!" muttered Varvara, going into the house.

Dyudya came out of the house with his accounts in his hands, sat down on the step, and began reckoning how much the traveller owed him for the night's lodging, oats, and watering his horses.

"You charge pretty heavily for the oats, my good man," said Matvey Savitch.

"If it's too much, don't take them. There's no compulsion, merchant."

When the travellers were ready to start, they were detained for a minute. Kuzka had lost his cap.

"Little swine, where did you put it?" Matvey Savitch roared angrily. "Where is it?"

Kuzka's face was working with terror; he ran up and down near the cart, and not finding it there, ran to the gate and then to the shed. The old woman and Sofya helped him look.

"I'll pull your ears off!" yelled Matvey Savitch. "Dirty brat!"

The cap was found at the bottom of the cart.

Kuzka brushed the hay off it with his sleeve, put it on, and timidly he crawled into the cart, still with an expression of terror on his face as though he were afraid of a blow from behind.

Matvey Savitch crossed himself. The driver gave a tug at the reins and the cart rolled out of the yard.

The Grasshopper

I

All Olga Ivanovna's friends and acquaintances were at her wedding.

"Look at him; isn't it true that there is something in him?" she said to her friends, with a nod towards her husband, as though she wanted to explain why she was marrying a simple, very ordinary, and in no way remarkable man.

Her husband, Osip Stepanitch Dymov, was a doctor, and only of the rank of a titular councillor. He was on the staff of two hospitals: in one a ward-surgeon and in the other a dissecting demonstrator. Every day from nine to twelve he saw patients and was busy in his ward, and after twelve o'clock he went by tram to the other hospital, where he dissected. His private practice was a small one, not worth more than five hundred roubles a year. That was all. What more could one say about him? Meanwhile, Olga Ivanovna and her friends and acquaintances were not quite ordinary people. Every one of them was remarkable in some way, and more or less famous; already had made a reputation and was looked upon as a celebrity; or if not yet a celebrity, gave brilliant promise of becoming one. There was an actor from the Dramatic Theatre, who was a great talent of established reputation, as well as an elegant, intelligent, and modest man, and a capital elocutionist, and who taught Olga Ivanovna to recite; there was a singer from the opera, a good-natured, fat man who assured Olga Ivanovna, with a sigh, that she was ruining herself, that if she would take herself in hand and not be lazy she might make a remarkable singer; then there were several artists, and chief among them Ryabovsky, a very handsome, fair young man of five-and-twenty who painted genre pieces, animal studies, and landscapes, was successful at exhibitions, and had sold his last picture for five hundred roubles. He touched up Olga Ivanovna's sketches, and used to say she might do something. Then a violoncellist, whose instrument used to sob, and who openly declared that of all the ladies of his acquaintance the only one who could accompany him was Olga Ivanovna; then there was a literary man, young but already well known, who had written stories, novels, and plays. Who else? Why, Vassily Vassilyitch, a landowner and amateur illustrator and vignettist, with a great feeling for the old Russian style, the old ballad and epic. On paper, on china, and on smoked plates, he produced literally marvels. In the midst of this free artistic company, spoiled by fortune, though refined and modest, who recalled the existence of doctors only in times of illness, and to whom the name of Dymov sounded in no way different from Sidorov or Tarasov—in the midst of this company Dymov seemed strange, not wanted, and small, though he was tall and broad-shouldered. He looked as though he had on somebody else's coat, and his beard was like a shopman's. Though if he had been a writer or an artist, they would have said that his beard reminded them of Zola.

An artist said to Olga Ivanovna that with her flaxen hair and in her wedding-dress she was very much like a graceful cherry-tree when it is covered all over with delicate white blossoms in spring.

"Oh, let me tell you," said Olga Ivanovna, taking his arm, "how it was it all came to pass so suddenly. Listen, listen! . . . I must tell you that my father was on the same staff at the hospital as Dymov. When my poor father was taken ill, Dymov watched for days and nights together at his bedside. Such self-sacrifice! Listen, Ryabovsky! You, my writer, listen; it is very interesting! Come nearer. Such self-sacrifice, such genuine sympathy! I sat up with my father, and did not sleep for nights, either. And all at once—the princess had won the hero's heart—my

Dymov fell head over ears in love. Really, fate is so strange at times! Well, after my father's death he came to see me sometimes, met me in the street, and one fine evening, all at once he made me an offer . . . like snow upon my head. . . . I lay awake all night, crying, and fell hellishly in love myself. And here, as you see, I am his wife. There really is something strong, powerful, bearlike about him, isn't there? Now his face is turned three-quarters towards us in a bad light, but when he turns round look at his forehead. Ryabovsky, what do you say to that forehead? Dymov, we are talking about you!" she called to her husband. "Come here; hold out your honest hand to Ryabovsky. . . . That's right, be friends."

Dymov, with a naïve and good-natured smile, held out his hand to Ryabovsky, and said:

"Very glad to meet you. There was a Ryabovsky in my year at the medical school. Was he a relation of yours?"

II

Olga Ivanovna was twenty-two, Dymov was thirty-one. They got on splendidly together when they were married. Olga Ivanovna hung all her drawing-room walls with her own and other people's sketches, in frames and without frames, and near the piano and furniture arranged picturesque corners with Japanese parasols, easels, daggers, busts, photographs, and rags of many colours. . . . In the dining-room she papered the walls with peasant woodcuts, hung up bark shoes and sickles, stood in a corner a scythe and a rake, and so achieved a dining-room in the Russian style. In her bedroom she draped the ceiling and the walls with dark cloths to make it like a cavern, hung a Venetian lantern over the beds, and at the door set a figure with a halberd. And every one thought that the young people had a very charming little home.

When she got up at eleven o'clock every morning, Olga Ivanovna played the piano or, if it were sunny, painted something in oils. Then between twelve and one she drove to her dressmaker's. As Dymov and she had very little money, only just enough, she and her dressmaker were often put to clever shifts to enable her to appear constantly in new dresses and make a sensation with them. Very often out of an old dyed dress, out of bits of tulle, lace, plush, and silk, costing nothing, perfect marvels were created, something bewitching—not a dress, but a dream. From the dressmaker's Olga Ivanovna usually drove to some actress of her acquaintance to hear the latest theatrical gossip, and incidentally to try and get hold of tickets for the first night of some new play or for a benefit performance. From the actress's she had to go to some artist's studio or to some exhibition or to see some celebrity—either to pay a visit or to give an invitation or simply to have a chat. And everywhere she met with a gay and friendly welcome, and was assured that she was good, that she was sweet, that she was rare.... Those whom she called great and famous received her as one of themselves, as an equal, and predicted with one voice that, with her talents, her taste, and her intelligence, she would do great things if she concentrated herself. She sang, she played the piano, she painted in oils, she carved, she took part in amateur performances; and all this not just anyhow, but all with talent, whether she made lanterns for an illumination or dressed up or tied somebody's cravat—everything she did was exceptionally graceful, artistic, and charming. But her talents showed themselves in nothing so clearly as in her faculty for quickly becoming acquainted and on intimate terms with celebrated people. No sooner did any one become ever so little celebrated, and set people talking about him, than she made his acquaintance, got on friendly terms the same day, and invited him to her house. Every new acquaintance she made was a veritable fête for her. She adored celebrated people, was proud of them, dreamed of them every night. She craved for them, and never could satisfy her craving. The old ones departed and were forgotten, new ones came to replace them, but to these, too, she soon grew accustomed or was disappointed in them, and began eagerly seeking for fresh great men, finding them and seeking for them again. What for?

Between four and five she dined at home with her husband. His simplicity, good sense, and kindheartedness touched her and moved her up to enthusiasm. She was constantly jumping up, impulsively hugging his head and showering kisses on it.

"You are a clever, generous man, Dymov," she used to say, "but you have one very serious defect. You take absolutely no interest in art. You don't believe in music or painting."

"I don't understand them," he would say mildly. "I have spent all my life in working at natural science and medicine, and I have never had time to take an interest in the arts."

"But, you know, that's awful, Dymov!"

"Why so? Your friends don't know anything of science or medicine, but you don't reproach them with it. Every one has his own line. I don't understand landscapes and operas, but the way I look at it is that if one set of sensible people devote their whole lives to them, and other sensible people pay immense sums for them, they must be of use. I don't understand them, but not understanding does not imply disbelieving in them."

"Let me shake your honest hand!"

After dinner Olga Ivanovna would drive off to see her friends, then to a theatre or to a concert, and she returned home after midnight. So it was every day.

On Wednesdays she had "At Homes." At these "At Homes" the hostess and her guests did not play cards and did not dance, but entertained themselves with various arts. An actor from the Dramatic Theatre recited, a singer sang, artists sketched in the albums of which Olga Ivanovna had a great number, the violoncellist played, and the hostess herself sketched, carved, sang, and played accompaniments. In the intervals between the recitations, music, and singing, they talked and argued about literature, the theatre, and painting. There were no ladies, for Olga Ivanovna considered all ladies wearisome and vulgar except actresses and her dressmaker. Not one of these entertainments passed without the hostess starting at every ring at the bell, and saying, with a triumphant expression, "It is he," meaning by "he," of course, some new celebrity. Dymov was not in the drawing-room, and no one remembered his existence. But exactly at half-past eleven the door leading into the dining-room opened, and Dymov would appear with his good-natured, gentle smile and say, rubbing his hands:

"Come to supper, gentlemen."

They all went into the dining-room, and every time found on the table exactly the same things: a dish of oysters, a piece of ham or veal, sardines, cheese, caviare, mushrooms, vodka, and two decanters of wine.

"My dear *maître d' hôtel*!" Olga Ivanovna would say, clasping her hands with enthusiasm, "you are simply fascinating! My friends, look at his forehead! Dymov, turn your profile. Look! he has the face of a Bengal tiger and an expression as kind and sweet as a gazelle. Ah, the darling!"

The visitors ate, and, looking at Dymov, thought, "He really is a nice fellow"; but they soon forgot about him, and went on talking about the theatre, music, and painting.

The young people were happy, and their life flowed on without a hitch.

The third week of their honeymoon was spent, however, not quite happily—sadly, indeed. Dymov caught erysipelas in the hospital, was in bed for six days, and had to have his beautiful black hair cropped. Olga Ivanovna sat beside him and wept bitterly, but when he was better she put a white handkerchief on his shaven head and began to paint him as a Bedouin. And they were both in good spirits. Three days after he had begun to go back to the hospital he had another mischance.

"I have no luck, little mother," he said one day at dinner. "I had four dissections to do today, and I cut two of my fingers at one. And I did not notice it till I got home."

Olga Ivanovna was alarmed. He smiled, and told her that it did not matter, and that he often cut his hands when he was dissecting.

"I get absorbed, little mother, and grow careless."

Olga Ivanovna dreaded symptoms of blood-poisoning, and prayed about it every night, but all went well. And again life flowed on peaceful and happy, free from grief and anxiety. The present was happy, and to follow it spring was at hand, already smiling in the distance, and promising a thousand delights. There would be no end to their happiness. In April, May and June a summer villa a good distance out of town; walks, sketching, fishing, nightingales; and then from July right on to autumn an artist's tour on the Volga, and in this tour Olga Ivanovna would take part as an indispensable member of the society. She had already had made for her two travelling dresses of linen, had bought paints, brushes, canvases, and a new palette for the journey. Almost every day Ryabovsky visited her to see what progress she was making in her painting; when she showed him her painting, he used to thrust his hands deep into his pockets, compress his lips, sniff, and say:

"Ye—es...! That cloud of yours is screaming: it's not in the evening light. The foreground is somehow chewed up, and there is something, you know, not the thing.... And your cottage is weighed down and whines pitifully. That corner ought to have been taken more in shadow, but on the whole it is not bad; I like it."

And the more incomprehensible he talked, the more readily Olga Ivanovna understood him.

III

After dinner on the second day of Trinity week, Dymov bought some sweets and some savouries and went down to the villa to see his wife. He had not seen her for a fortnight, and missed her terribly. As he sat in the train and afterwards as he looked for his villa in a big wood, he felt all the while hungry and weary, and dreamed of how he would have supper in freedom with his wife, then tumble into bed and to sleep. And he was delighted as he looked at his parcel, in which there was caviare, cheese, and white salmon.

The sun was setting by the time he found his villa and recognized it. The old servant told him that her mistress was not at home, but that most likely she would soon be in. The villa, very uninviting in appearance, with low ceilings papered with writing-paper and with uneven floors full of crevices, consisted only of three rooms. In one there was a bed, in the second there were canvases, brushes, greasy papers, and men's overcoats and hats lying about on the chairs and in the windows, while in the third Dymov found three unknown men; two were dark-haired and had beards, the other was clean-shaven and fat, apparently an actor. There was a samovar boiling on the table.

"What do you want?" asked the actor in a bass voice, looking at Dymov ungraciously. "Do you want Olga Ivanovna? Wait a minute; she will be here directly."

Dymov sat down and waited. One of the dark-haired men, looking sleepily and listlessly at him, poured himself out a glass of tea, and asked:

"Perhaps you would like some tea?"

Dymov was both hungry and thirsty, but he refused tea for fear of spoiling his supper. Soon he heard footsteps and a familiar laugh; a door slammed, and Olga Ivanovna ran into the room, wearing a wide-brimmed hat and carrying a box in her hand; she was followed by Ryabovsky, rosy and good-humoured, carrying a big umbrella and a camp-stool.

"Dymov!" cried Olga Ivanovna, and she flushed crimson with pleasure. "Dymov!" she repeated, laying her head and both arms on his bosom. "Is that you? Why haven't you come for so long? Why? Why?"

"When could I, little mother? I am always busy, and whenever I am free it always happens somehow that the train does not fit."

"But how glad I am to see you! I have been dreaming about you the whole night, the whole night, and I was afraid you must be ill. Ah! if you only knew how sweet you are! You have come in the nick of time! You will be my salvation! You are the only person who can save me! There is to be a most original wedding here tomorrow," she went on, laughing, and tying her husband's cravat. "A young telegraph clerk at the station, called Tchikeldyeev, is going to be married. He is a handsome young man and—well, not stupid, and you know there is something strong, bearlike in his face . . . you might paint him as a young Norman. We summer visitors take a great interest in him, and have promised to be at his wedding. . . . He is a lonely, timid man, not well off, and of course it would be a shame not to be sympathetic to him. Fancy! the wedding will be after the service; then we shall all walk from the church to the bride's lodgings . . . you see the wood, the birds singing, patches of sunlight on the grass, and all of us spots of different colours against the bright green background—very original, in the style of the French impressionists. But, Dymov, what am I to go to the church in?" said Olga Ivanovna, and she looked as though she were going to cry. "I have nothing here, literally nothing! no dress, no flowers, no gloves . . . you must save me. Since you have come, fate itself bids you save me. Take the keys, my precious, go home and get my pink dress from the wardrobe. You remember it; it hangs in front. . . . Then, in the storeroom, on the floor, on the right side, you will see two cardboard boxes. When you open the top one you will see tulle, heaps of tulle and rags of all sorts, and under them flowers. Take out all the flowers carefully, try not to crush them, darling; I will choose among them later. . . . And buy me some gloves."

"Very well," said Dymov; "I will go tomorrow and send them to you."

"Tomorrow?" asked Olga Ivanovna, and she looked at him surprised. "You won't have time tomorrow. The first train goes tomorrow at nine, and the wedding's at eleven. No, darling, it must be today; it absolutely must be today. If you won't be able to come tomorrow, send them by a messenger. Come, you must run along. . . . The passenger train will be in directly; don't miss it, darling."

"Very well."

"Oh, how sorry I am to let you go!" said Olga Ivanovna, and tears came into her eyes. "And why did I promise that telegraph clerk, like a silly?"

Dymov hurriedly drank a glass of tea, took a cracknel, and, smiling gently, went to the station. And the caviare, the cheese, and the white salmon were eaten by the two dark gentlemen and the fat actor.

IV

On a still moonlight night in July Olga Ivanovna was standing on the deck of a Volga steamer and looking alternately at the water and at the picturesque banks. Beside her was standing Ryabovsky, telling her the black shadows on the water were not shadows, but a dream, that it would be sweet to sink into forgetfulness, to die, to become a memory in the sight of that enchanted water with the fantastic glimmer, in sight of the fathomless sky and the mournful, dreamy shores that told of the vanity of our life and of the existence of something higher, blessed, and eternal. The past was vulgar and uninteresting, the future was trivial, and that marvellous night, unique in a lifetime, would soon be over, would blend with eternity; then, why live?

And Olga Ivanovna listened alternately to Ryabovsky's voice and the silence of the night, and thought of her being immortal and never dying. The turquoise colour of the water, such as she had never seen before, the sky, the river-banks, the black shadows, and the unaccountable joy that flooded her soul, all told her that she would make a great artist, and that somewhere in the distance, in the infinite space beyond the moonlight, success, glory, the love of the people, lay awaiting her. . . . When she gazed steadily without blinking into the distance, she seemed to see crowds of people, lights, triumphant strains of music, cries of enthusiasm, she herself in a white dress, and flowers showered upon her from all sides. She thought, too, that beside her, leaning with his elbows on the rail of the steamer, there was standing a real great man, a genius, one of God's elect. . . . All that he had created up to the present was fine, new, and extraordinary, but what he would create in time, when with maturity his rare talent reached its full development, would be astounding, immeasurably sublime; and that could be seen by his face, by his manner of expressing himself and his attitude to nature. He talked of shadows, of the tones of evening, of the moonlight, in a special way, in a language of his own, so that one could not help feeling the fascination of his power over nature. He was very handsome, original, and his life, free, independent, aloof from all common cares, was like the life of a bird.

"It's growing cooler," said Olga Ivanovna, and she gave a shudder.

Ryabovsky wrapped her in his cloak, and said mournfully:

"I feel that I am in your power; I am a slave. Why are you so enchanting today?"

He kept staring intently at her, and his eyes were terrible. And she was afraid to look at him.

"I love you madly," he whispered, breathing on her cheek. "Say one word to me and I will not go on living; I will give up art . . ." he muttered in violent emotion. "Love me, love . . ."

"Don't talk like that," said Olga Ivanovna, covering her eyes. "It's dreadful! How about Dymov?"

"What of Dymov? Why Dymov? What have I to do with Dymov? The Volga, the moon, beauty, my love, ecstasy, and there is no such thing as Dymov. . . . Ah! I don't know . . . I don't care about the past; give me one moment, one instant!"

Olga Ivanovna's heart began to throb. She tried to think about her husband, but all her past, with her wedding, with Dymov, and with her "At Homes," seemed to her petty, trivial, dingy, unnecessary, and far, far away. . . . Yes, really, what of Dymov? Why Dymov? What had she to do with Dymov? Had he any existence in nature, or was he only a dream?

"For him, a simple and ordinary man, the happiness he has had already is enough," she thought, covering her face with her hands. "Let them condemn me, let them curse me, but in spite of them all I will go to my ruin; I will go to my ruin! . . . One must experience everything in life. My God! how terrible and how glorious!"

"Well? Well?" muttered the artist, embracing her, and greedily kissing the hands with which she feebly tried to thrust him from her. "You love me? Yes? Yes? Oh, what a night! marvellous night!"

"Yes, what a night!" she whispered, looking into his eyes, which were bright with tears.

Then, she looked round quickly, put her arms round him, and kissed him on the lips.

"We are nearing Kineshmo!" said some one on the other side of the deck.

They heard heavy footsteps; it was a waiter from the refreshment-bar.

"Waiter," said Olga Ivanovna, laughing and crying with happiness, "bring us some wine."

The artist, pale with emotion, sat on the seat, looking at Olga Ivanovna with adoring, grateful eyes; then he closed his eyes, and said, smiling languidly:

"I am tired."

And he leaned his head against the rail.

V

On the second of September the day was warm and still, but overcast. In the early morning a light mist had hung over the Volga, and after nine o'clock it had begun to spout with rain. And there seemed no hope of the sky clearing. Over their morning tea Ryabovsky told Olga

Ivanovna that painting was the most ungrateful and boring art, that he was not an artist, that none but fools thought that he had any talent, and all at once, for no rhyme or reason, he snatched up a knife and with it scraped over his very best sketch. After his tea he sat plunged in gloom at the window and gazed at the Volga. And now the Volga was dingy, all of one even colour without a gleam of light, cold-looking. Everything, everything recalled the approach of dreary, gloomy autumn. And it seemed as though nature had removed now from the Volga the sumptuous green covers from the banks, the brilliant reflections of the sunbeams, the transparent blue distance, and all its smart gala array, and had packed it away in boxes till the coming spring, and the crows were flying above the Volga and crying tauntingly, "Bare, bare!"

Ryabovsky heard their cawing, and thought he had already gone off and lost his talent, that everything in this world was relative, conditional, and stupid, and that he ought not to have taken up with this woman. . . . In short, he was out of humour and depressed.

Olga Ivanovna sat behind the screen on the bed, and, passing her fingers through her lovely flaxen hair, pictured herself first in the drawing-room, then in the bedroom, then in her husband's study; her imagination carried her to the theatre, to the dressmaker, to her distinguished friends. Were they getting something up now? Did they think of her? The season had begun by now, and it would be time to think about her "At Homes." And Dymov? Dear Dymov! with what gentleness and childlike pathos he kept begging her in his letters to make haste and come home! Every month he sent her seventy-five roubles, and when she wrote him that she had lent the artists a hundred roubles, he sent that hundred too. What a kind, generous-hearted man! The travelling wearied Olga Ivanovna; she was bored; and she longed to get away from the peasants, from the damp smell of the river, and to cast off the feeling of physical uncleanliness of which she was conscious all the time, living in the peasants' huts and wandering from village to village. If Ryabovsky had not given his word to the artists that he would stay with them till the twentieth of September, they might have gone away that very day. And how nice that would have been!

"My God!" moaned Ryabovsky. "Will the sun ever come out? I can't go on with a sunny landscape without the sun. . . ."

"But you have a sketch with a cloudy sky," said Olga Ivanovna, coming from behind the screen. "Do you remember, in the right foreground forest trees, on the left a herd of cows and geese? You might finish it now."

"Aie!" the artist scowled. "Finish it! Can you imagine I am such a fool that I don't know what I want to do?"

"How you have changed to me!" sighed Olga Ivanovna.

"Well, a good thing too!"

Olga Ivanovna's face quivered; she moved away to the stove and began to cry.

"Well, that's the last straw—crying! Give over! I have a thousand reasons for tears, but I am not crying."

"A thousand reasons!" cried Olga Ivanovna. "The chief one is that you are weary of me. Yes!" she said, and broke into sobs. "If one is to tell the truth, you are ashamed of our love. You keep trying to prevent the artists from noticing it, though it is impossible to conceal it, and they have known all about it for ever so long."

"Olga, one thing I beg you," said the artist in an imploring voice, laying his hand on his heart—"one thing; don't worry me! I want nothing else from you!"

"But swear that you love me still!"

"This is agony!" the artist hissed through his teeth, and he jumped up. "It will end by my throwing myself in the Volga or going out of my mind! Let me alone!"

"Come, kill me, kill me!" cried Olga Ivanovna. "Kill me!"

She sobbed again, and went behind the screen. There was a swish of rain on the straw thatch of the hut. Ryabovsky clutched his head and strode up and down the hut; then with a resolute face, as though bent on proving something to somebody, put on his cap, slung his gun over his shoulder, and went out of the hut.

After he had gone, Olga Ivanovna lay a long time on the bed, crying. At first she thought it would be a good thing to poison herself, so that when Ryabovsky came back he would find her dead; then her imagination carried her to her drawing-room, to her husband's study, and she imagined herself sitting motionless beside Dymov and enjoying the physical peace and cleanliness, and in the evening sitting in theatre, listening to Mazini. And a yearning for civilization, for the noise and bustle of the town, for celebrated people sent a pang to her heart. A peasant woman came into the hut and began in a leisurely way lighting the stove to get the dinner. There was a smell of charcoal fumes, and the air was filled with bluish smoke. The artists came in, in muddy high boots and with faces wet with rain, examined their sketches, and comforted themselves by saying that the Volga had its charms even in bad weather. On the wall the cheap clock went "tic-tic-tic." . . . The flies, feeling chilled, crowded round the ikon in the corner, buzzing, and one could hear the cockroaches scurrying about among the thick portfolios under the seats. . . .

Ryabovsky came home as the sun was setting. He flung his cap on the table, and, without removing his muddy boots, sank pale and exhausted on the bench and closed his eyes.

"I am tired . . ." he said, and twitched his eyebrows, trying to raise his eyelids.

To be nice to him and to show she was not cross, Olga Ivanovna went up to him, gave him a silent kiss, and passed the comb through his fair hair. She meant to comb it for him.

"What's that?" he said, starting as though something cold had touched him, and he opened his eyes. "What is it? Please let me alone."

He thrust her off, and moved away. And it seemed to her that there was a look of aversion and annoyance on his face.

At that time the peasant woman cautiously carried him, in both hands, a plate of cabbage-soup. And Olga Ivanovna saw how she wetted her fat fingers in it. And the dirty peasant woman, standing with her body thrust forward, and the cabbage-soup which Ryabovsky began eating greedily, and the hut, and their whole way of life, which she at first had so loved for its simplicity and artistic disorder, seemed horrible to her now. She suddenly felt insulted, and said coldly:

"We must part for a time, or else from boredom we shall quarrel in earnest. I am sick of this; I am going today."

"Going how? Astride on a broomstick?"

"Today is Thursday, so the steamer will be here at half-past nine."

"Eh? Yes, yes. . . . Well, go, then . . ." Ryabovsky said softly, wiping his mouth with a towel instead of a dinner napkin. "You are dull and have nothing to do here, and one would have to be a great egoist to try and keep you. Go home, and we shall meet again after the twentieth."

Olga Ivanovna packed in good spirits. Her cheeks positively glowed with pleasure. Could it really be true, she asked herself, that she would soon be writing in her drawing-room and sleeping in her bedroom, and dining with a cloth on the table? A weight was lifted from her heart, and she no longer felt angry with the artist.

"My paints and brushes I will leave with you, Ryabovsky," she said. "You can bring what's left. . . . Mind, now, don't be lazy here when I am gone; don't mope, but work. You are such a splendid fellow, Ryabovsky!"

At ten o'clock Ryabovsky gave her a farewell kiss, in order, as she thought, to avoid kissing her on the steamer before the artists, and went with her to the landing-stage. The steamer soon came up and carried her away.

She arrived home two and a half days later. Breathless with excitement, she went, without taking off her hat or waterproof, into the drawing-room and thence into the dining-room. Dymov, with his waistcoat unbuttoned and no coat, was sitting at the table sharpening a knife on a fork; before him lay a grouse on a plate. As Olga Ivanovna went into the flat she was convinced that it was essential to hide everything from her husband, and that she would have the strength and skill to do so; but now, when she saw his broad, mild, happy smile, and shining, joyful eyes, she felt that to deceive this man was as vile, as revolting, and as impossible and out of her power as to bear false witness, to steal, or to kill, and in a flash she resolved to tell him all that had happened. Letting him kiss and embrace her, she sank down on her knees before him and hid her face.

"What is it, what is it, little mother?" he asked tenderly. "Were you homesick?"

She raised her face, red with shame, and gazed at him with a guilty and imploring look, but fear and shame prevented her from telling him the truth.

"Nothing," she said; "it's just nothing. . . ."

"Let us sit down," he said, raising her and seating her at the table. "That's right, eat the grouse. You are starving, poor darling."

She eagerly breathed in the atmosphere of home and ate the grouse, while he watched her with tenderness and laughed with delight.

VI

Apparently, by the middle of the winter Dymov began to suspect that he was being deceived. As though his conscience was not clear, he could not look his wife straight in the face, did not smile with delight when he met her, and to avoid being left alone with her, he often brought in to dinner his colleague, Korostelev, a little close-cropped man with a wrinkled face, who kept buttoning and unbuttoning his reefer jacket with embarrassment when he talked with Olga Ivanovna, and then with his right hand nipped his left moustache. At dinner the two doctors talked about the fact that a displacement of the diaphragm was sometimes accompanied by irregularities of the heart, or that a great number of neurotic complaints were met with of late, or that Dymov had the day before found a cancer of the lower abdomen while dissecting a corpse with the diagnosis of pernicious anaemia. And it seemed as though they were talking of medicine to give Olga Ivanovna a chance of being silent—that is, of not lying. After dinner Korostelev sat down to the piano, while Dymov sighed and said to him:

"Ech, brother—well, well! Play something melancholy."

Hunching up his shoulders and stretching his fingers wide apart, Korostelev played some chords and began singing in a tenor voice, "Show me the abode where the Russian peasant would not groan," while Dymov sighed once more, propped his head on his fist, and sank into thought.

Olga Ivanovna had been extremely imprudent in her conduct of late. Every morning she woke up in a very bad humour and with the thought that she no longer cared for Ryabovsky, and that, thank God, it was all over now. But as she drank her coffee she reflected that Ryabovsky had robbed her of her husband, and that now she was left with neither her husband nor Ryabovsky; then she remembered talks she had heard among her acquaintances of a picture Ryabovsky was preparing for the exhibition, something striking, a mixture of genre and landscape, in the style of Polyenov, about which every one who had been into his studio went into raptures; and this, of course, she mused, he had created under her influence, and altogether, thanks to her influence, he had greatly changed for the better. Her influence was so beneficent and essential that if she were to leave him he might perhaps go to ruin. And she remembered, too, that the last time he had come to see her in a great-coat with flecks on it and a new tie, he had asked her languidly:

"Am I beautiful?"

And with his elegance, his long curls, and his blue eyes, he really was very beautiful (or perhaps it only seemed so), and he had been affectionate to her.

Considering and remembering many things Olga Ivanovna dressed and in great agitation drove to Ryabovsky's studio. She found him in high spirits, and enchanted with his really magnificent picture. He was dancing about and playing the fool and answering serious questions with jokes. Olga Ivanovna was jealous of the picture and hated it, but from politeness she stood before the picture for five minutes in silence, and, heaving a sigh, as though before a holy shrine, said softly:

"Yes, you have never painted anything like it before. Do you know, it is positively awe-inspiring?"

And then she began beseeching him to love her and not to cast her off, to have pity on her in her misery and her wretchedness. She shed tears, kissed his hands, insisted on his swearing that he loved her, told him that without her good influence he would go astray and be ruined. And, when she had spoilt his good-humour, feeling herself humiliated, she would drive off to her dressmaker or to an actress of her acquaintance to try and get theatre tickets.

If she did not find him at his studio she left a letter in which she swore that if he did not come to see her that day she would poison herself. He was scared, came to see her, and stayed to dinner. Regardless of her husband's presence, he would say rude things to her, and she would answer him in the same way. Both felt they were a burden to each other, that they were tyrants and enemies, and were wrathful, and in their wrath did not notice that their behaviour was unseemly, and that even Korostelev, with his close-cropped head, saw it all. After dinner Ryabovsky made haste to say good-bye and get away.

"Where are you off to?" Olga Ivanovna would ask him in the hall, looking at him with hatred.

Scowling and screwing up his eyes, he mentioned some lady of their acquaintance, and it was evident that he was laughing at her jealousy and wanted to annoy her. She went to her bedroom and lay down on her bed; from jealousy, anger, a sense of humiliation and shame, she bit the pillow and began sobbing aloud. Dymov left Korostelev in the drawing-room, went into the bedroom, and with a desperate and embarrassed face said softly:

"Don't cry so loud, little mother; there's no need. You must be quiet about it. You must not let people see. . . . You know what is done is done, and can't be mended."

Not knowing how to ease the burden of her jealousy, which actually set her temples throbbing with pain, and thinking still that things might be set right, she would wash, powder her tear-stained face, and fly off to the lady mentioned.

Not finding Ryabovsky with her, she would drive off to a second, then to a third. At first she was ashamed to go about like this, but afterwards she got used to it, and it would happen that in one evening she would make the round of all her female acquaintances in search of Ryabovsky, and they all understood it.

One day she said to Ryabovsky of her husband:

"That man crushes me with his magnanimity."

This phrase pleased her so much that when she met the artists who knew of her affair with Ryabovsky she said every time of her husband, with a vigorous movement of her arm:

"That man crushes me with his magnanimity."

Their manner of life was the same as it had been the year before. On Wednesdays they were "At Home"; an actor recited, the artists sketched. The violoncellist played, a singer sang, and invariably at half-past eleven the door leading to the dining-room opened and Dymov, smiling, said:

"Come to supper, gentlemen."

As before, Olga Ivanovna hunted celebrities, found them, was not satisfied, and went in pursuit of fresh ones. As before, she came back late every night; but now Dymov was not, as last year, asleep, but sitting in his study at work of some sort. He went to bed at three o'clock and got up at eight.

One evening when she was getting ready to go to the theatre and standing before the pier glass, Dymov came into her bedroom, wearing his dress-coat and a white tie. He was smiling gently and looked into his wife's face joyfully, as in old days; his face was radiant.

"I have just been defending my thesis," he said, sitting down and smoothing his knees.

"Defending?" asked Olga Ivanovna.

"Oh, oh!" he laughed, and he craned his neck to see his wife's face in the mirror, for she was still standing with her back to him, doing up her hair. "Oh, oh," he repeated, "do you know it's very possible they may offer me the Readership in General Pathology? It seems like it."

It was evident from his beaming, blissful face that if Olga Ivanovna had shared with him his joy and triumph he would have forgiven her everything, both the present and the future, and would have forgotten everything, but she did not understand what was meant by a "readership" or by "general pathology"; besides, she was afraid of being late for the theatre, and she said nothing.

He sat there another two minutes, and with a guilty smile went away.

VII

It had been a very troubled day.

Dymov had a very bad headache; he had no breakfast, and did not go to the hospital, but spent the whole time lying on his sofa in the study. Olga Ivanovna went as usual at midday to see Ryabovsky, to show him her still-life sketch, and to ask him why he had not been to see her the evening before. The sketch seemed to her worthless, and she had painted it only in order to have an additional reason for going to the artist.

She went in to him without ringing, and as she was taking off her goloshes in the entry she heard a sound as of something running softly in the studio, with a feminine rustle of skirts; and as she hastened to peep in she caught a momentary glimpse of a bit of brown petticoat, which vanished behind a big picture draped, together with the easel, with black calico, to the floor. There could be no doubt that a woman was hiding there. How often Olga Ivanovna herself had taken refuge behind that picture!

Ryabovsky, evidently much embarrassed, held out both hands to her, as though surprised at her arrival, and said with a forced smile:

"Aha! Very glad to see you! Anything nice to tell me?"

Olga Ivanovna's eyes filled with tears. She felt ashamed and bitter, and would not for a million roubles have consented to speak in the presence of the outsider, the rival, the deceitful woman who was standing now behind the picture, and probably giggling malignantly.

"I have brought you a sketch," she said timidly in a thin voice, and her lips quivered. "*Nature morte.*"

"Ah—ah! . . . A sketch?"

The artist took the sketch in his hands, and as he examined it walked, as it were mechanically, into the other room.

Olga Ivanovna followed him humbly.

"*Nature morte* . . . first-rate sort," he muttered, falling into rhyme. "Kurort . . . sport . . . port . . ."

From the studio came the sound of hurried footsteps and the rustle of a skirt.

So she had gone. Olga Ivanovna wanted to scream aloud, to hit the artist on the head with something heavy, but she could see nothing through her tears, was crushed by her shame, and felt herself, not Olga Ivanovna, not an artist, but a little insect.

"I am tired . . ." said the artist languidly, looking at the sketch and tossing his head as though struggling with drowsiness. "It's very nice, of course, but here a sketch today, a sketch last year, another sketch in a month . . . I wonder you are not bored with them. If I were you I should give up painting and work seriously at music or something. You're not an artist, you know, but a musician. But you can't think how tired I am! I'll tell them to bring us some tea, shall I?"

He went out of the room, and Olga Ivanovna heard him give some order to his footman. To avoid farewells and explanations, and above all to avoid bursting into sobs, she ran as fast as she could, before Ryabovsky came back, to the entry, put on her goloshes, and went out into the street; then she breathed easily, and felt she was free for ever from Ryabovsky and from painting and from the burden of shame which had so crushed her in the studio. It was all over!

She drove to her dressmaker's; then to see Barnay, who had only arrived the day before; from Barnay to a music-shop, and all the time she was thinking how she would write Ryabovsky a cold, cruel letter full of personal dignity, and how in the spring or the summer she would go with Dymov to the Crimea, free herself finally from the past there, and begin a new life.

On getting home late in the evening she sat down in the drawing-room, without taking off her things, to begin the letter. Ryabovsky had told her she was not an artist, and to pay him out she wrote to him now that he painted the same thing every year, and said exactly the same thing every day; that he was at a standstill, and that nothing more would come of him than had come already. She wanted to write, too, that he owed a great deal to her good influence, and that if he was going wrong it was only because her influence was paralysed by various dubious persons like the one who had been hiding behind the picture that day.

"Little mother!" Dymov called from the study, without opening the door.

"What is it?"

"Don't come in to me, but only come to the door—that's right. . . . The day before yesterday I must have caught diphtheria at the hospital, and now . . . I am ill. Make haste and send for Korostelev."

Olga Ivanovna always called her husband by his surname, as she did all the men of her acquaintance; she disliked his Christian name, Osip, because it reminded her of the Osip in Gogol and the silly pun on his name. But now she cried:

"Osip, it cannot be!"

"Send for him; I feel ill," Dymov said behind the door, and she could hear him go back to the sofa and lie down. "Send!" she heard his voice faintly.

"Good Heavens!" thought Olga Ivanovna, turning chill with horror. "Why, it's dangerous!"

For no reason she took the candle and went into the bedroom, and there, reflecting what she must do, glanced casually at herself in the pier glass. With her pale, frightened face, in a jacket with sleeves high on the shoulders, with yellow ruches on her bosom, and with stripes running in unusual directions on her skirt, she seemed to herself horrible and disgusting. She suddenly felt poignantly sorry for Dymov, for his boundless love for her, for his young life, and even for the desolate little bed in which he had not slept for so long; and she remembered his habitual, gentle, submissive smile. She wept bitterly, and wrote an imploring letter to Korostelev. It was two o'clock in the night.

VIII

When towards eight o'clock in the morning Olga Ivanovna, her head heavy from want of sleep and her hair unbrushed, came out of her bedroom, looking unattractive and with a guilty expression on her face, a gentleman with a black beard, apparently the doctor, passed by her into the entry. There was a smell of drugs. Korostelev was standing near the study door, twisting his left moustache with his right hand.

"Excuse me, I can't let you go in," he said surlily to Olga Ivanovna; "it's catching. Besides, it's no use, really; he is delirious, anyway."

"Has he really got diphtheria?" Olga Ivanovna asked in a whisper.

"People who wantonly risk infection ought to be hauled up and punished for it," muttered Korostelev, not answering Olga Ivanovna's question. "Do you know why he caught it? On Tuesday he was sucking up the mucus through a pipette from a boy with diphtheria. And what for? It was stupid. . . . Just from folly. . . ."

"Is it dangerous, very?" asked Olga Ivanovna.

"Yes; they say it is the malignant form. We ought to send for Shrek really."

A little red-haired man with a long nose and a Jewish accent arrived; then a tall, stooping, shaggy individual, who looked like a head deacon; then a stout young man with a red face and spectacles. These were doctors who came to watch by turns beside their colleague. Korostelev did not go home when his turn was over, but remained and wandered about the rooms like an uneasy spirit. The maid kept getting tea for the various doctors, and was constantly running to the chemist, and there was no one to do the rooms. There was a dismal stillness in the flat.

Olga Ivanovna sat in her bedroom and thought that God was punishing her for having deceived her husband. That silent, unrepining, uncomprehended creature, robbed by his mildness of all personality and will, weak from excessive kindness, had been suffering in obscurity somewhere on his sofa, and had not complained. And if he were to complain even in delirium, the doctors watching by his bedside would learn that diphtheria was not the only cause of his sufferings. They would ask Korostelev. He knew all about it, and it was not for nothing that he looked at his friend's wife with eyes that seemed to say that she was the real chief criminal and diphtheria was only her accomplice. She did not think now of the moonlight evening on the Volga, nor the words of love, nor their poetical life in the peasant's hut. She thought only that from an idle whim, from self-indulgence, she had sullied herself all over from head to foot in something filthy, sticky, which one could never wash off. . . .

"Oh, how fearfully false I've been!" she thought, recalling the troubled passion she had known with Ryabovsky. "Curse it all! . . ."

At four o'clock she dined with Korostelev. He did nothing but scowl and drink red wine, and did not eat a morsel. She ate nothing, either. At one minute she was praying inwardly and vowing to God that if Dymov recovered she would love him again and be a faithful wife to him. Then, forgetting herself for a minute, she would look at Korostelev, and think: "Surely it must be dull to be a humble, obscure person, not remarkable in any way, especially with such a wrinkled face and bad manners!" Then it seemed to her that God would strike her dead that minute for not having once been in her husband's study, for fear of infection. And altogether she had a dull, despondent feeling and a conviction that her life was spoilt, and that there was no setting it right anyhow. . . .

After dinner darkness came on. When Olga Ivanovna went into the drawing-room Korostelev was asleep on the sofa, with a gold-embroidered silk cushion under his head.

"Khee-poo-ah," he snored—"khee-poo-ah."

And the doctors as they came to sit up and went away again did not notice this disorder. The fact that a strange man was asleep and snoring in the drawing-room, and the sketches on the walls and the exquisite decoration of the room, and the fact that the lady of the house was dishevelled and untidy—all that aroused not the slightest interest now. One of the doctors chanced to laugh at something, and the laugh had a strange and timid sound that made one's heart ache.

When Olga Ivanovna went into the drawing-room next time, Korostelev was not asleep, but sitting up and smoking.

"He has diphtheria of the nasal cavity," he said in a low voice, "and the heart is not working properly now. Things are in a bad way, really."

"But you will send for Shrek?" said Olga Ivanovna.

"He has been already. It was he noticed that the diphtheria had passed into the nose. What's the use of Shrek! Shrek's no use at all, really. He is Shrek, I am Korostelev, and nothing more."

The time dragged on fearfully slowly. Olga Ivanovna lay down in her clothes on her bed, that had not been made all day, and sank into a doze. She dreamed that the whole flat was filled up from floor to ceiling with a huge piece of iron, and that if they could only get the iron out they would all be light-hearted and happy. Waking, she realized that it was not the iron but Dymov's illness that was weighing on her.

"Nature morte, port . . ." she thought, sinking into forgetfulness again. "Sport . . . Kurort . . . and what of Shrek? Shrek . . . trek . . . wreck. . . . And where are my friends now? Do they know that we are in trouble? Lord, save . . . spare! Shrek . . . trek . . ."

And again the iron was there. . . . The time dragged on slowly, though the clock on the lower storey struck frequently. And bells were continually ringing as the doctors arrived. . . . The housemaid came in with an empty glass on a tray, and asked, "Shall I make the bed, madam?" and getting no answer, went away.

The clock below struck the hour. She dreamed of the rain on the Volga; and again some one came into her bedroom, she thought a stranger. Olga Ivanovna jumped up, and recognized Korostelev.

"What time is it?" she asked.

"About three."

"Well, what is it?"

"What, indeed! . . . I've come to tell you he is passing. . . ."

He gave a sob, sat down on the bed beside her, and wiped away the tears with his sleeve. She could not grasp it at once, but turned cold all over and began slowly crossing herself.

"He is passing," he repeated in a shrill voice, and again he gave a sob. "He is dying because he sacrificed himself. What a loss for science!" he said bitterly. "Compare him with all of us. He was a great man, an extraordinary man! What gifts! What hopes we all had of him!" Korostelev went on, wringing his hands: "Merciful God, he was a man of science; we shall never look on his like again. Osip Dymov, what have you done—aie, aie, my God!"

Korostelev covered his face with both hands in despair, and shook his head.

"And his moral force," he went on, seeming to grow more and more exasperated against some one. "Not a man, but a pure, good, loving soul, and clean as crystal. He served science and died for science. And he worked like an ox night and day—no one spared him—and with his youth and his learning he had to take a private practice and work at translations at night to pay for these . . . vile rags!"

Korostelev looked with hatred at Olga Ivanovna, snatched at the sheet with both hands and angrily tore it, as though it were to blame.

"He did not spare himself, and others did not spare him. Oh, what's the use of talking!"

"Yes, he was a rare man," said a bass voice in the drawing-room.

Olga Ivanovna remembered her whole life with him from the beginning to the end, with all its details, and suddenly she understood that he really was an extraordinary, rare, and, compared with every one else she knew, a great man. And remembering how her father, now dead, and all the other doctors had behaved to him, she realized that they really had seen in him a future celebrity. The walls, the ceiling, the lamp, and the carpet on the floor, seemed to be winking at her sarcastically, as though they would say, "You were blind! you were blind!" With a wail she flung herself out of the bedroom, dashed by some unknown man in the drawing-room, and ran into her husband's study. He was lying motionless on the sofa, covered to the waist with a quilt. His face was fearfully thin and sunken, and was of a greyish-yellow colour such as is never seen in the living; only from the forehead, from the black eyebrows and from the familiar smile, could he be recognized as Dymov. Olga Ivanovna hurriedly felt his chest, his forehead, and his hands. The chest was still warm, but the forehead and hands were unpleasantly cold, and the half-open eyes looked, not at Olga Ivanovna, but at the quilt.

"Dymov!" she called aloud, "Dymov!" She wanted to explain to him that it had been a mistake, that all was not lost, that life might still be beautiful and happy, that he was an extraordinary, rare, great man, and that she would all her life worship him and bow down in homage and holy awe before him. . . .

"Dymov!" she called him, patting him on the shoulder, unable to believe that he would never wake again. "Dymov! Dymov!"

In the drawing-room Korostelev was saying to the housemaid:

"Why keep asking? Go to the church beadle and enquire where they live. They'll wash the body and lay it out, and do everything that is necessary."

After the Theatre

Nadya Zelenin had just come back with her mamma from the theatre where she had seen a performance of "Yevgeny Onyegin." As soon as she reached her own room she threw off her dress, let down her hair, and in her petticoat and white dressing-jacket hastily sat down to the table to write a letter like Tatyana's.

"I love you," she wrote, "but you do not love me, do not love me!"

She wrote it and laughed.

She was only sixteen and did not yet love anyone. She knew that an officer called Gorny and a student called Gruzdev loved her, but now after the opera she wanted to be doubtful of their love. To be unloved and unhappy—how interesting that was. There is something beautiful, touching, and poetical about it when one loves and the other is indifferent. Onyegin was interesting because he was not in love at all, and Tatyana was fascinating because she was so much in love; but if they had been equally in love with each other and had been happy, they would perhaps have seemed dull.

"Leave off declaring that you love me," Nadya went on writing, thinking of Gorny. "I cannot believe it. You are very clever, cultivated, serious, you have immense talent, and perhaps a brilliant future awaits you, while I am an uninteresting girl of no importance, and you know very well that I should be only a hindrance in your life. It is true that you were attracted by me and thought you had found your ideal in me, but that was a mistake, and now you are asking yourself in despair: 'Why did I meet that girl?' And only your goodness of heart prevents you from owning it to yourself. . . ."

Nadya felt sorry for herself, she began to cry, and went on:

"It is hard for me to leave my mother and my brother, or I should take a nun's veil and go whither chance may lead me. And you would be left free and would love another. Oh, if I were dead!"

She could not make out what she had written through her tears; little rainbows were quivering on the table, on the floor, on the ceiling, as though she were looking through a prism. She could not write, she sank back in her easy-chair and fell to thinking of Gorny.

My God! how interesting, how fascinating men were! Nadya recalled the fine expression, ingratiating, guilty, and soft, which came into the officer's face when one argued about music with him, and the effort he made to prevent his voice from betraying his passion. In a society where cold haughtiness and indifference are regarded as signs of good breeding and gentlemanly bearing, one must conceal one's passions. And he did try to conceal them, but he did not succeed, and everyone knew very well that he had a passionate love of music. The endless discussions about music and the bold criticisms of people who knew nothing about it kept him always on the strain; he was frightened, timid, and silent. He played the piano magnificently, like a professional pianist, and if he had not been in the army he would certainly have been a famous musician.

The tears on her eyes dried. Nadya remembered that Gorny had declared his love at a Symphony concert, and again downstairs by the hatstand where there was a tremendous draught blowing in all directions.

"I am very glad that you have at last made the acquaintance of Gruzdev, our student friend," she went on writing. "He is a very clever man, and you will be sure to like him. He came to see us yesterday and stayed till two o'clock. We were all delighted with him, and I regretted that you had not come. He said a great deal that was remarkable."

Nadya laid her arms on the table and leaned her head on them, and her hair covered the letter. She recalled that the student, too, loved her, and that he had as much right to a letter from her as Gorny. Wouldn't it be better after all to write to Gruzdev? There was a stir of joy in her bosom for no reason whatever; at first the joy was small, and rolled in her bosom like an india-rubber ball; then it became more massive, bigger, and rushed like a wave. Nadya forgot Gorny and Gruzdev; her thoughts were in a tangle and her joy grew and grew; from her bosom it passed into her arms and legs, and it seemed as though a light, cool breeze were breathing on her head and ruffling her hair. Her shoulders quivered with subdued laughter, the table and the lamp chimney shook, too, and tears from her eyes splashed on the letter. She could not stop laughing, and to prove to herself that she was not laughing about nothing she made haste to think of something funny.

"What a funny poodle," she said, feeling as though she would choke with laughter. "What a funny poodle!"

She thought how, after tea the evening before, Gruzdev had played with Maxim the poodle, and afterwards had told them about a very intelligent poodle who had run after a crow in the yard, and the crow had looked round at him and said: "Oh, you scamp!"

The poodle, not knowing he had to do with a learned crow, was fearfully confused and retreated in perplexity, then began barking. . . .

"No, I had better love Gruzdev," Nadya decided, and she tore up the letter to Gorny.

She fell to thinking of the student, of his love, of her love; but the thoughts in her head insisted on flowing in all directions, and she thought about everything—about her mother, about the street, about the pencil, about the piano. . . . She thought of them joyfully, and felt that everything was good, splendid, and her joy told her that this was not all, that in a little while it would be better still. Soon it would be spring, summer, going with her mother to Gorbiki. Gorny would come for his furlough, would walk about the garden with her and make love to her. Gruzdev would come too. He would play croquet and skittles with her, and would tell her wonderful things. She had a passionate longing for the garden, the darkness, the pure sky, the stars. Again her shoulders shook with laughter, and it seemed to her that there was a scent of wormwood in the room and that a twig was tapping at the window.

She went to her bed, sat down, and not knowing what to do with the immense joy which filled her with yearning, she looked at the holy image hanging at the back of her bed, and said:

"Oh, Lord God! Oh, Lord God!"

In Exile

Old Semyon, nicknamed Canny, and a young Tatar, whom no one knew by name, were sitting on the river-bank by the camp-fire; the other three ferrymen were in the hut. Semyon, an old man of sixty, lean and toothless, but broad-shouldered and still healthy-looking, was drunk; he would have gone in to sleep long before, but he had a bottle in his pocket and he was afraid that the fellows in the hut would ask him for vodka. The Tatar was ill and weary, and wrapping himself up in his rags was describing how nice it was in the Simbirsk province, and what a beautiful and clever wife he had left behind at home. He was not more than twenty-five, and now by the light of the camp-fire, with his pale and sick, mournful face, he looked like a boy.

"To be sure, it is not paradise here," said Canny. "You can see for yourself, the water, the bare banks, clay, and nothing else. . . . Easter has long passed and yet there is ice on the river, and this morning there was snow. . . ."

"It's bad! it's bad!" said the Tatar, and looked round him in terror.

The dark, cold river was flowing ten paces away; it grumbled, lapped against the hollow clay banks and raced on swiftly towards the far-away sea. Close to the bank there was the dark blur of a big barge, which the ferrymen called a "karbos." Far away on the further bank, lights, dying down and flickering up again, zigzagged like little snakes; they were burning last year's grass. And beyond the little snakes there was darkness again. There little icicles could be heard knocking against the barge. It was damp and cold. . . .

The Tatar glanced at the sky. There were as many stars as at home, and the same blackness all round, but something was lacking. At home in the Simbirsk province the stars were quite different, and so was the sky.

"It's bad! it's bad!" he repeated.

"You will get used to it," said Semyon, and he laughed. "Now you are young and foolish, the milk is hardly dry on your lips, and it seems to you in your foolishness that you are more wretched than anyone; but the time will come when you will say to yourself: 'I wish no one a better life than mine.' You look at me. Within a week the floods will be over and we shall set up the ferry; you will all go wandering off about Siberia while I shall stay and shall begin going from bank to bank. I've been going like that for twenty-two years, day and night. The pike and the salmon are under the water while I am on the water. And thank God for it, I want nothing; God give everyone such a life."

The Tatar threw some dry twigs on the camp-fire, lay down closer to the blaze, and said:

"My father is a sick man. When he dies my mother and wife will come here. They have promised."

"And what do you want your wife and mother for?" asked Canny. "That's mere foolishness, my lad. It's the devil confounding you, damn his soul! Don't you listen to him, the cursed one. Don't let him have his way. He is at you about the women, but you spite him; say, 'I don't want them!' He is on at you about freedom, but you stand up to him and say: 'I don't want it!' I want nothing, neither father nor mother, nor wife, nor freedom, nor post, nor paddock; I want nothing, damn their souls!"

Semyon took a pull at the bottle and went on:

"I am not a simple peasant, not of the working class, but the son of a deacon, and when I was free I lived at Kursk; I used to wear a frock-coat, and now I have brought myself to such a pass that I can sleep naked on the ground and eat grass. And I wish no one a better life. I want nothing and I am afraid of nobody, and the way I look at it is that there is nobody richer and freer than I am. When they sent me here from Russia from the first day I stuck it out; I want nothing! The devil was at me about my wife and about my home and about freedom, but I told him: 'I want nothing.' I stuck to it, and here you see I live well, and I don't complain, and if anyone gives way to the devil and listens to him, if but once, he is lost, there is no salvation for him: he is sunk in the bog to the crown of his head and will never get out.

"It is not only a foolish peasant like you, but even gentlemen, well-educated people, are lost. Fifteen years ago they sent a gentleman here from Russia. He hadn't shared something with his brothers and had forged something in a will. They did say he was a prince or a baron, but maybe he was simply an official—who knows? Well, the gentleman arrived here, and first thing he bought himself a house and land in Muhortinskoe. 'I want to live by my own work,' says he, 'in the sweat of my brow, for I am not a gentleman now,' says he, 'but a settler.' 'Well,' says I, 'God help you, that's the right thing.' He was a young man then, busy and careful; he used to mow himself and catch fish and ride sixty miles on horseback. Only this is what happened: from the very first year he took to riding to Gyrino for the post; he used to stand on my ferry and sigh: 'Ech, Semyon, how long it is since they sent me any money from home!' 'You don't want money, Vassily Sergeyitch,' says I. 'What use is it to you? You cast away the past, and forget it as though it had never been at all, as though it had been a dream, and begin to live anew. Don't listen to the devil,' says I; 'he will bring you to no good, he'll draw you into a snare. Now you want money,' says I, 'but in a very little while you'll be wanting something else, and then more and more. If you want to be happy,' says I, 'the chief thing is not to want anything. Yes. . . . If,' says I, 'if Fate has wronged you and me cruelly, it's no good asking for her favor and bowing down to her, but you despise her and laugh at her, or else she will laugh at you.' That's what I said to him. . . .

"Two years later I ferried him across to this side, and he was rubbing his hands and laughing. 'I am going to Gyrino to meet my wife,' says he. 'She was sorry for me,' says he; 'she has come. She is good and kind.' And he was breathless with joy. So a day later he came with his wife. A beautiful young lady in a hat; in her arms was a baby girl. And lots of luggage of all sorts. And my Vassily Sergeyitch was fussing round her; he couldn't take his eyes off her and couldn't say enough in praise of her. 'Yes, brother Semyon, even in Siberia people can live!' 'Oh, all right,' thinks I, 'it will be a different tale presently.' And from that time forward he went almost every week to inquire whether money had not come from Russia. He wanted a lot of money. 'She is losing her youth and beauty here in Siberia for my sake,' says he, 'and sharing my bitter lot with me, and so I ought,' says he, 'to provide her with every comfort. . . .'

"To make it livelier for the lady he made acquaintance with the officials and all sorts of riff-raff. And of course he had to give food and drink to all that crew, and there had to be a piano and a shaggy lapdog on the sofa—plague take it! . . . Luxury, in fact, self-indulgence. The lady did not stay with him long. How could she? The clay, the water, the cold, no vegetables for you, no fruit. All around you ignorant and drunken people and no sort of manners, and she was a spoilt lady from Petersburg or Moscow. . . . To be sure she moped. Besides, her husband, say what you like, was not a gentleman now, but a settler—not the same rank.

"Three years later, I remember, on the eve of the Assumption, there was shouting from the further bank. I went over with the ferry, and what do I see but the lady, all wrapped up, and with her a young gentleman, an official. A sledge with three horses. . . . I ferried them across here, they got in and away like the wind. They were soon lost to sight. And towards morning Vassily Sergeyitch galloped down to the ferry. 'Didn't my wife come this way with a gentleman in spectacles, Semyon?' 'She did,' said I; 'you may look for the wind in the fields!' He galloped in pursuit of them. For five days and nights he was riding after them. When I ferried him over to the other side afterwards, he flung himself on the ferry and beat his head on the boards of the ferry and howled. 'So that's how it is,' says I. I laughed, and reminded him 'people can live even in Siberia!' And he beat his head harder than ever. . . .

"Then he began longing for freedom. His wife had slipped off to Russia, and of course he was drawn there to see her and to get her away from her lover. And he took, my lad, to galloping almost every day, either to the post or the town to see the commanding officer; he kept sending in petitions for them to have mercy on him and let him go back home; and he used to say that he had spent some two hundred roubles on telegrams alone. He sold his land and mortgaged his house to the Jews. He grew gray and bent, and yellow in the face, as though he was in consumption. If he talked to you he would go, khee—khee—khee,... and there were tears in his eyes. He kept rushing about like this with petitions for eight years, but now he has grown brighter and more cheerful again: he has found another whim to give way to. You see, his daughter has grown up. He looks at her, and she is the apple of his eye. And to tell the truth she is all right, good-looking, with black eyebrows and a lively disposition. Every Sunday he used to ride with her to church in Gyrino. They used to stand on the ferry, side by side, she would laugh and he could not take his eyes off her. 'Yes, Semyon,' says he, 'people can live even in Siberia. Even in Siberia there is happiness. Look,' says he, 'what a daughter I have got! I warrant you wouldn't find another like her for a thousand versts round.' 'Your daughter is all right,' says I, 'that's true, certainly.' But to myself I thought: 'Wait a bit, the wench is young, her blood is dancing, she wants to live, and there is no life here.' And she did begin to pine, my lad.... She faded and faded, and now she can hardly crawl about. Consumption.

"So you see what Siberian happiness is, damn its soul! You see how people can live in Siberia.... He has taken to going from one doctor to another and taking them home with him. As soon as he hears that two or three hundred miles away there is a doctor or a sorcerer, he will drive to fetch him. A terrible lot of money he spent on doctors, and to my thinking he had better have spent the money on drink.... She'll die just the same. She is certain to die, and then it will be all over with him. He'll hang himself from grief or run away to Russia—that's a sure thing. He'll run away and they'll catch him, then he will be tried, sent to prison, he will have a taste of the lash...."

"Good! good!" said the Tatar, shivering with cold.

"What is good?" asked Canny.

"His wife, his daughter.... What of prison and what of sorrow!—anyway, he did see his wife and his daughter.... You say, want nothing. But 'nothing' is bad! His wife lived with him three years—that was a gift from God. 'Nothing' is bad, but three years is good. How not understand?"

Shivering and hesitating, with effort picking out the Russian words of which he knew but few, the Tatar said that God forbid one should fall sick and die in a strange land, and be buried in the cold and dark earth; that if his wife came to him for one day, even for one hour, that for such happiness he would be ready to bear any suffering and to thank God. Better one day of happiness than nothing.

Then he described again what a beautiful and clever wife he had left at home. Then, clutching his head in both hands, he began crying and assuring Semyon that he was not guilty, and was suffering for nothing. His two brothers and an uncle had carried off a peasant's horses, and had beaten the old man till he was half dead, and the commune had not judged fairly, but had contrived a sentence by which all the three brothers were sent to Siberia, while the uncle, a rich man, was left at home.

"You will get used to it!" said Semyon.

The Tatar was silent, and stared with tear-stained eyes at the fire; his face expressed bewilderment and fear, as though he still did not understand why he was here in the darkness and the wet, beside strangers, and not in the Simbirsk province.

Canny lay near the fire, chuckled at something, and began humming a song in an undertone.

"What joy has she with her father?" he said a little later. "He loves her and he rejoices in her, that's true; but, mate, you must mind your ps and qs with him, he is a strict old man, a harsh old man. And young wenches don't want strictness. They want petting and ha-ha-ha! and ho-ho-ho! and scent and pomade. Yes. . . . Ech! life, life," sighed Semyon, and he got up heavily. "The vodka is all gone, so it is time to sleep. Eh? I am going, my lad. . . ."

Left alone, the Tatar put on more twigs, lay down and stared at the fire; he began thinking of his own village and of his wife. If his wife could only come for a month, for a day; and then if she liked she might go back again. Better a month or even a day than nothing. But if his wife kept her promise and came, what would he have to feed her on? Where could she live here?

"If there were not something to eat, how could she live?" the Tatar asked aloud.

He was paid only ten kopecks for working all day and all night at the oar; it is true that travelers gave him tips for tea and for vodka, but the men shared all they received among themselves, and gave nothing to the Tatar, but only laughed at him. And from poverty he was hungry, cold, and frightened.... Now, when his whole body was aching and shivering, he ought to go into the hut and lie down to sleep; but he had nothing to cover him there, and it was colder than on the river-bank; here he had nothing to cover him either, but at least he could make up the fire....

In another week, when the floods were quite over and they set the ferry going, none of the ferrymen but Semyon would be wanted, and the Tatar would begin going from village to village begging for alms and for work. His wife was only seventeen; she was beautiful, spoilt, and shy; could she possibly go from village to village begging alms with her face unveiled? No, it was terrible even to think of that....

It was already getting light; the barge, the bushes of willow on the water, and the waves could be clearly discerned, and if one looked round there was the steep clay slope; at the bottom of it the hut thatched with dingy brown straw, and the huts of the village lay clustered higher up. The cocks were already crowing in the village.

The rusty red clay slope, the barge, the river, the strange, unkind people, hunger, cold, illness, perhaps all that was not real. Most likely it was all a dream, thought the Tatar. He felt that he was asleep and heard his own snoring.... Of course he was at home in the Simbirsk province, and he had only to call his wife by name for her to answer; and in the next room was his mother.... What terrible dreams there are, though! What are they for? The Tatar smiled and opened his eyes. What river was this, the Volga?

Snow was falling.

"Boat!" was shouted on the further side. "Boat!"

The Tatar woke up, and went to wake his mates and row over to the other side. The ferrymen came on to the river-bank, putting on their torn sheepskins as they walked, swearing with voices husky from sleepiness and shivering from the cold. On waking from their sleep, the river, from which came a breath of piercing cold, seemed to strike them as revolting and horrible. They jumped into the barge without hurrying themselves. . . . The Tatar and the three ferrymen took the long, broad-bladed oars, which in the darkness looked like the claws of crabs; Semyon leaned his stomach against the tiller. The shout on the other side still continued, and two shots were fired from a revolver, probably with the idea that the ferrymen were asleep or had gone to the pot-house in the village.

"All right, you have plenty of time," said Semyon in the tone of a man convinced that there was no necessity in this world to hurry—that it would lead to nothing, anyway.

The heavy, clumsy barge moved away from the bank and floated between the willow-bushes, and only the willows slowly moving back showed that the barge was not standing still but moving. The ferrymen swung the oars evenly in time; Semyon lay with his stomach on the tiller and, describing a semicircle in the air, flew from one side to the other. In the darkness it looked as though the men were sitting on some antediluvian animal with long paws, and were moving on it through a cold, desolate land, the land of which one sometimes dreams in nightmares.

They passed beyond the willows and floated out into the open. The creak and regular splash of the oars was heard on the further shore, and a shout came: "Make haste! make haste!"

Another ten minutes passed, and the barge banged heavily against the landing-stage.

"And it keeps sprinkling and sprinkling," muttered Semyon, wiping the snow from his face; "and where it all comes from God only knows."

On the bank stood a thin man of medium height, in a jacket lined with fox-fur and in a white lambskin cap. He was standing at a little distance from his horses and not moving; he had a gloomy, concentrated expression, as though he were trying to remember something and angry with his untrustworthy memory. When Semyon went up to him and took off his cap, smiling, he said:

"I am hastening to Anastasyevka. My daughter's worse again, and they say that there is a new doctor at Anastasyevka."

They dragged the carriage on to the barge and floated back. The man whom Semyon addressed as Vassily Sergeyitch stood all the time motionless, tightly compressing his thick lips and staring off into space; when his coachman asked permission to smoke in his presence he made no answer, as though he had not heard. Semyon, lying with his stomach on the tiller, looked mockingly at him and said:

"Even in Siberia people can live—can li-ive!"

There was a triumphant expression on Canny's face, as though he had proved something and was delighted that things had happened as he had foretold. The unhappy helplessness of the man in the foxskin coat evidently afforded him great pleasure.

"It's muddy driving now, Vassily Sergeyitch," he said when the horses were harnessed again on the bank. "You should have put off going for another fortnight, when it will be drier. Or else not have gone at all. . . . If any good would come of your going—but as you know yourself, people have been driving about for years and years, day and night, and it's always been no use. That's the truth."

Vassily Sergeyitch tipped him without a word, got into his carriage and drove off.

"There, he has galloped off for a doctor!" said Semyon, shrinking from the cold. "But looking for a good doctor is like chasing the wind in the fields or catching the devil by the tail, plague take your soul! What a queer chap, Lord forgive me a sinner!"

The Tatar went up to Canny, and, looking at him with hatred and repulsion, shivering, and mixing Tatar words with his broken Russian, said: "He is good . . . good; but you are bad! You are bad! The gentleman is a good soul, excellent, and you are a beast, bad! The gentleman is alive, but you are a dead carcass. . . . God created man to be alive, and to have joy and grief and sorrow; but you want nothing, so you are not alive, you are stone, clay! A stone wants nothing and you want nothing. You are a stone, and God does not love you, but He loves the gentleman!"

Everyone laughed; the Tatar frowned contemptuously, and with a wave of his hand wrapped himself in his rags and went to the campfire. The ferrymen and Semyon sauntered to the hut.

"It's cold," said one ferryman huskily as he stretched himself on the straw with which the damp clay floor was covered.

"Yes, it's not warm," another assented. "It's a dog's life. . . ."

They all lay down. The door was thrown open by the wind and the snow drifted into the hut; nobody felt inclined to get up and shut the door: they were cold, and it was too much trouble.

"I am all right," said Semyon as he began to doze. "I wouldn't wish anyone a better life."

"You are a tough one, we all know. Even the devils won't take you!"

Sounds like a dog's howling came from outside.

"What's that? Who's there?"

"It's the Tatar crying."

"I say. . . . He's a queer one!"

"He'll get u-used to it!" said Semyon, and at once fell asleep.

The others were soon asleep too. The door remained unclosed.

Neighbours

Pyotr Mihalitch Ivashin was very much out of humour: his sister, a young girl, had gone away to live with Vlassitch, a married man. To shake off the despondency and depression which pursued him at home and in the fields, he called to his aid his sense of justice, his genuine and noble ideas—he had always defended free-love!—but this was of no avail, and he always came back to the same conclusion as their foolish old nurse, that his sister had acted wrongly and that Vlassitch had abducted his sister. And that was distressing.

His mother did not leave her room all day long; the old nurse kept sighing and speaking in whispers; his aunt had been on the point of taking her departure every day, and her trunks were continually being brought down to the hall and carried up again to her room. In the house, in the yard, and in the garden it was as still as though there were some one dead in the house. His aunt, the servants, and even the peasants, so it seemed to Pyotr Mihalitch, looked at him enigmatically and with perplexity, as though they wanted to say "Your sister has been seduced; why are you doing nothing?" And he reproached himself for inactivity, though he did not know precisely what action he ought to have taken.

So passed six days. On the seventh—it was Sunday afternoon—a messenger on horseback brought a letter. The address was in a familiar feminine handwriting: "Her Excy. Anna Nikolaevna Ivashin." Pyotr Mihalitch fancied that there was something defiant, provocative, in the handwriting and in the abbreviation "Excy." And advanced ideas in women are obstinate, ruthless, cruel.

"She'd rather die than make any concession to her unhappy mother, or beg her forgiveness," thought Pyotr Mihalitch, as he went to his mother with the letter.

His mother was lying on her bed, dressed. Seeing her son, she rose impulsively, and straightening her grey hair, which had fallen from under her cap, asked quickly:

"What is it? What is it?"

"This has come . . ." said her son, giving her the letter.

Zina's name, and even the pronoun "she" was not uttered in the house. Zina was spoken of impersonally: "this has come," "Gone away," and so on. . . . The mother recognised her daughter's handwriting, and her face grew ugly and unpleasant, and her grey hair escaped again from her cap.

"No!" she said, with a motion of her hands, as though the letter scorched her fingers. "No, no, never! Nothing would induce me!"

The mother broke into hysterical sobs of grief and shame; she evidently longed to read the letter, but her pride prevented her. Pyotr Mihalitch realised that he ought to open the letter himself and read it aloud, but he was overcome by anger such as he had never felt before; he ran out into the yard and shouted to the messenger:

"Say there will be no answer! There will be no answer! Tell them that, you beast!"

And he tore up the letter; then tears came into his eyes, and feeling that he was cruel, miserable, and to blame, he went out into the fields.

He was only twenty-seven, but he was already stout. He dressed like an old man in loose, roomy clothes, and suffered from asthma. He already seemed to be developing the characteristics of an elderly country bachelor. He never fell in love, never thought of marriage, and loved no one but his mother, his sister, his old nurse, and the gardener, Vassilitch. He was fond of good fare, of his nap after dinner, and of talking about politics and exalted subjects. He had in his day taken his degree at the university, but he now looked upon his studies as though in them he had discharged a duty incumbent upon young men between the ages of eighteen and twenty-five; at any rate, the ideas which now strayed every day through his mind had nothing in common with the university or the subjects he had studied there.

In the fields it was hot and still, as though rain were coming. It was steaming in the wood, and there was a heavy fragrant scent from the pines and rotting leaves. Pyotr Mihalitch stopped several times and wiped his wet brow. He looked at his winter corn and his spring oats, walked round the clover-field, and twice drove away a partridge with its chicks which had strayed in from the wood. And all the while he was thinking that this insufferable state of things could not go on for ever, and that he must end it one way or another. End it stupidly, madly, but he must end it.

"But how? What can I do?" he asked himself, and looked imploringly at the sky and at the trees, as though begging for their help.

But the sky and the trees were mute. His noble ideas were no help, and his common sense whispered that the agonising question could have no solution but a stupid one, and that to-day's scene with the messenger was not the last one of its kind. It was terrible to think what was in store for him!

As he returned home the sun was setting. By now it seemed to him that the problem was incapable of solution. He could not accept the accomplished fact, and he could not refuse to accept it, and there was no intermediate course. When, taking off his hat and fanning himself with his handkerchief, he was walking along the road, and had only another mile and a half to go before he would reach home, he heard bells behind him. It was a very choice and successful combination of bells, which gave a clear crystal note. No one had such bells on his horses but the police captain, Medovsky, formerly an officer in the hussars, a man in broken-down health, who had been a great rake and spendthrift, and was a distant relation of Pyotr Mihalitch. He was like one of the family at the Ivashins' and had a tender, fatherly affection for Zina, as well as a great admiration for her.

"I was coming to see you," he said, overtaking Pyotr Mihalitch. "Get in; I'll give you a lift."

He was smiling and looked cheerful. Evidently he did not yet know that Zina had gone to live with Vlassitch; perhaps he had been told of it already, but did not believe it. Pyotr Mihalitch felt in a difficult position.

"You are very welcome," he muttered, blushing till the tears came into his eyes, and not knowing how to lie or what to say. "I am delighted," he went on, trying to smile, "but . . . Zina is away and mother is ill."

"How annoying!" said the police captain, looking pensively at Pyotr Mihalitch. "And I was meaning to spend the evening with you. Where has Zinaida Mihalovna gone?"

"To the Sinitskys', and I believe she meant to go from there to the monastery. I don't quite know."

The police captain talked a little longer and then turned back. Pyotr Mihalitch walked home, and thought with horror what the police captain's feelings would be when he learned the truth. And Pyotr Mihalitch imagined his feelings, and actually experiencing them himself, went into the house.

"Lord help us," he thought, "Lord help us!"

At evening tea the only one at the table was his aunt. As usual, her face wore the expression that seemed to say that though she was a weak, defenceless woman, she would allow no one to insult her. Pyotr Mihalitch sat down at the other end of the table (he did not like his aunt) and began drinking tea in silence.

"Your mother has had no dinner again to-day," said his aunt. "You ought to do something about it, Petrusha. Starving oneself is no help in sorrow."

It struck Pyotr Mihalitch as absurd that his aunt should meddle in other people's business and should make her departure depend on Zina's having gone away. He was tempted to say something rude to her, but restrained himself. And as he restrained himself he felt the time had come for action, and that he could not bear it any longer. Either he must act at once or fall on the ground, and scream and bang his head upon the floor. He pictured Vlassitch and Zina, both of them progressive and self-satisfied, kissing each other somewhere under a maple tree, and all the anger and bitterness that had been accumulating in him for the last seven days fastened upon Vlassitch.

"One has seduced and abducted my sister," he thought, "another will come and murder my mother, a third will set fire to the house and sack the place.... And all this under the mask of friendship, lofty ideas, unhappiness!"

"No, it shall not be!" Pyotr Mihalitch cried suddenly, and he brought his fist down on the table.

He jumped up and ran out of the dining-room. In the stable the steward's horse was standing ready saddled. He got on it and galloped off to Vlassitch.

There was a perfect tempest within him. He felt a longing to do something extraordinary, startling, even if he had to repent of it all his life afterwards. Should he call Vlassitch a blackguard, slap him in the face, and then challenge him to a duel? But Vlassitch was not one of those men who do fight duels; being called a blackguard and slapped in the face would only make him more unhappy, and would make him shrink into himself more than ever. These unhappy, defenceless people are the most insufferable, the most tiresome creatures in the world. They can do anything with impunity. When the luckless man responds to well-deserved reproach by looking at you with eyes full of deep and guilty feeling, and with a sickly smile bends his head submissively, even justice itself could not lift its hand against him.

"No matter. I'll horsewhip him before her eyes and tell him what I think of him," Pyotr Mihalitch decided.

He was riding through his wood and waste land, and he imagined Zina would try to justify her conduct by talking about the rights of women and individual freedom, and about there being no difference between legal marriage and free union. Like a woman, she would argue about what she did not understand. And very likely at the end she would ask, "How do you come in? What right have you to interfere?"

"No, I have no right," muttered Pyotr Mihalitch. "But so much the better.... The harsher I am, the less right I have to interfere, the better."

It was sultry. Clouds of gnats hung over the ground and in the waste places the peewits called plaintively. Everything betokened rain, but he could not see a cloud in the sky. Pyotr Mihalitch crossed the boundary of his estate and galloped over a smooth, level field. He often went along this road and knew every bush, every hollow in it. What now in the far distance looked in the dusk like a dark cliff was a red church; he could picture it all down to the smallest detail, even the plaster on the gate and the calves that were always grazing in the church enclosure. Three-quarters of a mile to the right of the church there was a copse like a dark blur—it was Count Koltonovitch's. And beyond the church Vlassitch's estate began.

From behind the church and the count's copse a huge black storm-cloud was rising, and there were ashes of white lightning.

"Here it is!" thought Pyotr Mihalitch. "Lord help us, Lord help us!"

The horse was soon tired after its quick gallop, and Pyotr Mihalitch was tired too. The storm-cloud looked at him angrily and seemed to advise him to go home. He felt a little scared.

"I will prove to them they are wrong," he tried to reassure himself. "They will say that it is free-love, individual freedom; but freedom means self-control and not subjection to passion. It's not liberty but license!"

He reached the count's big pond; it looked dark blue and frowning under the cloud, and a smell of damp and slime rose from it. Near the dam, two willows, one old and one young, drooped tenderly towards one another. Pyotr Mihalitch and Vlassitch had been walking near this very spot only a fortnight before, humming a students' song:

" 'Youth is wasted, life is nought, when the heart is cold and loveless.' "

A wretched song!

It was thundering as Pyotr Mihalitch rode through the copse, and the trees were bending and rustling in the wind. He had to make haste. It was only three-quarters of a mile through a meadow from the copse to Vlassitch's house. Here there were old birch-trees on each side of the road. They had the same melancholy and unhappy air as their owner Vlassitch, and looked as tall and lanky as he. Big drops of rain pattered on the birches and on the grass; the wind had suddenly dropped, and there was a smell of wet earth and poplars. Before him he saw Vlassitch's fence with a row of yellow acacias, which were tall and lanky too; where the fence was broken he could see the neglected orchard.

Pyotr Mihalitch was not thinking now of the horsewhip or of a slap in the face, and did not know what he would do at Vlassitch's. He felt nervous. He felt frightened on his own account and on his sister's, and was terrified at the thought of seeing her. How would she behave with her brother? What would they both talk about? And had he not better go back before it was too late? As he made these reflections, he galloped up the avenue of lime-trees to the house, rode round the big clumps of lilacs, and suddenly saw Vlassitch.

Vlassitch, wearing a cotton shirt, and top-boots, bending forward, with no hat on in the rain, was coming from the corner of the house to the front door. He was followed by a workman with a hammer and a box of nails. They must have been mending a shutter which had been banging in the wind. Seeing Pyotr Mihalitch, Vlassitch stopped.

"It's you!" he said, smiling. "That's nice."

"Yes, I've come, as you see," said Pyotr Mihalitch, brushing the rain off himself with both hands.

"Well, that's capital! I'm very glad," said Vlassitch, but he did not hold out his hand: evidently he did not venture, but waited for Pyotr Mihalitch to hold out his. "It will do the oats good," he said, looking at the sky.

"Yes."

They went into the house in silence. To the right of the hall was a door leading to another hall and then to the drawing-room, and on the left was a little room which in winter was used by the steward. Pyotr Mihalitch and Vlassitch went into this little room.

"Where were you caught in the rain?"

"Not far off, quite close to the house."

Pyotr Mihalitch sat down on the bed. He was glad of the noise of the rain and the darkness of the room. It was better: it made it less dreadful, and there was no need to see his companion's face. There was no anger in his heart now, nothing but fear and vexation with himself. He felt he had made a bad beginning, and that nothing would come of this visit.

Both were silent for some time and affected to be listening to the rain.

"Thank you, Petrusha," Vlassitch began, clearing his throat. "I am very grateful to you for coming. It's generous and noble of you. I understand it, and, believe me, I appreciate it. Believe me."

He looked out of the window and went on, standing in the middle of the room:

"Everything happened so secretly, as though we were concealing it all from you. The feeling that you might be wounded and angry has been a blot on our happiness all these days. But let me justify myself. We kept it secret not because we did not trust you. To begin with, it all happened suddenly, by a kind of inspiration; there was no time to discuss it. Besides, it's such a private, delicate matter, and it was awkward to bring a third person in, even some one as intimate as you. Above all, in all this we reckoned on your generosity. You are a very noble and generous person. I am infinitely grateful to you. If you ever need my life, come and take it."

Vlassitch talked in a quiet, hollow bass, always on the same droning note; he was evidently agitated. Pyotr Mihalitch felt it was his turn to speak, and that to listen and keep silent would really mean playing the part of a generous and noble simpleton, and that had not been his idea in coming. He got up quickly and said, breathlessly in an undertone:

"Listen, Grigory. You know I liked you and could have desired no better husband for my sister; but what has happened is awful! It's terrible to think of it!"

"Why is it terrible?" asked Vlassitch, with a quiver in his voice. "It would be terrible if we had done wrong, but that isn't so."

"Listen, Grigory. You know I have no prejudices; but, excuse my frankness, to my mind you have both acted selfishly. Of course, I shan't say so to my sister—it will distress her; but you ought to know: mother is miserable beyond all description."

"Yes, that's sad," sighed Vlassitch. "We foresaw that, Petrusha, but what could we have done? Because one's actions hurt other people, it doesn't prove that they are wrong. What's to be done! Every important step one takes is bound to distress somebody. If you went to fight for freedom, that would distress your mother, too. What's to be done! Any one who puts the peace of his family before everything has to renounce the life of ideas completely."

There was a vivid flash of lightning at the window, and the lightning seemed to change the course of Vlassitch's thoughts. He sat down beside Pyotr Mihalitch and began saying what was utterly beside the point.

"I have such a reverence for your sister, Petrusha," he said. "When I used to come and see you, I felt as though I were going to a holy shrine, and I really did worship Zina. Now my reverence for her grows every day. For me she is something higher than a wife—yes, higher!" Vlassitch waved his hands. "She is my holy of holies. Since she is living with me, I enter my house as though it were a temple. She is an extraordinary, rare, most noble woman!"

"Well, he's off now!" thought Pyotr Mihalitch; he disliked the word "woman."

"Why shouldn't you be married properly?" he asked. "How much does your wife want for a divorce?"

"Seventy-five thousand."

"It's rather a lot. But if we were to negotiate with her?"

"She won't take a farthing less. She is an awful woman, brother," sighed Vlassitch. "I've never talked to you about her before—it was unpleasant to think of her; but now that the subject has come up, I'll tell you about her. I married her on the impulse of the moment—a fine, honourable impulse. An officer in command of a battalion of our regiment—if you care to hear the details—had an affair with a girl of eighteen; that is, to put it plainly, he seduced her, lived with her for two months, and abandoned her. She was in an awful position, brother. She was ashamed to go home to her parents; besides, they wouldn't have received her. Her lover had abandoned her; there was nothing left for her but to go to the barracks and sell herself. The other officers in the regiment were indignant. They were by no means saints themselves, but the baseness of it was so striking. Besides, no one in the regiment could endure the man. And to spite him, you understand, the indignant lieutenants and ensigns began getting up a subscription for the unfortunate girl. And when we subalterns met together and began to subscribe five or ten roubles each, I had a sudden inspiration. I felt it was an opportunity to do something fine. I hastened to the girl and warmly expressed my sympathy. And while I was on my way to her, and while I was talking to her, I loved her fervently as a woman insulted and injured. Yes.... Well, a week later I made her an offer. The colonel and my comrades thought my marriage out of keeping with the dignity of an officer. That roused me more than ever. I wrote a long letter, do you know, in which I proved that my action ought to be inscribed in the annals of the regiment in letters of gold, and so on. I sent the letter to my colonel and copies to my comrades. Well, I was excited, and, of course, I could not avoid being rude. I was asked to leave the regiment. I have a rough copy of it put away somewhere; I'll give it to you to read sometime. It was written with great feeling. You will see what lofty and noble sentiments I was experiencing. I resigned my commission and came here with my wife. My father had left a few debts, I had no money, and from the first day my wife began making acquaintances, dressing herself smartly, and playing cards, and I was obliged to mortgage the estate. She led a bad life, you understand, and you are the only one of the neighbours who hasn't been her lover. After two years I gave her all I had to set me free and she went off to town. Yes.... And now I pay her twelve hundred roubles a year. She is an awful woman! There is a fly, brother, which lays an egg in the back of a spider so that the spider can't shake it off: the grub fastens upon the spider and drinks its heart's blood. That was how this woman fastened upon me and sucks the blood of my heart. She hates and despises me for being so stupid; that is, for marrying a woman like her. My chivalry seems to her despicable. 'A wise man cast me off,' she says, 'and a fool picked me up.' To her thinking no one but a pitiful idiot could have behaved as I did. And that is insufferably bitter to me, brother. Altogether, I may say in parenthesis, fate has been hard upon me, very hard."

Pyotr Mihalitch listened to Vlassitch and wondered in perplexity what it was in this man that had so charmed his sister. He was not young—he was forty-one—lean and lanky, narrow-chested, with a long nose, and grey hairs in his beard. He talked in a droning voice, had a sickly smile, and waved his hands awkwardly as he talked. He had neither health, nor pleasant, manly manners, nor *savoir-faire,* nor gaiety, and in all his exterior there was something colourless and indefinite. He dressed without taste, his surroundings were depressing, he did not care for poetry or painting because "they have no answer to give to the questions of the day"—that is, he did not understand them; music did not touch him. He was a poor farmer.

His estate was in a wretched condition and was mortgaged; he was paying twelve per cent. on the second mortgage and owed ten thousand on personal securities as well. When the time came to pay the interest on the mortgage or to send money to his wife, he asked every one to lend him money with as much agitation as though his house were on fire, and, at the same time losing his head, he would sell the whole of his winter store of fuel for five roubles and a stack of straw for three roubles, and then have his garden fence or old cucumber-frames chopped up to heat his stoves. His meadows were ruined by pigs, the peasants' cattle strayed in the undergrowth in his woods, and every year the old trees were fewer and fewer: beehives and rusty pails lay about in his garden and kitchen-garden. He had neither talents nor abilities, nor even ordinary capacity for living like other people. In practical life he was a weak, naïve man, easy to deceive and to cheat, and the peasants with good reason called him "simple."

He was a Liberal, and in the district was regarded as a "Red," but even his progressiveness was a bore. There was no originality nor moving power about his independent views: he was revolted, indignant, and delighted always on the same note; it was always spiritless and ineffective. Even in moments of strong enthusiasm he never raised his head or stood upright. But the most tiresome thing of all was that he managed to express even his best and finest ideas so that they seemed in him commonplace and out of date. It reminded one of something old one had read long ago, when slowly and with an air of profundity he would begin discoursing of his noble, lofty moments, of his best years; or when he went into raptures over the younger generation, which has always been, and still is, in advance of society; or abused Russians for donning their dressing-gowns at thirty and forgetting the principles of their *alma mater.* If you stayed the night with him, he would put Pissarev or Darwin on your bedroom table; if you said you had read it, he would go and bring Dobrolubov.

In the district this was called free-thinking, and many people looked upon this free-thinking as an innocent and harmless eccentricity; it made him profoundly unhappy, however. It was for him the maggot of which he had just been speaking; it had fastened upon him and was sucking his life-blood. In his past there had been the strange marriage in the style of Dostoevsky; long letters and copies written in a bad, unintelligible hand-writing, but with great feeling, endless misunderstandings, explanations, disappointments, then debts, a second mortgage, the allowance to his wife, the monthly borrowing of money—and all this for no benefit to any one, either himself or others. And in the present, as in the past, he was still in a nervous flurry, on the lookout for heroic actions, and poking his nose into other people's affairs; as before, at every favourable opportunity there were long letters and copies, wearisome, stereotyped conversations about the village community, or the revival of handicrafts or the establishment of cheese factories—conversations as like one another as though he had prepared them, not in his living brain, but by some mechanical process. And finally this scandal with Zina of which one could not see the end!

And meanwhile Zina was young—she was only twenty-two—good-looking, elegant, gay; she was fond of laughing, chatter, argument, a passionate musician; she had good taste in dress, in furniture, in books, and in her own home she would not have put up with a room like this, smelling of boots and cheap vodka. She, too, had advanced ideas, but in her free-thinking one felt the overflow of energy, the vanity of a young, strong, spirited girl, passionately eager to be better and more original than others.... How had it happened that she had fallen in love with Vlassitch?

"He is a Quixote, an obstinate fanatic, a maniac," thought Pyotr Mihalitch, "and she is as soft, yielding, and weak in character as I am.... She and I give in easily, without resistance. She loves him; but, then, I, too, love him in spite of everything."

Pyotr Mihalitch considered Vlassitch a good, straightforward man, but narrow and one-sided. In his perturbations and his sufferings, and in fact in his whole life, he saw no lofty aims, remote or immediate; he saw nothing but boredom and incapacity for life. His self-sacrifice and all that Vlassitch himself called heroic actions or noble impulses seemed to him a useless waste of force, unnecessary blank shots which consumed a great deal of powder. And Vlassitch's fanatical belief in the extraordinary loftiness and faultlessness of his own way of thinking struck him as naïve and even morbid; and the fact that Vlassitch all his life had contrived to mix the trivial with the exalted, that he had made a stupid marriage and looked upon it as an act of heroism, and then had affairs with other women and regarded that as a triumph of some idea or other was simply incomprehensible.

Nevertheless, Pyotr Mihalitch was fond of Vlassitch; he was conscious of a sort of power in him, and for some reason he had never had the heart to contradict him.

Vlassitch sat down quite close to him for a talk in the dark, to the accompaniment of the rain, and he had cleared his throat as a prelude to beginning on something lengthy, such as the history of his marriage. But it was intolerable for Pyotr Mihalitch to listen to him; he was tormented by the thought that he would see his sister directly.

"Yes, you've had bad luck," he said gently; "but, excuse me, we've been wandering from the point. That's not what we are talking about."

"Yes, yes, quite so. Well, let us come back to the point," said Vlassitch, and he stood up. "I tell you, Petrusha, our conscience is clear. We are not married, but there is no need for me to prove to you that our marriage is perfectly legitimate. You are as free in your ideas as I am, and, happily, there can be no disagreement between us on that point. As for our future, that ought not to alarm you. I'll work in the sweat of my brow, I'll work day and night—in fact, I will strain every nerve to make Zina happy. Her life will be a splendid one! You may ask, am I able to do it. I am, brother! When a man devotes every minute to one thought, it's not difficult for him to attain his object. But let us go to Zina; it will be a joy to her to see you."

Pyotr Mihalitch's heart began to beat. He got up and followed Vlassitch into the hall, and from there into the drawing-room. There was nothing in the huge gloomy room but a piano and a long row of old chairs ornamented with bronze, on which no one ever sat. There was a candle alight on the piano. From the drawing-room they went in silence into the dining-room. This room, too, was large and comfortless; in the middle of the room there was a round table with two leaves with six thick legs, and only one candle. A clock in a large mahogany case like an ikon stand pointed to half-past two.

Vlassitch opened the door into the next room and said:

"Zina, here is Petrusha come to see us!"

At once there was the sound of hurried footsteps and Zina came into the dining-room. She was tall, plump, and very pale, and, just as when he had seen her for the last time at home, she was wearing a black skirt and a red blouse, with a large buckle on her belt. She flung one arm round her brother and kissed him on the temple.

"What a storm!" she said. "Grigory went off somewhere and I was left quite alone in the house."

She was not embarrassed, and looked at her brother as frankly and candidly as at home; looking at her, Pyotr Mihalitch, too, lost his embarrassment.

"But you are not afraid of storms," he said, sitting down at the table.

"No," she said, "but here the rooms are so big, the house is so old, and when there is thunder it all rattles like a cupboard full of crockery. It's a charming house altogether," she went on, sitting down opposite her brother. "There's some pleasant memory in every room. In my room, only fancy, Grigory's grandfather shot himself."

"In August we shall have the money to do up the lodge in the garden," said Vlassitch.

"For some reason when it thunders I think of that grandfather," Zina went on. "And in this dining-room somebody was flogged to death."

"That's an actual fact," said Vlassitch, and he looked with wide-open eyes at Pyotr Mihalitch. "Sometime in the forties this place was let to a Frenchman called Olivier. The portrait of his daughter is lying in an attic now—a very pretty girl. This Olivier, so my father told me, despised Russians for their ignorance and treated them with cruel derision. Thus, for instance, he insisted on the priest walking without his hat for half a mile round his house, and on the church bells being rung when the Olivier family drove through the village. The serfs and altogether the humble of this world, of course, he treated with even less ceremony. Once there came along this road one of the simple-hearted sons of wandering Russia, somewhat after the style of Gogol's divinity student, Homa Brut. He asked for a night's lodging, pleased the bailiffs, and was given a job at the office of the estate. There are many variations of the story. Some say the divinity student stirred up the peasants, others that Olivier's daughter fell in love with him. I don't know which is true, only one fine evening Olivier called him in here and cross-examined him, then ordered him to be beaten. Do you know, he sat here at this table drinking claret while the stable-boys beat the man. He must have tried to wring something out of him. Towards morning the divinity student died of the torture and his body was hidden. They say it was thrown into Koltovitch's pond. There was an inquiry, but the Frenchman paid some thousands to some one in authority and went away to Alsace. His lease was up just then, and so the matter ended."

"What scoundrels!" said Zina, shuddering.

"My father remembered Olivier and his daughter well. He used to say she was remarkably beautiful and eccentric. I imagine the divinity student had done both—stirred up the peasants and won the daughter's heart. Perhaps he wasn't a divinity student at all, but some one travelling incognito."

Zina grew thoughtful; the story of the divinity student and the beautiful French girl had evidently carried her imagination far away. It seemed to Pyotr Mihalitch that she had not changed in the least during the last week, except that she was a little paler. She looked calm and just as usual, as though she had come with her brother to visit Vlassitch. But Pyotr Mihalitch felt that some change had taken place in himself. Before, when she was living at home, he could have spoken to her about anything, and now he did not feel equal to asking her the simple question, "How do you like being here?" The question seemed awkward and unnecessary. Probably the same change had taken place in her. She was in no haste to turn the conversation to her mother, to her home, to her relations with Vlassitch; she did not defend herself, she did not say that free unions are better than marriages in the church; she was not agitated, and calmly brooded over the story of Olivier. . . . And why had they suddenly begun talking of Olivier?

"You are both of you wet with the rain," said Zina, and she smiled joyfully; she was touched by this point of resemblance between her brother and Vlassitch.

And Pyotr Mihalitch felt all the bitterness and horror of his position. He thought of his deserted home, the closed piano, and Zina's bright little room into which no one went now; he thought there were no prints of little feet on the garden-paths, and that before tea no one went off, laughing gaily, to bathe. What he had clung to more and more from his childhood upwards, what he had loved thinking about when he used to sit in the stuffy class-room or the lecture theatre—brightness, purity, and joy, everything that filled the house with life and light, had gone never to return, had vanished, and was mixed up with a coarse, clumsy story of some battalion officer, a chivalrous lieutenant, a depraved woman and a grandfather who had shot himself. . . . And to begin to talk about his mother or to think that the past could ever return would mean not understanding what was clear.

Pyotr Mihalitch's eyes filled with tears and his hand began to tremble as it lay on the table. Zina guessed what he was thinking about, and her eyes, too, glistened and looked red.

"Grigory, come here," she said to Vlassitch.

They walked away to the window and began talking of something in a whisper. From the way that Vlassitch stooped down to her and the way she looked at him, Pyotr Mihalitch realised again that everything was irreparably over, and that it was no use to talk of anything. Zina went out of the room.

"Well, brother!" Vlassitch began, after a brief silence, rubbing his hands and smiling. "I called our life happiness just now, but that was, so to speak, poetical license. In reality, there has not been a sense of happiness so far. Zina has been thinking all the time of you, of her mother, and has been worrying; looking at her, I, too, felt worried. Hers is a bold, free nature, but, you know, it's difficult when you're not used to it, and she is young, too. The servants call her 'Miss'; it seems a trifle, but it upsets her. There it is, brother."

Zina brought in a plateful of strawberries. She was followed by a little maidservant, looking crushed and humble, who set a jug of milk on the table and made a very low bow: she had something about her that was in keeping with the old furniture, something petrified and dreary.

The sound of the rain had ceased. Pyotr Mihalitch ate strawberries while Vlassitch and Zina looked at him in silence. The moment of the inevitable but useless conversation was approaching, and all three felt the burden of it. Pyotr Mihalitch's eyes filled with tears again; he pushed away his plate and said that he must be going home, or it would be getting late, and perhaps it would rain again. The time had come when common decency required Zina to speak of those at home and of her new life.

"How are things at home?" she asked rapidly, and her pale face quivered. "How is mother?"

"You know mother . . ." said Pyotr Mihalitch, not looking at her.

"Petrusha, you've thought a great deal about what has happened," she said, taking hold of her brother's sleeve, and he knew how hard it was for her to speak. "You've thought a great deal: tell me, can we reckon on mother's accepting Grigory . . . and the whole position, one day?"

She stood close to her brother, face to face with him, and he was astonished that she was so beautiful, and that he seemed not to have noticed it before. And it seemed to him utterly absurd that his sister, so like his mother, pampered, elegant, should be living with Vlassitch and in Vlassitch's house, with the petrified servant, and the table with six legs—in the house where a man had been flogged to death, and that she was not going home with him, but was staying here to sleep.

"You know mother," he said, not answering her question. "I think you ought to have . . . to do something, to ask her forgiveness or something. . . ."

"But to ask her forgiveness would mean pretending we had done wrong. I'm ready to tell a lie to comfort mother, but it won't lead anywhere. I know mother. Well, what will be, must be!" said Zina, growing more cheerful now that the most unpleasant had been said. "We'll wait for five years, ten years, and be patient, and then God's will be done."

She took her brother's arm, and when she walked through the dark hall she squeezed close to him. They went out on the steps. Pyotr Mihalitch said good-bye, got on his horse, and set off at a walk; Zina and Vlassitch walked a little way with him. It was still and warm, with a delicious smell of hay; stars were twinkling brightly between the clouds. Vlassitch's old garden, which had seen so many gloomy stories in its time, lay slumbering in the darkness, and for some reason it was mournful riding through it.

"Zina and I to-day after dinner spent some really exalted moments," said Vlassitch. "I read aloud to her an excellent article on the question of emigration. You must read it, brother! You really must. It's remarkable for its lofty tone. I could not resist writing a letter to the editor to be forwarded to the author. I wrote only a single line: 'I thank you and warmly press your noble hand.' "

Pyotr Mihalitch was tempted to say, "Don't meddle in what does not concern you," but he held his tongue.

Vlassitch walked by his right stirrup and Zina by the left; both seemed to have forgotten that they had to go home. It was damp, and they had almost reached Koltovitch's copse. Pyotr Mihalitch felt that they were expecting something from him, though they hardly knew what it was, and he felt unbearably sorry for them. Now as they walked by the horse with submissive faces, lost in thought, he had a deep conviction that they were unhappy, and could not be happy, and their love seemed to him a melancholy, irreparable mistake. Pity and the sense that he could do nothing to help them reduced him to that state of spiritual softening when he was ready to make any sacrifice to get rid of the painful feeling of sympathy.

"I'll come over sometimes for a night," he said.

But it sounded as though he were making a concession, and did not satisfy him. When they stopped near Koltovitch's copse to say good-bye, he bent down to Zina, touched her shoulder, and said:

"You are right, Zina! You have done well." To avoid saying more and bursting into tears, he lashed his horse and galloped into the wood. As he rode into the darkness, he looked round and saw Vlassitch and Zina walking home along the road—he taking long strides, while she walked with a hurried, jerky step beside him—talking eagerly about something.

"I am an old woman!" thought Pyotr Mihalitch. "I went to solve the question and I have only made it more complicated—there it is!"

He was heavy at heart. When he got out of the copse he rode at a walk and then stopped his horse near the pond. He wanted to sit and think without moving. The moon was rising and was reflected in a streak of red on the other side of the pond. There were low rumbles of thunder in the distance. Pyotr Mihalitch looked steadily at the water and imagined his sister's despair, her martyr-like pallor, the tearless eyes with which she would conceal her humiliation from others. He imagined her with child, imagined the death of their mother, her funeral, Zina's horror. . . . The proud, superstitious old woman would be sure to die of grief. Terrible pictures of the future rose before him on the background of smooth, dark water, and among pale feminine figures he saw himself, a weak, cowardly man with a guilty face.

A hundred paces off on the right bank of the pond, something dark was standing motionless: was it a man or a tall post? Pyotr Mihalitch thought of the divinity student who had been killed and thrown into the pond.

"Olivier behaved inhumanly, but one way or another he did settle the question, while I have settled nothing and have only made it worse," he thought, gazing at the dark figure that looked like a ghost. "He said and did what he thought right while I say and do what I don't think right; and I don't know really what I do think. . . ."

He rode up to the dark figure: it was an old rotten post, the relic of some shed.

From Koltovitch's copse and garden there came a strong fragrant scent of lilies of the valley and honey-laden flowers. Pyotr Mihalitch rode along the bank of the pond and looked mournfully into the water. And thinking about his life, he came to the conclusion he had never said or acted upon what he really thought, and other people had repaid him in the same way. And so the whole of life seemed to him as dark as this water in which the night sky was reflected and water-weeds grew in a tangle. And it seemed to him that nothing could ever set it right.

Terror

My Friend's Story

Dmitri Petrovitch Silin had taken his degree and entered the government service in Petersburg, but at thirty he gave up his post and went in for agriculture. His farming was fairly successful, and yet it always seemed to me that he was not in his proper place, and that he would do well to go back to Petersburg. When sunburnt, grey with dust, exhausted with toil, he met me near the gates or at the entrance, and then at supper struggled with sleepiness and his wife took him off to bed as though he were a baby; or when, overcoming his sleepiness, he began in his soft, cordial, almost imploring voice, to talk about his really excellent ideas, I saw him not as a farmer nor an agriculturist, but only as a worried and exhausted man, and it was clear to me that he did not really care for farming, but that all he wanted was for the day to be over and "Thank God for it."

I liked to be with him, and I used to stay on his farm for two or three days at a time. I liked his house, and his park, and his big fruit garden, and the river—and his philosophy, which was clear, though rather spiritless and rhetorical. I suppose I was fond of him on his own account, though I can't say that for certain, as I have not up to now succeeded in analysing my feelings at that time. He was an intelligent, kind-hearted, genuine man, and not a bore, but I remember that when he confided to me his most treasured secrets and spoke of our relation to each other as friendship, it disturbed me unpleasantly, and I was conscious of awkwardness. In his affection for me there was something inappropriate, tiresome, and I should have greatly preferred commonplace friendly relations.

The fact is that I was extremely attracted by his wife, Marya Sergeyevna. I was not in love with her, but I was attracted by her face, her eyes, her voice, her walk. I missed her when I did not see her for a long time, and my imagination pictured no one at that time so eagerly as that young, beautiful, elegant woman. I had no definite designs in regard to her, and did not dream of anything of the sort, yet for some reason, whenever we were left alone, I remembered that her husband looked upon me as his friend, and I felt awkward. When she played my favourite pieces on the piano or told me something interesting, I listened with pleasure, and yet at the same time for some reason the reflection that she loved her husband, that he was my friend, and that she herself looked upon me as his friend, obtruded themselves upon me, my spirits flagged, and I became listless, awkward, and dull. She noticed this change and would usually say:

"You are dull without your friend. We must send out to the fields for him."

And when Dmitri Petrovitch came in, she would say:

"Well, here is your friend now. Rejoice."

So passed a year and a half.

It somehow happened one July Sunday that Dmitri Petrovitch and I, having nothing to do, drove to the big village of Klushino to buy things for supper. While we were going from one shop to another the sun set and the evening came on—the evening which I shall probably never forget in my life. After buying cheese that smelt like soap, and petrified sausages that smelt of tar, we went to the tavern to ask whether they had any beer. Our coachman went off to the blacksmith to get our horses shod, and we told him we would wait for him near the church. We walked, talked, laughed over our purchases, while a man who was known in the district by a very strange nickname, "Forty Martyrs," followed us all the while in silence with a mysterious air like a detective. This Forty Martyrs was no other than Gavril Syeverov, or more simply Gavryushka, who had been for a short time in my service as a footman and had been dismissed by me for drunkenness. He had been in Dmitri Petrovitch's service, too, and by him had been dismissed for the same vice. He was an inveterate drunkard, and indeed his whole life was as drunk and disorderly as himself. His father had been a priest and his mother of noble rank, so by birth he belonged to the privileged class; but however carefully I scrutinized his exhausted, respectful, and always perspiring face, his red beard now turning grey, his pitifully torn reefer jacket and his red shirt, I could not discover in him the faintest trace of anything we associate with privilege. He spoke of himself as a man of education, and used to say that he had been in a clerical school, but had not finished his studies there, as he had been expelled for smoking; then he had sung in the bishop's choir and lived for two years in a monastery, from which he was also expelled, but this time not for smoking but for "his weakness." He had walked all over two provinces, had presented petitions to the Consistory, and to various government offices, and had been four times on his trial. At last, being stranded in our district, he had served as a footman, as a forester, as a kennelman, as a sexton, had married a cook who was a widow and rather a loose character, and had so hopelessly sunk into a menial position, and had grown so used to filth and dirt, that he even spoke of his privileged origin with a certain scepticism, as of some myth. At the time I am describing, he was hanging about without a job, calling himself a carrier and a huntsman, and his wife had disappeared and made no sign.

From the tavern we went to the church and sat in the porch, waiting for the coachman. Forty Martyrs stood a little way off and put his hand before his mouth in order to cough in it respectfully if need be. By now it was dark; there was a strong smell of evening dampness, and the moon was on the point of rising. There were only two clouds in the clear starry sky exactly over our heads: one big one and one smaller; alone in the sky they were racing after one another like mother and child, in the direction where the sunset was glowing.

"What a glorious day!" said Dmitri Petrovitch.

"In the extreme . . ." Forty Martyrs assented, and he coughed respectfully into his hand. "How was it, Dmitri Petrovitch, you thought to visit these parts?" he asked in an ingratiating voice, evidently anxious to get up a conversation.

Dmitri Petrovitch made no answer. Forty Martyrs heaved a deep sigh and said softly, not looking at us:

"I suffer solely through a cause to which I must answer to Almighty God. No doubt about it, I am a hopeless and incompetent man; but believe me, on my conscience, I am without a crust of bread and worse off than a dog. . . . Forgive me, Dmitri Petrovitch."

Silin was not listening, but sat musing with his head propped on his fists. The church stood at the end of the street on the high river-bank, and through the trellis gate of the enclosure we could see the river, the water-meadows on the near side of it, and the crimson glare of a camp fire about which black figures of men and horses were moving. And beyond the fire, further away, there were other lights, where there was a little village. They were singing there. On the river, and here and there on the meadows, a mist was rising. High narrow coils of mist, thick and white as milk, were trailing over the river, hiding the reflection of the stars and hovering over the willows. Every minute they changed their form, and it seemed as though some were embracing, others were bowing, others lifting up their arms to heaven with wide sleeves like priests, as though they were praying. . . . Probably they reminded Dmitri Petrovitch of ghosts and of the dead, for he turned facing me and asked with a mournful smile:

"Tell me, my dear fellow, why is it that when we want to tell some terrible, mysterious, and fantastic story, we draw our material, not from life, but invariably from the world of ghosts and of the shadows beyond the grave."

"We are frightened of what we don't understand."

"And do you understand life? Tell me: do you understand life better than the world beyond the grave?"

Dmitri Petrovitch was sitting quite close to me, so that I felt his breath upon my cheek. In the evening twilight his pale, lean face seemed paler than ever and his lark beard was black as soot. His eyes were sad, truthful, and a little frightened, as though he were about to tell me something horrible. He looked into my eyes and went on in his habitual imploring voice:

"Our life and the life beyond the grave are equally incomprehensible and horrible. If any one is afraid of ghosts he ought to be afraid, too, of me, and of those lights and of the sky, seeing that, if you come to reflect, all that is no less fantastic and beyond our grasp than apparitions from the other world. Prince Hamlet did not kill himself because he was afraid of the visions that might haunt his dreams after death. I like that famous soliloquy of his, but, to be candid, it never touched my soul. I will confess to you as a friend that in moments of depression I have sometimes pictured to myself the hour of my death. My fancy invented thousands of the gloomiest visions, and I have succeeded in working myself up to an agonizing exaltation, to a state of nightmare, and I assure you that that did not seem to me more terrible than reality. What I mean is, apparitions are terrible, but life is terrible, too. I don't understand life and I am afraid of it, my dear boy; I don't know. Perhaps I am a morbid person, unhinged. It seems to a sound, healthy man that he understands everything he sees and hears, but that 'seeming' is lost to me, and from day to day I am poisoning myself with terror. There is a disease, the fear of open spaces, but my disease is the fear of life. When I lie on the grass and watch a little beetle which was born yesterday and understands nothing, it seems to me that its life consists of nothing else but fear, and in it I see myself."

"What is it exactly you are frightened of?" I asked.

"I am afraid of everything. I am not by nature a profound thinker, and I take little interest in such questions as the life beyond the grave, the destiny of humanity, and, in fact, I am rarely carried away to the heights. What chiefly frightens me is the common routine of life from which none of us can escape. I am incapable of distinguishing what is true and what is false in my actions, and they worry me. I recognize that education and the conditions of life have imprisoned me in a narrow circle of falsity, that my whole life is nothing else than a daily effort to deceive myself and other people, and to avoid noticing it; and I am frightened at the thought that to the day of my death I shall not escape from this falsity. To-day I do something and to-morrow I do not understand why I did it. I entered the service in Petersburg and took fright; I came here to work on the land, and here, too, I am frightened. . . . I see that we know very little and so make mistakes every day.

We are unjust, we slander one another and spoil each other's lives, we waste all our powers on trash which we do not need and which hinders us from living; and that frightens me, because I don't understand why and for whom it is necessary. I don't understand men, my dear fellow, and I am afraid of them. It frightens me to look at the peasants, and I don't know for what higher objects they are suffering and what they are living for. If life is an enjoyment, then they are unnecessary, superfluous people; if the object and meaning of life is to be found in poverty and unending, hopeless ignorance, I can't understand for whom and what this torture is necessary. I understand no one and nothing. Kindly try to understand this specimen, for instance," said Dmitri Petrovitch, pointing to Forty Martyrs. "Think of him!"

Noticing that we were looking at him, Forty Martyrs coughed deferentially into his fist and said:

"I was always a faithful servant with good masters, but the great trouble has been spirituous liquor. If a poor fellow like me were shown consideration and given a place, I would kiss the ikon. My word's my bond."

The sexton walked by, looked at us in amazement, and began pulling the rope. The bell, abruptly breaking upon the stillness of the evening, struck ten with a slow and prolonged note.

"It's ten o'clock, though," said Dmitri Petrovitch. "It's time we were going. Yes, my dear fellow," he sighed, "if only you knew how afraid I am of my ordinary everyday thoughts, in which one would have thought there should be nothing dreadful. To prevent myself thinking I distract my mind with work and try to tire myself out that I may sleep sound at night. Children, a wife—all that seems ordinary with other people; but how that weighs upon me, my dear fellow!"

He rubbed his face with his hands, cleared his throat, and laughed.

"If I could only tell you how I have played the fool in my life!" he said. "They all tell me that I have a sweet wife, charming children, and that I am a good husband and father. They think I am very happy and envy me. But since it has come to that, I will tell you in secret: my happy family life is only a grievous misunderstanding, and I am afraid of it."

His pale face was distorted by a wry smile. He put his arm round my waist and went on in an undertone:

"You are my true friend; I believe in you and have a deep respect for you. Heaven gave us friendship that we may open our hearts and escape from the secrets that weigh upon us. Let me take advantage of your friendly feeling for me and tell you the whole truth. My home life, which seems to you so enchanting, is my chief misery and my chief terror. I got married in a strange and stupid way. I must tell you that I was madly in love with Masha before I married her, and was courting her for two years. I asked her to marry me five times, and she refused me because she did not care for me in the least. The sixth, when burning with passion I crawled on my knees before her and implored her to take a beggar and marry me, she consented.... What she said to me was: 'I don't love you, but I will be true to you....' I accepted that condition with rapture. At the time I understood what that meant, but I swear to God I don't understand it now. 'I don't love you, but I will be true to you.' What does that mean? It's a fog, a darkness. I love her now as intensely as I did the day we were married, while she, I believe, is as indifferent as ever, and I believe she is glad when I go away from home. I don't know for certain whether she cares for me or not—I don't know, I don't know; but, as you see, we live under the same roof, call each other 'thou,' sleep together, have children, our property is in common.... What does it mean, what does it mean? What is the object of it? And do you understand it at all, my dear fellow? It's cruel torture! Because I don't understand our relations, I hate, sometimes her, sometimes myself, sometimes both at once. Everything is in a tangle in my brain; I torment myself and grow stupid. And as though to spite me, she grows more beautiful every day, she is getting more wonderful. . . . I fancy her hair is marvellous, and her smile is like no other woman's. I love her, and I know that my love is hopeless. Hopeless love for a woman by whom one has two children! Is that intelligible? And isn't it terrible? Isn't it more terrible than ghosts?"

He was in the mood to have talked on a good deal longer, but luckily we heard the coachman's voice. Our horses had arrived. We got into the carriage, and Forty Martyrs, taking off his cap, helped us both into the carriage with an expression that suggested that he had long been waiting for an opportunity to come in contact with our precious persons.

"Dmitri Petrovitch, let me come to you," he said, blinking furiously and tilting his head on one side. "Show divine mercy! I am dying of hunger!"

"Very well," said Silin. "Come, you shall stay three days, and then we shall see."

"Certainly, sir," said Forty Martyrs, overjoyed. "I'll come today, sir."

It was a five miles' drive home. Dmitri Petrovitch, glad that he had at last opened his heart to his friend, kept his arm round my waist all the way; and speaking now, not with bitterness and not with apprehension, but quite cheerfully, told me that if everything had been satisfactory in his home life, he should have returned to Petersburg and taken up scientific work there. The movement which had driven so many gifted young men into the country was, he said, a deplorable movement. We had plenty of rye and wheat in Russia, but absolutely no cultured people. The strong and gifted among the young ought to take up science, art, and politics; to do otherwise meant being wasteful. He generalized with pleasure and expressed regret that he would be parting from me early next morning, as he had to go to a sale of timber.

And I felt awkward and depressed, and it seemed to me that I was deceiving the man. And at the same time it was pleasant to me. I gazed at the immense crimson moon which was rising, and pictured the tall, graceful, fair woman, with her pale face, always well-dressed and fragrant with some special scent, rather like musk, and for some reason it pleased me to think she did not love her husband.

On reaching home, we sat down to supper. Marya Sergeyevna, laughing, regaled us with our purchases, and I thought that she certainly had wonderful hair and that her smile was unlike any other woman's. I watched her, and I wanted to detect in every look and movement that she did not love her husband, and I fancied that I did see it.

Dmitri Petrovitch was soon struggling with sleep. After supper he sat with us for ten minutes and said:

"Do as you please, my friends, but I have to be up at three o'clock tomorrow morning. Excuse my leaving you."

He kissed his wife tenderly, pressed my hand with warmth and gratitude, and made me promise that I would certainly come the following week. That he might not oversleep next morning, he went to spend the night in the lodge.

Marya Sergeyevna always sat up late, in the Petersburg fashion, and for some reason on this occasion I was glad of it.

"And now," I began when we were left alone, "and now you'll be kind and play me something."

I felt no desire for music, but I did not know how to begin the conversation. She sat down to the piano and played, I don't remember what. I sat down beside her and looked at her plump white hands and tried to read something on her cold, indifferent face. Then she smiled at something and looked at me.

"You are dull without your friend," she said.

I laughed.

"It would be enough for friendship to be here once a month, but I turn up oftener than once a week."

Saying this, I got up and walked from one end of the room to the other. She too got up and walked away to the fireplace.

"What do you mean to say by that?" she said, raising her large, clear eyes and looking at me.

I made no answer.

"What you say is not true," she went on, after a moment's thought. "You only come here on account of Dmitri Petrovitch. Well, I am very glad. One does not often see such friendships nowadays."

"Aha!" I thought, and, not knowing what to say, I asked: "Would you care for a turn in the garden?"

"No."

I went out upon the verandah. Nervous shudders were running over my head and I felt chilly with excitement. I was convinced now that our conversation would be utterly trivial, and that there was nothing particular we should be able to say to one another, but that, that night, what I did not dare to dream of was bound to happen—that it was bound to be that night or never.

"What lovely weather!" I said aloud.

"It makes absolutely no difference to me," she answered.

I went into the drawing-room. Marya Sergeyevna was standing, as before, near the fireplace, with her hands behind her back, looking away and thinking of something.

"Why does it make no difference to you?" I asked.

"Because I am bored. You are only bored without your friend, but I am always bored. However . . . that is of no interest to you."

I sat down to the piano and struck a few chords, waiting to hear what she would say.

"Please don't stand on ceremony," she said, looking angrily at me, and she seemed as though on the point of crying with vexation. "If you are sleepy, go to bed. Because you are Dmitri Petrovitch's friend, you are not in duty bound to be bored with his wife's company. I don't want a sacrifice. Please go."

I did not, of course, go to bed. She went out on the verandah while I remained in the drawing-room and spent five minutes turning over the music. Then I went out, too. We stood close together in the shadow of the curtains, and below us were the steps bathed in moonlight. The black shadows of the trees stretched across the flower beds and the yellow sand of the paths.

"I shall have to go away tomorrow, too," I said.

"Of course, if my husband's not at home you can't stay here," she said sarcastically. "I can imagine how miserable you would be if you were in love with me! Wait a bit: one day I shall throw myself on your neck. . . . I shall see with what horror you will run away from me. That would be interesting."

Her words and her pale face were angry, but her eyes were full of tender passionate love. I already looked upon this lovely creature as my property, and then for the first time I noticed that she had golden eyebrows, exquisite eyebrows. I had never seen such eyebrows before. The thought that I might at once press her to my heart, caress her, touch her wonderful hair, seemed to me such a miracle that I laughed and shut my eyes.

"It's bed-time now. . . . A peaceful night," she said.

"I don't want a peaceful night," I said, laughing, following her into the drawing-room. "I shall curse this night if it is a peaceful one."

Pressing her hand, and escorting her to the door, I saw by her face that she understood me, and was glad that I understood her, too.

I went to my room. Near the books on the table lay Dmitri Petrovitch's cap, and that reminded me of his affection for me. I took my stick and went out into the garden. The mist had risen here, too, and the same tall, narrow, ghostly shapes which I had seen earlier on the river were trailing round the trees and bushes and wrapping about them. What a pity I could not talk to them!

In the extraordinary transparent air, each leaf, each drop of dew stood out distinctly; it was all smiling at me in the stillness half asleep, and as I passed the green seats I recalled the words in some play of Shakespeare's: "How sweetly falls the moonlight on yon seat!"

There was a mound in the garden; I went up it and sat down. I was tormented by a delicious feeling. I knew for certain that in a moment I should hold in my arms, should press to my heart her magnificent body, should kiss her golden eyebrows; and I wanted to disbelieve it, to tantalize myself, and was sorry that she had cost me so little trouble and had yielded so soon.

But suddenly I heard heavy footsteps. A man of medium height appeared in the avenue, and I recognized him at once as Forty Martyrs. He sat down on the bench and heaved a deep sigh, then crossed himself three times and lay down. A minute later he got up and lay on the other side. The gnats and the dampness of the night prevented his sleeping.

"Oh, life!" he said. "Wretched, bitter life!"

Looking at his bent, wasted body and hearing his heavy, noisy sighs, I thought of an unhappy, bitter life of which the confession had been made to me that day, and I felt uneasy and frightened at my blissful mood. I came down the knoll and went to the house.

"Life, as he thinks, is terrible," I thought, "so don't stand on ceremony with it, bend it to your will, and until it crushes you, snatch all you can wring from it."

Marya Sergeyevna was standing on the verandah. I put my arms round her without a word, and began greedily kissing her eyebrows, her temples, her neck. . . .

In my room she told me she had loved me for a long time, more than a year. She vowed eternal love, cried and begged me to take her away with me. I repeatedly took her to the window to look at her face in the moonlight, and she seemed to me a lovely dream, and I made haste to hold her tight to convince myself of the truth of it. It was long since I had known such raptures.... Yet somewhere far away at the bottom of my heart I felt an awkwardness, and I was ill at ease. In her love for me there was something incongruous and burdensome, just as in Dmitri Petrovitch's friendship. It was a great, serious passion with tears and vows, and I wanted nothing serious in it—no tears, no vows, no talk of the future. Let that moonlight night flash through our lives like a meteor and—*basta!*

At three o'clock she went out of my room, and, while I was standing in the doorway, looking after her, at the end of the corridor Dmitri Petrovitch suddenly made his appearance; she started and stood aside to let him pass, and her whole figure was expressive of repulsion. He gave a strange smile, coughed, and came into my room.

"I forgot my cap here yesterday," he said without looking at me.

He found it and, holding it in both hands, put it on his head; then he looked at my confused face, at my slippers, and said in a strange, husky voice unlike his own:

"I suppose it must be my fate that I should understand nothing.... If you understand anything, I congratulate you. It's all darkness before my eyes."

And he went out, clearing his throat. Afterwards from the window I saw him by the stable, harnessing the horses with his own hands. His hands were trembling, he was in nervous haste and kept looking round at the house; probably he was feeling terror. Then he got into the gig, and, with a strange expression as though afraid of being pursued, lashed the horses.

Shortly afterwards I set off, too. The sun was already rising, and the mist of the previous day clung timidly to the bushes and the hillocks. On the box of the carriage was sitting Forty Martyrs; he had already succeeded in getting drunk and was muttering tipsy nonsense.

"I am a free man," he shouted to the horses. "Ah, my honeys, I am a nobleman in my own right, if you care to know!"

The terror of Dmitri Petrovitch, the thought of whom I could not get out of my head, infected me. I thought of what had happened and could make nothing of it. I looked at the rooks, and it seemed so strange and terrible that they were flying.

"Why have I done this?" I kept asking myself in bewilderment and despair. "Why has it turned out like this and not differently? To whom and for what was it necessary that she should love me in earnest, and that he should come into my room to fetch his cap? What had a cap to do with it?"

I set off for Petersburg that day, and I have not seen Dmitri Petrovitch nor his wife since. I am told that they are still living together.

The Helpmate

[His Wife]

"I've asked you not to tidy my table," said Nikolay Yevgrafitch. "There's no finding anything when you've tidied up. Where's the telegram? Where have you thrown it? Be so good as to look for it. It's from Kazan, dated yesterday."

The maid—a pale, very slim girl with an indifferent expression—found several telegrams in the basket under the table, and handed them to the doctor without a word; but all these were telegrams from patients. Then they looked in the drawing-room, and in Olga Dmitrievna's room.

It was past midnight. Nikolay Yevgrafitch knew his wife would not be home very soon, not till five o'clock at least. He did not trust her, and when she was long away he could not sleep, was worried, and at the same time he despised his wife, and her bed, and her looking-glass, and her boxes of sweets, and the hyacinths, and the lilies of the valley which were sent her every day by some one or other, and which diffused the sickly fragrance of a florist's shop all over the house. On such nights he became petty, ill-humoured, irritable, and he fancied now that it was very necessary for him to have the telegram he had received the day before from his brother, though it contained nothing but Christmas greetings.

On the table of his wife's room under the box of stationery he found a telegram, and glanced at it casually. It was addressed to his wife, care of his mother-in-law, from Monte Carlo, and signed Michel. . . . The doctor did not understand one word of it, as it was in some foreign language, apparently English.

"Who is this Michel? Why Monte Carlo? Why directed care of her mother?"

During the seven years of his married life he had grown used to being suspicious, guessing, catching at clues, and it had several times occurred to him, that his exercise at home had qualified him to become an excellent detective. Going into his study and beginning to reflect, he recalled at once how he had been with his wife in Petersburg a year and a half ago, and had lunched with an old school-fellow, a civil engineer, and how that engineer had introduced to him and his wife a young man of two or three and twenty, called Mihail Ivanovitch, with rather a curious short surname—Riss. Two months later the doctor had seen the young man's photograph in his wife's album, with an inscription in French: "In remembrance of the present and in hope of the future." Later on he had met the young man himself at his mother-in-law's. And that was at the time when his wife had taken to being very often absent and coming home at four or five o'clock in the morning, and was constantly asking him to get her a passport for abroad, which he kept refusing to do; and a continual feud went on in the house which made him feel ashamed to face the servants.

Six months before, his colleagues had decided that he was going into consumption, and advised him to throw up everything and go to the Crimea. When she heard of this, Olga Dmitrievna affected to be very much alarmed; she began to be affectionate to her husband, and kept assuring him that it would be cold and dull in the Crimea, and that he had much better go to Nice, and that she would go with him, and there would nurse him, look after him, take care of him.

Now, he understood why his wife was so particularly anxious to go to Nice: her Michel lived at Monte Carlo.

He took an English dictionary, and translating the words, and guessing their meaning, by degrees he put together the following sentence: "I drink to the health of my beloved darling, and kiss her little foot a thousand times, and am impatiently expecting her arrival." He pictured the pitiable, ludicrous part he would play if he had agreed to go to Nice with his wife. He felt so mortified that he almost shed tears and began pacing to and fro through all the rooms of the flat in great agitation. His pride, his plebeian fastidiousness, was revolted. Clenching his fists and scowling with disgust, he wondered how he, the son of a village priest, brought up in a clerical school, a plain, straightforward man, a surgeon by profession—how could he have let himself be enslaved, have sunk into such shameful bondage to this weak, worthless, mercenary, low creature.

" 'Little foot'!" he muttered to himself, crumpling up the telegram; " 'little foot'!"

Of the time when he fell in love and proposed to her, and the seven years that he had been living with her, all that remained in his memory was her long, fragrant hair, a mass of soft lace, and her little feet, which certainly were very small, beautiful feet; and even now it seemed as though he still had from those old embraces the feeling of lace and silk upon his hands and face—and nothing more. Nothing more—that is, not counting hysterics, shrieks, reproaches, threats, and lies—brazen, treacherous lies. He remembered how in his father's house in the village a bird would sometimes chance to fly in from the open air into the house and would struggle desperately against the window-panes and upset things; so this woman from a class utterly alien to him had flown into his life and made complete havoc of it. The best years of his life had been spent as though in hell, his hopes for happiness shattered and turned into a mockery, his health gone, his rooms as vulgar in their atmosphere as a cocotte's, and of the ten thousand he earned every year he could never save ten roubles to send his old mother in the village, and his debts were already about fifteen thousand. It seemed that if a band of brigands had been living in his rooms his life would not have been so hopelessly, so irremediably ruined as by the presence of this woman.

He began coughing and gasping for breath. He ought to have gone to bed and got warm, but he could not. He kept walking about the rooms, or sat down to the table, nervously fidgeting with a pencil and scribbling mechanically on a paper.

"Trying a pen. . . . A little foot."

By five o'clock he grew weaker and threw all the blame on himself. It seemed to him now that if Olga Dmitrievna had married some one else who might have had a good influence over her—who knows?—she might after all have become a good, straightforward woman. He was a poor psychologist, and knew nothing of the female heart; besides, he was churlish, uninteresting. . . .

"I haven't long to live now," he thought. "I am a dead man, and ought not to stand in the way of the living. It would be strange and stupid to insist upon one's rights now. I'll have it out with her; let her go to the man she loves. . . . I'll give her a divorce. I'll take the blame on myself."

Olga Dmitrievna came in at last, and she walked into the study and sank into a chair just as she was in her white cloak, hat, and overboots.

"The nasty, fat boy," she said with a sob, breathing hard. "It's really dishonest; it's disgusting." She stamped. "I can't put up with it; I can't, I can't!"

"What's the matter?" asked Nikolay Yevgrafitch, going up to her.

"That student, Azarbekov, was seeing me home, and he lost my bag, and there was fifteen roubles in it. I borrowed it from mamma."

She was crying in a most genuine way, like a little girl, and not only her handkerchief, but even her gloves, were wet with tears.

"It can't be helped!" said the doctor. "If he's lost it, he's lost it, and it's no good worrying over it. Calm yourself; I want to talk to you."

"I am not a millionaire to lose money like that. He says he'll pay it back, but I don't believe him; he's poor . . ."

Her husband begged her to calm herself and to listen to him, but she kept on talking of the student and of the fifteen roubles she had lost.

"Ach! I'll give you twenty-five roubles to-morrow if you'll only hold your tongue!" he said irritably.

"I must take off my things!" she said, crying. "I can't talk seriously in my fur coat! How strange you are!"

He helped her off with her coat and overboots, detecting as he did so the smell of the white wine she liked to drink with oysters (in spite of her etherealness she ate and drank a great deal). She went into her room and came back soon after, having changed her things and powdered her face, though her eyes still showed traces of tears. She sat down, retreating into her light, lacy dressing-gown, and in the mass of billowy pink her husband could see nothing but her hair, which she had let down, and her little foot wearing a slipper.

"What do you want to talk about?" she asked, swinging herself in a rocking-chair.

"I happened to see this;" and he handed her the telegram.

She read it and shrugged her shoulders.

"Well?" she said, rocking herself faster. "That's the usual New Year's greeting and nothing else. There are no secrets in it."

"You are reckoning on my not knowing English. No, I don't know it; but I have a dictionary. That telegram is from Riss; he drinks to the health of his beloved and sends you a thousand kisses. But let us leave that," the doctor went on hurriedly. "I don't in the least want to reproach you or make a scene. We've had scenes and reproaches enough; it's time to make an end of them.... This is what I want to say to you: you are free, and can live as you like."

There was a silence. She began crying quietly.

"I set you free from the necessity of lying and keeping up pretences," Nikolay Yevgrafitch continued. "If you love that young man, love him; if you want to go abroad to him, go. You are young, healthy, and I am a wreck, and haven't long to live. In short... you understand me."

He was agitated and could not go on. Olga Dmitrievna, crying and speaking in a voice of self-pity, acknowledged that she loved Riss, and used to drive out of town with him and see him in his rooms, and now she really did long to go abroad.

"You see, I hide nothing from you," she added, with a sigh. "My whole soul lies open before you. And I beg you again, be generous, get me a passport."

"I repeat, you are free."

She moved to another seat nearer him to look at the expression of his face. She did not believe him and wanted now to understand his secret meaning. She never did believe any one, and however generous were their intentions, she always suspected some petty or ignoble motive or selfish object in them. And when she looked searchingly into his face, it seemed to him that there was a gleam of green light in her eyes as in a cat's.

"When shall I get the passport?" she asked softly.

He suddenly had an impulse to say "Never"; but he restrained himself and said:

"When you like."

"I shall only go for a month."

"You'll go to Riss for good. I'll get you a divorce, take the blame on myself, and Riss can marry you."

"But I don't want a divorce!" Olga Dmitrievna retorted quickly, with an astonished face. "I am not asking you for a divorce! Get me a passport, that's all."

"But why don't you want the divorce?" asked the doctor, beginning to feel irritated. "You are a strange woman. How strange you are! If you are fond of him in earnest and he loves you too, in your position you can do nothing better than get married. Can you really hesitate between marriage and adultery?"

"I understand you," she said, walking away from him, and a spiteful, vindictive expression came into her face. "I understand you perfectly. You are sick of me, and you simply want to get rid of me, to force this divorce on me. Thank you very much; I am not such a fool as you think. I won't accept the divorce and I won't leave you—I won't, I won't! To begin with, I don't want to lose my position in society," she continued quickly, as though afraid of being prevented from speaking. "Secondly, I am twenty-seven and Riss is only twenty-three; he'll be tired of me in a year and throw me over. And what's more, if you care to know, I'm not certain that my feeling will last long . . . so there! I'm not going to leave you."

"Then I'll turn you out of the house!" shouted Nikolay Yevgrafitch, stamping. "I shall turn you out, you vile, loathsome woman!"

"We shall see!" she said, and went out.

It was broad daylight outside, but the doctor still sat at the table moving the pencil over the paper and writing mechanically.

"My dear Sir. . . . Little foot."

Or he walked about and stopped in the drawing-room before a photograph taken seven years ago, soon after his marriage, and looked at it for a long time. It was a family group: his father-in-law, his mother-in-law, his wife Olga Dmitrievna when she was twenty, and himself in the rôle of a happy young husband. His father-in-law, a clean-shaven, dropsical privy councillor, crafty and avaricious; his mother-in-law, a stout lady with small predatory features like a weasel, who loved her daughter to distraction and helped her in everything; if her daughter were strangling some one, the mother would not have protested, but would only have screened her with her skirts. Olga Dmitrievna, too, had small predatory-looking features, but more expressive and bolder than her mother's; she was not a weasel, but a beast on a bigger scale! And Nikolay Yevgrafitch himself in the photograph looked such a guileless soul, such a kindly, good fellow, so open and simple-hearted; his whole face was relaxed in the naïve, good-natured smile of a divinity student, and he had had the simplicity to believe that that company of beasts of prey into which destiny had chanced to thrust him would give him romance and happiness and all he had dreamed of when as a student he used to sing the song "Youth is wasted, life is nought, when the heart is cold and loveless."

And once more he asked himself in perplexity how he, the son of a village priest, with his democratic bringing up—a plain, blunt, straightforward man—could have so helplessly surrendered to the power of this worthless, false, vulgar, petty creature, whose nature was so utterly alien to him.

When at eleven o'clock he put on his coat to go to the hospital the servant came into his study.

"What is it?" he asked.

"The mistress has got up and asks you for the twenty-five roubles you promised her yesterday."

The Two Volodyas

"Let me; I want to drive myself! I'll sit by the driver!" Sofya Lvovna said in a loud voice. "Wait a minute, driver; I'll get up on the box beside you."

She stood up in the sledge, and her husband, Vladimir Nikititch, and the friend of her childhood, Vladimir Mihalovitch, held her arms to prevent her falling. The three horses were galloping fast.

"I said you ought not to have given her brandy," Vladimir Nikititch whispered to his companion with vexation. "What a fellow you are, really!"

The Colonel knew by experience that in women like his wife, Sofya Lvovna, after a little too much wine, turbulent gaiety was followed by hysterical laughter and then tears. He was afraid that when they got home, instead of being able to sleep, he would have to be administering compresses and drops.

"Wo!" cried Sofya Lvovna. "I want to drive myself!"

She felt genuinely gay and triumphant. For the last two months, ever since her wedding, she had been tortured by the thought that she had married Colonel Yagitch from worldly motives and, as it is said, *par dépit;* but that evening, at the restaurant, she had suddenly become convinced that she loved him passionately. In spite of his fifty-four years, he was so slim, agile, supple, he made puns and hummed to the gipsies' tunes so charmingly. Really, the older men were nowadays a thousand times more interesting than the young. It seemed as though age and youth had changed parts. The Colonel was two years older than her father, but could there be any importance in that if, honestly speaking, there were infinitely more vitality, go, and freshness in him than in herself, though she was only twenty-three?

"Oh, my darling!" she thought. "You are wonderful!"

She had become convinced in the restaurant, too, that not a spark of her old feeling remained. For the friend of her childhood, Vladimir Mihalovitch, or simply Volodya, with whom only the day before she had been madly, miserably in love, she now felt nothing but complete indifference. All that evening he had seemed to her spiritless, torpid, uninteresting, and insignificant, and the *sangfroid* with which he habitually avoided paying at restaurants on this occasion revolted her, and she had hardly been able to resist saying, "If you are poor, you should stay at home." The Colonel paid for all.

Perhaps because trees, telegraph posts, and drifts of snow kept flitting past her eyes, all sorts of disconnected ideas came rushing into her mind. She reflected: the bill at the restaurant had been a hundred and twenty roubles, and a hundred had gone to the gipsies, and to-morrow she could fling away a thousand roubles if she liked; and only two months ago, before her wedding, she had not had three roubles of her own, and had to ask her father for every trifle. What a change in her life!

Her thoughts were in a tangle. She recalled, how, when she was a child of ten, Colonel Yagitch, now her husband, used to make love to her aunt, and every one in the house said that he had ruined her. And her aunt had, in fact, often come down to dinner with her eyes red from crying, and was always going off somewhere; and people used to say of her that the poor thing could find no peace anywhere. He had been very handsome in those days, and had an extraordinary reputation as a lady-killer. So much so that he was known all over the town, and it was said of him that he paid a round of visits to his adorers every day like a doctor visiting his patients. And even now, in spite of his grey hair, his wrinkles, and his spectacles, his thin face looked handsome, especially in profile.

Sofya Lvovna's father was an army doctor, and had at one time served in the same regiment with Colonel Yagitch. Volodya's father was an army doctor too, and he, too, had once been in the same regiment as her father and Colonel Yagitch. In spite of many amatory adventures, often very complicated and disturbing, Volodya had done splendidly at the university, and had taken a very good degree. Now he was specialising in foreign literature, and was said to be writing a thesis. He lived with his father, the army doctor, in the barracks, and had no means of his own, though he was thirty. As children Sofya and he had lived under the same roof, though in different flats. He often came to play with her, and they had dancing and French lessons together. But when he grew up into a graceful, remarkably handsome young man, she began to feel shy of him, and then fell madly in love with him, and had loved him right up to the time when she was married to Yagitch. He, too, had been renowned for his success with women almost from the age of fourteen, and the ladies who deceived their husbands on his account excused themselves by saying that he was only a boy. Some one had told a story of him lately that when he was a student living in lodgings so as to be near the university, it always happened if one knocked at his door, that one heard his footstep, and then a whispered apology: "*Pardon, je ne suis pas seul.*" Yagitch was delighted with him, and blessed him as a worthy successor, as Derchavin blessed Pushkin; he appeared to be fond of him. They would play billiards or picquet by the hour together without uttering a word, if Yagitch drove out on any expedition he always took Volodya with him, and Yagitch was the only person Volodya initiated into the mysteries of his thesis. In earlier days, when Yagitch was rather younger, they had often been in the position of rivals, but they had never been jealous of one another. In the circle in which they moved Yagitch was nicknamed Big Volodya, and his friend Little Volodya.

Besides Big Volodya, Little Volodya, and Sofya Lvovna, there was a fourth person in the sledge—Margarita Alexandrovna, or, as every one called her, Rita, a cousin of Madame Yagitch—a very pale girl over thirty, with black eyebrows and a pince-nez, who was for ever smoking cigarettes, even in the bitterest frost, and who always had her knees and the front of her blouse covered with cigarette ash. She spoke through her nose, drawling every word, was of a cold temperament, could drink any amount of wine and liquor without being drunk, and used to tell scandalous anecdotes in a languid and tasteless way. At home she spent her days reading thick magazines, covering them with cigarette ash, or eating frozen apples.

"Sonia, give over fooling," she said, drawling. "It's really silly."

As they drew near the city gates they went more slowly, and began to pass people and houses. Sofya Lvovna subsided, nestled up to her husband, and gave herself up to her thoughts. Little Volodya sat opposite. By now her light-hearted and cheerful thoughts were mingled with gloomy ones. She thought that the man sitting opposite knew that she loved him, and no doubt he believed the gossip that she married the Colonel *par dépit.* She had never told him of her love; she had not wanted him to know, and had done her best to hide her feeling, but from her face she knew that he understood her perfectly—and her pride suffered. But what was most humiliating in her position was that, since her wedding, Volodya had suddenly begun to pay her attention, which he had never done before, spending hours with her, sitting silent or chattering about trifles; and even now in the sledge, though he did not talk to her, he touched her foot with his and pressed her hand a little. Evidently that was all he wanted, that she should be married; and it was evident that he despised her and that she only excited in him an interest of a special kind as though she were an immoral and disreputable woman. And when the feeling of triumph and love for her husband were mingled in her soul with humiliation and wounded pride, she was overcome by a spirit of defiance, and longed to sit on the box, to shout and whistle to the horses.

Just as they passed the nunnery the huge hundred-ton bell rang out. Rita crossed herself.

"Our Olga is in that nunnery," said Sofya Lvovna, and she, too, crossed herself and shuddered.

"Why did she go into the nunnery?" said the Colonel.

"*Par dépit,*" Rita answered crossly, with obvious allusion to Sofya's marrying Yagitch. "*Par dépit* is all the fashion nowadays. Defiance of all the world. She was always laughing, a desperate flirt, fond of nothing but balls and young men, and all of a sudden off she went—to surprise every one!"

"That's not true," said Volodya, turning down the collar of his fur coat and showing his handsome face. "It wasn't a case of *par dépit;* it was simply horrible, if you like. Her brother Dmitri was sent to penal servitude, and they don't know where he is now. And her mother died of grief."

He turned up his collar again.

"Olga did well," he added in a muffled voice. "Living as an adopted child, and with such a paragon as Sofya Lvovna,—one must take that into consideration too!"

Sofya Lvovna heard a tone of contempt in his voice, and longed to say something rude to him, but she said nothing. The spirit of defiance came over her again; she stood up again and shouted in a tearful voice:

"I want to go to the early service! Driver, back! I want to see Olga."

They turned back. The nunnery bell had a deep note, and Sofya Lvovna fancied there was something in it that reminded her of Olga and her life. The other church bells began ringing too. When the driver stopped the horses, Sofya Lvovna jumped out of the sledge and, unescorted and alone, went quickly up to the gate.

"Make haste, please!" her husband called to her. "It's late already."

She went in at the dark gateway, then by the avenue that led from the gate to the chief church. The snow crunched under her feet, and the ringing was just above her head, and seemed to vibrate through her whole being. Here was the church door, then three steps down, and an ante-room with ikons of the saints on both sides, a fragrance of juniper and incense, another door, and a dark figure opening it and bowing very low. The service had not yet begun. One nun was walking by the ikon-screen and lighting the candles on the tall standard candlesticks, another was lighting the chandelier. Here and there, by the columns and the side chapels, there stood black, motionless figures. "I suppose they must remain standing as they are now till the morning," thought

Sofya Lvovna, and it seemed to her dark, cold, and dreary—drearier than a graveyard. She looked with a feeling of dreariness at the still, motionless figures and suddenly felt a pang at her heart. For some reason, in one short nun, with thin shoulders and a black kerchief on her head, she recognised Olga, though when Olga went into the nunnery she had been plump and had looked taller. Hesitating and extremely agitated, Sofya Lvovna went up to the nun, and looking over her shoulder into her face, recognised her as Olga.

"Olga!" she cried, throwing up her hands, and could not speak from emotion. "Olga!"

The nun knew her at once; she raised her eyebrows in surprise, and her pale, freshly washed face, and even, it seemed, the white headcloth that she wore under her wimple, beamed with pleasure.

"What a miracle from God!" she said, and she, too, threw up her thin, pale little hands.

Sofya Lvovna hugged her and kissed her warmly, and was afraid as she did so that she might smell of spirits.

"We were just driving past, and we thought of you," she said, breathing hard, as though she had been running. "Dear me! How pale you are! I . . . I'm very glad to see you. Well, tell me how are you? Are you dull?"

Sofya Lvovna looked round at the other nuns, and went on in a subdued voice:

"There've been so many changes at home . . . you know, I'm married to Colonel Yagitch. You remember him, no doubt. . . . I am very happy with him."

"Well, thank God for that. And is your father quite well?"

"Yes, he is quite well. He often speaks of you. You must come and see us during the holidays, Olga, won't you?"

"I will come," said Olga, and she smiled. "I'll come on the second day."

Sofya Lvovna began crying, she did not know why, and for a minute she shed tears in silence, then she wiped her eyes and said:

"Rita will be very sorry not to have seen you. She is with us too. And Volodya's here. They are close to the gate. How pleased they'd be if you'd come out and see them. Let's go out to them; the service hasn't begun yet."

"Let us," Olga agreed. She crossed herself three times and went out with Sofya Lvovna to the entrance.

"So you say you're happy, Sonitchka?" she asked when they came out at the gate.

"Very."

"Well, thank God for that."

The two Volodyas, seeing the nun, got out of the sledge and greeted her respectfully. Both were visibly touched by her pale face and her black monastic dress, and both were pleased that she had remembered them and come to greet them. That she might not be cold, Sofya Lvovna wrapped her up in a rug and put one half of her fur coat round her. Her tears had relieved and purified her heart, and she was glad that this noisy, restless, and, in reality, impure night should unexpectedly end so purely and serenely. And to keep Olga by her a little longer she suggested:

"Let us take her for a drive! Get in, Olga; we'll go a little way."

The men expected the nun to refuse—saints don't dash about in three-horse sledges; but to their surprise, she consented and got into the sledge. And while the horses were galloping to the city gate all were silent, and only tried to make her warm and comfortable, and each of them was thinking of what she had been in the past and what she was now. Her face was now passionless, inexpressive, cold, pale, and transparent, as though there were water, not blood, in her veins. And two or three years ago she had been plump and rosy, talking about her suitors and laughing at every trifle.

Near the city gate the sledge turned back; when it stopped ten minutes later near the nunnery, Olga got out of the sledge. The bell had begun to ring more rapidly.

"The Lord save you," said Olga, and she bowed low as nuns do.

"Mind you come, Olga."

"I will, I will."

She went and quickly disappeared through the gateway. And when after that they drove on again, Sofya Lvovna felt very sad. Every one was silent. She felt dispirited and weak all over. That she should have made a nun get into a sledge and drive in a company hardly sober seemed to her now stupid, tactless, and almost sacrilegious. As the intoxication passed off, the desire to deceive herself passed away also. It was clear to her now that she did not love her husband, and never could love him, and that it all had been foolishness and nonsense. She had married him from interested motives, because, in the words of her school friends, he was madly rich, and because she was afraid of becoming an old maid like Rita, and because she was sick of her father, the doctor, and wanted to annoy Volodya. If she could have imagined when she got married, that it would be so oppressive, so dreadful, and so hideous, she would not have consented to the marriage for all the wealth in the world. But now there was no setting it right. She must make up her mind to it.

They reached home. Getting into her warm, soft bed, and pulling the bed-clothes over her, Sofya Lvovna recalled the dark church, the smell of incense, and the figures by the columns, and she felt frightened at the thought that these figures would be standing there all the while she was asleep. The early service would be very, very long; then there would be "the hours," then the mass, then the service of the day. . . .

"But of course there is a God—there certainly is a God; and I shall have to die, so that sooner or later one must think of one's soul, of eternal life, like Olga. Olga is saved now; she has settled all questions for herself. . . . But if there is no God? Then her life is wasted. But how is it wasted? Why is it wasted?"

And a minute later the thought came into her mind again:

"There is a God; death must come; one must think of one's soul. If Olga were to see death before her this minute she would not be afraid. She is prepared. And the great thing is that she has already solved the problem of life for herself. There is a God . . . yes. . . . But is there no other solution except going into a monastery? To go into the monastery means to renounce life, to spoil it . . ."

Sofya Lvovna began to feel rather frightened; she hid her head under her pillow.

"I mustn't think about it," she whispered. "I mustn't . . ."

Yagitch was walking about on the carpet in the next room with a soft jingle of spurs, thinking about something. The thought occurred to Sofya Lvovna that this man was near and dear to her only for one reason—that his name, too, was Vladimir. She sat up in bed and called tenderly:

"Volodya!"

"What is it?" her husband responded.

"Nothing."

She lay down again. She heard a bell, perhaps the same nunnery bell. Again she thought of the vestibule and the dark figures, and thoughts of God and of inevitable death strayed through her mind, and she covered her ears that she might not hear the bell. She thought that before old age and death there would be a long, long life before her, and that day by day she would have to put up with being close to a man she did not love, who had just now come into the bedroom and was getting into bed, and would have to stifle in her heart her hopeless love for the other young, fascinating, and, as she thought, exceptional man. She looked at her husband and tried to say good-night to him, but suddenly burst out crying instead. She was vexed with herself.

"Well, now then for the music!" said Yagitch.

She was not pacified till ten o'clock in the morning. She left off crying and trembling all over, but she began to have a splitting headache. Yagitch was in haste to go to the late mass, and in the next room was grumbling at his orderly, who was helping him to dress. He came into the bedroom once with the soft jingle of his spurs to fetch something, and then a second time wearing his epaulettes, and his orders on his breast, limping slightly from rheumatism; and it struck Sofya Lvovna that he looked and walked like a bird of prey.

She heard Yagitch ring the telephone bell.

"Be so good as to put me on to the Vassilevsky barracks," he said; and a minute later: "Vassilevsky barracks? Please ask Doctor Salimovitch to come to the telephone . . ." And a minute later: "With whom am I speaking? Is it you, Volodya? Delighted. Ask your father to come to us at once, dear boy; my wife is rather shattered after yesterday. Not at home, you say? H'm! . . . Thank you. Very good. I shall be much obliged. . . . *Merci.*"

Yagitch came into the bedroom for the third time, bent down to his wife, made the sign of the cross over her, gave her his hand to kiss (the women who had been in love with him used to kiss his hand and he had got into the habit of it), and saying that he should be back to dinner, went out.

At twelve o'clock the maid came in to announce that Vladimir Mihalovitch had arrived. Sofya Lvovna, staggering with fatigue and headache, hurriedly put on her marvellous new lilac dressing-gown trimmed with fur, and hastily did up her hair after a fashion. She was conscious of an inexpressible tenderness in her heart, and was trembling with joy and with fear that he might go away. She wanted nothing but to look at him.

Volodya came dressed correctly for calling, in a swallow-tail coat and white tie. When Sofya Lvovna came in he kissed her hand and expressed his genuine regret that she was ill. Then when they had sat down, he admired her dressing-gown.

"I was upset by seeing Olga yesterday," she said. "At first I felt it dreadful, but now I envy her. She is like a rock that cannot be shattered; there is no moving her. But was there no other solution for her, Volodya? Is burying oneself alive the only solution of the problem of life? Why, it's death, not life!"

At the thought of Olga, Volodya's face softened.

"Here, you are a clever man, Volodya," said Sofya Lvovna. "Show me how to do what Olga has done. Of course, I am not a believer and should not go into a nunnery, but one can do something equivalent. Life isn't easy for me," she added after a brief pause. "Tell me what to do. . . . Tell me something I can believe in. Tell me something, if it's only one word."

"One word? By all means: tararaboomdeeay."

"Volodya, why do you despise me?" she asked hotly. "You talk to me in a special, fatuous way, if you'll excuse me, not as one talks to one's friends and women one respects. You are so good at your work, you are fond of science; why do you never talk of it to me? Why is it? Am I not good enough?"

Volodya frowned with annoyance and said:

"Why do you want science all of a sudden? Don't you perhaps want constitutional government? Or sturgeon and horse-radish?"

"Very well, I am a worthless, trivial, silly woman with no convictions. I have a mass, a mass of defects. I am neurotic, corrupt, and I ought to be despised for it. But you, Volodya, are ten years older than I am, and my husband is thirty years older. I've grown up before your eyes, and if you would, you could have made anything you liked of me—an angel. But you"—her voice quivered—"treat me horribly. Yagitch has married me in his old age, and you . . ."

"Come, come," said Volodya, sitting nearer her and kissing both her hands. "Let the Schopenhauers philosophise and prove whatever they like, while we'll kiss these little hands."

"You despise me, and if only you knew how miserable it makes me," she said uncertainly, knowing beforehand that he would not believe her. "And if you only knew how I want to change, to begin another life! I think of it with enthusiasm!" and tears of enthusiasm actually came into her eyes. "To be good, honest, pure, not to be lying; to have an object in life."

"Come, come, come, please don't be affected! I don't like it!" said Volodya, and an ill-humoured expression came into his face. "Upon my word, you might be on the stage. Let us behave like simple people."

To prevent him from getting cross and going away, she began defending herself, and forced herself to smile to please him; and again she began talking of Olga, and of how she longed to solve the problem of her life and to become something real.

"Ta-ra-ra-boomdee-ay," he hummed. "Tara-ra-boom-dee-ay!"

And all at once he put his arm round her waist, while she, without knowing what she was doing, laid her hands on his shoulders and for a minute gazed with ecstasy, almost intoxication, at his clever, ironical face, his brow, his eyes, his handsome beard.

"You have known that I love you for ever so long," she confessed to him, and she blushed painfully, and felt that her lips were twitching with shame. "I love you. Why do you torture me?"

She shut her eyes and kissed him passionately on the lips, and for a long while, a full minute, could not take her lips away, though she knew it was unseemly, that he might be thinking the worse of her, that a servant might come in.

"Oh, how you torture me!" she repeated.

When half an hour later, having got all that he wanted, he was sitting at lunch in the dining-room, she was kneeling before him, gazing greedily into his face, and he told her that she was like a little dog waiting for a bit of ham to be thrown to it. Then he sat her on his knee, and dancing her up and down like a child, hummed:

"Tara-raboom-dee-ay. . . . Tara-raboomdee-ay."

And when he was getting ready to go she asked him in a passionate whisper:

"When? To-day? Where?" And held out both hands to his mouth as though she wanted to seize his answer in them.

"To-day it will hardly be convenient," he said after a minute's thought. "To-morrow, perhaps."

And they parted. Before dinner Sofya Lvovna went to the nunnery to see Olga, but there she was told that Olga was reading the psalter somewhere over the dead. From the nunnery she went to her father's and found that he, too, was out. Then she took another sledge and drove aimlessly about the streets till evening. And for some reason she kept thinking of the aunt whose eyes were red with crying, and who could find no peace anywhere.

And at night they drove out again with three horses to a restaurant out of town and listened to the gipsies. And driving back past the nunnery again, Sofya Lvovna thought of Olga, and she felt aghast at the thought that for the girls and women of her class there was no solution but to go on driving about and telling lies, or going into a nunnery to mortify the flesh. . . . And next day she met her lover, and again Sofya Lvovna drove about the town alone in a hired sledge thinking about her aunt.

A week later Volodya threw her over. And after that life went on as before, uninteresting, miserable, and sometimes even agonising. The Colonel and Volodya spent hours playing billiards and picquet, Rita told anecdotes in the same languid, tasteless way, and Sofya Lvovna went about alone in hired sledges and kept begging her husband to take her for a good drive with three horses.

Going almost every day to the nunnery, she wearied Olga, complaining of her unbearable misery, weeping, and feeling as she did so that she brought with her into the cell something impure, pitiful, shabby. And Olga repeated to her mechanically as though a lesson learnt by rote, that all this was of no consequence, that it would all pass and God would forgive her.

Rothschild's Fiddle

The town was a little one, worse than a village, and it was inhabited by scarcely any but old people who died with an infrequency that was really annoying. In the hospital and in the prison fortress very few coffins were needed. In fact business was bad. If Yakov Ivanov had been an undertaker in the chief town of the province he would certainly have had a house of his own, and people would have addressed him as Yakov Matveyitch; here in this wretched little town people called him simply Yakov; his nickname in the street was for some reason Bronze, and he lived in a poor way like a humble peasant, in a little old hut in which there was only one room, and in this room he and Marfa, the stove, a double bed, the coffins, his bench, and all their belongings were crowded together.

Yakov made good, solid coffins. For peasants and working people he made them to fit himself, and this was never unsuccessful, for there were none taller and stronger than he, even in the prison, though he was seventy. For gentry and for women he made them to measure, and used an iron foot-rule for the purpose. He was very unwilling to take orders for children's coffins, and made them straight off without measurements, contemptuously, and when he was paid for the work he always said:

"I must confess I don't like trumpery jobs."

Apart from his trade, playing the fiddle brought him in a small income.

The Jews' orchestra conducted by Moisey Ilyitch Shahkes, the tinsmith, who took more than half their receipts for himself, played as a rule at weddings in the town. As Yakov played very well on the fiddle, especially Russian songs, Shahkes sometimes invited him to join the orchestra at a fee of half a rouble a day, in addition to tips from the visitors. When Bronze sat in the orchestra first of all his face became crimson and perspiring; it was hot, there was a suffocating smell of garlic, the fiddle squeaked, the double bass wheezed close to his right ear, while the flute wailed at his left, played by a gaunt, red-haired Jew who had a perfect network of red and blue veins all over his face, and who bore the name of the famous millionaire Rothschild. And this accursed Jew contrived to play even the liveliest things plaintively. For no apparent reason Yakov little by little became possessed by hatred and contempt for the Jews, and especially for Rothschild; he began to pick quarrels with him, rail at him in unseemly language and once even tried to strike him, and Rothschild was offended and said, looking at him ferociously:

"If it were not that I respect you for your talent, I would have sent you flying out of the window."

Then he began to weep. And because of this Yakov was not often asked to play in the orchestra; he was only sent for in case of extreme necessity in the absence of one of the Jews.

Yakov was never in a good temper, as he was continually having to put up with terrible losses. For instance, it was a sin to work on Sundays or Saints' days, and Monday was an unlucky day, so that in the course of the year there were some two hundred days on which, whether he liked it or not, he had to sit with his hands folded. And only think, what a loss that meant. If anyone in the town had a wedding without music, or if Shahkes did not send for Yakov, that was a loss, too. The superintendent of the prison was ill for two years and was wasting away, and Yakov was impatiently waiting for him to die, but the superintendent went away to the chief town of the province to be doctored, and there took and died. There's a loss for you, ten roubles at least, as there would have been an expensive coffin to make, lined with brocade. The thought of his losses haunted Yakov, especially at night; he laid his fiddle on the bed beside him, and when all sorts of nonsensical ideas came into his mind he touched a string; the fiddle gave out a sound in the darkness, and he felt better.

On the sixth of May of the previous year Marfa had suddenly been taken ill. The old woman's breathing was laboured, she drank a great deal of water, and she staggered as she walked, yet she lighted the stove in the morning and even went herself to get water. Towards evening she lay down. Yakov played his fiddle all day; when it was quite dark he took the book in which he used every day to put down his losses, and, feeling dull, he began adding up the total for the year. It came to more than a thousand roubles. This so agitated him that he flung the reckoning beads down, and trampled them under his feet. Then he picked up the reckoning beads, and again spent a long time clicking with them and heaving deep, strained sighs. His face was crimson and wet with perspiration. He thought that if he had put that lost thousand roubles in the bank, the interest for a year would have been at least forty roubles, so that forty roubles was a loss too. In fact, wherever one turned there were losses and nothing else.

"Yakov!" Marfa called unexpectedly. "I am dying."

He looked round at his wife. Her face was rosy with fever, unusually bright and joyful-looking. Bronze, accustomed to seeing her face always pale, timid, and unhappy-looking, was bewildered. It looked as if she really were dying and were glad that she was going away for ever from that hut, from the coffins, and from Yakov. . . . And she gazed at the ceiling and moved her lips, and her expression was one of happiness, as though she saw death as her deliverer and were whispering with him.

It was daybreak; from the windows one could see the flush of dawn. Looking at the old woman, Yakov for some reason reflected that he had not once in his life been affectionate to her, had had no feeling for her, had never once thought to buy her a kerchief, or to bring her home some dainty from a wedding, but had done nothing but shout at her, scold her for his losses, shake his fists at her; it is true he had never actually beaten her, but he had frightened her, and at such times she had always been numb with terror. Why, he had forbidden her to drink tea because they spent too much without that, and she drank only hot water. And he understood why she had such a strange, joyful face now, and he was overcome with dread.

As soon as it was morning he borrowed a horse from a neighbour and took Marfa to the hospital. There were not many patients there, and so he had not long to wait, only three hours. To his great satisfaction the patients were not being received by the doctor, who was himself ill, but by the assistant, Maxim Nikolaitch, an old man of whom everyone in the town used to say that, though he drank and was quarrelsome, he knew more than the doctor.

"I wish you good-day," said Yakov, leading his old woman into the consulting room. "You must excuse us, Maxim Nikolaitch, we are always troubling you with our trumpery affairs. Here you see my better half is ailing, the partner of my life, as they say, excuse the expression. . . ."

Knitting his grizzled brows and stroking his whiskers the assistant began to examine the old woman, and she sat on a stool, a wasted, bent figure with a sharp nose and open mouth, looking like a bird that wants to drink.

"H——m . . . Ah! . . ." the assistant said slowly, and he heaved a sigh. "Influenza and possibly fever. There's typhus in the town now. Well, the old woman has lived her life, thank God. . . . How old is she?"

"She'll be seventy in another year, Maxim Nikolaitch."

"Well, the old woman has lived her life, it's time to say good-bye."

"You are quite right in what you say, of course, Maxim Nikolaitch," said Yakov, smiling from politeness, "and we thank you feelingly for your kindness, but allow me to say every insect wants to live."

"To be sure," said the assistant, in a tone which suggested that it depended upon him whether the woman lived or died. "Well, then, my good fellow, put a cold compress on her head, and give her these powders twice a day, and so good-bye. Bonjour."

From the expression of his face Yakov saw that it was a bad case, and that no sort of powders would be any help; it was clear to him that

Marfa would die very soon, if not to-day, to-morrow. He nudged the assistant's elbow, winked at him, and said in a low voice:

"If you would just cup her, Maxim Nikolaitch."

"I have no time, I have no time, my good fellow. Take your old woman and go in God's name. Good-bye."

"Be so gracious," Yakov besought him. "You know yourself that if, let us say, it were her stomach or her inside that were bad, then powders or drops, but you see she had got a chill! In a chill the first thing is to let blood, Maxim Nikolaitch."

But the assistant had already sent for the next patient, and a peasant woman came into the consulting room with a boy.

"Go along, go along," he said to Yakov, frowning. "It's no use to—"

"In that case put on leeches, anyway! Make us pray for you for ever."

The assistant flew into a rage and shouted:

"You speak to me again! You blockhead. . . ."

Yakov flew into a rage too, and he turned crimson all over, but he did not utter a word. He took Marfa on his arm and led her out of the room. Only when they were sitting in the cart he looked morosely and ironically at the hospital, and said:

"A nice set of artists they have settled here! No fear, but he would have cupped a rich man, but even a leech he grudges to the poor. The Herods!"

When they got home and went into the hut, Marfa stood for ten minutes holding on to the stove. It seemed to her that if she were to lie down Yakov would talk to her about his losses, and scold her for lying down and not wanting to work. Yakov looked at her drearily and thought that to-morrow was St. John the Divine's, and next day St. Nikolay the Wonder-worker's, and the day after that was Sunday, and then Monday, an unlucky day. For four days he would not be able to work, and most likely Marfa would die on one of those days; so he would have to make the coffin to-day. He picked up his iron rule, went up to the old woman and took her measure. Then she lay down, and he crossed himself and began making the coffin.

When the coffin was finished Bronze put on his spectacles and wrote in his book: "Marfa Ivanov's coffin, two roubles, forty kopecks."

And he heaved a sigh. The old woman lay all the time silent with her eyes closed. But in the evening, when it got dark, she suddenly called the old man.

"Do you remember, Yakov," she asked, looking at him joyfully. "Do you remember fifty years ago God gave us a little baby with flaxen hair? We used always to be sitting by the river then, singing songs . . . under the willows," and laughing bitterly, she added: "The baby girl died."

Yakov racked his memory, but could not remember the baby or the willows.

"It's your fancy," he said.

The priest arrived; he administered the sacrament and extreme unction. Then Marfa began muttering something unintelligible, and towards morning she died. Old women, neighbours, washed her, dressed her, and laid her in the coffin. To avoid paying the sacristan, Yakov read the psalms over the body himself, and they got nothing out of him for the grave, as the grave-digger was a crony of his. Four peasants carried the coffin to the graveyard, not for money, but from respect. The coffin was followed by old women, beggars, and a couple of crazy saints, and the people who met it crossed themselves piously. . . . And Yakov was very much pleased that it was so creditable, so decorous, and so cheap, and no offence to anyone. As he took his last leave of Marfa he touched the coffin and thought: "A good piece of work!"

But as he was going back from the cemetery he was overcome by acute depression. He didn't feel quite well: his breathing was laboured and feverish, his legs felt weak, and he had a craving for drink. And thoughts of all sorts forced themselves on his mind. He remembered again that all his life he had never felt for Marfa, had never been affectionate to her. The fifty-two years they had lived in the same hut had dragged on a long, long time, but it had somehow happened that in all that time he had never once thought of her, had paid no attention to her, as though she had been a cat or a dog. And yet, every day, she had lighted the stove, had cooked and baked, had gone for the water, had chopped the wood, had slept with him in the same bed, and when he came home drunk from the weddings always reverently hung his fiddle on the wall and put him to bed, and all this in silence, with a timid, anxious expression.

Rothschild, smiling and bowing, came to meet Yakov.

"I was looking for you, uncle," he said. "Moisey Ilyitch sends you his greetings and bids you come to him at once."

Yakov felt in no mood for this. He wanted to cry.

"Leave me alone," he said, and walked on.

"How can you," Rothschild said, fluttered, running on in front. "Moisey Ilyitch will be offended! He bade you come at once!"

Yakov was revolted at the Jew's gasping for breath and blinking, and having so many red freckles on his face. And it was disgusting to look at his green coat with black patches on it, and all his fragile, refined figure.

"Why are you pestering me, garlic?" shouted Yakov. "Don't persist!"

The Jew got angry and shouted too:

"Not so noisy, please, or I'll send you flying over the fence!"

"Get out of my sight!" roared Yakov, and rushed at him with his fists. "One can't live for you scabby Jews!"

Rothschild, half dead with terror, crouched down and waved his hands over his head, as though to ward off a blow; then he leapt up and ran away as fast as his legs could carry him: as he ran he gave little skips and kept clasping his hands, and Yakov could see how his long thin spine wriggled. Some boys, delighted at the incident, ran after him shouting "Jew! Jew!" Some dogs joined in the chase barking. Someone burst into a roar of laughter, then gave a whistle; the dogs barked with even more noise and unanimity. Then a dog must have bitten Rothschild, as a desperate, sickly scream was heard.

Yakov went for a walk on the grazing ground, then wandered on at random in the outskirts of the town, while the street boys shouted:

"Here's Bronze! Here's Bronze!"

He came to the river, where the curlews floated in the air uttering shrill cries and the ducks quacked. The sun was blazing hot, and there was a glitter from the water, so that it hurt the eyes to look at it. Yakov walked by a path along the bank and saw a plump, rosy-cheeked lady come out of the bathing-shed, and thought about her: "Ugh! you otter!"

Not far from the bathing-shed boys were catching crayfish with bits of meat; seeing him, they began shouting spitefully, "Bronze! Bronze!" And then he saw an old spreading willow-tree with a big hollow in it, and a crow's nest on it. . . . And suddenly there rose up vividly in Yakov's memory a baby with flaxen hair, and the willow-tree Marfa had spoken of. Why, that is it, the same willow-tree—green, still, and sorrowful. . . . How old it has grown, poor thing!

He sat down under it and began to recall the past. On the other bank, where now there was the water meadow, in those days there stood a big birch-wood, and yonder on the bare hillside that could be seen on the horizon an old, old pine forest used to be a bluish patch in the distance. Big boats used to sail on the river. But now it was all smooth and unruffled, and on the other bank there stood now only one birch-tree, youthful and slender like a young lady, and there was nothing on the river but ducks and geese, and it didn't look as though there had ever been boats on it. It seemed as though even the geese were fewer than of old. Yakov shut his eyes, and in his imagination huge flocks of white geese soared, meeting one another.

He wondered how it had happened that for the last forty or fifty years of his life he had never once been to the river, or if he had been by it he had not paid attention to it. Why, it was a decent sized river, not a trumpery one; he might have gone in for fishing and sold the fish to merchants, officials, and the bar-keeper at the station, and then have put money in the bank; he might have sailed in a boat from one house to another, playing the fiddle, and people of all classes would have paid to hear him; he might have tried getting big boats afloat again—that would be better than making coffins; he might have bred geese, killed them and sent them in the winter to Moscow. Why, the feathers alone would very likely mount up to ten roubles in the year. But he had wasted his time, he had done nothing of this. What losses! Ah! What losses! And if he had gone in for all those things at once—catching fish and playing the fiddle, and running boats and killing geese—what a fortune he would have made! But nothing of this had happened, even in his dreams; life had passed uselessly without any pleasure, had been wasted for nothing, not even a pinch of snuff; there was nothing left in front, and if one looked back—there was nothing there but losses, and such terrible ones, it made one cold all over. And why was it a man could not live so as to avoid these losses and misfortunes? One wondered why they had cut down the birch copse and the pine forest. Why was he walking with no reason on the grazing ground? Why do people always do what isn't needful? Why had Yakov all his life scolded, bellowed, shaken his fists, ill-treated his wife, and, one might ask, what necessity was there for him to frighten and insult the Jew that day? Why did people in general hinder each other from living? What losses were due to it! what terrible losses! If it were not for hatred and malice people would get immense benefit from one another.

In the evening and the night he had visions of the baby, of the willow, of fish, of slaughtered geese, and Marfa looking in profile like a bird that wants to drink, and the pale, pitiful face of Rothschild, and faces moved down from all sides and muttered of losses. He tossed from side to side, and got out of bed five times to play the fiddle.

In the morning he got up with an effort and went to the hospital. The same Maxim Nikolaitch told him to put a cold compress on his head, and gave him some powders, and from his tone and expression of face Yakov realized that it was a bad case and that no powders would be any use. As he went home afterwards, he reflected that death would be nothing but a benefit; he would not have to eat or drink, or pay taxes or offend people, and, as a man lies in his grave not for one year but for hundreds and thousands, if one reckoned it up the gain would be enormous. A man's life meant loss: death meant gain. This reflection was, of course, a just one, but yet it was bitter and mortifying; why was the order of the world so strange, that life, which is given to man only once, passes away without benefit?

He was not sorry to die, but at home, as soon as he saw his fiddle, it sent a pang to his heart and he felt sorry. He could not take the fiddle with him to the grave, and now it would be left forlorn, and the same thing would happen to it as to the birch copse and the pine forest. Everything in this world was wasted and would be wasted! Yakov went out of the hut and sat in the doorway, pressing the fiddle to his bosom. Thinking of his wasted, profitless life, he began to play, he did not know what, but it was plaintive and touching, and tears trickled down his cheeks. And the harder he thought, the more mournfully the fiddle wailed.

The latch clicked once and again, and Rothschild appeared at the gate. He walked across half the yard boldly, but seeing Yakov he stopped short, and seemed to shrink together, and probably from terror, began making signs with his hands as though he wanted to show on his fingers what o'clock it was.

"Come along, it's all right," said Yakov in a friendly tone, and he beckoned him to come up. "Come along!"

Looking at him mistrustfully and apprehensively, Rothschild began to advance, and stopped seven feet off.

"Be so good as not to beat me," he said, ducking. "Moisey Ilyitch has sent me again. 'Don't be afraid,' he said; 'go to Yakov again and tell him,' he said, 'we can't get on without him.' There is a wedding on Wednesday. . . . Ye—es! Mr. Shapovalov is marrying his daughter to a good man. . . . And it will be a grand wedding, oo-oo!" added the Jew, screwing up one eye.

"I can't come," said Yakov, breathing hard. "I'm ill, brother."

And he began playing again, and the tears gushed from his eyes on to the fiddle. Rothschild listened attentively, standing sideways to him and folding his arms on his chest. The scared and perplexed expression on his face, little by little, changed to a look of woe and suffering; he rolled his eyes as though he were experiencing an agonizing ecstasy, and articulated, "Vachhh!" and tears slowly ran down his cheeks and trickled on his greenish coat.

And Yakov lay in bed all the rest of the day grieving. In the evening, when the priest confessing him asked, Did he remember any special sin he had committed? straining his failing memory he thought again of Marfa's unhappy face, and the despairing shriek of the Jew when the dog bit him, and said, hardly audibly, "Give the fiddle to Rothschild."

"Very well," answered the priest.

And now everyone in the town asks where Rothschild got such a fine fiddle. Did he buy it or steal it? Or perhaps it had come to him as a pledge. He gave up the flute long ago, and now plays nothing but the fiddle. As plaintive sounds flow now from his bow, as came once from his flute, but when he tries to repeat what Yakov played, sitting in the doorway, the effect is something so sad and sorrowful that his audience weep, and he himself rolls his eyes and articulates "Vachhh! . . ." And this new air was so much liked in the town that the merchants and officials used to be continually sending for Rothschild and making him play it over and over again a dozen times.

The Student

At first the weather was fine and still. The thrushes were calling, and in the swamps close by something alive droned pitifully with a sound like blowing into an empty bottle. A snipe flew by, and the shot aimed at it rang out with a gay, resounding note in the spring air. But when it began to get dark in the forest a cold, penetrating wind blew inappropriately from the east, and everything sank into silence. Needles of ice stretched across the pools, and it felt cheerless, remote, and lonely in the forest. There was a whiff of winter.

Ivan Velikopolsky, the son of a sacristan, and a student of the clerical academy, returning home from shooting, walked all the time by the path in the water-side meadow. His fingers were numb and his face was burning with the wind. It seemed to him that the cold that had suddenly come on had destroyed the order and harmony of things, that nature itself felt ill at ease, and that was why the evening darkness was falling more rapidly than usual. All around it was deserted and peculiarly gloomy. The only light was one gleaming in the widows' gardens near the river; the village, over three miles away, and everything in the distance all round was plunged in the cold evening mist. The student remembered that, as he went out from the house, his mother was sitting barefoot on the floor in the entry, cleaning the samovar, while his father lay on the stove coughing; as it was Good Friday nothing had been cooked, and the student was terribly hungry. And now, shrinking from the cold, he thought that just such a wind had blown in the days of Rurik and in the time of Ivan the Terrible and Peter, and in their time there had been just the same desperate poverty and hunger, the same thatched roofs with holes in them, ignorance, misery, the same desolation around, the same darkness, the same feeling of oppression—all these had existed, did exist, and would exist, and the lapse of a thousand years would make life no better. And he did not want to go home.

The gardens were called the widows' because they were kept by two widows, mother and daughter. A camp fire was burning brightly with a crackling sound, throwing out light far around on the ploughed earth. The widow Vasilisa, a tall, fat old woman in a man's coat, was standing by and looking thoughtfully into the fire; her daughter Lukerya, a little pock-marked woman with a stupid-looking face, was sitting on the ground, washing a caldron and spoons. Apparently they had just had supper. There was a sound of men's voices; it was the labourers watering their horses at the river.

"Here you have winter back again," said the student, going up to the camp fire. "Good evening."

Vasilisa started, but at once recognized him and smiled cordially.

"I did not know you; God bless you," she said. "You'll be rich."

They talked. Vasilisa, a woman of experience, who had been in service with the gentry, first as a wet-nurse, afterwards as a children's nurse, expressed herself with refinement, and a soft, sedate smile never left her face; her daughter Lukerya, a village peasant woman, who had been crushed by her husband, simply screwed up her eyes at the student and said nothing, and she had a strange expression like that of a deaf mute.

"At just such a fire the Apostle Peter warmed himself," said the student, stretching out his hands to the fire, "so it must have been cold then, too. Ah, what a terrible night it must have been, granny! An utterly dismal long night!"

He looked round at the darkness, shook his head abruptly and asked:

"No doubt you have been at the reading of the Twelve Gospels?"

"Yes, I have," answered Vasilisa.

"If you remember at the Last Supper Peter said to Jesus, 'I am ready to go with Thee into darkness and unto death.' And our Lord answered him thus: 'I say unto thee, Peter, before the cock croweth thou wilt have denied Me thrice.' After the supper Jesus went through the agony of death in the garden and prayed, and poor Peter was weary in spirit and faint, his eyelids were heavy and he could not struggle against sleep. He fell asleep. Then you heard how Judas the same night kissed Jesus and betrayed Him to His tormentors. They took Him bound to the high priest and beat Him, while Peter, exhausted, worn out with misery and alarm, hardly awake, you know, feeling that something awful was just going to happen on earth, followed behind.... He loved Jesus passionately, intensely, and now he saw from far off how He was beaten...."

Lukerya left the spoons and fixed an immovable stare upon the student.

"They came to the high priest's," he went on; "they began to question Jesus, and meantime the labourers made a fire in the yard as it was cold, and warmed themselves. Peter, too, stood with them near the fire and warmed himself as I am doing. A woman, seeing him, said: 'He was with Jesus, too'—that is as much as to say that he, too, should be taken to be questioned. And all the labourers that were standing near the fire must have looked sourly and suspiciously at him, because he was confused and said: 'I don't know Him.' A little while after again someone recognized him as one of Jesus' disciples and said: 'Thou, too, art one of them,' but again he denied it. And for the third time someone turned to him: 'Why, did I not see thee with Him in the garden to-day?' For the third time he denied it. And immediately after that time the cock crowed, and Peter, looking from afar off at Jesus, remembered the words He had said to him in the evening.... He remembered, he came to himself, went out of the yard and wept bitterly—bitterly. In the Gospel it is written: 'He went out and wept bitterly.' I imagine it: the still, still, dark, dark garden, and in the stillness, faintly audible, smothered sobbing...."

The student sighed and sank into thought. Still smiling, Vasilisa suddenly gave a gulp, big tears flowed freely down her cheeks, and she screened her face from the fire with her sleeve as though ashamed of her tears, and Lukerya, staring immovably at the student, flushed crimson, and her expression became strained and heavy like that of someone enduring intense pain.

The labourers came back from the river, and one of them riding a horse was quite near, and the light from the fire quivered upon him. The student said good-night to the widows and went on. And again the darkness was about him and his fingers began to be numb. A cruel wind was blowing, winter really had come back and it did not feel as though Easter would be the day after to-morrow.

Now the student was thinking about Vasilisa: since she had shed tears all that had happened to Peter the night before the Crucifixion must have some relation to her. . . .

He looked round. The solitary light was still gleaming in the darkness and no figures could be seen near it now. The student thought again that if Vasilisa had shed tears, and her daughter had been troubled, it was evident that what he had just been telling them about, which had happened nineteen centuries ago, had a relation to the present—to both women, to the desolate village, to himself, to all people. The old woman had wept, not because he could tell the story touchingly, but because Peter was near to her, because her whole being was interested in what was passing in Peter's soul.

And joy suddenly stirred in his soul, and he even stopped for a minute to take breath. "The past," he thought, "is linked with the present by an unbroken chain of events flowing one out of another." And it seemed to him that he had just seen both ends of that chain; that when he touched one end the other quivered.

When he crossed the river by the ferry boat and afterwards, mounting the hill, looked at his village and towards the west where the cold purple sunset lay a narrow streak of light, he thought that truth and beauty which had guided human life there in the garden and in the yard of the high priest had continued without interruption to this day, and had evidently always been the chief thing in human life and in all earthly life, indeed; and the feeling of youth, health, vigour—he was only twenty-two—and the inexpressible sweet expectation of happiness, of unknown mysterious happiness, took possession of him little by little, and life seemed to him enchanting, marvellous, and full of lofty meaning.

The Teacher of Literature

I

There was the thud of horses' hoofs on the wooden floor; they brought out of the stable the black horse, Count Nulin; then the white, Giant; then his sister Maika. They were all magnificent, expensive horses. Old Shelestov saddled Giant and said, addressing his daughter Masha:

"Well, Marie Godefroi, come, get on! Hopla!"

Masha Shelestov was the youngest of the family; she was eighteen, but her family could not get used to thinking that she was not a little girl, and so they still called her Manya and Manyusa; and after there had been a circus in the town which she had eagerly visited, every one began to call her Marie Godefroi.

"Hop-la!" she cried, mounting Giant. Her sister Varya got on Maika, Nikitin on Count Nulin, the officers on their horses, and the long picturesque cavalcade, with the officers in white tunics and the ladies in their riding habits, moved at a walking pace out of the yard.

Nikitin noticed that when they were mounting the horses and afterwards riding out into the street, Masha for some reason paid attention to no one but himself. She looked anxiously at him and at Count Nulin and said:

"You must hold him all the time on the curb, Sergey Vassilitch. Don't let him shy. He's pretending."

And either because her Giant was very friendly with Count Nulin, or perhaps by chance, she rode all the time beside Nikitin, as she had done the day before, and the day before that. And he looked at her graceful little figure sitting on the proud white beast, at her delicate profile, at the chimney-pot hat, which did not suit her at all and made her look older than her age—looked at her with joy, with tenderness, with rapture; listened to her, taking in little of what she said, and thought:

"I promise on my honour, I swear to God, I won't be afraid and I'll speak to her today."

It was seven o'clock in the evening—the time when the scent of white acacia and lilac is so strong that the air and the very trees seem heavy with the fragrance. The band was already playing in the town gardens. The horses made a resounding thud on the pavement, on all sides there were sounds of laughter, talk, and the banging of gates. The soldiers they met saluted the officers, the schoolboys bowed to Nikitin, and all the people who were hurrying to the gardens to hear the band were pleased at the sight of the party. And how warm it was! How soft-looking were the clouds scattered carelessly about the sky, how kindly and comforting the shadows of the poplars and the acacias, which stretched across the street and reached as far as the balconies and second stories of the houses on the other side.

They rode on out of the town and set off at a trot along the high-road. Here there was no scent of lilac and acacia, no music of the band, but there was the fragrance of the fields, there was the green of young rye and wheat, the marmots were squeaking, the rooks were cawing. Wherever one looked it was green, with only here and there black patches of bare ground, and far away to the left in the cemetery a white streak of apple-blossom.

They passed the slaughter-houses, then the brewery, and overtook a military band hastening to the suburban gardens.

"Polyansky has a very fine horse, I don't deny that," Masha said to Nikitin, with a glance towards the officer who was riding beside Varya.

"But it has blemishes. That white patch on its left leg ought not to be there, and, look, it tosses its head. You can't train it not to now; it will toss its head till the end of its days."

Masha was as passionate a lover of horses as her father. She felt a pang when she saw other people with fine horses, and was pleased when she saw defects in them. Nikitin knew nothing about horses; it made absolutely no difference to him whether he held his horse on the bridle or on the curb, whether he trotted or galloped; he only felt that his position was strained and unnatural, and that consequently the officers who knew how to sit in their saddles must please Masha more than he could. And he was jealous of the officers.

As they rode by the suburban gardens some one suggested their going in and getting some seltzer-water. They went in. There were no trees but oaks in the gardens; they had only just come into leaf, so that through the young foliage the whole garden could still be seen with its platform, little tables, and swings, and the crows' nests were visible, looking like big hats. The party dismounted near a table and asked for seltzer-water. People they knew, walking about the garden, came up to them. Among them the army doctor in high boots, and the conductor of the band, waiting for the musicians. The doctor must have taken Nikitin for a student, for he asked:

"Have you come for the summer holidays?"

"No, I am here permanently," answered Nikitin. "I am a teacher at the school."

"You don't say so?" said the doctor, with surprise. "So young and already a teacher?"

"Young, indeed! My goodness, I'm twenty-six!"

"You have a beard and moustache, but yet one would never guess you were more than twenty-two or twenty-three. How young-looking you are!"

"What a beast!" thought Nikitin. "He, too, takes me for a whippersnapper!"

He disliked it extremely when people referred to his youth, especially in the presence of women or the schoolboys. Ever since he had come to the town as a master in the school he had detested his own youthful appearance. The schoolboys were not afraid of him, old people called him "young man," ladies preferred dancing with him to listening to his long arguments, and he would have given a great deal to be ten years older.

From the garden they went on to the Shelestovs' farm. There they stopped at the gate and asked the bailiff's wife, Praskovya, to bring some new milk. Nobody drank the milk; they all looked at one another, laughed, and galloped back. As they rode back the band was playing in the suburban garden; the sun was setting behind the cemetery, and half the sky was crimson from the sunset.

Masha again rode beside Nikitin. He wanted to tell her how passionately he loved her, but he was afraid he would be overheard by the officers and Varya, and he was silent. Masha was silent, too, and he felt why she was silent and why she was riding beside him, and was so happy that the earth, the sky, the lights of the town, the black outline of the brewery—all blended for him into something very pleasant and comforting, and it seemed to him as though Count Nulin were stepping on air and would climb up into the crimson sky.

They arrived home. The samovar was already boiling on the table, old Shelestov was sitting with his friends, officials in the Circuit Court, and as usual he was criticizing something.

"It's loutishness!" he said. "Loutishness and nothing more. Yes!"

Since Nikitin had been in love with Masha, everything at the Shelestovs' pleased him: the house, the garden, and the evening tea, and the wickerwork chairs, and the old nurse, and even the word "loutishness," which the old man was fond of using. The only thing he did not like was the number of cats and dogs and the Egyptian pigeons, who moaned disconsolately in a big cage in the verandah. There were so many house-dogs and yard-dogs that he had only learnt to recognize two of them in the course of his acquaintance with the Shelestovs: Mushka and Som. Mushka was a little mangy dog with a shaggy face, spiteful and spoiled. She hated Nikitin: when she saw him she put her head on one side, showed her teeth, and began: "Rrr . . . nga-nga-nga . . . rrr . . . !" Then she would get under his chair, and when he would try to drive her away she would go off into piercing yaps, and the family would say: "Don't be frightened. She doesn't bite. She is a good dog."

Som was a tall black dog with long legs and a tail as hard as a stick.

At dinner and tea he usually moved about under the table, and thumped on people's boots and on the legs of the table with his tail. He was a good-natured, stupid dog, but Nikitin could not endure him because he had the habit of putting his head on people's knees at dinner and messing their trousers with saliva. Nikitin had more than once tried to hit him on his head with a knife-handle, to flip him on the nose, had abused him, had complained of him, but nothing saved his trousers.

After their ride the tea, jam, rusks, and butter seemed very nice. They all drank their first glass in silence and with great relish; over the second they began an argument. It was always Varya who started the arguments at tea; she was good-looking, handsomer than Masha, and was considered the cleverest and most cultured person in the house, and she behaved with dignity and severity, as an eldest daughter should who has taken the place of her dead mother in the house. As the mistress of the house, she felt herself entitled to wear a dressing-gown in the presence of her guests, and to call the officers by their surnames; she looked on Masha as a little girl, and talked to her as though she were a schoolmistress. She used to speak of herself as an old maid—so she was certain she would marry.

Every conversation, even about the weather, she invariably turned into an argument. She had a passion for catching at words, pouncing on contradictions, quibbling over phrases. You would begin talking to her, and she would stare at you and suddenly interrupt: "Excuse me, excuse me, Petrov, the other day you said the very opposite!"

Or she would smile ironically and say: "I notice, though, you begin to advocate the principles of the secret police. I congratulate you."

If you jested or made a pun, you would hear her voice at once: "That's stale," "That's pointless." If an officer ventured on a joke, she would make a contemptuous grimace and say, "An army joke!"

And she rolled the *r* so impressively that Mushka invariably answered from under a chair, "Rrr . . . nga-nga-nga . . . !"

On this occasion at tea the argument began with Nikitin's mentioning the school examinations.

"Excuse me, Sergey Vassilitch," Varya interrupted him. "You say it's difficult for the boys. And whose fault is that, let me ask you? For instance, you set the boys in the eighth class an essay on 'Pushkin as a Psychologist.' To begin with, you shouldn't set such a difficult subject; and, secondly, Pushkin was not a psychologist. Shtchedrin now, or Dostoevsky let us say, is a different matter, but Pushkin is a great poet and nothing more."

"Shtchedrin is one thing, and Pushkin is another," Nikitin answered sulkily.

"I know you don't think much of Shtchedrin at the high school, but that's not the point. Tell me, in what sense is Pushkin a psychologist?"

"Why, do you mean to say he was not a psychologist? If you like, I'll give you examples."

And Nikitin recited several passages from "Onyegin" and then from "Boris Godunov."

"I see no psychology in that." Varya sighed. "The psychologist is the man who describes the recesses of the human soul, and that's fine poetry and nothing more."

"I know the sort of psychology you want," said Nikitin, offended. "You want some one to saw my finger with a blunt saw while I howl at the top of my voice—that's what you mean by psychology."

"That's poor! But still you haven't shown me in what sense Pushkin is a psychologist?"

When Nikitin had to argue against anything that seemed to him narrow, conventional, or something of that kind, he usually leaped up from his seat, clutched at his head with both hands, and began with a moan, running from one end of the room to another. And it was the same now: he jumped up, clutched his head in his hands, and with a moan walked round the table, then he sat down a little way off.

The officers took his part. Captain Polyansky began assuring Varya that Pushkin really was a psychologist, and to prove it quoted two lines from Lermontov; Lieutenant Gernet said that if Pushkin had not been a psychologist they would not have erected a monument to him in Moscow.

"That's loutishness!" was heard from the other end of the table. "I said as much to the governor: 'It's loutishness, your Excellency,' I said."

"I won't argue any more," cried Nikitin. "It's unending. . . . Enough! Ach, get away, you nasty dog!" he cried to Som, who laid his head and paw on his knee.

"Rrr . . . nga-nga-nga!" came from under the table.

"Admit that you are wrong!" cried Varya. "Own up!"

But some young ladies came in, and the argument dropped of itself. They all went into the drawing-room. Varya sat down at the piano and began playing dances. They danced first a waltz, then a polka, then a quadrille with a grand chain which Captain Polyansky led through all the rooms, then a waltz again.

During the dancing the old men sat in the drawing-room, smoking and looking at the young people. Among them was Shebaldin, the director of the municipal bank, who was famed for his love of literature and dramatic art. He had founded the local Musical and Dramatic Society, and took part in the performances himself, confining himself, for some reason, to playing comic footmen or to reading in a sing-song voice "The Woman who was a Sinner." His nickname in the town was "the Mummy," as he was tall, very lean and scraggy, and always had a solemn air and a fixed, lustreless eye. He was so devoted to the dramatic art that he even shaved his moustache and beard, and this made him still more like a mummy.

After the grand chain, he shuffled up to Nikitin sideways, coughed, and said:

"I had the pleasure of being present during the argument at tea. I fully share your opinion. We are of one mind, and it would be a great pleasure to me to talk to you. Have you read Lessing on the dramatic art of Hamburg?"

"No, I haven't."

Shebaldin was horrified, and waved his hands as though he had burnt his fingers, and saying nothing more, staggered back from Nikitin. Shebaldin's appearance, his question, and his surprise, struck Nikitin as funny, but he thought none the less:

"It really is awkward. I am a teacher of literature, and to this day I've not read Lessing. I must read him."

Before supper the whole company, old and young, sat down to play "fate." They took two packs of cards: one pack was dealt round to the company, the other was laid on the table face downwards.

"The one who has this card in his hand," old Shelestov began solemnly, lifting the top card of the second pack, "is fated to go into the nursery and kiss nurse."

The pleasure of kissing the nurse fell to the lot of Shebaldin. They all crowded round him, took him to the nursery, and laughing and clapping their hands, made him kiss the nurse. There was a great uproar and shouting.

"Not so ardently!" cried Shelestov with tears of laughter. "Not so ardently!"

It was Nikitin's "fate" to hear the confessions of all. He sat on a chair in the middle of the drawing-room. A shawl was brought and put over his head. The first who came to confess to him was Varya.

"I know your sins," Nikitin began, looking in the darkness at her stern profile. "Tell me, madam, how do you explain your walking with Polyansky every day? Oh, it's not for nothing she walks with an hussar!"

"That's poor," said Varya, and walked away.

Then under the shawl he saw the shine of big motionless eyes, caught the lines of a dear profile in the dark, together with a familiar, precious fragrance which reminded Nikitin of Masha's room.

"Marie Godefroi," he said, and did not know his own voice, it was so soft and tender, "what are your sins?"

Masha screwed up her eyes and put out the tip of her tongue at him, then she laughed and went away. And a minute later she was standing in the middle of the room, clapping her hands and crying:

"Supper, supper, supper!"

And they all streamed into the dining-room. At supper Varya had another argument, and this time with her father. Polyansky ate stolidly, drank red wine, and described to Nikitin how once in a winter campaign he had stood all night up to his knees in a bog; the enemy was so near that they were not allowed to speak or smoke, the night was cold and dark, a piercing wind was blowing. Nikitin listened and stole sideglances at Masha. She was gazing at him immovably, without blinking, as though she was pondering something or was lost in a reverie. . . . It was pleasure and agony to him both at once.

"Why does she look at me like that?" was the question that fretted him. "It's awkward. People may notice it. Oh, how young, how naïve she is!"

The party broke up at midnight. When Nikitin went out at the gate, a window opened on the first-floor, and Masha showed herself at it.

"Sergey Vassilitch!" she called.

"What is it?"

"I tell you what . . ." said Masha, evidently thinking of something to say. "I tell you what. . . . Polyansky said he would come in a day or two with his camera and take us all. We must meet here."

"Very well."

Masha vanished, the window was slammed, and some one immediately began playing the piano in the house.

"Well, it is a house!" thought Nikitin while he crossed the street. "A house in which there is no moaning except from Egyptian pigeons, and they only do it because they have no other means of expressing their joy!"

But the Shelestovs were not the only festive household. Nikitin had not gone two hundred paces before he heard the strains of a piano from another house. A little further he met a peasant playing the balalaika at the gate. In the gardens the band struck up a potpourri of Russian songs.

Nikitin lived nearly half a mile from the Shelestovs' in a flat of eight rooms at the rent of three hundred roubles a year, which he shared with his colleague Ippolit Ippolititch, a teacher of geography and history. When Nikitin went in this Ippolit Ippolititch, a snub-nosed, middle-aged man with a reddish beard, with a coarse, good-natured, unintellectual face like a workman's, was sitting at the table correcting his pupils' maps. He considered that the most important and necessary part of the study of geography was the drawing of maps, and of the study of history the learning of dates: he would sit for nights together correcting in blue pencil the maps drawn by the boys and girls he taught, or making chronological tables.

"What a lovely day it has been!" said Nikitin, going in to him. "I wonder at you—how can you sit indoors?"

Ippolit Ippolititch was not a talkative person; he either remained silent or talked of things which everybody knew already. Now what he answered was:

"Yes, very fine weather. It's May now; we soon shall have real summer. And summer's a very different thing from winter. In the winter you have to heat the stoves, but in summer you can keep warm without. In summer you have your window open at night and still are warm, and in winter you are cold even with the double frames in."

Nikitin had not sat at the table for more than one minute before he was bored.

"Good-night!" he said, getting up and yawning. "I wanted to tell you something romantic concerning myself, but you are—geography! If one talks to you of love, you will ask one at once, 'What was the date of the Battle of Kalka?' Confound you, with your battles and your capes in Siberia!"

"What are you cross about?"

"Why, it is vexatious!"

And vexed that he had not spoken to Masha, and that he had no one to talk to of his love, he went to his study and lay down upon the sofa. It was dark and still in the study. Lying gazing into the darkness, Nikitin for some reason began thinking how in two or three years he would go to Petersburg, how Masha would see him off at the station and would cry; in Petersburg he would get a long letter from her in which she would entreat him to come home as quickly as possible. And he would write to her.... He would begin his letter like that: "My dear little rat!"

"Yes, my dear little rat!" he said, and he laughed.

He was lying in an uncomfortable position. He put his arms under his head and put his left leg over the back of the sofa. He felt more comfortable. Meanwhile a pale light was more and more perceptible at the windows, sleepy cocks crowed in the yard. Nikitin went on thinking how he would come back from Petersburg, how Masha would meet him at the station, and with a shriek of delight would fling herself on his neck; or, better still, he would cheat her and come home by stealth late at night: the cook would open the door, then he would go on tiptoe to the bedroom, undress noiselessly, and jump into bed! And she would wake up and be overjoyed.

It was beginning to get quite light. By now there were no windows, no study. On the steps of the brewery by which they had ridden that day Masha was sitting, saying something. Then she took Nikitin by the arm and went with him to the suburban garden. There he saw the oaks and the crows' nests like hats. One of the nests rocked; out of it peeped Shebaldin, shouting loudly: "You have not read Lessing!"

Nikitin shuddered all over and opened his eyes. Ippolit Ippolititch was standing before the sofa, and throwing back his head, was putting on his cravat.

"Get up; it's time for school," he said. "You shouldn't sleep in your clothes; it spoils your clothes. You should sleep in your bed, undressed."

And as usual he began slowly and emphatically saying what everybody knew.

Nikitin's first lesson was on Russian language in the second class. When at nine o'clock punctually he went into the classroom, he saw written on the blackboard two large letters—*M. S.* That, no doubt, meant Masha Shelestov.

"They've scented it out already, the rascals . . ." thought Nikitin. "How is it they know everything?"

The second lesson was in the fifth class. And there two letters, *M. S.*, were written on the blackboard; and when he went out of the classroom at the end of the lesson, he heard the shout behind him as though from a theatre gallery:

"Hurrah for Masha Shelestov!"

His head was heavy from sleeping in his clothes, his limbs were weighted down with inertia. The boys, who were expecting every day to break up before the examinations, did nothing, were restless, and so bored that they got into mischief. Nikitin, too, was restless, did not notice their pranks, and was continually going to the window. He could see the street brilliantly lighted up with the sun; above the houses the blue limpid sky, the birds, and far, far away, beyond the gardens and the houses, vast indefinite distance, the forests in the blue haze, the smoke from a passing train. . . .

Here two officers in white tunics, playing with their whips, passed in the street in the shade of the acacias. Here a lot of Jews, with grey beards, and caps on, drove past in a waggonette. . . . The governess walked by with the director's granddaughter. Some ran by in the company of two other dogs. . . . And then Varya, wearing a simple grey dress and red stockings, carrying the "Vyestnik Evropi" in her hand, passed by. She must have been to the town library. . . .

And it would be a long time before lessons were over at three o'clock! And after school he could not go home nor to the Shelestovs', but must go to give a lesson at Wolf's. This Wolf, a wealthy Jew who had turned Lutheran, did not send his children to the high school, but had them taught at home by the high-school masters, and paid five roubles a lesson.

He was bored, bored, bored.

At three o'clock he went to Wolf's and spent there, as it seemed to him, an eternity. He left there at five o'clock, and before seven he had to be at the high school again to a meeting of the masters—to draw up the plan for the *viva voce* examination of the fourth and sixth classes.

When late in the evening he left the high school and went to the Shelestovs', his heart was beating and his face was flushed. A month before, even a week before, he had, every time that he made up his mind to speak to her, prepared a whole speech, with an introduction and a conclusion. Now he had not one word ready; everything was in a muddle in his head, and all he knew was that today he would *certainly* declare himself, and that it was utterly impossible to wait any longer.

"I will ask her to come to the garden," he thought; "we'll walk about a little and I'll speak."

There was not a soul in the hall; he went into the dining-room and then into the drawing-room. . . . There was no one there either. He could hear Varya arguing with some one upstairs and the clink of the dressmaker's scissors in the nursery.

There was a little room in the house which had three names: the little room, the passage room, and the dark room. There was a big cupboard in it where they kept medicines, gunpowder, and their hunting gear. Leading from this room to the first floor was a narrow wooden staircase where cats were always asleep. There were two doors in it—one leading to the nursery, one to the drawing-room. When Nikitin went into this room to go upstairs, the door from the nursery opened and shut with such a bang that it made the stairs and the cupboard tremble; Masha, in a dark dress, ran in with a piece of blue material in her hand, and, not noticing Nikitin, darted towards the stairs.

"Stay . . ." said Nikitin, stopping her. "Good-evening, Godefroi. . . . Allow me. . . ."

He gasped, he did not know what to say; with one hand he held her hand and with the other the blue material. And she was half frightened, half surprised, and looked at him with big eyes.

"Allow me . . ." Nikitin went on, afraid she would go away. "There's something I must say to you. . . . Only . . . it's inconvenient here. I cannot, I am incapable. . . . Understand, Godefroi, I can't—that's all. . . ."

The blue material slipped on to the floor, and Nikitin took Masha by the other hand. She turned pale, moved her lips, then stepped back from Nikitin and found herself in the corner between the wall and the cupboard.

"On my honour, I assure you . . ." he said softly. "Masha, on my honour. . . ."

She threw back her head and he kissed her lips, and that the kiss might last longer he put his fingers to her cheeks; and it somehow happened that he found himself in the corner between the cupboard and the wall, and she put her arms round his neck and pressed her head against his chin.

Then they both ran into the garden. The Shelestovs had a garden of nine acres. There were about twenty old maples and lime-trees in it; there was one fir-tree, and all the rest were fruit-trees: cherries, apples, pears, horse-chestnuts, silvery olive-trees. . . . There were heaps of flowers, too.

Nikitin and Masha ran along the avenues in silence, laughed, asked each other from time to time disconnected questions which they did not answer. A crescent moon was shining over the garden, and drowsy tulips and irises were stretching up from the dark grass in its faint light, as though entreating for words of love for them, too.

When Nikitin and Masha went back to the house, the officers and the young ladies were already assembled and dancing the mazurka. Again Polyansky led the grand chain through all the rooms, again after dancing they played "fate." Before supper, when the visitors had gone into the dining-room, Masha, left alone with Nikitin, pressed close to him and said:

"You must speak to papa and Varya yourself; I am ashamed."

After supper he talked to the old father. After listening to him, Shelestov thought a little and said:

"I am very grateful for the honour you do me and my daughter, but let me speak to you as a friend. I will speak to you, not as a father, but as one gentleman to another. Tell me, why do you want to be married so young? Only peasants are married so young, and that, of course, is loutishness. But why should you? Where's the satisfaction of putting on the fetters at your age?"

"I am not young!" said Nikitin, offended. "I am in my twenty-seventh year."

"Papa, the farrier has come!" cried Varya from the other room.

And the conversation broke off. Varya, Masha, and Polyansky saw Nikitin home. When they reached his gate, Varya said:

"Why is it your mysterious Metropolit Metropolititch never shows himself anywhere? He might come and see us."

The mysterious Ippolit Ippolititch was sitting on his bed, taking off his trousers, when Nikitin went in to him.

"Don't go to bed, my dear fellow," said Nikitin breathlessly. "Stop a minute; don't go to bed!"

Ippolit Ippolititch put on his trousers hurriedly and asked in a flutter:

"What is it?"

"I am going to be married."

Nikitin sat down beside his companion, and looking at him wonderingly, as though surprised at himself, said:

"Only fancy, I am going to be married! To Masha Shelestov! I made an offer today."

"Well? She seems a good sort of girl. Only she is very young."

"Yes, she is young," sighed Nikitin, and shrugged his shoulders with a careworn air. "Very, very young!"

"She was my pupil at the high school. I know her. She wasn't bad at geography, but she was no good at history. And she was inattentive in class, too."

Nikitin for some reason felt suddenly sorry for his companion, and longed to say something kind and comforting to him.

"My dear fellow, why don't you get married?" he asked. "Why don't you marry Varya, for instance? She is a splendid, first-rate girl! It's true she is very fond of arguing, but a heart . . . what a heart! She was just asking about you. Marry her, my dear boy! Eh?"

He knew perfectly well that Varya would not marry this dull, snub-nosed man, but still persuaded him to marry her—why?

"Marriage is a serious step," said Ippolit Ippolititch after a moment's thought. "One has to look at it all round and weigh things thoroughly; it's not to be done rashly. Prudence is always a good thing, and especially in marriage, when a man, ceasing to be a bachelor, begins a new life."

And he talked of what every one has known for ages. Nikitin did not stay to listen, said good-night, and went to his own room. He undressed quickly and quickly got into bed, in order to be able to think the sooner of his happiness, of Masha, of the future; he smiled, then suddenly recalled that he had not read Lessing.

"I must read him," he thought. "Though, after all, why should I? Bother him!"

And exhausted by his happiness, he fell asleep at once and went on smiling till the morning.

He dreamed of the thud of horses' hoofs on a wooden floor; he dreamed of the black horse Count Nulin, then of the white Giant and its sister Maika, being led out of the stable.

II

"It was very crowded and noisy in the church, and once some one cried out, and the head priest, who was marrying Masha and me, looked through his spectacles at the crowd, and said severely: 'Don't move about the church, and don't make a noise, but stand quietly and pray. You should have the fear of God in your hearts.'

"My best men were two of my colleagues, and Masha's best men were Captain Polyansky and Lieutenant Gernet. The bishop's choir sang superbly. The sputtering of the candles, the brilliant light, the gorgeous dresses, the officers, the numbers of gay, happy faces, and a special ethereal look in Masha, everything together—the surroundings and the words of the wedding prayers—moved me to tears and filled me with triumph. I thought how my life had blossomed, how poetically it was shaping itself! Two years ago I was still a student, I was living in cheap furnished rooms, without money, without relations, and, as I fancied then, with nothing to look forward to. Now I am a teacher in the high school in one of the best provincial towns, with a secure income, loved, spoiled. It is for my sake, I thought, this crowd is collected, for my sake three candelabra have been lighted, the deacon is booming, the choir is doing its best; and it's for my sake that this young creature, whom I soon shall call my wife, is so young, so elegant, and so joyful. I recalled our first meetings, our rides into the country, my declaration of love and the weather, which, as though expressly, was so exquisitely fine all the summer; and the happiness which at one time in my old rooms seemed to me possible only in novels and stories, I was now experiencing in reality—I was now, as it were, holding it in my hands.

"After the ceremony they all crowded in disorder round Masha and me, expressed their genuine pleasure, congratulated us and wished us joy. The brigadier-general, an old man of seventy, confined himself to congratulating Masha, and said to her in a squeaky, aged voice, so loud that it could be heard all over the church:

" 'I hope that even after you are married you may remain the rose you are now, my dear.'

"The officers, the director, and all the teachers smiled from politeness, and I was conscious of an agreeable artificial smile on my face, too. Dear Ippolit Ippolititch, the teacher of history and geography, who always says what every one has heard before, pressed my hand warmly and said with feeling:

" 'Hitherto you have been unmarried and have lived alone, and now you are married and no longer single.'

"From the church we went to a two-storied house which I am receiving as part of the dowry. Besides that house Masha is bringing me twenty thousand roubles, as well as a piece of waste land with a shanty on it, where I am told there are numbers of hens and ducks which are not looked after and are turning wild. When I got home from the church, I stretched myself at full length on the low sofa in my new study and began to smoke; I felt snug, cosy, and comfortable, as I never had in my life before. And meanwhile the wedding party were shouting 'Hurrah!' while a wretched band in the hall played flourishes and all sorts of trash. Varya, Masha's sister, ran into the study with a wineglass in her hand, and with a queer, strained expression, as though her mouth were full of water; apparently she had meant to go on further, but she suddenly burst out laughing and sobbing, and the wineglass crashed on the floor. We took her by the arms and led her away.

" 'Nobody can understand!' she muttered afterwards, lying on the old nurse's bed in a back room. 'Nobody, nobody! My God, nobody can understand!'

"But every one understood very well that she was four years older than her sister Masha, and still unmarried, and that she was crying, not from envy, but from the melancholy consciousness that her time was passing, and perhaps had passed. When they danced the quadrille, she was back in the drawing-room with a tear-stained and heavily powdered face, and I saw Captain Polyansky holding a plate of ice before her while she ate it with a spoon.

"It is past five o'clock in the morning. I took up my diary to describe my complete and perfect happiness, and thought I would write a good six pages, and read it tomorrow to Masha; but, strange to say, everything is muddled in my head and as misty as a dream, and I can remember vividly nothing but that episode with Varya, and I want to write, 'Poor Varya!' I could go on sitting here and writing 'Poor Varya!' By the way, the trees have begun rustling; it will rain. The crows are cawing, and my Masha, who has just gone to sleep, has for some reason a sorrowful face."

For a long while afterwards Nikitin did not write his diary. At the beginning of August he had the school examinations, and after the fifteenth the classes began. As a rule he set off for school before nine in the morning, and before ten o'clock he was looking at his watch and pining for his Masha and his new house. In the lower forms he would set some boy to dictate, and while the boys were writing, would sit in the window with his eyes shut, dreaming; whether he dreamed of the future or recalled the past, everything seemed to him equally delightful, like a fairy tale. In the senior classes they were reading aloud Gogol or Pushkin's prose works, and that made him sleepy; people, trees, fields, horses, rose before his imagination, and he would say with a sigh, as though fascinated by the author:

"How lovely!"

At the midday recess Masha used to send him lunch in a snow-white napkin, and he would eat it slowly, with pauses, to prolong the enjoyment of it; and Ippolit Ippolititch, whose lunch as a rule consisted of nothing but bread, looked at him with respect and envy, and gave expression to some familiar fact, such as:

"Men cannot live without food."

After school Nikitin went straight to give his private lessons, and when at last by six o'clock he got home, he felt excited and anxious, as though he had been away for a year. He would run upstairs breathless, find Masha, throw his arms round her, and kiss her and swear that he loved her, that he could not live without her, declare that he had missed her fearfully, and ask her in trepidation how she was and why she looked so depressed. Then they would dine together. After dinner he would lie on the sofa in his study and smoke, while she sat beside him and talked in a low voice.

His happiest days now were Sundays and holidays, when he was at home from morning till evening. On those days he took part in the naïve but extraordinarily pleasant life which reminded him of a pastoral idyl. He was never weary of watching how his sensible and practical Masha was arranging her nest, and anxious to show that he was of some use in the house, he would do something useless—for instance, bring the chaise out of the stable and look at it from every side. Masha had installed a regular dairy with three cows, and in her cellar she had many jugs of milk and pots of sour cream, and she kept it all for butter. Sometimes, by way of a joke, Nikitin would ask her for a glass of milk, and she would be quite upset because it was against her rules; but he would laugh and throw his arms round her, saying:

"There, there; I was joking, my darling! I was joking!"

Or he would laugh at her strictness when, finding in the cupboard some stale bit of cheese or sausage as hard as a stone, she would say seriously:

"They will eat that in the kitchen."

He would observe that such a scrap was only fit for a mousetrap, and she would reply warmly that men knew nothing about housekeeping, and that it was just the same to the servants if you were to send down a hundredweight of savouries to the kitchen. He would agree, and embrace her enthusiastically. Everything that was just in what she said seemed to him extraordinary and amazing; and what did not fit in with his convictions seemed to him naïve and touching.

Sometimes he was in a philosophical mood, and he would begin to discuss some abstract subject while she listened and looked at his face with curiosity.

"I am immensely happy with you, my joy," he used to say, playing with her fingers or plaiting and unplaiting her hair. "But I don't look upon this happiness of mine as something that has come to me by chance, as though it had dropped from heaven. This happiness is a perfectly natural, consistent, logical consequence. I believe that man is the creator of his own happiness, and now I am enjoying just what I have myself created. Yes, I speak without false modesty: I have created this happiness myself and I have a right to it. You know my past. My unhappy childhood, without father or mother; my depressing youth, poverty—all this was a struggle, all this was the path by which I made my way to happiness. . . ."

In October the school sustained a heavy loss: Ippolit Ippolititch was taken ill with erysipelas on the head and died. For two days before his death he was unconscious and delirious, but even in his delirium he said nothing that was not perfectly well known to every one.

"The Volga flows into the Caspian Sea. . . . Horses eat oats and hay. . . ."

There were no lessons at the high school on the day of his funeral.

His colleagues and pupils were the coffin-bearers, and the school choir sang all the way to the grave the anthem "Holy God." Three priests, two deacons, all his pupils and the staff of the boys' high school, and the bishop's choir in their best kaftans, took part in the procession. And passers-by who met the solemn procession, crossed themselves and said:

"God grant us all such a death."

Returning home from the cemetery much moved, Nikitin got out his diary from the table and wrote:

"We have just consigned to the tomb Ippolit Ippolititch Ryzhitsky. Peace to your ashes, modest worker! Masha, Varya, and all the women at the funeral, wept from genuine feeling, perhaps because they knew this uninteresting, humble man had never been loved by a woman. I wanted to say a warm word at my colleague's grave, but I was warned that this might displease the director, as he did not like our poor friend. I believe that this is the first day since my marriage that my heart has been heavy."

There was no other event of note in the scholastic year.

The winter was mild, with wet snow and no frost; on Epiphany Eve, for instance, the wind howled all night as though it were autumn, and water trickled off the roofs; and in the morning, at the ceremony of the blessing of the water, the police allowed no one to go on the river, because they said the ice was swelling up and looked dark. But in spite of bad weather Nikitin's life was as happy as in summer. And, indeed, he acquired another source of pleasure; he learned to play *vint.* Only one thing troubled him, moved him to anger, and seemed to prevent him from being perfectly happy: the cats and dogs which formed part of his wife's dowry. The rooms, especially in the morning, always smelt like a menagerie, and nothing could destroy the odour; the cats frequently fought with the dogs. The spiteful beast Mushka was fed a dozen times a day; she still refused to recognize Nikitin and growled at him: "Rrr . . . nga-nga-nga!"

One night in Lent he was returning home from the club where he had been playing cards. It was dark, raining, and muddy. Nikitin had an unpleasant feeling at the bottom of his heart and could not account for it. He did not know whether it was because he had lost twelve roubles at cards, or whether because one of the players, when they were settling up, had said that of course Nikitin had pots of money, with obvious reference to his wife's portion. He did not regret the twelve roubles, and there was nothing offensive in what had been said; but, still, there was the unpleasant feeling. He did not even feel a desire to go home.

"Foo, how horrid!" he said, standing still at a lamp-post.

It occurred to him that he did not regret the twelve roubles because he got them for nothing. If he had been a working man he would have known the value of every farthing, and would not have been so careless whether he lost or won. And his good-fortune had all, he reflected, come to him by chance, for nothing, and really was as superfluous for him as medicine for the healthy. If, like the vast majority of people, he had been harassed by anxiety for his daily bread, had been struggling for existence, if his back and chest had ached from work, then supper, a warm snug home, and domestic happiness, would have been the necessity, the compensation, the crown of his life; as it was, all this had a strange, indefinite significance for him.

"Foo, how horrid!" he repeated, knowing perfectly well that these reflections were in themselves a bad sign.

When he got home Masha was in bed: she was breathing evenly and smiling, and was evidently sleeping with great enjoyment. Near her the white cat lay curled up, purring. While Nikitin lit the candle and lighted his cigarette, Masha woke up and greedily drank a glass of water.

"I ate too many sweets," she said, and laughed. "Have you been home?" she asked after a pause.

"No."

Nikitin knew already that Captain Polyansky, on whom Varya had been building great hopes of late, was being transferred to one of the western provinces, and was already making his farewell visits in the town, and so it was depressing at his father-in-law's.

"Varya looked in this evening," said Masha, sitting up. "She did not say anything, but one could see from her face how wretched she is, poor darling! I can't bear Polyansky. He is fat and bloated, and when he walks or dances his cheeks shake. . . . He is not a man I would choose. But, still, I did think he was a decent person."

"I think he is a decent person now," said Nikitin.

"Then why has he treated Varya so badly?"

"Why badly?" asked Nikitin, beginning to feel irritation against the white cat, who was stretching and arching its back. "As far as I know, he has made no proposal and has given her no promises."

"Then why was he so often at the house? If he didn't mean to marry her, he oughtn't to have come."

Nikitin put out the candle and got into bed. But he felt disinclined to lie down and to sleep. He felt as though his head were immense and empty as a barn, and that new, peculiar thoughts were wandering about in it like tall shadows. He thought that, apart from the soft light of the ikon lamp, that beamed upon their quiet domestic happiness, that apart from this little world in which he and this cat lived so peacefully and happily, there was another world. . . . And he had a passionate, poignant longing to be in that other world, to work himself at some factory or big workshop, to address big audiences, to write, to publish, to raise a stir, to exhaust himself, to suffer. . . . He wanted something that would engross him till he forgot himself, ceased to care for the personal happiness which yielded him only sensations so monotonous. And suddenly there rose vividly before his imagination the figure of Shebaldin with his clean-shaven face, saying to him with horror: "You haven't even read Lessing! You are quite behind the times! How you have gone to seed!"

Masha woke up and again drank some water. He glanced at her neck, at her plump shoulders and throat, and remembered the word the brigadier-general had used in church—"rose."

"Rose," he muttered, and laughed.

His laugh was answered by a sleepy growl from Mushka under the bed: "Rrr . . . nga-nga-nga . . . !"

A heavy anger sank like a cold weight on his heart, and he felt tempted to say something rude to Masha, and even to jump up and hit her; his heart began throbbing.

"So then," he asked, restraining himself, "since I went to your house, I was bound in duty to marry you?"

"Of course. You know that very well."

"That's nice." And a minute later he repeated: "That's nice."

To relieve the throbbing of his heart, and to avoid saying too much, Nikitin went to his study and lay down on the sofa, without a pillow; then he lay on the floor on the carpet.

"What nonsense it is!" he said to reassure himself. "You are a teacher, you are working in the noblest of callings. . . . What need have you of any other world? What rubbish!"

But almost immediately he told himself with conviction that he was not a real teacher, but simply a government employé, as commonplace and mediocre as the Czech who taught Greek. He had never had a vocation for teaching, he knew nothing of the theory of teaching, and never had been interested in the subject; he did not know how to treat children; he did not understand the significance of what he taught, and perhaps did not teach the right things. Poor Ippolit Ippolititch had been frankly stupid, and all the boys, as well as his colleagues, knew what he was and what to expect from him; but he, Nikitin, like the Czech, knew how to conceal his stupidity and cleverly deceived every one by pretending that, thank God, his teaching was a success. These new ideas frightened Nikitin; he rejected them, called them stupid, and believed that all this was due to his nerves, that he would laugh at himself.

And he did, in fact, by the morning laugh at himself and call himself an old woman; but it was clear to him that his peace of mind was lost, perhaps, for ever, and that in that little two-story house happiness was henceforth impossible for him. He realized that the illusion had evaporated, and that a new life of unrest and clear sight was beginning which was incompatible with peace and personal happiness.

Next day, which was Sunday, he was at the school chapel, and there met his colleagues and the director. It seemed to him that they were entirely preoccupied with concealing their ignorance and discontent with life, and he, too, to conceal his uneasiness, smiled affably and talked of trivialities. Then he went to the station and saw the mail train come in and go out, and it was agreeable to him to be alone and not to have to talk to any one.

At home he found Varya and his father-in-law, who had come to dinner. Varya's eyes were red with crying, and she complained of a headache, while Shelestov ate a great deal, saying that young men nowadays were unreliable, and that there was very little gentlemanly feeling among them.

"It's loutishness!" he said. "I shall tell him so to his face: 'It's loutishness, sir,' I shall say."

Nikitin smiled affably and helped Masha to look after their guests, but after dinner he went to his study and shut the door.

The March sun was shining brightly in at the windows and shedding its warm rays on the table. It was only the twentieth of the month, but already the cabmen were driving with wheels, and the starlings were noisy in the garden. It was just the weather in which Masha would come in, put one arm round his neck, tell him the horses were saddled or the chaise was at the door, and ask him what she should put on to keep warm. Spring was beginning as exquisitely as last spring, and it promised the same joys. . . . But Nikitin was thinking that it would be nice to take a holiday and go to Moscow, and stay at his old lodgings there. In the next room they were drinking coffee and talking of Captain Polyansky, while he tried not to listen and wrote in his diary: "Where am I, my God? I am surrounded by vulgarity and vulgarity. Wearisome, insignificant people, pots of sour cream, jugs of milk, cockroaches, stupid women. . . . There is nothing more terrible, mortifying, and distressing than vulgarity. I must escape from here, I must escape today, or I shall go out of my mind!"

At a Country House

Pavel Ilyitch Rashevitch walked up and down, stepping softly on the floor covered with little Russian plaids, and casting a long shadow on the wall and ceiling while his guest, Meier, the deputy examining magistrate, sat on the sofa with one leg drawn up under him smoking and listening. The clock already pointed to eleven, and there were sounds of the table being laid in the room next to the study.

"Say what you like," Rashevitch was saying, "from the standpoint of fraternity, equality, and the rest of it, Mitka, the swineherd, is perhaps a man the same as Goethe and Frederick the Great; but take your stand on a scientific basis, have the courage to look facts in the face, and it will be obvious to you that blue blood is not a mere prejudice, that it is not a feminine invention. Blue blood, my dear fellow, has an historical justification, and to refuse to recognize it is, to my thinking, as strange as to refuse to recognize the antlers on a stag. One must reckon with facts! You are a law student and have confined your attention to the humane studies, and you can still flatter yourself with illusions of equality, fraternity, and so on; I am an incorrigible Darwinian, and for me words such as lineage, aristocracy, noble blood, are not empty sounds."

Rashevitch was roused and spoke with feeling. His eyes sparkled, his pince-nez would not stay on his nose, he kept nervously shrugging his shoulders and blinking, and at the word "Darwinian" he looked jauntily in the looking-glass and combed his grey beard with both hands. He was wearing a very short and shabby reefer jacket and narrow trousers; the rapidity of his movements, his jaunty air, and his abbreviated jacket all seemed out of keeping with him, and his big comely head, with long hair suggestive of a bishop or a veteran poet, seemed to have been fixed on to the body of a tall, lanky, affected youth. When he stood with his legs wide apart, his long shadow looked like a pair of scissors.

He was fond of talking, and he always fancied that he was saying something new and original. In the presence of Meier he was conscious of an unusual flow of spirits and rush of ideas. He found the examining magistrate sympathetic, and was stimulated by his youth, his health, his good manners, his dignity, and, above all, by his cordial attitude to himself and his family. Rashevitch was not a favourite with his acquaintances; as a rule they fought shy of him, and, as he knew, declared that he had driven his wife into her grave with his talking, and they called him, behind his back, a spiteful creature and a toad. Meier, a man new to the district and unprejudiced, visited him often and readily and had even been known to say that Rashevitch and his daughters were the only people in the district with whom he felt as much at home as with his own people. Rashevitch liked him too, because he was a young man who might be a good match for his elder daughter, Genya.

And now, enjoying his ideas and the sound of his own voice, and looking with pleasure at the plump but well-proportioned, neatly cropped, correct Meier, Rashevitch dreamed of how he would arrange his daughter's marriage with a good man, and then how all his worries over the estate would pass to his son-in-law. Hateful worries! The interest owing to the bank had not been paid for the last two quarters, and fines and arrears of all sorts had mounted up to more than two thousand.

"To my mind there can be no doubt," Rashevitch went on, growing more and more enthusiastic, "that if a Richard Cœur-de-Lion, or Frederick Barbarossa, for instance, is brave and noble those qualities will pass by heredity to his son, together with the convolutions and bumps of the brain, and if that courage and nobility of soul are preserved in the son by means of education and exercise, and if he marries a princess who is also noble and brave, those qualities will be transmitted to his grandson, and so on, until they become a generic characteristic and pass organically into the flesh and blood. Thanks to a strict sexual selection, to the fact that high-born families have instinctively guarded themselves against marriage with their inferiors, and young men of high rank have not married just anybody, lofty, spiritual qualities have been transmitted from generation to generation in their full purity, have been preserved, and as time goes on have, through exercise, become more exalted and lofty. For the fact that there is good in humanity we are indebted to nature, to the normal, natural, consistent order of things, which has throughout the ages scrupulously segregated blue blood from plebeian. Yes, my dear boy, no low lout, no cook's son has given us literature, science, art, law, conceptions of honour and duty. . . . For all these things mankind is indebted exclusively to the aristocracy, and from that point of view, the point of view of natural history, an inferior Sobakevitch by the very fact of his blue blood is superior and more useful than the very best merchant, even though the latter may have built fifteen museums. Say what you like! And when I refuse to shake hands with a low lout or a cook's son, or to let him sit down to table with me, by that very act I am safeguarding what is the best thing on earth, and am carrying out one of Mother Nature's finest designs for leading us up to perfection. . . ."

Rashevitch stood still, combing his beard with both hands; his shadow, too, stood still on the wall, looking like a pair of scissors.

"Take Mother-Russia now," he went on, thrusting his hands in his pockets and standing first on his heels and then on his toes. "Who are her best people? Take our first-rate painters, writers, composers. . . . Who are they? They were all of aristocratic origin. Pushkin, Lermontov, Turgenev, Gontcharov, Tolstoy, they were not sexton's children."

"Gontcharov was a merchant," said Meier.

"Well, the exception only proves the rule. Besides, Gontcharov's genius is quite open to dispute. But let us drop names and turn to facts. What would you say, my good sir, for instance, to this eloquent fact:

when one of the mob forces his way where he has not been permitted before, into society, into the world of learning, of literature, into the Zemstvo or the law courts, observe, Nature herself, first of all, champions the higher rights of humanity, and is the first to wage war on the rabble. As soon as the plebeian forces himself into a place he is not fit for he begins to ail, to go into consumption, to go out of his mind, and to degenerate, and nowhere do we find so many puny, neurotic wrecks, consumptives, and starvelings of all sorts as among these darlings. They die like flies in autumn. If it were not for this providential degeneration there would not have been a stone left standing of our civilization, the rabble would have demolished everything. Tell me, if you please, what has the inroad of the barbarians given us so far? What has the rabble brought with it?" Rashevitch assumed a mysterious, frightened expression, and went on: "Never has literature and learning been at such low ebb among us as now. The men of to-day, my good sir, have neither ideas nor ideals, and all their sayings and doings are permeated by one spirit—to get all they can and to strip someone to his last thread. All these men of to-day who give themselves out as honest and progressive people can be bought at a rouble a piece, and the distinguishing mark of the 'intellectual' of to-day is that you have to keep strict watch over your pocket when you talk to him, or else he will run off with your purse." Rashevitch winked and burst out laughing. "Upon my soul, he will!" he said, in a thin, gleeful voice. "And morals! What of their morals?" Rashevitch looked round towards the door. "No one is surprised nowadays when a wife robs and leaves her husband. What's that, a trifle! Nowadays, my dear boy, a chit of a girl of twelve is scheming to get a lover, and all these amateur theatricals and literary evenings are only invented to make it easier to get a rich merchant to take a girl on as his mistress. . . . Mothers sell their daughters, and people make no bones about asking a husband at what price he sells his wife, and one can haggle over the bargain, you know, my dear. . . ."

Meier, who had been sitting motionless and silent all the time, suddenly got up from the sofa and looked at his watch.

"I beg your pardon, Pavel Ilyitch," he said, "it is time for me to be going."

But Pavel Ilyitch, who had not finished his remarks, put his arm round him and, forcibly reseating him on the sofa, vowed that he would not let him go without supper. And again Meier sat and listened, but he looked at Rashevitch with perplexity and uneasiness, as though he were only now beginning to understand him. Patches of red came into his face. And when at last a maidservant came in to tell them that the young ladies asked them to go to supper, he gave a sigh of relief and was the first to walk out of the study.

At the table in the next room were Rashevitch's daughters, Genya and Iraida, girls of four-and-twenty and two-and-twenty respectively, both very pale, with black eyes, and exactly the same height. Genya had her hair down, and Iraida had hers done up high on her head. Before eating anything they each drank a wineglassful of bitter liqueur, with an air as though they had drunk it by accident for the first time in their lives and both were overcome with confusion and burst out laughing.

"Don't be naughty, girls," said Rashevitch.

Genya and Iraida talked French with each other, and Russian with their father and their visitor. Interrupting one another, and mixing up French words with Russian, they began rapidly describing how just at this time in August, in previous years, they had set off to the boarding school and what fun it had been. Now there was nowhere to go, and they had to stay at their home in the country, summer and winter without change. Such dreariness!

"Don't be naughty, girls," Rashevitch said again.

He wanted to be talking himself. If other people talked in his presence, he suffered from a feeling like jealousy.

"So that's how it is, my dear boy," he began, looking affectionately at Meier. "In the simplicity and goodness of our hearts, and from fear of being suspected of being behind the times, we fraternize with, excuse me, all sorts of riff-raff, we preach fraternity and equality with money-lenders and innkeepers; but if we would only think, we should see how criminal that good-nature is. We have brought things to such a pass, that the fate of civilization is hanging on a hair. My dear fellow, what our forefathers gained in the course of ages will be to-morrow, if not to-day, outraged and destroyed by these modern Huns. . . ."

After supper they all went into the drawing-room. Genya and Iraida lighted the candles on the piano, got out their music. . . . But their father still went on talking, and there was no telling when he would leave off. They looked with misery and vexation at their egoist-father, to whom the pleasure of chattering and displaying his intelligence was evidently more precious and important than his daughters' happiness. Meier, the only young man who ever came to their house, came—they knew—for the sake of their charming, feminine society, but the irrepressible old man had taken possession of him, and would not let him move a step away.

"Just as the knights of the west repelled the invasions of the Mongols, so we, before it is too late, ought to unite and strike together against our foe," Rashevitch went on in the tone of a preacher, holding up his right hand. "May I appear to the riff-raff not as Pavel Ilyitch, but as a mighty, menacing Richard Cœur-de-Lion. Let us give up sloppy sentimentality; enough of it! Let us all make a compact, that as soon as a plebeian comes near us we fling some careless phrase straight in his ugly face: 'Paws off! Go back to your kennel, you cur!' straight in his ugly face," Rashevitch went on gleefully, flicking his crooked finger in front of him. "In his ugly face!"

"I can't do that," Meier brought out, turning away.

"Why not?" Rashevitch answered briskly, anticipating a prolonged and interesting argument. "Why not?"

"Because I am of the artisan class myself!"

As he said this Meier turned crimson, and his neck seemed to swell, and tears actually gleamed in his eyes.

"My father was a simple workman," he said, in a rough, jerky voice, "but I see no harm in that."

Rashevitch was fearfully confused. Dumb-foundered, as though he had been caught in the act of a crime, he gazed helplessly at Meier, and did not know what to say. Genya and Iraida flushed crimson, and bent over their music; they were ashamed of their tactless father. A minute passed in silence, and there was a feeling of unbearable discomfort, when all at once with a sort of painful stiffness and inappropriateness, there sounded in the air the words:

"Yes, I am of the artisan class, and I am proud of it!"

Thereupon Meier, stumbling awkwardly among the furniture, took his leave, and walked rapidly into the hall, though his carriage was not yet at the door.

"You'll have a dark drive to-night," Rashevitch muttered, following him. "The moon does not rise till late to-night."

They stood together on the steps in the dark, and waited for the horses to be brought. It was cool.

"There's a falling star," said Meier, wrapping himself in his overcoat.

"There are a great many in August."

When the horses were at the door, Rashevitch gazed intently at the sky, and said with a sigh:

"A phenomenon worthy of the pen of Flammarion. . . ."

After seeing his visitor off, he walked up and down the garden, gesticulating in the darkness, reluctant to believe that such a queer, stupid misunderstanding had only just occurred. He was ashamed and vexed with himself. In the first place it had been extremely incautious and tactless on his part to raise the damnable subject of blue blood, without finding out beforehand what his visitor's position was. Something of the same sort had happened to him before; he had, on one occasion in a railway carriage, begun abusing the Germans, and it had afterwards appeared that all the persons he had been conversing with were German. In the second place he felt that Meier would never come and see him again. These intellectuals who have risen from the people are morbidly sensitive, obstinate and slow to forgive.

"It's bad, it's bad," muttered Rashevitch, spitting; he had a feeling of discomfort and loathing as though he had eaten soap. "Ah, it's bad!"

He could see from the garden, through the drawing-room window, Genya by the piano, very pale, and looking scared, with her hair down. She was talking very, very rapidly. . . . Iraida was walking up and down the room, lost in thought; but now she, too, began talking rapidly with her face full of indignation. They were both talking at once. Rashevitch could not hear a word, but he guessed what they were talking about. Genya was probably complaining that her father drove away every decent person from the house with his talk, and to-day he had driven away from them their one acquaintance, perhaps a suitor, and now the poor young man would not have one place in the whole district where he could find rest for his soul. And judging by the despairing way in which she threw up her arms, Iraida was talking probably on the subject of their dreary existence, their wasted youth. . . .

When he reached his own room, Rashevitch sat down on his bed and began to undress. He felt oppressed, and he was still haunted by the same feeling as though he had eaten soap. He was ashamed. As he undressed he looked at his long, sinewy, elderly legs, and remembered that in the district they called him the "toad," and after every long conversation he always felt ashamed. Somehow or other, by some fatality, it always happened that he began mildly, amicably, with good intentions, calling himself an old student, an idealist, a Quixote, but without being himself aware of it, gradually passed into abuse and slander, and what was most surprising, with perfect sincerity criticized science, art and morals, though he had not read a book for the last twenty years, had been nowhere farther than their provincial town, and did not really know what was going on in the world. If he sat down to write anything, if it were only a letter of congratulation, there would somehow be abuse in the letter. And all this was strange, because in reality he was a man of feeling, given to tears. Could he be possessed by some devil which hated and slandered in him, apart from his own will?

"It's bad," he sighed, as he lay down under the quilt. "It's bad."

His daughters did not sleep either. There was a sound of laughter and screaming, as though someone was being pursued; it was Genya in hysterics. A little later Iraida was sobbing too. A maidservant ran barefoot up and down the passage several times. . . .

"What a business! Good Lord! . . ." muttered Rashevitch, sighing and tossing from side to side. "It's bad."

He had a nightmare. He dreamt he was standing naked, as tall as a giraffe, in the middle of the room, and saying, as he flicked his finger before him:

"In his ugly face! his ugly face! his ugly face!"

He woke up in a fright, and first of all remembered that a misunderstanding had happened in the evening, and that Meier would certainly not come again. He remembered, too, that he had to pay the interest at the bank, to find husbands for his daughters, that one must have food and drink, and close at hand were illness, old age, unpleasantnesses, that soon it would be winter, and that there was no wood. . . .

It was past nine o'clock in the morning. Rashevitch slowly dressed, drank his tea and ate two hunks of bread and butter. His daughters did not come down to breakfast; they did not want to meet him, and that wounded him. He lay down on his sofa in his study, then sat down to his table and began writing a letter to his daughters. His hand shook and his eyes smarted. He wrote that he was old, and no use to anyone and that nobody loved him, and he begged his daughters to forget him, and when he died to bury him in a plain, deal coffin without ceremony, or to send his body to Harkov to the dissecting theatre. He felt that every line he wrote reeked of malice and affectation, but he could not stop, and went on writing and writing.

"The toad!" he suddenly heard from the next room; it was the voice of his elder daughter, a voice with a hiss of indignation. "The toad!"

"The toad!" the younger one repeated like an echo. "The toad!"

The Head-Gardener's Story

A sale of flowers was taking place in Count N.'s greenhouses. The purchasers were few in number—a landowner who was a neighbor of mine, a young timber-merchant, and myself. While the workmen were carrying out our magnificent purchases and packing them into the carts, we sat at the entry of the greenhouse and chatted about one thing and another. It is extremely pleasant to sit in a garden on a still April morning, listening to the birds, and watching the flowers brought out into the open air and basking in the sunshine.

The head-gardener, Mihail Karlovitch, a venerable old man with a full shaven face, wearing a fur waist-coat and no coat, superintended the packing of the plants himself, but at the same time he listened to our conversation in the hope of hearing something new. He was an intelligent, very good-hearted man, respected by everyone. He was for some reason looked upon by everyone as a German, though he was in reality on his father's side Swedish, on his mother's side Russian, and attended the Orthodox church. He knew Russian, Swedish, and German. He had read a good deal in those languages, and nothing one could do gave him greater pleasure than lending him some new book or talking to him, for instance, about Ibsen.

He had his weaknesses, but they were innocent ones: he called himself the head-gardener, though there were no under-gardeners; the expression of his face was unusually dignified and haughty; he could not endure to be contradicted, and liked to be listened to with respect and attention.

"That young fellow there I can recommend to you as an awful rascal," said my neighbor, pointing to a laborer with a swarthy, gipsy face, who drove by with the water-barrel. "Last week he was tried in the town for burglary and was acquitted; they pronounced him mentally deranged, and yet look at him, he is the picture of health. Scoundrels are very often acquitted nowadays in Russia on grounds of abnormality and aberration, yet these acquittals, these unmistakable proofs of an indulgent attitude to crime, lead to no good. They demoralize the masses, the sense of justice is blunted in all as they become accustomed to seeing vice unpunished, and you know in our age one may boldly say in the words of Shakespeare that in our evil and corrupt age virtue must ask forgiveness of vice."

"That's very true," the merchant assented. "Owing to these frequent acquittals, murder and arson have become much more common. Ask the peasants."

Mihail Karlovitch turned towards us and said:

"As far as I am concerned, gentlemen, I am always delighted to meet with these verdicts of not guilty. I am not afraid for morality and justice when they say 'Not guilty,' but on the contrary I feel pleased. Even when my conscience tells me the jury have made a mistake in acquitting the criminal, even then I am triumphant. Judge for yourselves, gentlemen; if the judges and the jury have more faith in *man* than in evidence, material proofs, and speeches for the prosecution, is not that faith *in man* in itself higher than any ordinary considerations? Such faith is only attainable by those few who understand and feel Christ."

"A fine thought," I said.

"But it's not a new one. I remember a very long time ago I heard a legend on that subject. A very charming legend," said the gardener, and he smiled. "I was told it by my grandmother, my father's mother, an excellent old lady. She told me it in Swedish, and it does not sound so fine, so classical, in Russian."

But we begged him to tell it and not to be put off by the coarseness of the Russian language. Much gratified, he deliberately lighted his pipe, looked angrily at the laborers, and began:

"There settled in a certain little town a solitary, plain, elderly gentleman called Thomson or Wilson—but that does not matter; the surname is not the point. He followed an honorable profession: he was a doctor. He was always morose and unsociable, and only spoke when required by his profession. He never visited anyone, never extended his acquaintance beyond a silent bow, and lived as humbly as a hermit. The fact was, he was a learned man, and in those days learned men were not like other people. They spent their days and nights in contemplation, in reading and in healing disease, looked upon everything else as trivial, and had no time to waste a word. The inhabitants of the town understood this, and tried not to worry him with their visits and empty chatter. They were very glad that God had sent them at last a man who could heal diseases, and were proud that such a remarkable man was living in their town. 'He knows everything,' they said about him.

"But that was not enough. They ought to have also said, 'He loves everyone.' In the breast of that learned man there beat a wonderful angelic heart. Though the people of that town were strangers and not his own people, yet he loved them like children, and did not spare himself for them. He was himself ill with consumption, he had a cough, but when he was summoned to the sick he forgot his own illness, he did not spare himself and, gasping for breath, climbed up the hills however high they might be. He disregarded the sultry heat and the cold, despised thirst and hunger. He would accept no money and, strange to say, when one of his patients died, he would follow the coffin with the relations, weeping.

"And soon he became so necessary to the town that the inhabitants wondered how they could have got on before without the man. Their gratitude knew no bounds. Grown-up people and children, good and bad alike, honest men and cheats—all, in fact, respected him and knew his value. In the little town and all the surrounding neighborhood there was no man who would allow himself to do anything disagreeable to him; indeed, they would never have dreamed of it. When he came out of his lodging, he never fastened the doors or windows, in complete confidence that there was no thief who could bring himself to do him wrong. He often had in the course of his medical duties to walk along the highroads, through the forests and mountains haunted by numbers of hungry vagrants; but he felt that he was in perfect security.

"One night he was returning from a patient when robbers fell upon him in the forest, but when they recognized him, they took off their hats respectfully and offered him something to eat. When he answered that he was not hungry, they gave him a warm wrap and accompanied him as far as the town, happy that fate had given them the chance in some small way to show their gratitude to the benevolent man. Well, to be sure, my grandmother told me that even the horses and the cows and the dogs knew him and expressed their joy when they met him.

"And this man who seemed by his sanctity to have guarded himself from every evil, to whom even brigands and frenzied men wished nothing but good, was one fine morning found murdered. Covered with blood, with his skull broken, he was lying in a ravine, and his pale face wore an expression of amazement. Yes, not horror but amazement was the emotion that had been fixed upon his face when he saw the murderer before him. You can imagine the grief that overwhelmed the inhabitants of the town and the surrounding districts. All were in despair, unable to believe their eyes, wondering who could have killed the man. The judges who conducted the inquiry and examined the doctor's body said: 'Here we have all the signs of a murder, but as there is not a man in the world capable of murdering our doctor, obviously it was not a case of murder, and the combination of evidence is due to simple chance. We must suppose that in the darkness he fell into the ravine of himself and was mortally injured.'

"The whole town agreed with this opinion. The doctor was buried, and nothing more was said about a violent death. The existence of a man who could have the baseness and wickedness to kill the doctor seemed incredible. There is a limit even to wickedness, isn't there?

"All at once, would you believe it, chance led them to discovering the murderer. A vagrant who had been many times convicted, notorious for his vicious life, was seen selling for drink a snuff-box and watch that had belonged to the doctor. When he was questioned he was confused, and answered with an obvious lie. A search was made, and in his bed was found a shirt with stains of blood on the sleeves, and a doctor's lancet set in gold. What more evidence was wanted? They put the criminal in prison. The inhabitants were indignant, and at the same time said:

" 'It's incredible! It can't be so! Take care that a mistake is not made; it does happen, you know, that evidence tells a false tale.'

"At his trial the murderer obstinately denied his guilt. Everything was against him, and to be convinced of his guilt was as easy as to believe that this earth is black; but the judges seem to have gone mad: they weighed every proof ten times, looked distrustfully at the witnesses, flushed crimson and sipped water. . . . The trial began early in the morning and was only finished in the evening.

" 'Accused!' the chief judge said, addressing the murderer, 'the court has found you guilty of murdering Dr. So-and-so, and has sentenced you to. . . .'

"The chief judge meant to say 'to the death penalty,' but he dropped from his hands the paper on which the sentence was written, wiped the cold sweat from his face, and cried out:

" 'No! May God punish me if I judge wrongly, but I swear he is not guilty. I cannot admit the thought that there exists a man who would dare to murder our friend the doctor! A man could not sink so low!'

" 'There cannot be such a man!' the other judges assented.

" 'No,' the crowd cried. 'Let him go!'

"The murderer was set free to go where he chose, and not one soul blamed the court for an unjust verdict. And my grandmother used to say that for such faith in humanity God forgave the sins of all the inhabitants of that town. He rejoices when people believe that man is His image and semblance, and grieves if, forgetful of human dignity, they judge worse of men than of dogs. The sentence of acquittal may bring harm to the inhabitants of the town, but on the other hand, think of the beneficial influence upon them of that faith in man—a faith which does not remain dead, you know; it raises up generous feelings in us, and always impels us to love and respect every man. Every man! And that is important."

Mihail Karlovitch had finished. My neighbor would have urged some objection, but the head-gardener made a gesture that signified that he did not like objections; then he walked away to the carts, and, with an expression of dignity, went on looking after the packing.

Whitebrow

[Patch]

A hungry she-wolf got up to go hunting. Her cubs, all three of them, were sound asleep, huddled in a heap and keeping each other warm. She licked them and went off.

It was already March, a month of spring, but at night the trees snapped with the cold, as they do in December, and one could hardly put one's tongue out without its being nipped. The wolf-mother was in delicate health and nervous; she started at the slightest sound, and kept hoping that no one would hurt the little ones at home while she was away. The smell of the tracks of men and horses, logs, piles of faggots, and the dark road with horse-dung on it frightened her; it seemed to her that men were standing behind the trees in the darkness, and that dogs were howling somewhere beyond the forest.

She was no longer young and her scent had grown feebler, so that it sometimes happened that she took the track of a fox for that of a dog, and even at times lost her way, a thing that had never been in her youth. Owing to the weakness of her health she no longer hunted calves and big sheep as she had in old days, and kept her distance now from mares with colts; she fed on nothing but carrion; fresh meat she tasted very rarely, only in the spring when she would come upon a hare and take away her young, or make her way into a peasant's stall where there were lambs.

Some three miles from her lair there stood a winter hut on the posting road. There lived the keeper Ignat, an old man of seventy, who was always coughing and talking to himself; at night he was usually asleep, and by day he wandered about the forest with a single-barrelled gun, whistling to the hares. He must have worked among machinery in early days, for before he stood still he always shouted to himself: "Stop the machine!" and before going on: "Full speed!" He had a huge black dog of indeterminate breed, called Arapka. When it ran too far ahead he used to shout to it: "Reverse action!" Sometimes he used to sing, and as he did so staggered violently, and often fell down (the wolf thought the wind blew him over), and shouted: "Run off the rails!"

The wolf remembered that, in the summer and autumn, a ram and two ewes were pasturing near the winter hut, and when she had run by not so long ago she fancied that she had heard bleating in the stall. And now, as she got near the place, she reflected that it was already March, and, by that time, there would certainly be lambs in the stall. She was tormented by hunger, she thought with what greediness she would eat a lamb, and these thoughts made her teeth snap, and her eyes glitter in the darkness like two sparks of light.

Ignat's hut, his barn, cattle-stall, and well were surrounded by high snowdrifts. All was still. Arapka was, most likely, asleep in the barn.

The wolf clambered over a snowdrift on to the stall, and began scratching away the thatched roof with her paws and her nose. The straw was rotten and decaying, so that the wolf almost fell through; all at once a smell of warm steam, of manure, and of sheep's milk floated straight to her nostrils. Down below, a lamb, feeling the cold, bleated softly. Leaping through the hole, the wolf fell with her four paws and chest on something soft and warm, probably a sheep, and at the same moment, something in the stall suddenly began whining, barking, and going off into a shrill little yap; the sheep huddled against the wall, and the wolf, frightened, snatched the first thing her teeth fastened on, and dashed away. . . .

She ran at her utmost speed, while Arapka, who by now had scented the wolf, howled furiously, the frightened hens cackled, and Ignat, coming out into the porch, shouted: "Full speed! Blow the whistle!"

And he whistled like a steam-engine, and then shouted: "Ho-ho-ho-ho!" and all this noise was repeated by the forest echo. When, little by little, it all died away, the wolf somewhat recovered herself, and began to notice that the prey she held in her teeth and dragged along the snow was heavier and, as it were, harder than lambs usually were at that season; and it smelt somehow different, and uttered strange sounds. . . . The wolf stopped and laid her burden on the snow, to rest and begin eating it, then all at once she leapt back in disgust. It was not a lamb, but a black puppy, with a big head and long legs, of a large breed, with a white patch on his brow, like Arapka's. Judging from his manners he was a simple, ignorant, yard-dog. He licked his crushed and wounded back, and, as though nothing was the matter, wagged his tail and barked at the wolf. She growled like a dog, and ran away from him. He ran after her. She looked round and snapped her teeth. He stopped in perplexity, and, probably deciding that she was playing with him, craned his head in the direction he had come from, and went off into a shrill, gleeful bark, as though inviting his mother Arapka to play with him and the wolf.

It was already getting light, and when the wolf reached her home in the thick aspen wood, each aspen tree could be seen distinctly, and the wood-cocks were already awake, and the beautiful male birds often flew up, disturbed by the incautious gambols and barking of the puppy.

"Why does he run after me?" thought the wolf with annoyance. "I suppose he wants me to eat him."

She lived with her cubs in a shallow hole; three years before, a tall old pine tree had been torn up by the roots in a violent storm, and the hole had been formed by it. Now there were dead leaves and moss at the bottom, and around it lay bones and bullocks' horns, with which the little ones played. They were by now awake, and all three of them, very much alike, were standing in a row at the edge of their hole, looking at their returning mother, and wagging their tails. Seeing them, the puppy stopped a little way off, and stared at them for a very long time; seeing that they, too, were looking very attentively at him, he began barking angrily, as at strangers.

By now it was daylight and the sun had risen, the snow sparkled all around, but still the puppy stood a little way off and barked. The cubs sucked their mother, pressing her thin belly with their paws, while she gnawed a horse's bone, dry and white; she was tormented by hunger, her head ached from the dog's barking, and she felt inclined to fall on the uninvited guest and tear him to pieces.

At last the puppy was hoarse and exhausted; seeing they were not afraid of him, and not even attending to him, he began somewhat timidly approaching the cubs, alternately squatting down and bounding a few steps forward. Now, by daylight, it was easy to have a good look at him.... His white forehead was big, and on it was a hump such as is only seen on very stupid dogs; he had little, blue, dingy-looking eyes, and the expression of his whole face was extremely stupid. When he reached the cubs he stretched out his broad paws, laid his head upon them, and began:

"Mnya, myna . . . nga—nga—nga . . . !"

The cubs did not understand what he meant, but they wagged their tails. Then the puppy gave one of the cubs a smack on its big head with his paw. The cub, too, gave him a smack on the head. The puppy stood sideways to him, and looked at him askance, wagging his tail, then dashed off, and ran round several times on the frozen snow. The cubs ran after him, he fell on his back and kicked up his legs, and all three of them fell upon him, squealing with delight, and began biting him, not to hurt but in play. The crows sat on the high pine tree, and looked down on their struggle, and were much troubled by it. They grew noisy and merry. The sun was hot, as though it were spring; and the woodcocks, continually flitting through the pine tree that had been blown down by the storm, looked as though made of emerald in the brilliant sunshine.

As a rule, wolf-mothers train their children to hunt by giving them prey to play with; and now watching the cubs chasing the puppy over the frozen snow and struggling with him, the mother thought:

"Let them learn."

When they had played long enough, the cubs went into the hole and lay down to sleep. The puppy howled a little from hunger, then he, too, stretched out in the sunshine. And when they woke up they began playing again.

All day long, and in the evening, the wolf-mother was thinking how the lamb had bleated in the cattle-shed the night before, and how it had smelt of sheep's milk, and she kept snapping her teeth from hunger, and never left off greedily gnawing the old bone, pretending to herself that it was the lamb. The cubs sucked their mother, and the puppy, who was hungry, ran round them and sniffed at the snow.

"I'll eat him . . ." the mother-wolf decided.

She went up to him, and he licked her nose and yapped at her, thinking that she wanted to play with him. In the past she had eaten dogs, but the dog smelt very doggy, and in the delicate state of her health she could not endure the smell; she felt disgusted and walked away. . . .

Towards night it grew cold. The puppy felt depressed and went home.

When the wolf-cubs were fast asleep, their mother went out hunting again. As on the previous night she was alarmed at every sound, and she was frightened by the stumps, the logs, the dark juniper bushes, which stood out singly, and in the distance were like human beings. She ran on the ice-covered snow, keeping away from the road. . . . All at once she caught a glimpse of something dark, far away on the road. She strained her eyes and ears: yes, something really was walking on in front, she could even hear the regular thud of footsteps. Surely not a badger? Cautiously holding her breath, and keeping always to one side, she over-took the dark patch, looked round, and recognised it. It was the puppy with the white brow, going with a slow, lingering step homewards.

"If only he doesn't hinder me again," thought the wolf, and ran quickly on ahead.

But the homestead was by now near. Again she clambered on to the cattle-shed by the snowdrift. The gap she had made yesterday had been already mended with straw, and two new rafters stretched across the roof. The wolf began rapidly working with her legs and nose, looking round to see whether the puppy were coming, but the smell of the warm steam and manure had hardly reached her nose before she heard a gleeful burst of barking behind her. It was the puppy. He leapt up to the wolf on the roof, then into the hole, and, feeling himself at home in the warmth, recognising his sheep, he barked louder than ever. . . .

Arapka woke up in the barn, and, scenting a wolf, howled, the hens began cackling, and by the time Ignat appeared in the porch with his single-barrelled gun the frightened wolf was already far away.

"Fuite!" whistled Ignat. "Fuite! Full steam ahead!"

He pulled the trigger—the gun missed fire; he pulled the trigger again—again it missed fire; he tried a third time—and a great blaze of flame flew out of the barrel and there was a deafening boom, boom. It kicked him violently on the shoulder, and, taking his gun in one hand and his axe in the other, he went to see what the noise was about.

A little later he went back to the hut.

"What was it?" a pilgrim, who was staying the night at the hut and had been awakened by the noise, asked in a husky voice.

"It's all right," answered Ignat. "Nothing of consequence. Our Whitebrow has taken to sleeping with the sheep in the warm. Only he hasn't the sense to go in at the door, but always tries to wriggle in by the roof. The other night he tore a hole in the roof and went off on the spree, the rascal, and now he has come back and scratched away the roof again."

"Stupid dog."

"Yes, there is a spring snapped in his brain. I do detest fools," sighed Ignat, clambering on to the stove. "Come, man of God, it's early yet to get up. Let us sleep full steam! . . ."

In the morning he called Whitebrow, smacked him hard about the ears, and then showing him a stick, kept repeating to him:

"Go in at the door! Go in at the door! Go in at the door!"

"Anna on the Neck"

I

After the wedding they had not even light refreshments; the happy pair simply drank a glass of champagne, changed into their travelling things, and drove to the station. Instead of a gay wedding ball and supper, instead of music and dancing, they went on a journey to pray at a shrine a hundred and fifty miles away. Many people commended this, saying that Modest Alexeitch was a man high up in the service and no longer young, and that a noisy wedding might not have seemed quite suitable; and music is apt to sound dreary when a government official of fifty-two marries a girl who is only just eighteen. People said, too, that Modest Alexeitch, being a man of principle, had arranged this visit to the monastery expressly in order to make his young bride realize that even in marriage he put religion and morality above everything.

The happy pair were seen off at the station. The crowd of relations and colleagues in the service stood, with glasses in their hands, waiting for the train to start to shout "Hurrah!" and the bride's father, Pyotr Leontyitch, wearing a top-hat and the uniform of a teacher, already drunk and very pale, kept craning towards the window, glass in hand and saying in an imploring voice:

"Anyuta! Anya, Anya! one word!"

Anna bent out of the window to him, and he whispered something to her, enveloping her in a stale smell of alcohol, blew into her ear—she could make out nothing—and made the sign of the cross over her face, her bosom, and her hands; meanwhile he was breathing in gasps and tears were shining in his eyes. And the schoolboys, Anna's brothers, Petya and Andrusha, pulled at his coat from behind, whispering in confusion:

"Father, hush! . . . Father, that's enough. . . ."

When the train started, Anna saw her father run a little way after the train, staggering and spilling his wine, and what a kind, guilty, pitiful face he had:

"Hurra—ah!" he shouted.

The happy pair were left alone. Modest Alexeitch looked about the compartment, arranged their things on the shelves, and sat down, smiling, opposite his young wife. He was an official of medium height, rather stout and puffy, who looked exceedingly well nourished, with long whiskers and no moustache. His clean-shaven, round, sharply defined chin looked like the heel of a foot. The most characteristic point in his face was the absence of moustache, the bare, freshly shaven place, which gradually passed into the fat cheeks, quivering like jelly. His deportment was dignified, his movements were deliberate, his manner was soft.

"I cannot help remembering now one circumstance," he said, smiling. "When, five years ago, Kosorotov received the order of St. Anna of the second grade, and went to thank His Excellency, His Excellency expressed himself as follows: 'So now you have three Annas: one in your buttonhole and two on your neck.' And it must be explained that at that time Kosorotov's wife, a quarrelsome and frivolous person, had just returned to him, and that her name was Anna. I trust that when I receive the Anna of the second grade His Excellency will not have occasion to say the same thing to me."

He smiled with his little eyes. And she, too, smiled, troubled at the thought that at any moment this man might kiss her with his thick damp lips, and that she had no right to prevent his doing so. The soft movements of his fat person frightened her; she felt both fear and disgust. He got up, without haste took off the order from his neck, took off his coat and waistcoat, and put on his dressing-gown.

"That's better," he said, sitting down beside Anna.

Anna remembered what agony the wedding had been, when it had seemed to her that the priest, and the guests, and every one in church had been looking at her sorrowfully and asking why, why was she, such a sweet, nice girl, marrying such an elderly, uninteresting gentleman. Only that morning she was delighted that everything had been satisfactorily arranged, but at the time of the wedding, and now in the railway carriage, she felt cheated, guilty, and ridiculous. Here she had married a rich man and yet she had no money, her wedding-dress had been bought on credit, and when her father and brothers had been saying good-bye, she could see from their faces that they had not a farthing. Would they have any supper that day? And tomorrow? And for some reason it seemed to her that her father and the boys were sitting tonight hungry without her, and feeling the same misery as they had the day after their mother's funeral.

"Oh, how unhappy I am!" she thought. "Why am I so unhappy?"

With the awkwardness of a man with settled habits, unaccustomed to deal with women, Modest Alexeitch touched her on the waist and patted her on the shoulder, while she went on thinking about money, about her mother and her mother's death. When her mother died, her father, Pyotr Leontyitch, a teacher of drawing and writing in the high school, had taken to drink, impoverishment had followed, the boys had not had boots or goloshes, their father had been hauled up before the magistrate, the warrant officer had come and made an inventory of the furniture.... What a disgrace! Anna had had to look after her drunken father, darn her brothers' stockings, go to market, and when she was complimented on her youth, her beauty, and her elegant manners, it seemed to her that every one was looking at her cheap hat and the holes in her boots that were inked over. And at night there had been tears and a haunting dread that her father would soon, very soon, be dismissed from the school for his weakness, and that he would not survive it, but would die, too, like their mother. But ladies of their acquaintance had taken the matter in hand and looked about for a good match for Anna. This Modest Alexeitch, who was neither young nor good-looking but had money, was soon found. He had a hundred thousand in the bank and the family estate, which he had let on lease. He was a man of principle and stood well with His Excellency; it would be nothing to him, so they told Anna, to get a note from His Excellency to the directors of the high school, or even to the Education Commissioner, to prevent Pyotr Leontyitch from being dismissed.

While she was recalling these details, she suddenly heard strains of music which floated in at the window, together with the sound of voices. The train was stopping at a station. In the crowd beyond the platform an accordion and a cheap squeaky fiddle were being briskly played, and the sound of a military band came from beyond the villas and the tall birches and poplars that lay bathed in the moonlight; there must have been a dance in the place. Summer visitors and townspeople, who used to come out here by train in fine weather for a breath of fresh air, were parading up and down on the platform. Among them was the wealthy owner of all the summer villas—a tall, stout, dark man called Artynov. He had prominent eyes and looked like an Armenian. He wore a strange costume; his shirt was unbuttoned, showing his chest; he wore high boots with spurs, and a black cloak hung from his shoulders and dragged on the ground like a train. Two boarhounds followed him with their sharp noses to the ground.

Tears were still shining in Anna's eyes, but she was not thinking now of her mother, nor of money, nor of her marriage; but shaking hands with school-boys and officers she knew, she laughed gaily and said quickly:

"How do you do? How are you?"

She went out on to the platform between the carriages into the moonlight, and stood so that they could all see her in her new splendid dress and hat.

"Why are we stopping here?" she asked.

"This is a junction. They are waiting for the mail train to pass."

Seeing that Artynov was looking at her, she screwed up her eyes coquettishly and began talking aloud in French; and because her voice sounded so pleasant, and because she heard music and the moon was reflected in the pond, and because Artynov, the notorious Don Juan and spoiled child of fortune, was looking at her eagerly and with curiosity, and because every one was in good spirits—she suddenly felt joyful, and when the train started and the officers of her acquaintance saluted her, she was humming the polka the strains of which reached her from the military band playing beyond the trees; and she returned to her compartment feeling as though it had been proved to her at the station that she would certainly be happy in spite of everything.

The happy pair spent two days at the monastery, then went back to town. They lived in a rent-free flat. When Modest Alexeitch had gone to the office, Anna played the piano, or shed tears of depression, or lay down on a couch and read novels or looked through fashion papers. At dinner Modest Alexevitch ate a great deal and talked about politics, about appointments, transfers, and promotions in the service, about the necessity of hard work, and said that, family life not being a pleasure but a duty, if you took care of the kopecks the roubles would take care of themselves, and that he put religion and morality before everything else in the world. And holding his knife in his fist as though it were a sword, he would say:

"Every one ought to have his duties!"

And Anna listened to him, was frightened, and could not eat, and she usually got up from the table hungry. After dinner her husband lay down for a nap and snored loudly, while Anna went to see her own people. Her father and the boys looked at her in a peculiar way, as though just before she came in they had been blaming her for having married for money a tedious, wearisome man she did not love; her rustling skirts, her bracelets, and her general air of a married lady, offended them and made them uncomfortable. In her presence they felt a little embarrassed and did not know what to talk to her about; but yet they still loved her as before, and were not used to having dinner without her. She sat down with them to cabbage soup, porridge, and fried potatoes, smelling of mutton dripping. Pyotr Leontyitch filled his glass from the decanter with a trembling hand and drank it off hurriedly, greedily, with repulsion, then poured out a second glass and then a third. Petya and Andrusha, thin, pale boys with big eyes, would take the decanter and say desperately:

"You mustn't, father. . . . Enough, father. . . ."

And Anna, too, was troubled and entreated him to drink no more; and he would suddenly fly into a rage and beat the table with his fists:

"I won't allow any one to dictate to me!" he would shout. "Wretched boys! wretched girl! I'll turn you all out!"

But there was a note of weakness, of good-nature in his voice, and no one was afraid of him. After dinner he usually dressed in his best. Pale, with a cut on his chin from shaving, craning his thin neck, he would stand for half an hour before the glass, prinking, combing his hair, twisting his black moustache, sprinkling himself with scent, tying his cravat in a bow; then he would put on his gloves and his top-hat, and go off to give his private lessons. Or if it was a holiday he would stay at home and paint, or play the harmonium, which wheezed and growled; he would try to wrest from it pure harmonious sounds and would sing to it; or would storm at the boys:

"Wretches! Good-for-nothing boys! You have spoiled the instrument!"

In the evening Anna's husband played cards with his colleagues, who lived under the same roof in the government quarters. The wives of these gentlemen would come in—ugly, tastelessly dressed women, as coarse as cooks—and gossip would begin in the flat as tasteless and unattractive as the ladies themselves. Sometimes Modest Alexeitch would take Anna to the theatre. In the intervals he would never let her stir a step from his side, but walked about arm in arm with her through the corridors and the foyer. When he bowed to some one, he immediately whispered to Anna: "A civil councillor . . . visits at His Excellency's"; or, "A man of means . . . has a house of his own." When they passed the buffet Anna had a great longing for something sweet; she was fond of chocolate and apple cakes, but she had no money, and she did not like to ask her husband. He would take a pear, pinch it with his fingers, and ask uncertainly:

"How much?"

"Twenty-five kopecks!"

"I say!" he would reply, and put it down; but as it was awkward to leave the buffet without buying anything, he would order some seltzer-water and drink the whole bottle himself, and tears would come into his eyes. And Anna hated him at such times.

And suddenly flushing crimson, he would say to her rapidly:

"Bow to that old lady!"

"But I don't know her."

"No matter. That's the wife of the director of the local treasury! Bow, I tell you," he would grumble insistently. "Your head won't drop off."

Anna bowed and her head certainly did not drop off, but it was agonizing. She did everything her husband wanted her to, and was furious with herself for having let him deceive her like the veriest idiot. She had only married him for his money, and yet she had less money now than before her marriage. In old days her father would sometimes give her twenty kopecks, but now she had not a farthing. To take money by stealth or ask for it, she could not; she was afraid of her husband, she trembled before him. She felt as though she had been afraid of him for years. In her childhood the director of the high school had always seemed the most impressive and terrifying force in the world, sweeping down like a thunderstorm or a steam-engine ready to crush her; another similar force of which the whole family talked, and of which they were for some reason afraid, was His Excellency; then there were a dozen others, less formidable, and among them the teachers at the high school, with shaven upper lips, stern, implacable; and now finally, there was Modest Alexeitch, a man of principle, who even resembled the director in the face. And in Anna's imagination all these forces blended together into one, and, in the form of a terrible, huge white bear, menaced the weak and erring such as her father. And she was afraid to say anything in opposition to her husband, and gave a forced smile, and tried to make a show of pleasure when she was coarsely caressed and defiled by embraces that excited her terror.

Only once Pyotr Leontyitch had the temerity to ask for a loan of fifty roubles in order to pay some very irksome debt, but what an agony it had been!

"Very good; I'll give it to you," said Modest Alexeitch after a moment's thought; "but I warn you I won't help you again till you give up drinking. Such a failing is disgraceful in a man in the government service! I must remind you of the well-known fact that many capable people have been ruined by that passion, though they might possibly, with temperance, have risen in time to a very high position."

And long-winded phrases followed: "inasmuch as . . . ," "following upon which proposition . . . ," "in view of the aforesaid contention . . ."; and Pyotr Leontyitch was in agonies of humiliation and felt an intense craving for alcohol.

And when the boys came to visit Anna, generally in broken boots and threadbare trousers, they, too, had to listen to sermons.

"Every man ought to have his duties!" Modest Alexeitch would say to them.

And he did not give them money. But he did give Anna bracelets, rings, and brooches, saying that these things would come in useful for a rainy day. And he often unlocked her drawer and made an inspection to see whether they were all safe.

II

Meanwhile winter came on. Long before Christmas there was an announcement in the local papers that the usual winter ball would take place on the twenty-ninth of December in the Hall of Nobility. Every evening after cards Modest Alexeitch was excitedly whispering with his colleagues' wives and glancing at Anna, and then paced up and down the room for a long while, thinking. At last, late one evening, he stood still, facing Anna, and said:

"You ought to get yourself a ball dress. Do you understand? Only please consult Marya Grigoryevna and Natalya Kuzminishna."

And he gave her a hundred roubles. She took the money, but she did not consult any one when she ordered the ball dress; she spoke to no one but her father, and tried to imagine how her mother would have dressed for a ball. Her mother had always dressed in the latest fashion and had always taken trouble over Anna, dressing her elegantly like a doll, and had taught her to speak French and dance the mazurka superbly (she had been a governess for five years before her marriage). Like her mother, Anna could make a new dress out of an old one, clean gloves with benzine, hire jewels; and, like her mother, she knew how to screw up her eyes, lisp, assume graceful attitudes, fly into raptures when necessary, and throw a mournful and enigmatic look into her eyes. And from her father she had inherited the dark colour of her hair and eyes, her highly-strung nerves, and the habit of always making herself look her best.

When, half an hour before setting off for the ball, Modest Alexeitch went into her room without his coat on, to put his order round his neck before her pier-glass, dazzled by her beauty and the splendour of her fresh, ethereal dress, he combed his whiskers complacently and said:

"So that's what my wife can look like . . . so that's what you can look like! Anyuta!" he went on, dropping into a tone of solemnity, "I have made your fortune, and now I beg you to do something for mine. I beg you to get introduced to the wife of His Excellency! For God's sake, do! Through her I may get the post of senior reporting clerk!"

They went to the ball. They reached the Hall of Nobility, the entrance with the hall porter. They came to the vestibule with the hatstands, the fur coats; footmen scurrying about, and ladies with low necks putting up their fans to screen themselves from the draughts. There was a smell of gas and of soldiers. When Anna, walking upstairs on her husband's arm, heard the music and saw herself full length in the looking-glass in the full glow of the lights, there was a rush of joy in her heart, and she felt the same presentment of happiness as in the moonlight at the station. She walked in proudly, confidently, for the first time feeling herself not a girl but a lady, and unconsciously imitating her mother in her walk and in her manner. And for the first time in her life she felt rich and free. Even her husband's presence did not oppress her, for as she crossed the threshold of the hall she had guessed instinctively that the proximity of an old husband did not detract from her in the least, but, on the contrary, gave her that shade of piquant mystery that is so attractive to men. The orchestra was already playing and the dances had begun. After their flat Anna was overwhelmed by the lights, the bright colours, the music, the noise, and looking round the room, thought, "Oh, how lovely!" She at once distinguished in the crowd all her acquaintances, every one she had met before at parties or on picnics—all the officers, the teachers, the lawyers, the officials, the landowners, His Excellency, Artynov, and the ladies of the highest standing, dressed up and very *décolletées,* handsome and ugly, who had already taken up their positions in the stalls and pavilions of the charity bazaar, to begin selling things for the benefit of the poor. A huge officer in epaulettes—she had been introduced to him in Staro-Kievsky Street when she was a schoolgirl, but now she could not remember his name—seemed to spring from out of the ground, begging her for a waltz, and she flew away from her husband, feeling as though she were floating away in a sailing-boat in a violent storm, while her husband was left far away on the shore. She danced passionately, with fervour, a waltz, then a polka and a quadrille, being snatched by one partner as soon as she was left by another, dizzy with music and the noise, mixing Russian with French, lisping, laughing, and with no thought of her husband or anything else. She excited great admiration among the men—that was evident, and indeed it could not have been otherwise; she was breathless with excitement, felt thirsty, and convulsively clutched her fan. Pyotr Leontyitch, her father, in a crumpled dress-coat that smelt of benzine, came up to her, offering her a plate of pink ice.

"You are enchanting this evening," he said, looking at her rapturously, "and I have never so much regretted that you were in such a hurry to get married. . . . What was it for? I know you did it for our sake, but . . ." With a shaking hand he drew out a roll of notes and said: "I got the money for my lessons today, and can pay your husband what I owe him."

She put the plate back into his hand, and was pounced upon by some one and borne off to a distance. She caught a glimpse over her partner's shoulder of her father gliding over the floor, putting his arm round a lady and whirling down the ballroom with her.

"How sweet he is when he is sober!" she thought.

She danced the mazurka with the same huge officer; he moved gravely, as heavily as a dead carcase in a uniform, twitched his shoulders and his chest, stamped his feet very languidly—he felt fearfully disinclined to dance. She fluttered round him, provoking him by her beauty, her bare neck; her eyes glowed defiantly, her movements were passionate, while he became more and more indifferent, and held out his hands to her as graciously as a king.

"Bravo, bravo!" said people watching them.

But little by little the huge officer, too, broke out; he grew lively, excited, and, overcome by her fascination, was carried away and danced lightly, youthfully, while she merely moved her shoulders and looked slyly at him as though she were now the queen and he were her slave; and at that moment it seemed to her that the whole room was looking at them, and that everybody was thrilled and envied them. The huge officer had hardly had time to thank her for the dance, when the crowd suddenly parted and the men drew themselves up in a strange way, with their hands at their sides. His Excellency, with two stars on his dress-coat, was walking up to her. Yes, His Excellency was walking straight towards her, for he was staring directly at her with a sugary smile, while he licked his lips as he always did when he saw a pretty woman.

"Delighted, delighted . . ." he began. "I shall order your husband to be clapped in a lock-up for keeping such a treasure hidden from us till now. I've come to you with a message from my wife," he went on, offering her his arm. "You must help us. . . . M-m-yes. . . . We ought to give you the prize for beauty as they do in America. . . . M-m-yes. . . . The Americans. . . . My wife is expecting you impatiently."

He led her to a stall and presented her to a middle-aged lady, the lower part of whose face was disproportionately large, so that she looked as though she were holding a big stone in her mouth.

"You must help us," she said through her nose in a sing-song voice. "All the pretty women are working for our charity bazaar, and you are the only one enjoying yourself. Why won't you help us?"

She went away, and Anna took her place by the cups and the silver samovar. She was soon doing a lively trade. Anna asked no less than a rouble for a cup of tea, and made the huge officer drink three cups. Artynov, the rich man with prominent eyes, who suffered from asthma, came up, too; he was not dressed in the strange costume in which Anna had seen him in the summer at the station, but wore a dress-coat like every one else. Keeping his eyes fixed on Anna, he drank a glass of champagne and paid a hundred roubles for it, then drank some tea and gave another hundred—all this without saying a word, as he was short of breath through asthma. . . . Anna invited purchasers and got money out of them, firmly convinced by now that her smiles and glances could not fail to afford these people great pleasure. She realized now that she was created exclusively for this noisy, brilliant, laughing life, with its music, its dancers, its adorers, and her old terror of a force that was sweeping down upon her and menacing to crush her seemed to her ridiculous: she was afraid of no one now, and only regretted that her mother could not be there to rejoice at her success.

Pyotr Leontyitch, pale by now but still steady on his legs, came up to the stall and asked for a glass of brandy. Anna turned crimson, expecting him to say something inappropriate (she was already ashamed of having such a poor and ordinary father); but he emptied his glass, took ten roubles out of his roll of notes, flung it down, and walked away with dignity without uttering a word. A little later she saw him dancing in the grand chain, and by now he was staggering and kept shouting something, to the great confusion of his partner; and Anna remembered how at the ball three years before he had staggered and shouted in the same way, and it had ended in the police-sergeant's taking him home to bed, and next day the director had threatened to dismiss him from his post. How inappropriate that memory was!

When the samovars were put out in the stalls and the exhausted ladies handed over their takings to the middle-aged lady with the stone in her mouth, Artynov took Anna on his arm to the hall where supper was served to all who had assisted at the bazaar. There were some twenty people at supper, not more, but it was very noisy. His Excellency proposed a toast:

"In this magnificent dining-room it will be appropriate to drink to the success of the cheap dining-rooms, which are the object of today's bazaar."

The brigadier-general proposed the toast: "To the power by which even the artillery is vanquished," and all the company clinked glasses with the ladies. It was very, very gay.

When Anna was escorted home it was daylight and the cooks were going to market. Joyful, intoxicated, full of new sensations, exhausted, she undressed, dropped into bed, and at once fell asleep. . . .

It was past one in the afternoon when the servant waked her and announced that M. Artynov had called. She dressed quickly and went down into the drawing-room. Soon after Artynov, His Excellency called to thank her for her assistance in the bazaar. With a sugary smile, chewing his lips, he kissed her hand, and asking her permission to come again, took his leave, while she remained standing in the middle of the drawing-room, amazed, enchanted, unable to believe that this change in her life, this marvellous change, had taken place so quickly; and at that moment Modest Alexeitch walked in . . . and he, too, stood before her now with the same ingratiating, sugary, cringingly respectful expression which she was accustomed to see on his face in the presence of the great and powerful; and with rapture, with indignation, with contempt, convinced that no harm would come to her from it, she said, articulating distinctly each word:

"Be off, you blockhead!"

From this time forward Anna never had one day free, as she was always taking part in picnics, expeditions, performances. She returned home every day after midnight, and went to bed on the floor in the drawing-room, and afterwards used to tell every one, touchingly, how she slept under flowers. She needed a very great deal of money, but she was no longer afraid of Modest Alexeitch, and spent his money as though it were her own; and she did not ask, did not demand it, simply sent him in the bills. "Give bearer two hundred roubles," or "Pay one hundred roubles at once."

At Easter Modest Alexeitch received the Anna of the second grade. When he went to offer his thanks, His Excellency put aside the paper he was reading and settled himself more comfortably in his chair.

"So now you have three Annas," he said, scrutinizing his white hands and pink nails—"one on your buttonhole and two on your neck."

Modest Alexeitch put two fingers to his lips as a precaution against laughing too loud and said:

"Now I have only to look forward to the arrival of a little Vladimir. I make bold to beg your Excellency to stand godfather."

He was alluding to Vladimir of the fourth grade, and was already imagining how he would tell everywhere the story of this pun, so happy in its readiness and audacity, and he wanted to say something equally happy, but His Excellency was buried again in his newspaper, and merely gave him a nod.

And Anna went on driving about with three horses, going out hunting with Artynov, playing in one-act dramas, going out to supper, and was more and more rarely with her own family; they dined now alone. Pyotr Leontyitch was drinking more heavily than ever; there was no money, and the harmonium had been sold long ago for debt. The boys did not let him go out alone in the street now, but looked after him for fear he might fall down; and whenever they met Anna driving in Staro-Kievsky Street with a pair of horses and Artynov on the box instead of a coachman, Pyotr Leontyitch took off his top-hat, and was about to shout to her, but Petya and Andrusha took him by the arm, and said imploringly:

"You mustn't, father. Hush, father!"

Ariadne

On the deck of a steamer sailing from Odessa to Sevastopol, a rather good-looking gentleman, with a little round beard, came up to me to smoke, and said:

"Notice those Germans sitting near the shelter? Whenever Germans or Englishmen get together, they talk about the crops, the price of wool, or their personal affairs. But for some reason or other when we Russians get together we never discuss anything but women and abstract subjects—but especially women."

This gentleman's face was familiar to me already. We had returned from abroad the evening before in the same train, and at Volotchisk when the luggage was being examined by the Customs, I saw him standing with a lady, his travelling companion, before a perfect mountain of trunks and baskets filled with ladies' clothes, and I noticed how embarrassed and downcast he was when he had to pay duty on some piece of silk frippery, and his companion protested and threatened to make a complaint. Afterwards, on the way to Odessa, I saw him carrying little pies and oranges to the ladies' compartment.

It was rather damp; the vessel swayed a little, and the ladies had retired to their cabins.

The gentleman with the little round beard sat down beside me and continued:

"Yes, when Russians come together they discuss nothing but abstract subjects and women. We are so intellectual, so solemn, that we utter nothing but truths and can discuss only questions of a lofty order. The Russian actor does not know how to be funny; he acts with profundity even in a farce. We're just the same: when we have got to talk of trifles we treat them only from an exalted point of view. It comes from a lack of boldness, sincerity, and simplicity. We talk so often about women, I fancy, because we are dissatisfied. We take too ideal a view of women, and make demands out of all proportion with what reality can give us; we get something utterly different from what we want, and the result is dissatisfaction, shattered hopes, and inward suffering, and if any one is suffering, he's bound to talk of it. It does not bore you to go on with this conversation?"

"No, not in the least."

"In that case, allow me to introduce myself," said my companion, rising from his seat a little: "Ivan Ilyitch Shamohin, a Moscow landowner of a sort. . . . You I know very well."

He sat down and went on, looking at me with a genuine and friendly expression:

"A mediocre philosopher, like Max Nordau, would explain these incessant conversations about women as a form of erotic madness, or would put it down to our having been slave-owners and so on; I take quite a different view of it. I repeat, we are dissatisfied because we are idealists. We want the creatures who bear us and our children to be superior to us and to everything in the world. When we are young we adore and poeticize those with whom we are in love: love and happiness with us are synonyms. Among us in Russia marriage without love is despised, sensuality is ridiculed and inspires repulsion, and the greatest success is enjoyed by those tales and novels in which women are beautiful, poetical, and exalted; and if the Russian has been for years in ecstasies over Raphael's Madonna, or is eager for the emancipation of women, I assure you there is no affectation about it. But the trouble is that when we have been married or been intimate with a woman for some two or three years, we begin to feel deceived and disillusioned: we pair off with others, and again—disappointment, again—repulsion, and in the long run we become convinced that women are lying, trivial, fussy, unfair, undeveloped, cruel—in fact, far from being superior, are immeasurably inferior to us men. And in our dissatisfaction and disappointment there is nothing left for us but to grumble and talk about what we've been so cruelly deceived in."

While Shamohin was talking I noticed that the Russian language and our Russian surroundings gave him great pleasure. This was probably because he had been very homesick abroad. Though he praised the Russians and ascribed to them a rare idealism, he did not disparage foreigners, and that I put down to his credit. It could be seen, too, that there was some uneasiness in his soul, that he wanted to talk more of himself than of women, and that I was in for a long story in the nature of a confession. And when we had asked for a bottle of wine and had each of us drunk a glass, this was how he did in fact begin:

"I remember in a novel of Weltmann's some one says, 'So that's the story!' and some one else answers, 'No, that's not the story—that's only the introduction to the story.' In the same way what I've said so far is only the introduction; what I really want to tell you is my own love story. Excuse me, I must ask you again; it won't bore you to listen?"

I told him it would not, and he went on:

The scene of my story is laid in the Moscow province in one of its northern districts. The scenery there, I must tell you, is exquisite. Our homestead is on the high bank of a rapid stream, where the water chatters noisily day and night: imagine a big old garden, neat flower-beds, beehives, a kitchen-garden, and below it a river with leafy willows, which, when there is a heavy dew on them, have a lustreless look as though they had turned grey; and on the other side a meadow, and beyond the meadow on the upland a terrible, dark pine forest. In that forest delicious, reddish agarics grow in endless profusion, and elks still live in its deepest recesses. When I am nailed up in my coffin I believe I shall still dream of those early mornings, you know, when the sun hurts your eyes: or the wonderful spring evenings when the nightingales and the landrails call in the garden and beyond the garden, and sounds of the harmonica float across from the village, while they play the piano indoors and the stream babbles . . . when there is such music, in fact, that one wants at the same time to cry and to sing aloud.

We have not much arable land, but our pasture makes up for it, and with the forest yields about two thousand roubles a year. I am the only son of my father; we are both modest persons, and with my father's pension that sum was amply sufficient for us.

The first three years after finishing at the university I spent in the country, looking after the estate and constantly expecting to be elected on some local assembly; but what was most important, I was violently in love with an extraordinarily beautiful and fascinating girl. She was the sister of our neighbour, Kotlovitch, a ruined landowner who had on his estate pine-apples, marvellous peaches, lightning conductors, a fountain in the courtyard, and at the same time not a farthing in his pocket. He did nothing and knew how to do nothing. He was as flabby as though he had been made of boiled turnip; he used to doctor the peasants by homœopathy and was interested in spiritualism. He was, however, a man of great delicacy and mildness, and by no means a fool, but I have no fondness for these gentlemen who converse with spirits and cure peasant women by magnetism. In the first place, the ideas of people who are not intellectually free are always in a muddle, and it's extremely difficult to talk to them; and, secondly, they usually love no one, and have nothing to do with women, and their mysticism has an unpleasant effect on sensitive people. I did not care for his appearance either. He was tall, stout, white-skinned, with a little head, little shining eyes, and chubby white fingers. He did not shake hands, but kneaded one's hands in his. And he was always apologising. If he asked for anything it was "Excuse me"; if he gave you anything it was "Excuse me" too.

As for his sister, she was a character out of a different opera. I must explain that I had not been acquainted with the Kotlovitches in my childhood and early youth, for my father had been a professor at N., and we had for many years lived away. When I did make their acquaintance the girl was twenty-two, had left school long before, and had spent two or three years in Moscow with a wealthy aunt who brought her out into society. When I was introduced and first had to talk to her, what struck me most of all was her rare and beautiful name—Ariadne. It suited her so wonderfully! She was a brunette, very thin, very slender, supple, elegant, and extremely graceful, with refined and exceedingly noble features. Her eyes were shining, too, but her brother's shone with a cold sweetness, mawkish as sugar-candy, while hers had the glow of youth, proud and beautiful. She conquered me on the first day of our acquaintance, and indeed it was inevitable. My first impression was so overwhelming that to this day I cannot get rid of my illusions; I am still tempted to imagine that nature had some grand, marvellous design when she created that girl.

Ariadne's voice, her walk, her hat, even her footprints on the sandy bank where she used to angle for gudgeon, filled me with delight and a passionate hunger for life. I judged of her spiritual being from her lovely face and lovely figure, and every word, every smile of Ariadne's bewitched me, conquered me and forced me to believe in the loftiness of her soul. She was friendly, ready to talk, gay and simple in her manners. She had a poetic belief in God, made poetic reflections about death, and there was such a wealth of varying shades in her spiritual organisation that even her faults seemed in her to carry with them peculiar, charming qualities. Suppose she wanted a new horse and had no money—what did that matter? Something might be sold or pawned, or if the steward swore that nothing could possibly be sold or pawned, the iron roofs might be torn off the lodges and taken to the factory, or at the very busiest time the farm-horses might be driven to the market and sold there for next to nothing. These unbridled desires reduced the whole household to despair at times, but she expressed them with such refinement that everything was forgiven her; all things were permitted her as to a goddess or to Cæsar's wife. My love was pathetic and was soon noticed by every one—my father, the neighbours, and the peasants—and they all sympathised with me. When I stood the workmen vodka, they would bow and say: "May the Kotlovitch young lady be your bride, please God!"

And Ariadne herself knew that I loved her. She would often ride over on horseback or drive in the char-à-banc to see us, and would spend whole days with me and my father. She made great friends with the old man, and he even taught her to bicycle, which was his favourite amusement.

I remember helping her to get on the bicycle one evening, and she looked so lovely that I felt as though I were burning my hands when I touched her. I shuddered with rapture, and when the two of them, my old father and she, both looking so handsome and elegant, bicycled side by side along the main road, a black horse ridden by the steward dashed aside on meeting them, and it seemed to me that it dashed aside because it too was overcome by her beauty. My love, my worship, touched Ariadne and softened her; she had a passionate longing to be captivated like me and to respond with the same love. It was so poetical!

But she was incapable of really loving as I did, for she was cold and already somewhat corrupted. There was a demon in her, whispering to her day and night that she was enchanting, adorable; and, having no definite idea for what object she was created, or for what purpose life had been given her, she never pictured herself in the future except as very wealthy and distinguished; she had visions of balls, races, liveries, of sumptuous drawing-rooms, of a salon of her own, and of a perfect swarm of counts, princes, ambassadors, celebrated painters and artists, all of them adoring her and in ecstasies over her beauty and her dresses. . . .

This thirst for personal success, and this continual concentration of the mind in one direction, makes people cold, and Ariadne was cold—to me, to nature, and to music. Meanwhile time was passing, and still there were no ambassadors on the scene. Ariadne went on living with her brother, the spiritualist: things went from bad to worse, so that she had nothing to buy hats and dresses with, and had to resort to all sorts of tricks and dodges to conceal her poverty.

As luck would have it, a certain Prince Maktuev, a wealthy man but an utterly insignificant person, had paid his addresses to her when she was living at her aunt's in Moscow. She had refused him, point-blank. But now she was fretted by the worm of repentance that she had refused him; just as a peasant pouts with repulsion at a mug of kvass with cockroaches in it but yet drinks it, so she frowned disdainfully at the recollection of the prince, and yet she would say to me: "Say what you like, there is something inexplicable, fascinating, in a title. . . ."

She dreamed of a title, of a brilliant position, and at the same time she did not want to let me go. However one may dream of ambassadors one's heart is not a stone, and one has wistful feelings for one's youth. Ariadne tried to fall in love, made a show of being in love, and even swore that she loved me. But I am a highly strung and sensitive man; when I am loved I feel it even at a distance, without vows and assurances; at once I felt as it were a coldness in the air, and when she talked to me of love, it seemed to me as though I were listening to the singing of a metal nightingale. Ariadne was herself aware that she was lacking in something. She was vexed and more than once I saw her cry. Another time—can you imagine it?—all of a sudden she embraced me and kissed me. It happened in the evening on the river-bank, and I saw by her eyes that she did not love me, but was embracing me from curiosity, to test herself and to see what came of it. And I felt dreadful. I took her hands and said to her in despair: "These caresses without love cause me suffering!"

"What a queer fellow you are!" she said with annoyance, and walked away.

Another year or two might have passed, and in all probability I should have married her, and so my story would have ended, but fate was pleased to arrange our romance differently. It happened that a new personage appeared on our horizon. Ariadne's brother had a visit from an old university friend called Mihail Ivanitch Lubkov, a charming man of whom coachmen and footmen used to say: "An entertaining gentleman." He was a man of medium height, lean and bald, with a face like a good-natured bourgeois, not interesting, but pale and presentable, with a stiff, well-kept moustache, with a neck like gooseskin, and a big Adam's apple. He used to wear pince-nez on a wide black ribbon, lisped, and could not pronounce either *r* or *l*. He was always in good spirits, everything amused him.

He had made an exceedingly foolish marriage at twenty, and had acquired two houses in Moscow as part of his wife's dowry. He began doing them up and building a bath-house, and was completely ruined.

Now his wife and four children lodged in Oriental Buildings in great poverty, and he had to support them—and this amused him. He was thirty-six and his wife was by now forty-two, and that, too, amused him. His mother, a conceited, sulky personage, with aristocratic pretensions, despised his wife and lived apart with a perfect menagerie of cats and dogs, and he had to allow her seventy-five roubles a month also; he was, too, a man of taste, liked lunching at the Slavyansky Bazaar and dining at the Hermitage; he needed a great deal of money, but his uncle only allowed him two thousand roubles a year, which was not enough, and for days together he would run about Moscow with his tongue out, as the saying is, looking for some one to borrow from—and this, too, amused him. He had come to Kotlovitch to find in the lap of nature, as he said, a rest from family life. At dinner, at supper, and on our walks, he talked about his wife, about his mother, about his creditors, about the bailiffs, and laughed at them; he laughed at himself and assured us that, thanks to his talent for borrowing, he had made a great number of agreeable acquaintances. He laughed without ceasing and we laughed too. Moreover, in his company we spent our time differently. I was more inclined to quiet, so to say idyllic pleasures; I liked fishing, evening walks, gathering mushrooms; Lubkov preferred picnics, fireworks, hunting. He used to get up picnics three times a week, and Ariadne, with an earnest and inspired face, used to write a list of oysters, champagne, sweets, and used to send me into Moscow to get them, without inquiring, of course, whether I had money. And at the picnics there were toasts and laughter, and again mirthful descriptions of how old his wife was, what fat lap-dogs his mother had, and what charming people his creditors were. . . .

Lubkov was fond of nature, but he regarded it as something long familiar and at the same time, in reality, infinitely beneath himself and created for his pleasure. He would sometimes stand still before some magnificent landscape and say: "It would be nice to have tea here."

One day, seeing Ariadne walking in the distance with a parasol, he nodded towards her and said:

"She's thin, and that's what I like; I don't like fat women."

This made me wince. I asked him not to speak like that about women before me. He looked at me in surprise and said:

"What is there amiss in my liking thin women and not caring for fat ones?"

I made no answer. Afterwards, being in very good spirits and a trifle elevated, he said:

"I've noticed Ariadne Grigoryevna likes you. I can't understand why you don't go in and win."

His words made me feel uncomfortable, and with some embarrassment I told him how I looked at love and women.

"I don't know," he sighed; "to my thinking, a woman's a woman and a man's a man. Ariadne Grigoryevna may be poetical and exalted, as you say, but it doesn't follow that she must be superior to the laws of nature. You see for yourself that she has reached the age when she must have a husband or a lover. I respect women as much as you do, but I don't think certain relations exclude poetry. Poetry's one thing and love is another. It's just the same as it is in farming. The beauty of nature is one thing and the income from your forests or fields is quite another."

When Ariadne and I were fishing, Lubkov would lie on the sand close by and make fun of me, or lecture me on the conduct of life.

"I wonder, my dear sir, how you can live without a love affair," he would say. "You are young, handsome, interesting—in fact, you're a man not to be sniffed at, yet you live like a monk. Och! I can't stand these fellows who are old at twenty-eight! I'm nearly ten years older than you are, and yet which of us is the younger? Ariadne Grigoryevna, which?"

"You, of course," Ariadne answered him.

And when he was bored with our silence and the attention with which we stared at our floats he went home, and she said, looking at me angrily:

"You're really not a man, but a mush, God forgive me! A man ought to be able to be carried away by his feelings, he ought to be able to be mad, to make mistakes, to suffer! A woman will forgive you audacity and insolence, but she will never forgive your reasonableness!"

She was angry in earnest, and went on:

"To succeed, a man must be resolute and bold. Lubkov is not so handsome as you are, but he is more interesting. He will always succeed with women because he's not like you; he's a man. . . ."

And there was actually a note of exasperation in her voice.

One day at supper she began saying, not addressing me, that if she were a man she would not stagnate in the country, but would travel, would spend the winter somewhere abroad—in Italy, for instance. Oh, Italy! At this point my father unconsciously poured oil on the flames; he began telling us at length about Italy, how splendid it was there, the exquisite scenery, the museums. Ariadne suddenly conceived a burning desire to go to Italy. She positively brought her fist down on the table and her eyes flashed as she said: "I must go!"

After that came conversations every day about Italy: how splendid it would be in Italy—ah, Italy!—oh, Italy! And when Ariadne looked at me over her shoulder, from her cold and obstinate expression I saw that in her dreams she had already conquered Italy with all its salons, celebrated foreigners and tourists, and there was no holding her back now. I advised her to wait a little, to put off her tour for a year or two, but she frowned disdainfully and said:

"You're as prudent as an old woman!"

Lubkov was in favour of the tour. He said it could be done very cheaply, and he, too, would go to Italy and have a rest there from family life.

I behaved, I confess, as naïvely as a schoolboy. Not from jealousy, but from a foreboding of something terrible and extraordinary, I tried as far as possible not to leave them alone together, and they made fun of me. For instance, when I went in they would pretend they had just been kissing one another, and so on.

But lo and behold, one fine morning, her plump, white-skinned brother, the spiritualist, made his appearance and expressed his desire to speak to me alone.

He was a man without will; in spite of his education and his delicacy he could never resist reading another person's letter, if it lay before him on the table. And now he admitted that he had by chance read a letter of Lubkov's to Ariadne.

"From that letter I learned that she is very shortly going abroad. My dear fellow, I am very much upset! Explain it to me for goodness' sake. I can make nothing of it!"

As he said this he breathed hard, breathing straight in my face and smelling of boiled beef.

"Excuse me for revealing the secret of this letter to you, but you are Ariadne's friend, she respects you. Perhaps you know something of it. She wants to go away, but with whom? Mr. Lubkov is proposing to go with her. Excuse me, but this is very strange of Mr. Lubkov; he is a married man, he has children, and yet he is making a declaration of love; he is writing to Ariadne 'darling.' Excuse me, but it is so strange!"

I turned cold all over; my hands and feet went numb and I felt an ache in my chest, as if a three-cornered stone had been driven into it. Kotlovitch sank helplessly into an easy-chair, and his hands fell limply at his sides.

"What can I do?" I inquired.

"Persuade her. . . . Impress her mind. . . . Just consider, what is Lubkov to her? Is he a match for her? Oh, good God! How awful it is, how awful it is!" he went on, clutching his head. "She has had such splendid offers—Prince Maktuev and . . . and others. The prince adores her, and only last Wednesday week his late grandfather, Ilarion, declared positively that Ariadne would be his wife—positively! His grandfather Ilarion is dead, but he is a wonderfully intelligent person; we call up his spirit every day."

After this conversation I lay awake all night and thought of shooting myself. In the morning I wrote five letters and tore them all up. Then I sobbed in the barn. Then I took a sum of money from my father and set off for the Caucasus without saying good-bye.

Of course, a woman's a woman and a man's a man, but can all that be as simple in our day as it was before the Flood, and can it be that I, a cultivated man endowed with a complex spiritual organisation, ought to explain the intense attraction I feel towards a woman simply by the fact that her bodily formation is different from mine? Oh, how awful that would be! I want to believe that in his struggle with nature the genius of man has struggled with physical love too, as with an enemy, and that, if he has not conquered it, he has at least succeeded in tangling it in a net-work of illusions of brotherhood and love; and for me, at any rate, it is no longer a simple instinct of my animal nature as with a dog or a toad, but is real love, and every embrace is spiritualised by a pure impulse of the heart and respect for the woman. In reality, a disgust for the animal instinct has been trained for ages in hundreds of generations; it is inherited by me in my blood and forms part of my nature, and if I poetize love, is not that as natural and inevitable in our day as my ears' not being able to move and my not being covered with fur? I fancy that's how the majority of civilised people look at it, so that the absence of the moral, poetical element in love is treated in these days as a phenomenon, as a sign of atavism; they say it is a symptom of degeneracy, of many forms of insanity. It is true that, in poetizing love, we assume in those we love qualities that are lacking in them, and that is a source of continual mistakes and continual miseries for us. But to my thinking it is better, even so; that is, it is better to suffer than to find complacency on the basis of woman being woman and man being man.

In Tiflis I received a letter from my father. He wrote that Ariadne Grigoryevna had on such a day gone abroad, intending to spend the whole winter away. A month later I returned home. It was by now autumn. Every week Ariadne sent my father extremely interesting letters on scented paper, written in an excellent literary style. It is my opinion that every woman can be a writer. Ariadne described in great detail how it had not been easy for her to make it up with her aunt and induce the latter to give her a thousand roubles for the journey, and what a long time she had spent in Moscow trying to find an old lady, a distant relation, in order to persuade her to go with her. Such a profusion of detail suggested fiction, and I realised, of course, that she had no chaperon with her.

Soon afterwards I, too, had a letter from her, also scented and literary. She wrote that she had missed me, missed my beautiful, intelligent, loving eyes. She reproached me affectionately for wasting my youth, for stagnating in the country when I might, like her, be living in paradise under the palms, breathing the fragrance of the orange-trees. And she signed herself "Your forsaken Ariadne." Two days later came another letter in the same style, signed "Your forgotten Ariadne." My mind was confused. I loved her passionately, I dreamed of her every night, and then this "your forsaken," "your forgotten"—what did it mean? What was it for? And then the dreariness of the country, the long evenings, the disquieting thoughts of Lubkov.... The uncertainty tortured me, and poisoned my days and nights; it became unendurable. I could not bear it and went abroad.

Ariadne summoned me to Abbazzia. I arrived there on a bright warm day after rain; the rain-drops were still hanging on the trees and glistening on the huge, barrack-like *dépendance* where Ariadne and Lubkov were living.

They were not at home. I went into the park; wandered about the avenues, then sat down. An Austrian General, with his hands behind him, walked past me, with red stripes on his trousers such as our generals wear. A baby was wheeled by in a perambulator and the wheels squeaked on the damp sand. A decrepit old man with jaundice passed, then a crowd of Englishwomen, a Catholic priest, then the Austrian General again. A military band, only just arrived from Fiume, with glittering brass instruments, sauntered by to the bandstand—they began playing.

Have you ever been at Abbazzia? It's a filthy little Slav town with only one street, which stinks, and in which one can't walk after rain without goloshes. I had read so much and always with such intense feeling about this earthly paradise that when afterwards, holding up my trousers, I cautiously crossed the narrow street, and in my ennui bought some hard pears from an old peasant woman who, recognising me as a Russian, said: "Tcheeteery" for "tchetyry" (four)—"davadtsat" for "dvadtsat" (twenty), and when I wondered in perplexity where to go and what to do here, and when I inevitably met Russians as disappointed as I was, I began to feel vexed and ashamed. There is a calm bay there full of steamers and boats with coloured sails. From there I could see Fiume and the distant islands covered with lilac mist, and it would have been picturesque if the view over the bay had not been hemmed in by the hotels and their *dépendances*—buildings in an absurd, trivial style of architecture, with which the whole of that green shore has been covered by greedy money grubbers, so that for the most part you see nothing in this little paradise but windows, terraces, and little squares with tables and waiters' black coats. There is a park such as you find now in every watering-place abroad. And the dark, motionless, silent foliage of the palms, and the bright yellow sand in the avenue, and the bright green seats, and the glitter of the braying military horns—all this sickened me in ten minutes! And yet one is obliged for some reason to spend ten days, ten weeks, there!

Having been dragged reluctantly from one of these watering-places to another, I have been more and more struck by the inconvenient and niggardly life led by the wealthy and well-fed, the dulness and feebleness of their imagination, the lack of boldness in their tastes and desires. And how much happier are those tourists, old and young, who, not having the money to stay in hotels, live where they can, admire the view of the sea from the tops of the mountains, lying on the green grass, walk instead of riding, see the forests and villages at close quarters, observe the customs of the country, listen to its songs, fall in love with its women. . . .

While I was sitting in the park, it began to get dark, and in the twilight my Ariadne appeared, elegant and dressed like a princess; after her walked Lubkov, wearing a new loose-fitting suit, bought probably in Vienna.

"Why are you cross with me?" he was saying. "What have I done to you?"

Seeing me, she uttered a cry of joy, and probably, if we had not been in the park, would have thrown herself on my neck. She pressed my hands warmly and laughed; and I laughed too and almost cried with emotion. Questions followed, of the village, of my father, whether I had seen her brother, and so on. She insisted on my looking her straight in the face, and asked if I remembered the gudgeon, our little quarrels, the picnics. . . .

"How nice it all was really!" she sighed. "But we're not having a slow time here either. We have a great many acquaintances, my dear, my best of friends! To-morrow I will introduce you to a Russian family here, but please buy yourself another hat." She scrutinised me and frowned. "Abbazzia is not the country," she said; "here one must be *comme il faut*."

Then we went to the restaurant. Ariadne was laughing and mischievous all the time; she kept calling me "dear," "good," "clever," and seemed as though she could not believe her eyes that I was with her. We sat on till eleven o'clock, and parted very well satisfied both with the supper and with each other.

Next day Ariadne presented me to the Russian family as: "The son of a distinguished professor whose estate is next to ours."

She talked to this family about nothing but estates and crops, and kept appealing to me. She wanted to appear to be a very wealthy landowner, and did, in fact, succeed in doing so. Her manner was superb like that of a real aristocrat, which indeed she was by birth.

"But what a person my aunt is!" she said suddenly, looking at me with a smile. "We had a slight tiff, and she has bolted off to Meran. What do you say to that?"

Afterwards when we were walking in the park I asked her:

"What aunt were you talking of just now? What aunt is that?"

"That was a saving lie," laughed Ariadne. "They must not know I'm without a chaperon."

After a moment's silence she came closer to me and said:

"My dear, my dear, do be friends with Lubkov. He is so unhappy! His wife and mother are simply awful."

She used the formal mode of address in speaking to Lubkov, and when she was going up to bed she said good-night to him exactly as she did to me, and their rooms were on different floors. All this made me hope that it was all nonsense, and that there was no sort of love affair between them, and I felt at ease when I met him. And when one day he asked me for the loan of three hundred roubles, I gave it to him with the greatest pleasure.

Every day we spent in enjoying ourselves and in nothing but enjoying ourselves; we strolled in the park, we ate, we drank. Every day there were conversations with the Russian family. By degrees I got used to the fact that if I went into the park I should be sure to meet the old man with jaundice, the Catholic priest, and the Austrian General, who always carried a pack of little cards, and wherever it was possible sat down and played patience, nervously twitching his shoulders. And the band played the same thing over and over again.

At home in the country I used to feel ashamed to meet the peasants when I was fishing or on a picnic party on a working day; here too I was ashamed at the sight of the footmen, the coachmen, and the workmen who met us. It always seemed to me they were looking at me and thinking: "Why are you doing nothing?" And I was conscious of this feeling of shame every day from morning to night. It was a strange, unpleasant, monotonous time; it was only varied by Lubkov's borrowing from me now a hundred, now fifty guldens, and being suddenly revived by the money as a morphia-maniac is by morphia, beginning to laugh loudly at his wife, at himself, at his creditors.

At last it began to be rainy and cold. We went to Italy, and I telegraphed to my father begging him for mercy's sake to send me eight hundred roubles to Rome. We stayed in Venice, in Bologna, in Florence, and in every town invariably put up at an expensive hotel, where we were charged separately for lights, and for service, and for heating, and for bread at lunch, and for the right of having dinner by ourselves. We ate enormously. In the morning they gave us *café complet;* at one o'clock lunch: meat, fish, some sort of omelette, cheese, fruits, and wine. At six o'clock dinner of eight courses with long intervals, during which we drank beer and wine. At nine o'clock tea. At midnight Ariadne would declare she was hungry, and ask for ham and boiled eggs. We would eat to keep her company.

In the intervals between meals we used to rush about the museums and exhibitions in continual anxiety for fear we should be late for dinner or lunch. I was bored at the sight of the pictures; I longed to be at home to rest; I was exhausted, looked about for a chair and hypocritically repeated after other people: "How exquisite, what atmosphere!" Like overfed boa constrictors, we noticed only the most glaring objects. The shop windows hypnotised us; we went into ecstasies over imitation brooches and bought a mass of useless trumpery.

The same thing happened in Rome, where it rained and there was a cold wind. After a heavy lunch we went to look at St. Peter's, and thanks to our replete condition and perhaps the bad weather, it made no sort of impression on us, and detecting in each other an indifference to art, we almost quarrelled.

The money came from my father. I went to get it, I remember, in the morning. Lubkov went with me.

"The present cannot be full and happy when one has a past," said he. "I have heavy burdens left on me by the past. However, if only I get the money, it's no great matter, but if not, I'm in a fix. Would you believe it, I have only eight francs left, yet I must send my wife a hundred and my mother another. And we must live here too. Ariadne's like a child; she won't enter into the position, and flings away money like a duchess. Why did she buy a watch yesterday? And, tell me, what object is there in our going on playing at being good children? Why, our hiding our relations from the servants and our friends costs us from ten to fifteen francs a day, as I have to have a separate room. What's the object of it?"

I felt as though a sharp stone had been turned round in my chest. There was no uncertainty now; it was all clear to me. I turned cold all over, and at once made a resolution to give up seeing them, to run away from them, to go home at once. . . .

"To get on terms with a woman is easy enough," Lubkov went on. "You have only to undress her; but afterwards what a bore it is, what a silly business!"

When I counted over the money I received he said:

"If you don't lend me a thousand francs, I am faced with complete ruin. Your money is the only resource left to me."

I gave him the money, and he at once revived and began laughing about his uncle, a queer fish, who could never keep his address secret from his wife. When I reached the hotel I packed and paid my bill. I had still to say good-bye to Ariadne.

I knocked at the door.

"Entrez!"

In her room was the usual morning disorder: tea-things on the table, an unfinished roll, an eggshell; a strong overpowering reek of scent. The bed had not been made, and it was evident that two had slept in it.

Ariadne herself had only just got out of bed and was now with her hair down in a flannel dressing-jacket.

I said good-morning to her, and then sat in silence for a minute while she tried to put her hair tidy, and then I asked her, trembling all over:

"Why . . . why . . . did you send for me here?"

Evidently she guessed what I was thinking; she took me by the hand and said:

"I want you to be here, you are so pure."

I felt ashamed of my emotion, of my trembling. And I was afraid I might begin sobbing, too! I went out without saying another word, and within an hour I was sitting in the train. All the journey, for some reason, I imagined Ariadne with child, and she seemed disgusting to me, and all the women I saw in the trains and at the stations looked to me, for some reason, as if they too were with child, and they too seemed disgusting and pitiable. I was in the position of a greedy, passionate miser who should suddenly discover that all his gold coins were false. The pure, gracious images which my imagination, warmed by love, had cherished for so long, my plans, my hopes, my memories, my ideas of love and of woman—all now were jeering and putting out their tongues at me. "Ariadne," I kept asking with horror, "that young, intellectual, extraordinarily beautiful girl, the daughter of a senator, carrying on an intrigue with such an ordinary, uninteresting vulgarian? But why should she not love Lubkov?" I answered myself. "In what is he inferior to me? Oh, let her love any one she likes, but why lie to me? But why is she bound to be open with me?" And so I went on over and over again till I was stupefied.

It was cold in the train; I was travelling first class, but even so there were three on a side, there were no double windows, the outer door opened straight into the compartment, and I felt as though I were in the stocks, cramped, abandoned, pitiful, and my legs were fearfully numb, and at the same time I kept recalling how fascinating she had been that morning in her dressing-jacket and with her hair down, and I was suddenly overcome by such acute jealousy that I leapt up in anguish, so that my neighbours stared at me in wonder and positive alarm.

At home I found deep snow and twenty degrees of frost. I'm fond of the winter; I'm fond of it because at that time, even in the hardest frosts, it's particularly snug at home. It's pleasant to put on one's fur jacket and felt overboots on a clear frosty day, to do something in the garden or in the yard, or to read in a well warmed room, to sit in my father's study before the open fire, to wash in my country bath-house.... Only if there is no mother in the house, no sister and no children, it is somehow dreary on winter evenings, and they seem extraordinarily long and quiet. And the warmer and snugger it is, the more acutely is this lack felt. In the winter when I came back from abroad, the evenings were endlessly long, I was intensely depressed, so depressed that I could not even read; in the daytime I was coming and going, clearing away the snow in the garden or feeding the chickens and the calves, but in the evening it was all up with me.

I had never cared for visitors before, but now I was glad of them, for I knew there was sure to be talk of Ariadne. Kotlovitch, the spiritualist, used often to come to talk about his sister, and sometimes he brought with him his friend Prince Maktuev, who was as much in love with Ariadne as I was. To sit in Ariadne's room, to finger the keys of her piano, to look at her music was a necessity for the prince—he could not live without it; and the spirit of his grandfather Ilarion was still predicting that sooner or later she would be his wife. The prince usually stayed a long time with us, from lunch to midnight, saying nothing all the time; in silence he would drink two or three bottles of beer, and from time to time, to show that he too was taking part in the conversation, he would laugh an abrupt, melancholy, foolish laugh. Before going home he would always take me aside and ask me in an undertone: "When did you see Ariadne Grigoryevna last? Was she quite well? I suppose she's not tired of being out there?"

Spring came on. There was the harrowing to do and then the sowing of spring corn and clover. I was sad, but there was the feeling of spring. One longed to accept the inevitable. Working in the fields and listening to the larks, I asked myself: "Couldn't I have done with this question of personal happiness once and for all? Couldn't I lay aside my fancy and marry a simple peasant girl?"

Suddenly when we were at our very busiest, I got a letter with the Italian stamp, and the clover and the beehives and the calves and the peasant girl all floated away like smoke. This time Ariadne wrote that she was profoundly, infinitely unhappy. She reproached me for not holding out a helping hand to her, for looking down upon her from the heights of my virtue and deserting her at the moment of danger. All this was written in a large, nervous handwriting with blots and smudges, and it was evident that she wrote in haste and distress. In conclusion she besought me to come and save her. Again my anchor was hauled up and I was carried away. Ariadne was in Rome. I arrived late in the evening, and when she saw me, she sobbed and threw herself on my neck. She had not changed at all that winter, and was just as young and charming. We had supper together and afterwards drove about Rome until dawn, and all the time she kept telling me about her doings. I asked where Lubkov was.

"Don't remind me of that creature!" she cried. "He is loathsome and disgusting to me!"

"But I thought you loved him," I said.

"Never," she said. "At first he struck me as original and aroused my pity, that was all. He is insolent and takes a woman by storm. And that's attractive. But we won't talk about him. That is a melancholy page in my life. He has gone to Russia to get money. Serve him right! I told him not to dare to come back."

She was living then, not at an hotel, but in a private lodging of two rooms which she had decorated in her own taste, frigidly and luxuriously. After Lubkov had gone away she had borrowed from her acquaintances about five thousand francs, and my arrival certainly was the one salvation for her. I had reckoned on taking her back to the country, but I did not succeed in that. She was homesick for her native place, but her recollections of the poverty she had been through there, of privations, of the rusty roof on her brother's house, roused a shudder of disgust, and when I suggested going home to her, she squeezed my hands convulsively and said:

"No, no, I shall die of boredom there!"

Then my love entered upon its final phase.

"Be the darling that you used to be; love me a little," said Ariadne, bending over to me. "You're sulky and prudent, you're afraid to yield to impulse, and keep thinking of consequences, and that's dull. Come, I beg you, I beseech you, be nice to me!... My pure one, my holy one, my dear one, I love you so!"

I became her lover. For a month anyway I was like a madman, conscious of nothing but rapture. To hold in one's arms a young and lovely body, with bliss to feel her warmth every time one waked up from sleep, and to remember that she was there—she, my Ariadne!—oh, it was not easy to get used to that! But yet I did get used to it, and by degrees became capable of reflecting on my new position. First of all, I realised, as before, that Ariadne did not love me. But she wanted to be really in love, she was afraid of solitude, and, above all, I was healthy, young, vigorous; she was sensual, like all cold people, as a rule—and we both made a show of being united by a passionate, mutual love. Afterwards I realised something else, too.

We stayed in Rome, in Naples, in Florence; we went to Paris, but there we thought it cold and went back to Italy. We introduced ourselves everywhere as husband and wife, wealthy landowners. People readily made our acquaintance and Ariadne had great social success everywhere. As she took lessons in painting, she was called an artist, and only imagine, that quite suited her, though she had not the slightest trace of talent.

She would sleep every day till two or three o'clock; she had her coffee and lunch in bed. At dinner she would eat soup, lobster, fish, meat, asparagus, game, and after she had gone to bed I used to bring up something, for instance roast beef, and she would eat it with a melancholy, careworn expression, and if she waked in the night she would eat apples and oranges.

The chief, so to say fundamental, characteristic of the woman was an amazing duplicity. She was continually deceitful every minute, apparently apart from any necessity, as it were by instinct, by an impulse such as makes the sparrow chirrup and the cockroach waggle its antennæ. She was deceitful with me, with the footman, with the porter, with the tradesmen in the shops, with her acquaintances; not one conversation, not one meeting, took place without affectation and pretence. A man had only to come into our room—whoever it might be, a waiter, or a baron—for her eyes, her expression, her voice to change, even the contour of her figure was transformed. At the very first glance at her then, you would have said there were no more wealthy and fashionable people in Italy than we. She never met an artist or a musician without telling him all sorts of lies about his remarkable talent.

"You have such a talent!" she would say, in honeyed cadences, "I'm really afraid of you. I think you must see right through people."

And all this simply in order to please, to be successful, to be fascinating! She waked up every morning with the one thought of "pleasing"! It was the aim and object of her life. If I had told her that in such a house, in such a street, there lived a man who was not attracted by her, it would have caused her real suffering. She wanted every day to enchant, to captivate, to drive men crazy. The fact that I was in her power and reduced to a complete nonentity before her charms gave her the same sort of satisfaction that visitors used to feel in tournaments. My subjection was not enough, and at nights, stretched out like a tigress, uncovered—she was always too hot—she would read the letters sent her by Lubkov; he besought her to return to Russia, vowing if she did not he would rob or murder some one to get the money to come to her. She hated him, but his passionate, slavish letters excited her. She had an extraordinary opinion of her own charms; she imagined that if somewhere, in some great assembly, men could have seen how beautifully she was made and the colour of her skin, she would have vanquished all Italy, the whole world. Her talk of her figure, of her skin, offended me, and observing this, she would, when she was angry, to vex me, say all sorts of vulgar things, taunting me. One day when we were at the summer villa of a lady of our acquaintance, and she lost her temper, she even went so far as to say: "If you don't leave off boring me with your sermons, I'll undress this minute and lie naked here on these flowers."

Often looking at her asleep, or eating, or trying to assume a naïve expression, I wondered why that extraordinary beauty, grace, and intelligence had been given her by God. Could it simply be for lolling in bed, eating and lying, lying endlessly? And was she intelligent really? She was afraid of three candles in a row, of the number thirteen, was terrified of spells and bad dreams. She argued about free love and freedom in general like a bigoted old woman, declared that Boleslav Markevitch was a better writer than Turgenev. But she was diabolically cunning and sharp, and knew how to seem a highly educated, advanced person in company.

Even at a good-humoured moment, she could always insult a servant or kill an insect without a pang; she liked bull-fights, liked to read about murders, and was angry when prisoners were acquitted.

For the life Ariadne and I were leading, we had to have a great deal of money. My poor father sent me his pension, all the little sums he received, borrowed for me wherever he could, and when one day he answered me: "Non habeo," I sent him a desperate telegram in which I besought him to mortgage the estate. A little later I begged him to get money somehow on a second mortgage. He did this too without a murmur and sent me every farthing. Ariadne despised the practical side of life; all this was no concern of hers, and when flinging away thousands of francs to satisfy her mad desires I groaned like an old tree, she would be singing "Addio bella Napoli" with a light heart.

Little by little I grew cold to her and began to be ashamed of our tie. I am not fond of pregnancy and confinements, but now I sometimes dreamed of a child who would have been at least a formal justification of our life. That I might not be completely disgusted with myself, I began reading and visiting museums and galleries, gave up drinking and took to eating very little. If one keeps oneself well in hand from morning to night, one's heart seems lighter. I began to bore Ariadne too. The people with whom she won her triumphs were, by the way, all of the middling sort; as before, there were no ambassadors, there was no salon, the money did not run to it, and this mortified her and made her sob, and she announced to me at last that perhaps she would not be against our returning to Russia.

And here we are on our way. For the last few months she has been zealously corresponding with her brother; she evidently has some secret projects, but what they are—God knows! I am sick of trying to fathom her underhand schemes! But we're going, not to the country, but to Yalta and afterwards to the Caucasus. She can only exist now at watering-places, and if you knew how I hate all these watering-places, how suffocated and ashamed I am in them. If I could be in the country now! If I could only be working now, earning my bread by the sweat of my brow, atoning for my follies. I am conscious of a superabundance of energy and I believe that if I were to put that energy to work I could redeem my estate in five years. But now, as you see, there is a complication. Here we're not abroad, but in mother Russia; we shall have to think of lawful wedlock. Of course, all attraction is over; there is no trace left of my old love, but, however that may be, I am bound in honour to marry her.

—

Shamohin, excited by his story, went below with me and we continued talking about women. It was late. It appeared that he and I were in the same cabin.

"So far it is only in the village that woman has not fallen behind man," said Shamohin. "There she thinks and feels just as man does, and struggles with nature in the name of culture as zealously as he. In the towns the woman of the bourgeois or intellectual class has long since fallen behind, and is returning to her primitive condition. She is half a human beast already, and, thanks to her, a great deal of what had been won by human genius has been lost again; the woman gradually disappears and in her place is the primitive female. This dropping-back on the part of the educated woman is a real danger to culture; in her retrogressive movement she tries to drag man after her and prevents him from moving forward. That is incontestable."

I asked: "Why generalise? Why judge of all women from Ariadne alone? The very struggle of women for education and sexual equality, which I look upon as a struggle for justice, precludes any hypothesis of a retrograde movement."

But Shamohin scarcely listened to me and he smiled distrustfully. He was a passionate, convinced misogynist, and it was impossible to alter his convictions.

"Oh, nonsense!" he interrupted. "When once a woman sees in me, not a man, not an equal, but a male, and her one anxiety all her life is to attract me—that is, to take possession of me—how can one talk of their rights? Oh, don't you believe them; they are very, very cunning! We men make a great stir about their emancipation, but they don't care about their emancipation at all, they only pretend to care about it; they are horribly cunning things, horribly cunning!"

I began to feel sleepy and weary of discussion. I turned over with my face to the wall.

"Yes," I heard as I fell asleep—"yes, and it's our education that's at fault, sir. In our towns, the whole education and bringing up of women in its essence tends to develop her into the human beast—that is, to make her attractive to the male and able to vanquish him. Yes, indeed"—Shamohin sighed—"little girls ought to be taught and brought up with boys, so that they might be always together. A woman ought to be trained so that she may be able, like a man, to recognise when she's wrong, or she always thinks she's in the right. Instil into a little girl from her cradle that a man is not first of all a cavalier or a possible lover, but her neighbour, her equal in everything. Train her to think logically, to generalise, and do not assure her that her brain weighs less than a man's and that therefore she can be indifferent to the sciences, to the arts, to the tasks of culture in general. The apprentice to the shoemaker or the house painter has a brain of smaller size than the grown-up man too, yet he works, suffers, takes his part in the general struggle for existence. We must give up our attitude to the physiological aspect, too—to pregnancy and childbirth, seeing that in the first place women don't have babies every month; secondly, not all women have babies; and, thirdly, a normal countrywoman works in the fields up to the day of her confinement and it does her no harm. Then there ought to be absolute equality in everyday life. If a man gives a lady his chair or picks up the handkerchief she has dropped, let her repay him in the same way. I have no objection if a girl of good family helps me to put on my coat or hands me a glass of water—"

I heard no more, for I fell asleep.

Next morning when we were approaching Sevastopol, it was damp, unpleasant weather; the ship rocked. Shamohin sat on deck with me, brooding and silent. When the bell rang for tea, men with their coat-collars turned up and ladies with pale, sleepy faces began going below; a young and very beautiful lady, the one who had been so angry with the Customs officers at Volotchisk, stopped before Shamohin and said with the expression of a naughty, fretful child:

"Jean, your birdie's been sea-sick."

Afterwards when I was at Yalta I saw the same beautiful lady dashing about on horseback with a couple of officers hardly able to keep up with her. And one morning I saw her in an overall and a Phrygian cap, sketching on the sea-front with a great crowd admiring her a little way off. I too was introduced to her. She pressed my hand with great warmth, and looking at me ecstatically, thanked me in honeyed cadences for the pleasure I had given her by my writings.

"Don't you believe her," Shamohin whispered to me, "she has never read a word of them."

When I was walking on the sea-front in the early evening Shamohin met me with his arms full of big parcels of fruits and dainties.

"Prince Maktuev is here!" he said joyfully. "He came yesterday with her brother, the spiritualist! Now I understand what she was writing to him about! Oh, Lord!" he went on, gazing up to heaven, and pressing his parcels to his bosom. "If she hits it off with the prince, it means freedom, then I can go back to the country with my father!"

And he ran on.

"I begin to believe in spirits," he called to me, looking back. "The spirit of grandfather Ilarion seems to have prophesied the truth! Oh, if only it is so!"

—

The day after this meeting I left Yalta and how Shamohin's story ended I don't know.

An Artist's Story

[The House with a Mezzanine]

I

It was six or seven years ago when I was living in one of the districts of the province of T——, on the estate of a young landowner called Byelokurov, who used to get up very early, wear a peasant tunic, drink beer in the evenings, and continually complain to me that he never met with sympathy from any one. He lived in the lodge in the garden, and I in the old seigniorial house, in a big room with columns, where there was no furniture except a wide sofa on which I used to sleep, and a table on which I used to lay out patience. There was always, even in still weather, a droning noise in the old Amos stoves, and in thunderstorms the whole house shook and seemed to be cracking into pieces; and it was rather terrifying, especially at night, when all the ten big windows were suddenly lit up by lightning.

Condemned by destiny to perpetual idleness, I did absolutely nothing. For hours together I gazed out of window at the sky, at the birds, at the avenue, read everything that was brought me by post, slept. Sometimes I went out of the house and wandered about till late in the evening.

One day as I was returning home, I accidentally strayed into a place I did not know. The sun was already sinking, and the shades of evening lay across the flowering rye. Two rows of old, closely planted, very tall fir-trees stood like two dense walls forming a picturesque, gloomy avenue. I easily climbed over the fence and walked along the avenue, slipping over the fir-needles which lay two inches deep on the ground. It was still and dark, and only here and there on the high tree-tops the vivid golden light quivered and made rainbows in the spiders' webs. There was a strong, almost stifling smell of resin. Then I turned into a long avenue of limes. Here, too, all was desolation and age; last year's leaves rusted mournfully under my feet and in the twilight shadows lurked between the trees. From the old orchard on the right came the faint, reluctant note of the golden oriole, who must have been old too. But at last the limes ended. I walked by an old white house of two storeys with a terrace, and there suddenly opened before me a view of a courtyard, a large pond with a bathing-house, a group of green willows, and a village on the further bank, with a high, narrow belfry on which there glittered a cross reflecting the setting sun.

For a moment it breathed upon me the fascination of something near and very familiar, as though I had seen that landscape at some time in my childhood.

At the white stone gates which led from the yard to the fields, old-fashioned solid gates with lions on them, were standing two girls. One of them, the elder, a slim, pale, very handsome girl with a perfect haystack of chestnut hair and a little obstinate mouth, had a severe expression and scarcely took notice of me, while the other, who was still very young, not more than seventeen or eighteen, and was also slim and pale, with a large mouth and large eyes, looked at me with astonishment as I passed by, said something in English, and was overcome with embarrassment. And it seemed to me that these two charming faces, too, had long been familiar to me. And I returned home feeling as though I had had a delightful dream.

One morning soon afterwards, as Byelokurov and I were walking near the house, a carriage drove unexpectedly into the yard, rustling over the grass, and in it was sitting one of those girls. It was the elder one. She had come to ask for subscriptions for some villagers whose cottages had been burnt down. Speaking with great earnestness and precision, and not looking at us, she told us how many houses in the village of Siyanovo had been burnt, how many men, women, and children were left homeless, and what steps were proposed, to begin with, by the Relief Committee, of which she was now a member. After handing us the subscription list for our signatures, she put it away and immediately began to take leave of us.

"You have quite forgotten us, Pyotr Petrovitch," she said to Byelokurov as she shook hands with him. "Do come, and if Monsieur N. (she mentioned my name) cares to make the acquaintance of admirers of his work, and will come and see us, mother and I will be delighted."

I bowed.

When she had gone Pyotr Petrovitch began to tell me about her. The girl was, he said, of good family, and her name was Lidia Voltchaninov, and the estate on which she lived with her mother and sister, like the village on the other side of the pond, was called Shelkovka. Her father had once held an important position in Moscow, and had died with the rank of privy councillor. Although they had ample means, the Voltchaninovs lived on their estate summer and winter without going away. Lidia was a teacher in the Zemstvo school in her own village, and received a salary of twenty-five roubles a month. She spent nothing on herself but her salary, and was proud of earning her own living.

"An interesting family," said Byelokurov. "Let us go over one day. They will be delighted to see you."

One afternoon on a holiday we thought of the Voltchaninovs, and went to Shelkovka to see them. They—the mother and two daughters—were at home. The mother, Ekaterina Pavlovna, who at one time had been handsome, but now, asthmatic, depressed, vague, and over-feeble for her years, tried to entertain me with conversation about painting. Having heard from her daughter that I might come to Shelkovka, she had hurriedly recalled two or three of my landscapes which she had seen in exhibitions in Moscow, and now asked what I meant to express by them. Lidia, or as they called her Lida, talked more to Byelokurov than to me. Earnest and unsmiling, she asked him why he was not on the Zemstvo, and why he had not attended any of its meetings.

"It's not right, Pyotr Petrovitch," she said reproachfully. "It's not right. It's too bad."

"That's true, Lida—that's true," the mother assented. "It isn't right."

"Our whole district is in the hands of Balagin," Lida went on, addressing me. "He is the chairman of the Zemstvo Board, and he has distributed all the posts in the district among his nephews and sons-in-law; and he does as he likes. He ought to be opposed. The young men ought to make a strong party, but you see what the young men among us are like. It's a shame, Pyotr Petrovitch!"

The younger sister, Genya, was silent while they were talking of the Zemstvo. She took no part in serious conversation. She was not looked upon as quite grown up by her family, and, like a child, was always called by the nickname of Misuce, because that was what she had called her English governess when she was a child. She was all the time looking at me with curiosity, and when I glanced at the photographs in the album, she explained to me: "That's uncle . . . that's god-father," moving her finger across the photograph. As she did so she touched me with her shoulder like a child, and I had a close view of her delicate, undeveloped chest, her slender shoulders, her plait, and her thin little body tightly drawn in by her sash.

We played croquet and lawn tennis, we walked about the garden, drank tea, and then sat a long time over supper. After the huge empty room with columns, I felt, as it were, at home in this small snug house where there were no oleographs on the walls and where the servants were spoken to with civility. And everything seemed to me young and pure, thanks to the presence of Lida and Misuce, and there was an atmosphere of refinement over everything. At supper Lida talked to Byelokurov again of the Zemstvo, of Balagin, and of school libraries. She was an energetic, genuine girl, with convictions, and it was interesting to listen to her, though she talked a great deal and in a loud voice—perhaps because she was accustomed to talking at school. On the other hand, Pyotr Petrovitch, who had retained from his student days the habit of turning every conversation into an argument, was tedious, flat, long-winded, and unmistakably anxious to appear clever and advanced. Gesticulating, he upset a sauce-boat with his sleeve, making a huge pool on the tablecloth, but no one except me appeared to notice it.

It was dark and still as we went home.

"Good breeding is shown, not by not upsetting the sauce, but by not noticing it when somebody else does," said Byelokurov, with a sigh. "Yes, a splendid, intellectual family! I've dropped out of all decent society; it's dreadful how I've dropped out of it! It's all through work, work, work!"

He talked of how hard one had to work if one wanted to be a model farmer. And I thought what a heavy, sluggish fellow he was! Whenever he talked of anything serious he articulated "Er-er" with intense effort, and worked just as he talked—slowly, always late and behindhand. I had little faith in his business capacity if only from the fact that when I gave him letters to post he carried them about in his pocket for weeks together.

"The hardest thing of all," he muttered as he walked beside me—"the hardest thing of all is that, work as one may, one meets with no sympathy from any one. No sympathy!"

II

I took to going to see the Voltchaninovs. As a rule I sat on the lower step of the terrace; I was fretted by dissatisfaction with myself; I was sorry at the thought of my life passing so rapidly and uninterestingly, and felt as though I would like to tear out of my breast the heart which had grown so heavy. And meanwhile I heard talk on the terrace, the rustling of dresses, the pages of a book being turned. I soon grew accustomed to the idea that during the day Lida received patients, gave out books, and often went into the village with a parasol and no hat, and in the evening talked aloud of the Zemstvo and schools. This slim, handsome, invariably austere girl, with her small well-cut mouth, always said dryly when the conversation turned on serious subjects:

"That's of no interest to you."

She did not like me. She disliked me because I was a landscape painter and did not in my pictures portray the privations of the peasants, and because, as she fancied, I was indifferent to what she put such faith in. I remember when I was travelling on the banks of Lake Baikal, I met a Buriat girl on horseback, wearing a shirt and trousers of blue Chinese canvas; I asked her if she would sell me her pipe. While we talked she looked contemptuously at my European face and hat, and in a moment she was bored with talking to me; she shouted to her horse and galloped on. And in just the same way Lida despised me as an alien. She never outwardly expressed her dislike for me, but I felt it, and sitting on the lower step of the terrace, I felt irritated, and said that doctoring peasants when one was not a doctor was deceiving them, and that it was easy to be benevolent when one had six thousand acres.

Meanwhile her sister Misuce had no cares, and spent her life in complete idleness just as I did. When she got up in the morning she immediately took up a book and sat down to read on the terrace in a deep arm-chair, with her feet hardly touching the ground, or hid herself with her book in the lime avenue, or walked out into the fields. She spent the whole day reading, poring greedily over her book, and only from the tired, dazed look in her eyes and the extreme paleness of her face one could divine how this continual reading exhausted her brain. When I arrived she would flush a little, leave her book, and looking into my face with her big eyes, would tell me eagerly of anything that had happened—for instance, that the chimney had been on fire in the servants' hall, or that one of the men had caught a huge fish in the pond. On ordinary days she usually went about in a light blouse and a dark blue skirt. We went for walks together, picked cherries for making jam, went out in the boat. When she jumped up to reach a cherry or sculled in the boat, her thin, weak arms showed through her transparent sleeves. Or I painted a sketch, and she stood beside me watching rapturously.

One Sunday at the end of July I came to the Voltchaninovs about nine o'clock in the morning. I walked about the park, keeping a good distance from the house, looking for white mushrooms, of which there was a great number that summer, and noting their position so as to come and pick them afterwards with Genya. There was a warm breeze. I saw Genya and her mother both in light holiday dresses coming home from church, Genya holding her hat in the wind. Afterwards I heard them having tea on the terrace.

For a careless person like me, trying to find justification for my perpetual idleness, these holiday mornings in our country-houses in the summer have always had a particular charm. When the green garden, still wet with dew, is all sparkling in the sun and looks radiant with happiness, when there is a scent of mignonette and oleander near the house, when the young people have just come back from church and are having breakfast in the garden, all so charmingly dressed and gay, and one knows that all these healthy, well-fed, handsome people are going to do nothing the whole long day, one wishes that all life were like that. Now, too, I had the same thought, and walked about the garden prepared to walk about like that, aimless and unoccupied, the whole day, the whole summer.

Genya came out with a basket; she had a look in her face as though she knew she would find me in the garden, or had a presentiment of it. We gathered mushrooms and talked, and when she asked a question she walked a little ahead so as to see my face.

"A miracle happened in the village yesterday," she said. "The lame woman Pelagea has been ill the whole year. No doctors or medicines did her any good; but yesterday an old woman came and whispered something over her, and her illness passed away."

"That's nothing much," I said. "You mustn't look for miracles only among sick people and old women. Isn't health a miracle? And life itself? Whatever is beyond understanding is a miracle."

"And aren't you afraid of what is beyond understanding?"

"No. Phenomena I don't understand I face boldly, and am not overwhelmed by them. I am above them. Man ought to recognise himself as superior to lions, tigers, stars, superior to everything in nature, even what seems miraculous and is beyond his understanding, or else he is not a man, but a mouse afraid of everything."

Genya believed that as an artist I knew a very great deal, and could guess correctly what I did not know. She longed for me to initiate her into the domain of the Eternal and the Beautiful—into that higher world in which, as she imagined, I was quite at home. And she talked to me of God, of the eternal life, of the miraculous. And I, who could never admit that my self and my imagination would be lost forever after death, answered: "Yes, men are immortal"; "Yes, there is eternal life in store for us." And she listened, believed, and did not ask for proofs.

As we were going home she stopped suddenly and said:

"Our Lida is a remarkable person—isn't she? I love her very dearly, and would be ready to give my life for her any minute. But tell me"—Genya touched my sleeve with her finger—"tell me, why do you always argue with her? Why are you irritated?"

"Because she is wrong."

Genya shook her head and tears came into her eyes.

"How incomprehensible that is!" she said.

At that minute Lida had just returned from somewhere, and standing with a whip in her hand, a slim, beautiful figure in the sunlight, at the steps, she was giving some orders to one of the men. Talking loudly, she hurriedly received two or three sick villagers; then with a busy and anxious face she walked about the rooms, opening one cupboard after another, and went upstairs. It was a long time before they could find her and call her to dinner, and she came in when we had finished our soup. All these tiny details I remember with tenderness, and that whole day I remember vividly, though nothing special happened. After dinner Genya lay in a long arm-chair reading, while I sat upon the bottom step of the terrace. We were silent. The whole sky was overcast with clouds, and it began to spot with fine rain. It was hot; the wind had dropped, and it seemed as though the day would never end. Ekaterina Pavlovna came out on the terrace, looking drowsy and carrying a fan.

"Oh, mother," said Genya, kissing her hand, "it's not good for you to sleep in the day."

They adored each other. When one went into the garden, the other would stand on the terrace, and, looking towards the trees, call "Aa—oo, Genya!" or "Mother, where are you?" They always said their prayers together, and had the same faith; and they understood each other perfectly even when they did not speak. And their attitude to people was the same. Ekaterina Pavlovna, too, grew quickly used to me and fond of me, and when I did not come for two or three days, sent to ask if I were well. She, too, gazed at my sketches with enthusiasm, and with the same openness and readiness to chatter as Misuce, she told me what had happened, and confided to me her domestic secrets.

She had a perfect reverence for her elder daughter. Lida did not care for endearments, she talked only of serious matters; she lived her life apart, and to her mother and sister was as sacred and enigmatic a person as the admiral, always sitting in his cabin, is to the sailors.

"Our Lida is a remarkable person," the mother would often say. "Isn't she?"

Now, too, while it was drizzling with rain, we talked of Lida.

"She is a remarkable girl," said her mother, and added in an undertone, like a conspirator, looking about her timidly: "You wouldn't easily find another like her; only, do you know, I am beginning to be a little uneasy. The school, the dispensary, books—all that's very good, but why go to extremes? She is three-and-twenty, you know; it's time for her to think seriously of herself. With her books and her dispensary she will find life has slipped by without having noticed it. . . . She must be married."

Genya, pale from reading, with her hair disarranged, raised her head and said as it were to herself, looking at her mother:

"Mother, everything is in God's hands."

And again she buried herself in her book.

Byelokurov came in his tunic and embroidered shirt. We played croquet and tennis, then when it got dark, sat a long time over supper and talked again about schools, and about Balagin, who had the whole district under his thumb. As I went away from the Voltchaninovs that evening, I carried away the impression of a long, long idle day, with a melancholy consciousness that everything ends in this world, however long it may be.

Genya saw us out to the gate, and perhaps because she had been with me all day, from morning till night, I felt dull without her, and that all that charming family were near and dear to me, and for the first time that summer I had a yearning to paint.

"Tell me, why do you lead such a dreary, colourless life?" I asked Byelokurov as I went home. "My life is dreary, difficult, and monotonous because I am an artist, a strange person. From my earliest days

I've been wrung by envy, self-dissatisfaction, distrust in my work. I'm always poor, I'm a wanderer, but you—you're a healthy, normal man, a landowner, and a gentleman. Why do you live in such an uninteresting way? Why do you get so little out of life? Why haven't you, for instance, fallen in love with Lida or Genya?"

"You forget that I love another woman," answered Byelokurov.

He was referring to Liubov Ivanovna, the lady who shared the lodge with him. Every day I saw this lady, very plump, rotund, and dignified, not unlike a fat goose, walking about the garden, in the Russian national dress and beads, always carrying a parasol; and the servant was continually calling her in to dinner or to tea. Three years before she had taken one of the lodges for a summer holiday, and had settled down at Byelokurov's apparently forever. She was ten years older than he was, and kept a sharp hand over him, so much so that he had to ask her permission when he went out of the house. She often sobbed in a deep masculine note, and then I used to send word to her that if she did not leave off, I should give up my rooms there; and she left off.

When we got home Byelokurov sat down on the sofa and frowned thoughtfully, and I began walking up and down the room, conscious of a soft emotion as though I were in love. I wanted to talk about the Voltchaninovs.

"Lida could only fall in love with a member of the Zemstvo, as devoted to schools and hospitals as she is," I said. "Oh, for the sake of a girl like that one might not only go into the Zemstvo, but even wear out iron shoes, like the girl in the fairy tale. And Misuce? What a sweet creature she is, that Misuce!"

Byelokurov, drawling out "Er—er," began a long-winded disquisition on the malady of the age—pessimism. He talked confidently, in a tone that suggested that I was opposing him. Hundreds of miles of desolate, monotonous, burnt-up steppe cannot induce such deep depression as one man when he sits and talks, and one does not know when he will go.

"It's not a question of pessimism or optimism," I said irritably; "it's simply that ninety-nine people out of a hundred have no sense."

Byelokurov took this as aimed at himself, was offended, and went away.

III

"The prince is staying at Malozyomovo, and he asks to be remembered to you," said Lida to her mother. She had just come in, and was taking off her gloves. "He gave me a great deal of interesting news. . . . He promised to raise the question of a medical relief centre at Malozyomovo again at the provincial assembly, but he says there is very little hope of it." And turning to me, she said: "Excuse me, I always forget that this cannot be interesting to you."

I felt irritated.

"Why not interesting to me?" I said, shrugging my shoulders. "You do not care to know my opinion, but I assure you the question has great interest for me."

"Yes?"

"Yes. In my opinion a medical relief centre at Malozyomovo is quite unnecessary."

My irritation infected her; she looked at me, screwing up her eyes, and asked:

"What is necessary? Landscapes?"

"Landscapes are not, either. Nothing is."

She finished taking off her gloves, and opened the newspaper, which had just been brought from the post. A minute later she said quietly, evidently restraining herself:

"Last week Anna died in childbirth, and if there had been a medical relief centre near, she would have lived. And I think even landscape-painters ought to have some opinions on the subject."

"I have a very definite opinion on that subject, I assure you," I answered; and she screened herself with the newspaper, as though unwilling to listen to me. "To my mind, all these schools, dispensaries, libraries, medical relief centres, under present conditions, only serve to aggravate the bondage of the people. The peasants are fettered by a great chain, and you do not break the chain, but only add fresh links to it—that's my view of it."

She raised her eyes to me and smiled ironically, and I went on trying to formulate my leading idea.

"What matters is not that Anna died in childbirth, but that all these

Annas, Mavras, Pelageas, toil from early morning till dark, fall ill from working beyond their strength, all their lives tremble for their sick and hungry children, all their lives are being doctored, and in dread of death and disease, fade and grow old early, and die in filth and stench. Their children begin the same story over again as soon as they grow up, and so it goes on for hundreds of years and milliards of men live worse than beasts—in continual terror, for a mere crust of bread. The whole horror of their position lies in their never having time to think of their souls, of their image and semblance. Cold, hunger, animal terror, a burden of toil, like avalanches of snow, block for them every way to spiritual activity—that is, to what distinguishes man from the brutes and what is the only thing which makes life worth living. You go to their help with hospitals and schools, but you don't free them from their fetters by that; on the contrary, you bind them in closer bonds, as, by introducing new prejudices, you increase the number of their wants, to say nothing of the fact that they've got to pay the Zemstvo for blisters and books, and so toil harder than ever."

"I am not going to argue with you," said Lida, putting down the paper. "I've heard all that before. I will only say one thing: one cannot sit with one's hands in one's lap. It's true that we are not saving humanity, and perhaps we make a great many mistakes; but we do what we can, and we are right. The highest and holiest task for a civilised being is to serve his neighbours, and we try to serve them as best we can. You don't like it, but one can't please every one."

"That's true, Lida," said her mother—"that's true."

In Lida's presence she was always a little timid, and looked at her nervously as she talked, afraid of saying something superfluous or inopportune. And she never contradicted her, but always assented: "That's true, Lida—that's true."

"Teaching the peasants to read and write, books of wretched precepts and rhymes, and medical relief centres, cannot diminish either ignorance or the death-rate, just as the light from your windows cannot light up this huge garden," said I. "You give nothing. By meddling in these people's lives you only create new wants in them, and new demands on their labour."

"Ach! Good heavens! But one must do something!" said Lida with vexation, and from her tone one could see that she thought my arguments worthless and despised them.

"The people must be freed from hard physical labour," said I. "We must lighten their yoke, let them have time to breathe, that they may not spend all their lives at the stove, at the wash-tub, and in the fields, but may also have time to think of their souls, of God—may have time to develop their spiritual capacities. The highest vocation of man is spiritual activity—the perpetual search for truth and the meaning of life. Make coarse animal labour unnecessary for them, let them feel themselves free, and then you will see what a mockery these dispensaries and books are. Once a man recognises his true vocation, he can only be satisfied by religion, science, and art, and not by these trifles."

"Free them from labour?" laughed Lida. "But is that possible?"

"Yes. Take upon yourself a share of their labour. If all of us, townspeople and country people, all without exception, would agree to divide between us the labour which mankind spends on the satisfaction of their physical needs, each of us would perhaps need to work only for two or three hours a day. Imagine that we all, rich and poor, work only for three hours a day, and the rest of our time is free. Imagine further that in order to depend even less upon our bodies and to labour less, we invent machines to replace our work, we try to cut down our needs to the minimum. We would harden ourselves and our children that they should not be afraid of hunger and cold, and that we shouldn't be continually trembling for their health like Anna, Mavra, and Pelagea. Imagine that we don't doctor ourselves, don't keep dispensaries, tobacco factories, distilleries—what a lot of free time would be left us after all! All of us together would devote our leisure to science and art. Just as the peasants sometimes work, the whole community together mending the roads, so all of us, as a community, would search for truth and the meaning of life, and I am convinced that the truth would be discovered very quickly; man would escape from this continual, agonising, oppressive dread of death, and even from death itself."

"You contradict yourself, though," said Lida. "You talk about science, and are yourself opposed to elementary education."

"Elementary education when a man has nothing to read but the signs on public houses and sometimes books which he cannot understand—such education has existed among us since the times of Rurik; Gogol's Petrushka has been reading for ever so long, yet as the village was in the days of Rurik so it has remained. What is needed is not elementary education, but freedom for a wide development of spiritual capacities. What are wanted are not schools, but universities."

"You are opposed to medicine, too."

"Yes. It would be necessary only for the study of diseases as natural phenomena, and not for the cure of them. If one must cure, it should not be diseases, but the causes of them. Remove the principal cause—physical labour, and then there will be no disease. I don't believe in a science that cures disease," I went on excitedly. "When science and art are real, they aim not at temporary private ends, but at eternal and universal—they seek for truth and the meaning of life, they seek for God, for the soul, and when they are tied down to the needs and evils of the day, to dispensaries and libraries, they only complicate and hamper life. We have plenty of doctors, chemists, lawyers, plenty of people can read and write, but we are quite without biologists, mathematicians, philosophers, poets. The whole of our intelligence, the whole of our spiritual energy, is spent on satisfying temporary, passing needs. Scientific men, writers, artists, are hard at work; thanks to them, the conveniences of life are multiplied from day to day. Our physical demands increase, yet truth is still a long way off, and man still remains the most rapacious and dirty animal; everything is tending to the degeneration of the majority of mankind, and the loss forever of all fitness for life. In such conditions an artist's work has no meaning, and the more talented he is, the stranger and the more unintelligible is his position, as when one looks into it, it is evident that he is working for the amusement of a rapacious and unclean animal, and is supporting the existing order. And I don't care to work and I won't work.... Nothing is any use; let the earth sink to perdition!"

"Misuce, go out of the room!" said Lida to her sister, apparently thinking my words pernicious to the young girl.

Genya looked mournfully at her mother and sister, and went out of the room.

"These are the charming things people say when they want to justify their indifference," said Lida. "It is easier to disapprove of schools and hospitals, than to teach or heal."

"That's true, Lida—that's true," the mother assented.

"You threaten to give up working," said Lida. "You evidently set a high value on your work. Let us give up arguing; we shall never agree, since I put the most imperfect dispensary or library of which you have just spoken so contemptuously on a higher level than any landscape." And turning at once to her mother, she began speaking in quite a different tone: "The prince is very much changed, and much thinner than when he was with us last. He is being sent to Vichy."

She told her mother about the prince in order to avoid talking to me. Her face glowed, and to hide her feeling she bent low over the table as though she were short-sighted, and made a show of reading the newspaper. My presence was disagreeable to her. I said good-bye and went home.

IV

It was quite still out of doors; the village on the further side of the pond was already asleep; there was not a light to be seen, and only the stars were faintly reflected in the pond. At the gate with the lions on it Genya was standing motionless, waiting to escort me.

"Every one is asleep in the village," I said to her, trying to make out her face in the darkness, and I saw her mournful dark eyes fixed upon me. "The publican and the horse-stealers are asleep, while we, well-bred people, argue and irritate each other."

It was a melancholy August night—melancholy because there was already a feeling of autumn; the moon was rising behind a purple cloud, and it shed a faint light upon the road and on the dark fields of winter corn by the sides. From time to time a star fell. Genya walked beside me along the road, and tried not to look at the sky, that she might not see the falling stars, which for some reason frightened her.

"I believe you are right," she said, shivering with the damp night air. "If people, all together, could devote themselves to spiritual ends, they would soon know everything."

"Of course. We are higher beings, and if we were really to recognise the whole force of human genius and lived only for higher ends, we should in the end become like gods. But that will never be—mankind will degenerate till no traces of genius remain."

When the gates were out of sight, Genya stopped and shook hands with me.

"Good-night," she said, shivering; she had nothing but her blouse over her shoulders and was shrinking with cold. "Come to-morrow."

I felt wretched at the thought of being left alone, irritated and dissatisfied with myself and other people; and I, too, tried not to look at the falling stars.

"Stay another minute," I said to her, "I entreat you."

I loved Genya. I must have loved her because she met me when I came and saw me off when I went away; because she looked at me tenderly and enthusiastically. How touchingly beautiful were her pale face, slender neck, slender arms, her weakness, her idleness, her reading. And intelligence? I suspected in her intelligence above the average. I was fascinated by the breadth of her views, perhaps because they were different from those of the stern, handsome Lida, who disliked me. Genya liked me, because I was an artist. I had conquered her heart by my talent, and had a passionate desire to paint for her sake alone; and I dreamed of her as of my little queen who with me would possess those trees, those fields, the mists, the dawn, the exquisite and beautiful scenery in the midst of which I had felt myself hopelessly solitary and useless.

"Stay another minute," I begged her. "I beseech you."

I took off my overcoat and put it over her chilly shoulders; afraid of looking ugly and absurd in a man's overcoat, she laughed, threw it off, and at that instant I put my arms round her and covered her face, shoulders, and hands with kisses.

"Till to-morrow," she whispered, and softly, as though afraid of breaking upon the silence of the night, she embraced me. "We have no secrets from one another. I must tell my mother and my sister at once. . . . It's so dreadful! Mother is all right; mother likes you—but Lida!"

She ran to the gates.

"Good-bye!" she called.

And then for two minutes I heard her running. I did not want to go home, and I had nothing to go for. I stood still for a little time hesitating, and made my way slowly back, to look once more at the house in which she lived, the sweet, simple old house, which seemed to be watching me from the windows of its upper storey, and understanding all about it. I walked by the terrace, sat on the seat by the tennis ground, in the dark under the old elm-tree, and looked from there at the house. In the windows of the top storey where Misuce slept there appeared a bright light, which changed to a soft green—they had covered the lamp with the shade. Shadows began to move. . . . I was full of tenderness, peace, and satisfaction with myself—satisfaction at having been able to be carried away by my feelings and having fallen in love, and at the same time I felt uncomfortable at the thought that only a few steps away from me, in one of the rooms of that house there was Lida, who disliked and perhaps hated me. I went on sitting there wondering whether Genya would come out; I listened and fancied I heard voices talking upstairs.

About an hour passed. The green light went out, and the shadows were no longer visible. The moon was standing high above the house, and lighting up the sleeping garden and the paths; the dahlias and the roses in front of the house could be seen distinctly, and looked all the same colour. It began to grow very cold. I went out of the garden, picked up my coat on the road, and slowly sauntered home.

When next day after dinner I went to the Voltchaninovs, the glass door into the garden was wide open. I sat down on the terrace, expecting Genya every minute, to appear from behind the flower-beds on the lawn, or from one of the avenues, or that I should hear her voice from the house. Then I walked into the drawing-room, the dining-room. There was not a soul to be seen. From the dining-room I walked along the long corridor to the hall and back. In this corridor there were several doors, and through one of them I heard the voice of Lida:

" 'God . . . sent . . . a crow,' " she said in a loud, emphatic voice, probably dictating—" 'God sent a crow a piece of cheese. . . . A crow . . . a piece of cheese.' . . . Who's there?" she called suddenly, hearing my steps.

"It's I."

"Ah! Excuse me, I cannot come out to you this minute; I'm giving Dasha her lesson."

"Is Ekaterina Pavlovna in the garden?"

"No, she went away with my sister this morning to our aunt in the province of Penza. And in the winter they will probably go abroad," she added after a pause. " 'God sent . . . the crow . . . a piece . . . of cheese.' . . . Have you written it?"

I went into the hall, and stared vacantly at the pond and the village, and the sound reached me of "A piece of cheese. . . . God sent the crow a piece of cheese."

And I went back by the way I had come here for the first time—first from the yard into the garden past the house, then into the avenue of lime-trees. . . . At this point I was overtaken by a small boy who gave me a note:

"I told my sister everything and she insists on my parting from you," I read. "I could not wound her by disobeying. God will give you happiness. Forgive me. If only you knew how bitterly my mother and I are crying!"

Then there was the dark fir avenue, the broken-down fence. . . . On the field where then the rye was in flower and the corncrakes were calling, now there were cows and hobbled horses. On the slope there were bright green patches of winter corn. A sober workaday feeling came over me and I felt ashamed of all I had said at the Voltchaninovs', and felt bored with life as I had been before. When I got home, I packed and set off that evening for Petersburg.

—

I never saw the Voltchaninovs again. Not long ago, on my way to the Crimea, I met Byelokurov in the train. As before, he was wearing a jerkin and an embroidered shirt, and when I asked how he was, he replied that, God be praised, he was well. We began talking. He had sold his old estate and bought another smaller one, in the name of Liubov Ivanovna. He could tell me little about the Voltchaninovs. Lida, he said, was still living in Shelkovka and teaching in the school; she had by degrees succeeded in gathering round her a circle of people sympathetic to her who made a strong party, and at the last election had turned out Balagin, who had till then had the whole district under his thumb. About Genya he only told me that she did not live at home, and that he did not know where she was.

I am beginning to forget the old house, and only sometimes when I am painting or reading I suddenly, apropos of nothing, remember the green light in the window, the sound of my footsteps as I walked home through the fields in the night, with my heart full of love, rubbing my hands in the cold. And still more rarely, at moments when I am sad and depressed by loneliness, I have dim memories, and little by little I begin to feel that she is thinking of me, too—that she is waiting for me, and that we shall meet. . . .

Misuce, where are you?

The Petchenyeg

Ivan Abramitch Zhmuhin, a retired Cossack officer, who had once served in the Caucasus, but now lived on his own farm, and who had once been young, strong, and vigorous, but now was old, dried up, and bent, with shaggy eyebrows and a greenish-grey moustache, was returning from the town to his farm one hot summer's day. In the town he had confessed and received absolution, and had made his will at the notary's (a fortnight before he had had a slight stroke), and now all the while he was in the railway carriage he was haunted by melancholy, serious thoughts of approaching death, of the vanity of vanities, of the transitoriness of all things earthly. At the station of Provalye—there is such a one on the Donetz line—a fair-haired, plump, middle-aged gentleman with a shabby portfolio stepped into the carriage and sat down opposite. They got into conversation.

"Yes," said Ivan Abramitch, looking pensively out of window, "it is never too late to marry. I myself married when I was forty-eight; I was told it was late, but it has turned out that it was not late or early, but simply that it would have been better not to marry at all. Everyone is soon tired of his wife, but not everyone tells the truth, because, you know, people are ashamed of an unhappy home life and conceal it. It's

'Manya this' and 'Manya that' with many a man by his wife's side, but if he had his way he'd put that Manya in a sack and drop her in the water. It's dull with one's wife, it's mere foolishness. And it's no better with one's children, I make bold to assure you. I have two of them, the rascals. There's nowhere for them to be taught out here in the steppe; I haven't the money to send them to school in Novo Tcherkask, and they live here like young wolves. Next thing they will be murdering someone on the highroad."

The fair-haired gentleman listened attentively, answered questions briefly in a low voice, and was apparently a gentleman of gentle and modest disposition. He mentioned that he was a lawyer, and that he was going to the village Dyuevka on business.

"Why, merciful heavens, that is six miles from me!" said Zhmuhin in a tone of voice as though someone were disputing with him. "But excuse me, you won't find horses at the station now. To my mind, the very best thing you can do, you know, is to come straight to me, stay the night, you know, and in the morning drive over with my horses."

The lawyer thought a moment and accepted the invitation.

When they reached the station the sun was already low over the steppe. They said nothing all the way from the station to the farm: the jolting prevented conversation. The trap bounded up and down, squeaked, and seemed to be sobbing, and the lawyer, who was sitting very uncomfortably, stared before him, miserably hoping to see the farm. After they had driven five or six miles there came into view in the distance a low-pitched house and a yard enclosed by a fence made of dark, flat stones standing on end; the roof was green, the stucco was peeling off, and the windows were little narrow slits like screwed-up eyes. The farm stood in the full sunshine, and there was no sign either of water or trees anywhere round. Among the neighbouring landowners and the peasants it was known as the Petchenyegs' farm. Many years before, a land surveyor, who was passing through the neighbourhood and put up at the farm, spent the whole night talking to Ivan Abramitch, was not favourably impressed, and as he was driving away in the morning said to him grimly:

"You are a Petchenyeg,* my good sir!"

From this came the nickname, the Petchenyegs' farm, which stuck to the place even more when Zhmuhin's boys grew up and began to make raids on the orchards and kitchen-gardens. Ivan Abramitch was called "You Know," as he usually talked a very great deal and frequently made use of that expression.

In the yard near a barn Zhmuhin's sons were standing, one a young man of nineteen, the other a younger lad, both barefoot and bareheaded. Just at the moment when the trap drove into the yard the younger one flung high up a hen which, cackling, described an arc in the air; the elder shot at it with a gun and the hen fell dead on the earth.

"Those are my boys learning to shoot birds flying," said Zhmuhin.

In the entry the travellers were met by a little thin woman with a pale face, still young and beautiful; from her dress she might have been taken for a servant.

"And this, allow me to introduce her," said Zhmuhin, "is the mother of my young cubs. Come, Lyubov Osipovna," he said, addressing her, "you must be spry, mother, and get something for our guest. Let us have supper. Look sharp!"

The house consisted of two parts: in one was the parlour and beside it old Zhmuhin's bedroom, both stuffy rooms with low ceilings and multitudes of flies and wasps, and in the other was the kitchen in which the cooking and washing was done and the labourers had their meals; here geese and turkey-hens were sitting on their eggs under the benches, and here were the beds of Lyubov Osipovna and her two sons. The furniture in the parlour was unpainted and evidently roughly made by a carpenter; guns, game-bags, and whips were hanging on the walls, and all this old rubbish was covered with the rust of years and looked grey with dust. There was not one picture; in the corner was a dingy board which had at one time been an ikon.

A young Little Russian woman laid the table and handed ham, then

* The Petchenyegs were a tribe of wild Mongolian nomads who made frequent inroads upon the Russians in the tenth and eleventh centuries.—*Translator's Note.*

beetroot soup. The visitor refused vodka and ate only bread and cucumbers.

"How about ham?" asked Zhmuhin.

"Thank you, I don't eat it," answered the visitor, "I don't eat meat at all."

"Why is that?"

"I am a vegetarian. Killing animals is against my principles."

Zhmuhin thought a minute and then said slowly with a sigh:

"Yes . . . to be sure. . . . I saw a man who did not eat meat in town, too. It's a new religion they've got now. Well, it's good. We can't go on always shooting and slaughtering, you know; we must give it up some day and leave even the beasts in peace. It's a sin to kill, it's a sin, there is no denying it. Sometimes one kills a hare and wounds him in the leg, and he cries like a child. . . . So it must hurt him!"

"Of course it hurts him; animals suffer just like human beings."

"That's true," Zhmuhin assented. "I understand that very well," he went on, musing, "only there is this one thing I don't understand: suppose, you know, everyone gave up eating meat, what would become of the domestic animals—fowls and geese, for instance?"

"Fowls and geese would live in freedom like wild birds."

"Now I understand. To be sure, crows and jackdaws get on all right without us. Yes. . . . Fowls and geese and hares and sheep, all will live in freedom, rejoicing, you know, and praising God; and they will not fear us, peace and concord will come. Only there is one thing, you know, I can't understand," Zhmuhin went on, glancing at the ham. "How will it be with the pigs? What is to be done with them?"

"They will be like all the rest—that is, they will live in freedom."

"Ah! Yes. But allow me to say, if they were not slaughtered they would multiply, you know, and then good-bye to the kitchen-gardens and the meadows. Why, a pig, if you let it free and don't look after it, will ruin everything in a day. A pig is a pig, and it is not for nothing it is called a pig. . . ."

They finished supper. Zhmuhin got up from the table and for a long while walked up and down the room, talking and talking. . . . He was fond of talking of something important or serious and was fond of meditating, and in his old age he had a longing to reach some haven, to be reassured, that he might not be so frightened of dying. He had a longing for meekness, spiritual calm, and confidence in himself, such as this guest of theirs had, who had satisfied his hunger on cucumbers and bread, and believed that doing so made him more perfect; he was sitting on a chest, plump and healthy, keeping silent and patiently enduring his boredom, and in the dusk when one glanced at him from the entry he looked like a big round stone which one could not move from its place. If a man has something to lay hold of in life he is all right.

Zhmuhin went through the entry to the porch, and then he could be heard sighing and saying reflectively to himself: "Yes. . . . To be sure. . . ." By now it was dark, and here and there stars could be seen in the sky. They had not yet lighted up indoors. Someone came into the parlour as noiselessly as a shadow and stood still near the door. It was Lyubov Osipovna, Zhmuhin's wife.

"Are you from the town?" she asked timidly, not looking at her visitor.

"Yes, I live in the town."

"Perhaps you are something in the learned way, sir; be so kind as to advise us. We ought to send in a petition."

"To whom?" asked the visitor.

"We have two sons, kind gentleman, and they ought to have been sent to school long ago, but we never see anyone and have no one to advise us. And I know nothing. For if they are not taught they will have to serve in the army as common Cossacks. It's not right, sir! They can't read and write, they are worse than peasants, and Ivan Abramitch himself can't stand them and won't let them indoors. But they are not to blame. The younger one, at any rate, ought to be sent to school, it is such a pity!" she said slowly, and there was a quiver in her voice; and it seemed incredible that a woman so small and so youthful could have grown-up children. "Oh, it's such a pity!"

"You don't know anything about it, mother, and it is not your affair," said Zhmuhin, appearing in the doorway. "Don't pester our guest with your wild talk. Go away, mother!"

Lyubov Osipovna went out, and in the entry repeated once more in a thin little voice: "Oh, it's such a pity!"

A bed was made up for the visitor on the sofa in the parlour, and that it might not be dark for him they lighted the lamp before the ikon. Zhmuhin went to bed in his own room. And as he lay there he thought of his soul, of his age, of his recent stroke which had so frightened him and made him think of death. He was fond of philosophizing when he was in quietness by himself, and then he fancied that he was a very earnest, deep thinker, and that nothing in this world interested him but serious questions. And now he kept thinking and he longed to pitch upon some one significant thought unlike others, which would be a guide to him in life, and he wanted to think out principles of some sort for himself so as to make his life as deep and earnest as he imagined that he felt himself to be. It would be a good thing for an old man like him to abstain altogether from meat, from superfluities of all sorts. The time when men give up killing each other and animals would come sooner or later, it could not but be so, and he imagined that time to himself and clearly pictured himself living in peace with all the animals, and suddenly he thought again of the pigs, and everything was in a tangle in his brain.

"It's a queer business, Lord have mercy upon us," he muttered, sighing heavily. "Are you asleep?" he asked.

"No."

Zhmuhin got out of bed and stopped in the doorway with nothing but his shirt on, displaying to his guest his sinewy legs, that looked as dry as sticks.

"Nowadays, you know," he began, "all sorts of telegraphs, telephones, and marvels of all kinds, in fact, have come in, but people are no better than they were. They say that in our day, thirty or forty years ago, men were coarse and cruel; but isn't it just the same now? We certainly did not stand on ceremony in our day. I remember in the Caucasus when we were stationed by a little river with nothing to do for four whole months—I was an under-officer at that time—something queer happened, quite in the style of a novel. Just on the banks of that river, you know, where our division was encamped, a wretched prince whom we had killed not long before was buried. And at night, you know, the princess used to come to his grave and weep. She would wail and wail, and moan and moan, and make us so depressed we couldn't sleep, and that's the fact. We couldn't sleep one night, we couldn't sleep a second; well, we got sick of it. And from a common-sense point of view you really can't go without your sleep for the devil knows what (excuse the expression). We took that princess and gave her a good thrashing, and she gave up coming. There's an instance for you. Nowadays, of course, there is not the same class of people, and they are not given to thrashing and they live in cleaner style, and there is more learning, but, you know, the soul is just the same: there is no change. Now, look here, there's a landowner living here among us; he has mines, you know; all sorts of tramps without passports who don't know where to go work for him. On Saturdays he has to settle up with the workmen, but he doesn't care to pay them, you know, he grudges the money. So he's got hold of a foreman who is a tramp too, though he does wear a hat. 'Don't you pay them anything,' he says, 'not a kopeck; they'll beat you, and let them beat you,' says he, 'but you put up with it, and I'll pay you ten roubles every Saturday for it.' So on the Saturday evening the workmen come to settle up in the usual way; the foreman says to them: 'Nothing!' Well, word for word, as the master said, they begin swearing and using their fists. . . . They beat him and they kick him . . . you know, they are a set of men brutalized by hunger—they beat him till he is senseless, and then they go each on his way. The master gives orders for cold water to be poured on the foreman, then flings ten roubles in his face. And he takes it and is pleased too, for indeed he'd be ready to be hanged for three roubles, let alone ten. Yes . . . and on Monday a new gang of workmen arrive; they work, for they have nowhere to go. . . . On Saturday it is the same story over again."

The visitor turned over on the other side with his face to the back of the sofa and muttered something.

"And here's another instance," Zhmuhin went on. "We had the Siberian plague here, you know—the cattle die off like flies, I can tell you—and the veterinary surgeons came here, and strict orders were given that the dead cattle were to be buried at a distance deep in the earth, that lime was to be thrown over them, and so on, you know, on scientific principles. My horse died too. I buried it with every precaution, and threw over three hundred-weight of lime over it. And what do you think? My fine fellows—my precious sons, I mean—dug it up, skinned it, and sold the hide for three roubles; there's an instance for you. So people have grown no better, and however you feed a wolf he will always look towards the forest; there it is. It gives one something to think about, eh? How do you look at it?"

On one side a flash of lightning gleamed through a chink in the window-blinds. There was the stifling feeling of a storm coming, the gnats were biting, and Zhmuhin, as he lay in his bedroom meditating, sighed and groaned and said to himself: "Yes, to be sure—" and there was no possibility of getting to sleep. Somewhere far, far away there was a growl of thunder.

"Are you asleep?"

"No," answered the visitor.

Zhmuhin got up, and thudding with his heels walked through the parlour and the entry to the kitchen to get a drink of water.

"The worst thing in the world, you know, is stupidity," he said a little later, coming back with a dipper. "My Lyubov Osipovna is on her knees saying her prayers. She prays every night, you know, and bows down to the ground, first that her children may be sent to school; she is afraid her boys will go into the army as simple Cossacks, and that they will be whacked across their backs with sabres. But for teaching one must have money, and where is one to get it? You may break the floor beating your head against it, but if you haven't got it you haven't. And the other reason she prays is because, you know, every woman imagines there is no one in the world as unhappy as she is. I am a plain-spoken man, and I don't want to conceal anything from you. She comes of a poor family, a village priest's daughter. I married her when she was seventeen, and they accepted my offer chiefly because they hadn't enough to eat; it was nothing but poverty and misery, while I have anyway land, you see—a farm—and after all I am an officer; it was a step up for her to marry me, you know. On the very first day when she was married she cried, and she has been crying ever since, all these twenty years; she has got a watery eye. And she's always sitting and thinking, and what do you suppose she is thinking about? What can a woman think about? Why, nothing. I must own I don't consider a woman a human being."

The visitor got up abruptly and sat on the bed.

"Excuse me, I feel stifled," he said; "I will go outside."

Zhmuhin, still talking about women, drew the bolt in the entry and they both went out. A full moon was floating in the sky just over the yard, and in the moonlight the house and barn looked whiter than by day; and on the grass brilliant streaks of moonlight, white too, stretched between the black shadows. Far away on the right could be seen the steppe, above it the stars were softly glowing—and it was all mysterious, infinitely far away, as though one were gazing into a deep abyss; while on the left heavy storm-clouds, black as soot, were piling up one upon another above the steppe; their edges were lighted up by the moon, and it looked as though there were mountains there with white snow on their peaks, dark forests, the sea. There was a flash of lightning, a faint rumble of thunder, and it seemed as though a battle were being fought in the mountains. . . .

Quite close to the house a little night-owl screeched monotonously: "Asleep! asleep!"

"What time is it now?" asked the visitor.

"Just after one."

"How long it is still to dawn!"

They went back to the house and lay down again. It was time to sleep, and one can usually sleep so splendidly before rain; but the old man had a hankering after serious, weighty thoughts; he wanted not simply to think but to meditate, and he meditated how good it would be, as death was near at hand, for the sake of his soul to give up the idleness which so imperceptibly swallowed up day after day, year after year, leaving no trace; to think out for himself some great exploit—for instance, to walk on foot far, far away, or to give up meat like this young man. And again he pictured to himself the time when animals would not be killed, pictured it clearly and distinctly as though he were living through that time himself; but suddenly it was all in a tangle again in his head and all was muddled.

The thunderstorm had passed over, but from the edges of the storm-clouds came rain softly pattering on the roof. Zhmuhin got up, stretching and groaning with old age, and looked into the parlour. Noticing that his visitor was not asleep, he said:

"When we were in the Caucasus, you know, there was a colonel there who was a vegetarian, too; he didn't eat meat, never went shooting, and would not let his servants catch fish. Of course, I understand that every animal ought to live in freedom and enjoy its life; only I don't understand how a pig can go about where it likes without being looked after. . . ."

The visitor got up and sat down. His pale, haggard face expressed weariness and vexation; it was evident that he was exhausted, and only his gentleness and the delicacy of his soul prevented him from expressing his vexation in words.

"It's getting light," he said mildly. "Please have the horse brought round for me."

"Why so? Wait a little and the rain will be over."

"No, I entreat you," said the visitor in horror, with a supplicating voice; "it is essential for me to go at once."

And he began hurriedly dressing.

By the time the horse was harnessed the sun was rising. It had just left off raining, the clouds were racing swiftly by, and the patches of blue were growing bigger and bigger in the sky. The first rays of the sun were timidly reflected below in the big puddles. The visitor walked through the entry with his portfolio to get into the trap, and at that moment Zhmuhin's wife, pale, and it seemed paler than the day before, with tear-stained eyes, looked at him intently without blinking, with the naïve expression of a little girl, and it was evident from her dejected face that she was envying him his freedom—oh, with what joy she would have gone away from there!—and she wanted to say something to him, most likely to ask advice about her children. And what a pitiable figure she was! This was not a wife, not the head of a house, not even a servant, but more like a dependent, a poor relation not wanted by anyone, a nonentity. . . . Her husband, fussing about, talking unceasingly, was seeing his visitor off, continually running in front of him, while she huddled up to the wall with a timid, guilty air, waiting for a convenient minute to speak.

"Please come again another time," the old man kept repeating incessantly; "what we have we are glad to offer, you know."

The visitor hurriedly got into the trap, evidently with relief, as though he were afraid every minute that they would detain him. The trap lurched about as it had the day before, squeaked, and furiously rattled the pail that was tied on at the back. He glanced round at Zhmuhin with a peculiar expression; it looked as though he wanted to call him a Petchenyeg, as the surveyor had once done, or some such name, but his gentleness got the upper hand. He controlled himself and said nothing. But in the gateway he suddenly could not restrain himself; he got up and shouted loudly and angrily: "You have bored me to death."

And he disappeared through the gate.

Near the barn Zhmuhin's sons were standing; the elder held a gun, while the younger had in his hands a grey cockerel with a bright red comb. The younger flung up the cockerel with all his might; the bird flew upwards higher than the house and turned over in the air like a pigeon. The elder boy fired and the cockerel fell like a stone.

The old man, overcome with confusion, not knowing how to explain the visitor's strange, unexpected shout, went slowly back into the house. And sitting down at the table he spent a long while meditating on the intellectual tendencies of the day, on the universal immorality, on the telegraph, on the telephone, on velocipedes, on how unnecessary it all was; little by little he regained his composure, then slowly had a meal, drank five glasses of tea, and lay down for a nap.

At Home

I

The Don railway. A quiet, cheerless station, white and solitary in the steppe, with its walls baking in the sun, without a speck of shade, and, it seems, without a human being. The train goes on after leaving one here; the sound of it is scarcely audible and dies away at last. Outside the station it is a desert, and there are no horses but one's own. One gets into the carriage—which is so pleasant after the train—and is borne along the road through the steppe, and by degrees there are unfolded before one views such as one does not see near Moscow—immense, endless, fascinating in their monotony. The steppe, the steppe, and nothing more; in the distance an ancient barrow or a windmill; ox-wagons laden with coal trail by.... Solitary birds fly low over the plain, and a drowsy feeling comes with the monotonous beat of their wings. It is hot. Another hour or so passes, and still the steppe, the steppe, and still in the distance the barrow. The driver tells you something, some long unnecessary tale, pointing into the distance with his whip. And tranquillity takes possession of the soul; one is loth to think of the past....

A carriage with three horses had been sent to fetch Vera Ivanovna Kardin. The driver put in her luggage and set the harness to rights.

"Everything just as it always has been," said Vera, looking about her.

"I was a little girl when I was here last, ten years ago. I remember old Boris came to fetch me then. Is he still living, I wonder?"

The driver made no reply, but, like a Little Russian, looked at her angrily and clambered on to the box.

It was a twenty-mile drive from the station, and Vera, too, abandoned herself to the charm of the steppe, forgot the past, and thought only of the wide expanse, of the freedom. Healthy, clever, beautiful, and young—she was only three-and-twenty—she had hitherto lacked nothing in her life but just this space and freedom.

The steppe, the steppe. . . . The horses trotted, the sun rose higher and higher; and it seemed to Vera that never in her childhood had the steppe been so rich, so luxuriant in June; the wild flowers were green, yellow, lilac, white, and a fragrance rose from them and from the warmed earth; and there were strange blue birds along the roadside. . . . Vera had long got out of the habit of praying, but now, struggling with drowsiness, she murmured:

"Lord, grant that I may be happy here."

And there was peace and sweetness in her soul, and she felt as though she would have been glad to drive like that all her life, looking at the steppe.

Suddenly there was a deep ravine overgrown with oak saplings and alder-trees; there was a moist feeling in the air—there must have been a spring at the bottom. On the near side, on the very edge of the ravine, a covey of partidges rose noisily. Vera remembered that in old days they used to go for evening walks to this ravine; so it must be near home! And now she could actually see the poplars, the barn, black smoke rising on one side—they were burning old straw. And there was Auntie Dasha coming to meet her and waving her handkerchief; grandfather was on the terrace. Oh dear, how happy she was!

"My darling, my darling!" cried her aunt, shrieking as though she were in hysterics. "Our real mistress has come! You must understand you are our mistress, you are our queen! Here everything is yours! My darling, my beauty, I am not your aunt, but your willing slave!"

Vera had no relations but her aunt and her grandfather; her mother had long been dead; her father, an engineer, had died three months before at Kazan, on his way from Siberia. Her grandfather had a big grey beard. He was stout, red-faced, and asthmatic, and walked leaning on a cane and sticking his stomach out. Her aunt, a lady of forty-two, drawn in tightly at the waist and fashionably dressed with sleeves high on the shoulder, evidently tried to look young and was still anxious to be charming; she walked with tiny steps with a wriggle of her spine.

"Will you love us?" she said, embracing Vera, "You are not proud?"

At her grandfather's wish there was a thanksgiving service, then they spent a long while over dinner—and Vera's new life began. She was given the best room. All the rugs in the house had been put in it, and a great many flowers; and when at night she lay down in her snug, wide, very soft bed and covered herself with a silk quilt that smelt of old clothes long stored away, she laughed with pleasure. Auntie Dasha came in for a minute to wish her good-night.

"Here you are home again, thank God," she said, sitting down on the bed. "As you see, we get along very well and have everything we want. There's only one thing: your grandfather is in a poor way! A terribly poor way! He is short of breath and he has begun to lose his memory. And you remember how strong, how vigorous, he used to be! There was no doing anything with him. . . . In old days, if the servants didn't please him or anything else went wrong, he would jump up at once and shout: 'Twenty-five strokes! The birch!' But now he has grown milder and you never hear him. And besides, times are changed, my precious; one mayn't beat them nowadays. Of course, they oughtn't to be beaten, but they need looking after."

"And are they beaten now, auntie?" asked Vera.

"The steward beats them sometimes, but I never do, bless their hearts! And your grandfather sometimes lifts his stick from old habit, but he never beats them."

Auntie Dasha yawned and crossed herself over her mouth and her right ear.

"It's not dull here?" Vera inquired.

"What shall I say? There are no landowners living here now, but there have been works built near, darling, and there are lots of engineers, doctors, and mine managers. Of course, we have theatricals and concerts, but we play cards more than anything. They come to us, too. Dr. Neshtchapov from the works comes to see us—such a handsome, interesting man! He fell in love with your photograph. I made up my mind: he is Verotchka's destiny, I thought. He's young, handsome, he has means—a good match, in fact. And of course you're a match for any one. You're of good family. The place is mortgaged, it's true, but it's in good order and not neglected; there is my share in it, but it will all come to you; I am your willing slave. And my brother, your father, left you fifteen thousand roubles. . . . But I see you can't keep your eyes open. Sleep, my child."

Next day Vera spent a long time walking round the house. The garden, which was old and unattractive, lying inconveniently upon the slope, had no paths, and was utterly neglected; probably the care of it was regarded as an unnecessary item in the management. There were numbers of grass-snakes. Hoopoes flew about under the trees calling "Oo-too-toot!" as though they were trying to remind her of something. At the bottom of the hill there was a river overgrown with tall reeds, and half a mile beyond the river was the village. From the garden Vera went out into the fields; looking into the distance, thinking of her new life in her own home, she kept trying to grasp what was in store for her. The space, the lovely peace of the steppe, told her that happiness was near at hand, and perhaps was here already; thousands of people, in fact, would have said: "What happiness to be young, healthy, well-educated, to be living on one's own estate!" And at the same time the endless plain, all alike, without one living soul, frightened her, and at moments it was clear to her that its peaceful green vastness would swallow up her life and reduce it to nothingness. She was very young, elegant, fond of life; she had finished her studies at an aristocratic boarding-school, had learnt three languages, had read a great deal, had travelled with her father—and could all this have been meant to lead to nothing but settling down in a remote country-house in the steppe, and wandering day after day from the garden into the fields and from the fields into the garden to while away the time, and then sitting at home listening to her grandfather's breathing? But what could she do? Where could she go? She could find no answer, and as she was returning home she doubted whether she would be happy here, and thought that driving from the station was far more interesting than living here.

Dr. Neshtchapov drove over from the works. He was a doctor, but three years previously he had taken a share in the works, and had become one of the partners; and now he no longer looked upon medicine as his chief vocation, though he still practised. In appearance he was a pale, dark man in a white waistcoat, with a good figure; but to guess what there was in his heart and his brain was difficult. He kissed Auntie Dasha's hand on greeting her, and was continually leaping up to set a chair or give his seat to some one. He was very silent and grave all the while, and, when he did speak, it was for some reason impossible to hear and understand his first sentence, though he spoke correctly and not in a low voice.

"You play the piano?" he asked Vera, and immediately leapt up, as she had dropped her handkerchief.

He stayed from midday to midnight without speaking, and Vera found him very unattractive. She thought that a white waistcoat in the country was bad form, and his elaborate politeness, his manners, and his pale, serious face with dark eyebrows, were mawkish; and it seemed to her that he was perpetually silent, probably because he was stupid. When he had gone her aunt said enthusiastically:

"Well? Isn't he charming?"

II

Auntie Dasha looked after the estate. Tightly laced, with jingling bracelets on her wrists, she went into the kitchen, the granary, the cattle-yard, tripping along with tiny steps, wriggling her spine; and whenever she talked to the steward or to the peasants, she used, for some reason, to put on a pince-nez. Vera's grandfather always sat in the same place, playing patience or dozing. He ate a very great deal at dinner and supper; they gave him the dinner cooked to-day and what was left from yesterday, and cold pie left from Sunday, and salt meat from the servants' dinner, and he ate it all greedily. And every dinner left on Vera such an impression, that when she saw afterwards a flock of sheep driven by, or flour being brought from the mill, she thought, "Grandfather will eat that." For the most part he was silent, absorbed in eating or in patience; but it sometimes happened at dinner that at the sight of Vera he would be touched and say tenderly:

"My only grandchild! Verotchka!"

And tears would glisten in his eyes. Or his face would turn suddenly crimson, his neck would swell, he would look with fury at the servants, and ask, tapping with his stick:

"Why haven't you brought the horse-radish?"

In winter he led a perfectly inactive existence; in summer he sometimes drove out into the fields to look at the oats and the hay; and when he came back he would flourish his stick and declare that everything was neglected now that he was not there to look after it.

"Your grandfather is out of humour," Auntie Dasha would whisper. "But it's nothing now to what it used to be in the old days: 'Twenty-five strokes! The birch!' "

Her aunt complained that every one had grown lazy, that no one did anything, and that the estate yielded no profit. Indeed, there was no systematic farming; they ploughed and sowed a little simply from habit, and in reality did nothing and lived in idleness. Meanwhile there was a running to and fro, reckoning and worrying all day long; the bustle in the house began at five o'clock in the morning; there were continual sounds of "Bring it," "Fetch it," "Make haste," and by the evening the servants were utterly exhausted. Auntie Dasha changed her cooks and her housemaids every week; sometimes she discharged them for immorality; sometimes they went of their own accord, complaining that they were worked to death. None of the village people would come to the house as servants; Auntie Dasha had to hire them from a distance. There was only one girl from the village living in the house, Alyona, and she stayed because her whole family—old people and children—were living upon her wages. This Alyona, a pale, rather stupid little thing, spent the whole day turning out the rooms, waiting at table, heating the stoves, sewing, washing; but it always seemed as though she were only pottering about, treading heavily with her boots, and were nothing but a hindrance in the house. In her terror that she might be dismissed and sent home, she often dropped and broke the crockery, and they stopped the value of it out of her wages, and then her mother and grandmother would come and bow down at Auntie Dasha's feet.

Once a week or sometimes oftener visitors would arrive. Her aunt would come to Vera and say:

"You should sit a little with the visitors, or else they'll think that you are stuck up."

Vera would go in to the visitors and play *vint* with them for hours together, or play the piano for the visitors to dance; her aunt, in high spirits and breathless from dancing, would come up and whisper to her:

"Be nice to Marya Nikiforovna."

On the sixth of December, St. Nikolay's Day, a large party of about thirty arrived all at once; they played *vint* until late at night, and many of them stayed the night. In the morning they sat down to cards again, then they had dinner, and when Vera went to her room after dinner to rest from conversation and tobacco smoke, there were visitors there too, and she almost wept in despair. And when they began to get ready to go in the evening, she was so pleased they were going at last, that she said:

"Do stay a little longer."

She felt exhausted by the visitors and constrained by their presence; yet every day, as soon as it began to grow dark, something drew her out of the house, and she went out to pay visits either at the works or at some neighbours', and then there were cards, dancing, forfeits, suppers. . . . The young people in the works or in the mines sometimes sang Little Russian songs, and sang them very well. It made one sad to hear them sing. Or they all gathered together in one room and talked in the dusk of the mines, of the treasures that had once been buried in the steppes, of Saur's Grave. . . . Later on, as they talked, a shout of "Help!" sometimes reached them. It was a drunken man going home, or some one was being robbed by the pit near by. Or the wind howled in the chimneys, the shutters banged; then, soon afterwards, they would hear the uneasy church bell, as the snow-storm began.

At all the evening parties, picnics, and dinners, Auntie Dasha was invariably the most interesting woman and the doctor the most interesting man. There was very little reading either at the works or at the country-houses; they played only marches and polkas; and the young people always argued hotly about things they did not understand, and the effect was crude. The discussions were loud and heated, but, strange to say, Vera had nowhere else met people so indifferent and careless as these. They seemed to have no fatherland, no religion, no public interests. When they talked of literature or debated some abstract question, it could be seen from Dr. Neshtchapov's face that the question had no interest for him whatever, and that for long, long years he had read nothing and cared to read nothing. Serious and expressionless, like a badly painted portrait, for ever in his white waistcoat, he was silent and incomprehensible as before; but the ladies, young and old, thought him interesting and were enthusiastic over his manners. They envied Vera, who appeared to attract him very much. And Vera always came away from the visits with a feeling of vexation, vowing inwardly to remain at home; but the day passed, the evening came, and she hurried off to the works again, and it was like that almost all the winter.

She ordered books and magazines, and used to read them in her room. And she read at night, lying in bed. When the clock in the corridor struck two or three, and her temples were beginning to ache from reading, she sat up in bed and thought, "What am I to do? Where am I to go?" Accursed, importunate question, to which there were a number of ready-made answers, and in reality no answer at all.

Oh, how noble, how holy, how picturesque it must be to serve the people, to alleviate their sufferings, to enlighten them! But she, Vera, did not know the people. And how could she go to them? They were strange and uninteresting to her; she could not endure the stuffy smell of the huts, the pot-house oaths, the unwashed children, the women's talk of illnesses. To walk over the snow-drifts, to feel cold, then to sit in a stifling hut, to teach children she disliked—no, she would rather die! And to teach the peasants' children while Auntie Dasha made money out of the pot-houses and fined the peasants—it was too great a farce! What a lot of talk there was of schools, of village libraries, of universal education; but if all these engineers, these mine-owners and ladies of her acquaintance, had not been hypocrites, and really had believed that enlightenment was necessary, they would not have paid the schoolmasters fifteen roubles a month as they did now, and would not have let them go hungry. And the schools and the talk about ignorance—it was all only to stifle the voice of conscience because they were ashamed to own fifteen or thirty thousand acres and to be indifferent to the peasants' lot. Here the ladies said about Dr. Neshtchapov that he was a kind man and had built a school at the works. Yes, he had built a school out of the old bricks at the works for some eight hundred roubles, and they sang the prayer for "long life" to him when the building was opened, but there was no chance of his giving up his shares, and it certainly never entered his head that the peasants were human beings like himself, and that they, too, needed university teaching, and not merely lessons in these wretched schools.

And Vera felt full of anger against herself and every one else. She took up a book again and tried to read it, but soon afterwards sat down and thought again. To become a doctor? But to do that one must pass an examination in Latin; besides, she had an invincible repugnance to corpses and disease. It would be nice to become a mechanic, a judge, a commander of a steamer, a scientist; to do something into which she could put all her powers, physical and spiritual, and to be tired out and sleep soundly at night; to give up her life to something that would make her an interesting person, able to attract interesting people, to love, to have a real family of her own. . . . But what was she to do? How was she to begin?

One Sunday in Lent her aunt came into her room early in the morning to fetch her umbrella. Vera was sitting up in bed clasping her head in her hands, thinking.

"You ought to go to church, darling," said her aunt, "or people will think you are not a believer."

Vera made no answer.

"I see you are dull, poor child," said Auntie Dasha, sinking on her knees by the bedside; she adored Vera. "Tell me the truth, are you bored?"

"Dreadfully."

"My beauty, my queen, I am your willing slave, I wish you nothing but good and happiness. . . . Tell me, why don't you want to marry

Nestchapov? What more do you want, my child? You must forgive me, darling; you can't pick and choose like this, we are not princes. . . . Time is passing, you are not seventeen. . . . And I don't understand it! He loves you, idolises you!"

"Oh, mercy!" said Vera with vexation. "How can I tell? He sits dumb and never says a word."

"He's shy, darling. . . . He's afraid you'll refuse him!"

And when her aunt had gone away, Vera remained standing in the middle of her room uncertain whether to dress or to go back to bed. The bed was hateful; if one looked out of the window there were the bare trees, the grey snow, the hateful jackdaws, the pigs that her grandfather would eat. . . .

"Yes, after all, perhaps I'd better get married!" she thought.

III

For two days Auntie Dasha went about with a tear-stained and heavily powdered face, and at dinner she kept sighing and looking towards the ikon. And it was impossible to make out what was the matter with her. But at last she made up her mind, went in to Vera, and said in a casual way:

"The fact is, child, we have to pay interest on the bank loan, and the tenant hasn't paid his rent. Will you let me pay it out of the fifteen thousand your papa left you?"

All day afterwards Auntie Dasha spent in making cherry jam in the garden. Alyona, with her cheeks flushed with the heat, ran to and from the garden to the house and back again to the cellar.

When Auntie Dasha was making jam with a very serious face as though she were performing a religious rite, and her short sleeves displayed her strong, little, despotic hands and arms, and when the servants ran about incessantly, bustling about the jam which they would never taste, there was always a feeling of martyrdom in the air. . . .

The garden smelt of hot cherries. The sun had set, the charcoal stove had been carried away, but the pleasant, sweetish smell still lingered in the air. Vera sat on a bench in the garden and watched a new labourer, a young soldier, not of the neighbourhood, who was, by her express orders, making new paths. He was cutting the turf with a spade and heaping it up on a barrow.

"Where were you serving?" Vera asked him.

"At Berdyansk."

"And where are you going now? Home?"

"No," answered the labourer. "I have no home."

"But where were you born and brought up?"

"In the province of Oryol. Till I went into the army I lived with my mother, in my step-father's house; my mother was the head of the house, and people looked up to her, and while she lived I was cared for. But while I was in the army I got a letter telling me my mother was dead. . . . And now I don't seem to care to go home. It's not my own father, so it's not like my own home."

"Then your father is dead?"

"I don't know. I am illegitimate."

At that moment Auntie Dasha appeared at the window and said:

"*Il ne faut pas parler aux gens.* . . . Go into the kitchen, my good man. You can tell your story there," she said to the soldier.

And then came as yesterday and every day supper, reading, a sleepless night, and endless thinking about the same thing. At three o'clock the sun rose; Alyona was already busy in the corridor, and Vera was not asleep yet and was trying to read. She heard the creak of the barrow: it was the new labourer at work in the garden. . . . Vera sat at the open window with a book, dozed, and watched the soldier making the paths for her, and that interested her. The paths were as even and level as a leather strap, and it was pleasant to imagine what they would be like when they were strewn with yellow sand.

She could see her aunt come out of the house soon after five o'clock, in a pink wrapper and curl-papers. She stood on the steps for three minutes without speaking, and then said to the soldier:

"Take your passport and go in peace. I can't have any one illegitimate in my house."

An oppressive, angry feeling sank like a stone on Vera's heart. She was indignant with her aunt, she hated her; she was so sick of her aunt that her heart was full of misery and loathing. But what was she to do? To stop her mouth? To be rude to her? But what would be the use? Suppose she struggled with her, got rid of her, made her harmless, prevented her grandfather from flourishing his stick—what would be the use of it? It would be like killing one mouse or one snake in the boundless steppe. The vast expanse, the long winters, the monotony and dreariness of life, instil a sense of helplessness; the position seems hopeless, and one wants to do nothing—everything is useless.

Alyona came in, and bowing low to Vera, began carrying out the arm-chairs to beat the dust out of them.

"You have chosen a time to clean up," said Vera with annoyance. "Go away."

Alyona was overwhelmed, and in her terror could not understand what was wanted of her. She began hurriedly tidying up the dressing-table.

"Go out of the room, I tell you," Vera shouted, turning cold; she had never had such an oppressive feeling before. "Go away!"

Alyona uttered a sort of moan, like a bird, and dropped Vera's gold watch on the carpet.

"Go away!" Vera shrieked in a voice not her own, leaping up and trembling all over. "Send her away; she worries me to death!" she went on, walking rapidly after Alyona down the passage, stamping her feet. "Go away! Birch her! Beat her!"

Then suddenly she came to herself, and just as she was, unwashed, uncombed, in her dressing-gown and slippers, she rushed out of the house. She ran to the familiar ravine and hid herself there among the sloe-trees, so that she might see no one and be seen by no one. Lying there motionless on the grass, she did not weep, she was not horror-stricken, but gazing at the sky open-eyed, she reflected coldly and clearly that something had happened which she could never forget and for which she could never forgive herself all her life.

"No, I can't go on like this," she thought. "It's time to take myself in hand, or there'll be no end to it. . . . I can't go on like this. . . ."

At midday Dr. Neshtchapov drove by the ravine on his way to the house. She saw him and made up her mind that she would begin a new life, and that she would make herself begin it, and this decision calmed her. And following with her eyes the doctor's well-built figure, she said, as though trying to soften the crudity of her decision:

"He's a nice man. . . . We shall get through life somehow."

She returned home. While she was dressing, Auntie Dasha came into the room, and said:

"Alyona upset you, darling; I've sent her home to the village. Her mother's given her a good beating and has come here, crying."

"Auntie," said Vera quickly, "I'm going to marry Dr. Neshtchapov. Only talk to him yourself . . . I can't."

And again she went out into the fields. And wandering aimlessly about, she made up her mind that when she was married she would look after the house, doctor the peasants, teach in the school, that she would do all the things that other women of her circle did. And this perpetual dissatisfaction with herself and every one else, this series of crude mistakes which stand up like a mountain before one whenever one looks back upon one's past, she would accept as her real life to which she was fated, and she would expect nothing better. . . . Of course there was nothing better! Beautiful nature, dreams, music, told one story, but reality another. Evidently truth and happiness existed somewhere outside real life. . . . One must give up one's own life and merge oneself into this luxuriant steppe, boundless and indifferent as eternity, with its flowers, its ancient barrows, and its distant horizon, and then it would be well with one. . . .

A month later Vera was living at the works.

The Schoolmistress

[In the Cart]

At half-past eight they drove out of the town.

The highroad was dry, a lovely April sun was shining warmly, but the snow was still lying in the ditches and in the woods. Winter, dark, long, and spiteful, was hardly over; spring had come all of a sudden. But neither the warmth nor the languid transparent woods, warmed by the breath of spring, nor the black flocks of birds flying over the huge puddles that were like lakes, nor the marvelous fathomless sky, into which it seemed one would have gone away so joyfully, presented anything new or interesting to Marya Vassilyevna who was sitting in the cart. For thirteen years she had been schoolmistress, and there was no reckoning how many times during all those years she had been to the town for her salary; and whether it were spring as now, or a rainy autumn evening, or winter, it was all the same to her, and she always—invariably—longed for one thing only, to get to the end of her journey as quickly as could be.

She felt as though she had been living in that part of the country for ages and ages, for a hundred years, and it seemed to her that she knew every stone, every tree on the road from the town to her school. Her past was here, her present was here, and she could imagine no other future than the school, the road to the town and back again, and again the school and again the road. . . .

She had got out of the habit of thinking of her past before she became a schoolmistress, and had almost forgotten it. She had once had a father and mother; they had lived in Moscow in a big flat near the Red Gate, but of all that life there was left in her memory only something vague and fluid like a dream. Her father had died when she was ten years old, and her mother had died soon after. . . . She had a brother, an officer; at first they used to write to each other, then her brother had given up answering her letters, he had got out of the way of writing. Of her old belongings, all that was left was a photograph of her mother, but it had grown dim from the dampness of the school, and now nothing could be seen but the hair and the eyebrows.

When they had driven a couple of miles, old Semyon, who was driving, turned round and said:

"They have caught a government clerk in the town. They have taken him away. The story is that with some Germans he killed Alexeyev, the Mayor, in Moscow."

"Who told you that?"

"They were reading it in the paper, in Ivan Ionov's tavern."

And again they were silent for a long time. Marya Vassilyevna thought of her school, of the examination that was coming soon, and of the girl and four boys she was sending up for it. And just as she was thinking about the examination, she was overtaken by a neighbouring landowner called Hanov in a carriage with four horses, the very man who had been examiner in her school the year before. When he came up to her he recognized her and bowed.

"Good-morning," he said to her. "You are driving home, I suppose."

This Hanov, a man of forty with a listless expression and a face that showed signs of wear, was beginning to look old, but was still handsome and admired by women. He lived in his big homestead alone, and was not in the service; and people used to say of him that he did nothing at home but walk up and down the room whistling, or play chess with his old footman. People said, too, that he drank heavily. And indeed at the examination the year before the very papers he brought with him smelt of wine and scent. He had been dressed all in new clothes on that occasion, and Marya Vassilyevna thought him very attractive, and all the while she sat beside him she had felt embarrassed. She was accustomed to see frigid and sensible examiners at the school, while this one did not remember a single prayer, or know what to ask questions about, and was exceedingly courteous and delicate, giving nothing but the highest marks.

"I am going to visit Bakvist," he went on, addressing Marya Vassilyevna, "but I am told he is not at home."

They turned off the highroad into a by-road to the village, Hanov leading the way and Semyon following. The four horses moved at a walking pace, with effort dragging the heavy carriage through the mud. Semyon tacked from side to side, keeping to the edge of the road, at one time through a snowdrift, at another through a pool, often jumping out of the cart and helping the horse. Marya Vassilyevna was still thinking about the school, wondering whether the arithmetic questions at the examination would be difficult or easy. And she felt annoyed with the Zemstvo board at which she had found no one the day before. How unbusiness-like! Here she had been asking them for the last two years to dismiss the watchman, who did nothing, was rude to her, and hit the schoolboys; but no one paid any attention. It was hard to find the president at the office, and when one did find him he would say with tears in his eyes that he hadn't a moment to spare; the inspector visited the school at most once in three years, and knew nothing whatever about his work, as he had been in the Excise Duties Department, and had received the post of school inspector through influence. The School Council met very rarely, and there was no knowing where it met; the school guardian was an almost illiterate peasant, the head of a tanning business, unintelligent, rude, and a great friend of the watchman's—and goodness knows to whom she could appeal with complaints or inquiries. . . .

"He really is handsome," she thought, glancing at Hanov.

The road grew worse and worse. . . . They drove into the wood. Here there was no room to turn round, the wheels sank deeply in, water splashed and gurgled through them, and sharp twigs struck them in the face.

"What a road!" said Hanov, and he laughed.

The schoolmistress looked at him and could not understand why this queer man lived here. What could his money, his interesting appearance, his refined bearing do for him here, in this mud, in this God-forsaken, dreary place? He got no special advantages out of life, and here, like Semyon, was driving at a jog-trot on an appalling road and enduring the same discomforts. Why live here if one could live in Petersburg or abroad? And one would have thought it would be nothing for a rich man like him to make a good road instead of this bad one, to avoid enduring this misery and seeing the despair on the faces of his coachman and Semyon; but he only laughed, and apparently did not mind, and wanted no better life. He was kind, soft, naïve, and he did not understand this coarse life, just as at the examination he did not know the prayers. He subscribed nothing to the schools but globes, and genuinely regarded himself as a useful person and a prominent worker in the cause of popular education. And what use were his globes here?

"Hold on, Vassilyevna!" said Semyon.

The cart lurched violently and was on the point of upsetting; something heavy rolled on to Marya Vassilyevna's feet—it was her parcel of purchases. There was a steep ascent uphill through the clay; here in the winding ditches rivulets were gurgling. The water seemed to have gnawed away the road; and how could one get along here! The horses breathed hard. Hanov got out of his carriage and walked at the side of the road in his long overcoat. He was hot.

"What a road!" he said, and laughed again. "It would soon smash up one's carriage."

"Nobody obliges you to drive about in such weather," said Semyon surlily. "You should stay at home."

"I am dull at home, grandfather. I don't like staying at home."

Beside old Semyon he looked graceful and vigorous, but yet in his walk there was something just perceptible which betrayed in him a being already touched by decay, weak, and on the road to ruin. And all at once there was a whiff of spirits in the wood. Marya Vassilyevna was filled with dread and pity for this man going to his ruin for no visible cause or reason, and it came into her mind that if she had been his wife or sister she would have devoted her whole life to saving him from ruin. His wife! Life was so ordered that here he was living in his great house alone, and she was living in a God-forsaken village alone, and yet for some reason the mere thought that he and she might be close to one another and equals seemed impossible and absurd. In reality, life was arranged and human relations were complicated so utterly beyond all understanding that when one thought about it one felt uncanny and one's heart sank.

"And it is beyond all understanding," she thought, "why God gives beauty, this graciousness, and sad, sweet eyes to weak, unlucky, useless people—why they are so charming."

"Here we must turn off to the right," said Hanov, getting into his carriage. "Good-by! I wish you all things good!"

And again she thought of her pupils, of the examination, of the watchman, of the School Council; and when the wind brought the sound of the retreating carriage these thoughts were mingled with others. She longed to think of beautiful eyes, of love, of the happiness which would never be. . . .

His wife? It was cold in the morning, there was no one to heat the stove, the watchman disappeared; the children came in as soon as it was light, bringing in snow and mud and making a noise: it was all so inconvenient, so comfortless. Her abode consisted of one little room and the kitchen close by. Her head ached every day after her work, and after dinner she had heart-burn. She had to collect money from the school-children for wood and for the watchman, and to give it to the school guardian, and then to entreat him—that overfed, insolent peasant—for God's sake to send her wood. And at night she dreamed of examinations, peasants, snowdrifts. And this life was making her grow old and coarse, making her ugly, angular, and awkward, as though she were made of lead. She was always afraid, and she would get up from her seat and not venture to sit down in the presence of a member of the Zemstvo or the school guardian. And she used formal, deferential expressions when she spoke of any one of them. And no one thought her attractive, and life was passing drearily, without affection, without friendly sympathy, without interesting acquaintances. How awful it would have been in her position if she had fallen in love!

"Hold on, Vassilyevna!"

Again a sharp ascent uphill. . . .

She had become a schoolmistress from necessity, without feeling any vocation for it; and she had never thought of a vocation, of serving the cause of enlightenment; and it always seemed to her that what was most important in her work was not the children, nor enlightenment, but the examinations. And what time had she for thinking of vocation, of serving the cause of enlightenment? Teachers, badly paid doctors, and their assistants, with their terribly hard work, have not even the comfort of thinking that they are serving an idea or the people, as their heads are always stuffed with thoughts of their daily bread, of wood for the fire, of bad roads, of illnesses. It is a hard-working, an uninteresting life, and only silent, patient cart-horses like Marya Vassilyevna could put up with it for long; the lively, nervous, impressionable people who talked about a vocation and serving the idea were soon weary of it and gave up the work.

Semyon kept picking out the driest and shortest way, first by a meadow, then by the backs of the village huts; but in one place the peasants would not let them pass, in another it was the priest's land and they could not cross it, in another Ivan Ionov had bought a plot from the landowner and had dug a ditch round it. They kept having to turn back.

They reached Nizhneye Gorodistche. Near the tavern on the dung-strewn earth, where the snow was still lying, there stood wagons that had brought great bottles of crude sulphuric acid. There were a great many people in the tavern, all drivers, and there was a smell of vodka, tobacco, and sheepskins. There was a loud noise of conversation and the banging of the swing-door. Through the wall, without ceasing for a moment, came the sound of a concertina being played in the shop. Marya Vassilyevna sat down and drank some tea, while at the next table peasants were drinking vodka and beer, perspiring from the tea they had just swallowed and the stifling fumes of the tavern.

"I say, Kuzma!" voices kept shouting in confusion. "What there!" "The Lord bless us!" "Ivan Dementyitch, I can tell you that!" "Look out, old man!"

A little pock-marked man with a black beard, who was quite drunk, was suddenly surprised by something and began using bad language.

"What are you swearing at, you there?" Semyon, who was sitting some way off, responded angrily. "Don't you see the young lady?"

"The young lady!" someone mimicked in another corner.

"Swinish crow!"

"We meant nothing . . ." said the little man in confusion. "I beg your pardon. We pay with our money and the young lady with hers. Good-morning!"

"Good-morning," answered the schoolmistress.

"And we thank you most feelingly."

Marya Vassilyevna drank her tea with satisfaction, and she, too, began turning red like the peasants, and fell to thinking again about firewood, about the watchman. . . .

"Stay, old man," she heard from the next table, "it's the schoolmistress from Vyazovye. . . . We know her; she's a good young lady."

"She's all right!"

The swing-door was continually banging, some coming in, others going out. Marya Vassilyevna sat on, thinking all the time of the same things, while the concertina went on playing and playing. The patches of sunshine had been on the floor, then they passed to the counter, to the wall, and disappeared altogether; so by the sun it was past midday. The peasants at the next table were getting ready to go. The little man, somewhat unsteadily, went up to Marya Vassilyevna and held out his hand to her; following his example, the others shook hands, too, at parting, and went out one after another, and the swing-door squeaked and slammed nine times.

"Vassilyevna, get ready," Semyon called to her.

They set off. And again they went at a walking pace.

"A little while back they were building a school here in their Nizhneye Gorodistche," said Semyon, turning round. "It was a wicked thing that was done!"

"Why, what?"

"They say the president put a thousand in his pocket, and the school guardian another thousand in his, and the teacher five hundred."

"The whole school only cost a thousand. It's wrong to slander people, grandfather. That's all nonsense."

"I don't know, . . . I only tell you what folks say."

But it was clear that Seymon did not believe the schoolmistress. The peasants did not believe her. They always thought she received too large a salary, twenty-one roubles a month (five would have been enough), and that of the money that she collected from the children for the firewood and the watchman the greater part she kept for herself. The guardian thought the same as the peasants, and he himself made a profit off the firewood and received payments from the peasants for being a guardian—without the knowledge of the authorities.

The forest, thank God! was behind them, and now it would be flat, open ground all the way to Vyazovye, and there was not far to go now. They had to cross the river and then the railway line, and then Vyazovye was in sight.

"Where are you driving?" Marya Vassilyevna asked Semyon. "Take the road to the right to the bridge."

"Why, we can go this way as well. It's not deep enough to matter."

"Mind you don't drown the horse."

"What?"

"Look, Hanov is driving to the bridge," said Marya Vassilyevna, seeing the four horses far away to the right. "It is he, I think."

"It is. So he didn't find Bakvist at home. What a pig-headed fellow he is. Lord have mercy upon us! He's driven over there, and what for? It's fully two miles nearer this way."

They reached the river. In the summer it was a little stream easily crossed by wading. It usually dried up in August, but now, after the spring floods, it was a river forty feet in breadth, rapid, muddy, and cold; on the bank and right up to the water there were fresh tracks of wheels, so it had been crossed here.

"Go on!" shouted Semyon angrily and anxiously, tugging violently at the reins and jerking his elbows as a bird does its wings. "Go on!"

The horse went on into the water up to his belly and stopped, but at once went on again with an effort, and Marya Vassilyevna was aware of a keen chilliness in her feet.

"Go on!" she, too, shouted, getting up. "Go on!"

They got out on the bank.

"Nice mess it is, Lord have mercy upon us!" muttered Seymon, setting straight the harness. "It's a perfect plague with this Zemstvo. . . ."

Her shoes and goloshes were full of water, the lower part of her dress and of her coat and one sleeve were wet and dripping: the sugar and flour had got wet, and that was worst of all, and Marya Vassilyevna could only clasp her hands in despair and say:

"Oh, Semyon, Semyon! How tiresome you are, really! . . ."

The barrier was down at the railway crossing. A train was coming out of the station. Marya Vassilyevna stood at the crossing waiting till it should pass, and shivering all over with cold. Vyazovye was in sight now, and the school with the green roof, and the church with its crosses flashing in the evening sun: and the station windows flashed too, and a pink smoke rose from the engine . . . and it seemed to her that everything was trembling with cold.

Here was the train; the windows reflected the gleaming light like the crosses on the church: it made her eyes ache to look at them. On the little platform between two first-class carriages a lady was standing, and Marya Vassilyevna glanced at her as she passed. Her mother! What a resemblance! Her mother had had just such luxuriant hair, just such a brow and bend of the head. And with amazing distinctness, for the first time in those thirteen years, there rose before her mind a vivid picture of her mother, her father, her brother, their flat in Moscow, the aquarium with little fish, everything to the tiniest detail; she heard the sound of the piano, her father's voice; she felt as she had been then, young, good-looking, well-dressed, in a bright warm room among her own people. A feeling of joy and happiness suddenly came over her, she pressed her hands to her temples in an ecstacy, and called softly, beseechingly:

"Mother!"

And she began crying, she did not know why. Just at that instant Hanov drove up with his team of four horses, and seeing him she imagined happiness such as she had never had, and smiled and nodded to him as an equal and a friend, and it seemed to her that her happiness, her triumph, was glowing in the sky and on all sides, in the windows and on the trees. Her father and mother had never died, she had never been a schoolmistress, it was a long, tedious, strange dream, and now she had awakened. . . .

"Vassilyevna, get in!"

And at once it all vanished. The barrier was slowly raised. Marya Vassilyevna, shivering and numb with cold, got into the cart. The carriage with the four horses crossed the railway line; Semyon followed it. The signalman took off his cap.

"And here is Vyazovye. Here we are."

The Man in a Case

At the furthest end of the village of Mironositskoe some belated sportsmen lodged for the night in the elder Prokofy's barn. There were two of them, the veterinary surgeon Ivan Ivanovitch and the schoolmaster Burkin. Ivan Ivanovitch had a rather strange double-barrelled surname—Tchimsha-Himalaisky—which did not suit him at all, and he was called simply Ivan Ivanovitch all over the province. He lived at a stud-farm near the town, and had come out shooting now to get a breath of fresh air. Burkin, the high-school teacher, stayed every summer at Count P——'s, and had been thoroughly at home in this district for years.

They did not sleep. Ivan Ivanovitch, a tall, lean old fellow with long moustaches, was sitting outside the door, smoking a pipe in the moonlight. Burkin was lying within on the hay, and could not be seen in the darkness.

They were telling each other all sorts of stories. Among other things, they spoke of the fact that the elder's wife, Mavra, a healthy and by no means stupid woman, had never been beyond her native village, had never seen a town nor a railway in her life, and had spent the last ten years sitting behind the stove, and only at night going out into the street.

"What is there wonderful in that!" said Burkin. "There are plenty of people in the world, solitary by temperament, who try to retreat into their shell like a hermit crab or a snail. Perhaps it is an instance of atavism, a return to the period when the ancestor of man was not yet a social animal and lived alone in his den, or perhaps it is only one of the diversities of human character—who knows? I am not a natural science man, and it is not my business to settle such questions; I only mean to say that people like Mavra are not uncommon. There is no need to look far; two months ago a man called Byelikov, a colleague of mine, the Greek master, died in our town. You have heard of him, no doubt. He was remarkable for always wearing goloshes and a warm wadded coat, and carrying an umbrella even in the very finest weather. And his umbrella was in a case, and his watch was in a case made of grey chamois leather, and when he took out his penknife to sharpen his pencil, his penknife, too, was in a little case; and his face seemed to be in a case too, because he always hid it in his turned-up collar. He wore dark spectacles and flannel vests, stuffed up his ears with cotton-wool, and when he got into a cab always told the driver to put up the hood. In short, the man displayed a constant and insurmountable impulse to wrap himself in a covering, to make himself, so to speak, a case which would isolate him and protect him from external influences. Reality irritated him, frightened him, kept him in continual agitation, and, perhaps to justify his timidity, his aversion for the actual, he always praised the past and what had never existed; and even the classical languages which he taught were in reality for him goloshes and umbrellas in which he sheltered himself from real life.

" 'Oh, how sonorous, how beautiful is the Greek language!' he would say, with a sugary expression; and as though to prove his words he would screw up his eyes and, raising his finger, would pronounce 'Anthropos!'

"And Byelikov tried to hide his thoughts also in a case. The only things that were clear to his mind were government circulars and newspaper articles in which something was forbidden. When some proclamation prohibited the boys from going out in the streets after nine o'clock in the evening, or some article declared carnal love unlawful, it was to his mind clear and definite; it was forbidden, and that was enough. For him there was always a doubtful element, something vague and not fully expressed, in any sanction or permission. When a dramatic club or a reading-room or a tea-shop was licensed in the town, he would shake his head and say softly:

" 'It is all right, of course; it is all very nice, but I hope it won't lead to anything!'

"Every sort of breach of order, deviation or departure from rule, depressed him, though one would have thought it was no business of his. If one of his colleagues was late for church or if rumours reached him of some prank of the high-school boys, or one of the mistresses was seen late in the evening in the company of an officer, he was much disturbed, and said he hoped that nothing would come of it. At the teachers' meetings he simply oppressed us with his caution, his circumspection, and his characteristic reflection on the ill-behaviour of the young people in both male and female high-schools, the uproar in the classes. . . .

"Oh, he hoped it would not reach the ears of the authorities; oh, he hoped nothing would come of it; and he thought it would be a very good thing if Petrov were expelled from the second class and Yegorov from the fourth. And, do you know, by his sighs, his despondency, his black spectacles on his pale little face, a little face like a pole-cat's, you know, he crushed us all, and we gave way, reduced Petrov's and Yegorov's marks for conduct, kept them in, and in the end expelled them both. He had a strange habit of visiting our lodgings. He would come to a teacher's, would sit down, and remain silent, as though he were carefully inspecting something. He would sit like this in silence for an hour or two and then go away. This he called 'maintaining good relations with his colleagues'; and it was obvious that coming to see us and sitting there was tiresome to him, and that he came to see us simply because he considered it his duty as our colleague. We teachers were afraid of him. And even the headmaster was afraid of him. Would you believe it, our teachers were all intellectual, right-minded people, brought up on Turgenev and Shtchedrin, yet this little chap, who always went about with goloshes and an umbrella, had the whole high-school under his thumb for fifteen long years! High-school, indeed—he had the whole town under his thumb! Our ladies did not get up private theatricals on Saturdays for fear he should hear of it, and the clergy dared not eat meat or play cards in his presence. Under the influence of people like Byelikov we have got into the way of being afraid of everything in our town for the last ten or fifteen years. They are afraid to speak aloud, afraid to send letters, afraid to make acquaintances, afraid to read books, afraid to help the poor, to teach people to read and write. . . ."

Ivan Ivanovitch cleared his throat, meaning to say something, but first lighted his pipe, gazed at the moon, and then said, with pauses:

"Yes, intellectual, right minded people read Shtchedrin and Turgenev, Buckle, and all the rest of them, yet they knocked under and put up with it . . . that's just how it is."

"Byelikov lived in the same house as I did," Burkin went on, "on the same storey, his door facing mine; we often saw each other, and I knew how he lived when he was at home. And at home it was the same story: dressing-gown, nightcap, blinds, bolts, a perfect succession of prohibitions and restrictions of all sorts, and—'Oh, I hope nothing will come of it!' Lenten fare was bad for him, yet he could not eat meat, as people might perhaps say Byelikov did not keep the fasts, and he ate fresh-water fish with butter—not a Lenten dish, yet one could not say that it was meat. He did not keep a female servant for fear people might think evil of him, but had as cook an old man of sixty, called Afanasy, half-witted and given to tippling, who had once been an officer's servant and could cook after a fashion. This Afanasy was usually standing at the door with his arms folded; with a deep sigh, he would mutter always the same thing:

" 'There are plenty of *them* about nowadays!'

"Byelikov had a little bedroom like a box; his bed had curtains. When he went to bed he covered his head over; it was hot and stuffy; the wind battered on the closed doors; there was a droning noise in the stove and a sound of sighs from the kitchen—ominous sighs. . . . And he felt frightened under the bed-clothes. He was afraid that something might happen, that Afanasy might murder him, that thieves might break in, and so he had troubled dreams all night, and in the morning, when we went together to the high-school, he was depressed and pale, and it was evident that the high-school full of people excited dread and aversion in his whole being, and that to walk beside me was irksome to a man of his solitary temperament.

" 'They make a great noise in our classes,' he used to say, as though trying to find an explanation for his depression. 'It's beyond anything.'

"And the Greek master, this man in a case—would you believe it?—almost got married."

Ivan Ivanovitch glanced quickly into the barn, and said:

"You are joking!"

"Yes, strange as it seems, he almost got married. A new teacher of history and geography, Mihail Savvitch Kovalenko, a Little Russian, was appointed. He came, not alone, but with his sister Varinka. He was a tall, dark young man with huge hands, and one could see from his face that he had a bass voice, and, in fact, he had a voice that seemed to come out of a barrel—'boom, boom, boom!' And she was not so young, about thirty, but she, too, was tall, well-made, with black eyebrows and red cheeks—in fact, she was a regular sugar-plum, and so sprightly, so noisy; she was always singing Little Russian songs and laughing. For the least thing she would go off into a ringing laugh—'Ha-ha-ha!' We made our first thorough acquaintance with the Kovalenkos at the headmaster's name-day party. Among the glum and intensely bored teachers who came even to the name-day party as a duty we suddenly saw a new Aphrodite risen from the waves; she walked with her arms akimbo, laughed, sang, danced.... She sang with feeling 'The Winds do Blow,' then another song, and another, and she fascinated us all—all, even Byelikov. He sat down by her and said with a honeyed smile:

" 'The Little Russian reminds one of the ancient Greek in its softness and agreeable resonance.'

"That flattered her, and she began telling him with feeling and earnestness that they had a farm in the Gadyatchsky district, and that her mamma lived at the farm, and that they had such pears, such melons, such *kabaks*! The Little Russians call pumpkins *kabaks* (*i.e.*, pothouses), while their pothouses they call *shinki*, and they make a beetroot soup with tomatoes and aubergines in it, 'which was so nice—awfully nice!'

"We listened and listened, and suddenly the same idea dawned upon us all:

" 'It would be a good thing to make a match of it,' the headmaster's wife said to me softly.

"We all for some reason recalled the fact that our friend Byelikov was not married, and it now seemed to us strange that we had hitherto failed to observe, and had in fact completely lost sight of, a detail so important in his life. What was his attitude to woman? How had he settled this vital question for himself? This had not interested us in the least till then; perhaps we had not even admitted the idea that a man who went out in all weathers in goloshes and slept under curtains could be in love.

" 'He is a good deal over forty and she is thirty,' the headmaster's wife went on, developing her idea. 'I believe she would marry him.'

"All sorts of things are done in the provinces through boredom, all sorts of unnecessary and nonsensical things! And that is because what is necessary is not done at all. What need was there, for instance, for us to make a match for this Byelikov, whom one could not even imagine married? The headmaster's wife, the inspector's wife, and all our high-school ladies, grew livelier and even better-looking, as though they had suddenly found a new object in life. The headmaster's wife would take a box at the theatre, and we beheld sitting in her box Varinka, with such a fan, beaming and happy, and beside her Byelikov, a little bent figure, looking as though he had been extracted from his house by pincers. I would give an evening party, and the ladies would insist on my inviting Byelikov and Varinka. In short, the machine was set in motion. It appeared that Varinka was not averse to matrimony. She had not a very cheerful life with her brother; they could do nothing but quarrel and scold one another from morning till night. Here is a scene, for instance. Kovalenko would be coming along the street, a tall, sturdy young ruffian, in an embroidered shirt, his love-locks falling on his forehead under his cap, in one hand a bundle of books, in the other a thick knotted stick, followed by his sister, also with books in her hand.

" 'But you haven't read it, Mihalik!' she would be arguing loudly. 'I tell you, I swear you have not read it at all!'

" 'And I tell you I have read it,' cries Kovalenko, thumping his stick on the pavement.

" 'Oh, my goodness, Mihalik! why are you so cross? We are arguing about principles.'

" 'I tell you that I have read it!' Kovalenko would shout, more loudly than ever.

"And at home, if there was an outsider present, there was sure to be a skirmish. Such a life must have been wearisome, and of course she must have longed for a home of her own. Besides, there was her age to be considered; there was no time left to pick and choose; it was a case of marrying anybody, even a Greek master. And, indeed, most of our young ladies don't mind whom they marry so long as they do get married. However that may be, Varinka began to show an unmistakable partiality for Byelikov.

"And Byelikov? He used to visit Kovalenko just as he did us. He would arrive, sit down, and remain silent. He would sit quiet, and Varinka would sing to him 'The Winds do Blow,' or would look pensively at him with her dark eyes, or would suddenly go off into a peal—'Ha-ha-ha!'

"Suggestion plays a great part in love affairs, and still more in getting married. Everybody—both his colleagues and the ladies—began assuring Byelikov that he ought to get married, that there was nothing left for him in life but to get married; we all congratulated him, with solemn countenances delivered ourselves of various platitudes, such as 'Marriage is a serious step.' Besides, Varinka was good-looking and interesting; she was the daughter of a civil councillor, and had a farm; and what was more, she was the first woman who had been warm and friendly in her manner to him. His head was turned, and he decided that he really ought to get married."

"Well, at that point you ought to have taken away his goloshes and umbrella," said Ivan Ivanovitch.

"Only fancy! that turned out to be impossible. He put Varinka's portrait on his table, kept coming to see me and talking about Varinka, and home life, saying marriage was a serious step. He was frequently at Kovalenko's, but he did not alter his manner of life in the least; on the contrary, indeed, his determination to get married seemed to have a depressing effect on him. He grew thinner and paler, and seemed to retreat further and further into his case.

" 'I like Varvara Savvishna,' he used to say to me, with a faint and wry smile, 'and I know that every one ought to get married, but... you know all this has happened so suddenly. . . . One must think a little.'

" 'What is there to think over?' I used to say to him. 'Get married—that is all.'

" 'No; marriage is a serious step. One must first weigh the duties before one, the responsibilities... that nothing may go wrong afterwards. It worries me so much that I don't sleep at night. And I must confess I am afraid: her brother and she have a strange way of thinking; they look at things strangely, you know, and her disposition is very impetuous. One may get married, and then, there is no knowing, one may find oneself in an unpleasant position.'

"And he did not make an offer; he kept putting it off, to the great vexation of the headmaster's wife and all our ladies; he went on weighing his future duties and responsibilities, and meanwhile he went for a walk with Varinka almost every day—possibly he thought that this was necessary in his position—and came to see me to talk about family life. And in all probability in the end he would have proposed to her, and would have made one of those unnecessary, stupid marriages such as are made by thousands among us from being bored and having nothing to do, if it had not been for a *kolossalische scandal.* I must mention that Varinka's brother, Kovalenko, detested Byelikov from the first day of their acquaintance, and could not endure him.

" 'I don't understand,' he used to say to us, shrugging his shoulders—'I don't understand how you can put up with that sneak, that nasty phiz. Ugh! how can you live here! The atmosphere is stifling and unclean! Do you call yourselves schoolmasters, teachers? You are paltry government clerks. You keep, not a temple of science, but a department for red tape and loyal behaviour, and it smells as sour as a police-station. No, my friends; I will stay with you for a while, and then I will go to my farm and there catch crabs and teach the Little Russians. I shall go, and you can stay here with your Judas—damn his soul!'

"Or he would laugh till he cried, first in a loud bass, then in a shrill, thin laugh, and ask me, waving his hands:

" 'What does he sit here for? What does he want? He sits and stares.'

"He even gave Byelikov a nickname, 'The Spider.' And it will readily be understood that we avoided talking to him of his sister's being about to marry 'The Spider.'

"And on one occasion, when the headmaster's wife hinted to him what a good thing it would be to secure his sister's future with such a reliable, universally respected man as Byelikov, he frowned and muttered:

" 'It's not my business; let her marry a reptile if she likes. I don't like meddling in other people's affairs.'

"Now hear what happened next. Some mischievous person drew a caricature of Byelikov walking along in his goloshes with his trousers tucked up, under his umbrella, with Varinka on his arm; below, the inscription 'Anthropos in love.' The expression was caught to a marvel, you know. The artist must have worked for more than one night, for the teachers of both the boys' and girls' high-schools, the teachers of the seminary, the government officials, all received a copy. Byelikov received one, too. The caricature made a very painful impression on him.

"We went out together; it was the first of May, a Sunday, and all of us, the boys and the teachers, had agreed to meet at the high-school and then to go for a walk together to a wood beyond the town. We set off, and he was green in the face and gloomier than a storm-cloud.

" 'What wicked, ill-natured people there are!' he said, and his lips quivered.

"I felt really sorry for him. We were walking along, and all of a sudden—would you believe it?—Kovalenko came bowling along on a bicycle, and after him, also on a bicycle, Varinka, flushed and exhausted, but good-humoured and gay.

" 'We are going on ahead,' she called. 'What lovely weather! Awfully lovely!'

"And they both disappeared from our sight. Byelikov turned white instead of green, and seemed petrified. He stopped short and stared at me. . . .

" 'What is the meaning of it? Tell me, please!' he asked. 'Can my eyes have deceived me? Is it the proper thing for high-school masters and ladies to ride bicycles?'

" 'What is there improper about it?' I said. 'Let them ride and enjoy themselves.'

" 'But how can that be?' he cried, amazed at my calm. 'What are you saying?'

"And he was so shocked that he was unwilling to go on, and returned home.

"Next day he was continually twitching and nervously rubbing his hands, and it was evident from his face that he was unwell. And he left before his work was over, for the first time in his life. And he ate no dinner. Towards evening he wrapped himself up warmly, though it was quite warm weather, and sallied out to the Kovalenkos'. Varinka was out; he found her brother, however.

" 'Pray sit down,' Kovalenko said coldly, with a frown. His face looked sleepy; he had just had a nap after dinner, and was in a very bad humour.

"Byelikov sat in silence for ten minutes, and then began:

" 'I have come to see you to relieve my mind. I am very, very much troubled. Some scurrilous fellow has drawn an absurd caricature of me and another person, in whom we are both deeply interested. I regard it as a duty to assure you that I have had no hand in it. . . . I have given no sort of ground for such ridicule—on the contrary, I have always behaved in every way like a gentleman.'

"Kovalenko sat sulky and silent. Byelikov waited a little, and went on slowly in a mournful voice:

" 'And I have something else to say to you. I have been in the service for years, while you have only lately entered it, and I consider it my duty as an older colleague to give you a warning. You ride on a bicycle, and that pastime is utterly unsuitable for an educator of youth.'

" 'Why so?' asked Kovalenko in his bass.

" 'Surely that needs no explanation, Mihail Savvitch—surely you can understand that? If the teacher rides a bicycle, what can you expect the pupils to do? You will have them walking on their heads next! And so long as there is no formal permission to do so, it is out of the question. I was horrified yesterday! When I saw your sister everything seemed dancing before my eyes. A lady or a young girl on a bicycle—it's awful!'

" 'What is it you want exactly?'

" 'All I want is to warn you, Mihail Savvitch. You are a young man, you have a future before you, you must be very, very careful in your behaviour, and you are so careless—oh, so careless! You go about in an embroidered shirt, are constantly seen in the street carrying books, and now the bicycle, too. The headmaster will learn that you and your sister ride the bicycle, and then it will reach the higher authorities. . . . Will that be a good thing?'

" 'It's no business of anybody else if my sister and I do bicycle!' said Kovalenko, and he turned crimson. 'And damnation take any one who meddles in my private affairs!'

"Byelikov turned pale and got up.

" 'If you speak to me in that tone I cannot continue,' he said. 'And I beg you never to express yourself like that about our superiors in my presence; you ought to be respectful to the authorities.'

" 'Why, have I said any harm of the authorities?' asked Kovalenko, looking at him wrathfully. 'Please leave me alone. I am an honest man, and do not care to talk to a gentleman like you. I don't like sneaks!'

"Byelikov flew into a nervous flutter, and began hurriedly putting on his coat, with an expression of horror on his face. It was the first time in his life he had been spoken to so rudely.

" 'You can say what you please,' he said, as he went out from the entry to the landing on the staircase. 'I ought only to warn you: possibly some one may have overheard us, and that our conversation may not be misunderstood and harm come of it, I shall be compelled to inform our headmaster of our conversation . . . in its main features. I am bound to do so.'

" 'Inform him? You can go and make your report!'

"Kovalenko seized him from behind by the collar and gave him a push, and Byelikov rolled downstairs, thudding with his goloshes. The staircase was high and steep, but he rolled to the bottom unhurt, got up, and touched his nose to see whether his spectacles were all right. But just as he was falling down the stairs Varinka came in, and with her two ladies; they stood below staring, and to Byelikov this was more terrible than anything. I believe he would rather have broken his neck or both legs than have been an object of ridicule. Why, now the whole town would hear of it; it would come to the headmaster's ears, would reach the higher authorities—oh, it might lead to something! There would be another caricature, and it would all end in his being asked to resign his post. . . .

"When he got up, Varinka recognized him, and, looking at his ridiculous face, his crumpled overcoat, and his goloshes, not understanding what had happened and supposing that he had slipped down by accident, could not restrain herself, and laughed loud enough to be heard by all the flats:

" 'Ha-ha-ha!'

"And this pealing, ringing 'Ha-ha-ha!' was the last straw that put an end to everything: to the proposed match and to Byelikov's earthly existence. He did not hear what Varinka said to him; he saw nothing. On reaching home, the first thing he did was to remove her portrait from the table; then he went to bed, and he never got up again.

"Three days later Afanasy came to me and asked whether we should not send for the doctor, as there was something wrong with his master. I went in to Byelikov. He lay silent behind the curtain, covered with a quilt; if one asked him a question, he said 'Yes' or 'No' and not another sound. He lay there while Afanasy, gloomy and scowling, hovered about him, sighing heavily, and smelling like a pothouse.

"A month later Byelikov died. We all went to his funeral—that is, both the high-schools and the seminary. Now when he was lying in his coffin his expression was mild, agreeable, even cheerful, as though he were glad that he had at last been put into a case which he would never leave again. Yes, he had attained his ideal! And, as though in his honour, it was dull, rainy weather on the day of his funeral, and we all wore goloshes and took our umbrellas. Varinka, too, was at the funeral, and when the coffin was lowered into the grave she burst into tears. I have noticed that Little Russian women are always laughing or crying—no intermediate mood.

"One must confess that to bury people like Byelikov is a great pleasure. As we were returning from the cemetery we wore discreet Lenten faces; no one wanted to display this feeling of pleasure—a feeling like that we had experienced long, long ago as children when our elders had gone out and we ran about the garden for an hour or two, enjoying complete freedom. Ah, freedom, freedom! The merest hint, the faintest hope of its possibility gives wings to the soul, does it not?

"We returned from the cemetery in a good humour. But not more than a week had passed before life went on as in the past, as gloomy, oppressive, and senseless—a life not forbidden by government prohibition, but not fully permitted, either: it was no better. And, indeed, though we had buried Byelikov, how many such men in cases were left, how many more of them there will be!"

"That's just how it is," said Ivan Ivanovitch and he lighted his pipe.

"How many more of them there will be!" repeated Burkin.

The schoolmaster came out of the barn. He was a short, stout man, completely bald, with a black beard down to his waist. The two dogs came out with him.

"What a moon!" he said, looking upwards.

It was midnight. On the right could be seen the whole village, a long street stretching far away for four miles. All was buried in deep silent slumber; not a movement, not a sound; one could hardly believe that nature could be so still. When on a moonlight night you see a broad village street, with its cottages, haystacks, and slumbering willows, a feeling of calm comes over the soul; in this peace, wrapped away from care, toil, and sorrow in the darkness of night, it is mild, melancholy, beautiful, and it seems as though the stars look down upon it kindly and with tenderness, and as though there were no evil on earth and all were well. On the left the open country began from the end of the village; it could be seen stretching far away to the horizon, and there was no movement, no sound in that whole expanse bathed in moonlight.

"Yes, that is just how it is," repeated Ivan Ivanovitch; "and isn't our living in town, airless and crowded, our writing useless papers, our playing *vint*—isn't that all a sort of case for us? And our spending our whole lives among trivial, fussy men and silly, idle women, our talking and our listening to all sorts of nonsense—isn't that a case for us, too? If you like, I will tell you a very edifying story."

"No; it's time we were asleep," said Burkin.

"Tell it tomorrow."

They went into the barn and lay down on the hay. And they were both covered up and beginning to doze when they suddenly heard light footsteps—patter, patter. . . . Some one was walking not far from the barn, walking a little and stopping, and a minute later, patter, patter again. . . . The dogs began growling.

"That's Mavra," said Burkin.

The footsteps died away.

"You see and hear that they lie," said Ivan Ivanovitch, turning over on the other side, "and they call you a fool for putting up with their lying. You endure insult and humiliation, and dare not openly say that you are on the side of the honest and the free, and you lie and smile yourself; and all that for the sake of a crust of bread, for the sake of a warm corner, for the sake of a wretched little worthless rank in the service. No, one can't go on living like this."

"Well, you are off on another tack now, Ivan Ivanovitch," said the schoolmaster. "Let us go to sleep!"

And ten minutes later Burkin was asleep. But Ivan Ivanovitch kept sighing and turning over from side to side; then he got up, went outside again, and, sitting in the doorway, lighted his pipe.

Gooseberries

The whole sky had been overcast with rain-clouds from early morning; it was a still day, not hot, but heavy, as it is in grey dull weather when the clouds have been hanging over the country for a long while, when one expects rain and it does not come. Ivan Ivanovitch, the veterinary surgeon, and Burkin, the high-school teacher, were already tired from walking, and the fields seemed to them endless. Far ahead of them they could just see the windmills of the village of Mironositskoe; on the right stretched a row of hillocks which disappeared in the distance behind the village, and they both knew that this was the bank of the river, that there were meadows, green willows, homesteads there, and that if one stood on one of the hillocks one could see from it the same vast plain, telegraph-wires, and a train which in the distance looked like a crawling caterpillar, and that in clear weather one could even see the town. Now, in still weather, when all nature seemed mild and dreamy, Ivan Ivanovitch and Burkin were filled with love of that countryside, and both thought how great, how beautiful a land it was.

"Last time we were in Prokofy's barn," said Burkin, "you were about to tell me a story."

"Yes; I meant to tell you about my brother."

Ivan Ivanovitch heaved a deep sigh and lighted a pipe to begin to tell his story, but just at that moment the rain began. And five minutes later heavy rain came down, covering the sky, and it was hard to tell when it would be over. Ivan Ivanovitch and Burkin stopped in hesitation; the dogs, already drenched, stood with their tails between their legs gazing at them feelingly.

"We must take shelter somewhere," said Burkin. "Let us go to Alehin's; it's close by."

"Come along."

They turned aside and walked through mown fields, sometimes going straight forward, sometimes turning to the right, till they came out on the road. Soon they saw poplars, a garden, then the red roofs of barns; there was a gleam of the river, and the view opened on to a broad expanse of water with a windmill and a white bath-house: this was Sofino, where Alehin lived.

The watermill was at work, drowning the sound of the rain; the dam was shaking. Here wet horses with drooping heads were standing near their carts, and men were walking about covered with sacks. It was damp, muddy, and desolate; the water looked cold and malignant. Ivan Ivanovitch and Burkin were already conscious of a feeling of wetness, messiness, and discomfort all over; their feet were heavy with mud, and when, crossing the dam, they went up to the barns, they were silent, as though they were angry with one another.

In one of the barns there was the sound of a winnowing machine, the door was open, and clouds of dust were coming from it. In the doorway was standing Alehin himself, a man of forty, tall and stout, with long hair, more like a professor or an artist than a landowner. He had on a white shirt that badly needed washing, a rope for a belt, drawers instead of trousers, and his boots, too, were plastered up with mud and straw. His eyes and nose were black with dust. He recognized Ivan Ivanovitch and Burkin, and was apparently much delighted to see them.

"Go into the house, gentlemen," he said, smiling; "I'll come directly, this minute."

It was a big two-storeyed house. Alehin lived in the lower storey, with arched ceilings and little windows, where the bailiffs had once lived; here everything was plain, and there was a smell of rye bread, cheap vodka, and harness. He went upstairs into the best rooms only on rare occasions, when visitors came. Ivan Ivanovitch and Burkin were met in the house by a maid-servant, a young woman so beautiful that they both stood still and looked at one another.

"You can't imagine how delighted I am to see you, my friends," said Alehin, going into the hall with them. "It is a surprise! Pelagea," he said, addressing the girl, "give our visitors something to change into. And, by the way, I will change too. Only I must first go and wash, for I almost think I have not washed since spring. Wouldn't you like to come into the bath-house? and meanwhile they will get things ready here."

Beautiful Pelagea, looking so refined and soft, brought them towels and soap, and Alehin went to the bath-house with his guests.

"It's a long time since I had a wash," he said, undressing. "I have got a nice bath-house, as you see—my father built it—but I somehow never have time to wash."

He sat down on the steps and soaped his long hair and his neck, and the water round him turned brown.

"Yes, I must say," said Ivan Ivanovitch meaningly, looking at his head.

"It's a long time since I washed . . ." said Alehin with embarrassment, giving himself a second soaping, and the water near him turned dark blue, like ink.

Ivan Ivanovitch went outside, plunged into the water with a loud splash, and swam in the rain, flinging his arms out wide. He stirred the water into waves which set the white lilies bobbing up and down; he swam to the very middle of the millpond and dived, and came up a minute later in another place, and swam on, and kept on diving, trying to touch the bottom.

"Oh, my goodness!" he repeated continually, enjoying himself thoroughly. "Oh, my goodness!" He swam to the mill, talked to the peasants there, then returned and lay on his back in the middle of the pond, turning his face to the rain. Burkin and Alehin were dressed and ready to go, but he still went on swimming and diving. "Oh, my goodness! . . ." he said. "Oh, Lord, have mercy on me! . . ."

"That's enough!" Burkin shouted to him.

They went back to the house. And only when the lamp was lighted in the big drawing-room upstairs, and Burkin and Ivan Ivanovitch, attired in silk dressing-gowns and warm slippers, were sitting in arm-chairs; and Alehin, washed and combed, in a new coat, was walking about the drawing-room, evidently enjoying the feeling of warmth, cleanliness, dry clothes, and light shoes; and when lovely Pelagea, stepping noiselessly on the carpet and smiling softly, handed tea and jam on a tray—only then Ivan Ivanovitch began on his story, and it seemed as though not only Burkin and Alehin were listening, but also the ladies, young and old, and the officers who looked down upon them sternly and calmly from their gold frames.

"There are two of us brothers," he began—"I, Ivan Ivanovitch, and my brother, Nikolay Ivanovitch, two years younger. I went in for a learned profession and became a veterinary surgeon, while Nikolay sat in a government office from the time he was nineteen. Our father, Tchimsha-Himalaisky, was a kantonist, but he rose to be an officer and left us a little estate and the rank of nobility. After his death the little estate went in debts and legal expenses; but, anyway, we had spent our childhood running wild in the country. Like peasant children, we passed our days and nights in the fields and the woods, looked after horses, stripped the bark off the trees, fished, and so on. . . . And, you know, whoever has once in his life caught perch or has seen the migrating of the thrushes in autumn, watched how they float in flocks over the village on bright, cool days, he will never be a real townsman, and will have a yearning for freedom to the day of his death. My brother was miserable in the government office. Years passed by, and he went on sitting in the same place, went on writing the same papers and thinking of one and the same thing—how to get into the country. And this yearning by degrees passed into a definite desire, into a dream of buying himself a little farm somewhere on the banks of a river or a lake.

"He was a gentle, good-natured fellow, and I was fond of him, but I never sympathized with this desire to shut himself up for the rest of his life in a little farm of his own. It's the correct thing to say that a man needs no more than six feet of earth. But six feet is what a corpse needs, not a man. And they say, too, now, that if our intellectual classes are attracted to the land and yearn for a farm, it's a good thing. But these farms are just the same as six feet of earth. To retreat from town, from the struggle, from the bustle of life, to retreat and bury oneself in one's farm—it's not life, it's egoism, laziness, it's monasticism of a sort, but monasticism without good works. A man does not need six feet of earth or a farm, but the whole globe, all nature, where he can have room to display all the qualities and peculiarities of his free spirit.

"My brother Nikolay, sitting in his government office, dreamed of how he would eat his own cabbages, which would fill the whole yard with such a savoury smell, take his meals on the green grass, sleep in the sun, sit for whole hours on the seat by the gate gazing at the fields and the forest. Gardening books and the agricultural hints in calendars were his delight, his favourite spiritual sustenance; he enjoyed reading newspapers, too, but the only things he read in them were the advertisements of so many acres of arable land and a grass meadow with farm-houses and buildings, a river, a garden, a mill and millponds, for sale. And his imagination pictured the garden-paths, flowers and fruit, starling cotes, the carp in the pond, and all that sort of thing, you know. These imaginary pictures were of different kinds according to the advertisements which he came across, but for some reason in every one of them he had always to have gooseberries. He could not imagine a homestead, he could not picture an idyllic nook, without gooseberries.

" 'Country life has its conveniences,' he would sometimes say. 'You sit on the verandah and you drink tea, while your ducks swim on the pond, there is a delicious smell everywhere, and . . . and the gooseberries are growing.'

"He used to draw a map of his property, and in every map there were the same things—(*a*) house for the family, (*b*) servants' quarters, (*c*) kitchen-garden, (*d*) gooseberry-bushes. He lived parsimoniously, was frugal in food and drink, his clothes were beyond description; he looked like a beggar, but kept on saving and putting money in the bank. He grew fearfully avaricious. I did not like to look at him, and I used to give him something and send him presents for Christmas and Easter, but he used to save that too. Once a man is absorbed by an idea there is no doing anything with him.

"Years passed: he was transferred to another province. He was over forty, and he was still reading the advertisements in the papers and saving up. Then I heard he was married. Still with the same object of buying a farm and having gooseberries, he married an elderly and ugly widow without a trace of feeling for her, simply because she had filthy lucre. He went on living frugally after marrying her, and kept her short of food, while he put her money in the bank in his name.

"Her first husband had been a postmaster, and with him she was accustomed to pies and home-made wines, while with her second husband she did not get enough black bread; she began to pine away with this sort of life, and three years later she gave up her soul to God. And I need hardly say that my brother never for one moment imagined that he was responsible for her death. Money, like vodka, makes a man queer. In our town there was a merchant who, before he died, ordered a plateful of honey and ate up all his money and lottery tickets with the honey, so that no one might get the benefit of it. While I was inspecting cattle at a railway-station, a cattle-dealer fell under an engine and had his leg cut off. We carried him into the waiting-room, the blood was flowing—it was a horrible thing—and he kept asking them to look for his leg and was very much worried about it; there were twenty roubles in the boot on the leg that had been cut off, and he was afraid they would be lost."

"That's a story from a different opera," said Burkin.

"After his wife's death," Ivan Ivanovitch went on, after thinking for half a minute, "my brother began looking out for an estate for himself. Of course, you may look about for five years and yet end by making a mistake, and buying something quite different from what you have dreamed of. My brother Nikolay bought through an agent a mortgaged estate of three hundred and thirty acres, with a house for the family, with servants' quarters, with a park, but with no orchard, no gooseberry-bushes, and no duck-pond; there was a river, but the water in it was the colour of coffee, because on one side of the estate there was a brickyard and on the other a factory for burning bones. But Nikolay Ivanovitch did not grieve much; he ordered twenty gooseberry-bushes, planted them, and began living as a country gentleman.

"Last year I went to pay him a visit. I thought I would go and see what it was like. In his letters my brother called his estate 'Tchumbaroklov Waste, alias Himalaiskoe.' I reached 'alias Himalaiskoe' in the afternoon. It was hot. Everywhere there were ditches, fences, hedges, fir-trees planted in rows, and there was no knowing how to get to the yard, where to put one's horse. I went up to the house, and was met by a fat red dog that looked like a pig. It wanted to bark, but it was too lazy. The cook, a fat, barefooted woman, came out of the kitchen, and she, too, looked like a pig, and said that her master was resting after dinner. I went in to see my brother. He was sitting up in bed with a quilt over his legs; he had grown older, fatter, wrinkled; his cheeks, his nose, and his mouth all stuck out—he looked as though he might begin grunting into the quilt at any moment.

"We embraced each other, and shed tears of joy and of sadness at the thought that we had once been young and now were both grey-headed and near the grave. He dressed, and led me out to show me the estate.

" 'Well, how are you getting on here?' I asked.

" 'Oh, all right, thank God; I am getting on very well.'

"He was no more a poor timid clerk, but a real landowner, a gentleman. He was already accustomed to it, had grown used to it, and liked it. He ate a great deal, went to the bath-house, was growing stout, was already at law with the village commune and both factories, and was very much offended when the peasants did not call him 'Your Honour.' And he concerned himself with the salvation of his soul in a substantial, gentlemanly manner, and performed deeds of charity, not simply, but with an air of consequence. And what deeds of charity! He treated the peasants for every sort of disease with soda and castor oil, and on his name-day had a thanksgiving service in the middle of the village, and then treated the peasants to a gallon of vodka—he thought that was the thing to do. Oh, those horrible gallons of vodka! One day the fat landowner hauls the peasants up before the district captain for trespass, and next day, in honour of a holiday, treats them to a gallon of vodka, and they drink and shout 'Hurrah!' and when they are drunk bow down to his feet. A change of life for the better, and being well-fed and idle develop in a Russian the most insolent self-conceit. Nikolay Ivanovitch, who at one time in the government office was afraid to have any views of his own, now could say nothing that was not gospel truth, and uttered such truths in the tone of a prime minister. 'Education is essential, but for the peasants it is premature.' 'Corporal punishment is harmful as a rule, but in some cases it is necessary and there is nothing to take its place.'

" 'I know the peasants and understand how to treat them,' he would say. 'The peasants like me. I need only to hold up my little finger and the peasants will do anything I like.'

"And all this, observe, was uttered with a wise, benevolent smile. He repeated twenty times over 'We noblemen,' 'I as a noble'; obviously he did not remember that our grandfather was a peasant, and our father a soldier. Even our surname Tchimsha-Himalaisky, in reality so incongruous, seemed to him now melodious, distinguished, and very agreeable.

"But the point just now is not he, but myself. I want to tell you about the change that took place in me during the brief hours I spent at his country place. In the evening, when we were drinking tea, the cook put on the table a plateful of gooseberries. They were not bought, but his own gooseberries, gathered for the first time since the bushes were planted. Nikolay Ivanovitch laughed and looked for a minute in silence at the gooseberries, with tears in his eyes; he could not speak for excitement. Then he put one gooseberry in his mouth, looked at me with the triumph of a child who has at last received his favourite toy, and said:

" 'How delicious!'

"And he ate them greedily, continually repeating, 'Ah, how delicious! Do taste them!'

"They were sour and unripe, but, as Pushkin says:

" 'Dearer to us the falsehood that exalts
Than hosts of baser truths.'

"I saw a happy man whose cherished dream was so obviously fulfilled, who had attained his object in life, who had gained what he wanted, who was satisfied with his fate and himself. There is always, for some reason, an element of sadness mingled with my thoughts of human happiness, and, on this occasion, at the sight of a happy man I was overcome by an oppressive feeling that was close upon despair. It was particularly oppressive at night. A bed was made up for me in the room next to my brother's bedroom, and I could hear that he was awake, and that he kept getting up and going to the plate of gooseberries and taking one. I reflected how many satisfied, happy people there really are! What a suffocating force it is! You look at life: the insolence and idleness of the strong, the ignorance and brutishness of the weak, incredible poverty all about us, overcrowding, degeneration, drunkenness, hypocrisy, lying.... Yet all is calm and stillness in the houses and in the streets; of the fifty thousand living in a town, there is not one who would cry out, who would give vent to his indignation aloud. We see the people going to market for provisions, eating by day, sleeping by night, talking their silly nonsense, getting married, growing old, serenely escorting their dead to the cemetery; but we do not see and we do not hear those who suffer, and what is terrible in life goes on somewhere behind the scenes. . . . Everything is quiet and peaceful, and nothing protests but mute statistics: so many people gone out of their minds, so many gallons of vodka drunk, so many children dead from malnutrition.... And this order of things is evidently necessary; evidently the happy man only feels at ease because the unhappy bear their burdens in silence, and without that silence happiness would be impossible. It's a case of general hypnotism. There ought to be behind the door of every happy, contented man some one standing with a hammer continually reminding him with a tap that there are unhappy people; that however happy he may be, life will show him her laws sooner or later, trouble will come for him—disease, poverty, losses, and no one will see or hear, just as now he neither sees nor hears others. But there is no man with a hammer; the happy man lives at his ease, and trivial daily cares faintly agitate him like the wind in the aspen-tree—and all goes well.

"That night I realized that I, too, was happy and contented," Ivan Ivanovitch went on, getting up. "I, too, at dinner and at the hunt liked to lay down the law on life and religion, and the way to manage the peasantry. I, too, used to say that science was light, that culture was essential, but for the simple people reading and writing was enough for the time. Freedom is a blessing, I used to say; we can no more do without it than without air, but we must wait a little. Yes, I used to talk like that, and now I ask, 'For what reason are we to wait?' " asked Ivan Ivanovitch, looking angrily at Burkin. "Why wait, I ask you? What grounds have we for waiting? I shall be told, it can't be done all at once; every idea takes shape in life gradually, in its due time. But who is it says that? Where is the proof that it's right? You will fall back upon the natural order of things, the uniformity of phenomena; but is there order and uniformity in the fact that I, a living, thinking man, stand over a chasm and wait for it to close of itself, or to fill up with mud at the very time when perhaps I might leap over it or build a bridge across it? And again, wait for the sake of what? Wait till there's no strength to live? And meanwhile one must live, and one wants to live!

"I went away from my brother's early in the morning, and ever since then it has been unbearable for me to be in town. I am oppressed by its peace and quiet; I am afraid to look at the windows, for there is no spectacle more painful to me now than the sight of a happy family sitting round the table drinking tea. I am old and am not fit for the struggle; I am not even capable of hatred; I can only grieve inwardly, feel irritated and vexed; but at night my head is hot from the rush of ideas, and I cannot sleep. . . . Ah, if I were young!"

Ivan Ivanovitch walked backwards and forwards in excitement, and repeated: "If I were young!"

He suddenly went up to Alehin and began pressing first one of his hands and then the other.

"Pavel Konstantinovitch," he said in an imploring voice, "don't be calm and contented, don't let yourself be put to sleep! While you are young, strong, confident, be not weary in well-doing! There is no happiness, and there ought not to be; but if there is a meaning and an object in life, that meaning and object is not our happiness, but something greater and more rational. Do good!"

And all this Ivan Ivanovitch said with a pitiful, imploring smile, as though he were asking him a personal favour.

Then all three sat in arm-chairs at different ends of the drawing-room and were silent. Ivan Ivanovitch's story had not satisfied either Burkin or Alehin. When the generals and ladies gazed down from their gilt frames, looking in the dusk as though they were alive, it was dreary to listen to the story of the poor clerk who ate gooseberries. They felt inclined, for some reason, to talk about elegant people, about women. And their sitting in the drawing-room where everything—the chandeliers in their covers, the arm-chairs, and the carpet under their feet—reminded them that those very people who were now looking down from their frames had once moved about, sat, drunk tea in this room, and the fact that lovely Pelagea was moving noiselessly about was better than any story.

Alehin was fearfully sleepy; he had got up early, before three o'clock in the morning, to look after his work, and now his eyes were closing; but he was afraid his visitors might tell some interesting story after he had gone, and he lingered on. He did not go into the question whether what Ivan Ivanovitch had just said was right and true. His visitors did not talk of groats, nor of hay, nor of tar, but of something that had no direct bearing on his life, and he was glad and wanted them to go on.

"It's bed-time, though," said Burkin, getting up. "Allow me to wish you good-night."

Alehin said good-night and went downstairs to his own domain, while the visitors remained upstairs. They were both taken for the night to a big room where there stood two old wooden beds decorated with carvings, and in the corner was an ivory crucifix. The big cool beds, which had been made by the lovely Pelagea, smelt agreeably of clean linen.

Ivan Ivanovitch undressed in silence and got into bed.

"Lord forgive us sinners!" he said, and put his head under the quilt.

His pipe lying on the table smelt strongly of stale tobacco, and Burkin could not sleep for a long while, and kept wondering where the oppressive smell came from.

The rain was pattering on the window-panes all night.

About Love

At lunch next day there were very nice pies, crayfish, and mutton cutlets; and while we were eating, Nikanor, the cook, came up to ask what the visitors would like for dinner. He was a man of medium height, with a puffy face and little eyes; he was close-shaven, and it looked as though his moustaches had not been shaved, but had been pulled out by the roots. Alehin told us that the beautiful Pelagea was in love with this cook. As he drank and was of a violent character, she did not want to marry him, but was willing to live with him without. He was very devout, and his religious convictions would not allow him to "live in sin"; he insisted on her marrying him, and would consent to nothing else, and when he was drunk he used to abuse her and even beat her. Whenever he got drunk she used to hide upstairs and sob, and on such occasions Alehin and the servants stayed in the house to be ready to defend her in case of necessity.

We began talking about love.

"How love is born," said Alehin, "why Pelagea does not love somebody more like herself in her spiritual and external qualities, and why she fell in love with Nikanor, that ugly snout—we all call him 'The Snout'—how far questions of personal happiness are of consequence in love—all that is unknown; one can take what view one likes of it. So far only one incontestable truth has been uttered about love: 'This is a great mystery.' Everything else that has been written or said about love is not a conclusion, but only a statement of questions which have remained unanswered. The explanation which would seem to fit one case does not apply in a dozen others, and the very best thing, to my mind, would be to explain every case individually without attempting to generalize. We ought, as the doctors say, to individualize each case."

"Perfectly true," Burkin assented.

"We Russians of the educated class have a partiality for these questions that remain unanswered. Love is usually poeticized, decorated with roses, nightingales; we Russians decorate our loves with these momentous questions, and select the most uninteresting of them, too. In Moscow, when I was a student, I had a friend who shared my life, a charming lady, and every time I took her in my arms she was thinking what I would allow her a month for housekeeping and what was the price of beef a pound. In the same way, when we are in love we are never tired of asking ourselves questions: whether it is honourable or dishonourable, sensible or stupid, what this love is leading up to, and so on. Whether it is a good thing or not I don't know, but that it is in the way, unsatisfactory, and irritating, I do know."

It looked as though he wanted to tell some story. People who lead a solitary existence always have something in their hearts which they are eager to talk about. In town bachelors visit the baths and the restaurants on purpose to talk, and sometimes tell the most interesting things to bath attendants and waiters; in the country, as a rule, they unbosom themselves to their guests. Now from the window we could see a grey sky, trees drenched in the rain; in such weather we could go nowhere, and there was nothing for us to do but to tell stories and to listen.

"I have lived at Sofino and been farming for a long time," Alehin began, "ever since I left the University. I am an idle gentleman by education, a studious person by disposition; but there was a big debt owing on the estate when I came here, and as my father was in debt partly because he had spent so much on my education, I resolved not to go away, but to work till I paid off the debt. I made up my mind to this and set to work, not, I must confess, without some repugnance. The land here does not yield much, and if one is not to farm at a loss one must employ serf labour or hired labourers, which is almost the same thing, or put it on a peasant footing—that is, work the fields oneself and with one's family. There is no middle path. But in those days I did not go into such subtleties. I did not leave a clod of earth unturned; I gathered together all the peasants, men and women, from the neighbouring villages; the work went on at a tremendous pace. I myself ploughed and sowed and reaped, and was bored doing it, and frowned with disgust, like a village cat driven by hunger to eat cucumbers in the kitchen-garden. My body ached, and I slept as I walked. At first it seemed to me that I could easily reconcile this life of toil with my cultured habits; to do so, I thought, all that is necessary is to maintain a certain external order in life. I established myself upstairs here in the best rooms, and ordered them to bring me there coffee and liquor after lunch and dinner, and when I went to bed I read every night the *Vyestnik Evropi*. But one day our priest, Father Ivan, came and drank up all my liquor at one sitting; and the *Vyestnik Evropi* went to the priest's daughters; as in the summer, especially at the hay-making, I did not succeed in getting to my bed at all, and slept in the sledge in the barn, or somewhere in the forester's lodge, what chance was there of reading? Little by little I moved downstairs, began dining in the servants' kitchen, and of my former luxury nothing is left but the servants who were in my father's service, and whom it would be painful to turn away.

"In the first years I was elected here an honourary justice of the peace. I used to have to go to the town and take part in the sessions of the congress and of the circuit court, and this was a pleasant change for me. When you live here for two or three months without a break, especially in the winter, you begin at last to pine for a black coat. And in the circuit court there were frock-coats, and uniforms, and dress-coats, too, all lawyers, men who have received a general education; I had some one to talk to. After sleeping in the sledge and dining in the kitchen, to sit in an arm-chair in clean linen, in thin boots, with a chain on one's waistcoat, is such luxury!

"I received a warm welcome in the town. I made friends eagerly.

And of all my acquaintanceships the most intimate and, to tell the truth, the most agreeable to me was my acquaintance with Luganovitch, the vice-president of the circuit court. You both know him: a most charming personality. It all happened just after a celebrated case of incendiarism; the preliminary investigation lasted two days; we were exhausted. Luganovitch looked at me and said:

" 'Look here, come round to dinner with me.'

"This was unexpected, as I knew Luganovitch very little, only officially, and I had never been to his house. I only just went to my hotel room to change and went off to dinner. And here it was my lot to meet Anna Alexyevna, Luganovitch's wife. At that time she was still very young, not more than twenty-two, and her first baby had been born just six months before. It is all a thing of the past; and now I should find it difficult to define what there was so exceptional in her, what it was in her attracted me so much; at the time, at dinner, it was all perfectly clear to me. I saw a lovely young, good, intelligent, fascinating woman, such as I had never met before; and I felt her at once some one close and already familiar, as though that face, those cordial, intelligent eyes, I had seen somewhere in my childhood, in the album which lay on my mother's chest of drawers.

"Four Jews were charged with being incendiaries, were regarded as a gang of robbers, and, to my mind, quite groundlessly. At dinner I was very much excited, I was uncomfortable, and I don't know what I said, but Anna Alexyevna kept shaking her head and saying to her husband:

" 'Dmitry, how is this?'

"Luganovitch is a good-natured man, one of those simple-hearted people who firmly maintain the opinion that once a man is charged before a court he is guilty, and to express doubt of the correctness of a sentence cannot be done except in legal form on paper, and not at dinner and in private conversation.

" 'You and I did not set fire to the place,' he said softly, 'and you see we are not condemned, and not in prison.'

"And both husband and wife tried to make me eat and drink as much as possible. From some trifling details, from the way they made the coffee together, for instance, and from the way they understood each other at half a word, I could gather that they lived in harmony and comfort, and that they were glad of a visitor. After dinner they played a duet on the piano; then it got dark, and I went home. That was at the beginning of spring.

"After that I spent the whole summer at Sofino without a break, and I had no time to think of the town, either, but the memory of the graceful fair-haired woman remained in my mind all those days; I did not think of her, but it was as though her light shadow were lying on my heart.

"In the late autumn there was a theatrical performance for some charitable object in the town. I went into the governor's box (I was invited to go there in the interval); I looked, and there was Anna Alexyevna sitting beside the governor's wife; and again the same irresistible, thrilling impression of beauty and sweet, caressing eyes, and again the same feeling of nearness. We sat side by side, then went to the foyer.

" 'You've grown thinner,' she said; 'have you been ill?'

" 'Yes, I've had rheumatism in my shoulder, and in rainy weather I can't sleep.'

" 'You look dispirited. In the spring, when you came to dinner, you were younger, more confident. You were full of eagerness, and talked a great deal then; you were very interesting, and I really must confess I was a little carried away by you. For some reason you often came back to my memory during the summer, and when I was getting ready for the theatre today I thought I should see you.'

"And she laughed.

" 'But you look dispirited today,' she repeated; 'it makes you seem older.'

"The next day I lunched at the Luganovitchs'. After lunch they drove out to their summer villa, in order to make arrangements there for the winter, and I went with them. I returned with them to the town, and at midnight drank tea with them in quiet domestic surroundings, while the fire glowed, and the young mother kept going to see if her baby girl was asleep. And after that, every time I went to town I never failed to visit the Luganovitchs. They grew used to me, and I grew used to them. As a rule I went in unannounced, as though I were one of the family.

" 'Who is there?' I would hear from a faraway room, in the drawling voice that seemed to me so lovely.

" 'It is Pavel Konstantinovitch,' answered the maid or the nurse.

"Anna Alexyevna would come out to me with an anxious face, and would ask every time:

" 'Why is it so long since you have been? Has anything happened?'

"Her eyes, the elegant refined hand she gave me, her indoor dress, the way she did her hair, her voice, her step, always produced the same impression on me of something new and extraordinary in my life, and very important. We talked together for hours, were silent, thinking each our own thoughts, or she played for hours to me on the piano. If there were no one at home I stayed and waited, talked to the nurse, played with the child, or lay on the sofa in the study and read; and when Anna Alexyevna came back I met her in the hall, took all her parcels from her, and for some reason I carried those parcels every time with as much love, with as much solemnity, as a boy.

"There is a proverb that if a peasant woman has no troubles she will buy a pig. The Luganovitchs had no troubles, so they made friends with me. If I did not come to the town I must be ill or something must have happened to me, and both of them were extremely anxious. They were worried that I, an educated man with a knowledge of languages, should, instead of devoting myself to science or literary work, live in the country, rush round like a squirrel in a rage, work hard with never a penny to show for it. They fancied that I was unhappy, and that I only talked, laughed, and ate to conceal my sufferings, and even at cheerful moments when I felt happy I was aware of their searching eyes fixed upon me. They were particularly touching when I really was depressed, when I was being worried by some creditor or had not money enough to pay interest on the proper day. The two of them, husband and wife, would whisper together at the window; then he would come to me and say with a grave face:

" 'If you really are in need of money at the moment, Pavel Konstantinovitch, my wife and I beg you not to hesitate to borrow from us.'

"And he would blush to his ears with emotion. And it would happen that, after whispering in the same way at the window, he would come up to me, with red ears, and say:

" 'My wife and I earnestly beg you to accept this present.'

"And he would give me studs, a cigar-case, or a lamp, and I would send them game, butter, and flowers from the country. They both, by the way, had considerable means of their own. In early days I often borrowed money, and was not very particular about it—borrowed wherever I could—but nothing in the world would have induced me to borrow from the Luganovitchs. But why talk of it?

"I was unhappy. At home, in the fields, in the barn, I thought of her; I tried to understand the mystery of a beautiful, intelligent young woman's marrying some one so uninteresting, almost an old man (her husband was over forty), and having children by him; to understand the mystery of this uninteresting, good, simple-hearted man, who argued with such wearisome good sense, at balls and evening parties kept near the more solid people, looking listless and superfluous, with a submissive, uninterested expression, as though he had been brought there for sale, who yet believed in his right to be happy, to have children by her; and I kept trying to understand why she had met him first and not me, and why such a terrible mistake in our lives need have happened.

"And when I went to the town I saw every time from her eyes that she was expecting me, and she would confess to me herself that she had had a peculiar feeling all that day and had guessed that I should come. We talked a long time, and were silent, yet we did not confess our love to each other, but timidly and jealously concealed it. We were afraid of everything that might reveal our secret to ourselves. I loved her tenderly, deeply, but I reflected and kept asking myself what our love could lead to if we had not the strength to fight against it. It seemed to be incredible that my gentle, sad love could all at once coarsely break up the even tenor of the life of her husband, her children, and all the household in which I was so loved and trusted. Would it be honourable? She would go away with me, but where? Where could I take her? It would have been a different matter if I had had a beautiful, interesting life—if, for instance, I had been struggling for the emancipation of my country, or had been a celebrated man of science, an artist or a painter; but as it was it would mean taking her from one everyday humdrum life to another as humdrum or perhaps more so. And how long would our happiness last? What would happen to her in case I was ill, in case I died, or if we simply grew cold to one another?

"And she apparently reasoned in the same way. She thought of her husband, her children, and of her mother, who loved the husband like a son. If she abandoned herself to her feelings she would have to lie, or else to tell the truth, and in her position either would have been equally terrible and inconvenient. And she was tormented by the question whether her love would bring me happiness—would she not complicate my life, which, as it was, was hard enough and full of all sorts of trouble? She fancied she was not young enough for me, that she was not industrious nor energetic enough to begin a new life, and she often talked to her husband of the importance of my marrying a girl of intelligence and merit who would be a capable housewife and a help to me—and she would immediately add that it would be difficult to find such a girl in the whole town.

—

"Meanwhile the years were passing. Anna Alexyevna already had two children. When I arrived at the Luganovitchs' the servants smiled cordially, the children shouted that Uncle Pavel Konstantinovitch had come, and hung on my neck; every one was overjoyed. They did not understand what was passing in my soul, and thought that I, too, was happy. Every one looked on me as a noble being. And grown-ups and children alike felt that a noble being was walking about their rooms, and that gave a peculiar charm to their manner towards me, as though in my presence their life, too, was purer and more beautiful. Anna Alexyevna and I used to go to the theatre together, always walking there; we used to sit side by side in the stalls, our shoulders touching. I would take the opera-glass from her hands without a word, and feel at that minute that she was near me, that she was mine, that we could not live without each other; but by some strange misunderstanding, when we came out of the theatre we always said good-bye and parted as though we were strangers. Goodness knows what people were saying about us in the town already, but there was not a word of truth in it all!

"In the latter years Anna Alexyevna took to going away for frequent visits to her mother or to her sister; she began to suffer from low spirits, she began to recognize that her life was spoilt and unsatisfied, and at times she did not care to see her husband nor her children. She was already being treated for neurasthenia.

"We were silent and still silent, and in the presence of outsiders she displayed a strange irritation in regard to me; whatever I talked about, she disagreed with me, and if I had an argument she sided with my opponent. If I dropped anything, she would say coldly:

" 'I congratulate you.'

"If I forgot to take the opera-glass when we were going to the theatre, she would say afterwards:

" 'I knew you would forget it.'

"Luckily or unluckily, there is nothing in our lives that does not end sooner or later. The time of parting came, as Luganovitch was appointed president in one of the western provinces. They had to sell their furniture, their horses, their summer villa. When they drove out to the villa, and afterwards looked back as they were going away, to look for the last time at the garden, at the green roof, every one was sad, and I realized that I had to say good-bye not only to the villa. It was arranged that at the end of August we should see Anna Alexyevna off to the Crimea, where the doctors were sending her, and that a little later Luganovitch and the children would set off for the western province.

"We were a great crowd to see Anna Alexyevna off. When she had said good-bye to her husband and her children and there was only a minute left before the third bell, I ran into her compartment to put a basket, which she had almost forgotten, on the rack, and I had to say good-bye. When our eyes met in the compartment our spiritual fortitude deserted us both; I took her in my arms, she pressed her face to my breast, and tears flowed from her eyes. Kissing her face, her shoulders, her hands wet with tears—oh, how unhappy we were!—I confessed my love for her, and with a burning pain in my heart I realized how unnecessary, how petty, and how deceptive all that had hindered us from loving was. I understood that when you love you must either, in your reasonings about that love, start from what is highest, from what is more important than happiness or unhappiness, sin or virtue in their accepted meaning, or you must not reason at all.

"I kissed her for the last time, pressed her hand, and parted for ever. The train had already started. I went into the next compartment—it was empty—and until I reached the next station I sat there crying. Then I walked home to Sofino. . . ."

While Alehin was telling his story, the rain left off and the sun came out. Burkin and Ivan Ivanovitch went out on the balcony, from which there was a beautiful view over the garden and the mill-pond, which was shining now in the sunshine like a mirror. They admired it, and at the same time they were sorry that this man with the kind, clever eyes, who had told them this story with such genuine feeling, should be rushing round and round this huge estate like a squirrel on a wheel instead of devoting himself to science or something else which would have made his life more pleasant; and they thought what a sorrowful face Anna Alexyevna must have had when he said good-bye to her in the railway-carriage and kissed her face and shoulders. Both of them had met her in the town, and Burkin knew her and thought her beautiful.

Ionitch

I

When visitors to the provincial town S—— complained of the dreariness and monotony of life, the inhabitants of the town, as though defending themselves, declared that it was very nice in S——, that there was a library, a theatre, a club; that they had balls; and, finally, that there were clever, agreeable, and interesting families with whom one could make acquaintance. And they used to point to the family of the Turkins as the most highly cultivated and talented.

This family lived in their own house in the principal street, near the Governor's. Ivan Petrovitch Turkin himself—a stout, handsome, dark man with whiskers—used to get up amateur performances for benevolent objects, and used to take the part of an elderly general and cough very amusingly. He knew a number of anecdotes, charades, proverbs, and was fond of being humorous and witty, and he always wore an expression from which it was impossible to tell whether he were joking or in earnest. His wife, Vera Iosifovna—a thin, nice-looking lady who wore a pince-nez—used to write novels and stories, and was very fond of reading them aloud to her visitors. The daughter, Ekaterina Ivanovna, a young girl, used to play on the piano. In short, every member of the family had a special talent. The Turkins welcomed visitors, and good-humouredly displayed their talents with genuine simplicity. Their stone house was roomy and cool in summer; half of the windows looked into a shady old garden, where nightingales used to sing in the spring. When there were visitors in the house, there was a clatter of knives in the kitchen and a smell of fried onions in the yard—and that was always a sure sign of a plentiful and savoury supper to follow.

And as soon as Dmitri Ionitch Startsev was appointed the district doctor, and took up his abode at Dyalizh, six miles from S——, he, too, was told that as a cultivated man it was essential for him to make the acquaintance of the Turkins. In the winter he was introduced to Ivan Petrovitch in the street; they talked about the weather, about the theatre, about the cholera; an invitation followed. On a holiday in the spring—it was Ascension Day—after seeing his patients, Startsev set off for town in search of a little recreation and to make some purchases. He walked in a leisurely way (he had not yet set up his carriage), humming all the time:

" 'Before I'd drunk the tears from life's goblet. . . .' "

In town he dined, went for a walk in the gardens, then Ivan Petrovitch's invitation came into his mind, as it were of itself, and he decided to call on the Turkins and see what sort of people they were.

"How do you do, if you please?" said Ivan Petrovitch, meeting him on the steps. "Delighted, delighted to see such an agreeable visitor. Come along; I will introduce you to my better half. I tell him, Verotchka," he went on, as he presented the doctor to his wife—"I tell him that he has no human right to sit at home in a hospital; he ought to devote his leisure to society. Oughtn't he, darling?"

"Sit here," said Vera Iosifovna, making her visitor sit down beside her. "You can dance attendance on me. My husband is jealous—he is an Othello; but we will try and behave so well that he will notice nothing."

"Ah, you spoilt chicken!" Ivan Petrovitch muttered tenderly, and he kissed her on the forehead. "You have come just in the nick of time," he said, addressing the doctor again. "My better half has written a 'hugeous' novel, and she is going to read it aloud to-day."

"Petit Jean," said Vera Iosifovna to her husband, "dites que l'on nous donne du thé."

Startsev was introduced to Ekaterina Ivanovna, a girl of eighteen, very much like her mother, thin and pretty. Her expression was still childish and her figure was soft and slim; and her developed girlish bosom, healthy and beautiful, was suggestive of spring, real spring.

Then they drank tea with jam, honey, and sweetmeats, and with very nice cakes, which melted in the mouth. As the evening came on, other visitors gradually arrived, and Ivan Petrovitch fixed his laughing eyes on each of them and said:

"How do you do, if you please?"

Then they all sat down in the drawing-room with very serious faces, and Vera Iosifovna read her novel. It began like this: "The frost was intense. . . ." The windows were wide open; from the kitchen came the clatter of knives and the smell of fried onions. . . . It was comfortable in the soft deep arm-chair; the lights had such a friendly twinkle in the twilight of the drawing-room, and at the moment on a summer evening when sounds of voices and laughter floated in from the street and whiffs of lilac from the yard, it was difficult to grasp that the frost was intense, and that the setting sun was lighting with its chilly rays a solitary wayfarer on the snowy plain. Vera Iosifovna read how a beautiful young countess founded a school, a hospital, a library, in her village, and fell in love with a wandering artist; she read of what never happens in real life, and yet it was pleasant to listen—it was comfortable, and such agreeable, serene thoughts kept coming into the mind, one had no desire to get up.

"Not badsome . . ." Ivan Petrovitch said softly.

And one of the visitors hearing, with his thoughts far away, said hardly audibly:

"Yes . . . truly. . . ."

One hour passed, another. In the town gardens close by a band was playing and a chorus was singing. When Vera Iosifovna shut her manuscript book, the company was silent for five minutes, listening to "Lutchina" being sung by the chorus, and the song gave what was not in the novel and is in real life.

"Do you publish your stories in magazines?" Startsev asked Vera Iosifovna.

"No," she answered. "I never publish. I write it and put it away in my cupboard. Why publish?" she explained. "We have enough to live on."

And for some reason every one sighed.

"And now, Kitten, you play something," Ivan Petrovitch said to his daughter.

The lid of the piano was raised and the music lying ready was opened. Ekaterina Ivanovna sat down and banged on the piano with both hands, and then banged again with all her might, and then again and again; her shoulders and bosom shook. She obstinately banged on the same notes, and it sounded as if she would not leave off until she had hammered the keys into the piano. The drawing-room was filled with the din; everything was resounding; the floor, the ceiling, the furniture. . . . Ekaterina Ivanovna was playing a difficult passage, interesting simply on account of its difficulty, long and monotonous, and Startsev, listening, pictured stones dropping down a steep hill and going on dropping, and he wished they would leave off dropping; and at the same time Ekaterina Ivanovna, rosy from the violent exercise, strong and vigorous, with a lock of hair falling over her forehead, attracted him very much. After the winter spent at Dyalizh among patients and peasants, to sit in a drawing-room, to watch this young, elegant, and, in all probability, pure creature, and to listen to these noisy, tedious but still cultured sounds, was so pleasant, so novel. . . .

"Well, Kitten, you have played as never before," said Ivan Petrovitch, with tears in his eyes, when his daughter had finished and stood up. "Die, Denis; you won't write anything better."

All flocked round her, congratulated her, expressed astonishment, declared that it was long since they had heard such music, and she listened in silence with a faint smile, and her whole figure was expressive of triumph.

"Splendid, superb!"

"Splendid," said Startsev, too, carried away by the general enthusiasm. "Where have you studied?" he asked Ekaterina Ivanovna. "At the Conservatoire?"

"No, I am only preparing for the Conservatoire, and till now have been working with Madame Zavlovsky."

"Have you finished at the high school here?"

"Oh, no," Vera Iosifovna answered for her. "We have teachers for her at home; there might be bad influences at the high school or a boarding school, you know. While a young girl is growing up, she ought to be under no influence but her mother's."

"All the same, I'm going to the Conservatoire," said Ekaterina Ivanovna.

"No. Kitten loves her mamma. Kitten won't grieve papa and mamma."

"No, I'm going, I'm going," said Ekaterina Ivanovna, with playful caprice and stamping her foot.

And at supper it was Ivan Petrovitch who displayed his talents. Laughing only with his eyes, he told anecdotes, made epigrams, asked ridiculous riddles and answered them himself, talking the whole time in his extraordinary language, evolved in the course of prolonged practice in witticism and evidently now become a habit: "Badsome," "Hugeous," "Thank you most dumbly," and so on.

But that was not all. When the guests, replete and satisfied, trooped into the hall, looking for their coats and sticks, there bustled about them the footman Pavlusha, or, as he was called in the family, Pava—a lad of fourteen with shaven head and chubby cheeks.

"Come, Pava, perform!" Ivan Petrovitch said to him.

Pava struck an attitude, flung up his arm, and said in a tragic tone: "Unhappy woman, die!"

And every one roared with laughter.

"It's entertaining," thought Startsev, as he went out into the street.

He went to a restaurant and drank some beer, then set off to walk home to Dyalizh; he walked all the way singing:

" 'Thy voice to me so languid and caressing. . . .' "

On going to bed, he felt not the slightest fatigue after the six miles' walk. On the contrary, he felt as though he could with pleasure have walked another twenty.

"Not badsome," he thought, and laughed as he fell asleep.

II

Startsev kept meaning to go to the Turkins' again, but there was a great deal of work in the hospital, and he was unable to find free time. In this way more than a year passed in work and solitude. But one day a letter in a light blue envelope was brought him from the town. . . .

Vera Iosifovna had been suffering for some time from migraine, but now since Kitten frightened her every day by saying that she was going away to the Conservatoire, the attacks began to be more frequent. All the doctors of the town had been at the Turkins'; at last it was the district doctor's turn. Vera Iosifovna wrote him a touching letter in which she begged him to come and relieve her sufferings. Startsev went, and after that he began to be often, very often at the Turkins'. . . . He really did something for Vera Iosifovna, and she was already telling all her visitors that he was a wonderful and exceptional doctor. But it was not for the sake of her migraine that he visited the Turkins' now. . . .

It was a holiday. Ekaterina Ivanovna finished her long, wearisome exercises on the piano. Then they sat a long time in the dining-room, drinking tea, and Ivan Petrovitch told some amusing story. Then there was a ring and he had to go into the hall to welcome a guest; Startsev took advantage of the momentary commotion, and whispered to Ekaterina Ivanovna in great agitation:

"For God's sake, I entreat you, don't torment me; let us go into the garden!"

She shrugged her shoulders, as though perplexed and not knowing what he wanted of her, but she got up and went.

"You play the piano for three or four hours," he said, following her; "then you sit with your mother, and there is no possibility of speaking to you. Give me a quarter of an hour at least, I beseech you."

Autumn was approaching, and it was quiet and melancholy in the old garden; the dark leaves lay thick in the walks. It was already beginning to get dark early.

"I haven't seen you for a whole week," Startsev went on, "and if you only knew what suffering it is! Let us sit down. Listen to me."

They had a favourite place in the garden; a seat under an old spreading maple. And now they sat down on this seat.

"What do you want?" said Ekaterina Ivanovna drily, in a matter-of-fact tone.

"I have not seen you for a whole week; I have not heard you for so long. I long passionately, I thirst for your voice. Speak."

She fascinated him by her freshness, the naïve expression of her eyes and cheeks. Even in the way her dress hung on her, he saw something extraordinarily charming, touching in its simplicity and naïve grace; and at the same time, in spite of this naïveté, she seemed to him intelligent and developed beyond her years. He could talk with her about literature, about art, about anything he liked; could complain to her of life, of people, though it sometimes happened in the middle of serious conversation she would laugh inappropriately or run away into the house. Like almost all girls of her neighbourhood, she had read a great deal (as a rule, people read very little in S——, and at the lending library they said if it were not for the girls and the young Jews, they might as well shut up the library). This afforded Startsev infinite delight; he used to ask her eagerly every time what she had been reading the last few days, and listened enthralled while she told him.

"What have you been reading this week since I saw you last?" he asked now. "Do please tell me."

"I have been reading Pisemsky."

"What exactly?"

" 'A Thousand Souls,' " answered Kitten. "And what a funny name Pisemsky had—Alexey Feofilaktitch!"

"Where are you going?" cried Startsev in horror, as she suddenly got up and walked towards the house. "I must talk to you; I want to explain myself. . . . Stay with me just five minutes, I supplicate you!"

She stopped as though she wanted to say something, then awkwardly thrust a note into his hand, ran home and sat down to the piano again.

"Be in the cemetery," Startsev read, "at eleven o'clock to-night, near the tomb of Demetti."

"Well, that's not at all clever," he thought, coming to himself. "Why the cemetery? What for?"

It was clear: Kitten was playing a prank. Who would seriously dream of making an appointment at night in the cemetery far out of the town, when it might have been arranged in the street or in the town gardens? And was it in keeping with him—a district doctor, an intelligent, staid man—to be sighing, receiving notes, to hang about cemeteries, to do silly things that even schoolboys think ridiculous nowadays? What would this romance lead to? What would his colleagues say when they heard of it? Such were Startsev's reflections as he wandered round the tables at the club, and at half-past ten he suddenly set off for the cemetery.

By now he had his own pair of horses, and a coachman called Panteleimon, in a velvet waistcoat. The moon was shining. It was still warm, warm as it is in autumn. Dogs were howling in the suburb near the slaughter-house. Startsev left his horses in one of the side-streets at the end of the town, and walked on foot to the cemetery.

"We all have our oddities," he thought. "Kitten is odd, too; and—who knows?—perhaps she is not joking, perhaps she will come"; and he abandoned himself to this faint, vain hope, and it intoxicated him.

He walked for half a mile through the fields; the cemetery showed as a dark streak in the distance, like a forest or a big garden. The wall of white stone came into sight, the gate. . . . In the moonlight he could read on the gate: "The hour cometh." Startsev went in at the little gate, and before anything else he saw the white crosses and monuments on both sides of the broad avenue, and the black shadows of them and the poplars; and for a long way round it was all white and black, and the slumbering trees bowed their branches over the white stones. It seemed as though it were lighter here than in the fields; the maple-leaves stood out sharply like paws on the yellow sand of the avenue and on the stones, and the inscriptions on the tombs could be clearly read. For the first moments Startsev was struck now by what he saw for the first time in his life, and what he would probably never see again; a world not like anything else, a world in which the moonlight was as soft and beautiful, as though slumbering here in its cradle, where there was no life, none whatever; but in every dark poplar, in every tomb, there was felt the presence of a mystery that promised a life peaceful, beautiful, eternal. The stones and faded flowers, together with the autumn scent of the leaves, all told of forgiveness, melancholy, and peace.

All was silence around; the stars looked down from the sky in the profound stillness, and Startsev's footsteps sounded loud and out of place, and only when the church clock began striking and he imagined himself dead, buried there for ever, he felt as though some one were looking at him, and for a moment he thought that it was not peace and tranquillity, but stifled despair, the dumb dreariness of non-existence. . . .

Demetti's tomb was in the form of a shrine with an angel at the top. The Italian opera had once visited S—— and one of the singers had died; she had been buried here, and this monument put up to her. No one in the town remembered her, but the lamp at the entrance reflected the moonlight, and looked as though it were burning.

There was no one, and, indeed, who would come here at midnight? But Startsev waited, and as though the moonlight warmed his passion, he waited passionately, and, in imagination, pictured kisses and embraces. He sat near the monument for half an hour, then paced up and down the side avenues, with his hat in his hand, waiting and thinking of the many women and girls buried in these tombs who had been beautiful and fascinating, who had loved, at night burned with passion, yielding themselves to caresses. How wickedly Mother Nature jested at man's expense, after all! How humiliating it was to recognise it!

Startsev thought this, and at the same time he wanted to cry out that he wanted love, that he was eager for it at all costs. To his eyes they were not slabs of marble, but fair white bodies in the moonlight; he saw shapes hiding bashfully in the shadows of the trees, felt their warmth, and the languor was oppressive. . . .

And as though a curtain were lowered, the moon went behind a cloud, and suddenly all was darkness. Startsev could scarcely find the gate—by now it was as dark as it is on an autumn night. Then he wandered about for an hour and a half, looking for the side-street in which he had left his horses.

"I am tired; I can scarcely stand on my legs," he said to Panteleimon.

And settling himself with relief in his carriage, he thought: "Och! I ought not to get fat!"

III

The following evening he went to the Turkins' to make an offer. But it turned out to be an inconvenient moment, as Ekaterina Ivanovna was in her own room having her hair done by a hair-dresser. She was getting ready to go to a dance at the club.

He had to sit a long time again in the dining-room drinking tea. Ivan Petrovitch, seeing that his visitor was bored and preoccupied, drew some notes out of his waistcoat pocket, read a funny letter from a German steward, saying that all the ironmongery was ruined and the plasticity was peeling off the walls.

"I expect they will give a decent dowry," thought Startsev, listening absent-mindedly.

After a sleepless night, he found himself in a state of stupefaction, as though he had been given something sweet and soporific to drink; there was fog in his soul, but joy and warmth, and at the same time a sort of cold, heavy fragment of his brain was reflecting:

"Stop before it is too late! Is she the match for you? She is spoilt, whimsical, sleeps till two o'clock in the afternoon, while you are a deacon's son, a district doctor. . . ."

"What of it?" he thought. "I don't care."

"Besides, if you marry her," the fragment went on, "then her relations will make you give up the district work and live in the town."

"After all," he thought, "if it must be the town, the town it must be. They will give a dowry; we can establish ourselves suitably."

At last Ekaterina Ivanovna came in, dressed for the ball, with a low neck, looking fresh and pretty; and Startsev admired her so much, and went into such ecstasies, that he could say nothing, but simply stared at her and laughed.

She began saying good-bye, and he—he had no reason for staying now—got up, saying that it was time for him to go home; his patients were waiting for him.

"Well, there's no help for that," said Ivan Petrovitch. "Go, and you might take Kitten to the club on the way."

It was spotting with rain; it was very dark, and they could only tell where the horses were by Panteleimon's husky cough. The hood of the carriage was put up.

"I stand upright; you lie down right; he lies all right," said Ivan Petrovitch as he put his daughter into the carriage.

They drove off.

"I was at the cemetery yesterday," Startsev began. "How ungenerous and merciless it was on your part! . . ."

"You went to the cemetery?"

"Yes, I went there and waited almost till two o'clock. I suffered . . ."

"Well, suffer, if you cannot understand a joke."

Ekaterina Ivanovna, pleased at having so cleverly taken in a man who was in love with her, and at being the object of such intense love, burst out laughing and suddenly uttered a shriek of terror, for, at that very minute, the horses turned sharply in at the gate of the club, and the carriage almost tilted over. Startsev put his arm round Ekaterina Ivanovna's waist; in her fright she nestled up to him, and he could not restrain himself, and passionately kissed her on the lips and on the chin, and hugged her more tightly.

"That's enough," she said drily.

And a minute later she was not in the carriage, and a policeman near the lighted entrance of the club shouted in a detestable voice to Panteleimon:

"What are you stopping for, you crow? Drive on."

Startsev drove home, but soon afterwards returned. Attired in another man's dress suit and a stiff white tie which kept sawing at his neck and trying to slip away from the collar, he was sitting at midnight in the club drawing-room, and was saying with enthusiasm to Ekaterina Ivanovna:

"Ah, how little people know who have never loved! It seems to me that no one has ever yet written of love truly, and I doubt whether this tender, joyful, agonising feeling can be described, and any one who has once experienced it would not attempt to put it into words. What is the use of preliminaries and introductions? What is the use of unnecessary fine words? My love is immeasurable. I beg, I beseech you," Startsev brought out at last, "be my wife!"

"Dmitri Ionitch," said Ekaterina Ivanovna, with a very grave face, after a moment's thought—"Dmitri Ionitch, I am very grateful to you for the honour. I respect you, but . . ." she got up and continued standing, "but, forgive me, I cannot be your wife. Let us talk seriously. Dmitri Ionitch, you know I love art beyond everything in life. I adore music; I love it frantically; I have dedicated my whole life to it. I want to be an artist; I want fame, success, freedom, and you want me to go on living in this town, to go on living this empty, useless life, which has become insufferable to me. To become a wife—oh, no, forgive me! One must strive towards a lofty, glorious goal, and married life would put me in bondage for ever. Dmitri Ionitch" (she faintly smiled as she pronounced his name; she thought of "Alexey Feofilaktitch")—"Dmitri Ionitch, you are a good, clever, honourable man; you are better than any one. . . ." Tears came into her eyes. "I feel for you with my whole heart, but . . . but you will understand. . . ."

And she turned away and went out of the drawing-room to prevent herself from crying.

Startsev's heart left off throbbing uneasily. Going out of the club into the street, he first of all tore off the stiff tie and drew a deep breath. He was a little ashamed and his vanity was wounded—he had not expected a refusal—and could not believe that all his dreams, his hopes and yearnings, had led him up to such a stupid end, just as in some little play at an amateur performance, and he was sorry for his feeling, for that love of his, so sorry that he felt as though he could have burst into sobs or have violently belaboured Panteleimon's broad back with his umbrella.

For three days he could not get on with anything, he could not eat nor sleep; but when the news reached him that Ekaterina Ivanovna had gone away to Moscow to enter the Conservatoire, he grew calmer and lived as before.

Afterwards, remembering sometimes how he had wandered about the cemetery or how he had driven all over the town to get a dress suit, he stretched lazily and said:

"What a lot of trouble, though!"

IV

Four years had passed. Startsev already had a large practice in the town. Every morning he hurriedly saw his patients at Dyalizh, then he drove in to see his town patients. By now he drove, not with a pair, but with a team of three with bells on them, and he returned home late at night. He had grown broader and stouter, and was not very fond of walking, as he was somewhat asthmatic. And Panteleimon had grown stout, too, and the broader he grew, the more mournfully he sighed and complained of his hard luck: he was sick of driving!

Startsev used to visit various households and met many people, but did not become intimate with any one. The inhabitants irritated him by their conversation, their views of life, and even their appearance. Experience taught him by degrees that while he played cards or lunched with one of these people, the man was a peaceable, friendly, and even intelligent human being; that as soon as one talked of anything not eatable, for instance, of politics or science, he would be completely at a loss, or would expound a philosophy so stupid and ill-natured that there was nothing else to do but wave one's hand in despair and go away. Even when Startsev tried to talk to liberal citizens, saying, for instance, that humanity, thank God, was progressing, and that one day it would be possible to dispense with passports and capital punishment, the liberal citizen would look at him askance and ask him mistrustfully: "Then any one could murder any one he chose in the open street?" And when, at tea or supper, Startsev observed in company that one should work, and that one ought not to live without working, every one took this as a reproach, and began to get angry and argue aggressively. With all that, the inhabitants did nothing, absolutely nothing, and took no interest in anything, and it was quite impossible to think of anything to say. And Startsev avoided conversation, and confined himself to eating and playing *vint;* and when there was a family festivity in some household and he was invited to a meal, then he sat and ate in silence, looking at his plate. And everything that was said at the time was uninteresting, unjust, and stupid; he felt irritated and disturbed, but held his tongue, and, because he sat glumly silent and looked at his plate, he was nicknamed in the town "the haughty Pole," though he never had been a Pole.

All such entertainments as theatres and concerts he declined, but he played *vint* every evening for three hours with enjoyment. He had another diversion to which he took imperceptibly, little by little: in the evening he would take out of his pockets the notes he had gained by his practice, and sometimes there were stuffed in his pockets notes—yellow and green, and smelling of scent and vinegar and incense and fish oil—up to the value of seventy roubles; and when they amounted to some hundreds he took them to the Mutual Credit Bank and deposited the money there to his account.

He was only twice at the Turkins' in the course of the four years after Ekaterina Ivanovna had gone away, on each occasion at the invitation of Vera Iosifovna, who was still undergoing treatment for migraine. Every summer Ekaterina Ivanovna came to stay with her parents, but he did not once see her; it somehow never happened.

But now four years had passed. One still, warm morning a letter was brought to the hospital. Vera Iosifovna wrote to Dmitri Ionitch that she was missing him very much, and begged him to come and see them, and to relieve her sufferings; and, by the way, it was her birthday. Below was a postscript: "I join in mother's request.—K."

Startsev considered, and in the evening he went to the Turkins'.

"How do you do, if you please?" Ivan Petrovitch met him, smiling with his eyes only. "Bongjour."

Vera Iosifovna, white-haired and looking much older, shook Startsev's hand, sighed affectedly, and said:

"You don't care to pay attentions to me, doctor. You never come and see us; I am too old for you. But now some one young has come; perhaps she will be more fortunate."

And Kitten? She had grown thinner, paler, had grown handsomer and more graceful; but now she was Ekaterina Ivanovna, not Kitten; she had lost the freshness and look of childish naïveté. And in her expression and manners there was something new—guilty and diffident, as though she did not feel herself at home here in the Turkins' house.

"How many summers, how many winters!" she said, giving Startsev her hand, and he could see that her heart was beating with excitement; and looking at him intently and curiously, she went on: "How much stouter you are! You look sunburnt and more manly, but on the whole you have changed very little."

Now, too, he thought her attractive, very attractive, but there was something lacking in her, or else something superfluous—he could not himself have said exactly what it was, but something prevented him from feeling as before. He did not like her pallor, her new expression, her faint smile, her voice, and soon afterwards he disliked her clothes, too, the low chair in which she was sitting; he disliked something in the past when he had almost married her. He thought of his love, of the dreams and the hopes which had troubled him four years before—and he felt awkward.

They had tea with cakes. Then Vera Iosifovna read aloud a novel; she read of things that never happen in real life, and Startsev listened, looked at her handsome grey head, and waited for her to finish.

"People are not stupid because they can't write novels, but because they can't conceal it when they do," he thought.

"Not badsome," said Ivan Petrovitch.

Then Ekaterina Ivanovna played long and noisily on the piano, and when she finished she was profusely thanked and warmly praised.

"It's a good thing I did not marry her," thought Startsev.

She looked at him, and evidently expected him to ask her to go into the garden, but he remained silent.

"Let us have a talk," she said, going up to him. "How are you getting on? What are you doing? How are things? I have been thinking about you all these days," she went on nervously. "I wanted to write to you, wanted to come myself to see you at Dyalizh. I quite made up my mind to go, but afterwards I thought better of it. God knows what your attitude is towards me now; I have been looking forward to seeing you to-day with such emotion. For goodness' sake let us go into the garden."

They went into the garden and sat down on the seat under the old maple, just as they had done four years before. It was dark.

"How are you getting on?" asked Ekaterina Ivanovna.

"Oh, all right; I am jogging along," answered Startsev.

And he could think of nothing more. They were silent.

"I feel so excited!" said Ekaterina Ivanovna, and she hid her face in her hands. "But don't pay attention to it. I am so happy to be at home; I am so glad to see every one. I can't get used to it. So many memories! I thought we should talk without stopping till morning."

Now he saw her face near, her shining eyes, and in the darkness she looked younger than in the room, and even her old childish expression seemed to have come back to her. And indeed she was looking at him with naïve curiosity, as though she wanted to get a closer view and understanding of the man who had loved her so ardently, with such tenderness, and so unsuccessfully; her eyes thanked him for that love. And he remembered all that had been, every minute detail; how he had wandered about the cemetery, how he had returned home in the morning exhausted, and he suddenly felt sad and regretted the past. A warmth began glowing in his heart.

"Do you remember how I took you to the dance at the club?" he asked. "It was dark and rainy then...."

The warmth was glowing now in his heart, and he longed to talk, to rail at life....

"Ech!" he said with a sigh. "You ask how I am living. How do we live here? Why, not at all. We grow old, we grow stout, we grow slack. Day after day passes; life slips by without colour, without expressions, without thoughts. . . . In the daytime working for gain, and in the evening the club, the company of card-players, alcoholic, raucous-voiced gentlemen whom I can't endure. What is there nice in it?"

"Well, you have work—a noble object in life. You used to be so fond of talking of your hospital. I was such a queer girl then; I imagined myself such a great pianist. Nowadays all young ladies play the piano, and I played, too, like everybody else, and there was nothing special about me. I am just such a pianist as my mother is an authoress. And of course I didn't understand you then, but afterwards in Moscow I often thought of you. I thought of no one but you. What happiness to be a district doctor; to help the suffering; to be serving the people! What happiness!" Ekaterina Ivanovna repeated with enthusiasm. "When I thought of you in Moscow, you seemed to me so ideal, so lofty. . . ."

Startsev thought of the notes he used to take out of his pockets in the evening with such pleasure, and the glow in his heart was quenched.

He got up to go into the house. She took his arm.

"You are the best man I've known in my life," she went on. "We will see each other and talk, won't we? Promise me. I am not a pianist; I am not in error about myself now, and I will not play before you or talk of music."

When they had gone into the house, and when Startsev saw in the lamplight her face, and her sad, grateful, searching eyes fixed upon him, he felt uneasy and thought again:

"It's a good thing I did not marry her then."

He began taking leave.

"You have no human right to go before supper," said Ivan Petrovitch as he saw him off. "It's extremely perpendicular on your part. Well, now, perform!" he added, addressing Pava in the hall.

Pava, no longer a boy, but a young man with moustaches, threw himself into an attitude, flung up his arm, and said in a tragic voice:

"Unhappy woman, die!"

All this irritated Startsev. Getting into his carriage, and looking at the dark house and garden which had once been so precious and so dear, he thought of everything at once—Vera Iosifovna's novels and Kitten's noisy playing, and Ivan Petrovitch's jokes and Pava's tragic posturing, and thought if the most talented people in the town were so futile, what must the town be?

Three days later Pava brought a letter from Ekaterina Ivanovna.

"You don't come and see us—why?" she wrote to him. "I am afraid that you have changed towards us. I am afraid, and I am terrified at the very thought of it. Reassure me; come and tell me that everything is well.

"I must talk to you.—Your E. I."

—

He read this letter, thought a moment, and said to Pava:

"Tell them, my good fellow, that I can't come to-day; I am very busy. Say I will come in three days or so."

But three days passed, a week passed; he still did not go. Happening once to drive past the Turkins' house, he thought he must go in, if only for a moment, but on second thoughts . . . did not go in.

And he never went to the Turkins' again.

V

Several more years have passed. Startsev has grown stouter still, has grown corpulent, breathes heavily, and already walks with his head thrown back. When stout and red in the face, he drives with his bells and his team of three horses, and Panteleimon, also stout and red in the face with his thick beefy neck, sits on the box, holding his arms stiffly out before him as though they were made of wood, and shouts to those he meets: "Keep to the ri-i-ight!" it is an impressive picture; one might think it was not a mortal, but some heathen deity in his chariot. He has an immense practice in the town, no time to breathe, and already has an estate and two houses in the town, and he is looking out for a third more profitable; and when at the Mutual Credit Bank he is told of a house that is for sale, he goes to the house without ceremony, and, marching through all the rooms, regardless of half-dressed women and children who gaze at him in amazement and alarm, he prods at the doors with his stick, and says:

"Is that the study? Is that a bedroom? And what's here?"

And as he does so he breathes heavily and wipes the sweat from his brow.

He has a great deal to do, but still he does not give up his work as district doctor; he is greedy for gain, and he tries to be in all places at once. At Dyalizh and in the town he is called simply "Ionitch": "Where is Ionitch off to?" or "Should not we call in Ionitch to a consultation?"

Probably because his throat is covered with rolls of fat, his voice has changed; it has become thin and sharp. His temper has changed, too: he has grown ill-humoured and irritable. When he sees his patients he is usually out of temper; he impatiently taps the floor with his stick, and shouts in his disagreeable voice:

"Be so good as to confine yourself to answering my questions! Don't talk so much!"

He is solitary. He leads a dreary life; nothing interests him.

During all the years he had lived at Dyalizh his love for Kitten had been his one joy, and probably his last. In the evenings he plays *vint* at the club, and then sits alone at a big table and has supper. Ivan, the oldest and most respectable of the waiters, serves him, hands him Lafitte No. 17, and every one at the club—the members of the committee, the cook and waiters—know what he likes and what he doesn't like and do their very utmost to satisfy him, or else he is sure to fly into a rage and bang on the floor with his stick.

As he eats his supper, he turns round from time to time and puts in his spoke in some conversation:

"What are you talking about? Eh? Whom?"

And when at a neighbouring table there is talk of the Turkins, he asks:

"What Turkins are you speaking of? Do you mean the people whose daughter plays on the piano?"

That is all that can be said about him.

And the Turkins? Ivan Petrovitch has grown no older; he is not changed in the least, and still makes jokes and tells anecdotes as of old. Vera Iosifovna still reads her novels aloud to her visitors with eagerness and touching simplicity. And Kitten plays the piano for four hours every day. She has grown visibly older, is constantly ailing, and every autumn goes to the Crimea with her mother. When Ivan Petrovitch sees them off at the station, he wipes his tears as the train starts, and shouts:

"Good-bye, if you please."

And he waves his handkerchief.

A Doctor's Visit

The Professor received a telegram from the Lyalikovs' factory; he was asked to come as quickly as possible. The daughter of some Madame Lyalikov, apparently the owner of the factory, was ill, and that was all that one could make out of the long, incoherent telegram. And the Professor did not go himself, but sent instead his assistant, Korolyov.

It was two stations from Moscow, and there was a drive of three miles from the station. A carriage with three horses had been sent to the station to meet Korolyov; the coachman wore a hat with a peacock's feather on it, and answered every question in a loud voice like a soldier: "No, sir!" "Certainly, sir!"

It was Saturday evening; the sun was setting, the workpeople were coming in crowds from the factory to the station, and they bowed to the carriage in which Korolyov was driving. And he was charmed with the evening, the farmhouses and villas on the road, and the birch-trees, and the quiet atmosphere all around, when the fields and woods and the sun seemed preparing, like the workpeople now on the eve of the holiday, to rest, and perhaps to pray....

He was born and had grown up in Moscow; he did not know the country, and he had never taken any interest in factories, or been inside one, but he had happened to read about factories, and had been in the houses of manufacturers and had talked to them; and whenever he saw a factory far or near, he always thought how quiet and peaceable it was outside, but within there was always sure to be impenetrable ignorance and dull egoism on the side of the owners, wearisome, unhealthy toil on the side of the workpeople, squabbling, vermin, vodka. And now when the workpeople timidly and respectfully made way for the carriage, in their faces, their caps, their walk, he read physical impurity, drunkenness, nervous exhaustion, bewilderment.

They drove in at the factory gates. On each side he caught glimpses of the little houses of workpeople, of the faces of women, of quilts and linen on the railings. "Look out!" shouted the coachman, not pulling up the horses. It was a wide courtyard without grass, with five immense blocks of buildings with tall chimneys a little distance one from another, warehouses and barracks, and over everything a sort of grey powder as though from dust. Here and there, like oases in the desert, there were pitiful gardens, and the green and red roofs of the houses in which the managers and clerks lived. The coachman suddenly pulled up the horses, and the carriage stopped at the house, which had been newly painted grey; here was a flower garden, with a lilac bush covered with dust, and on the yellow steps at the front door there was a strong smell of paint.

"Please come in, doctor," said women's voices in the passage and the entry, and at the same time he heard sighs and whisperings. "Pray walk in.... We've been expecting you so long... we're in real trouble. Here, this way."

Madame Lyalikov—a stout elderly lady wearing a black silk dress with fashionable sleeves, but, judging from her face, a simple uneducated woman—looked at the doctor in a flutter, and could not bring herself to hold out her hand to him; she did not dare. Beside her stood a personage with short hair and a pince-nez; she was wearing a blouse of many colours, and was very thin and no longer young. The servants called her Christina Dmitryevna, and Korolyov guessed that this was the governess. Probably, as the person of most education in the house, she had been charged to meet and receive the doctor, for she began immediately, in great haste, stating the causes of the illness, giving trivial and tiresome details, but without saying who was ill or what was the matter.

The doctor and the governess were sitting talking while the lady of the house stood motionless at the door, waiting. From the conversation Korolyov learned that the patient was Madame Lyalikov's only daughter and heiress, a girl of twenty, called Liza; she had been ill for a long time, and had consulted various doctors, and the previous night she had suffered till morning from such violent palpitations of the heart, that no one in the house had slept, and they had been afraid she might die.

"She has been, one may say, ailing from a child," said Christina Dmitryevna in a sing-song voice, continually wiping her lips with her hand. "The doctors say it is nerves; when she was a little girl she was scrofulous, and the doctors drove it inwards, so I think it may be due to that."

They went to see the invalid. Fully grown up, big and tall, but ugly like her mother, with the same little eyes and disproportionate breadth of the lower part of the face, lying with her hair in disorder, muffled up to the chin, she made upon Korolyov at the first minute the impression of a poor, destitute creature, sheltered and cared for here out of charity, and he could hardly believe that this was the heiress of the five huge buildings.

"I am the doctor come to see you," said Korolyov. "Good evening."

He mentioned his name and pressed her hand, a large, cold, ugly hand; she sat up, and, evidently accustomed to doctors, let herself be sounded, without showing the least concern that her shoulders and chest were uncovered.

"I have palpitations of the heart," she said, "It was so awful all night. . . . I almost died of fright! Do give me something."

"I will, I will; don't worry yourself."

Korolyov examined her and shrugged his shoulders.

"The heart is all right," he said; "it's all going on satisfactorily; everything is in good order. Your nerves must have been playing pranks a little, but that's so common. The attack is over by now, one must suppose; lie down and go to sleep."

At that moment a lamp was brought into the bedroom. The patient screwed up her eyes at the light, then suddenly put her hands to her head and broke into sobs. And the impression of a destitute, ugly creature vanished, and Korolyov no longer noticed the little eyes or the heavy development of the lower part of the face. He saw a soft, suffering expression which was intelligent and touching: she seemed to him altogether graceful, feminine, and simple; and he longed to soothe her, not with drugs, not with advice, but with simple, kindly words. Her mother put her arms round her head and hugged her. What despair, what grief was in the old woman's face! She, her mother, had reared her and brought her up, spared nothing, and devoted her whole life to having her daughter taught French, dancing, music: had engaged a dozen teachers for her; had consulted the best doctors, kept a governess. And now she could not make out the reason of these tears, why there was all this misery, she could not understand, and was bewildered; and she had a guilty, agitated, despairing expression, as though she had omitted something very important, had left something undone, had neglected to call in somebody—and whom, she did not know.

"Lizanka, you are crying again . . . again," she said, hugging her daughter to her. "My own, my darling, my child, tell me what it is! Have pity on me! Tell me."

Both wept bitterly. Korolyov sat down on the side of the bed and took Liza's hand.

"Come, give over; it's no use crying," he said kindly. "Why, there is nothing in the world that is worth those tears. Come, we won't cry; that's no good. . . ."

And inwardly he thought:

"It's high time she was married. . . ."

"Our doctor at the factory gave her kalibromati," said the governess, "but I notice it only makes her worse. I should have thought that if she is given anything for the heart it ought to be drops. . . . I forget the name. . . . Convallaria, isn't it?"

And there followed all sorts of details. She interrupted the doctor, preventing his speaking, and there was a look of effort on her face, as though she supposed that, as the woman of most education in the house, she was duty bound to keep up a conversation with the doctor, and on no other subject but medicine.

Korolyov felt bored.

"I find nothing special the matter," he said, addressing the mother as he went out of the bedroom. "If your daughter is being attended by the factory doctor, let him go on attending her. The treatment so far has been perfectly correct, and I see no reason for changing your doctor. Why change? It's such an ordinary trouble; there's nothing seriously wrong."

He spoke deliberately as he put on his gloves, while Madame Lyalikov stood without moving, and looked at him with her tearful eyes.

"I have half an hour to catch the ten o'clock train," he said. "I hope I am not too late."

"And can't you stay?" she asked, and tears trickled down her cheeks again. "I am ashamed to trouble you, but if you would be so good. . . . For God's sake," she went on in an undertone, glancing towards the door, "do stay to-night with us! She is all I have . . . my only daughter. . . . She frightened me last night; I can't get over it. . . . Don't go away, for goodness' sake! . . ."

He wanted to tell her that he had a great deal of work in Moscow, that his family were expecting him home; it was disagreeable to him to spend the evening and the whole night in a strange house quite needlessly; but he looked at her face, heaved a sigh, and began taking off his gloves without a word.

All the lamps and candles were lighted in his honour in the drawing-room and the dining-room. He sat down at the piano and began turning over the music. Then he looked at the pictures on the walls, at the portraits. The pictures, oil-paintings in gold frames, were views of the Crimea—a stormy sea with a ship, a Catholic monk with a wine-glass; they were all dull, smooth daubs, with no trace of talent in them. There was not a single good-looking face among the portraits, nothing but broad cheekbones and astonished-looking eyes. Lyalikov, Liza's father, had a low forehead and a self-satisfied expression; his uniform sat like a sack on his bulky plebeian figure; on his breast was a medal and a Red Cross Badge. There was little sign of culture, and the luxury was senseless and haphazard, and was as ill fitting as that uniform. The floors irritated him with their brilliant polish, the lustres on the chandelier irritated him, and he was reminded for some reason of the story of the merchant who used to go to the baths with a medal on his neck. . . .

He heard a whispering in the entry; some one was softly snoring. And suddenly from outside came harsh, abrupt, metallic sounds, such as Korolyov had never heard before, and which he did not understand now; they roused strange, unpleasant echoes in his soul.

"I believe nothing would induce me to remain here to live . . ." he thought, and went back to the music-books again.

"Doctor, please come to supper!" the governess called him in a low voice.

He went into supper. The table was large and laid with a vast number of dishes and wines, but there were only two to supper: himself and Christina Dmitryevna. She drank Madeira, ate rapidly, and talked, looking at him through her pince-nez:

"Our workpeople are very contented. We have performances at the factory every winter; the workpeople act themselves. They have lectures with a magic lantern, a splendid tea-room, and everything they want. They are very much attached to us, and when they heard that Lizanka was worse they had a service sung for her. Though they have no education, they have their feelings, too."

"It looks as though you have no man in the house at all," said Korolyov.

"Not one. Pyotr Nikanoritch died a year and a half ago, and left us alone. And so there are the three of us. In the summer we live here, and in winter we live in Moscow, in Polianka. I have been living with them for eleven years—as one of the family."

At supper they served sterlet, chicken rissoles, and stewed fruit; the wines were expensive French wines.

"Please don't stand on ceremony, doctor," said Christina Dmitryevna, eating and wiping her mouth with her fist, and it was evident she found her life here exceedingly pleasant. "Please have some more."

After supper the doctor was shown to his room, where a bed had been made up for him, but he did not feel sleepy. The room was stuffy and it smelt of paint; he put on his coat and went out.

It was cool in the open air; there was already a glimmer of dawn, and all the five blocks of buildings, with their tall chimneys, barracks, and warehouses, were distinctly outlined against the damp air. As it was a holiday, they were not working, and the windows were dark, and in only one of the buildings was there a furnace burning; two windows were crimson, and fire mixed with smoke came from time to time from the chimney. Far away beyond the yard the frogs were croaking and the nightingales singing.

Looking at the factory buildings and the barracks, where the workpeople were asleep, he thought again what he always thought when he saw a factory. They may have performances for the workpeople, magic lanterns, factory doctors, and improvements of all sorts, but, all the same, the workpeople he had met that day on his way from the station did not look in any way different from those he had known long ago in his childhood, before there were factory performances and improvements. As a doctor accustomed to judging correctly of chronic complaints, the radical cause of which was incomprehensible and incurable, he looked upon factories as something baffling, the cause of which also was obscure and not removable, and all the improvements in the life of the factory hands he looked upon not as superfluous, but as comparable with the treatment of incurable illnesses.

"There is something baffling in it, of course . . ." he thought, looking at the crimson windows. "Fifteen hundred or two thousand workpeople are working without rest in unhealthy surroundings, making bad cotton goods, living on the verge of starvation, and only waking from this nightmare at rare intervals in the tavern; a hundred people act as overseers, and the whole life of that hundred is spent in imposing fines, in abuse, in injustice, and only two or three so-called owners enjoy the profits, though they don't work at all, and despise the wretched cotton. But what are the profits, and how do they enjoy them? Madame Lyalikov and her daughter are unhappy—it makes one wretched to look at them; the only one who enjoys her life is Christina Dmitryevna, a stupid, middle-aged maiden lady in pince-nez. And so it appears that all these five blocks of buildings are at work, and inferior cotton is sold in the Eastern markets, simply that Christina Dmitryevna may eat sterlet and drink Madeira."

Suddenly there came a strange noise, the same sound Korolyov had heard before supper. Some one was striking on a sheet of metal near one of the buildings; he struck a note, and then at once checked the vibrations, so that short, abrupt, discordant sounds were produced, rather like "Dair . . . dair . . . dair. . . ." Then there was half a minute of stillness, and from another building there came sounds equally abrupt and unpleasant, lower bass notes: "Drin . . . drin . . . drin. . . ." Eleven times. Evidently it was the watchman striking the hour.

Near the third building he heard: "Zhuk . . . zhuk . . . zhuk. . . ." And so near all the buildings, and then behind the barracks and beyond the gates. And in the stillness of the night it seemed as though these sounds were uttered by a monster with crimson eyes—the devil himself, who controlled the owners and the work-people alike, and was deceiving both.

Korolyov went out of the yard into the open country.

"Who goes there?" some one called to him at the gates in an abrupt voice.

"It's just like being in prison," he thought, and made no answer.

Here the nightingales and the frogs could be heard more distinctly, and one could feel it was a night in May. From the station came the noise of a train; somewhere in the distance drowsy cocks were crowing; but, all the same, the night was still, the world was sleeping tranquilly. In a field not far from the factory there could be seen the framework of a house and heaps of building material: Korolyov sat down on the planks and went on thinking.

"The only person who feels happy here is the governess, and the factory hands are working for her gratification. But that's only apparent: she is only the figurehead. The real person, for whom everything is being done, is the devil."

And he thought about the devil, in whom he did not believe, and he looked around at the two windows where the fires were gleaming. It seemed to him that out of those crimson eyes the devil himself was looking at him—that unknown force that had created the mutual relation of the strong and the weak, that coarse blunder which one could never correct. The strong must hinder the weak from living—such was the law of Nature; but only in a newspaper article or in a school book was that intelligible and easily accepted. In the hotchpotch which was everyday life, in the tangle of trivialities out of which human relations were woven, it was no longer a law, but a logical absurdity, when the strong and the weak were both equally victims of their mutual relations, unwillingly submitting to some directing force, unknown, standing outside life, apart from man.

So thought Korolyov, sitting on the planks, and little by little he was possessed by a feeling that this unknown and mysterious force was really close by and looking at him. Meanwhile the east was growing paler, time passed rapidly; when there was not a soul anywhere near, as though everything were dead, the five buildings and their chimneys against the grey background of the dawn had a peculiar look—not the same as by day; one forgot altogether that inside there were steam motors, electricity, telephones, and kept thinking of lake-dwellings, of the Stone Age, feeling the presence of a crude, unconscious force. . . .

And again there came the sound: "Dair . . . dair . . . dair . . . dair . . ." twelve times. Then there was stillness, stillness for half a minute, and at the other end of the yard there rang out:

"Drin . . . drin . . . drin. . . ."

"Horribly disagreeable," thought Korolyov.

"Zhuk . . . zhuk . . ." there resounded from a third place, abruptly, sharply, as though with annoyance—"Zhuk . . . zhuk. . . ."

And it took four minutes to strike twelve. Then there was a hush; and again it seemed as though everything were dead.

Korolyov sat a little longer, then went to the house, but sat up for a good while longer. In the adjoining rooms there was whispering, there was a sound of shuffling slippers and bare feet.

"Is she having another attack?" thought Korolyov.

He went out to have a look at the patient. By now it was quite light in the rooms, and a faint glimmer of sunlight, piercing through the morning mist, quivered on the floor and on the wall of the drawing-room. The door of Liza's room was open, and she was sitting in a low chair beside her bed, with her hair down, wearing a dressing-gown and wrapped in a shawl. The blinds were down on the windows.

"How do you feel?" asked Korolyov.

"Thank you."

He touched her pulse, then straightened her hair, that had fallen over her forehead.

"You are not asleep," he said. "It's beautiful weather outside. It's spring. The nightingales are singing, and you sit in the dark and think of something."

She listened and looked into his face; her eyes were sorrowful and intelligent, and it was evident she wanted to say something to him.

"Does this happen to you often?" he said.

She moved her lips, and answered:

"Often, I feel wretched almost every night."

At that moment the watchman in the yard began striking two o'-clock. They heard: "Dair . . . dair . . ." and she shuddered.

"Do those knockings worry you?" he asked.

"I don't know. Everything here worries me," she answered, and pondered. "Everything worries me. I hear sympathy in your voice; it seemed to me as soon as I saw you that I could tell you all about it."

"Tell me, I beg you."

"I want to tell you of my opinion. It seems to me that I have no illness, but that I am weary and frightened, because it is bound to be so and cannot be otherwise. Even the healthiest person can't help being uneasy if, for instance, a robber is moving about under his window. I am constantly being doctored," she went on, looking at her knees, and she gave a shy smile. "I am very grateful, of course, and I do not deny that the treatment is a benefit; but I should like to talk, not with a doctor, but with some intimate friend who would understand me and would convince me that I was right or wrong."

"Have you no friends?" asked Korolyov.

"I am lonely. I have a mother; I love her, but, all the same, I am lonely. That's how it happens to be. . . . Lonely people read a great deal, but say little and hear little. Life for them is mysterious; they are mystics and often see the devil where he is not. Lermontov's Tamara was lonely and she saw the devil."

"Do you read a great deal?"

"Yes. You see, my whole time is free from morning till night. I read by day, and by night my head is empty; instead of thoughts there are shadows in it."

"Do you see anything at night?" asked Korolyov.

"No, but I feel. . . ."

She smiled again, raised her eyes to the doctor, and looked at him so sorrowfully, so intelligently; and it seemed to him that she trusted him, and that she wanted to speak frankly to him, and that she thought the same as he did. But she was silent, perhaps waiting for him to speak.

And he knew what to say to her. It was clear to him that she needed as quickly as possible to give up the five buildings and the million if she had it—to leave that devil that looked out at night; it was clear to him, too, that she thought so herself, and was only waiting for some one she trusted to confirm her.

But he did not know how to say it. How? One is shy of asking men under sentence what they have been sentenced for; and in the same way it is awkward to ask very rich people what they want so much money for, why they make such a poor use of their wealth, why they don't give it up, even when they see in it their unhappiness; and if they begin a conversation about it themselves, it is usually embarrassing, awkward, and long.

"How is one to say it?" Korolyov wondered. "And is it necessary to speak?"

And he said what he meant in a roundabout way:

"You in the position of a factory owner and a wealthy heiress are dissatisfied; you don't believe in your right to it; and here now you can't sleep. That, of course, is better than if you were satisfied, slept soundly, and thought everything was satisfactory. Your sleeplessness does you credit; in any case, it is a good sign. In reality, such a conversation as this between us now would have been unthinkable for our parents. At night they did not talk, but slept sound; we, our generation, sleep badly, are restless, but talk a great deal, and are always trying to settle whether we are right or not. For our children or grandchildren that question—whether they are right or not—will have been settled. Things will be clearer for them than for us. Life will be good in fifty years' time; it's only a pity we shall not last out till then. It would be interesting to have a peep at it."

"What will our children and grandchildren do?" asked Liza.

"I don't know. . . . I suppose they will throw it all up and go away."

"Go where?"

"Where? . . . Why, where they like," said Korolyov; and he laughed. "There are lots of places a good, intelligent person can go to."

He glanced at his watch.

"The sun has risen, though," he said. "It is time you were asleep. Undress and sleep soundly. Very glad to have made your acquaintance," he went on, pressing her hand. "You are a good, interesting woman. Good-night!"

He went to his room and went to bed.

In the morning when the carriage was brought round they all came out on to the steps to see him off. Liza, pale and exhausted, was in a white dress as though for a holiday, with a flower in her hair; she looked at him, as yesterday, sorrowfully and intelligently, smiled and talked, and all with an expression as though she wanted to tell him something special, important—him alone. They could hear the larks trilling and the church bells pealing. The windows in the factory buildings were sparkling gaily, and, driving across the yard and afterwards along the road to the station, Korolyov thought neither of the workpeople nor of lake dwellings, nor of the devil, but thought of the time, perhaps close at hand, when life would be as bright and joyous as that still Sunday morning; and he thought how pleasant it was on such a morning in the spring to drive with three horses in a good carriage, and to bask in the sunshine.

A Dreary Story

From the Notebook of an Old Man

I

There is in Russia an emeritus Professor Nikolay Stepanovitch, a chevalier and privy councillor; he has so many Russian and foreign decorations that when he has occasion to put them on the students nickname him "The Ikonstand." His acquaintances are of the most aristocratic; for the last twenty-five or thirty years, at any rate, there has not been one single distinguished man of learning in Russia with whom he has not been intimately acquainted. There is no one for him to make friends with nowadays; but if we turn to the past, the long list of his famous friends winds up with such names as Pirogov, Kavelin, and the poet Nekrasov, all of whom bestowed upon him a warm and sincere affection. He is a member of all the Russian and of three foreign universities. And so on, and so on. All that and a great deal more that might be said makes up what is called my "name."

That is my name as known to the public. In Russia it is known to every educated man, and abroad it is mentioned in the lecture-room with the addition "honoured and distinguished." It is one of those fortunate names to abuse which or to take which in vain, in public or in print, is considered a sign of bad taste. And that is as it should be. You see, my name is closely associated with the conception of a highly distinguished man of great gifts and unquestionable usefulness. I have the industry and power of endurance of a camel, and that is important, and I have talent, which is even more important. Moreover, while I am on this subject, I am a well-educated, modest, and honest fellow. I have never poked my nose into literature or politics; I have never sought popularity in polemics with the ignorant; I have never made speeches either at public dinners or at the funerals of my friends. . . . In fact, there is no slur on my learned name, and there is no complaint one can make against it. It is fortunate.

The bearer of that name, that is I, see myself as a man of sixty-two, with a bald head, with false teeth, and with an incurable tic douloureux. I am myself as dingy and unsightly as my name is brilliant and splendid. My head and my hands tremble with weakness; my neck, as Turgenev says of one of his heroines, is like the handle of a double bass; my chest is hollow; my shoulders narrow; when I talk or lecture, my mouth turns down at one corner; when I smile, my whole face is covered with aged-looking, deathly wrinkles. There is nothing impressive about my pitiful figure; only, perhaps, when I have an attack of tic douloureux my face wears a peculiar expression, the sight of which must have roused in every one the grim and impressive thought, "Evidently that man will soon die."

I still, as in the past, lecture fairly well; I can still, as in the past, hold the attention of my listeners for a couple of hours. My fervour, the literary skill of my exposition, and my humour, almost efface the defects of my voice, though it is harsh, dry, and monotonous as a praying beggar's. I write poorly. That bit of my brain which presides over the faculty of authorship refuses to work. My memory has grown weak; there is a lack of sequence in my ideas, and when I put them on paper it always seems to me that I have lost the instinct for their organic connection; my construction is monotonous; my language is poor and timid. Often I write what I do not mean; I have forgotten the beginning when I am writing the end. Often I forget ordinary words, and I always have to waste a great deal of energy in avoiding superfluous phrases and unnecessary parentheses in my letters, both unmistakable proofs of a decline in mental activity. And it is noteworthy that the simpler the letter the more painful the effort to write it. At a scientific article I feel far more intelligent and at ease than at a letter of congratulation or a minute of proceedings. Another point: I find it easier to write German or English than to write Russian.

As regards my present manner of life, I must give a foremost place to the insomnia from which I have suffered of late. If I were asked what constituted the chief and fundamental feature of my existence now, I should answer, Insomnia. As in the past, from habit I undress and go to bed exactly at midnight. I fall asleep quickly, but before two o'clock I wake up and feel as though I had not slept at all. Sometimes I get out of bed and light a lamp. For an hour or two I walk up and down the room looking at the familiar photographs and pictures. When I am weary of walking about, I sit down to my table. I sit motionless, thinking of nothing, conscious of no inclination; if a book is lying before me, I mechanically move it closer and read it without any interest—in that way not long ago I mechanically read through in one night a whole novel, with the strange title "The Song the Lark was Singing"; or to occupy my attention I force myself to count to a thousand; or I imagine the face of one of my colleagues and begin trying to remember in what year and under what circumstances he entered the service. I like listening to sounds. Two rooms away from me my daughter Liza says something rapidly in her sleep, or my wife crosses the drawing-room with a candle and invariably drops the matchbox; or a warped cupboard creaks; or the burner of the lamp suddenly begins to hum—and all these sounds, for some reason, excite me.

To lie awake at night means to be at every moment conscious of being abnormal, and so I look forward with impatience to the morning and the day when I have a right to be awake. Many wearisome hours pass before the cock crows in the yard. He is my first bringer of good tidings. As soon as he crows I know that within an hour the porter will wake up below, and, coughing angrily, will go upstairs to fetch something. And then a pale light will begin gradually glimmering at the windows, voices will sound in the street. . . .

The day begins for me with the entrance of my wife. She comes in to me in her petticoat, before she has done her hair, but after she has washed, smelling of flower-scented eau-de-Cologne, looking as though she had come in by chance. Every time she says exactly the same thing: "Excuse me, I have just come in for a minute.... Have you had a bad night again?"

Then she puts out the lamp, sits down near the table, and begins talking. I am no prophet, but I know what she will talk about. Every morning it is exactly the same thing. Usually, after anxious inquiries concerning my health, she suddenly mentions our son who is an officer serving at Warsaw. After the twentieth of each month we send him fifty roubles, and that serves as the chief topic of our conversation.

"Of course it is difficult for us," my wife would sigh, "but until he is completely on his own feet it is our duty to help him. The boy is among strangers, his pay is small.... However, if you like, next month we won't send him fifty, but forty. What do you think?"

Daily experience might have taught my wife that constantly talking of our expenses does not reduce them, but my wife refuses to learn by experience, and regularly every morning discusses our officer son, and tells me that bread, thank God, is cheaper, while sugar is a halfpenny dearer—with a tone and an air as though she were communicating interesting news.

I listen, mechanically assent, and probably because I have had a bad night, strange and inappropriate thoughts intrude themselves upon me. I gaze at my wife and wonder like a child. I ask myself in perplexity, is it possible that this old, very stout, ungainly woman, with her dull expression of petty anxiety and alarm about daily bread, with eyes dimmed by continual brooding over debts and money difficulties, who can talk of nothing but expenses and who smiles at nothing but things getting cheaper—is it possible that this woman is no other than the slender Varya whom I fell in love with so passionately for her fine, clear intelligence, for her pure soul, her beauty, and, as Othello his Desdemona, for her "sympathy" for my studies? Could that woman be no other than the Varya who had once borne me a son?

I look with strained attention into the face of this flabby, spiritless, clumsy old woman, seeking in her my Varya, but of her past self nothing is left but her anxiety over my health and her manner of calling my salary "our salary," and my cap "our cap." It is painful for me to look at her, and, to give her what little comfort I can, I let her say what she likes, and say nothing even when she passes unjust criticisms on other people or pitches into me for not having a private practice or not publishing text-books.

Our conversation always ends in the same way. My wife suddenly remembers with dismay that I have not had my tea.

"What am I thinking about, sitting here?" she says, getting up. "The samovar has been on the table ever so long, and here I stay gossiping. My goodness! how forgetful I am growing!"

She goes out quickly, and stops in the doorway to say:

"We owe Yegor five months' wages. Did you know it? You mustn't let the servants' wages run on; how many times I have said it! It's much easier to pay ten roubles a month than fifty roubles every five months!"

As she goes out, she stops to say:

"The person I am sorriest for is our Liza. The girl studies at the Conservatoire, always mixes with people of good position, and goodness knows how she is dressed. Her fur coat is in such a state she is ashamed to show herself in the street. If she were somebody else's daughter it wouldn't matter, but of course every one knows that her father is a distinguished professor, a privy councillor."

And having reproached me with my rank and reputation, she goes away at last. That is how my day begins. It does not improve as it goes on.

As I am drinking my tea, my Liza comes in wearing her fur coat and her cap, with her music in her hand, already quite ready to go to the Conservatoire. She is two-and-twenty. She looks younger, is pretty, and rather like my wife in her young days. She kisses me tenderly on my forehead and on my hand, and says:

"Good-morning, papa; are you quite well?"

As a child she was very fond of ice-cream, and I used often to take her to a confectioner's. Ice-cream was for her the type of everything delightful. If she wanted to praise me she would say: "You are as nice as cream, papa." We used to call one of her little fingers "pistachio ice," the next, "cream ice," the third "raspberry," and so on. Usually when she came in to say good-morning to me I used to sit her on my knee, kiss her little fingers, and say:

"Creamy ice . . . pistachio . . . lemon. . . ."

And now, from old habit, I kiss Liza's fingers and mutter: "Pistachio . . . cream . . . lemon . . ." but the effect is utterly different. I am cold as ice and I am ashamed. When my daughter comes in to me and touches my forehead with her lips I start as though a bee had stung me on the head, give a forced smile, and turn my face away. Ever since I have been suffering from sleeplessness, a question sticks in my brain like a nail. My daughter often sees me, an old man and a distinguished man, blush painfully at being in debt to my footman; she sees how often anxiety over petty debts forces me to lay aside my work and to walk up and down the room for hours together, thinking; but why is it she never comes to me in secret to whisper in my ear: "Father, here is my watch, here are my bracelets, my earrings, my dresses. . . . Pawn them all; you want money . . ."? How is it that, seeing how her mother and I are placed in a false position and do our utmost to hide our poverty from people, she does not give up her expensive pleasure of music lessons? I would not accept her watch nor her bracelets, nor the sacrifice of her lessons—God forbid! That isn't what I want.

I think at the same time of my son, the officer at Warsaw. He is a clever, honest, and sober fellow. But that is not enough for me. I think if I had an old father, and if I knew there were moments when he was put to shame by his poverty, I should give up my officer's commission to somebody else, and should go out to earn my living as a workman. Such thoughts about my children poison me. What is the use of them? It is only a narrow-minded or embittered man who can harbour evil thoughts about ordinary people because they are not heroes. But enought of that!

At a quarter to ten I have to go and give a lecture to my dear boys. I dress and walk along the road which I have known for thirty years, and which has its history for me. Here is the big grey house with the chemist's shop; at this point there used to stand a little house, and in it was a beershop; in that beershop I thought out my thesis and wrote my first love-letter to Varya. I wrote it in pencil, on a page headed "Historia morbi." Here there is a grocer's shop; at one time it was kept by a little Jew, who sold me cigarettes on credit; then by a fat peasant woman, who liked the students because "every one of them has a mother"; now there is a red-haired shopkeeper sitting in it, a very stolid man who drinks tea from a copper teapot. And here are the gloomy gates of the University, which have long needed doing up; I see the bored porter in his sheep-skin, the broom, the drifts of snow.... On a boy coming fresh from the provinces and imagining that the temple of science must really be a temple, such gates cannot make a healthy impression. Altogether the dilapidated condition of the University buildings, the gloominess of the corridors, the griminess of the walls, the lack of light, the dejected aspect of the steps, the hat-stands and the benches, take a prominent position among predisposing causes in the history of Russian pessimism.... Here is our garden ... I fancy it has grown neither better nor worse since I was a student. I don't like it. It would be far more sensible if there were tall pines and fine oaks growing here instead of sickly-looking lime-trees, yellow acacias, and skimpy pollard lilacs. The student whose state of mind is in the majority of cases created by his surroundings, ought in the place where he is studying to see facing him at every turn nothing but what is lofty, strong and elegant.... God preserve him from gaunt trees, broken windows, grey walls, and doors covered with torn American leather!

When I go to my own entrance the door is flung wide open, and I am met by my colleague, contemporary, and namesake, the porter Nikolay. As he lets me in he clears his throat and says:

"A frost, your Excellency!"

Or, if my great-coat is wet:

"Rain, your Excellency!"

Then he runs on ahead of me and opens all the doors on my way. In my study he carefully takes off my fur coat, and while doing so manages to tell me some bit of University news. Thanks to the close intimacy existing between all the University porters and beadles, he knows everything that goes on in the four faculties, in the office, in the rector's private room, in the library. What does he not know? When in an evil day a rector or dean, for instance, retires, I hear him in conversation with the young porters mention the candidates for the post, explain that such a one would not be confirmed by the minister, that another would himself refuse to accept it, then drop into fantastic details concerning mysterious papers received in the office, secret conversations alleged to have taken place between the minister and the trustee, and so on. With the exception of these details, he almost always turns out to be right. His estimates of the candidates, though original, are very correct, too. If one wants to know in what year some one read his thesis, entered the service, retired, or died, then summon to your assistance the vast memory of that soldier, and he will not only tell you the year, the month and the day, but will furnish you also with the details that accompanied this or that event. Only one who loves can remember like that.

He is the guardian of the University traditions. From the porters who were his predecessors he has inherited many legends of University life, has added to that wealth much of his own gained during his time of service, and if you care to hear he will tell you many long and intimate stories. He can tell one about extraordinary sages who knew *everything,* about remarkable students who did not sleep for weeks, about numerous martyrs and victims of science; with him good triumphs over evil, the weak always vanquishes the strong, the wise man the fool, the humble the proud, the young the old. There is no need to take all these fables and legends for sterling coin; but filter them, and you will have left what is wanted: our fine traditions and the names of real heroes, recognized as such by all.

In our society the knowledge of the learned world consists of anecdotes of the extraordinary absentmindedness of certain old professors, and two or three witticisms variously ascribed to Gruber, to me, and to Babukin. For the educated public that is not much. If it loved science, learned men, and students, as Nikolay does, its literature would long ago have contained whole epics, records of sayings and doings such as, unfortunately, it cannot boast of now.

After telling me a piece of news, Nikolay assumes a severe expression, and conversation about business begins. If any outsider could at such times overhear Nikolay's free use of our terminology, he might perhaps imagine that he was a learned man disguised as a soldier. And, by the way, the rumours of the erudition of the University porters are greatly exaggerated. It is true that Nikolay knows more than a hundred Latin words, knows how to put the skeleton together, sometimes prepares the apparatus and amuses the students by some long, learned quotation, but the by no means complicated theory of the circulation of the blood, for instance, is as much a mystery to him now as it was twenty years ago.

At the table in my study, bending low over some book or preparation, sits Pyotr Ignatyevitch, my demonstrator, a modest and industrious but by no means clever man of five-and-thirty, already bald and corpulent; he works from morning to night, reads a lot, remembers well everything he has read—and in that way he is not a man, but pure gold; in all else he is a carthorse or, in other words, a learned dullard. The carthorse characteristics that show his lack of talent are these: his outlook is narrow and sharply limited by his specialty; outside his special branch he is simple as a child.

"Fancy! what a misfortune! They say Skobelev is dead."

Nikolay crosses himself, but Pyotr Ignatyevitch turns to me and asks:

"What Skobelev is that?"

Another time—somewhat earlier—I told him that Professor Perov was dead. Good Pyotr Ignatyevitch asked:

"What did he lecture on?"

I believe if Patti had sung in his very ear, if a horde of Chinese had invaded Russia, if there had been an earthquake, he would not have stirred a limb, but screwing up his eye, would have gone on calmly looking through his microscope. What is he to Hecuba or Hecuba to him, in fact? I would give a good deal to see how this dry stick sleeps with his wife at night.

Another characteristic is his fanatical faith in the infallibility of science, and, above all, of everything written by the Germans. He believes in himself, in his preparations; knows the object of life, and knows nothing of the doubts and disappointments that turn the hair of talent grey. He has a slavish reverence for authorities and a complete lack of any desire for independent thought. To change his convictions is difficult, to argue with him impossible. How is one to argue with a man who is firmly persuaded that medicine is the finest of sciences, that doctors are the best of men, and that the traditions of the medical profession are superior to those of any other? Of the evil past of medicine only one tradition has been preserved—the white tie still worn by doctors; for a learned—in fact, for any educated man the only traditions that can exist are those of the University as a whole, with no distinction between medicine, law, etc. But it would be hard for Pyotr Ignatyevitch to accept these facts, and he is ready to argue with you till the day of judgment.

I have a clear picture in my mind of his future. In the course of his life he will prepare many hundreds of chemicals of exceptional purity; he will write a number of dry and very accurate memoranda, will make some dozen conscientious translations, but he won't do anything striking. To do that one must have imagination, inventiveness, the gift of insight, and Pyotr Ignatyevitch has nothing of the kind. In short, he is not a master in science, but a journeyman.

Pyotr Ignatyevitch, Nikolay, and I, talk in subdued tones. We are not quite ourselves. There is always a peculiar feeling when one hears through the doors a murmur as of the sea from the lecture-theatre. In the course of thirty years I have not grown accustomed to this feeling, and I experience it every morning. I nervously button up my coat, ask Nikolay unnecessary questions, lose my temper.... It is just as though I were frightened; it is not timidity, though, but something different which I can neither describe nor find a name for.

Quite unnecessarily, I look at my watch and say: "Well, it's time to go in."

And we march into the room in the following order: foremost goes Nikolay, with the chemicals and apparatus or with a chart; after him I come; and then the carthorse follows humbly, with hanging head; or, when necessary, a dead body is carried in first on a stretcher, followed by Nikolay, and so on. On my entrance the students all stand up, then they sit down, and the sound as of the sea is suddenly hushed. Stillness reigns.

I know what I am going to lecture about, but I don't know how I am going to lecture, where I am going to begin or with what I am going to end. I haven't a single sentence ready in my head. But I have only to look round the lecture-hall (it is built in the form of an amphitheatre) and utter the stereotyped phrase, "Last lecture we stopped at..." when sentences spring up from my soul in a long string, and I am carried away by my own eloquence. I speak with irresistible rapidity and passion, and it seems as though there were no force which could check the flow of my words. To lecture well—that is, with profit to the listeners and without boring them—one must have, besides talent, experience and a special knack; one must possess a clear conception of one's own powers, of the audience to which one is lecturing, and of the subject of one's lecture. Moreover, one must be a man who knows what he is doing; one must keep a sharp lookout, and not for one second lose sight of what lies before one.

A good conductor, interpreting the thought of the composer, does twenty things at once: reads the score, waves his baton, watches the singer, makes a motion sideways, first to the drum then to the wind-instruments, and so on. I do just the same when I lecture. Before me a hundred and fifty faces, all unlike one another; three hundred eyes all looking straight into my face. My object is to dominate this many-headed monster. If every moment as I lecture I have a clear vision of the degree of its attention and its power of comprehension, it is in my power. The other foe I have to overcome is in myself. It is the infinite variety of forms, phenomena, laws, and the multitude of ideas of my own and other people's conditioned by them. Every moment I must have the skill to snatch out of that vast mass of material what is most important and necessary, and, as rapidly as my words flow, clothe my thought in a form in which it can be grasped by the monster's intelligence, and may arouse its attention, and at the same time one must keep a sharp lookout that one's thoughts are conveyed, not just as they come, but in a certain order, essential for the correct composition of the picture I wish to sketch. Further, I endeavour to make my diction literary, my definitions brief and precise, my wording, as far as possible, simple and eloquent. Every minute I have to pull myself up and remember that I have only an hour and forty minutes at my disposal. In short, one has one's work cut out. At one and the same minute one has to play the part of savant and teacher and orator, and it's a bad thing if the orator gets the upper hand of the savant or of the teacher in one, or *vice versa.*

You lecture for a quarter of an hour, for half an hour, when you notice that the students are beginning to look at the ceiling, at Pyotr Ignatyevitch; one is feeling for his handkerchief, another shifts in his seat, another smiles at his thoughts. . . . That means that their attention is flagging. Something must be done. Taking advantage of the first opportunity, I make some pun. A broad grin comes on to a hundred and fifty faces, the eyes shine brightly, the sound of the sea is audible for a brief moment. . . . I laugh too. Their attention is refreshed, and I can go on.

No kind of sport, no kind of game or diversion, has ever given me such enjoyment as lecturing. Only at lectures have I been able to abandon myself entirely to passion, and have understood that inspiration is not an invention of the poets, but exists in real life, and I imagine Hercules after the most piquant of his exploits felt just such voluptuous exhaustion as I experience after every lecture.

That was in old times. Now at lectures I feel nothing but torture. Before half an hour is over I am conscious of an overwhelming weakness in my legs and my shoulders. I sit down in my chair, but I am not accustomed to lecture sitting down; a minute later I get up and go on standing, then sit down again. There is a dryness in my mouth, my voice grows husky, my head begins to go round. . . . To conceal my condition from my audience I continually drink water, cough, often blow my nose as though I were hindered by a cold, make puns inappropriately, and in the end break off earlier than I ought to. But above all I am ashamed.

My conscience and my intelligence tell me that the very best thing I could do now would be to deliver a farewell lecture to the boys, to say my last word to them, to bless them, and give up my post to a man younger and stronger than me. But, God, be my judge, I have not manly courage enough to act according to my conscience.

Unfortunately, I am not a philosopher and not a theologian. I know perfectly well that I cannot live more than another six months; it might be supposed that I ought now to be chiefly concerned with the question of the shadowy life beyond the grave, and the visions that will visit my slumbers in the tomb. But for some reason my soul refuses to recognize these questions, though my mind is fully alive to their importance. Just as twenty, thirty years ago, so now, on the threshold of death, I am interested in nothing but science. As I yield up my last breath I shall still believe that science is the most important, the most splendid, the most essential thing in the life of man; that it always has been and will be the highest manifestation of love, and that only by means of it will man conquer himself and nature. This faith is perhaps naïve and may rest on false assumptions, but it is not my fault that I believe that and nothing else; I cannot overcome in myself this belief.

But that is not the point. I only ask people to be indulgent to my weakness, and to realize that to tear from the lecture-theatre and his pupils a man who is more interested in the history of the development of the bone medulla than in the final object of creation would be equivalent to taking him and nailing him up in his coffin without waiting for him to be dead.

Sleeplessness and the consequent strain of combating increasing weakness leads to something strange in me. In the middle of my lecture tears suddenly rise in my throat, my eyes begin to smart, and I feel a passionate, hysterical desire to stretch out my hands before me and break into loud lamentation. I want to cry out in a loud voice that I, a famous man, have been sentenced by fate to the death penalty, that within some six months another man will be in control here in the lecture-theatre. I want to shriek that I am poisoned; new ideas such as I have not known before have poisoned the last days of my life, and are still stinging my brain like mosquitoes. And at that moment my position seems to me so awful that I want all my listeners to be horrified, to leap up from their seats and to rush in panic terror, with desperate screams, to the exit.

It is not easy to get through such moments.

II

After my lecture I sit at home and work. I read journals and monographs, or prepare my next lecture; sometimes I write something. I work with interruptions, as I have from time to time to see visitors.

There is a ring at the bell. It is a colleague come to discuss some business matter with me. He comes in to me with his hat and his stick, and, holding out both these objects to me, says:

"Only for a minute! Only for a minute! Sit down, *collega*! Only a couple of words."

To begin with, we both try to show each other that we are extraordinarily polite and highly delighted to see each other. I make him sit down in an easy-chair, and he makes me sit down; as we do so, we cautiously pat each other on the back, touch each other's buttons, and it looks as though we were feeling each other and afraid of scorching our fingers. Both of us laugh, though we say nothing amusing. When we are seated we bow our heads towards each other and begin talking in subdued voices. However affectionately disposed we may be to one another, we cannot help adorning our conversation with all sorts of Chinese mannerisms, such as "As you so justly observed," or "I have already had the honour to inform you"; we cannot help laughing if one of us makes a joke, however unsuccessfully. When we have finished with business my colleague gets up impulsively and, waving his hat in the direction of my work, begins to say good-bye. Again we paw one another and laugh. I see him into the hall; when I assist my colleague to put on his coat, while he does all he can to decline this high honour. Then when Yegor opens the door my colleague declares that I shall catch cold, while I make a show of being ready to go even into the street with him. And when at last I go back into my study my face still goes on smiling, I suppose from inertia.

A little later another ring at the bell. Somebody comes into the hall, and is a long time coughing and taking off his things. Yegor announces a student. I tell him to ask him in. A minute later a young man of agreeable appearance comes in. For the last year he and I have been on strained relations; he answers me disgracefully at the examinations, and I mark him one. Every year I have some seven such hopefuls whom, to express it in the students' slang, I "chivy" or "floor." Those of them who fail in their examination through incapacity or illness usually bear their cross patiently and do not haggle with me; those who come to the house and haggle with me are always youths of sanguine temperament, broad natures, whose failure at examinations spoils their appetites and hinders them from visiting the opera with their usual regularity. I let the first class off easily, but the second I chivy through a whole year.

"Sit down," I say to my visitor; "what have you to tell me?"

"Excuse me, professor, for troubling you," he begins, hesitating, and not looking me in the face. "I would not have ventured to trouble you if it had not been . . . I have been up for your examination five times, and have been ploughed. . . . I beg you, be so good as to mark me for a pass, because . . ."

The argument which all the sluggards bring forward on their own behalf is always the same; they have passed well in all their subjects and have only come to grief in mine, and that is the more surprising because they have always been particularly interested in my subject and knew it so well; their failure has always been entirely owing to some incomprehensible misunderstanding.

"Excuse me, my friend," I say to the visitor; "I cannot mark you for a pass. Go and read up the lectures and come to me again. Then we shall see."

A pause. I feel an impulse to torment the student a little for liking beer and the opera better than science, and I say, with a sigh:

"To my mind, the best thing you can do now is to give up medicine altogether. If, with your abilities, you cannot succeed in passing the examination, it's evident that you have neither the desire nor the vocation for a doctor's calling."

The sanguine youth's face lengthens.

"Excuse me, professor," he laughs, "but that would be odd of me, to say the least of it. After studying for five years, all at once to give it up."

"Oh, well! Better to have lost your five years than have to spend the rest of your life in doing work you do not care for."

But at once I feel sorry for him, and I hasten to add:

"However, as you think best. And so read a little more and come again."

"When?" the idle youth asks in a hollow voice.

"When you like. Tomorrow if you like."

And in his good-natured eyes I read:

"I can come all right, but of course you will plough me again, you beast!"

"Of course," I say, "you won't know more science for going in for my examination another fifteen times, but it is training your character, and you must be thankful for that."

Silence follows. I get up and wait for my visitor to go, but he stands and looks towards the window, fingers his beard, and thinks. It grows boring.

The sanguine youth's voice is pleasant and mellow, his eyes are clever and ironical, his face is genial, though a little bloated from frequent indulgence in beer and overlong lying on the sofa; he looks as though he could tell me a lot of interesting things about the opera, about his affairs of the heart, and about comrades whom he likes. Unluckily, it is not the thing to discuss these subjects, or else I should have been glad to listen to him.

"Professor, I give you my word of honour that if you mark me for a pass I . . . I'll . . ."

As soon as we reach the "word of honour" I wave my hands and sit down to the table. The student ponders a minute longer, and says dejectedly:

"In that case, good-bye. . . . I beg your pardon."

"Good-bye, my friend. Good luck to you."

He goes irresolutely into the hall, slowly puts on his outdoor things, and, going out into the street, probably ponders for some time longer; unable to think of anything, except "old devil," inwardly addressed to me, he goes into a wretched restaurant to dine and drink beer, and then home to bed. "Peace be to thy ashes, honest toiler."

A third ring at the bell. A young doctor, in a pair of new black trousers, gold spectacles, and of course a white tie, walks in. He introduces himself. I beg him to be seated, and ask what I can do for him. Not without emotion, the young devotee of science begins telling me that he has passed his examination as a doctor of medicine, and that he has now only to write his dissertation. He would like to work with me under my guidance, and he would be greatly obliged to me if I would give him a subject for his dissertation.

"Very glad to be of use to you, colleague," I say, "but just let us come to an understanding as to the meaning of a dissertation. That word is taken to mean a composition which is a product of independent creative effort. Is that not so? A work written on another man's subject and under another man's guidance is called something different. . . ."

The doctor says nothing. I fly into a rage and jump up from my seat.

"Why is it you all come to me?" I cry angrily. "Do I keep a shop? I don't deal in subjects. For the thousand and oneth time I ask you all to leave me in peace! Excuse my brutality, but I am quite sick of it!"

The doctor remains silent, but a faint flush is apparent on his cheekbones. His face expresses a profound reverence for my fame and my learning, but from his eyes I can see he feels a contempt for my voice, my pitiful figure, and my nervous gesticulation. I impress him in my anger as a queer fish.

"I don't keep a shop," I go on angrily. "And it is a strange thing! Why don't you want to be independent? Why have you such a distaste for independence?"

I say a great deal, but he still remains silent. By degrees I calm down, and of course give in. The doctor gets a subject from me for his theme not worth a halfpenny, writes under my supervision a dissertation of no use to any one, with dignity defends it in a dreary discussion, and receives a degree of no use to him.

The rings at the bell may follow one another endlessly, but I will confine my description here to four of them. The bell rings for the fourth time, and I hear familiar footsteps, the rustle of a dress, a dear voice. . . .

Eighteen years ago a colleague of mine, an oculist, died leaving a little daughter Katya, a child of seven, and sixty thousand roubles. In his will he made me the child's guardian. Till she was ten years old Katya lived with us as one of the family, then she was sent to a boarding-school, and only spent the summer holidays with us. I never had time to look after her education. I only superintended it at leisure moments, and so I can say very little about her childhood.

The first thing I remember, and like so much in remembrance, is the extraordinary trustfulness with which she came into our house and let herself be treated by the doctors, a trustfulness which was always shining in her little face. She would sit somewhere out of the way, with her face tied up, invariably watching something with attention; whether she watched me writing or turning over the pages of a book, or watched my wife bustling about, or the cook scrubbing a potato in the kitchen, or the dog playing, her eyes invariably expressed the same thought—that is, "Everything that is done in this world is nice and sensible." She was curious, and very fond of talking to me. Sometimes she would sit at the table opposite me, watching my movements and asking questions. It interested her to know what I was reading, what I did at the University, whether I was not afraid of the dead bodies, what I did with my salary.

"Do the students fight at the University?" she would ask.

"They do, dear."

"And do you make them go down on their knees?"

"Yes, I do."

And she thought it funny that the students fought and I made them go down on their knees, and she laughed. She was a gentle, patient, good child. It happened not infrequently that I saw something taken away from her, saw her punished without reason, or her curiosity repressed; at such times a look of sadness was mixed with the invariable expression of trustfulness on her face—that was all. I did not know how to take her part; only when I saw her sad I had an inclination to draw her to me and to commiserate her like some old nurse: "My poor little orphan one!"

I remember, too, that she was fond of fine clothes and of sprinkling herself with scent. In that respect she was like me. I, too, am fond of pretty clothes and nice scent.

I regret that I had not time nor inclination to watch over the rise and development of the passion which took complete possession of Katya when she was fourteen or fifteen. I mean her passionate love for the theatre. When she used to come from boarding-school and stay with us for the summer holidays, she talked of nothing with such pleasure and such warmth as of plays and actors. She bored us with her continual talk of the theatre. My wife and children would not listen to her. I was the only one who had not the courage to refuse to attend to her. When she had a longing to share her transports, she used to come into my study and say in an imploring tone:

"Nikolay Stepanovitch, do let me talk to you about the theatre!"

I pointed to the clock, and said:

"I'll give you half an hour—begin."

Later on she used to bring with her dozens of portraits of actors and actresses which she worshipped; then she attempted several times to take part in private theatricals, and the upshot of it all was that when she left school she came to me and announced that she was born to be an actress.

I had never shared Katya's inclinations for the theatre. To my mind, if a play is good there is no need to trouble the actors in order that it may make the right impression; it is enough to read it. If the play is poor, no acting will make it good.

In my youth I often visited the theatre, and now my family takes a box twice a year and carries me off for a little distraction. Of course, that is not enough to give me the right to judge of the theatre. In my opinion the theatre has become no better than it was thirty or forty years ago. Just as in the past, I can never find a glass of clean water in the corridors or foyers of the theatre. Just as in the past, the attendants fine me twenty kopecks for my fur coat, though there is nothing reprehensible in wearing a warm coat in winter. As in the past, for no sort of reason, music is played in the intervals, which adds something new and uncalled-for to the impression made by the play. As in the past, men go in the intervals and drink spirits in the buffet. If no progress can be seen in trifles, I should look for it in vain in what is more important. When an actor wrapped from head to foot in stage traditions and conventions tries to recite a simple ordinary speech, "To be or not to be," not simply, but invariably with the accompaniment of hissing and convulsive movements all over his body, or when he tries to convince me at all costs that Tchatsky, who talks so much with fools and is so fond of folly, is a very clever man, and that "Woe from Wit" is not a dull play, the stage gives me the same feeling of conventionality which bored me so much forty years ago when I was regaled with the classical howling and beating on the breast. And every time I come out of the theatre more conservative than I go in.

The sentimental and confiding public may be persuaded that the stage, even in its present form, is a school; but any one who is familiar with a school in its true sense will not be caught with that bait. I cannot say what will happen in fifty or a hundred years, but in its actual condition the theatre can serve only as an entertainment. But this entertainment is too costly to be frequently enjoyed. It robs the state of thousands of healthy and talented young men and women, who, if they had not devoted themselves to the theatre, might have been good doctors, farmers, schoolmistresses, officers; it robs the public of the evening hours—the best time for intellectual work and social intercourse. I say nothing of the waste of money and the moral damage to the spectator when he sees murder, fornication, or false witness unsuitably treated on the stage.

Katya was of an entirely different opinion. She assured me that the theatre, even in its present condition, was superior to the lecture-hall, to books, or to anything in the world. The stage was a power that united in itself all the arts, and actors were missionaries. No art nor science was capable of producing so strong and so certain an effect on the soul of man as the stage, and it was with good reason that an actor of medium quality enjoys greater popularity than the greatest savant or artist. And no sort of public service could provide such enjoyment and gratification as the theatre.

And one fine day Katya joined a troupe of actors, and went off, I believe to Ufa, taking away with her a good supply of money, a store of rainbow hopes, and the most aristocratic views of her work.

Her first letters on the journey were marvellous. I read them, and was simply amazed that those small sheets of paper could contain so much youth, purity of spirit, holy innocence, and at the same time subtle and apt judgments which would have done credit to a fine masculine intellect. It was more like a rapturous pæan of praise she sent me than a mere description of the Volga, the country, the towns she visited, her companions, her failures and successes; every sentence was fragrant with that confiding trustfulness I was accustomed to read in her face—and at the same time there were a great many grammatical mistakes, and there was scarcely any punctuation at all.

Before six months had passed I received a highly poetical and enthusiastic letter beginning with the words, "I have come to love . . ." This letter was accompanied by a photograph representing a young man with a shaven face, a wide-brimmed hat, and a plaid flung over his shoulder. The letters that followed were as splendid as before, but now commas and stops made their appearance in them, the grammatical mistakes disappeared, and there was a distinctly masculine flavour about them. Katya began writing to me how splendid it would be to build a great theatre somewhere on the Volga, on a cooperative system, and to attract to the enterprise the rich merchants and the steamer owners; there would be a great deal of money in it; there would be vast audiences; the actors would play on co-operative terms. . . . Possibly all this was really excellent, but it seemed to me that such schemes could only originate from a man's mind.

However that may have been, for a year and a half everything seemed to go well: Katya was in love, believed in her work, and was happy; but then I began to notice in her letters unmistakable signs of falling off. It began with Katya's complaining of her companions—this was the first and most ominous symptom; if a young scientific or literary man begins his career with bitter complaints of scientific and literary men, it is a sure sign that he is worn out and not fit for his work. Katya wrote to me that her companions did not attend the rehearsals and never knew their parts; that one could see in every one of them an utter disrespect for the public in the production of absurd plays, and in their behaviour on the stage; that for the benefit of the Actors' Fund, which they only talked about, actresses of the serious drama demeaned themselves by singing chansonettes, while tragic actors sang comic songs making fun of deceived husbands and the pregnant condition of unfaithful wives, and so on. In fact, it was amazing that all this had not yet ruined the provincial stage, and that it could still maintain itself on such a rotten and unsubstantial footing.

In answer I wrote Katya a long and, I must confess, a very boring letter. Among other things, I wrote to her:

"I have more than once happened to converse with old actors, very worthy men, who showed a friendly disposition towards me; from my conversations with them I could understand that their work was controlled not so much by their own intelligence and free choice as by fashion and the mood of the public. The best of them had had to play in their day in tragedy, in operetta, in Parisian farces, and in extravaganzas, and they always seemed equally sure that they were on the right path and that they were of use. So, as you see, the cause of the evil must be sought, not in the actors, but, more deeply, in the art itself and in the attitude of the whole of society to it."

This letter of mine only irritated Katya. She answered me:

"You and I are singing parts out of different operas. I wrote to you, not of the worthy men who showed a friendly disposition to you, but of a band of knaves who have nothing worthy about them. They are a horde of savages who have got on the stage simply because no one would have taken them elsewhere, and who call themselves artists simply because they are impudent. There are numbers of dull-witted creatures, drunkards, intriguing schemers and slanderers, but there is not one person of talent among them. I cannot tell you how bitter it is to me that the art I love has fallen into the hands of people I detest; how bitter it is that the best men look on at evil from afar, not caring to come closer, and, instead of intervening, write ponderous commonplaces and utterly useless sermons. . . ." And so on, all in the same style.

A little time passed, and I got this letter: "I have been brutally deceived. I cannot go on living. Dispose of my money as you think best. I loved you as my father and my only friend. Good-bye."

It turned out that *he,* too, belonged to the "horde of savages." Later on, from certain hints, I gathered that there had been an attempt at suicide. I believe Katya tried to poison herself. I imagine that she must have been seriously ill afterwards, as the next letter I got was from Yalta, where she had most probably been sent by the doctors. Her last letter contained a request to send her a thousand roubles to Yalta as quickly as possible, and ended with these words:

"Excuse the gloominess of this letter; yesterday I buried my child." After spending about a year in the Crimea, she returned home.

She had been about four years on her travels, and during those four years, I must confess, I had played a rather strange and unenviable part in regard to her. When in earlier days she had told me she was going on the stage, and then wrote to me of her love; when she was periodically overcome by extravagance, and I continually had to send her first one and then two thousand roubles; when she wrote to me of her intention of suicide, and then of the death of her baby, every time I lost my head, and all my sympathy for her sufferings found no expression except that, after prolonged reflection, I wrote long, boring letters which I might just as well not have written. And yet I took a father's place with her and loved her like a daughter!

Now Katya is living less than half a mile off. She has taken a flat of five rooms, and has installed herself fairly comfortably and in the taste of the day. If any one were to undertake to describe her surroundings, the most characteristic note in the picture would be indolence. For the indolent body there are soft lounges, soft stools; for indolent feet soft rugs; for indolent eyes faded, dingy, or flat colours; for the indolent soul the walls are hung with a number of cheap fans and trivial pictures, in which the originality of the execution is more conspicuous than the subject; and the room contains a multitude of little tables and shelves filled with utterly useless articles of no value, and shapeless rags in place of curtains.... All this, together with the dread of bright colours, of symmetry, and of empty space, bears witness not only to spiritual indolence, but also to a corruption of natural taste. For days together Katya lies on the lounge reading, principally novels and stories. She only goes out of the house once a day, in the afternoon, to see me.

I go on working while Katya sits silent not far from me on the sofa, wrapping herself in her shawl, as though she were cold. Either because I find her sympathetic or because I was used to her frequent visits when she was a little girl, her presence does not prevent me from concentrating my attention. From time to time I mechanically ask her some question; she gives very brief replies; or, to rest for a minute, I turn round and watch her as she looks dreamily at some medical journal or review. And at such moments I notice that her face has lost the old look of confiding trustfulness. Her expression now is cold, apathetic, and absent-minded, like that of passengers who had to wait too long for a train. She is dressed, as in old days, simply and beautifully, but carelessly; her dress and her hair show visible traces of the sofas and rocking-chairs in which she spends whole days at a stretch. And she has lost the curiosity she had in old days. She has ceased to ask me questions now, as though she had experienced everything in life and looked for nothing new from it.

Towards four o'clock there begins to be sounds of movement in the hall and in the drawing-room. Liza has come back from the Conservatoire, and has brought some girl-friends in with her. We hear them playing on the piano, trying their voices and laughing; in the dining-room Yegor is laying the table, with the clatter of crockery.

"Good-bye," said Katya. "I won't go in and see your people today. They must excuse me. I haven't time. Come and see me."

While I am seeing her to the door, she looks me up and down grimly, and says with vexation:

"You are getting thinner and thinner! Why don't you consult a doctor? I'll call at Sergey Fyodorovitch's and ask him to have a look at you."

"There's no need, Katya."

"I can't think where your people's eyes are! They are a nice lot, I must say!"

She puts on her fur coat abruptly, and as she does so two or three hairpins drop unnoticed on the floor from her carelessly arranged hair. She is too lazy and in too great a hurry to do her hair up; she carelessly stuffs the falling curls under her hat, and goes away.

When I go into the dining-room my wife asks me:

"Was Katya with you just now? Why didn't she come in to see us? It's really strange . . ."

"Mamma," Liza says to her reproachfully, "let her alone, if she doesn't want to. We are not going down on our knees to her."

"It's very neglectful, anyway. To sit for three hours in the study without remembering our existence! But of course she must do as she likes."

Varya and Liza both hate Katya. This hatred is beyond my comprehension, and probably one would have to be a woman in order to understand it. I am ready to stake my life that of the hundred and fifty young men I see every day in the lecture-theatre, and of the hundred elderly ones I meet every week, hardly one could be found capable of understanding their hatred and aversion for Katya's past—that is, for her having been a mother without being a wife, and for her having had an illegitimate child; and at the same time I cannot recall one woman or girl of my acquaintance who would not consciously or unconsciously harbour such feelings. And this is not because woman is purer or more virtuous than man: why, virtue and purity are not very different from vice if they are not free from evil feeling. I attribute this simply to the backwardness of woman. The mournful feeling of compassion and the pang of conscience experienced by a modern man at the sight of suffering is, to my mind, far greater proof of culture and moral elevation than hatred and aversion. Woman is as tearful and as coarse in her feelings now as she was in the Middle Ages, and to my thinking those who advise that she should be educated like a man are quite right.

My wife also dislikes Katya for having been an actress, for ingratitude, for pride, for eccentricity, and for the numerous vices which one woman can always find in another.

Besides my wife and daughter and me, there are dining with us two or three of my daughter's friends and Alexandr Adolfovitch Gnekker, her admirer and suitor. He is a fair-haired young man under thirty, of medium height, very stout and broad-shouldered, with red whiskers near his ears, and little waxed moustaches which make his plump smooth face look like a toy. He is dressed in a very short reefer jacket, a flowered waistcoat, breeches very full at the top and very narrow at the ankle, with a large check pattern on them, and yellow boots without heels. He has prominent eyes like a crab's, his cravat is like a crab's neck, and I even fancy there is a smell of crab-soup about the young man's whole person. He visits us every day, but no one in my family knows anything of his origin nor of the place of his education, nor of his means of livelihood. He neither plays nor sings, but has some connection with music and singing, sells somebody's pianos somewhere, is frequently at the Conservatoire, is acquainted with all the celebrities, and is a steward at the concerts; he criticizes music with great authority, and I have noticed that people are eager to agree with him.

Rich people always have dependents hanging about them; the arts and sciences have the same. I believe there is not an art nor a science in the world free from "foreign bodies" after the style of this Mr. Gnekker. I am not a musician, and possibly I am mistaken in regard to Mr. Gnekker, of whom, indeed, I know very little. But his air of authority and the dignity with which he takes his stand beside the piano when any one is playing or singing strike me as very suspicious.

You may be ever so much of a gentleman and a privy councillor, but if you have a daughter you cannot be secure of immunity from that petty bourgeois atmosphere which is so often brought into your house and into your mood by the attentions of suitors, by matchmaking and marriage. I can never reconcile myself, for instance, to the expression of triumph on my wife's face every time Gnekker is in our company, nor can I reconcile myself to the bottles of Lafitte, port and sherry which are only brought out on his account, that he may see with his own eyes the liberal and luxurious way in which we live. I cannot tolerate the habit of spasmodic laughter Liza has picked up at the Conservatoire, and her way of screwing up her eyes whenever there are men in the room. Above all, I cannot understand why a creature utterly alien to my habits, my studies, my whole manner of life, completely different from the people I like, should come and see me every day, and every day should dine with me. My wife and my servants mysteriously whisper that he is a suitor, but still I don't understand his presence; it rouses in me the same wonder and perplexity as if they were to set a Zulu beside me at the table. And it seems strange to me, too, that my daughter, whom I am used to thinking of as a child, should love that cravat, those eyes, those soft cheeks....

In the old days I used to like my dinner, or at least was indifferent about it; now it excites in me no feeling but weariness and irritation. Ever since I became an "Excellency" and one of the Deans of the Faculty my family has for some reason found it necessary to make a complete change in our menu and dining habits. Instead of the simple dishes to which I was accustomed when I was a student and when I was in practice, now they feed me with a purée with little white things like circles floating about in it, and kidneys stewed in madeira. My rank as a general and my fame have robbed me for ever of cabbage-soup and savoury pies, and goose with apple-sauce, and bream with boiled grain. They have robbed me of our maid-servant Agasha, a chatty and laughter-loving old woman, instead of whom Yegor, a dull-witted and conceited fellow with a white glove on his right hand, waits at dinner. The intervals between the courses are short, but they seem immensely long because there is nothing to occupy them. There is none of the gaiety of the old days, the spontaneous talk, the jokes, the laughter; there is nothing of mutual affection and the joy which used to animate the children, my wife, and me when in old days we met together at meals. For me, the celebrated man of science, dinner was a time of rest and reunion, and for my wife and children a fête—brief indeed, but bright and joyous—in which they knew that for half an hour I belonged, not to science, not to students, but to them alone. Our real exhilaration from one glass of wine is gone for ever, gone is Agasha, gone the bream with boiled grain, gone the uproar that greeted every little startling incident at dinner, such as the cat and dog fighting under the table, or Katya's bandage falling off her face into her soup-plate.

To describe our dinner nowadays is as uninteresting as to eat it. My wife's face wears a look of triumph and affected dignity, and her habitual expression of anxiety. She looks at our plates and says, "I see you don't care for the joint. Tell me; you don't like it, do you?" and I am obliged to answer: "There is no need for you to trouble, my dear; the meat is very nice." And she will say: "You always stand up for me, Nikolay Stepanovitch, and you never tell the truth. Why is Alexandr Adolfovitch eating so little?" And so on in the same style all through dinner. Liza laughs spasmodically and screws up her eyes. I watch them both, and it is only now at dinner that it becomes absolutely evident to me that the inner life of these two has slipped away out of my ken. I have a feeling as though I had once lived at home with a real wife and children and that now I am dining with visitors, in the house of a sham wife who is not the real one, and am looking at a Liza who is not the real Liza. A startling change has taken place in both of them; I have missed the long process by which that change was effected, and it is no wonder that I can make nothing of it. Why did that change take place? I don't know. Perhaps the whole trouble is that God has not given my wife and daughter the same strength of character as me. From childhood I have been accustomed to resisting external influences, and have steeled myself pretty thoroughly. Such catastrophes in life as fame, the rank of a general, the transition from comfort to living beyond our means, acquaintance with celebrities, etc., have scarcely affected me, and I have remained intact and unashamed; but on my wife and Liza, who have not been through the same hardening process and are weak, all this has fallen like an avalanche of snow, overwhelming them. Gnekker and the young ladies talk of fugues, of counterpoint, of singers and pianists, of Bach and Brahms, while my wife, afraid of their suspecting her of ignorance of music, smiles to them sympathetically and mutters: "That's exquisite . . . really! You don't say so! . . ." Gnekker eats with solid dignity, jests with solid dignity, and condescendingly listens to the remarks of the young ladies. From time to time he is moved to speak in bad French, and then, for some reason or other, he thinks it necessary to address me as "*Votre Excellence.*"

And I am glum. Evidently I am a constraint to them and they are a constraint to me. I have never in my earlier days had a close knowledge of class antagonism, but now I am tormented by something of that sort. I am on the lookout for nothing but bad qualities in Gnekker; I quickly find them, and am fretted at the thought that a man not of my circle is sitting here as my daughter's suitor. His presence has a bad influence on me in other ways, too. As a rule, when I am alone or in the society of people I like, I never think of my own achievements, or, if I do recall them, they seem to me as trivial as though I had only completed my studies yesterday; but in the presence of people like Gnekker my achievements in science seem to be a lofty mountain the top of which vanishes into the clouds, while at its foot Gnekkers are running about scarcely visible to the naked eye.

After dinner I go into my study and there smoke my pipe, the only one in the whole day, the sole relic of my old bad habit of smoking from morning till night. While I am smoking my wife comes in and sits down to talk to me. Just as in the morning, I know beforehand what our conversation is going to be about.

"I must talk to you seriously, Nikolay Stepanovitch," she begins. "I mean about Liza. . . . Why don't you pay attention to it?"

"To what?"

"You pretend to notice nothing. But that is not right. We can't shirk responsibility. . . . Gnekker has intentions in regard to Liza. . . . What do you say?"

"That he is a bad man I can't say, because I don't know him, but that I don't like him I have told you a thousand times already."

"But you can't . . . you can't!"

She gets up and walks about in excitement.

"You can't take up that attitude to a serious step," she says. "When it is a question of our daughter's happiness we must lay aside all personal feeling. I know you do not like him.... Very good... if we refuse him now, if we break it all off, how can you be sure that Liza will not have a grievance against us all her life? Suitors are not plentiful nowadays, goodness knows, and it may happen that no other match will turn up.... He is very much in love with Liza, and she seems to like him.... Of course, he has no settled position, but that can't be helped. Please God, in time he will get one. He is of good family and well off."

"'Where did you learn that?"

"He told us so. His father has a large house in Harkov and an estate in the neighbourhood. In short, Nikolay Stepanovitch, you absolutely must go to Harkov."

"What for?"

"You will find out all about him there.... You know the professors there; they will help you. I would go myself, but I am a woman. I cannot...."

"I am not going to Harkov," I say morosely.

My wife is frightened, and a look of intense suffering comes into her face.

"For God's sake, Nikolay Stepanovitch," she implores me, with tears in her voice—"for God's sake, take this burden off me! I am so worried!"

It is painful for me to look at her.

"Very well, Varya," I say affectionately, "if you wish it, then certainly I will go to Harkov and do all you want."

She presses her handkerchief to her eyes and goes off to her room to cry, and I am left alone.

A little later lights are brought in. The armchair and the lampshade cast familiar shadows that have long grown wearisome on the walls and on the floor, and when I look at them I feel as though the night had come and with it my accursed sleeplessness. I lie on my bed, then get up and walk about the room, then lie down again. As a rule it is after dinner, at the approach of evening, that my nervous excitement reaches its highest pitch. For no reason I begin crying and burying my head in the pillow. At such times I am afraid that some one may come in; I am afraid of suddenly dying; I am ashamed of my tears, and altogether there is something insufferable in my soul. I feel that I can no longer bear the sight of my lamp, of my books, of the shadows on the floor. I cannot bear the sound of the voices coming from the drawing-room. Some force unseen, uncomprehended, is roughly thrusting me out of my flat. I leap up hurriedly, dress, and cautiously, that my family may not notice, slip out into the street. Where am I to go?

The answer to that question has long been ready in my brain. To Katya.

III

As a rule she is lying on the sofa or in a lounge-chair reading. Seeing me, she raises her read languidly, sits up, and shakes hands.

"You are always lying down," I say, after pausing and taking breath. "That's not good for you. You ought to occupy yourself with something."

"What?"

"I say you ought to occupy yourself in some way."

"With what? A woman can be nothing but a simple workwoman or an actress."

"Well, if you can't be a workwoman, be an actress."

She says nothing.

"You ought to get married," I say, half in jest.

"There is no one to marry. There's no reason to, either."

"You can't live like this."

"Without a husband? Much that matters; I could have as many men as I like if I wanted to."

"That's ugly, Katya."

"What is ugly?"

"Why, what you have just said."

Noticing that I am hurt and wishing to efface the disagreeable impression, Katya says:

"Let us go; come this way."

She takes me into a very snug little room, and says, pointing to the writing-table:

"Look . . . I have got that ready for you. You shall work here. Come here every day and bring your work with you. They only hinder you there at home. Will you work here? Will you like to?"

Not to wound her by refusing, I answer that I will work here, and that I like the room very much. Then we both sit down in the snug little room and begin talking.

The warm, snug surroundings and the presence of a sympathetic person does not, as in old days, arouse in me a feeling of pleasure, but an intense impulse to complain and grumble. I feel for some reason that if I lament and complain I shall feel better.

"Things are in a bad way with me, my dear—very bad. . . ."

"What is it?"

"You see how it is, my dear; the best and holiest right of kings is the right of mercy. And I have always felt myself a king, since I have made unlimited use of that right. I have never judged, I have been indulgent, I have readily forgiven every one, right and left. Where others have protested and expressed indignation, I have only advised and persuaded. All my life it has been my endeavour that my society should not be a burden to my family, to my students, to my colleagues, to my servants. And I know that this attitude to people has had a good influence on all who have chanced to come into contact with me. But now I am not a king. Something is happening to me that is only excusable in a slave; day and night my brain is haunted by evil thoughts, and feelings such as I never knew before are brooding in my soul. I am full of hatred, and contempt, and indignation, and loathing, and dread. I have become execessively severe, exacting, irritable, ungracious, suspicious. Even things that in old days would have provoked me only to an unnecessary jest and a good-natured laugh now arouse an oppressive feeling in me. My reasoning, too, has undergone a change: in old days I despised money; now I harbour an evil feeling, not towards money, but towards the rich as though they were to blame: in old days I hated violence and tyranny, but now I hate the men who make use of violence, as though they were alone to blame, and not all of us who do not know how to educate each other. What is the meaning of it? If these new ideas and new feelings have come from a change of convictions, what is that change due to? Can the world have grown worse and I better, or was I blind before and indifferent? If this change is the result of a general decline of physical and intellectual powers—I am ill, you know, and every day I am losing weight—my position is pitiable; it means that my new ideas are morbid and abnormal; I ought to be ashamed of them and think them of no consequence. . . ."

"Illness has nothing to do with it," Katya interrupts me; "it's simply that your eyes are opened, that's all. You have seen what in old days, for some reason, you refused to see. To my thinking, what you ought to do first of all, is to break with your family for good, and go away."

"You are talking nonsense."

"You don't love them; why should you force your feelings? Can you call them a family? Nonentities! If they died today, no one would notice their absence tomorrow."

Katya despises my wife and Liza as much as they hate her. One can hardly talk at this date of people's having a right to despise one another. But if one looks at it from Katya's standpoint and recognizes such a right, one can see she has as much right to despise my wife and Liza as they have to hate her.

"Nonentities," she goes on. "Have you had dinner today? How was it they did not forget to tell you it was ready? How is it they still remember your existence?"

"Katya," I say sternly, "I beg you to be silent."

"You think I enjoy talking about them? I should be glad not to know them at all. Listen, my dear: give it all up and go away. Go abroad. The sooner the better."

"What nonsense! What about the University?"

"The University, too. What is it to you? There's no sense in it, anyway. You have been lecturing for thirty years, and where are your pupils? Are many of them celebrated scientific men? Count them up! And to multiply the doctors who exploit ignorance and pile up hundreds of thousands for themselves, there is no need to be a good and talented man. You are not wanted."

"Good heavens! how harsh you are!" I cry in horror. "How harsh you are! Be quiet or I will go away! I don't know how to answer the harsh things you say!"

The maid comes in and summons us to tea. At the samovar our conversation, thank God, changes. After having had my grumble out, I have a longing to give way to another weakness of old age, reminiscences. I tell Katya about my past, and to my great astonishment tell her incidents which, till then, I did not suspect of being still preserved in my memory, and she listens to me with tenderness, with pride, holding her breath. I am particularly fond of telling her how I was educated in a seminary and dreamed of going to the University.

"At times I used to walk about our seminary garden . . ." I would tell her. "If from some far-away tavern the wind floated sounds of a song and the squeaking of an accordion, or a sledge with bells dashed by the garden-fence, it was quite enough to send a rush of happiness, filling not only my heart, but even my stomach, my legs, my arms. . . . I would listen to the accordion or the bells dying away in the distance and imagine myself a doctor, and paint pictures, one better than another. And here, as you see, my dreams have come true. I have had more than I dared to dream of. For thirty years I have been the favourite professor, I have had splendid comrades, I have enjoyed fame and honour. I have loved, married from passionate love, have had children. In fact, looking back upon it, I see my whole life as a fine composition arranged with talent. Now all that is left to me is not to spoil the end. For that I must die like a man. If death is really a thing to dread, I must meet it as a teacher, a man of science, and a citizen of a Christian country ought to meet it, with courage and untroubled soul. But I am spoiling the end; I am sinking, I fly to you, I beg for help, and you tell me 'Sink; that is what you ought to do.' "

But here there comes a ring at the front-door. Katya and I recognize it, and say:

"It must be Mihail Fyodorovitch."

And a minute later my colleague, the philologist Mihail Fyodorovitch, a tall, well-built man of fifty, clean-shaven, with thick grey hair and black eyebrows, walks in. He is a good-natured man and an excellent comrade. He comes of a fortunate and talented old noble family which has played a prominent part in the history of literature and enlightenment. He is himself intelligent, talented, and very highly educated, but has his oddities. To a certain extent we are all odd and all queer fish, but in his oddities there is something exceptional, apt to cause anxiety among his acquaintances. I know a good many people for whom his oddities completely obscure his good qualities.

Coming in to us, he slowly takes off his gloves and says in his velvety bass:

"Good-evening. Are you having tea? That's just right. It's diabolically cold."

Then he sits down to the table, takes a glass, and at once begins talking. What is most characteristic in his manner of talking is the continually jesting tone, a sort of mixture of philosophy and drollery as in Shakespeare's gravediggers. He is always talking about serious things, but he never speaks seriously. His judgments are always harsh and railing, but, thanks to his soft, even, jesting tone, the harshness and abuse do not jar upon the ear, and one soon grows used to them. Every evening he brings with him five or six anecdotes from the University, and he usually begins with them when he sits down to table.

"Oh, Lord!" he sighs, twitching his black eyebrows ironically. "What comic people there are in the world!"

"Well?" asks Katya.

"As I was coming from my lecture this morning I met that old idiot N. N—— on the stairs. . . . He was going along as usual, sticking out his chin like a horse, looking for some one to listen to his grumblings at his migraine, at his wife, and his students who won't attend his lectures. 'Oh,' I thought, 'he has seen me—I am done for now; it is all up. . . .' "

And so on in the same style. Or he will begin like this:

"I was yesterday at our friend Z. Z——'s public lecture. I wonder how it is our alma mater—don't speak of it after dark—dare display in public such noodles and patent dullards as that Z. Z——. Why, he is a European fool! Upon my word, you could not find another like him all over Europe! He lectures—can you imagine?—as though he were sucking a sugar-stick—sue, sue, sue; . . . he is in a nervous funk; he can hardly decipher his own manuscript; his poor little thoughts crawl along like a bishop on a bicycle, and, what's worse, you can never make out what he is trying to say. The deadly dulness is awful, the very flies expire. It can only be compared with the boredom in the assembly-hall at the yearly meeting when the traditional address is read—damn it!"

And at once an abrupt transition:

"Three years ago—Nikolay Stepanovitch here will remember it—I had to deliver that address. It was hot, stifling, my uniform cut me under the arms—it was deadly! I read for half an hour, for an hour, for an hour and a half, for two hours. . . . 'Come,' I thought; 'thank God, there are only ten pages left!' And at the end there were four pages that there was no need to read, and I reckoned to leave them out. 'So there are only six really,' I thought; 'that is, only six pages left to read.' But, only fancy, I chanced to glance before me, and, sitting in the front row, side by side, were a general with a ribbon on his breast and a bishop. The poor beggars were numb with boredom; they were staring with their eyes wide open to keep awake, and yet they were trying to put on an expression of attention and to pretend that they understood what I was saying and liked it. 'Well,' I thought, 'since you like it you shall have it! I'll pay you out;' so I just gave them those four pages too."

As is usual with ironical people, when he talks nothing in his face smiles but his eyes and eyebrows. At such times there is no trace of hatred or spite in his eyes, but a great deal of humour, and that peculiar fox-like slyness which is only to be noticed in very observant people. Since I am speaking about his eyes, I notice another peculiarity in them. When he takes a glass from Katya, or listens to her speaking, or looks after her as she goes out of the room for a moment, I notice in his eyes something gentle, beseeching, pure. . . .

The maid-servant takes away the samovar and puts on the table a large piece of cheese, some fruit, and a bottle of Crimean champagne—a rather poor wine of which Katya had grown fond in the Crimea. Mihail Fyodorovitch takes two packs of cards off the whatnot and begins to play patience. According to him, some varieties of patience require great concentration and attention, yet while he lays out the cards he does not leave off distracting his attention with talk. Katya watches his cards attentively, and more by gesture than by words helps him in his play. She drinks no more than a couple of wine-glasses of wine the whole evening; I drink four glasses, and the rest of the bottle falls to the share of Mihail Fyodorovitch, who can drink a great deal and never get drunk.

Over our patience we settle various questions, principally of the higher order, and what we care for most of all—that is, science and learning—is more roughly handled than anything.

"Science, thank God, has outlived its day," says Mihail Fyodorovitch emphatically. "Its song is sung. Yes, indeed. Mankind begins to feel impelled to replace it by something different. It has grown on the soil of superstition, been nourished by superstition, and is now just as much the quintessence of superstition as its defunct granddames, alchemy, metaphysics, and philosophy. And, after all, what has it given to mankind? Why, the difference between the learned Europeans and the Chinese who have no science is trifling, purely external. The Chinese know nothing of science, but what have they lost thereby?"

"Flies know nothing of science, either," I observe, "but what of that?"

"There is no need to be angry, Nikolay Stepanovitch. I only say this here between ourselves.... I am more careful than you think, and I am not going to say this in public—God forbid! The superstition exists in the multitude that the arts and sciences are superior to agriculture, commerce, superior to handicrafts. Our sect is maintained by that superstition, and it is not for you and me to destroy it. God forbid!"

After patience the younger generation comes in for a dressing too.

"Our audiences have degenerated," sighs Mihail Fyodorovitch. "Not to speak of ideals and all the rest of it, if only they were capable of work and rational thought! In fact, it's a case of 'I look with mournful eyes on the young men of today.' "

"Yes; they have degenerated horribly," Katya agrees. "Tell me, have you had one man of distinction among them for the last five or ten years?"

"I don't know how it is with the other professors, but I can't remember any among mine."

"I have seen in my day many of your students and young scientific men and many actors—well, I have never once been so fortunate as to meet—I won't say a hero or a man of talent, but even an interesting man. It's all the same grey mediocrity, puffed up with self-conceit."

All this talk of degeneration always affects me as though I had accidentally overheard offensive talk about my own daughter. It offends me that these charges are wholesale, and rest on such worn-out commonplaces, on such wordy vapourings as degeneration and absence of ideals, or on references to the splendours of the past. Every accusation, even if it is uttered in ladies' society, ought to be formulated with all possible definiteness, or it is not an accusation, but idle disparagement, unworthy of decent people.

I am an old man, I have been lecturing for thirty years, but I notice neither degeneration nor lack of ideals, and I don't find that the present is worse than the past. My porter Nikolay, whose experience of this subject has its value, says that the students of today are neither better nor worse than those of the past.

If I were asked what I don't like in my pupils of today, I should answer the question, not straight off and not at length, but with sufficient definiteness. I know their failings, and so have no need to resort to vague generalities. I don't like their smoking, using spirituous beverages, marrying late, and often being so irresponsible and careless that they will let one of their number be starving in their midst while they neglect to pay their subscriptions to the Students' Aid Society. They don't know modern languages, and they don't express themselves correctly in Russian; no longer ago than yesterday my colleague, the professor of hygiene, complained to me that he had to give twice as many lectures, because the students had a very poor knowledge of physics and were utterly ignorant of meteorology. They are readily carried away by the influence of the last new writers, even when they are not first-rate, but they take absolutely no interest in classics such as Shakespeare, Marcus Aurelius, Epictetus, or Pascal, and this inability to distinguish the great from the small betrays their ignorance of practical life more than anything. All difficult questions that have more or less a social character (for instance the migration question) they settle by studying monographs on the subject, but not by way of scientific investigation or experiment, though that method is at their disposal and is more in keeping with their calling. They gladly become ward-surgeons, assistants, demonstrators, external teachers, and are ready to fill such posts until they are forty, though independence, a sense of freedom and personal initiative, are no less necessary in science than, for instance, in art or commerce. I have pupils and listeners, but no successors and helpers, and so I love them and am touched by them, but am not proud of them. And so on, and so on....

Such shortcomings, however numerous they may be, can only give rise to a pessimistic or fault-finding temper in a faint-hearted and timid man. All these failings have a casual, transitory character, and are completely dependent on conditions of life; in some ten years they will have disappeared or given place to other fresh defects, which are all inevitable and will in their turn alarm the faint-hearted. The students' sins often vex me, but that vexation is nothing in comparison with the joy I have been experiencing now for the last thirty years when I talk to my pupils, lecture to them, watch their relations, and compare them with people not of their circle.

Mihail Fyodorovitch speaks evil of everything. Katya listens, and neither of them notices into what depths the apparently innocent diversion of finding fault with their neighbours is gradually drawing them. They are not conscious how by degrees simple talk passes into malicious mockery and jeering, and how they are both beginning to drop into the habits and methods of slander.

"Killing types one meets with," says Mihail Fyodorovitch. "I went yesterday to our friend Yegor Petrovitch's, and there I found a studious gentleman, one of your medicals in his third year, I believe. Such a face! . . . in the Dobrolubov style, the imprint of profound thought on his brow; we got into talk. 'Such doings, young man,' said I. 'I've read,' said I, 'that some German—I've forgotten his name—has created from the human brain a new kind of alkaloid, idiotine.' What do you think? He believed it, and there was positively an expression of respect on his face, as though to say, 'See what we fellows can do!' And the other day I went to the theatre. I took my seat. In the next row directly in front of me were sitting two men: one of 'us fellows' and apparently a law student, the other a shaggy-looking figure, a medical student. The latter was as drunk as a cobbler. He did not look at the stage at all. He was dozing with his nose on his shirt-front. But as soon as an actor begins loudly reciting a monologue, or simply raises his voice, our friend starts, pokes his neighbour in the ribs, and asks, 'What is he saying? Is it elevating?' 'Yes,' answers one of our fellows. "B-r-r-ravo!' roars the medical student. 'Elevating! Bravo!' He had gone to the theatre, you see, the drunken blockhead, not for the sake of art, the play, but for elevation! He wanted noble sentiments."

Katya listens and laughs. She has a strange laugh; she catches her breath in rhythmically regular gasps, very much as though she were playing the accordion, and nothing in her face is laughing but her nostrils. I grow depressed and don't know what to say. Beside myself, I fire up, leap up from my seat, and cry:

"Do leave off! Why are you sitting here like two toads, poisoning the air with your breath? Give over!"

And without waiting for them to finish their gossip I prepare to go home. And, indeed, it is high time: it is past ten.

"I will stay a little longer," says Mihail Fyodorovitch. "Will you allow me, Ekaterina Vladimirovna?"

"I will," answers Katya.

"*Bene*! In that case have up another little bottle."

They both accompany me with candles to the hall, and while I put on my fur coat, Mihail Fyodorovitch says:

"You have grown dreadfully thin and older looking, Nikolay Stepanovitch. What's the matter with you? Are you ill?"

"Yes; I am not very well."

"And you are not doing anything for it . . ." Katya puts in grimly.

"Why don't you? You can't go on like that! God helps those who help themselves, my dear fellow. Remember me to your wife and daughter, and make my apologies for not having been to see them. In a day or two, before I go abroad, I shall come to say good-bye. I shall be sure to. I am going away next week."

I come away from Katya, irritated and alarmed by what has been said about my being ill, and dissatisfied with myself. I ask myself whether I really ought not to consult one of my colleagues. And at once I imagine how my colleague, after listening to me, would walk away to the window without speaking, would think a moment, then would turn round to me and, trying to prevent my reading the truth in his face, would say in a careless tone: "So far I see nothing serious, but at the same time, *collega,* I advise you to lay aside your work. . . ." And that would deprive me of my last hope.

Who is without hope? Now that I am diagnosing my illness and prescribing for myself, from time to time I hope that I am deceived by my own illness, that I am mistaken in regard to the albumen and the sugar I find, and in regard to my heart, and in regard to the swellings I have twice noticed in the mornings; when with the fervour of the hypochondriac I look through the textbooks of therapeutics and take a different medicine every day, I keep fancying that I shall hit upon something comforting. All that is petty.

Whether the sky is covered with clouds or the moon and the stars are shining, I turn my eyes towards it every evening and think that death is taking me soon. One would think that my thoughts at such times ought to be deep as the sky, brilliant, striking. . . . But no! I think about myself, about my wife, about Liza, Gnekker, the students, people in general; my thoughts are evil, petty, I am insincere with myself, and at such times my theory of life may be expressed in the words the celebrated Araktcheev said in one of his intimate letters: "Nothing good can exist in the world without evil, and there is more evil than good." That is, everything is disgusting; there is nothing to live for, and the sixty-two years I have already lived must be reckoned as wasted. I catch myself in these thoughts, and try to persuade myself that they are accidental, temporary, and not deeply rooted in me, but at once I think:

"If so, what drives me every evening to those two toads?"

And I vow to myself that I will never go to Katya's again, though I know I shall go next evening.

Ringing the bell at the door and going upstairs, I feel that I have no family now and no desire to bring it back again. It is clear that the new Araktcheev thoughts are not casual, temporary visitors, but have possession of my whole being. With my conscience ill at ease, dejected, languid, hardly able to move my limbs, feeling as though tons were added to my weight, I get into bed and quickly drop asleep.

And then—insomnia!

IV

Summer comes on and life is changed.

One fine morning Liza comes in to me and says in a jesting tone:

"Come, your Excellency! We are ready."

My Excellency is conducted into the street, and seated in a cab. As I go along, having nothing to do, I read the signboards from right to left. The word "Traktir" reads "Ritkart"; that would just suit some baron's family: Baroness Ritkart. Farther on I drive through fields, by the graveyard, which makes absolutely no impression on me, though I shall soon lie in it; then I drive by forests and again by fields. There is nothing of interest. After two hours of driving, my Excellency is conducted into the lower storey of a summer villa and installed in a small, very cheerful little room with light blue hangings.

At night there is sleeplessness as before, but in the morning I do not put a good face upon it and listen to my wife, but lie in bed. I do not sleep, but lie in the drowsy, half-conscious condition in which you know you are not asleep, but dreaming. At midday I get up and from habit sit down at my table, but I do not work now; I amuse myself with French books in yellow covers, sent me by Katya. Of course, it would be more patriotic to read Russian authors, but I must confess I cherish no particular liking for them. With the exception of two or three of the older writers, all our literature of today strikes me as not being literature, but a special sort of home industry, which exists simply in order to be encouraged, though people do not readily make use of its products. The very best of these home products cannot be called remarkable and cannot be sincerely praised without qualification. I must say the same of all the literary novelties I have read during the last ten or fifteen years; not one of them is remarkable, and not one of them can be praised without a "but." Cleverness, a good tone, but no talent; talent, a good tone, but no cleverness; or talent, cleverness, but not a good tone.

I don't say the French books have talent, cleverness, and a good tone. They don't satisfy me, either. But they are not so tedious as the Russian, and it is not unusual to find in them the chief element of artistic creation—the feeling of personal freedom which is lacking in the Russian authors. I don't remember one new book in which the author does not try from the first page to entangle himself in all sorts of conditions and contracts with his conscience. One is afraid to speak of the naked body; another ties himself up hand and foot in psychological analysis; a third must have a "warm attitude to man"; a fourth purposely scrawls whole descriptions of nature that he may not be suspected of writing with a purpose. . . . One is bent upon being middleclass in his work, another must be a nobleman, and so on. There is intentionalness, circumspection, and self-will, but they have neither the independence nor the manliness to write as they like, and therefore there is no creativeness.

All this applies to what is called belles-lettres.

As for serious treatises in Russian on sociology, for instance, on art, and so on, I do not read them simply from timidity. In my childhood and early youth I had for some reason a terror of doorkeepers and attendants at the theatre, and that terror has remained with me to this day. I am afraid of them even now. It is said that we are only afraid of what we do not understand. And, indeed, it is very difficult to understand why doorkeepers and theatre attendants are so dignified, haughty, and majestically rude. I feel exactly the same terror when I read serious articles. Their extraordinary dignity, their bantering lordly tone, their familiar manner to foreign authors, their ability to split straws with dignity—all that is beyond my understanding; it is intimidating and utterly unlike the quiet, gentlemanly tone to which I am accustomed when I read the works of our medical and scientific writers. It oppresses me to read not only the articles written by serious Russians, but even works translated or edited by them. The pretentious, edifying tone of the preface; the redundancy of remarks made by the translator, which prevent me from concentrating my attention; the question marks and "sic" in parenthesis scattered all over the book or article by the liberal translator, are to my mind an outrage on the author and on my independence as a reader.

Once I was summoned as an expert to a circuit court; in an interval one of my fellow-experts drew my attention to the rudeness of the public prosecutor to the defendants, among whom there were two ladies of good education. I believe I did not exaggerate at all when I told him that the prosecutor's manner was no ruder than that of the authors of serious articles to one another. Their manners are, indeed, so rude that I cannot speak of them without distaste. They treat one another and the writers they criticize either with superfluous respect, at the sacrifice of their own dignity, or, on the contrary, with far more ruthlessness than I have shown in my notes and my thoughts in regard to my future son-in-law Gnekker. Accusations of irrationality, of evil intentions, and, indeed, of every sort of crime, form an habitual ornament of serious articles. And that, as young medical men are fond of saying in their monographs, is the *ultima ratio*! Such ways must infallibly have an effect on the morals of the younger generation of writers, and so I am not at all surprised that in the new works with which our literature has been enriched during the last ten or fifteen years the heroes drink too much vodka and the heroines are not over-chaste.

I read French books, and I look out of the window which is open; I can see the spikes of my garden-fence, two or three scraggy trees, and beyond the fence the road, the fields, and beyond them a broad stretch of pine-wood. Often I admire a boy and girl, both flaxen-headed and ragged, who clamber on the fence and laugh at my baldness. In their shining little eyes I read, "Go up, go up, thou baldhead!" They are almost the only people who care nothing for my celebrity or my rank.

Visitors do not come to me every day now. I will only mention the visits of Nikolay and Pyotr Ignatyevitch. Nikolay usually comes to me on holidays, with some pretext of business, though really to see me. He arrives very much exhilarated, a thing which never occurs to him in the winter.

"What have you to tell me?" I ask, going out to him in the hall.

"Your Excellency!" he says, pressing his hand to his heart and looking at me with the ecstasy of a lover—"your Excellency! God be my witness! Strike me dead on the spot! *Gaudeamus egitur juventus*!"

And he greedily kisses me on the shoulder, on the sleeve, and on the buttons.

"Is everything going well?" I ask him.

"Your Excellency! So help me God! . . ."

He persists in grovelling before me for no sort of reason, and soon bores me, so I send him away to the kitchen, where they give him dinner.

Pyotr Ignatyevitch comes to see me on holidays, too, with the special object of seeing me and sharing his thoughts with me. He usually sits down near my table, modest, neat, and reasonable, and does not venture to cross his legs or put his elbows on the table. All the time, in a soft, even, little voice, in rounded bookish phrases, he tells me various, to his mind, very interesting and piquant items of news which he has read in the magazines and journals. They are all alike and may be reduced to this type: "A Frenchman has made a discovery; some one else, a German, has denounced him, proving that the discovery was made in 1870 by some American; while a third person, also a German, trumps them both by proving they both had made fools of themselves, mistaking bubbles of air for dark pigment under the microscope." Even when he wants to amuse me, Pyotr Ignatyevitch tells me things in the same lengthy, circumstantial manner as though he were defending a thesis, enumerating in detail the literary sources from which he is deriving his narrative, doing his utmost to be accurate as to the date and number of the journals and the name of every one concerned, invariably mentioning it in full—Jean Jacques Petit, never simply Petit. Sometimes he stays to dinner with us, and then during the whole of dinner-time he goes on telling me the same sort of piquant anecdotes, reducing every one at table to a state of dejected boredom. If Gnekker and Liza begin talking before him of fugues and counterpoint, Brahms and Bach, he drops his eyes modestly, and is overcome with embarrassment; he is ashamed that such trivial subjects should be discussed before such serious people as him and me.

In my present state of mind five minutes of him is enough to sicken me as though I had been seeing and hearing him for an eternity. I hate the poor fellow. His soft, smooth voice and bookish language exhaust me, and his stories stupefy me.... He cherishes the best of feelings for me, and talks to me simply in order to give me pleasure, and I repay him by looking at him as though I wanted to hypnotize him, and think, "Go, go, go!..." But he is not amenable to thought-suggestion, and sits on and on and on....

While he is with me I can never shake off the thought, "It's possible when I die he will be appointed to succeed me," and my poor lecture-hall presents itself to me as an oasis in which the spring is dried up; and I am ungracious, silent, and surly with Pyotr Ignatyevitch, as though he were to blame for such thoughts, and not I myself. When he begins, as usual, praising up the German savants, instead of making fun of him good-humouredly, as I used to do, I mutter sullenly:

"Asses, your Germans! . . ."

That is like the late Professor Nikita Krylov, who once, when he was bathing with Pirogov at Revel and vexed at the water's being very cold, burst out with, "Scoundrels, these Germans!" I behave badly with Pyotr Ignatyevitch, and only when he is going away, and from the window I catch a glimpse of his grey hat behind the garden-fence, I want to call out and say, "Forgive me, my dear fellow!"

Dinner is even drearier than in the winter. Gnekker, whom now I hate and despise, dines with us almost every day. I used to endure his presence in silence, now I aim biting remarks at him which make my wife and daughter blush. Carried away by evil feeling, I often say things that are simply stupid, and I don't know why I say them. So on one occasion it happened that I stared a long time at Gnekker, and, *à propos* of nothing, I fired off:

"An eagle may perchance swoop down below a cock,
But never will the fowl soar upwards to the clouds. . . ."

And the most vexatious thing is that the fowl Gnekker shows himself much cleverer than the eagle professor. Knowing that my wife and daughter are on his side, he takes up the line of meeting my gibes with condescending silence, as though to say:

"The old chap is in his dotage; what's the use of talking to him?"

Or he makes fun of me good-naturedly. It is wonderful how petty a man may become! I am capable of dreaming all dinner-time of how Gnekker will turn out to be an adventurer, how my wife and Liza will come to see their mistake, and how I will taunt them—and such absurd thoughts at the time when I am standing with one foot in the grave!

There are now, too, misunderstandings of which in the old days I had no idea except from hearsay. Though I am ashamed of it, I will describe one that occurred the other day after dinner.

I was sitting in my room smoking a pipe; my wife came in as usual, sat down, and began saying what a good thing it would be for me to go to Harkov now while it is warm and I have free time, and there find out what sort of person our Gnekker is.

"Very good; I will go," I assented.

My wife, pleased with me, got up and was going to the door, but turned back and said:

"By the way, I have another favour to ask of you. I know you will be angry, but it is my duty to warn you. . . . Forgive my saying it, Nikolay Stepanovitch, but all our neighbours and acquaintances have begun talking about your being so often at Katya's. She is clever and well-educated; I don't deny that her company may be agreeable; but at your age and with your social position it seems strange that you should find pleasure in her society. . . . Besides, she has such a reputation that . . ."

All the blood suddenly rushed to my brain, my eyes flashed fire, I leaped up and, clutching at my head and stamping my feet, shouted in a voice unlike my own:

"Let me alone! let me alone! let me alone!"

Probably my face was terrible, my voice was strange, for my wife suddenly turned pale and began shrieking aloud in a despairing voice that was utterly unlike her own. Liza, Gnekker, then Yegor, came running in at our shouts. . . .

"Let me alone!" I cried; "let me alone! Go away!"

My legs turned numb as though they had ceased to exist; I felt myself falling into some one's arms; for a little while I still heard weeping, then sank into a swoon which lasted two or three hours.

Now about Katya; she comes to see me every day towards evening, and of course neither the neighbours nor our acquaintances can avoid noticing it. She comes in for a minute and carries me off for a drive with her. She has her own horse and a new chaise bought this summer. Altogether she lives in an expensive style; she has taken a big detached villa with a large garden, and has taken all her town retinue with her—two maids, a coachman . . . I often ask her:

"Katya, what will you live on when you have spent your father's money?"

"Then we shall see," she answers.

"That money, my dear, deserves to be treated more seriously. It was earned by a good man, by honest labour."

"You have told me that already. I know it."

At first we drive through the open country, then through the pinewood which is visible from my window. Nature seems to me as beautiful as it always has been, though some evil spirit whispers to me that these pines and fir trees, birds, and white clouds on the sky, will not notice my absence when in three or four months I am dead. Katya loves driving, and she is pleased that it is fine weather and that I am sitting beside her. She is in good spirits and does not say harsh things.

"You are a very good man, Nikolay Stepanovitch," she says. "You are a rare specimen, and there isn't an actor who would understand how to play you. Me or Mihail Fyodorovitch, for instance, any poor actor could do, but not you. And I envy you, I envy you horribly! Do you know what I stand for? What?"

She ponders for a minute, and then asks me:

"Nikolay Stepanovitch, I am a negative phenomenon! Yes?"

"Yes," I answer.

"H'm! what am I to do?"

What answer was I to make her? It is easy to say "work," or "give your possessions to the poor," or "know yourself," and because it is so easy to say that, I don't know what to answer.

My colleagues when they teach therapeutics advise "the individual study of each separate case." One has but to obey this advice to gain the conviction that the methods recommended in the textbooks as the best and as providing a safe basis for treatment turn out to be quite unsuitable in individual cases. It is just the same in moral ailments.

But I must make some answer, and I say:

"You have too much free time, my dear; you absolutely must take up some occupation. After all, why shouldn't you be an actress again if it is your vocation?"

"I cannot!"

"Your tone and manner suggest that you are a victim. I don't like that, my dear; it is your own fault. Remember, you began with falling out with people and methods, but you have done nothing to make either better. You did not struggle with evil, but were cast down by it, and you are not the victim of the struggle, but of your own impotence. Well, of course you were young and inexperienced then; now it may all be different. Yes, really, go on the stage. You will work, you will serve a sacred art."

"Don't pretend, Nikolay Stepanovitch," Katya interrupts me. "Let us make a compact once for all; we will talk about actors, actresses, and authors, but we will let art alone. You are a splendid and rare person, but you don't know enough about art sincerely to think it sacred. You have no instinct or feeling for art. You have been hard at work all your life, and have not had time to acquire that feeling. Altogether . . . I don't like talk about art," she goes on nervously. "I don't like it! And, my goodness, how they have vulgarized it!"

"Who has vulgarized it?"

"They have vulgarized it by drunkenness, the newspapers by their familiar attitude, clever people by philosophy."

"Philosophy has nothing to do with it."

"Yes, it has. If any one philosophizes about it, it shows he does not understand it."

To avoid bitterness I hasten to change the subject, and then sit a long time silent. Only when we are driving out of the wood and turning towards Katya's villa I go back to my former question, and say:

"You have still not answered me, why you don't want to go on the stage."

"Nikolay Stepanovitch, this is cruel!" she cries, and suddenly flushes all over. "You want me to tell you the truth aloud? Very well, if . . . if you like it! I have no talent! No talent and . . . and a great deal of vanity! So there!"

After making this confession she turns her face away from me, and to hide the trembling of her hands tugs violently at the reins.

As we are driving towards her villa we see Mihail Fyodorovitch walking near the gate, impatiently awaiting us.

"That Mihail Fyodorovitch again!" says Katya with vexation. "Do rid me of him, please! I am sick and tired of him . . . bother him!"

Mihail Fyodorovitch ought to have gone abroad long ago, but he puts off going from week to week. Of late there have been certain changes in him. He looks, as it were, sunken, has taken to drinking until he is tipsy, a thing which never used to happen to him, and his black eyebrows are beginning to turn grey. When our chaise stops at the gate he does not conceal his joy and his impatience. He fussily helps me and Katya out, hurriedly asks questions, laughs, rubs his hands, and that gentle, imploring, pure expression, which I used to notice only in his eyes, is now suffused all over his face. He is glad and at the same time he is ashamed of his gladness, ashamed of his habit of spending every evening with Katya. And he thinks it necessary to explain his visit by some obvious absurdity such as: "I was driving by, and I thought I would just look in for a minute."

We all three go indoors; first we drink tea, then the familiar packs of cards, the big piece of cheese, the fruit, and the bottle of Crimean champagne are put upon the table. The subjects of our conversation are not new; they are just the same as in the winter. We fall foul of the University, the students, and literature and the theatre; the air grows thick and stifling with evil speaking, and poisoned by the breath, not of two toads as in the winter, but of three. Besides the velvety baritone laugh and the giggle like the gasp of a concertina, the maid who waits upon us hears an unpleasant cracked "He, he!" like the chuckle of a general in a vaudeville.

V

There are terrible nights with thunder, lightning, rain, and wind, such as are called among the people "sparrow nights." There has been one such night in my personal life. . . .

I woke up after midnight and leaped suddenly out of bed. It seemed to me for some reason that I was just immediately going to die. Why did it seem so? I had no sensation in my body that suggested my immediate death, but my soul was oppressed with terror, as though I had suddenly seen a vast menacing glow of fire.

I rapidly struck a light, drank some water straight out of the decanter, then hurried to the open window. The weather outside was magnificent. There was a smell of hay and some other very sweet scent. I could see the spikes of the fence, the gaunt, drowsy trees by the window, the road, the dark streak of woodland, there was a serene, very bright moon in the sky and not a single cloud, perfect stillness, not one leaf stirring. I felt that everything was looking at me and waiting for me to die. . . .

It was uncanny. I closed the window and ran to my bed. I felt for my pulse, and not finding it in my wrist, tried to find it in my temple, then in my chin, and again in my wrist, and everything I touched was cold and clammy with sweat. My breathing came more and more rapidly, my body was shivering, all my inside was in commotion; I had a sensation on my face and on my bald head as though they were covered with spiders' webs.

What should I do? Call my family? No; it would be no use. I could not imagine what my wife and Liza would do when they came in to me.

I hid my head under the pillow, closed my eyes, and waited and waited. . . . My spine was cold; it seemed to be drawn inwards, and I felt as though death were coming upon me stealthily from behind. . . .

"Kee-vee! kee-vee!" I heard a sudden shriek in the night's stillness, and did not know where it was—in my breast or in the street. "Kee-vee! kee-vee!"

"My God, how terrible!" I would have drunk some more water, but by then it was fearful to open my eyes and I was afraid to raise my head. I was possessed by unaccountable animal terror, and I cannot understand why I was so frightened: was it that I wanted to live, or that some new unknown pain was in store for me?

Upstairs, overhead, some one moaned or laughed. . . . I listened. Soon afterwards there was a sound of footsteps on the stairs. Some one came hurriedly down, then went up again. A minute later there was a sound of steps downstairs again; some one stopped near my door and listened.

"Who is there?" I cried.

The door opened. I boldly opened my eyes, and saw my wife. Her face was pale and her eyes were tear-stained.

"You are not asleep, Nikolay Stepanovitch?" she asked.

"What is it?"

"For God's sake, go up and have a look at Liza; there is something the matter with her. . . ."

"Very good, with pleasure," I muttered, greatly relieved at not being alone. "Very good, this minute. . . ."

I followed my wife, heard what she said to me, and was too agitated to understand a word. Patches of light from her candle danced about the stairs, our long shadows trembled. My feet caught in the skirts of my dressing-gown; I gasped for breath, and felt as though something were pursuing me and trying to catch me from behind.

"I shall die on the spot, here on the staircase," I thought. "On the spot. . . ." But we passed the staircase, the dark corridor with the Italian windows, and went into Liza's room. She was sitting on the bed in her nightdress, with her bare feet hanging down, and she was moaning.

"Oh, my God! Oh, my God!" she was muttering, screwing up her eyes at our candle. "I can't bear it."

"Liza, my child," I said, "what is it?"

Seeing me, she began crying out, and flung herself on my neck.

"My kind papa! . . ." she sobbed—"my dear, good papa . . . my darling, my pet, I don't know what is the matter with me. . . . I am miserable!"

She hugged me, kissed me, and babbled fond words I used to hear from her when she was a child.

"Calm yourself, my child. God be with you," I said. "There is no need to cry. I am miserable, too."

I tried to tuck her in; my wife gave her water, and we awkwardly stumbled by her bedside; my shoulder jostled against her shoulder, and meanwhile I was thinking how we used to give our children their bath together.

"Help her! help her!" my wife implored me. "Do something!"

What could I do? I could do nothing. There was some load on the girl's heart; but I did not understand, I knew nothing about it, and could only mutter:

"It's nothing, it's nothing; it will pass. Sleep, sleep!"

To make things worse, there was a sudden sound of dogs howling, at first subdued and uncertain, then loud, two dogs howling together. I had never attached significance to such omens as the howling of dogs or the shrieking of owls, but on that occasion it sent a pang to my heart, and I hastened to explain the howl to myself.

"It's nonsense," I thought, "the influence of one organism on another. The intensely strained condition of my nerves has infected my wife, Liza, the dog—that is all. . . . Such infection explains presentiments, forebodings. . . ."

When a little later I went back to my room to write a prescription for Liza, I no longer thought I should die at once, but only had such a weight, such a feeling of oppression in my soul that I felt actually sorry that I had not died on the spot. For a long time I stood motionless in the middle of the room, pondering what to prescribe for Liza. But the moans overhead ceased, and I decided to prescribe nothing, and yet I went on standing there. . . .

There was a deathlike stillness, such a stillness, as some author has expressed it, "it rang in one's ears." Time passed slowly; the streaks of moonlight on the window-sill did not shift their position, but seemed as though frozen. . . . It was still some time before dawn.

But the gate in the fence creaked, some one stole in and, breaking a twig from one of those scraggy trees, cautiously tapped on the window with it.

"Nikolay Stepanovitch," I heard a whisper. "Nikolay Stepanovitch."

I opened the window, and fancied I was dreaming: under the window, huddled against the wall, stood a woman in a black dress, with the moonlight bright upon her, looking at me with great eyes. Her face was pale, stern, and weird-looking in the moonlight, like marble, her chin was quivering.

"It is I," she said—"I . . . Katya."

In the moonlight all women's eyes look big and black, all people look taller and paler, and that was probably why I had not recognized her for the first minute.

"What is it?"

"Forgive me!" she said. "I suddenly felt unbearably miserable . . . I couldn't stand it, so came here. There was a light in your window and . . . and I ventured to knock. . . . I beg your pardon. . . . Ah! if you knew how miserable I am! What are you doing just now?"

"Nothing. . . . I can't sleep."

"I had a feeling that there was something wrong, but that is nonsense."

Her brows were lifted, her eyes shone with tears, and her whole face was lighted up with the familiar look of trustfulness which I had not seen for so long.

"Nikolay Stepanovitch," she said imploringly, stretching out both hands to me, "my precious friend, I beg you, I implore you.... If you don't despise my affection and respect for you, consent to what I ask of you."

"What is it?"

"Take my money from me!"

"Come! what an idea! What do I want with your money?"

"You'll go away somewhere for your health.... You ought to go for your health. Will you take it? Yes? Nikolay Stepanovitch darling, yes?"

She looked greedily into my face and repeated: "Yes, you will take it?"

"No, my dear, I won't take it . . ." I said. "Thank you."

She turned her back upon me and bowed her head. Probably I refused her in a tone which made further conversation about money impossible.

"Go home to bed," I said. "We will see each other tomorrow."

"So you don't consider me your friend?" she asked dejectedly.

"I don't say that. But your money would be no use to me now."

"I beg your pardon . . ." she said, dropping her voice a whole octave. "I understand you . . . to be indebted to a person like me . . . a retired actress.... But, good-bye...."

And she went away so quickly that I had not time even to say good-bye.

VI

I am in Harkov.

As it would be useless to contend against my present mood and, indeed, beyond my power, I have made up my mind that the last days of my life shall at least be irreproachable externally. If I am unjust in regard to my wife and daughter, which I fully recognize, I will try and do as she wishes; since she wants me to go to Harkov, I go to Harkov. Besides, I have become of late so indifferent to everything that it is really all the same to me where I go, to Harkov, or to Paris, or to Berditchev.

I arrived here at midday, and have put up at the hotel not far from the cathedral. The train was jolting, there were draughts, and now I am sitting on my bed, holding my head and expecting tic douloureux. I ought to have gone today to see some professors of my acquaintance, but I have neither strength nor inclination.

The old corridor attendant comes in and asks whether I have brought my bed-linen. I detain him for five minutes, and put several questions to him about Gnekker, on whose account I have come here. The attendant turns out to be a native of Harkov; he knows the town like the fingers of his hand, but does not remember any household of the surname of Gnekker. I question him about the estate—the same answer.

The clock in the corridor strikes one, then two, then three. . . . These last months in which I am waiting for death seem much longer than the whole of my life. And I have never before been so ready to resign myself to the slowness of time as now. In the old days, when one sat in the station and waited for a train, or presided in an examination-room, a quarter of an hour would seem an eternity. Now I can sit all night on my bed without moving, and quite unconcernedly reflect that tomorrow will be followed by another night as long and colourless, and the day after tomorrow.

In the corridor it strikes five, six, seven. . . . It grows dark.

There is a dull pain in my cheek, the tic beginning. To occupy myself with thoughts, I go back to my old point of view, when I was not so indifferent, and ask myself why I, a distinguished man, a privy councillor, am sitting in this little hotel room, on this bed with the unfamiliar grey quilt. Why am I looking at that cheap tin washing-stand and listening to the whirr of the wretched clock in the corridor? Is all this in keeping with my fame and my lofty position? And I answer these questions with a jeer. I am amused by the naïveté with which I used in my youth to exaggerate the value of renown and of the exceptional position which celebrities are supposed to enjoy. I am famous, my name is pronounced with reverence, my portrait has been both in the *Niva* and in the *Illustrated News of the World;* I have read my biography even in a German magazine. And what of all that? Here I am sitting utterly alone in a strange town, on a strange bed, rubbing my aching cheek with my hand. . . . Domestic worries, the hard-heartedness of creditors, the rudeness of the railway servants, the inconveniences of the passport system, the expensive and unwholesome food in the refreshment-rooms, the general rudeness and coarseness in social intercourse—all this, and a great deal more which would take too long to reckon up, affects me as much as any working man who is famous only in his alley. In what way does my exceptional position find expression? Admitting that I am celebrated a thousand times over, that I am a hero of whom my country is proud. They publish bulletins of my illness in every paper, letters of sympathy come to me by post from my colleagues, my pupils, the general public; but all that does not prevent me from dying in a strange bed, in misery, in utter loneliness. Of course, no one is to blame for that; but I in my foolishness dislike my popularity. I feel as though it had cheated me.

At ten o'clock I fall asleep, and in spite of the tic I sleep soundly, and should have gone on sleeping if I had not been awakened. Soon after one came a sudden knock at the door.

"Who is there?"

"A telegram."

"You might have waited till tomorrow," I say angrily, taking the telegram from the attendant. "Now I shall not get to sleep again."

"I am sorry. Your light was burning, so I thought you were not asleep."

I tear open the telegram and look first at the signature. From my wife.

"What does she want?"

"Gnekker was secretly married to Liza yesterday. Return."

—

I read the telegram, and my dismay does not last long. I am dismayed, not by what Liza and Gnekker have done, but by the indifference with which I hear of their marriage. They say philosophers and the truly wise are indifferent. It is false: indifference is the paralysis of the soul; it is premature death.

I go to bed again, and begin trying to think of something to occupy my mind. What am I to think about? I feel as though everything had been thought over already and there is nothing which could hold my attention now.

When daylight comes I sit up in bed with my arms round my knees, and to pass the time I try to know myself. "Know thyself" is excellent and useful advice; it is only a pity that the ancients never thought to indicate the means of following this precept.

When I have wanted to understand somebody or myself I have considered, not the actions, in which everything is relative, but the desires.

"Tell me what you want, and I will tell you what manner of man you are."

And now I examine myself: what do I want?

I want our wives, our children, our friends, our pupils, to love in us, not our fame, not the brand and not the label, but to love us as ordinary men. Anything else? I should like to have had helpers and successors. Anything else? I should like to wake up in a hundred years' time and to have just a peep out of one eye at what is happening in science. I should have liked to have lived another ten years. . . . What further? Why, nothing further. I think and think, and can think of nothing more. And however much I might think, and however far my thoughts might travel, it is clear to me that there is nothing vital, nothing of great importance in my desires. In my passion for science, in my desire to live, in this sitting on a strange bed, and in this striving to know myself—in all the thoughts, feelings, and ideas I form about everything, there is no common bond to connect it all into one whole. Every feeling and every thought exists apart in me; and in all my criticisms of science, the theatre, literature, my pupils, and in all the pictures my imagination draws, even the most skilful analyst could not find what is called a general idea, or the god of a living man.

And if there is not that, then there is nothing.

In a state so poverty-stricken, a serious ailment, the fear of death, the influences of circumstance and men were enough to turn upside down and scatter in fragments all which I had once looked upon as my theory of life, and in which I had seen the meaning and joy of my existence. So there is nothing surprising in the fact that I have overshadowed the last months of my life with thoughts and feelings only worthy of a slave and barbarian, and that now I am indifferent and take no heed of the dawn. When a man has not in him what is loftier and mightier than all external impressions a bad cold is really enough to upset his equilibrium and make him begin to see an owl in every bird, to hear a dog howling in every sound. And all his pessimism or optimism with his thoughts great and small have at such times significance as symptoms and nothing more.

I am vanquished. If it is so, it is useless to think, it is useless to talk. I will sit and wait in silence for what is to come.

In the morning the corridor attendant brings me tea and a copy of the local newspaper. Mechanically I read the advertisements on the first page, the leading article, the extracts from the newspapers and journals, the chronicle of events. . . . In the latter I find, among other things, the following paragraph: "Our distinguished savant, Professor Nikolay Stepanovitch So-and-so, arrived yesterday in Harkov, and is staying in the So-and-so Hotel."

Apparently, illustrious names are created to live on their own account, apart from those that bear them. Now my name is promenading tranquilly about Harkov; in another three months, printed in gold letters on my monument, it will shine bright as the sun itself, while I shall be already under the moss.

A light tap at the door. Somebody wants me.

"Who is there? Come in."

The door opens, and I step back surprised and hurriedly wrap my dressing-gown round me. Before me stands Katya.

"How do you do?" she says, breathless with running upstairs. "You didn't expect me? I have come here, too. . . . I have come, too!"

She sits down and goes on, hesitating and not looking at me.

"Why don't you speak to me? I have come, too . . . today. . . . I found out that you were in this hotel, and have come to you."

"Very glad to see you," I say, shrugging my shoulders, "but I am surprised. You seem to have dropped from the skies. What have you come for?"

"Oh . . . I've simply come."

Silence. Suddenly she jumps up impulsively and comes to me.

"Nikolay Stepanovitch," she says, turning pale and pressing her hands on her bosom—"Nikolay Stepanovitch, I cannot go on living like this! I cannot! For God's sake tell me quickly, this minute, what I am to do! Tell me, what am I to do?"

"What can I tell you?" I ask in perplexity. "I can do nothing."

"Tell me, I beseech you," she goes on, breathing hard and trembling all over. "I swear that I cannot go on living like this. It's too much for me!"

She sinks on a chair and begins sobbing. She flings her head back, wrings her hands, taps with her feet; her hat falls off and hangs bobbing on its elastic; her hair is ruffled.

"Help me! help me!" she implores me. "I cannot go on!"

She takes her handkerchief out of her travelling-bag, and with it pulls out several letters, which fall from her lap to the floor. I pick them up, and on one of them I recognize the handwriting of Mihail Fyodorovitch and accidentally read a bit of a word "passionat . . ."

"There is nothing I can tell you, Katya," I say.

"Help me!" she sobs, clutching at my hand and kissing it. "You are my father, you know, my only friend! You are clever, educated; you have lived so long; you have been a teacher! Tell me, what am I to do?"

"Upon my word, Katya, I don't know. . . ."

I am utterly at a loss and confused, touched by her sobs, and hardly able to stand.

"Let us have lunch, Katya," I say, with a forced smile. "Give over crying."

And at once I add in a sinking voice:

"I shall soon be gone, Katya. . . ."

"Only one word, only one word!" she weeps, stretching out her hands to me.

"What am I to do?"

"You are a queer girl, really . . ." I mutter. "I don't understand it! So sensible, and all at once . . . crying your eyes out. . . ."

A silence follows. Katya straightens her hair, puts on her hat, then crumples up the letters and stuffs them in her bag—and all this deliberately, in silence. Her face, her bosom, and her gloves are wet with tears, but her expression now is cold and forbidding. . . . I look at her, and feel ashamed that I am happier than she. The absence of what my philosophic colleagues call a general idea I have detected in myself only just before death, in the decline of my days, while the soul of this poor girl has known and will know no refuge all her life, all her life!

"Let us have lunch, Katya," I say.

"No, thank you," she answers coldly.

Another minute passes in silence.

"I don't like Harkov," I say; "it's so grey here—such a grey town."

"Yes, perhaps. . . . It's ugly. I am here not for long, passing through. I am going on today."

"Where?"

"To the Crimea . . . that is, to the Caucasus."

"Oh! For long?"

"I don't know."

Katya gets up, and, with a cold smile, holds out her hand without looking at me.

I want to ask her, "Then, you won't be at my funeral?" but she does not look at me; her hand is cold and, as it were, strange. I escort her to the door in silence. She goes out, walks down the long corridor without looking back; she knows that I am looking after her, and most likely she will look back at the turn.

No, she did not look back. I've seen her black dress for the last time: her steps have died away. Farewell, my treasure!

The Darling

Olenka, the daughter of the retired collegiate assessor, Plemyanniakov, was sitting in her back porch, lost in thought. It was hot, the flies were persistent and teasing, and it was pleasant to reflect that it would soon be evening. Dark rainclouds were gathering from the east, and bringing from time to time a breath of moisture in the air.

Kukin, who was the manager of an open-air theatre called the Tivoli, and who lived in the lodge, was standing in the middle of the garden looking at the sky.

"Again!" he observed despairingly. "It's going to rain again! Rain every day, as though to spite me. I might as well hang myself! It's ruin! Fearful losses every day."

He flung up his hands, and went on, addressing Olenka:

"There! that's the life we lead, Olga Semyonovna. It's enough to make one cry. One works and does one's utmost; one wears oneself out, getting no sleep at night, and racks one's brain what to do for the best. And then what happens? To begin with, one's public is ignorant, boorish. I give them the very best operetta, a dainty masque, first rate music-hall artists. But do you suppose that's what they want! They don't understand anything of that sort. They want a clown; what they ask for is vulgarity. And then look at the weather! Almost every evening it rains. It started on the tenth of May, and it's kept it up all May and June. It's simply awful! The public doesn't come, but I've to pay the rent just the same, and pay the artists."

The next evening the clouds would gather again, and Kukin would say with an hysterical laugh:

"Well, rain away, then! Flood the garden, drown me! Damn my luck in this world and the next! Let the artists have me up! Send me to prison!—to Siberia!—the scaffold! Ha, ha, ha!"

And next day the same thing.

Olenka listened to Kukin with silent gravity, and sometimes tears came into her eyes. In the end his misfortunes touched her; she grew to love him. He was a small thin man, with a yellow face, and curls combed forward on his forehead. He spoke in a thin tenor; as he talked his mouth worked on one side, and there was always an expression of despair on his face; yet he aroused a deep and genuine affection in her. She was always fond of some one, and could not exist without loving. In earlier days she had loved her papa, who now sat in a darkened room, breathing with difficulty; she had loved her aunt who used to come every other year from Bryansk; and before that, when she was at school, she had loved her French master. She was a gentle, soft-hearted, compassionate girl, with mild, tender eyes and very good health. At the sight of her full rosy cheeks, her soft white neck with a little dark mole on it, and the kind, naïve smile, which came into her face when she listened to anything pleasant, men thought, "Yes, not half bad," and smiled too, while lady visitors could not refrain from seizing her hand in the middle of a conversation, exclaiming in a gush of delight, "You darling!"

The house in which she had lived from her birth upwards, and which was left her in her father's will, was at the extreme end of the town, not far from the Tivoli. In the evenings and at night she could hear the band playing, and the crackling and banging of fireworks, and it seemed to her that it was Kukin struggling with his destiny, storming the entrenchments of his chief foe, the indifferent public; there was a sweet thrill at her heart, she had no desire to sleep, and when he returned home at daybreak, she tapped softly at her bedroom window, and showing him only her face and one shoulder through the curtain, she gave him a friendly smile. . . .

He proposed to her, and they were married. And when he had a closer view of her neck and her plump, fine shoulders, he threw up his hands, and said:

"You darling!"

He was happy, but as it rained on the day and night of his wedding, his face still retained an expression of despair.

They got on very well together. She used to sit in his office, to look after things in the Tivoli, to put down the accounts and pay the wages. And her rosy cheeks, her sweet, naïve, radiant smile, were to be seen now at the office window, now in the refreshment bar or behind the scenes of the theatre. And already she used to say to her acquaintances that the theatre was the chief and most important thing in life, and that it was only through the drama that one could derive true enjoyment and become cultivated and humane.

"But do you suppose the public understands that?" she used to say. "What they want is a clown. Yesterday we gave 'Faust Inside Out,' and almost all the boxes were empty; but if Vanitchka and I had been producing some vulgar thing, I assure you the theatre would have been packed. Tomorrow Vanitchka and I are doing 'Orpheus in Hell.' Do come."

And what Kukin said about the theatre and the actors she repeated. Like him she despised the public for their ignorance and their indifference to art; she took part in the rehearsals, she corrected the actors, she kept an eye on the behaviour of the musicians, and when there was an unfavourable notice in the local paper, she shed tears, and then went to the editor's office to set things right.

The actors were fond of her and used to call her "Vanitchka and I," and "the darling"; she was sorry for them and used to lend them small sums of money, and if they deceived her, she used to shed a few tears in private, but did not complain to her husband.

They got on well in the winter too. They took the theatre in the town for the whole winter, and let it for short terms to a Little Russian company, or to a conjurer, or to a local dramatic society. Olenka grew stouter, and was always beaming with satisfaction, while Kukin grew thinner and yellower, and continually complained of their terrible losses, although he had not done badly all the winter. He used to cough at night, and she used to give him hot raspberry tea or lime-flower water, to rub him with eau-de-Cologne and to wrap him in her warm shawls.

"You're such a sweet pet!" she used to say with perfect sincerity, stroking his hair. "You're such a pretty dear!"

Towards Lent he went to Moscow to collect a new troupe, and without him she could not sleep, but sat all night at her window, looking at the stars, and she compared herself with the hens, who are awake all night and uneasy when the cock is not in the hen-house. Kukin was detained in Moscow, and wrote that he would be back at Easter, adding some instructions about the Tivoli. But on the Sunday before Easter, late in the evening, came a sudden ominous knock at the gate; some one was hammering on the gate as though on a barrel—boom, boom, boom! The drowsy cook went flopping with her bare feet through the puddles, as she ran to open the gate.

"Please open," said some one outside in a thick bass. "There is a telegram for you."

Olenka had received telegrams from her husband before, but this time for some reason she felt numb with terror. With shaking hands she opened the telegram and read as follows:

> "IVAN PETROVITCH DIED SUDDENLY TO-DAY. AWAITING IMMATE INSTRUCTIONS FUFUNERAL TUESDAY."

That was how it was written in the telegram—"fufuneral," and the utterly incomprehensible word "immate." It was signed by the stage manager of the operatic company.

"My darling!" sobbed Olenka. "Vanitchka, my precious, my darling! Why did I ever meet you! Why did I know you and love you! Your poor heart-broken Olenka is all alone without you!"

Kukin's funeral took place on Tuesday in Moscow, Olenka returned home on Wednesday, and as soon as she got indoors she threw herself on her bed and sobbed so loudly that it could be heard next door, and in the street.

"Poor darling!" the neighbours said, as they crossed themselves. "Olga Semyonovna, poor darling! How she does take on!"

Three months later Olenka was coming home from mass, melancholy and in deep mourning. It happened that one of her neighbours, Vassily Andreitch Pustovalov, returning home from church, walked back beside her. He was the manager at Babakayev's, the timber merchant's. He wore a straw hat, a white waistcoat, and a gold watch-chain, and looked more like a country gentleman than a man in trade.

"Everything happens as it is ordained, Olga Semyonovna," he said gravely, with a sympathetic note in his voice; "and if any of our dear ones die, it must be because it is the will of God, so we ought to have fortitude and bear it submissively."

After seeing Olenka to her gate, he said good-bye and went on. All day afterwards she heard his sedately dignified voice, and whenever she shut her eyes she saw his dark beard. She liked him very much. And apparently she had made an impression on him too, for not long afterwards an elderly lady, with whom she was only slightly acquainted, came to drink coffee with her, and as soon as she was seated at table began to talk about Pustovalov, saying that he was an excellent man whom one could thoroughly depend upon, and that any girl would be glad to marry him. Three days later Pustovalov came himself. He did not stay long, only about ten minutes, and he did not say much, but when he left, Olenka loved him—loved him so much that she lay awake all night in a perfect fever, and in the morning she sent for the elderly lady. The match was quickly arranged, and then came the wedding.

Pustovalov and Olenka got on very well together when they were married.

Usually he sat in the office till dinner-time, then he went out on business, while Olenka took his place, and sat in the office till evening, making up accounts and booking orders.

"Timber gets dearer every year; the price rises twenty per cent," she would say to her customers and friends. "Only fancy we used to sell local timber, and now Vassitchka always has to go for wood to the

Mogilev district. And the freight!" she would add, covering her cheeks with her hands in horror. "The freight!"

It seemed to her that she had been in the timber trade for ages and ages, and that the most important and necessary thing in life was timber; and there was something intimate and touching to her in the very sound of words such as "baulk," "post," "beam," "pole," "scantling," "batten," "lath," "plank," etc.

At night when she was asleep she dreamed of perfect mountains of planks and boards, and long strings of wagons, carting timber somewhere far away. She dreamed that a whole regiment of six-inch beams forty feet high, standing on end, was marching upon the timber-yard; that logs, beams, and boards knocked together with the resounding crash of dry wood, kept falling and getting up again, piling themselves on each other. Olenka cried out in her sleep, and Pustovalov said to her tenderly: "Olenka, what's the matter, darling? Cross yourself!"

Her husband's ideas were hers. If he thought the room was too hot, or that business was slack, she thought the same. Her husband did not care for entertainments, and on holidays he stayed at home. She did likewise.

"You are always at home or in the office," her friends said to her. "You should go to the theatre, darling, or to the circus."

"Vassitchka and I have no time to go to theatres," she would answer sedately. "We have no time for nonsense. What's the use of these theatres?"

On Saturdays Pustovalov and she used to go to the evening service; on holidays to early mass, and they walked side by side with softened faces as they came home from church. There was a pleasant fragrance about them both, and her silk dress rustled agreeably. At home they drank tea, with fancy bread and jams of various kinds, and afterwards they ate pie. Every day at twelve o'clock there was a savoury smell of beet-root soup and of mutton or duck in their yard, and on fast-days of fish, and no one could pass the gate without feeling hungry. In the office the samovar was always boiling, and customers were regaled with tea and cracknels. Once a week the couple went to the baths and returned side by side, both red in the face.

"Yes, we have nothing to complain of, thank God," Olenka used to say to her acquaintances. "I wish every one were as well off as Vassitchka and I."

When Pustovalov went away to buy wood in the Mogilev district, she missed him dreadfully, lay awake and cried. A young veterinary surgeon in the army, called Smirnin, to whom they had let their lodge, used sometimes to come in in the evening. He used to talk to her and play cards with her, and this entertained her in her husband's absence. She was particularly interested in what he told her of his home life. He was married and had a little boy, but was separated from his wife because she had been unfaithful to him, and now he hated her and used to send her forty roubles a month for the maintenance of their son. And hearing of all this, Olenka sighed and shook her head. She was sorry for him.

"Well, God keep you," she used to say to him at parting, as she lighted him down the stairs with a candle. "Thank you for coming to cheer me up, and may the Mother of God give you health."

And she always expressed herself with the same sedateness and dignity, the same reasonableness, in imitation of her husband. As the veterinary surgeon was disappearing behind the door below, she would say:

"You know, Vladimir Platonitch, you'd better make it up with your wife. You should forgive her for the sake of your son. You may be sure the little fellow understands."

And when Pustovalov came back, she told him in a low voice about the veterinary surgeon and his unhappy home life, and both sighed and shook their heads and talked about the boy, who, no doubt, missed his father, and by some strange connection of ideas, they went up to the holy ikons, bowed to the ground before them and prayed that God would give them children.

And so the Pustovalovs lived for six years quietly and peaceably in love and complete harmony.

But behold! one winter day after drinking hot tea in the office, Vassily Andreitch went out into the yard without his cap on to see about sending off some timber, caught cold and was taken ill. He had the best doctors, but he grew worse and died after four months' illness. And Olenka was a widow once more.

"I've nobody, now you've left me, my darling," she sobbed, after her husband's funeral. "How can I live without you, in wretchedness and misery! Pity me, good people, all alone in the world!"

She went about dressed in black with long "weepers," and gave up wearing hat and gloves for good. She hardly ever went out, except to church, or to her husband's grave, and led the life of a nun. It was not till six months later that she took off the weepers and opened the shutters of the windows. She was sometimes seen in the mornings, going with her cook to market for provisions, but what went on in her house and how she lived now could only be surmised. People guessed, from seeing her drinking tea in her garden with the veterinary surgeon, who read the newspaper aloud to her, and from the fact that, meeting a lady she knew at the post-office, she said to her:

"There is no proper veterinary inspection in our town, and that's the cause of all sorts of epidemics. One is always hearing of people's getting infection from the milk supply, or catching diseases from horses and cows. The health of domestic animals ought to be as well cared for as the health of human beings."

She repeated the veterinary surgeon's words, and was of the same opinion as he about everything. It was evident that she could not live a year without some attachment, and had found new happiness in the lodge. In any one else this would have been censured, but no one could think ill of Olenka; everything she did was so natural. Neither she nor the veterinary surgeon said anything to other people of the change in their relations, and tried, indeed, to conceal it, but without success, for Olenka could not keep a secret. When he had visitors, men serving in his regiment, and she poured out tea or served the supper, she would begin talking of the cattle plague, of the foot and mouth disease, and of the municipal slaughter-houses. He was dreadfully embarrassed, and when the guests had gone, he would seize her by the hand and hiss angrily:

"I've asked you before not to talk about what you don't understand. When we veterinary surgeons are talking among ourselves, please don't put your word in. It's really annoying."

And she would look at him with astonishment and dismay, and ask him in alarm: "But, Voloditchka, what *am* I to talk about?"

And with tears in her eyes she would embrace him, begging him not to be angry, and they were both happy.

But this happiness did not last long. The veterinary surgeon departed, departed for ever with his regiment, when it was transferred to a distant place—to Siberia, it may be. And Olenka was left alone.

Now she was absolutely alone. Her father had long been dead, and his armchair lay in the attic, covered with dust and lame of one leg. She got thinner and plainer, and when people met her in the street they did not look at her as they used to, and did not smile to her; evidently her best years were over and left behind, and now a new sort of life had begun for her, which did not bear thinking about. In the evening Olenka sat in the porch, and heard the band playing and the fireworks popping in the Tivoli, but now the sound stirred no response. She looked into her yard without interest, thought of nothing, wished for nothing, and afterwards, when night came on she went to bed and dreamed of her empty yard. She ate and drank as it were unwillingly.

And what was worst of all, she had no opinions of any sort. She saw the objects about her and understood what she saw, but could not form any opinion about them, and did not know what to talk about. And how awful it is not to have any opinions! One sees a bottle, for instance, or the rain, or a peasant driving in his cart, but what the bottle is for, or the rain, or the peasant, and what is the meaning of it, one can't say, and could not even for a thousand roubles. When she had Kukin, or Pustovalov, or the veterinary surgeon, Olenka could explain everything, and give her opinion about anything you like, but now there was the same emptiness in her brain and in her heart as there was in her yard outside. And it was as harsh and as bitter as wormwood in the mouth.

Little by little the town grew in all directions. The road became a street, and where the Tivoli and the timber-yard had been, there were new turnings and houses. How rapidly time passes! Olenka's house grew dingy, the roof got rusty, the shed sank on one side, and the whole yard was overgrown with docks and stinging-nettles. Olenka herself had grown plain and elderly; in summer she sat in the porch, and her soul, as before, was empty and dreary and full of bitterness. In winter she sat at her window and looked at the snow. When she caught the scent of spring, or heard the chime of the church bells, a sudden rush of memories from the past came over her, there was a tender ache in her heart, and her eyes brimmed over with tears; but this was only for a minute, and then came emptiness again and the sense of the futility of life. The black kitten, Briska, rubbed against her and purred softly, but Olenka was not touched by these feline caresses. That was not what she needed. She wanted a love that would absorb her whole being, her whole soul and reason—that would give her ideas and an object in life, and would warm her old blood. And she would shake the kitten off her skirt and say with vexation:

"Get along; I don't want you!"

And so it was, day after day and year after year, and no joy, and no opinions. Whatever Mavra, the cook, said she accepted.

One hot July day, towards evening, just as the cattle were being driven away, and the whole yard was full of dust, some one suddenly knocked at the gate. Olenka went to open it herself and was dumbfounded when she looked out: she saw Smirnin, the veterinary surgeon, grey-headed, and dressed as a civilian. She suddenly remembered everything. She could not help crying and letting her head fall on his breast without uttering a word, and in the violence of her feeling she did not notice how they both walked into the house and sat down to tea.

"My dear Vladimir Platonitch! What fate has brought you?" she muttered, trembling with joy.

"I want to settle here for good, Olga Semyonovna," he told her. "I have resigned my post, and have come to settle down and try my luck on my own account. Besides, it's time for my boy to go to school. He's a big boy. I am reconciled with my wife, you know."

"Where is she?" asked Olenka.

"She's at the hotel with the boy, and I'm looking for lodgings."

"Good gracious, my dear soul! Lodgings? Why not have my house? Why shouldn't that suit you? Why, my goodness, I wouldn't take any rent!" cried Olenka in a flutter, beginning to cry again. "You live here, and the lodge will do nicely for me. Oh dear! how glad I am!"

Next day the roof was painted and the walls were whitewashed, and Olenka, with her arms akimbo, walked about the yard giving directions. Her face was beaming with her old smile, and she was brisk and alert as though she had waked from a long sleep. The veterinary's wife arrived—a thin, plain lady, with short hair and a peevish expression. With her was her little Sasha, a boy of ten, small for his age, blue-eyed, chubby, with dimples in his cheeks. And scarcely had the boy walked into the yard when he ran after the cat, and at once there was the sound of his gay, joyous laugh.

"Is that your puss, auntie?" he asked Olenka. "When she has little ones, do give us a kitten. Mamma is awfully afraid of mice."

Olenka talked to him, and gave him tea. Her heart warmed and there was a sweet ache in her bosom, as though the boy had been her own child. And when he sat at the table in the evening, going over his lessons, she looked at him with deep tenderness and pity as she murmured to herself:

"You pretty pet! . . . my precious! . . . Such a fair little thing, and so clever."

" 'An island is a piece of land which is entirely surrounded by water,' " he read aloud.

"An island is a piece of land," she repeated, and this was the first opinion to which she gave utterance with positive conviction after so many years of silence and dearth of ideas.

Now she had opinions of her own, and at supper she talked to Sasha's parents, saying how difficult the lessons were at the high schools, but that yet the high-school was better than a commercial one, since with a high-school education all careers were open to one, such as being a doctor or an engineer.

Sasha began going to the high school. His mother departed to Harkov to her sister's and did not return; his father used to go off every day to inspect cattle, and would often be away from home for three days together, and it seemed to Olenka as though Sasha was entirely abandoned, that he was not wanted at home, that he was being starved, and she carried him off to her lodge and gave him a little room there.

And for six months Sasha had lived in the lodge with her. Every morning Olenka came into his bedroom and found him fast asleep, sleeping noiselessly with his hand under his cheek. She was sorry to wake him.

"Sashenka," she would say mournfully, "get up, darling. It's time for school."

He would get up, dress and say his prayers, and then sit down to breakfast, drink three glasses of tea, and eat two large cracknels and half a buttered roll. All this time he was hardly awake and a little ill-humoured in consequence.

"You don't quite know your fable, Sashenka," Olenka would say, looking at him as though he were about to set off on a long journey. "What a lot of trouble I have with you! You must work and do your best, darling, and obey your teachers."

"Oh, do leave me alone!" Sasha would say.

Then he would go down the street to school, a little figure, wearing a big cap and carrying a satchel on his shoulder. Olenka would follow him noiselessly.

"Sashenka!" she would call after him, and she would pop into his hand a date or a caramel. When he reached the street where the school was, he would feel ashamed of being followed by a tall, stout woman; he would turn round and say:

"You'd better go home, auntie. I can go the rest of the way alone."

She would stand still and look after him fixedly till he had disappeared at the school-gate.

Ah, how she loved him! Of her former attachments not one had been so deep; never had her soul surrendered to any feeling so spontaneously, so disinterestedly, and so joyously as now that her maternal instincts were aroused. For this little boy with the dimple in his cheek and the big school cap, she would have given her whole life, she would have given it with joy and tears of tenderness. Why? Who can tell why?

When she had seen the last of Sasha, she returned home, contented and serene, brimming over with love; her face, which had grown younger during the last six months, smiled and beamed; people meeting her looked at her with pleasure.

"Good-morning, Olga Semyonovna, darling. How are you, darling?"

"The lessons at the high school are very difficult now," she would relate at the market. "It's too much; in the first class yesterday they gave him a fable to learn by heart, and a Latin translation and a problem. You know it's too much for a little chap."

And she would begin talking about the teachers, the lessons, and the school books, saying just what Sasha said.

At three o'clock they had dinner together: in the evening they learned their lessons together and cried. When she put him to bed, she would stay a long time making the Cross over him and murmuring a prayer; then she would go to bed and dream of that far-away misty future when Sasha would finish his studies and become a doctor or an engineer, would have a big house of his own with horses and a carriage, would get married and have children. . . . She would fall asleep still thinking of the same thing, and tears would run down her cheeks from her closed eyes, while the black cat lay purring beside her: "Mrr, mrr, mrr."

Suddenly there would come a loud knock at the gate.

Olenka would wake up breathless with alarm, her heart throbbing. Half a minute later would come another knock.

"It must be a telegram from Harkov," she would think, beginning to tremble from head to foot. "Sasha's mother is sending for him from Harkov. . . . Oh, mercy on us!"

She was in despair. Her head, her hands, and her feet would turn chill, and she would feel that she was the most unhappy woman in the world. But another minute would pass, voices would be heard: it would turn out to be the veterinary surgeon coming home from the club.

"Well, thank God!" she would think.

And gradually the load in her heart would pass off, and she would feel at ease. She would go back to bed thinking of Sasha, who lay sound asleep in the next room, sometimes crying out in his sleep:

"I'll give it you! Get away! Shut up!"

The New Villa

I

Two miles from the village of Obrutchanovo a huge bridge was being built. From the village, which stood up high on the steep river-bank, its trellis-like skeleton could be seen, and in foggy weather and on still winter days, when its delicate iron girders and all the scaffolding around was covered with hoar frost, it presented a picturesque and even fantastic spectacle. Kutcherov, the engineer who was building the bridge, a stout, broad-shouldered, bearded man in a soft crumpled cap drove through the village in his racing droshky or his open carriage. Now and then on holidays navvies working on the bridge would come to the village; they begged for alms, laughed at the women, and sometimes carried off something. But that was rare; as a rule the days passed quietly and peacefully as though no bridge-building were going on, and only in the evening, when camp fires gleamed near the bridge, the wind faintly wafted the songs of the navvies. And by day there was sometimes the mournful clang of metal, don-don-don.

It happened that the engineer's wife came to see him. She was pleased with the river-banks and the gorgeous view over the green valley with trees, churches, flocks, and she began begging her husband to buy a small piece of ground and to build them a cottage on it. Her husband agreed. They bought sixty acres of land, and on the high bank in a field, where in earlier days the cows of Obrutchanovo used to wander, they built a pretty house of two storeys with a terrace and a verandah, with a tower and a flagstaff on which a flag fluttered on Sundays—they built it in about three months, and then all the winter they were planting big trees, and when spring came and everything began to be green there were already avenues to the new house, a gardener and two labourers in white aprons were digging near it, there was a little fountain, and a globe of looking-glass flashed so brilliantly that it was painful to look at. The house had already been named the New Villa.

On a bright, warm morning at the end of May two horses were brought to Obrutchanovo to the village blacksmith, Rodion Petrov. They came from the New Villa. The horses were sleek, graceful beasts, as white as snow, and strikingly alike.

"Perfect swans!" said Rodion, gazing at them with reverent admiration.

His wife Stepanida, his children and grandchildren came out into the street to look at them. By degrees a crowd collected. The Lytchkovs, father and son, both men with swollen faces and entirely beardless, came up bareheaded. Kozov, a tall, thin old man with a long, narrow beard, came up leaning on a stick with a crook handle: he kept winking with his crafty eyes and smiling ironically as though he knew something.

"It's only that they are white; what is there in them?" he said. "Put mine on oats, and they will be just as sleek. They ought to be in a plough and with a whip, too. . . ."

The coachman simply looked at him with disdain, but did not utter a word. And afterwards, while they were blowing up the fire at the forge, the coachman talked while he smoked cigarettes. The peasants learned from him various details: his employers were wealthy people; his mistress, Elena Ivanovna, had till her marriage lived in Moscow in a poor way as a governess; she was kind-hearted, compassionate, and fond of helping the poor. On the new estate, he told them, they were not going to plough or to sow, but simply to live for their pleasure, live only to breathe the fresh air. When he had finished and led the horses back a crowd of boys followed him, the dogs barked, and Kozov, looking after him, winked sarcastically.

"Landowners, too-oo!" he said. "They have built a house and set up horses, but I bet they are nobodies—landowners, too-oo."

Kozov for some reason took a dislike from the first to the new house, to the white horses, and to the handsome, well-fed coachman. Kozov was a solitary man, a widower; he had a dreary life (he was prevented from working by a disease which he sometimes called a rupture and sometimes worms); he was maintained by his son, who worked at a confectioner's in Harkov and sent him money; and from early morning till evening he sauntered at leisure about the river or about the village; if he saw, for instance, a peasant carting a log, or fishing, he would say: "That log's dry wood—it is rotten," or, "They won't bite in weather like this." In times of drought he would declare that there would not be a drop of rain till the frost came; and when the rains came he would say that everything would rot in the fields, that everything was ruined. And as he said these things he would wink as though he knew something.

At the New Villa they burned Bengal lights and sent up fireworks in the evenings, and a sailing-boat with red lanterns floated by Obrutchanovo. One morning the engineer's wife, Elena Ivanovna, and her little daughter drove to the village in a carriage with yellow wheels and a pair of dark bay ponies; both mother and daughter were wearing broad-brimmed straw hats, bent down over their ears.

This was exactly at the time when they were carting manure, and the blacksmith Rodion, a tall, gaunt old man, bareheaded and barefooted, was standing near his dirty and repulsive-looking cart and, flustered, looked at the ponies, and it was evident by his face that he had never seen such little horses before.

"The Kutcherov lady has come!" was whispered around. "Look, the Kutcherov lady has come!"

Elena Ivanovna looked at the huts as though she were selecting one, and then stopped at the very poorest, at the windows of which there were so many children's heads—flaxen, red, and dark. Stepanida, Rodion's wife, a stout woman, came running out of the hut; her kerchief slipped off her grey head; she looked at the carriage facing the sun, and her face smiled and wrinkled up as though she were blind.

"This is for your children," said Elena Ivanovna, and she gave her three roubles.

Stepanida suddenly burst into tears and bowed down to the ground. Rodion, too, flopped to the ground, displaying his brownish bald head, and as he did so he almost caught his wife in the ribs with the fork. Elena Ivanovna was overcome with confusion and drove back.

II

The Lytchkovs, father and son, caught in their meadows two cart-horses, a pony, and a broad-faced Aalhaus bull-calf, and with the help of red-headed Volodka, son of the blacksmith Rodion, drove them to the village. They called the village elder, collected witnesses, and went to look at the damage.

"All right, let 'em!" said Kozov, winking, "le-et 'em! Let them get out of it if they can, the engineers! Do you think there is no such thing as law? All right! Send for the police inspector, draw up a statement! . . ."

"Draw up a statement," repeated Volodka.

"I don't want to let this pass!" shouted the younger Lytchkov. He shouted louder and louder, and his beardless face seemed to be more and more swollen. "They've set up a nice fashion! Leave them free, and they will ruin all the meadows! You've no sort of right to ill-treat people! We are not serfs now!"

"We are not serfs now!" repeated Volodka.

"We got on all right without a bridge," said the elder Lytchkov gloomily; "we did not ask for it. What do we want a bridge for? We don't want it!"

"Brothers, good Christians, we cannot leave it like this!"

"All right, let 'em!" said Kozov, winking. "Let them get out of it if they can! Landowners, indeed!"

They went back to the village, and as they walked the younger

Lytchkov beat himself on the breast with his fist and shouted all the way, and Volodka shouted, too, repeating his words. And meanwhile quite a crowd had gathered in the village round the thoroughbred bull-calf and the horses. The bull-calf was embarrassed and looked up from under his brows, but suddenly lowered his muzzle to the ground and took to his heels, kicking up his hind legs; Kozov was frightened and waved his stick at him, and they all burst out laughing. Then they locked up the beasts and waited.

In the evening the engineer sent five roubles for the damage, and the two horses, the pony and the bull-calf, without being fed or given water, returned home, their heads hanging with a guilty air as though they were convicted criminals.

On getting the five roubles the Lytchkovs, father and son, the village elder and Volodka, punted over the river in a boat and went to a hamlet on the other side where there was a tavern, and there had a long carousal. Their singing and the shouting of the younger Lytchkov could be heard from the village. Their women were uneasy and did not sleep all night. Rodion did not sleep either.

"It's a bad business," he said, sighing and turning from side to side. "The gentleman will be angry, and then there will be trouble. . . . They have insulted the gentleman. . . . Oh, they've insulted him. It's a bad business. . . ."

It happened that the peasants, Rodion amongst them, went into their forest to divide the clearings for mowing, and as they were returning home they were met by the engineer. He was wearing a red cotton shirt and high boots; a setter dog with its long tongue hanging out, followed behind him.

"Good-day, brothers," he said.

The peasants stopped and took off their hats.

"I have long wanted to have a talk with you, friends," he went on. "This is what it is. Ever since the early spring your cattle have been in my copse and garden every day. Everything is trampled down; the pigs have rooted up the meadow, are ruining everything in the kitchen garden, and all the undergrowth in the copse is destroyed. There is no getting on with your herdsmen; one asks them civilly, and they are rude. Damage is done on my estate every day and I do nothing—I don't fine you or make a complaint; meanwhile you impounded my horses and my bull calf and exacted five roubles. Was that right? Is that neighbourly?" he went on, and his face was so soft and persuasive, and his expression was not forbidding. "Is that the way decent people behave? A week ago one of your people cut down two oak saplings in my copse. You have dug up the road to Eresnevo, and now I have to go two miles round. Why do you injure me at every step? What harm have I done you? For God's sake, tell me! My wife and I do our utmost to live with you in peace and harmony; we help the peasants as we can. My wife is a kind, warm-hearted woman; she never refuses you help. That is her dream—to be of use to you and your children. You reward us with evil for our good. You are unjust, my friends. Think of that. I ask you earnestly to think it over. We treat you humanely; repay us in the same coin."

He turned and went away. The peasants stood a little longer, put on their caps and walked away. Rodion, who always understood everything that was said to him in some peculiar way of his own, heaved a sigh and said:

"We must pay. 'Repay in coin, my friends' . . . he said."

They walked to the village in silence. On reaching home Rodion said his prayer, took off his boots, and sat down on the bench beside his wife. Stepanida and he always sat side by side when they were at home, and always walked side by side in the street; they ate and they drank and they slept always together, and the older they grew the more they loved one another. It was hot and crowded in their hut, and there were children everywhere—on the floors, in the windows, on the stove. . . . In spite of her advanced years Stepanida was still bearing children, and now, looking at the crowd of children, it was hard to distinguish which were Rodion's and which were Volodka's. Volodka's wife, Lukerya, a plain young woman with prominent eyes and a nose like the beak of a bird, was kneading dough in a tub; Volodka was sitting on the stove with his legs hanging.

"On the road near Nikita's buckwheat . . . the engineer with his dog . . ." Rodion began, after a rest, scratching his ribs and his elbow.

" 'You must pay,' says he . . . 'coin,' says he. . . . Coin or no coin, we shall have to collect ten kopecks from every hut. We've offended the gentleman very much. I am sorry for him. . . ."

"We've lived without a bridge," said Volodka, not looking at anyone, "and we don't want one."

"What next; the bridge is a government business."

"We don't want it."

"Your opinion is not asked. What is it to you?"

" 'Your opinion is not asked,' " Volodka mimicked him. "We don't want to drive anywhere; what do we want with a bridge? If we have to, we can cross by the boat."

Someone from the yard outside knocked at the window so violently that it seemed to shake the whole hut.

"Is Volodka at home?" he heard the voice of the younger Lytchkov. "Volodka, come out, come along."

Volodka jumped down off the stove and began looking for his cap.

"Don't go, Volodka," said Rodion diffidently. "Don't go with them, son. You are foolish, like a little child; they will teach you no good; don't go!"

"Don't go, son," said Stepanida, and she blinked as though about to shed tears. "I bet they are calling you to the tavern."

" 'To the tavern,' " Volodka mimicked.

"You'll come back drunk again, you currish Herod," said Lukerya, looking at him angrily. "Go along, go along, and may you burn up with vodka, you tailless Satan!"

"You hold your tongue," shouted Volodka.

"They've married me to a fool, they've ruined me, a luckless orphan, you red-headed drunkard . . ." wailed Lukerya, wiping her face with a hand covered with dough. "I wish I had never set eyes on you."

Volodka gave her a blow on the ear and went off.

III

Elena Ivanovna and her little daughter visited the village on foot. They were out for a walk. It was a Sunday, and the peasant women and girls were walking up and down the street in their brightly-coloured dresses. Rodion and Stepanida, sitting side by side at their door, bowed and smiled to Elena Ivanovna and her little daughter as to acquaintances. From the windows more than a dozen children stared at them; their faces expressed amazement and curiosity, and they could be heard whispering:

"The Kutcherov lady has come! The Kutcherov lady!"

"Good-morning," said Elena Ivanovna, and she stopped; she paused, and then asked: "Well, how are you getting on?"

"We get along all right, thank God," answered Rodion, speaking rapidly. "To be sure we get along."

"The life we lead!" smiled Stepanida. "You can see our poverty yourself, dear lady! The family is fourteen souls in all, and only two bread-winners. We are supposed to be blacksmiths, but when they bring us a horse to shoe we have no coal, nothing to buy it with. We are worried to death, lady," she went on, and laughed. "Oh, oh, we are worried to death."

Elena Ivanovna sat down at the entrance and, putting her arm round her little girl, pondered something, and judging from the little girl's expression, melancholy thoughts were straying through her mind, too; as she brooded she played with the sumptuous lace on the parasol she had taken out of her mother's hands.

"Poverty," said Rodion, "a great deal of anxiety—you see no end to it. Here, God sends no rain . . . our life is not easy, there is no denying it."

"You have a hard time in this life," said Elena Ivanovna, "but in the other world you will be happy."

Rodion did not understand her, and simply coughed into his clenched hand by way of reply. Stepanida said:

"Dear lady, the rich men will be all right in the next world, too. The rich put up candles, pay for services; the rich give to beggars, but what can the poor man do? He has no time to make the sign of the cross. He is the beggar of beggars himself; how can he think of his soul? And many sins come from poverty; from trouble we snarl at one another like dogs, we haven't a good word to say to one another, and all sorts of things happen, dear lady—God forbid! It seems we have no luck in this world nor the next. All the luck has fallen to the rich."

She spoke gaily; she was evidently used to talking of her hard life. And Rodion smiled, too; he was pleased that his old woman was so clever, so ready of speech.

"It is only on the surface that the rich seem to be happy," said Elena Ivanovna. "Every man has his sorrow. Here my husband and I do not live poorly, we have means, but are we happy? I am young, but I have had four children; my children are always being ill. I am ill, too, and constantly being doctored."

"And what is your illness?" asked Rodion.

"A woman's complaint. I get no sleep; a continual headache gives me no peace. Here I am sitting and talking, but my head is bad, I am weak all over, and I should prefer the hardest labour to such a condition. My soul, too, is troubled; I am in continual fear for my children, my husband. Every family has its own trouble of some sort; we have ours. I am not of noble birth. My grandfather was a simple peasant, my father was a tradesman in Moscow; he was a plain, uneducated man, too, while my husband's parents were wealthy and distinguished. They did not want him to marry me, but he disobeyed them, quarrelled with them, and they have not forgiven us to this day. That worries my husband; it troubles him and keeps him in constant agitation; he loves his mother, loves her dearly. So I am uneasy, too, my soul is in pain."

Peasants, men and women, were by now standing round Rodion's hut and listening. Kozov came up, too, and stood twitching his long, narrow beard. The Lytchkovs, father and son, drew near.

"And say what you like, one cannot be happy and satisfied if one does not feel in one's proper place." Elena Ivanovna went on. "Each of you has his strip of land, each of you works and knows what he is working for; my husband builds bridges—in short, everyone has his place, while I, I simply walk about. I have not my bit to work. I don't work, and feel as though I were an outsider. I am saying all this that you may not judge from outward appearances; if a man is expensively dressed and has means it does not prove that he is satisfied with his life."

She got up to go away and took her daughter by the hand.

"I like your place here very much," she said, and smiled, and from that faint, diffident smile one could tell how unwell she really was, how young and how pretty; she had a pale, thinnish face with dark eyebrows and fair hair. And the little girl was just such another as her mother: thin, fair, and slender. There was a fragrance of scent about them.

"I like the river and the forest and the village," Elena Ivanovna went on; "I could live here all my life, and I feel as though here I should get strong and find my place. I want to help you—I want to dreadfully—to be of use, to be a real friend to you. I know your need, and what I don't know I feel, my heart guesses. I am sick, feeble, and for me perhaps it is not possible to change my life as I would. But I have children. I will try to bring them up that they may be of use to you, may love you. I shall impress upon them continually that their life does not belong to them, but to you. Only I beg you earnestly, I beseech you, trust us, live in friendship with us. My husband is a kind, good man. Don't worry him, don't irritate him. He is sensitive to every trifle, and yesterday, for instance, your cattle were in our vegetable garden, and one of your people broke down the fence to the bee-hives, and such an attitude to us drives my husband to despair. I beg you," she went on in an imploring voice, and she clasped her hands on her bosom—"I beg you to treat us as good neighbours; let us live in peace! There is a saying, you know, that even a bad peace is better than a good quarrel, and, 'Don't buy property, but buy neighbours.' I repeat my husband is a kind man and good; if all goes well we promise to do everything in our power for you; we will mend the roads, we will build a school for your children. I promise you."

"Of course we thank you humbly, lady," said Lytchkov the father, looking at the ground; "you are educated people; it is for you to know best. Only, you see, Voronov, a rich peasant at Eresnevo, promised to build a school; he, too, said, 'I will do this for you,' 'I will do that for you,' and he only put up the framework and refused to go on. And then they made the peasants put the roof on and finish it; it cost them a thousand roubles. Voronov did not care; he only stroked his beard, but the peasants felt it a bit hard."

"That was a crow, but now there's a rook, too," said Kozov, and he winked.

There was the sound of laughter.

"We don't want a school," said Volodka sullenly. "Our children go to Petrovskoe, and they can go on going there; we don't want it."

Elena Ivanovna seemed suddenly intimidated; her face looked paler and thinner, she shrank into herself as though she had been touched with something coarse, and walked away without uttering another word. And she walked more and more quickly, without looking round.

"Lady," said Rodion, walking after her, "lady, wait a bit; hear what I would say to you."

He followed her without his cap, and spoke softly as though begging. "Lady, wait and hear what I will say to you."

They had walked out of the village, and Elena Ivanovna stopped beside a cart in the shade of an old mountain ash.

"Don't be offended, lady," said Rodion. "What does it mean? Have patience. Have patience for a couple of years. You will live here, you will have patience, and it will all come round. Our folks are good and peaceable; there's no harm in them; it's God's truth I'm telling you. Don't mind Kozov and the Lytchkovs, and don't mind Volodka. He's a fool; he listens to the first that speaks. The others are quiet folks; they are silent. Some would be glad, you know, to say a word from the heart and to stand up for themselves, but cannot. They have a heart and a conscience, but no tongue. Don't be offended . . . have patience. . . . What does it matter?"

Elena Ivanovna looked at the broad, tranquil river, pondering, and tears flowed down her cheeks. And Rodion was troubled by those tears; he almost cried himself.

"Never mind . . ." he muttered. "Have patience for a couple of years. You can have the school, you can have the roads, only not all at once. If you went, let us say, to sow corn on that mound you would first have to weed it out, to pick out all the stones, and then to plough, and work and work . . . and with the people, you see, it is the same . . . you must work and work until you overcome them."

The crowd had moved away from Rodion's hut, and was coming along the street towards the mountain ash. They began singing songs and playing the concertina, and they kept coming closer and closer. . . .

"Mamma, let us go away from here," said the little girl, huddling up to her mother, pale and shaking all over; "let us go away, mamma!"

"Where?"

"To Moscow. . . . Let us go, mamma."

The child began crying.

Rodion was utterly overcome; his face broke into profuse perspiration; he took out of his pocket a little crooked cucumber, like a half-moon, covered with crumbs of rye bread, and began thrusting it into the little girl's hands.

"Come, come," he muttered, scowling severely; "take the little cucumber, eat it up. . . . You mustn't cry. Mamma will whip you. . . . She'll tell your father of you when you get home. Come, come. . . ."

They walked on, and he still followed behind them, wanting to say something friendly and persuasive to them. And seeing that they were both absorbed in their own thoughts and their own griefs, and not noticing him, he stopped and, shading his eyes from the sun, looked after them for a long time till they disappeared into their copse.

IV

The engineer seemed to grow irritable and petty, and in every trivial incident saw an act of robbery or outrage. His gate was kept bolted even by day, and at night two watchmen walked up and down the garden beating a board; and they gave up employing anyone from Obrutchanovo as a labourer. As ill-luck would have it someone (either a peasant or one of the workmen) took the new wheels off the cart and replaced them by old ones, then soon afterwards two bridles and a pair of pincers were carried off, and murmurs arose even in the village. People began to say that a search should be made at the Lytchkovs' and at Volodka's, and then the bridles and the pincers were found under the hedge in the engineer's garden; someone had thrown them down there.

It happened that the peasants were coming in a crowd out of the forest, and again they met the engineer on the road. He stopped, and without wishing them good-day he began, looking angrily first at one, then at another:

"I have begged you not to gather mushrooms in the park and near the yard, but to leave them for my wife and children, but your girls come before daybreak and there is not a mushroom left. . . . Whether one asks you or not it makes no difference. Entreaties, and friendliness, and persuasion I see are all useless."

He fixed his indignant eyes on Rodion and went on:

"My wife and I behaved to you as human beings, as to our equals, and you? But what's the use of talking! It will end by our looking down upon you. There is nothing left!"

And making an effort to restrain his anger, not to say too much, he turned and went on.

On getting home Rodion said his prayer, took off his boots, and sat down beside his wife.

"Yes . . ." he began with a sigh. "We were walking along just now, and Mr. Kutcherov met us. . . . Yes. . . . He saw the girls at daybreak. . . . 'Why don't they bring mushrooms,' he said . . . 'to my wife and children?' he said. . . . And then he looked at me and he said: 'I and my wife will look after you,' he said. I wanted to fall down at his feet, but I hadn't the courage. . . . God give him health. . . . God bless him! . . ."

Stepanida crossed herself and sighed.

"They are kind, simple-hearted people," Rodion went on. " 'We shall look after you.' . . . He promised me that before everyone. In our old age . . . it wouldn't be a bad thing. . . . I should always pray for them. . . . Holy Mother, bless them. . . ."

The Feast of the Exaltation of the Cross, the fourteenth of September, was the festival of the village church. The Lytchkovs, father and son, went across the river early in the morning and returned to dinner drunk; they spent a long time going about the village, alternately singing and swearing; then they had a fight and went to the New Villa to complain. First Lytchkov the father went into the yard with a long ashen stick in his hands. He stopped irresolutely and took off his hat. Just at that moment the engineer and his family were sitting on the verandah, drinking tea.

"What do you want?" shouted the engineer.

"Your honour . . ." Lytchkov began, and burst into tears. "Show the Divine mercy, protect me . . . my son makes my life a misery . . . your honour. . . ."

Lytchkov the son walked up, too; he, too, was bareheaded and had a stick in his hand; he stopped and fixed his drunken senseless eyes on the verandah.

"It is not my business to settle your affairs," said the engineer. "Go to the rural captain or the police officer."

"I have been everywhere. . . . I have lodged a petition . . ." said Lytchkov the father, and he sobbed. "Where can I go now? He can kill me now, it seems. He can do anything. Is that the way to treat a father? A father?"

He raised his stick and hit his son on the head; the son raised his stick and struck his father just on his bald patch such a blow that the stick bounced back. The father did not even flinch, but hit his son again and again on the head. And so they stood and kept hitting one another on the head, and it looked not so much like a fight as some sort of a game. And peasants, men and women, stood in a crowd at the gate and looked into the garden, and the faces of all were grave. They were the peasants who had come to greet them for the holiday, but seeing the Lytchkovs, they were ashamed and did not go in.

The next morning Elena Ivanovna went with the children to Moscow. And there was a rumour that the engineer was selling his house. . . .

V

The peasants had long ago grown used to the sight of the bridge, and it was difficult to imagine the river at that place without a bridge. The heap of rubble left from the building of it had long been overgrown with grass, the navvies were forgotten, and instead of the strains of the "Dubinushka" that they used to sing, the peasants heard almost every hour the sounds of a passing train.

The New Villa has long ago been sold; now it belongs to a government clerk who comes here from the town for the holidays with his family, drinks tea on the terrace, and then goes back to the town again. He wears a cockade on his cap; he talks and clears his throat as though he were a very important official, though he is only of the rank of a collegiate secretary, and when the peasants bow he makes no response.

In Obrutchanovo everyone has grown older; Kozov is dead. In Rodion's hut there are even more children. Volodka has grown a long red beard. They are still as poor as ever.

In the early spring the Obrutchanovo peasants were sawing wood near the station. And after work they were going home; they walked without haste one after the other. Broad saws curved over their shoulders; the sun was reflected in them. The nightingales were singing in the bushes on the bank, larks were trilling in the heavens. It was quiet at the New Villa; there was not a soul there, and only golden pigeons—golden because the sunlight was streaming upon them—were flying over the house. All of them—Rodion, the two Lytchkovs, and Volodka—thought of the white horses, the little ponies, the fireworks, the boat with the lanterns; they remembered how the engineer's wife, so beautiful and so grandly dressed, had come into the village and talked to them in such a friendly way. And it seemed as though all that had never been; it was like a dream or a fairy-tale.

They trudged along, tired out, and mused as they went. . . . In their village, they mused, the people were good, quiet, sensible, fearing God, and Elena Ivanovna, too, was quiet, kind, and gentle; it made one sad to look at her, but why had they not got on together? Why had they parted like enemies? How was it that some mist had shrouded from their eyes what mattered most, and had let them see nothing but damage done by cattle, bridles, pincers, and all those trivial things which now, as they remembered them, seemed so nonsensical? How was it that with the new owner they lived in peace, and yet had been on bad terms with the engineer?

And not knowing what answer to make to these questions they were all silent except Volodka, who muttered something.

"What is it?" Rodion asked.

"We lived without a bridge . . ." said Volodka gloomily. "We lived without a bridge, and did not ask for one . . . and we don't want it. . . ."

No one answered him and they walked on in silence with drooping heads.

On Official Duty

The deputy examining magistrate and the district doctor were going to an inquest in the village of Syrnya. On the road they were overtaken by a snowstorm; they spent a long time going round and round, and arrived, not at midday, as they had intended, but in the evening when it was dark. They put up for the night at the Zemstvo hut. It so happened that it was in this hut that the dead body was lying—the corpse of the Zemstvo insurance agent, Lesnitsky, who had arrived in Syrnya three days before and, ordering the samovar in the hut, had shot himself, to the great surprise of everyone; and the fact that he had ended his life so strangely, after unpacking his eatables and laying them out on the table, and with the samovar before him, led many people to suspect that it was a case of murder; an inquest was necessary.

In the outer room the doctor and the examining magistrate shook the snow off themselves and knocked it off their boots. And meanwhile the old village constable, Ilya Loshadin, stood by, holding a little tin lamp. There was a strong smell of paraffin.

"Who are you?" asked the doctor.

"Conshtable, . . ." answered the constable.

He used to spell it "conshtable" when he signed the receipts at the post office.

"And where are the witnesses?"

"They must have gone to tea, your honor."

On the right was the parlor, the travelers' or gentry's room; on the left the kitchen, with a big stove and sleeping shelves under the rafters. The doctor and the examining magistrate, followed by the constable, holding the lamp high above his head, went into the parlor. Here a still, long body covered with white linen was lying on the floor close to the table-legs. In the dim light of the lamp they could clearly see, besides the white covering, new rubber goloshes, and everything about it was uncanny and sinister: the dark walls, and the silence, and the goloshes, and the stillness of the dead body. On the table stood a samovar, cold long ago; and round it parcels, probably the eatables.

"To shoot oneself in the Zemstvo hut, how tactless!" said the doctor. "If one does want to put a bullet through one's brains, one ought to do it at home in some outhouse."

He sank on to a bench, just as he was, in his cap, his fur coat, and his felt overboots; his fellow-traveler, the examining magistrate, sat down opposite.

"These hysterical, neurasthenic people are great egoists," the doctor went on hotly. "If a neurasthenic sleeps in the same room with you, he rustles his newspaper; when he dines with you, he gets up a scene with his wife without troubling about your presence; and when he feels inclined to shoot himself, he shoots himself in a village in a Zemstvo hut, so as to give the maximum of trouble to everybody. These gentlemen in every circumstance of life think of no one but themselves! That's why the elderly so dislike our 'nervous age.' "

"The elderly dislike so many things," said the examining magistrate, yawning. "You should point out to the elder generation what the difference is between the suicides of the past and the suicides of today. In the old days the so-called gentleman shot himself because he had made away with Government money, but nowadays it is because he is sick of life, depressed. . . . Which is better?"

"Sick of life, depressed; but you must admit that he might have shot himself somewhere else."

"Such trouble!" said the constable, "such trouble! It's a real affliction. The people are very much upset, your honor; they haven't slept these three nights. The children are crying. The cows ought to be milked, but the women won't go to the stall—they are afraid . . . for fear the gentleman should appear to them in the darkness. Of course they are silly women, but some of the men are frightened too. As soon as it is dark they won't go by the hut one by one, but only in a flock together. And the witnesses too. . . ."

Dr. Startchenko, a middle-aged man in spectacles with a dark beard, and the examining magistrate Lyzhin, a fair man, still young, who had only taken his degree two years before and looked more like a student than an official, sat in silence, musing. They were vexed that they were late. Now they had to wait till morning, and to stay here for the night, though it was not yet six o'clock; and they had before them a long evening, a dark night, boredom, uncomfortable beds, beetles, and cold in the morning; and listening to the blizzard that howled in the chimney and in the loft, they both thought how unlike all this was the life which they would have chosen for themselves and of which they had once dreamed, and how far away they both were from their contemporaries, who were at that moment walking about the lighted streets in town without noticing the weather, or were getting ready for the theatre, or sitting in their studies over a book. Oh, how much they would have given now only to stroll along the Nevsky Prospect, or along Petrovka in Moscow, to listen to decent singing, to sit for an hour or so in a restaurant!

"Oo-oo-oo-oo!" sang the storm in the loft, and something outside slammed viciously, probably the signboard on the hut. "Oo-oo-oo-oo!"

"You can do as you please, but I have no desire to stay here," said Startchenko, getting up. "It's not six yet, it's too early to go to bed; I am off. Von Taunitz lives not far from here, only a couple of miles from Syrnya. I shall go to see him and spend the evening there. Constable, run and tell my coachman not to take the horses out. And what are you going to do?" he asked Lyzhin.

"I don't know; I expect I shall go to sleep."

The doctor wrapped himself in his fur coat and went out. Lyzhin could hear him talking to the coachman and the bells beginning to quiver on the frozen horses. He drove off.

"It is not nice for you, sir, to spend the night in here," said the constable; "come into the other room. It's dirty, but for one night it won't matter. I'll get a samovar from a peasant and heat it directly. I'll heap up some hay for you, and then you go to sleep, and God bless you, your honor."

A little later the examining magistrate was sitting in the kitchen drinking tea, while Loshadin, the constable, was standing at the door talking. He was an old man about sixty, short and very thin, bent and white, with a naïve smile on his face and watery eyes; and he kept smacking with his lips as though he were sucking a sweetmeat. He was wearing a short sheepskin coat and high felt boots, and held his stick in his hands all the time. The youth of the examining magistrate aroused his compassion, and that was probably why he addressed him familiarly.

"The elder gave orders that he was to be informed when the police superintendent or the examining magistrate came," he said, "so I suppose I must go now. . . . It's nearly three miles to the *volost,* and the storm, the snowdrifts, are something terrible—maybe one won't get there before midnight. Ough! how the wind roars!"

"I don't need the elder," said Lyzhin. "There is nothing for him to do here."

He looked at the old man with curiosity, and asked:

"Tell me, grandfather, how many years have you been constable?"

"How many? Why, thirty years. Five years after the Freedom I began going as constable, that's how I reckon it. And from that time I have been going every day since. Other people have holidays, but I am always going. When it's Easter and the church bells are ringing and Christ has risen, I still go about with my bag—to the treasury, to the post, to the police superintendent's lodgings, to the rural captain, to the tax inspector, to the municipal office, to the gentry, to the peasants, to all orthodox Christians. I carry parcels, notices, tax papers, letters, forms of different sorts, circulars, and to be sure, kind gentleman, there are all sorts of forms nowadays, so as to note down the numbers—yellow, white, and red—and every gentleman or priest or well-to-do peasant must write down a dozen times in the year how much he has sown and harvested, how many quarters or poods he has of rye, how many of oats, how many of hay, and what the weather's like, you know, and insects, too, of all sorts. To be sure you can write what you like, it's only a regulation, but one must go and give out the notices and then go again and collect them. Here, for instance, there's no need to cut open the gentleman; you know yourself it's a silly thing, it's only dirtying your hands, and here you have been put to trouble, your honor; you have come because it's the regulation; you can't help it. For thirty years I have been going round according to regulation. In the summer it is all right, it is warm and dry; but in winter and autumn it's uncomfortable. At times I have been almost drowned and almost frozen; all sorts of things have happened—wicked people set on me in the forest and took away my bag; I have been beaten, and I have been before a court of law."

"What were you accused of?"

"Of fraud."

"How do you mean?"

"Why, you see, Hrisanf Grigoryev, the clerk, sold the contractor some boards belonging to someone else—cheated him, in fact. I was mixed up in it. They sent me to the tavern for vodka; well, the clerk did not share with me—did not even offer me a glass; but as through my poverty I was—in appearance, I mean—not a man to be relied upon, not a man of any worth, we were both brought to trial; he was sent to prison, but, praise God! I was acquitted on all points. They read a notice, you know, in the court. And they were all in uniforms—in the court, I mean. I can tell you, your honor, my duties for anyone not used to them are terrible, absolutely killing; but to me it is nothing. In fact, my feet ache when I am not walking. And at home it is worse for me. At home one has to heat the stove for the clerk in the *volost* office, to fetch water for him, to clean his boots."

"And what wages do you get?" Lyzhin asked.

"Eighty-four roubles a year."

"I'll bet you get other little sums coming in. You do, don't you?"

"Other little sums? No, indeed! Gentlemen nowadays don't often give tips. Gentlemen nowadays are strict, they take offense at anything. If you bring them a notice they are offended, if you take off your cap before them they are offended. 'You have come to the wrong entrance,' they say. 'You are a drunkard,' they say. 'You smell of onion; you are a blockhead; you are the son of a bitch.' There are kind-hearted ones, of course; but what does one get from them? They only laugh and call one all sorts of names. Mr. Altuhin, for instance, he is a good-natured gentleman; and if you look at him he seems sober and in his right mind, but so soon as he sees me he shouts and does not know what he means himself. He gave me such a name. 'You,' said he, . . ." The constable uttered some word, but in such a low voice that it was impossible to make out what he said.

"What?" Lyzhin asked. "Say it again."

" 'Administration,' " the constable repeated aloud. "He has been calling me that for a long while, for the last six years. 'Hullo, Administration!' But I don't mind; let him, God bless him! Sometimes a lady will send one a glass of vodka and a bit of pie, and one drinks to her health. But peasants give more; peasants are more kind-hearted, they have the fear of God in their hearts: one will give a bit of bread, another a drop of cabbage soup, another will stand one a glass. The village elders treat one to tea in the tavern. Here the witnesses have gone to their tea. 'Loshadin,' they said, 'you stay here and keep watch for us,' and they gave me a kopeck each. You see, they are frightened, not being used to it, and yesterday they gave me fifteen kopecks and offered me a glass."

"And you, aren't you frightened?"

"I am, sir; but of course it is my duty, there is no getting away from it. In the summer I was taking a convict to the town, and he set upon me and gave me such a drubbing! And all around were fields, forest—how could I get away from him? It's just the same here. I remember the gentleman, Mr. Lesnitsky, when he was so high, and I knew his father and mother. I am from the village of Nedoshtchotova, and they, the Lesnitsky family, were not more than three-quarters of a mile from us and less than that, their ground next to ours, and Mr. Lesnitsky had a sister, a God-fearing and tender-hearted lady. Lord keep the soul of Thy servant Yulya, eternal memory to her! She was never married, and when she was dying she divided all her property; she left three hundred acres to the monastery, and six hundred to the commune of peasants of Nedoshtchotova to commemorate her soul; but her brother hid the will, they do say burnt it in the stove, and took all this land for himself. He thought, to be sure, it was for his benefit; but—nay, wait a bit, you won't get on in the world through injustice, brother. The gentleman did not go to confession for twenty years after. He kept away from the church, to be sure, and died impenitent. He burst. He was a very fat man, so he burst lengthways. Then everything was taken from the young master, from Seryozha, to pay the debts—everything there was. Well, he had not gone very far in his studies, he couldn't do anything, and the president of the Rural Board, his uncle—'I'll take him'—Seryozha, I mean—thinks he, 'for an agent; let him collect the insurance, that's not a difficult job,' and the gentleman was young and proud, he wanted to be living on a bigger scale and in better style and with more freedom. To be sure it was a come-down for him to be jolting about the district in a wretched cart and talking to the peasants; he would walk and keep looking on the ground, looking on the ground and saying nothing; if you called his name right in his ear, 'Sergey Sergeyitch!' he would look round like this, 'Eh?' and look down on the ground again, and now you see he has laid hands on himself. There's no sense in it, your honor, it's not right, and there's no making out what's the meaning of it, merciful Lord! Say your father was rich and you are poor; it is mortifying, there's no doubt about it, but there, you must make up your mind to it. I used to live in good style, too; I had two horses, your honor, three cows, I used to keep twenty head of sheep; but the time has come, and I am left with nothing but a wretched bag, and even that is not mine but Government property. And now in our Nedoshtchotova, if the truth is to be told, my house is the worst of the lot. Makey had four footmen, and now Makey is a footman himself. Petrak had four laborers, and now Petrak is a laborer himself."

"How was it you became poor?" asked the examining magistrate.

"My sons drink terribly. I could not tell you how they drink, you wouldn't believe it."

Lyzhin listened and thought how he, Lyzhin, would go back sooner or later to Moscow, while this old man would stay here for ever, and would always be walking and walking. And how many times in his life he would come across such battered, unkempt old men, not "men of any worth," in whose souls fifteen kopecks, glasses of vodka, and a profound belief that you can't get on in this life by dishonesty, were equally firmly rooted.

Then he grew tired of listening, and told the old man to bring him some hay for his bed. There was an iron bedstead with a pillow and a quilt in the traveler's room, and it could be fetched in; but the dead man had been lying by it for nearly three days (and perhaps sitting on it just before his death), and it would be disagreeable to sleep upon it now. . . .

"It's only half-past seven," thought Lyzhin, glancing at his watch. "How awful it is!"

He was not sleepy, but having nothing to do to pass away the time, he lay down and covered himself with a rug. Loshadin went in and out several times, clearing away the tea-things; smacking his lips and sighing, he kept tramping round the table; at last he took his little lamp and went out, and, looking at his long, gray-headed, bent figure from behind, Lyzhin thought:

"Just like a magician in an opera."

It was dark. The moon must have been behind the clouds, as the windows and the snow on the window-frames could be seen distinctly.

"Oo-oo-oo-oo!" sang the storm, "Oo-oo-oo-oo!"

"Ho-ho-ly sa-aints!" wailed a woman in the loft, or it sounded like it. "Ho-ho-ly sa-aints!"

"B-booh!" something outside banged against the wall. "Trah!"

The examining magistrate listened: there was no woman up there, it was the wind howling. It was rather cold, and he put his fur coat over his rug. As he got warm he thought how remote all this—the storm, and the hut, and the old man, and the dead body lying in the next room—how remote it all was from the life he desired for himself, and how alien it all was to him, how petty, how uninteresting. If this man had killed himself in Moscow or somewhere in the neighborhood, and he had had to hold an inquest on him there, it would have been interesting, important, and perhaps he might even have been afraid to sleep in the next room to the corpse. Here, nearly a thousand miles from Moscow, all this was seen somehow in a different light; it was not life, they were not human beings, but something only existing "according to the regulation," as Loshadin said; it would leave not the faintest trace in the memory, and would be forgotten as soon as he, Lyzhin, drove away from Syrnya. The fatherland, the real Russia, was Moscow, Petersburg; but here he was in the provinces, the colonies. When one dreamed of playing a leading part, of becoming a popular figure, of being, for instance, examining magistrate in particularly important cases or prosecutor in a circuit court, of being a society lion, one always thought of Moscow. To live, one must be in Moscow; here one cared for nothing, one grew easily resigned to one's insignificant position, and only expected one thing of life—to get away quickly, quickly. And Lyzhin mentally moved about the Moscow streets, went into the familiar houses, met his kindred, his comrades, and there was a sweet pang at his heart at the thought that he was only twenty-six, and that if in five or ten years he could break away from here and get to Moscow, even then it would not be too late and he would still have a whole life before him. And as he sank into unconsciousness, as his thoughts began to be confused, he imagined the long corridor of the court at Moscow, himself delivering a speech, his sisters, the orchestra which for some reason kept droning: "Oo-oo-oo-oo! Oo-oo-oo-oo!"

"Booh! Trah!" sounded again. "Booh!"

And he suddenly recalled how one day, when he was talking to the bookkeeper in the little office of the Rural Board, a thin, pale gentleman with black hair and dark eyes walked in; he had a disagreeable look in his eyes such as one sees in people who have slept too long after dinner, and it spoilt his delicate, intelligent profile; and the high boots he was wearing did not suit him, but looked clumsy. The bookkeeper had introduced him: "This is our insurance agent."

"So that was Lesnitsky, . . . this same man," . . . Lyzhin reflected now.

He recalled Lesnitsky's soft voice, imagined his gait, and it seemed to him that someone was walking beside him now with a step like Lesnitsky's.

All at once he felt frightened, his head turned cold.

"Who's there?" he asked in alarm.

"The conshtable!"

"What do you want here?"

"I have come to ask, your honor—you said this evening that you did not want the elder, but I am afraid he may be angry. He told me to go to him. Shouldn't I go?"

"That's enough, you bother me," said Lyzhin with vexation, and he covered himself up again.

"He may be angry. . . . I'll go, your honor. I hope you will be comfortable," and Loshadin went out.

In the passage there was coughing and subdued voices. The witnesses must have returned.

"We'll let those poor beggars get away early to-morrow, . . ." thought the examining magistrate; "we'll begin the inquest as soon as it is daylight."

He began sinking into forgetfulness when suddenly there were steps again, not timid this time but rapid and noisy. There was the slam of a door, voices, the scratching of a match. . . .

"Are you asleep? Are you asleep?" Dr. Startchenko was asking him hurriedly and angrily as he struck one match after another; he was covered with snow, and brought a chill air in with him. "Are you asleep? Get up! Let us go to Von Taunitz's. He has sent his own horses for you. Come along. There, at any rate, you will have supper, and sleep like a human being. You see I have come for you myself. The horses are splendid, we shall get there in twenty minutes."

"And what time is it now?"

"A quarter past ten."

Lyzhin, sleepy and discontented, put on his felt overboots, his fur-lined coat, his cap and hood, and went out with the doctor. There was not a very sharp frost, but a violent and piercing wind was blowing and driving along the street the clouds of snow which seemed to be racing away in terror: high drifts were heaped up already under the fences and at the doorways. The doctor and the examining magistrate got into the sledge, and the white coachman bent over them to button up the cover. They were both hot.

"Ready!"

They drove through the village. "Cutting a feathery furrow," thought the examining magistrate, listlessly watching the action of the trace horse's legs. There were lights in all the huts, as though it were the eve of a great holiday: the peasants had not gone to bed because they were afraid of the dead body. The coachman preserved a sullen silence, probably he had felt dreary while he was waiting by the Zemstvo hut, and now he, too, was thinking of the dead man.

"At the Von Taunitz's," said Startchenko, "they all set upon me when they heard that you were left to spend the night in the hut, and asked me why I did not bring you with me."

As they drove out of the village, at the turning the coachman suddenly shouted at the top of his voice: "Out of the way!"

They caught a glimpse of a man: he was standing up to his knees in the snow, moving off the road and staring at the horses. The examining magistrate saw a stick with a crook, and a beard and a bag, and he fancied that it was Loshadin, and even fancied that he was smiling. He flashed by and disappeared.

The road ran at first along the edge of the forest, then along a broad forest clearing; they caught glimpses of old pines and a young birch copse, and tall, gnarled young oak trees standing singly in the clearings where the wood had lately been cut; but soon it was all merged in the clouds of snow. The coachman said he could see the forest; the examining magistrate could see nothing but the trace horse. The wind blew on their backs.

All at once the horses stopped.

"Well, what is it now?" asked Startchenko crossly.

The coachman got down from the box without a word and began running round the sledge, treading on his heels; he made larger and larger circles, getting further and further away from the sledge, and it looked as though he were dancing; at last he came back and began to turn off to the right.

"You've got off the road, eh?" asked Startchenko.

"It's all ri-ight. . . ."

Then there was a little village and not a single light in it. Again the forest and the fields. Again they lost the road, and again the coachman got down from the box and danced round the sledge. The sledge flew along a dark avenue, flew swiftly on. And the heated trace horse's hoofs knocked against the sledge. Here there was a fearful roaring sound from the trees, and nothing could be seen, as though they were flying on into space; and all at once the glaring light at the entrance and the windows flashed upon their eyes, and they heard the good-natured, drawn-out barking of dogs. They had arrived.

While they were taking off their fur coats and their felt boots below, "Un Petit Verre de Clicquot" was being played upon the piano overhead, and they could hear the children beating time with their feet. Immediately on going in they were aware of the snug warmth and special smell of the old apartments of a mansion where, whatever the weather outside, life is so warm and clean and comfortable.

"That's capital!" said Von Taunitz, a fat man with an incredibly thick neck and with whiskers, as he shook the examining magistrate's hand. "That's capital! You are very welcome, delighted to make your acquaintance. We are colleagues to some extent, you know. At one time I was deputy prosecutor; but not for long, only two years. I came here to look after the estate, and here I have grown old—an old fogey, in fact. You are very welcome," he went on, evidently restraining his voice so as not to speak too loud; he was going upstairs with his guests. "I have no wife, she's dead. But here, I will introduce my daughters," and turning round, he shouted down the stairs in a voice of thunder: "Tell Ignat to have the sledge ready at eight o'clock tomorrow morning."

His four daughters, young and pretty girls, all wearing gray dresses and with their hair done up in the same style, and their cousin, also young and attractive, with her children, were in the drawingroom. Startchenko, who knew them already, began at once begging them to sing something, and two of the young ladies spent a long time declaring they could not sing and that they had no music; then the cousin sat down to the piano, and with trembling voices, they sang a duet from "The Queen of Spades." Again "Un Petit Verre de Clicquot" was played, and the children skipped about, beating time with their feet. And Startchenko pranced about too. Everybody laughed.

Then the children said good-night and went off to bed. The examining magistrate laughed, danced a quadrille, flirted, and kept wondering whether it was not all a dream? The kitchen of the Zemstvo hut, the heap of hay in the corner, the rustle of the beetles, the revolting poverty-stricken surroundings, the voices of the witnesses, the wind, the snow storm, the danger of being lost; and then all at once this splendid, brightly lighted room, the sounds of the piano, the lovely girls, the curly-headed children, the gay, happy laughter—such a transformation seemed to him like a fairy tale, and it seemed incredible that such transitions were possible at the distance of some two miles in the course of one hour. And dreary thoughts prevented him from enjoying himself, and he kept thinking this was not life here, but bits of life, fragments, that everything here was accidental, that one could draw no conclusions from it; and he even felt sorry for these girls, who were living and would end their lives in the wilds, in a province far away from the center of culture, where nothing is accidental, but everything is in accordance with reason and law, and where, for instance, every suicide is intelligible, so that one can explain why it has happened and what is its significance in the general scheme of things. He imagined that if the life surrounding him here in the wilds were not intelligible to him, and if he did not see it, it meant that it did not exist at all.

At supper the conversation turned on Lesnitsky.

"He left a wife and child," said Startchenko. "I would forbid neurasthenics and all people whose nervous system is out of order to marry, I would deprive them of the right and possibility of multiplying their kind. To bring into the world nervous, invalid children is a crime."

"He was an unfortunate young man," said Von Taunitz, sighing gently and shaking his head. "What a lot one must suffer and think about before one brings oneself to take one's own life, . . . a young life! Such a misfortune may happen in any family, and that is awful. It is hard to bear such a thing, insufferable. . . ."

And all the girls listened in silence with grave faces, looking at their father. Lyzhin felt that he, too, must say something, but he couldn't think of anything, and merely said:

"Yes, suicide is an undesirable phenomenon."

He slept in a warm room, in a soft bed covered with a quilt under which there were fine clean sheets, but for some reason did not feel comfortable: perhaps because the doctor and Von Taunitz were, for a long time, talking in the adjoining room, and overhead he heard, through the ceiling and in the stove, the wind roaring just as in the Zemstvo hut, and as plaintively howling: "Oo-oo-oo-oo!"

Von Taunitz's wife had died two years before, and he was still unable to resign himself to his loss and, whatever he was talking about, always mentioned his wife; and there was no trace of a prosecutor left about him now.

"Is it possible that I may some day come to such a condition?" thought Lyzhin, as he fell asleep, still hearing through the wall his host's subdued, as it were bereaved, voice.

The examining magistrate did not sleep soundly. He felt hot and uncomfortable, and it seemed to him in his sleep that he was not at Von Taunitz's, and not in a soft clean bed, but still in the hay at the Zemstvo hut, hearing the subdued voices of the witnesses; he fancied that Lesnitsky was close by, not fifteen paces away. In his dreams he remembered how the insurance agent, black-haired and pale, wearing dusty high boots, had come into the book-keeper's office. "This is our insurance agent. . . ."

Then he dreamed that Lesnitsky and Loshadin the constable were walking through the open country in the snow, side by side, supporting each other; the snow was whirling about their heads, the wind was blowing on their backs, but they walked on, singing: "We go on, and on, and on. . . ."

The old man was like a magician in an opera, and both of them were singing as though they were on the stage:

"We go on, and on, and on! . . . You are in the warmth, in the light and snugness, but we are walking in the frost and the storm, through the deep snow. . . . We know nothing of ease, we know nothing of joy. . . . We bear all the burden of this life, yours and ours. . . . Oo-oo-oo! We go on, and on, and on. . . ."

Lyzhin woke and sat up in bed. What a confused, bad dream! And why did he dream of the constable and the agent together? What nonsense! And now while Lyzhin's heart was throbbing violently and he was sitting on his bed, holding his head in his hands, it seemed to him that there really was something in common between the lives of the insurance agent and the constable. Don't they really go side by side holding each other up? Some tie unseen, but significant and essential, existed between them, and even between them and Von Taunitz and between all men—all men; in this life, even in the remotest desert, nothing is accidental, everything is full of one common idea, everything has one soul, one aim, and to understand it it is not enough to think, it is not enough to reason, one must have also, it seems, the gift of insight into life, a gift which is evidently not bestowed on all. And the unhappy man who had broken down, who had killed himself—the "neurasthenic," as the doctor called him—and the old peasant who spent every day of his life going from one man to another, were only accidental, were only fragments of life for one who thought of his own life as accidental, but were parts of one organism—marvelous and rational—for one who thought of his own life as part of that universal whole and understood it. So thought Lyzhin, and it was a thought that had long lain hidden in his soul, and only now it was unfolded broadly and clearly to his consciousness.

He lay down and began to drop asleep; and again they were going along together, singing: "We go on, and on, and on. . . . We take from life what is hardest and bitterest in it, and we leave you what is easy and joyful; and sitting at supper, you can coldly and sensibly discuss why we suffer and perish, and why we are not as sound and as satisfied as you."

What they were singing had occurred to his mind before, but the thought was somewhere in the background behind his other thoughts, and flickered timidly like a far-away light in foggy weather. And he felt that this suicide and the peasant's sufferings lay upon his conscience, too; to resign himself to the fact that these people, submissive to their fate, should take up the burden of what was hardest and gloomiest in life—how awful it was! To accept this, and to desire for himself a life full of light and movement among happy and contented people, and to be continually dreaming of such, means dreaming of fresh suicides of men crushed by toil and anxiety, or of men weak and outcast whom people only talk of sometimes at supper with annoyance or mockery, without going to their help. . . . And again:

"We go on, and on, and on ..." as though someone were beating with a hammer on his temples.

He woke early in the morning with a headache, roused by a noise; in the next room Von Taunitz was saying loudly to the doctor:

"It's impossible for you to go now. Look what's going on outside. Don't argue, you had better ask the coachman; he won't take you in such weather for a million."

"But it's only two miles," said the doctor in an imploring voice.

"Well, if it were only half a mile. If you can't, then you can't. Directly you drive out of the gates it is perfect hell, you would be off the road in a minute. Nothing will induce me to let you go, you can say what you like."

"It's bound to be quieter towards evening," said the peasant who was heating the stove.

And in the next room the doctor began talking of the rigorous climate and its influence on the character of the Russian, of the long winters which, by preventing movement from place to place, hinder the intellectual development of the people; and Lyzhin listened with vexation to these observations and looked out of window at the snow drifts which were piled on the fence. He gazed at the white dust which covered the whole visible expanse, at the trees which bowed their heads despairingly to right and then to left, listened to the howling and the banging, and thought gloomily:

"Well, what moral can be drawn from it? It's a blizzard and that is all about it. . . ."

At midday they had lunch, then wandered aimlessly about the house; they went to the windows.

"And Lesnitsky is lying there," thought Lyzhin, watching the whirling snow, which raced furiously round and round upon the drifts. "Lesnitsky is lying there, the witnesses are waiting. . . ."

They talked of the weather, saying that the snowstorm usually lasted two days and nights, rarely longer. At six o'clock they had dinner, then they played cards, sang, danced; at last they had supper. The day was over, they went to bed.

In the night, towards morning, it all subsided. When they got up and looked out of window, the bare willows with their weakly drooping branches were standing perfectly motionless; it was dull and still, as though nature now were ashamed of its orgy, of its mad nights, and the license it had given to its passions. The horses, harnessed tandem, had been waiting at the front door since five o'clock in the morning. When it was fully daylight the doctor and the examining magistrate put on their fur coats and felt boots, and, saying good-by to their host, went out.

At the steps beside the coachman stood the familiar figure of the constable, Ilya Loshadin, with an old leather bag across his shoulder and no cap on his head, covered with snow all over, and his face was red and wet with perspiration. The footman who had come out to help the gentlemen and cover their legs looked at him sternly and said:

"What are you standing here for, you old devil? Get away!"

"Your honor, the people are anxious," said Loshadin, smiling naïvely all over his face, and evidently pleased at seeing at last the people he had waited for so long. "The people are very uneasy, the children are crying. . . . They thought, your honor, that you had gone back to the town again. Show us the heavenly mercy, our benefactors! . . ."

The doctor and the examining magistrate said nothing, got into the sledge, and drove to Syrnya.

The Lady with the Dog

I

It was said that a new person had appeared on the sea-front: a lady with a little dog. Dmitri Dmitritch Gurov, who had by then been a fortnight at Yalta, and so was fairly at home there, had begun to take an interest in new arrivals. Sitting in Verney's pavilion, he saw, walking on the sea-front, a fair-haired young lady of medium height, wearing a *béret;* a white Pomeranian dog was running behind her.

And afterwards he met her in the public gardens and in the square several times a day. She was walking alone, always wearing the same *béret,* and always with the same white dog; no one knew who she was, and every one called her simply "the lady with the dog."

"If she is here alone without a husband or friends, it wouldn't be amiss to make her acquaintance," Gurov reflected.

He was under forty, but he had a daughter already twelve years old, and two sons at school. He had been married young, when he was a student in his second year, and by now his wife seemed half as old again as he. She was a tall, erect woman with dark eyebrows, staid and dignified, and, as she said of herself, intellectual. She read a great deal, used phonetic spelling, called her husband, not Dmitri, but Dimitri, and he secretly considered her unintelligent, narrow, inelegant, was afraid of her, and did not like to be at home. He had begun being unfaithful to her long ago—had been unfaithful to her often, and, probably on that account, almost always spoke ill of women, and when they were talked about in his presence, used to call them "the lower race."

It seemed to him that he had been so schooled by bitter experience that he might call them what he liked, and yet he could not get on for two days together without "the lower race." In the society of men he was bored and not himself, with them he was cold and uncommunicative; but when he was in the company of women he felt free, and knew what to say to them and how to behave; and he was at ease with them even when he was silent. In his appearance, in his character, in his whole nature, there was something attractive and elusive which allured women and disposed them in his favour; he knew that, and some force seemed to draw him, too, to them.

Experience often repeated, truly bitter experience, had taught him long ago that with decent people, especially Moscow people—always slow to move and irresolute—every intimacy, which at first so agreeably diversifies life and appears a light and charming adventure, inevitably grows into a regular problem of extreme intricacy, and in the long run the situation becomes unbearable. But at every fresh meeting with an interesting woman this experience seemed to slip out of his memory, and he was eager for life, and everything seemed simple and amusing.

One evening he was dining in the gardens, and the lady in the *béret* came up slowly to take the next table. Her expression, her gait, her dress, and the way she did her hair told him that she was a lady, that she was married, that she was in Yalta for the first time and alone, and that she was dull there. . . . The stories told of the immorality in such places as Yalta are to a great extent untrue; he despised them, and knew that such stories were for the most part made up by persons who would themselves have been glad to sin if they had been able; but when the lady sat down at the next table three paces from him, he remembered these tales of easy conquests, of trips to the mountains, and the tempting thought of a swift, fleeting love affair, a romance with an unknown woman, whose name he did not know, suddenly took possession of him.

He beckoned coaxingly to the Pomeranian, and when the dog came up to him he shook his finger at it. The Pomeranian growled: Gurov shook his finger at it again.

The lady looked at him and at once dropped her eyes.

"He doesn't bite," she said, and blushed.

"May I give him a bone?" he asked; and when she nodded he asked courteously, "Have you been long in Yalta?"

"Five days."

"And I have already dragged out a fortnight here."

There was a brief silence.

"Time goes fast, and yet it is so dull here!" she said, not looking at him.

"That's only the fashion to say it is dull here. A provincial will live in Belyov or Zhidra and not be dull, and when he comes here it's 'Oh, the dulness! Oh, the dust!' One would think he came from Grenada."

She laughed. Then both continued eating in silence, like strangers, but after dinner they walked side by side; and there sprang up between them the light jesting conversation of people who are free and satisfied, to whom it does not matter where they go or what they talk about. They walked and talked of the strange light on the sea: the water was of a soft warm lilac hue, and there was a golden streak from the moon upon it. They talked of how sultry it was after a hot day. Gurov told her that he came from Moscow, that he had taken his degree in Arts, but had a post in a bank; that he had trained as an opera-singer, but had given it up, that he owned two houses in Moscow. . . . And from her he learnt that she had grown up in Petersburg, but had lived in S—— since her marriage two years before, that she was staying another month in Yalta, and that her husband, who needed a holiday too, might perhaps come and fetch her. She was not sure whether her husband had a post in a Crown Department or under the Provincial Council—and was amused by her own ignorance. And Gurov learnt, too, that she was called Anna Sergeyevna.

Afterwards he thought about her in his room at the hotel—thought she would certainly meet him next day; it would be sure to happen. As he got into bed he thought how lately she had been a girl at school, doing lessons like his own daughter; he recalled the diffidence, the angularity, that was still manifest in her laugh and her manner of talking with a stranger. This must have been the first time in her life she had been alone in surroundings in which she was followed, looked at, and spoken to merely from a secret motive which she could hardly fail to guess. He recalled her slender, delicate neck, her lovely grey eyes.

"There's something pathetic about her, anyway," he thought, and fell asleep.

II

A week had passed since they had made acquaintance. It was a holiday. It was sultry indoors, while in the street the wind whirled the dust round and round, and blew people's hats off. It was a thirsty day, and Gurov often went into the pavilion, and pressed Anna Sergeyevna to have syrup and water or an ice. One did not know what to do with oneself.

In the evening when the wind had dropped a little, they went out on the groyne to see the steamer come in. There were a great many people walking about the harbour; they had gathered to welcome some one, bringing bouquets. And two peculiarities of a well-dressed Yalta crowd were very conspicuous: the elderly ladies were dressed like young ones, and there were great numbers of generals.

Owing to the roughness of the sea, the steamer arrived late, after the sun had set, and it was a long time turning about before it reached the groyne. Anna Sergeyevna looked through her lorgnette at the steamer and the passengers as though looking for acquaintances, and when she turned to Gurov her eyes were shining. She talked a great deal and asked disconnected questions, forgetting next moment what she had asked; then she dropped her lorgnette in the crush.

The festive crowd began to disperse; it was too dark to see people's faces. The wind had completely dropped, but Gurov and Anna Sergeyevna still stood as though waiting to see some one else come from the steamer. Anna Sergeyevna was silent now, and sniffed the flowers without looking at Gurov.

"The weather is better this evening," he said. "Where shall we go now? Shall we drive somewhere?"

She made no answer.

Then he looked at her intently, and all at once put his arm round her and kissed her on the lips, and breathed in the moisture and the fragrance of the flowers; and he immediately looked round him, anxiously wondering whether any one had seen them.

"Let us go to your hotel," he said softly. And both walked quickly.

The room was close and smelt of the scent she had bought at the Japanese shop. Gurov looked at her and thought: "What different people one meets in the world!" From the past he preserved memories of careless, good-natured women, who loved cheerfully and were grateful to him for the happiness he gave them, however brief it might be; and of women like his wife who loved without any genuine feeling, with superfluous phrases, affectedly, hysterically, with an expression that suggested that it was not love nor passion, but something more significant; and of two or three others, very beautiful, cold women, on whose faces he had caught a glimpse of a rapacious expression—an obstinate desire to snatch from life more than it could give, and these were capricious, unreflecting, domineering, unintelligent women not in their first youth, and when Gurov grew cold to them their beauty excited his hatred, and the lace on their linen seemed to him like scales.

But in this case there was still the diffidence, the angularity of inexperienced youth, an awkward feeling; and there was a sense of consternation as though some one had suddenly knocked at the door. The attitude of Anna Sergeyevna—"the lady with the dog"—to what had happened was somehow peculiar, very grave, as though it were her fall—so it seemed, and it was strange and inappropriate. Her face dropped and faded, and on both sides of it her long hair hung down mournfully; she mused in a dejected attitude like "the woman who was a sinner" in an old-fashioned picture.

"It's wrong," she said. "You will be the first to despise me now."

There was a water-melon on the table. Gurov cut himself a slice and began eating it without haste. There followed at least half an hour of silence.

Anna Sergeyevna was touching; there was about her the purity of a good, simple woman who had seen little of life. The solitary candle burning on the table threw a faint light on her face, yet it was clear that she was very unhappy.

"How could I despise you?" asked Gurov. "You don't know what you are saying."

"God forgive me," she said, and her eyes filled with tears. "It's awful."

"You seem to feel you need to be forgiven."

"Forgiven? No. I am a bad, low woman; I despise myself and don't attempt to justify myself. It's not my husband but myself I have deceived. And not only just now; I have been deceiving myself for a long time. My husband may be a good, honest man, but he is a flunkey! I don't know what he does there, what his work is, but I know he is a flunkey! I was twenty when I was married to him. I have been tormented by curiosity; I wanted something better. 'There must be a different sort of life,' I said to myself. I wanted to live! To live, to live! . . . I was fired by curiosity . . . you don't understand it, but, I swear to God, I could not control myself; something happened to me: I could not be restrained. I told my husband I was ill, and came here. . . . And here I have been walking about as though I were dazed, like a mad creature; . . . and now I have become a vulgar, contemptible woman whom any one may despise."

Gurov felt bored already, listening to her. He was irritated by the naïve tone, by this remorse, so unexpected and inopportune; but for the tears in her eyes, he might have thought she was jesting or playing a part.

"I don't understand," he said softly. "What is it you want?"

She hid her face on his breast and pressed close to him.

"Believe me, believe me, I beseech you . . ." she said. "I love a pure, honest life, and sin is loathsome to me. I don't know what I am doing. Simple people say: 'The Evil One has beguiled me.' And I may say of myself now that the Evil One has beguiled me."

"Hush, hush! . . ." he muttered.

He looked at her fixed, scared eyes, kissed her, talked softly and affectionately, and by degrees she was comforted, and her gaiety returned; they both began laughing.

Afterwards when they went out there was not a soul on the sea-front. The town with its cypresses had quite a deathlike air, but the sea still broke noisily on the shore; a single barge was rocking on the waves, and a lantern was blinking sleepily on it.

They found a cab and drove to Oreanda.

"I found out your surname in the hall just now: it was written on the board—Von Diderits," said Gurov. "Is your husband a German?"

"No; I believe his grandfather was a German, but he is an Orthodox Russian himself."

At Oreanda they sat on a seat not far from the church, looked down at the sea, and were silent. Yalta was hardly visible through the morning mist; white clouds stood motionless on the mountain-tops. The leaves did not stir on the trees, grasshoppers chirruped, and the monotonous hollow sound of the sea rising up from below, spoke of the peace, of the eternal sleep awaiting us. So it must have sounded when there was no Yalta, no Oreanda here; so it sounds now, and it will sound as indifferently and monotonously when we are all no more. And in this constancy, in this complete indifference to the life and death of each of us, there lies hid, perhaps, a pledge of our eternal salvation, of the unceasing movement of life upon earth, of unceasing progress towards perfection. Sitting beside a young woman who in the dawn seemed so lovely, soothed and spellbound in these magical surroundings—the sea, mountains, clouds, the open sky—Gurov thought how in reality everything is beautiful in this world when one reflects: everything except what we think or do ourselves when we forget our human dignity and the higher aims of our existence.

A man walked up to them—probably a keeper—looked at them and walked away. And this detail seemed mysterious and beautiful, too. They saw a steamer come from Theodosia, with its lights out in the glow of dawn.

"There is dew on the grass," said Anna Sergeyevna, after a silence.

"Yes. It's time to go home."

They went back to the town.

Then they met every day at twelve o'clock on the sea-front, lunched and dined together, went for walks, admired the sea. She complained that she slept badly, that her heart throbbed violently; asked the same questions, troubled now by jealousy and now by the fear that he did not respect her sufficiently. And often in the square or gardens, when there was no one near them, he suddenly drew her to him and kissed her passionately. Complete idleness, these kisses in broad daylight while he looked round in dread of some one's seeing them, the heat, the smell of the sea, and the continual passing to and fro before him of idle, well-dressed, well-fed people, made a new man of him; he told Anna Sergeyevna how beautiful she was, how fascinating. He was impatiently passionate, he would not move a step away from her, while she was often pensive and continually urged him to confess that he did not respect her, did not love her in the least, and thought of her as nothing but a common woman. Rather late almost every evening they drove somewhere out of town, to Oreanda or to the waterfall; and the expedition was always a success, the scenery invariably impressed them as grand and beautiful.

They were expecting her husband to come, but a letter came from him, saying that there was something wrong with his eyes, and he entreated his wife to come home as quickly as possible. Anna Sergeyevna made haste to go.

"It's a good thing I am going away," she said to Gurov. "It's the finger of destiny!"

She went by coach and he went with her. They were driving the whole day. When she had got into a compartment of the express, and when the second bell had rung, she said:

"Let me look at you once more . . . look at you once again. That's right."

She did not shed tears, but was so sad that she seemed ill, and her face was quivering.

"I shall remember you . . . think of you," she said. "God be with you; be happy. Don't remember evil against me. We are parting forever—it must be so, for we ought never to have met. Well, God be with you."

The train moved off rapidly, its lights soon vanished from sight, and a minute later there was no sound of it, as though everything had conspired together to end as quickly as possible that sweet delirium, that madness. Left alone on the platform, and gazing into the dark distance, Gurov listened to the chirrup of the grasshoppers and the hum of the telegraph wires, feeling as though he had only just waked up. And he thought, musing, that there had been another episode or adventure in his life, and it, too, was at an end, and nothing was left of it but a memory. . . . He was moved, sad, and conscious of a slight remorse. This young woman whom he would never meet again had not been happy with him; he was genuinely warm and affectionate with her, but yet in his manner, his tone, and his caresses there had been a shade of light irony, the coarse condescension of a happy man who was, besides, almost twice her age. All the time she had called him kind, exceptional, lofty; obviously he had seemed to her different from what he really was, so he had unintentionally deceived her. . . .

Here at the station was already a scent of autumn; it was a cold evening.

"It's time for me to go north," thought Gurov as he left the platform. "High time!"

III

At home in Moscow everything was in its winter routine; the stoves were heated, and in the morning it was still dark when the children were having breakfast and getting ready for school, and the nurse would light the lamp for a short time. The frosts had begun already. When the first snow has fallen, on the first day of sledge-driving it is pleasant to see the white earth, the white roofs, to draw soft, delicious breath, and the season brings back the days of one's youth. The old limes and birches, white with hoar-frost, have a good-natured expression; they are nearer to one's heart than cypresses and palms, and near them one doesn't want to be thinking of the sea and the mountains.

Gurov was Moscow born; he arrived in Moscow on a fine frosty day, and when he put on his fur coat and warm gloves, and walked along Petrovka, and when on Saturday evening he heard the ringing of the bells, his recent trip and the places he had seen lost all charm for him.

Little by little he became absorbed in Moscow life, greedily read three newspapers a day, and declared he did not read the Moscow papers on principle! He already felt a longing to go to restaurants, clubs, dinner-parties, anniversary celebrations, and he felt flattered at entertaining distinguished lawyers and artists, and at playing cards with a professor at the doctors' club. He could already eat a whole plateful of salt fish and cabbage. . . .

In another month, he fancied, the image of Anna Sergeyevna would be shrouded in a mist in his memory, and only from time to time would visit him in his dreams with a touching smile as others did. But more than a month passed, real winter had come, and everything was still clear in his memory as though he had parted with Anna Sergeyevna only the day before. And his memories glowed more and more vividly. When in the evening stillness he heard from his study the voices of his children, preparing their lessons, or when he listened to a song or the organ at the restaurant, or the storm howled in the chimney, suddenly everything would rise up in his memory: what had happened on the groyne, and the early morning with the mist on the mountains, and the steamer coming from Theodosia, and the kisses. He would pace a long time about his room, remembering it all and smiling; then his memories passed into dreams, and in his fancy the past was mingled with what was to come. Anna Sergeyevna did not visit him in dreams, but followed him about everywhere like a shadow and haunted him. When he shut his eyes he saw her as though she were living before him, and she seemed to him lovelier, younger, tenderer than she was; and he imagined himself finer than he had been in Yalta. In the evenings she peeped out at him from the bookcase, from the fireplace, from the corner—he heard her breathing, the caressing rustle of her dress. In the street he watched the women, looking for some one like her.

He was tormented by an intense desire to confide his memories to some one. But in his home it was impossible to talk of his love, and he had no one outside; he could not talk to his tenants nor to any one at the bank. And what had he to talk of? Had he been in love, then? Had there been anything beautiful, poetical, or edifying or simply interesting in his relations with Anna Sergeyevna? And there was nothing for him but to talk vaguely of love, of woman, and no one guessed what it meant; only his wife twitched her black eyebrows, and said: "The part of a lady-killer does not suit you at all, Dimitri."

One evening, coming out of the doctors' club with an official with whom he had been playing cards, he could not resist saying:

"If only you knew what a fascinating woman I made the acquaintance of in Yalta!"

The official got into his sledge and was driving away, but turned suddenly and shouted:

"Dmitri Dmitritch!"

"What?"

"You were right this evening: the sturgeon was a bit too strong!"

These words, so ordinary, for some reason moved Gurov to indignation, and struck him as degrading and unclean. What savage manners, what people! What senseless nights, what uninteresting, uneventful days! The rage for card-playing, the gluttony, the drunkenness, the continual talk always about the same thing. Useless pursuits and conversations always about the same things absorb the better part of one's time, the better part of one's strength, and in the end there is left a life grovelling and curtailed, worthless and trivial, and there is no escaping or getting away from it—just as though one were in a madhouse or a prison.

Gurov did not sleep all night, and was filled with indignation. And he had a headache all next day. And the next night he slept badly; he sat up in bed, thinking, or paced up and down his room. He was sick of his children, sick of the bank; he had no desire to go anywhere or to talk of anything.

In the holidays in December he prepared for a journey, and told his wife he was going to Petersburg to do something in the interests of a young friend—and he set off for S——. What for? He did not very well know himself. He wanted to see Anna Sergeyevna and to talk with her—to arrange a meeting, if possible.

He reached S—— in the morning, and took the best room at the hotel, in which the floor was covered with grey army cloth, and on the table was an inkstand, grey with dust and adorned with a figure on horseback, with its hat in its hand and its head broken off. The hotel porter gave him the necessary information; Von Diderits lived in a house of his own in Old Gontcharny Street—it was not far from the hotel: he was rich and lived in good style, and had his own horses; every one in the town knew him. The porter pronounced the name "Dridirits."

Gurov went without haste to Old Gontcharny Street and found the house. Just opposite the house stretched a long grey fence adorned with nails.

"One would run away from a fence like that," thought Gurov, looking from the fence to the windows of the house and back again.

He considered: to-day was a holiday, and the husband would probably be at home. And in any case it would be tactless to go into the house and upset her. If he were to send her a note it might fall into her husband's hands, and then it might ruin everything. The best thing was to trust to chance. And he kept walking up and down the street by the fence, waiting for the chance. He saw a beggar go in at the gate and dogs fly at him; then an hour later he heard a piano, and the sounds were faint and indistinct. Probably it was Anna Sergeyevna playing. The front door suddenly opened, and an old woman came out, followed by the familiar white Pomeranian. Gurov was on the point of calling to the dog, but his heart began beating violently, and in his excitement he could not remember the dog's name.

He walked up and down, and loathed the grey fence more and more, and by now he thought irritably that Anna Sergeyevna had forgotten him, and was perhaps already amusing herself with some one else, and that that was very natural in a young woman who had nothing to look at from morning till night but that confounded fence. He went back to his hotel room and sat for a long while on the sofa, not knowing what to do, then he had dinner and a long nap.

"How stupid and worrying it is!" he thought when he woke and looked at the dark windows: it was already evening. "Here I've had a good sleep for some reason. What shall I do in the night?"

He sat on the bed, which was covered by a cheap grey blanket, such as one sees in hospitals, and he taunted himself in his vexation:

"So much for the lady with the dog . . . so much for the adventure. . . . You're in a nice fix. . . ."

That morning at the station a poster in large letters had caught his eye. "The Geisha" was to be performed for the first time. He thought of this and went to the theatre.

"It's quite possible she may go to the first performance," he thought.

The theatre was full. As in all provincial theatres, there was a fog above the chandelier, the gallery was noisy and restless; in the front row the local dandies were standing up before the beginning of the performance, with their hands behind them; in the Governor's box the Governor's daughter, wearing a boa, was sitting in the front seat, while the Governor himself lurked modestly behind the curtain with only his hands visible; the orchestra was a long time tuning up; the stage curtain swayed. All the time the audience were coming in and taking their seats Gurov looked at them eagerly.

Anna Sergeyevna, too, came in. She sat down in the third row, and when Gurov looked at her his heart contracted, and he understood clearly that for him there was in the whole world no creature so near, so precious, and so important to him; she, this little woman, in no way remarkable, lost in a provincial crowd, with a vulgar lorgnette in her hand, filled his whole life now, was his sorrow and his joy, the one happiness that he now desired for himself, and to the sounds of the inferior orchestra, of the wretched provincial violins, he thought how lovely she was. He thought and dreamed.

A young man with small side-whiskers, tall and stooping, came in with Anna Sergeyevna and sat down beside her; he bent his head at every step and seemed to be continually bowing. Most likely this was the husband whom at Yalta, in a rush of bitter feeling, she had called a flunkey. And there really was in his long figure, his side-whiskers, and the small bald patch on his head, something of the flunkey's obsequiousness; his smile was sugary, and in his buttonhole there was some badge of distinction like the number on a waiter.

During the first interval the husband went away to smoke; she remained alone in her stall. Gurov, who was sitting in the stalls, too, went up to her and said in a trembling voice, with a forced smile:

"Good-evening."

She glanced at him and turned pale, then glanced again with horror, unable to believe her eyes, and tightly gripped the fan and the lorgnette in her hands, evidently struggling with herself not to faint. Both were silent. She was sitting, he was standing, frightened by her confusion and not venturing to sit down beside her. The violins and the flute began tuning up. He felt suddenly frightened; it seemed as though all the people in the boxes were looking at them. She got up and went quickly to the door; he followed her, and both walked senselessly along passages, and up and down stairs, and figures in legal, scholastic, and civil service uniforms, all wearing badges, flitted before their eyes. They caught glimpses of ladies, of fur coats hanging on pegs; the draughts blew on them, bringing a smell of stale tobacco. And Gurov, whose heart was beating violently, thought:

"Oh, heavens! Why are these people here and this orchestra! . . ."

And at that instant he recalled how when he had seen Anna Sergeyevna off at the station he had thought that everything was over and they would never meet again. But how far they were still from the end!

On the narrow, gloomy staircase over which was written "To the Amphitheatre," she stopped.

"How you have frightened me!" she said, breathing hard, still pale and overwhelmed. "Oh, how you have frightened me! I am half dead. Why have you come? Why?"

"But do understand, Anna, do understand . . ." he said hastily in a low voice. "I entreat you to understand. . . ."

She looked at him with dread, with entreaty, with love; she looked at him intently, to keep his features more distinctly in her memory.

"I am so unhappy," she went on, not heeding him. "I have thought of nothing but you all the time; I live only in the thought of you. And I wanted to forget, to forget you; but why, oh, why, have you come?"

On the landing above them two schoolboys were smoking and looking down, but that was nothing to Gurov; he drew Anna Sergeyevna to him, and began kissing her face, her cheeks, and her hands.

"What are you doing, what are you doing!" she cried in horror, pushing him away. "We are mad. Go away to-day; go away at once. . . . I beseech you by all that is sacred, I implore you. . . . There are people coming this way!"

Some one was coming up the stairs.

"You must go away," Anna Sergeyevna went on in a whisper. "Do you hear, Dmitri Dmitritch? I will come and see you in Moscow. I have never been happy; I am miserable now, and I never, never shall be happy, never! Don't make me suffer still more! I swear I'll come to Moscow. But now let us part. My precious, good, dear one, we must part!"

She pressed his hand and began rapidly going downstairs, looking round at him, and from her eyes he could see that she really was unhappy. Gurov stood for a little while, listened, then, when all sound had died away, he found his coat and left the theatre.

IV

And Anna Sergeyevna began coming to see him in Moscow. Once in two or three months she left S——, telling her husband that she was going to consult a doctor about an internal complaint—and her husband believed her, and did not believe her. In Moscow she stayed at the Slaviansky Bazaar hotel, and at once sent a man in a red cap to Gurov. Gurov went to see her, and no one in Moscow knew of it.

Once he was going to see her in this way on a winter morning (the messenger had come the evening before when he was out). With him walked his daughter, whom he wanted to take to school: it was on the way. Snow was falling in big wet flakes.

"It's three degrees above freezing-point, and yet it is snowing," said Gurov to his daughter. "The thaw is only on the surface of the earth; there is quite a different temperature at a greater height in the atmosphere."

"And why are there no thunderstorms in the winter, father?"

He explained that, too. He talked, thinking all the while that he was going to see *her*, and no living soul knew of it, and probably never would know. He had two lives: one, open, seen and known by all who cared to know, full of relative truth and of relative falsehood, exactly like the lives of his friends and acquaintances; and another life running its course in secret. And through some strange, perhaps accidental, conjunction of circumstances, everything that was essential, of interest and of value to him, everything in which he was sincere and did not deceive himself, everything that made the kernel of his life, was hidden from other people; and all that was false in him, the sheath in which he hid himself to conceal the truth—such, for instance, as his work in the bank, his discussions at the club, his "lower race," his presence with his wife at anniversary festivities—all that was open. And he judged of others by himself, not believing in what he saw, and always believing that every man had his real, most interesting life under the cover of secrecy and under the cover of night. All personal life rested on secrecy, and possibly it was partly on that account that civilised man was so nervously anxious that personal privacy should be respected.

After leaving his daughter at school, Gurov went on to the Slaviansky Bazaar. He took off his fur coat below, went upstairs, and softly knocked at the door. Anna Sergeyevna, wearing his favourite grey dress, exhausted by the journey and the suspense, had been expecting him since the evening before. She was pale; she looked at him, and did not smile, and he had hardly come in when she fell on his breast. Their kiss was slow and prolonged, although they had not met for two years.

"Well, how are you getting on there?" he asked. "What news?"

"Wait; I'll tell you directly. . . . I can't talk."

She could not speak; she was crying. She turned away from him, and pressed her handkerchief to her eyes.

"Let her have her cry out. I'll sit down and wait," he thought, and he sat down in an arm-chair.

Then he rang and asked for tea to be brought him, and while he drank his tea she remained standing at the window with her back to him. She was crying from emotion, from the miserable consciousness that their life was so hard for them; they could only meet in secret, hiding themselves from people, like thieves! Was not their life shattered?

"Come, do stop!" he said.

It was evident to him that this love of theirs would not soon be over, that he could not see the end of it. Anna Sergeyevna grew more and more attached to him. She adored him, and it was unthinkable to say to her that it was bound to have an end some day; besides, she would not have believed it!

He went up to her and took her by the shoulders to say something affectionate and cheering, and at that moment he saw himself in the looking-glass.

His hair was already beginning to turn grey. And it seemed strange to him that he had grown so much older, so much plainer during the last few years. The shoulders on which his hands rested were warm and quivering. He felt compassion for this life, still so warm and lovely, but probably already not far from beginning to fade and wither like his own. Why did she love him so much? He always seemed to women different from what he was, and they loved in him not himself, but the man created by their imagination, whom they had been eagerly seeking all their lives; and afterwards, when they noticed their mistake, they loved him all the same. And not one of them had been happy with him. Time passed, he had made their acquaintance, got on with them, parted, but he had never once loved; it was anything you like, but not love.

And only now when his head was grey he had fallen properly, really in love—for the first time in his life.

Anna Sergeyevna and he loved each other like people very close and akin, like husband and wife, like tender friends; it seemed to them that fate itself had meant them for one another, and they could not understand why he had a wife and she a husband; and it was as though they were a pair of birds of passage, caught and forced to live in different cages. They forgave each other for what they were ashamed of in their past, they forgave everything in the present, and felt that this love of theirs had changed them both.

In moments of depression in the past he had comforted himself with any arguments that came into his mind, but now he no longer cared for arguments; he felt profound compassion, he wanted to be sincere and tender. . . .

"Don't cry, my darling," he said. "You've had your cry; that's enough. . . . Let us talk now, let us think of some plan."

Then they spent a long while taking counsel together, talked of how to avoid the necessity for secrecy, for deception, for living in different towns and not seeing each other for long at a time. How could they be free from this intolerable bondage?

"How? How?" he asked, clutching his head. "How?"

And it seemed as though in a little while the solution would be found, and then a new and splendid life would begin; and it was clear to both of them that they had still a long, long road before them, and that the most complicated and difficult part of it was only just beginning.

At Christmas Time

I

"What shall I write?" said Yegor, and he dipped his pen in the ink.

Vasilisa had not seen her daughter for four years. Her daughter Yefimya had gone after her wedding to Petersburg, had sent them two letters, and since then seemed to vanish out of their lives; there had been no sight nor sound of her. And whether the old woman were milking her cow at dawn, or heating her stove, or dozing at night, she was always thinking of one and the same thing—what was happening to Yefimya, whether she were alive out yonder. She ought to have sent a letter, but the old father could not write, and there was no one to write.

But now Christmas had come, and Vasilisa could not bear it any longer, and went to the tavern to Yegor, the brother of the innkeeper's wife, who had sat in the tavern doing nothing ever since he came back from the army; people said that he could write letters very well if he were properly paid. Vasilisa talked to the cook at the tavern, then to the mistress of the house, then to Yegor himself. They agreed upon fifteen kopecks.

And now—it happened on the second day of the holidays, in the tavern kitchen—Yegor was sitting at the table, holding the pen in his hand. Vasilisa was standing before him, pondering with an expression of anxiety and woe on her face. Pyotr, her husband, a very thin old man with a brownish bald patch, had come with her; he stood looking straight before him like a blind man. On the stove a piece of pork was being braised in a saucepan; it was spurting and hissing, and seemed to be actually saying: "Flu-flu-flu." It was stifling.

"What am I to write?" Yegor asked again.

"What?" asked Vasilisa, looking at him angrily and suspiciously. "Don't worry me! You are not writing for nothing; no fear, you'll be paid for it. Come, write: 'To our dear son-in-law, Andrey Hrisanfitch, and to our only beloved daughter, Yefimya Petrovna, with our love we send a low bow and our parental blessing abiding for ever.' "

"Written; fire away."

" 'And we wish them a happy Christmas; we are alive and well, and I wish you the same, please the Lord . . . the Heavenly King.' "

Vasilisa pondered and exchanged glances with the old man.

" 'And I wish you the same, please the Lord . . . the Heavenly King,' " she repeated, beginning to cry.

She could say nothing more. And yet before, when she lay awake thinking at night, it had seemed to her that she could not get all she had to say into a dozen letters. Since the time when her daughter had gone away with her husband much water had flowed into the sea, the old people had lived feeling bereaved, and sighed heavily at night as though they had buried their daughter. And how many events had occurred in the village since then, how many marriages and deaths! How long the winters had been! How long the nights!

"It's hot," said Yegor, unbuttoning his waistcoat. "It must be seventy degrees. What more?" he asked.

The old people were silent.

"What does your son-in-law do in Petersburg?" asked Yegor.

"He was a soldier, my good friend," the old man answered in a weak voice. "He left the service at the same time as you did. He was a soldier, and now, to be sure, he is at Petersburg at a hydropathic establishment. The doctor treats the sick with water. So he, to be sure, is house-porter at the doctor's."

"Here it is written down," said the old woman, taking a letter out of her pocket. "We got it from Yefimya, goodness knows when. Maybe they are no longer in this world."

Yegor thought a little and began writing rapidly:

"At the present time"—he wrote—"since your destiny through your own doing allotted you to the Military Career, we counsel you to look into the Code of Disciplinary Offences and Fundamental Laws of the War Office, and you will see in that law the Civilization of the Officials of the War Office."

He wrote and kept reading aloud what was written, while Vasilisa considered what she ought to write: how great had been their want the year before, how their corn had not lasted even till Christmas, how they had to sell their cow. She ought to ask for money, ought to write that the old father was often ailing and would soon no doubt give up his soul to God . . . but how to express this in words? What must be said first and what afterwards?

"Take note," Yegor went on writing, "in volume five of the Army Regulations soldier is a common noun and a proper one, a soldier of the first rank is called a general, and of the last a private. . . ."

The old man stirred his lips and said softly:

"It would be all right to have a look at the grandchildren."

"What grandchildren?" asked the old woman, and she looked angrily at him; "perhaps there are none."

"Well, but perhaps there are. Who knows?"

"And thereby you can judge," Yegor hurried on, "what is the enemy without and what is the enemy within. The foremost of our enemies within is Bacchus." The pen squeaked, executing upon the paper flourishes like fish-hooks. Yegor hastened and read over every line several times. He sat on a stool sprawling his broad feet under the table, well-fed, bursting with health, with a coarse animal face and a red bull neck. He was vulgarity itself: coarse, conceited, invincible, proud of having been born and bred in a pot-house; and Vasilisa quite understood the vulgarity, but could not express it in words, and could only look angrily and suspiciously at Yegor. Her head was beginning to ache, and her thoughts were in confusion from the sound of his voice and his unintelligible words, from the heat and the stuffiness, and she said nothing and thought nothing, but simply waited for him to finish scribbling. But the old man looked with full confidence. He believed in his old woman who had brought him there, and in Yegor; and when he had mentioned the hydropathic establishment it could be seen that he believed in the establishment and the healing efficacy of water.

Having finished the letter, Yegor got up and read the whole of it through from the beginning. The old man did not understand, but he nodded his head trustfully.

"That's all right; it is smooth . . ." he said. "God give you health. That's all right. . . ."

They laid on the table three five-kopeck pieces and went out of the tavern; the old man looked immovably straight before him as though he were blind, and perfect trustfulness was written on his face; but as Vasilisa came out of the tavern she waved angrily at the dog, and said angrily:

"Ugh, the plague."

The old woman did not sleep all night; she was disturbed by thoughts, and at daybreak she got up, said her prayers, and went to the station to send off the letter.

It was between eight and nine miles to the station.

II

Dr. B. O. Mozelweiser's hydropathic establishment worked on New Year's Day exactly as on ordinary days; the only difference was that the porter, Andrey Hrisanfitch, had on a uniform with new braiding, his boots had an extra polish, and he greeted every visitor with "A Happy New Year to you!"

It was the morning; Andrey Hrisanfitch was standing at the door, reading the newspaper. Just at ten o'clock there arrived a general, one of the habitual visitors, and directly after him the postman; Andrey Hrisanfitch helped the general off with his great-coat, and said:

"A Happy New Year to your Excellency!"

"Thank you, my good fellow; the same to you."

And at the top of the stairs the general asked, nodding towards the door (he asked the same question every day and always forgot the answer):

"And what is there in that room?"

"The massage room, your Excellency."

When the general's steps had died away Andrey Hrisanfitch looked at the post that had come, and found one addressed to himself. He tore it open, read several lines, then, looking at the newspaper, he walked without haste to his own room, which was downstairs close by at the end of the passage. His wife Yefimya was sitting on the bed, feeding her baby; another child, the eldest, was standing by, laying its curly head on her knee; a third was asleep on the bed.

Going into the room, Andrey gave his wife the letter and said:

"From the country, I suppose."

Then he walked out again without taking his eyes from the paper. He could hear Yefimya with a shaking voice reading the first lines. She read them and could read no more; these lines were enough for her. She burst into tears, and hugging her eldest child, kissing him, she began saying—and it was hard to say whether she were laughing or crying:

"It's from granny, from grandfather," she said. "From the country.... The Heavenly Mother, Saints and Martyrs! The snow lies heaped up under the roofs now ... the trees are as white as white. The boys slide on little sledges ... and dear old bald grandfather is on the stove ... and there is a little yellow dog.... My own darlings!"

Andrey Hrisanfitch, hearing this, recalled that his wife had on three or four occasions given him letters and asked him to send them to the country, but some important business had always prevented him; he had not sent them, and the letters somehow got lost.

"And little hares run about in the fields," Yefimya went on chanting, kissing her boy and shedding tears. "Grandfather is kind and gentle; granny is good, too—kind-hearted. They are warm-hearted in the country, they are God-fearing ... and there is a little church in the village; the peasants sing in the choir. Queen of Heaven, Holy Mother and Defender, take us away from here!"

Andrey Hrisanfitch returned to his room to smoke a little till there was another ring at the door, and Yefimya ceased speaking, subsided, and wiped her eyes, though her lips were still quivering. She was very much frightened of him—oh, how frightened of him! She trembled and was reduced to terror by the sound of his steps, by the look in his eyes, and dared not utter a word in his presence.

Andrey Hrisanfitch lighted a cigarette, but at that very moment there was a ring from upstairs. He put out his cigarette, and, assuming a very grave face, hastened to his front door.

The general was coming downstairs, fresh and rosy from his bath.

"And what is there in that room?" he asked, pointing to a door.

Andrey Hrisanfitch put his hands down swiftly to the seams of his trousers, and pronounced loudly:

"Charcot douche, your Excellency!"

The Bishop

I

The evening service was being celebrated on the eve of Palm Sunday in the Old Petrovsky Convent. When they began distributing the palm it was close upon ten o'clock, the candles were burning dimly, the wicks wanted snuffing; it was all in a sort of mist. In the twilight of the church the crowd seemed heaving like the sea, and to Bishop Pyotr, who had been unwell for the last three days, it seemed that all the faces—old and young, men's and women's—were alike, that everyone who came up for the palm had the same expression in his eyes. In the mist he could not see the doors; the crowd kept moving and looked as though there were no end to it. The female choir was singing, a nun was reading the prayers for the day.

How stifling, how hot it was! How long the service went on! Bishop Pyotr was tired. His breathing was laboured and rapid, his throat was parched, his shoulders ached with weariness, his legs were trembling. And it disturbed him unpleasantly when a religious maniac uttered occasional shrieks in the gallery. And then all of a sudden, as though in a dream or delirium, it seemed to the bishop as though his own mother Marya Timofyevna, whom he had not seen for nine years, or some old woman just like his mother, came up to him out of the crowd, and, after taking a palm branch from him, walked away looking at him all the while good-humouredly with a kind, joyful smile until she was lost in the crowd. And for some reason tears flowed down his face. There was peace in his heart, everything was well, yet he kept gazing fixedly towards the left choir, where the prayers were being read, where in the dusk of evening you could not recognize anyone, and—wept. Tears glistened on his face and on his beard. Here someone close at hand was weeping, then someone else farther away, then others and still others, and little by little the church was filled with soft weeping. And a little later, within five minutes, the nuns' choir was singing; no one was weeping and everything was as before.

Soon the service was over. When the bishop got into his carriage to drive home, the gay, melodious chime of the heavy, costly bells was filling the whole garden in the moonlight. The white walls, the white crosses on the tombs, the white birch-trees and black shadows, and the far-away moon in the sky exactly over the convent, seemed now living their own life, apart and incomprehensible, yet very near to man. It was the beginning of April, and after the warm spring day it turned cool; there was a faint touch of frost, and the breath of spring could be felt in the soft, chilly air. The road from the convent to the town was sandy, the horses had to go at a walking pace, and on both sides of the carriage in the brilliant, peaceful moonlight there were people trudging along home from church through the sand. And all was silent, sunk in thought; everything around seemed kindly, youthful, akin, everything—trees and sky and even the moon, and one longed to think that so it would be always.

At last the carriage drove into the town and rumbled along the principal street. The shops were already shut, but at Erakin's, the millionaire shopkeeper's, they were trying the new electric lights, which flickered brightly, and a crowd of people were gathered round. Then came wide, dark, deserted streets, one after another; then the high-road, the open country, the fragrance of pines. And suddenly there rose up before the bishop's eyes a white turreted wall, and behind it a tall belfry in the full moonlight, and beside it five shining, golden cupolas: this was the Pankratievsky Monastery, in which Bishop Pyotr lived. And here, too, high above the monastery, was the silent, dreamy moon. The carriage drove in at the gate, crunching over the sand; here and there in the moonlight there were glimpses of dark monastic figures, and there was the sound of footsteps on the flag-stones. . . .

"You know, your holiness, your mamma arrived while you were away," the lay brother informed the bishop as he went into his cell.

"My mother? When did she come?"

"Before the evening service. She asked first where you were and then she went to the convent."

"Then it was her I saw in the church, just now! Oh, Lord!"

And the bishop laughed with joy.

"She bade me tell your holiness," the lay brother went on, "that she would come to-morrow. She had a little girl with her—her grandchild, I suppose. They are staying at Ovsyannikov's inn."

"What time is it now?"

"A little after eleven."

"Oh, how vexing!"

The bishop sat for a little while in the parlour, hesitating, and as it were refusing to believe it was so late. His arms and legs were stiff, his head ached. He was hot and uncomfortable. After resting a little he went into his bedroom, and there, too, he sat a little, still thinking of his mother; he could hear the lay brother going away, and Father Sisoy coughing the other side of the wall. The monastery clock struck a quarter.

The bishop changed his clothes and began reading the prayers before sleep. He read attentively those old, long familiar prayers, and at the same time thought about his mother. She had nine children and about forty grandchildren. At one time, she had lived with her husband, the deacon, in a poor village; she had lived there a very long time from the age of seventeen to sixty. The bishop remembered her from early childhood, almost from the age of three, and—how he had loved her! Sweet, precious childhood, always fondly remembered! Why did it, that long-past time that could never return, why did it seem brighter, fuller, and more festive than it had really been? When in his childhood or youth he had been ill, how tender and sympathetic his mother had been! And now his prayers mingled with the memories, which gleamed more and more brightly like a flame, and the prayers did not hinder his thinking of his mother.

When he had finished his prayers he undressed and lay down, and at once, as soon as it was dark, there rose before his mind his dead father, his mother, his native village Lesopolye . . . the creak of wheels, the bleat of sheep, the church bells on bright summer mornings, the gypsies under the window—oh, how sweet to think of it! He remembered the priest of Lesopolye, Father Simeon—mild, gentle, kindly; he was a lean little man, while his son, a divinity student, was a huge fellow and talked in a roaring bass voice. The priest's son had flown into a rage with the cook and abused her: "Ah, you Jehud's ass!" and Father Simeon overhearing it, said not a word, and was only ashamed because he could not remember where such an ass was mentioned in the Bible. After him the priest at Lesopolye had been Father Demyan, who used to drink heavily, and at times drank till he saw green snakes, and was even nicknamed Demyan Snakeseer. The schoolmaster at Lesopolye was Matvey Nikolaitch, who had been a divinity student, a kind and intelligent man, but he, too, was a drunkard; he never beat the schoolchildren, but for some reason he always had hanging on his wall a bunch of birch-twigs, and below it an utterly meaningless inscription in Latin: "Betula kinderbalsamica secuta." He had a shaggy black dog whom he called Syntax.

And his holiness laughed. Six miles from Lesopolye was the village Obnino with a wonder-working ikon. In the summer they used to carry the ikon in procession about the neighbouring villages and ring the bells the whole day long; first in one village and then in another, and it used to seem to the bishop then that joy was quivering in the air, and he (in those days his name was Pavlusha) used to follow the ikon, bareheaded and barefoot, with naïve faith, with a naïve smile, infinitely happy. In Obnino, he remembered now, there were always a lot of people, and the priest there, Father Alexey, to save time during mass, used to make his deaf nephew Ilarion read the names of those for whose health or whose souls' peace prayers were asked. Ilarion used to read them, now and then getting a five or ten kopeck piece for the service, and only when he was grey and bald, when life was nearly over, he suddenly saw written on one of the pieces of paper: "What a fool you are, Ilarion." Up to fifteen at least Pavlusha was undeveloped and idle at his lessons, so much so that they thought of taking him away from the clerical school and putting him into a shop; one day, going to the post at Obnino for letters, he had stared a long time at the post-office clerks and asked: "Allow me to ask, how do you get your salary, every month or every day?"

His holiness crossed himself and turned over on the other side, trying to stop thinking and go to sleep.

"My mother has come," he remembered and laughed.

The moon peeped in at the window, the floor was lighted up, and there were shadows on it. A cricket was chirping. Through the wall Father Sisoy was snoring in the next room, and his aged snore had a sound that suggested loneliness, forlornness, even vagrancy. Sisoy had once been housekeeper to the bishop of the diocese, and was called now "the former Father Housekeeper"; he was seventy years old, he lived in a monastery twelve miles from the town and stayed sometimes in the town, too. He had come to the Pankratievsky Monastery three days before, and the bishop had kept him that he might talk to him at his leisure about matters of business, about the arrangements here. . . .

At half-past one they began ringing for matins. Father Sisoy could be heard coughing, muttering something in a discontented voice, then he got up and walked barefoot about the rooms.

"Father Sisoy," the bishop called.

Sisoy went back to his room and a little later made his appearance in his boots, with a candle; he had on his cassock over his underclothes and on his head was an old faded skull-cap.

"I can't sleep," said the bishop, sitting up. "I must be unwell. And what it is I don't know. Fever!"

"You must have caught cold, your holiness. You must be rubbed with tallow." Sisoy stood a little and yawned. "O Lord, forgive me, a sinner."

"They had the electric lights on at Erakin's to-day," he said; "I don't like it!"

Father Sisoy was old, lean, bent, always dissatisfied with something, and his eyes were angry-looking and prominent as a crab's.

"I don't like it," he said, going away. "I don't like it. Bother it!"

II

Next day, Palm Sunday, the bishop took the service in the cathedral in the town, then he visited the bishop of the diocese, then visited a very sick old lady, the widow of a general, and at last drove home. Between one and two o'clock he had welcome visitors dining with him—his mother and his niece Katya, a child of eight years old. All dinner-time the spring sunshine was streaming in at the windows, throwing bright light on the white tablecloth and on Katya's red hair. Through the double windows they could hear the noise of the rooks and the notes of the starlings in the garden.

"It is nine years since we have met," said the old lady. "And when I looked at you in the monastery yesterday, good Lord! you've not changed a bit, except maybe you are thinner and your beard is a little longer. Holy Mother, Queen of Heaven! Yesterday at the evening service no one could help crying. I, too, as I looked at you, suddenly began crying, though I couldn't say why. His Holy Will!"

And in spite of the affectionate tone in which she said this, he could see she was constrained as though she were uncertain whether to address him formally or familiarly, to laugh or not, and that she felt herself more a deacon's widow than his mother. And Katya gazed without blinking at her uncle, his holiness, as though trying to discover what sort of a person he was. Her hair sprang up from under the comb and the velvet ribbon and stood out like a halo: she had a turned-up nose and sly eyes. The child had broken a glass before sitting down to dinner, and now her grandmother, as she talked, moved away from Katya first a wineglass and then a tumbler. The bishop listened to his mother and remembered how many, many years ago she used to take him and his brothers and sisters to relations whom she considered rich; in those days she was taken up with the care of her children, now with her grandchildren, and she had brought Katya. . . .

"Your sister, Varenka, has four children," she told him; "Katya, here, is the eldest. And your brother-in-law Father Ivan fell sick, God knows of what, and died three days before the Assumption; and my poor Varenka is left a beggar."

"And how is Nikanor getting on?" the bishop asked about his eldest brother.

"He is all right, thank God. Though he has nothing much, yet he can live. Only there is one thing: his son, my grandson Nikolasha, did not want to go into the Church; he has gone to the university to be a doctor. He thinks it is better; but who knows! His Holy Will!"

"Nikolasha cuts up dead people," said Katya, spilling water over her knees.

"Sit still, child," her grandmother observed calmly, and took the glass out of her hand. "Say a prayer, and go on eating."

"How long it is since we have seen each other!" said the bishop, and he tenderly stroked his mother's hand and shoulder; "and I missed you abroad, mother, I missed you dreadfully."

"Thank you."

"I used to sit in the evenings at the open window, lonely and alone; often there was music playing, and all at once I used to be overcome with homesickness and felt as though I would give everything only to be at home and see you."

His mother smiled, beamed, but at once she made a grave face and said:

"Thank you."

His mood suddenly changed. He looked at his mother and could not understand how she had come by that respectfulness, that timid expression of face: what was it for? And he did not recognize her. He felt sad and vexed. And then his head ached just as it had the day before; his legs felt fearfully tired, and the fish seemed to him stale and tasteless; he felt thirsty all the time. . . .

After dinner two rich ladies, landowners, arrived and sat for an hour and a half in silence with rigid countenances; the archimandrite, a silent, rather deaf man, came to see him about business. Then they began ringing for vespers; the sun was setting behind the wood and the day was over. When he returned from church, he hurriedly said his prayers, got into bed, and wrapped himself up as warm as possible.

It was disagreeable to remember the fish he had eaten at dinner. The moonlight worried him, and then he heard talking. In an adjoining room, probably in the parlour, Father Sisoy was talking politics:

"There's war among the Japanese now. They are fighting. The Japanese, my good soul, are the same as the Montenegrins; they are the same race. They were under the Turkish yoke together."

And then he heard the voice of Marya Timofyevna:

"So, having said our prayers and drunk tea, we went, you know, to Father Yegor at Novokatnoye, so . . ."

And she kept on saying, "having had tea" or "having drunk tea," and it seemed as though the only thing she had done in her life was to drink tea.

The bishop slowly, languidly, recalled the seminary, the academy. For three years he had been Greek teacher in the seminary: by that time he could not read without spectacles. Then he had become a monk; he had been made a school inspector. Then he had defended his thesis for his degree. When he was thirty-two he had been made rector of the seminary, and consecrated archimandrite: and then his life had been so easy, so pleasant; it seemed so long, so long, no end was in sight. Then he had begun to be ill, had grown very thin and almost blind, and by the advice of the doctors had to give up everything and go abroad.

"And what then?" asked Sisoy in the next room.

"Then we drank tea . . ." answered Marya Timofyevna.

"Good gracious, you've got a green beard," said Katya suddenly in surprise, and she laughed.

The bishop remembered that the grey-headed Father Sisoy's beard really had a shade of green in it, and he laughed.

"God have mercy upon us, what we have to put up with with this girl!" said Sisoy, aloud, getting angry. "Spoilt child! Sit quiet!"

The bishop remembered the perfectly new white church in which he had conducted the services while living abroad, he remembered the sound of the warm sea. In his flat he had five lofty light rooms; in his study he had a new writing-table, lots of books. He had read a great deal and often written. And he remembered how he had pined for his native land, how a blind beggar woman had played the guitar under his window every day and sung of love, and how, as he listened, he had always for some reason thought of the past. But eight years had passed and he had been called back to Russia, and now he was a suffragan bishop, and all the past had retreated far away into the mist as though it were a dream. . . .

Father Sisoy came into the bedroom with a candle.

"I say!" he said, wondering, "are you asleep already, your holiness?"

"What is it?"

"Why, it's still early, ten o'clock or less. I bought a candle to-day; I wanted to rub you with tallow."

"I am in a fever . . ." said the bishop, and he sat up. "I really ought to have something. My head is bad. . . ."

Sisoy took off the bishop's shirt and began rubbing his chest and back with tallow.

"That's the way . . . that's the way . . ." he said. "Lord Jesus Christ . . . that's the way. I walked to the town to-day; I was at what's-his-name's—the chief priest Sidonsky's. . . . I had tea with him. I don't like him. Lord Jesus Christ. . . . That's the way. I don't like him."

III

The bishop of the diocese, a very fat old man, was ill with rheumatism or gout, and had been in bed for over a month. Bishop Pyotr went to see him almost every day, and saw all who came to ask his help. And now that he was unwell he was struck by the emptiness, the triviality of everything which they asked and for which they wept; he was vexed at their ignorance, their timidity; and all this useless, petty business oppressed him by the mass of it, and it seemed to him that now he understood the diocesan bishop, who had once in his young days written on "The Doctrines of the Freedom of the Will," and now seemed to be all lost in trivialities, to have forgotten everything, and to have no thoughts of religion. The bishop must have lost touch with Russian life while he was abroad; he did not find it easy; the peasants seemed to him coarse, the women who sought his help dull and stupid, the seminarists and their teachers uncultivated and at times savage. And the documents coming in and going out were reckoned by tens of thousands;

and what documents they were! The higher clergy in the whole diocese gave the priests, young and old, and even their wives and children, marks for their behaviour—a five, a four, and sometimes even a three; and about this he had to talk and to read and write serious reports. And there was positively not one minute to spare; his soul was troubled all day long, and the bishop was only at peace when he was in church.

He could not get used, either, to the awe which, through no wish of his own, he inspired in people in spite of his quiet, modest disposition. All the people in the province seemed to him little, scared, and guilty when he looked at them. Everyone was timid in his presence, even the old chief priests; everyone "flopped" at his feet, and not long previously an old lady, a village priest's wife who had come to consult him, was so overcome by awe that she could not utter a single word, and went empty away. And he, who could never in his sermons bring himself to speak ill of people, never reproached anyone because he was so sorry for them, was moved to fury with the people who came to consult him, lost his temper and flung their petitions on the floor. The whole time he had been here, not one person had spoken to him genuinely, simply, as to a human being; even his old mother seemed now not the same! And why, he wondered, did she chatter away to Sisoy and laugh so much; while with him, her son, she was grave and usually silent and constrained, which did not suit her at all. The only person who behaved freely with him and said what he meant was old Sisoy, who had spent his whole life in the presence of bishops and had outlived eleven of them. And so the bishop was at ease with him, although, of course, he was a tedious and nonsensical man.

After the service on Tuesday, his holiness Pyotr was in the diocesan bishop's house receiving petitions there; he got excited and angry, and then drove home. He was as unwell as before; he longed to be in bed, but he had hardly reached home when he was informed that a young merchant called Erakin, who subscribed liberally to charities, had come to see him about a very important matter. The bishop had to see him. Erakin stayed about an hour, talked very loud, almost shouted, and it was difficult to understand what he said.

"God grant it may," he said as he went away. "Most essential! According to circumstances, your holiness! I trust it may!"

After him came the Mother Superior from a distant convent. And when she had gone they began ringing for vespers. He had to go to church.

In the evening the monks sang harmoniously, with inspiration. A young priest with a black beard conducted the service; and the bishop, hearing of the Bridegroom who comes at midnight and of the Heavenly Mansion adorned for the festival, felt no repentance for his sins, no tribulation, but peace at heart and tranquillity. And he was carried back in thought to the distant past, to his childhood and youth, when, too, they used to sing of the Bridegroom and of the Heavenly Mansion; and now that past rose up before him—living, fair, and joyful as in all likelihood it never had been. And perhaps in the other world, in the life to come, we shall think of the distant past, of our life here, with the same feeling. Who knows? The bishop was sitting near the altar. It was dark; tears flowed down his face. He thought that here he had attained everything a man in his position could attain; he had faith and yet everything was not clear, something was lacking still. He did not want to die; and he still felt that he had missed what was most important, something of which he had dimly dreamed in the past; and he was troubled by the same hopes for the future as he had felt in childhood, at the academy and abroad.

"How well they sing to-day!" he thought, listening to the singing. "How nice it is!"

IV

On Thursday he celebrated mass in the cathedral; it was the Washing of Feet. When the service was over and the people were going home, it was sunny, warm; the water gurgled in the gutters, and the unceasing trilling of the larks, tender, telling of peace, rose from the fields outside the town. The trees were already awakening and smiling a welcome, while above them the infinite, fathomless blue sky stretched into the distance, God knows whither.

On reaching home his holiness drank some tea, then changed his clothes, lay down on his bed, and told the lay brother to close the shutters on the windows. The bedroom was darkened. But what weariness, what pain in his legs and his back, a chill heavy pain, what a noise in his ears! He had not slept for a long time—for a very long time, as it seemed to him now, and some trifling detail which haunted his brain as soon as his eyes were closed prevented him from sleeping. As on the day before, sounds reached him from the adjoining rooms through the walls, voices, the jingle of glasses and teaspoons. . . . Marya Timofyevna was gaily telling Father Sisoy some story with quaint turns of speech, while the latter answered in a grumpy, ill-humoured voice: "Bother them! Not likely! What next!" And the bishop again felt vexed and then hurt that with other people his old mother behaved in a simple, ordinary way, while with him, her son, she was shy, spoke little, and did not say what she meant, and even, as he fancied, had during all those three days kept trying in his presence to find an excuse for standing up, because she was embarrassed at sitting before him. And his father? He, too, probably, if he had been living, would not have been able to utter a word in the bishop's presence. . . .

Something fell down on the floor in the adjoining room and was broken; Katya must have dropped a cup or a saucer, for Father Sisoy suddenly spat and said angrily:

"What a regular nuisance the child is! Lord forgive my transgressions! One can't provide enough for her."

Then all was quiet, the only sounds came from outside. And when the bishop opened his eyes he saw Katya in his room, standing motionless, staring at him. Her red hair, as usual, stood up from under the comb like a halo.

"Is that you, Katya?" he asked. "Who is it downstairs who keeps opening and shutting a door?"

"I don't hear it," answered Katya; and she listened.

"There, someone has just passed by."

"But that was a noise in your stomach, uncle."

He laughed and stroked her on the head.

"So you say Cousin Nikolasha cuts up dead people?" he asked after a pause.

"Yes, he is studying."

"And is he kind?"

"Oh, yes, he's kind. But he drinks vodka awfully."

"And what was it your father died of?"

"Papa was weak and very, very thin, and all at once his throat was bad. I was ill then, too, and brother Fedya; we all had bad throats. Papa died, uncle, and we got well."

Her chin began quivering, and tears gleamed in her eyes and trickled down her cheeks.

"Your holiness," she said in a shrill voice, by now weeping bitterly, "uncle, mother and all of us are left very wretched. . . . Give us a little money . . . do be kind . . . uncle darling. . . ."

He, too, was moved to tears, and for a long time was too much touched to speak. Then he stroked her on the head, patted her on the shoulder and said:

"Very good, very good, my child. When the holy Easter comes, we will talk it over. . . . I will help you. . . . I will help you. . . ."

His mother came in quietly, timidly, and prayed before the ikon. Noticing that he was not sleeping, she said:

"Won't you have a drop of soup?"

"No, thank you," he answered, "I am not hungry."

"You seem to be unwell, now I look at you. I should think so; you may well be ill! The whole day on your legs, the whole day. . . . And, my goodness, it makes one's heart ache even to look at you! Well, Easter is not far off; you will rest then, please God. Then we will have a talk, too, but now I'm not going to disturb you with my chatter. Come along, Katya; let his holiness sleep a little."

And he remembered how once very long ago, when he was a boy, she had spoken exactly like that, in the same jestingly respectful tone, with a Church dignitary. . . . Only from her extraordinarily kind eyes and the timid, anxious glance she stole at him as she went out of the room could one have guessed that this was his mother. He shut his eyes and seemed to sleep, but twice heard the clock strike and Father Sisoy coughing the other side of the wall. And once more his mother came in and looked timidly at him for a minute. Someone drove up to the steps, as he could hear, in a coach or in a chaise. Suddenly a knock, the door slammed, the lay brother came into the bedroom.

"Your holiness," he called.

"Well?"

"The horses are here; it's time for the evening service."

"What o'clock is it?"

"A quarter past seven."

He dressed and drove to the cathedral. During all the "Twelve Gospels" he had to stand in the middle of the church without moving, and the first gospel, the longest and the most beautiful, he read himself. A mood of confidence and courage came over him. That first gospel, "Now is the Son of Man glorified," he knew by heart; and as he read he raised his eyes from time to time, and saw on both sides a perfect sea of lights and heard the splutter of candles, but, as in past years, he could not see the people, and it seemed as though these were all the same people as had been round him in those days, in his childhood and his youth; that they would always be the same every year and till such time as God only knew.

His father had been a deacon, his grandfather a priest, his great-grandfather a deacon, and his whole family, perhaps from the days when Christianity had been accepted in Russia, had belonged to the priesthood; and his love for the Church services, for the priesthood, for the peal of the bells, was deep in him, ineradicable, innate. In church, particularly when he took part in the service, he felt vigorous, of good cheer, happy. So it was now. Only when the eighth gospel had been read, he felt that his voice had grown weak, even his cough was inaudible. His head had begun to ache intensely, and he was troubled by a fear that he might fall down. And his legs were indeed quite numb, so that by degrees he ceased to feel them and could not understand how or on what he was standing, and why he did not fall. . . .

It was a quarter to twelve when the service was over. When he reached home, the bishop undressed and went to bed at once without even saying his prayers. He could not speak and felt that he could not have stood up. When he had covered his head with the quilt he felt a sudden longing to be abroad, an insufferable longing! He felt that he would give his life not to see those pitiful cheap shutters, those low ceilings, not to smell that heavy monastery smell. If only there were one person to whom he could have talked, have opened his heart!

For a long while he heard footsteps in the next room and could not tell whose they were. At last the door opened, and Sisoy came in with a candle and a tea-cup in his hand.

"You are in bed already, your holiness?" he asked. "Here I have come to rub you with spirit and vinegar. A thorough rubbing does a great deal of good. Lord Jesus Christ! . . . That's the way . . . that's the way. . . . I've just been in our monastery. . . . I don't like it. I'm going away from here to-morrow, your holiness; I don't want to stay longer. Lord Jesus Christ. . . . That's the way. . . ."

Sisoy could never stay long in the same place, and he felt as though he had been a whole year in the Pankratievsky Monastery. Above all, listening to him it was difficult to understand where his home was, whether he cared for anyone or anything, whether he believed in God. . . . He did not know himself why he was a monk, and, indeed, he did not think about it, and the time when he had become a monk had long passed out of his memory; it seemed as though he had been born a monk.

"I'm going away to-morrow; God be with them all."

"I should like to talk to you. . . . I can't find the time," said the bishop softly with an effort. "I don't know anything or anybody here. . . ."

"I'll stay till Sunday if you like; so be it, but I don't want to stay longer. I am sick of them!"

"I ought not to be a bishop," said the bishop softly. "I ought to have been a village priest, a deacon . . . or simply a monk. . . . All this oppresses me . . . oppresses me."

"What? Lord Jesus Christ. . . . That's the way. Come, sleep well, your holiness! . . . What's the good of talking? It's no use. Good-night!"

The bishop did not sleep all night. And at eight o'clock in the morning he began to have hæmorrhage from the bowels. The lay brother was alarmed, and ran first to the archimandrite, then for the monastery doctor, Ivan Andreyitch, who lived in the town. The doctor, a stout old man with a long grey beard, made a prolonged examination of the bishop, and kept shaking his head and frowning, then said:

"Do you know, your holiness, you have got typhoid?"

After an hour or so of hæmorrhage the bishop looked much thinner, paler, and wasted; his face looked wrinkled, his eyes looked bigger, and he seemed older, shorter, and it seemed to him that he was thinner, weaker, more insignificant than anyone, that everything that had been had retreated far, far away and would never go on again or be repeated.

"How good," he thought, "how good!"

His old mother came. Seeing his wrinkled face and his big eyes, she was frightened, she fell on her knees by the bed and began kissing his face, his shoulders, his hands. And to her, too, it seemed that he was thinner, weaker, and more insignificant than anyone, and now she forgot that he was a bishop, and kissed him as though he were a child very near and very dear to her.

"Pavlusha, darling," she said; "my own, my darling son! . . . Why are you like this? Pavlusha, answer me!"

Katya, pale and severe, stood beside her, unable to understand what was the matter with her uncle, why there was such a look of suffering on her grandmother's face, why she was saying such sad and touching things. By now he could not utter a word, he could understand nothing, and he imagined he was a simple ordinary man, that he was walking quickly, cheerfully through the fields, tapping with his stick, while above him was the open sky bathed in sunshine, and that he was free now as a bird and could go where he liked!

"Pavlusha, my darling son, answer me," the old woman was saying. "What is it? My own!"

"Don't disturb his holiness," Sisoy said angrily, walking about the room. "Let him sleep . . . what's the use . . . it's no good. . . ."

Three doctors arrived, consulted together, and went away again. The day was long, incredibly long, then the night came on and passed slowly, slowly, and towards morning on Saturday the lay brother went in to the old mother who was lying on the sofa in the parlour, and asked her to go into the bedroom: the bishop had just breathed his last.

Next day was Easter Sunday. There were forty-two churches and six monasteries in the town; the sonorous, joyful clang of the bells hung over the town from morning till night unceasingly, setting the spring air aquiver; the birds were singing, the sun was shining brightly. The big market square was noisy, swings were going, barrel organs were playing, accordions were squeaking, drunken voices were shouting. After midday people began driving up and down the principal street.

In short, all was merriment, everything was satisfactory, just as it had been the year before, and as it will be in all likelihood next year.

A month later a new suffragan bishop was appointed, and no one thought anything more of Bishop Pyotr, and afterwards he was completely forgotten. And only the dead man's old mother, who is living to-day with her son-in-law the deacon in a remote little district town, when she goes out at night to bring her cow in and meets other women at the pasture, begins talking of her children and her grandchildren, and says that she had a son a bishop, and this she says timidly, afraid that she may not be believed. . . .

And, indeed, there are some who do not believe her.

Betrothed

[The Bride]

I

It was ten o'clock in the evening and the full moon was shining over the garden. In the Shumins' house an evening service celebrated at the request of the grandmother, Marfa Mihalovna, was just over, and now Nadya—she had gone into the garden for a minute—could see the table being laid for supper in the dining-room, and her grandmother bustling about in her gorgeous silk dress; Father Andrey, a chief priest of the cathedral, was talking to Nadya's mother, Nina Ivanovna, and now in the evening light through the window her mother for some reason looked very young; Andrey Andreitch, Father Andrey's son, was standing by listening attentively.

It was still and cool in the garden, and dark peaceful shadows lay on the ground. There was a sound of frogs croaking, far, far away beyond the town. There was a feeling of May, sweet May! One drew deep breaths and longed to fancy that not here but far away under the sky, above the trees, far away in the open country, in the fields and the woods, the life of spring was unfolding now, mysterious, lovely, rich and holy beyond the understanding of weak, sinful man. And for some reason one wanted to cry.

She, Nadya, was already twenty-three. Ever since she was sixteen she had been passionately dreaming of marriage and at last she was engaged to Andrey Andreitch, the young man who was standing on the other side of the window; she liked him, the wedding was already fixed for July 7, and yet there was no joy in her heart, she was sleeping badly, her spirits drooped. . . . She could hear from the open windows of the basement where the kitchen was the hurrying servants, the clatter of knives, the banging of the swing door; there was a smell of roast turkey and pickled cherries, and for some reason it seemed to her that it would be like that all her life, with no change, no end to it.

Some one came out of the house and stood on the steps; it was Alexandr Timofeitch, or, as he was always called, Sasha, who had come from Moscow ten days before and was staying with them. Years ago a distant relation of the grandmother, a gentleman's widow called Marya Petrovna, a thin, sickly little woman who had sunk into poverty, used to come to the house to ask for assistance. She had a son Sasha. It used for some reason to be said that he had talent as an artist, and when his mother died Nadya's grandmother had, for the salvation of her soul, sent him to the Komissarovsky school in Moscow; two years later he went into the school of painting, spent nearly fifteen years there, and only just managed to scrape through the leaving examination in the section of architecture. He did not set up as an architect, however, but took a job at a lithographer's. He used to come almost every year, usually very ill, to stay with Nadya's grandmother to rest and recover.

He was wearing now a frock-coat buttoned up, and shabby canvas trousers, crumpled into creases at the bottom. And his shirt had not been ironed and he had somehow all over a look of not being fresh. He was very thin, with big eyes, long thin fingers and a swarthy bearded face, and all the same he was handsome. With the Shumins he was like one of the family, and in their house felt he was at home. And the room in which he lived when he was there had for years been called Sasha's room. Standing on the steps he saw Nadya, and went up to her.

"It's nice here," he said.

"Of course it's nice, you ought to stay here till the autumn."

"Yes, I expect it will come to that. I dare say I shall stay with you till September."

He laughed for no reason, and sat down beside her.

"I'm sitting gazing at mother," said Nadya. "She looks so young from here! My mother has her weaknesses, of course," she added; after a pause, "but still she is an exceptional woman."

"Yes, she is very nice . . ." Sasha agreed. "Your mother, in her own way of course, is a very good and sweet woman, but . . . how shall I say? I went early this morning into your kitchen and there I found four servants sleeping on the floor, no bedsteads, and rags for bedding, stench, bugs, beetles . . . it is just as it was twenty years ago, no change at all. Well, Granny, God bless her, what else can you expect of Granny? But your mother speaks French, you know, and acts in private theatricals. One would think she might understand."

As Sasha talked, he used to stretch out two long wasted fingers before the listener's face.

"It all seems somehow strange to me here, now I am out of the habit of it," he went on. "There is no making it out. Nobody ever does anything. Your mother spends the whole day walking about like a duchess, Granny does nothing either, nor you either. And your Andrey Andreitch never does anything either."

Nadya had heard this the year before and, she fancied, the year before that too, and she knew that Sasha could not make any other criticism, and in old days this had amused her, but now for some reason she felt annoyed.

"That's all stale, and I have been sick of it for ages," she said and got up. "You should think of something a little newer."

He laughed and got up too, and they went together toward the house. She, tall, handsome, and well-made, beside him looked very healthy and smartly dressed; she was conscious of this and felt sorry for him and for some reason awkward.

"And you say a great deal you should not," she said. "You've just been talking about my Andrey, but you see you don't know him."

"My Andrey. . . . Bother him, your Andrey. I am sorry for your youth."

They were already sitting down to supper as the young people went into the dining-room. The grandmother, or Granny as she was called in the household, a very stout, plain old lady with bushy eyebrows and a little moustache, was talking loudly, and from her voice and manner of speaking it could be seen that she was the person of most importance in the house. She owned rows of shops in the market, and the old-fashioned house with columns and the garden, yet she prayed every morning that God might save her from ruin and shed tears as she did so. Her daughter-in-law, Nadya's mother, Nina Ivanovna, a fair-haired woman tightly laced in, with a pince-nez, and diamonds on every finger, Father Andrey, a lean, toothless old man whose face always looked as though he were just going to say something amusing, and his son, Andrey Andreitch, a stout and handsome young man with curly hair looking like an artist or an actor, were all talking of hypnotism.

"You will get well in a week here," said Granny, addressing Sasha. "Only you must eat more. What do you look like!" she sighed. "You are really dreadful! You are a regular prodigal son, that is what you are."

"After wasting his father's substance in riotous living," said Father Andrey slowly, with laughing eyes. "He fed with senseless beasts."

"I like my dad," said Andrey Andreitch, touching his father on the shoulder. "He is a splendid old fellow, a dear old fellow."

Everyone was silent for a space. Sasha suddenly burst out laughing and put his dinner napkin to his mouth.

"So you believe in hypnotism?" said Father Andrey to Nina Ivanovna.

"I cannot, of course, assert that I believe," answered Nina Ivanovna, assuming a very serious, even severe, expression; "but I must own that there is much that is mysterious and incomprehensible in nature."

"I quite agree with you, though I must add that religion distinctly curtails for us the domain of the mysterious."

A big and very fat turkey was served. Father Andrey and Nina Ivanovna went on with their conversation. Nina Ivanovna's diamonds glittered on her fingers, then tears began to glitter in her eyes, she grew excited.

"Though I cannot venture to argue with you," she said, "you must admit there are so many insoluble riddles in life!"

"Not one, I assure you."

After supper Andrey Andreitch played the fiddle and Nina Ivanovna accompanied him on the piano. Ten years before he had taken his degree at the university in the Faculty of Arts, but had never held any post, had no definite work, and only from time to time took part in concerts for charitable objects; and in the town he was regarded as a musician.

Andrey Andreitch played; they all listened in silence. The samovar was boiling quietly on the table and no one but Sasha was drinking tea. Then when it struck twelve a violin string suddenly broke; everyone laughed, bustled about, and began saying good-bye.

After seeing her fiancé out, Nadya went upstairs where she and her mother had their rooms (the lower storey was occupied by the grandmother). They began putting the lights out below in the dining-room, while Sasha still sat on drinking tea. He always spent a long time over tea in the Moscow style, drinking as much as seven glasses at a time. For a long time after Nadya had undressed and gone to bed she could hear the servants clearing away downstairs and Granny talking angrily. At last everything was hushed, and nothing could be heard but Sasha from time to time coughing on a bass note in his room below.

II

When Nadya woke up it must have been two o'clock, it was beginning to get light. A watchman was tapping somewhere far away. She was not sleepy, and her bed felt very soft and uncomfortable. Nadya sat up in her bed and fell to thinking as she had done every night in May. Her thoughts were the same as they had been the night before, useless, persistent thoughts, always alike, of how Andrey Andreitch had begun courting her and had made her an offer, how she had accepted him and then little by little had come to appreciate the kindly, intelligent man. But for some reason now when there was hardly a month left before the wedding, she began to feel dread and uneasiness as though something vague and oppressive were before her.

"Tick-tock, tick-tock . . ." the watchman tapped lazily. ". . . Tick-tock."

Through the big old-fashioned window she could see the garden and at a little distance bushes of lilac in full flower, drowsy and lifeless from the cold; and the thick white mist was floating softly up to the lilac, trying to cover it. Drowsy rooks were cawing in the far-away trees.

"My God, why is my heart so heavy?"

Perhaps every girl felt the same before her wedding. There was no knowing! Or was it Sasha's influence? But for several years past Sasha had been repeating the same thing, like a copybook, and when he talked he seemed naïve and queer. But why was it she could not get Sasha out of her head? Why was it?

The watchman left off tapping for a long while. The birds were twittering under the windows and the mist had disappeared from the garden. Everything was lighted up by the spring sunshine as by a smile. Soon the whole garden, warm and caressed by the sun, returned to life, and dewdrops like diamonds glittered on the leaves and the old neglected garden on that morning looked young and gaily decked.

Granny was already awake. Sasha's husky cough began. Nadya could hear them below, setting the samovar and moving the chairs. The hours passed slowly, Nadya had been up and walking about the garden for a long while and still the morning dragged on.

At last Nina Ivanovna appeared with a tear-stained face, carrying a glass of mineral water. She was interested in spiritualism and homeopathy, read a great deal, was fond of talking of the doubts to which she was subject, and to Nadya it seemed as though there were a deep mysterious significance in all that.

Now Nadya kissed her mother and walked beside her.

"What have you been crying about, mother?" she asked.

"Last night I was reading a story in which there is an old man and his daughter. The old man is in some office and his chief falls in love with his daughter. I have not finished it, but there was a passage which made it hard to keep from tears," said Nina Ivanovna and she sipped at her glass. "I thought of it this morning and shed tears again."

"I have been so depressed all these days," said Nadya after a pause. "Why is it I don't sleep at night!"

"I don't know, dear. When I can't sleep I shut my eyes very tightly, like this, and picture to myself Anna Karenin moving about and talking, or something historical from the ancient world. . . ."

Nadya felt that her mother did not understand her and was incapable of understanding. She felt this for the first time in her life, and it positively frightened her and made her want to hide herself; and she went away to her own room.

At two o'clock they sat down to dinner. It was Wednesday, a fast day, and so vegetable soup and bream with boiled grain were set before Granny.

To tease Granny Sasha ate his meat soup as well as the vegetable soup. He was making jokes all through dinner-time, but his jests were laboured and invariably with a moral bearing, and the effect was not at all amusing when before making some witty remark he raised his very long, thin, deathly-looking fingers; and when one remembered that he was very ill and would probably not be much longer in this world, one felt sorry for him and ready to weep.

After dinner Granny went off to her own room to lie down. Nina Ivanovna played on the piano for a little, and then she too went away.

"Oh, dear Nadya!" Sasha began his usual afternoon conversation, "if only you would listen to me! If only you would!"

She was sitting far back in an old-fashioned armchair, with her eyes shut, while he paced slowly about the room from corner to corner.

"If only you would go to the university," he said. "Only enlightened and holy people are interesting, it's only they who are wanted. The more of such people there are, the sooner the Kingdom of God will come on earth. Of your town then not one stone will be left, everything will be blown up from the foundations, everything will be changed as though by magic. And then there will be immense, magnificent houses here, wonderful gardens, marvellous fountains, remarkable people. . . . But that's not what matters most. What matters most is that the crowd, in our sense of the word, in the sense in which it exists now—that evil will not exist then, because every man will believe and every man will know what he is living for and no one will seek moral support in the crowd. Dear Nadya, darling girl, go away! Show them all that you are sick of this stagnant, grey, sinful life. Prove it to yourself at least!"

"I can't, Sasha, I'm going to be married."

"Oh nonsense! What's it for!"

They went out into the garden and walked up and down a little.

"And however that may be, my dear girl, you must think, you must realize how unclean, how immoral this idle life of yours is," Sasha went on. "Do understand that if, for instance, you and your mother and your grandmother do nothing, it means that someone else is working for you, you are eating up someone else's life, and is that clean, isn't it filthy?"

Nadya wanted to say "Yes, that is true"; she wanted to say that she understood, but tears came into her eyes, her spirits drooped, and shrinking into herself she went off to her room.

Towards evening Andrey Andreitch arrived and as usual played the fiddle for a long time. He was not given to much talk as a rule, and was fond of the fiddle, perhaps because one could be silent while playing. At eleven o'clock when he was about to go home and had put on his greatcoat, he embraced Nadya and began greedily kissing her face, her shoulders, and her hands.

"My dear, my sweet, my charmer," he muttered. "Oh how happy I am! I am beside myself with rapture!"

And it seemed to her as though she had heard that long, long ago, or had read it somewhere . . . in some old tattered novel thrown away long ago.

In the dining-room Sasha was sitting at the table drinking tea with the saucer poised on his five long fingers; Granny was laying out patience; Nina Ivanovna was reading. The flame crackled in the ikon lamp and everything, it seemed, was quiet and going well. Nadya said good-night, went upstairs to her room, got into bed and fell asleep at once. But just as on the night before, almost before it was light, she woke up. She was not sleepy, there was an uneasy, oppressive feeling in her heart. She sat up with her head on her knees and thought of her fiancé and her marriage. . . . She for some reason remembered that her mother had not loved her father and now had nothing and lived in complete dependence on her mother-in-law, Granny. And however much Nadya pondered she could not imagine why she had hitherto seen in her mother something special and exceptional, how it was she had not noticed that she was a simple, ordinary, unhappy woman.

And Sasha downstairs was not asleep, she could hear him coughing. He is a queer, naïve man, thought Nadya, and in all his dreams, in all those marvellous gardens and wonderful fountains one felt there was something absurd. But for some reason in his naïveté, in this very absurdity there was something so beautiful that as soon as she thought of the possibility of going to the university, it sent a cold thrill through her heart and her bosom and flooded them with joy and rapture.

"But better not think, better not think . . ." she whispered. "I must not think of it."

"Tick-tock," tapped the watchman somewhere far away. "Tick-tock . . . tick-tock. . . ."

III

In the middle of June Sasha suddenly felt bored and made up his mind to return to Moscow.

"I can't exist in this town," he said gloomily. "No water supply, no drains! It disgusts me to eat at dinner; the filth in the kitchen is incredible. . . ."

"Wait a little, prodigal son!" Granny tried to persuade him, speaking for some reason in a whisper, "the wedding is to be on the seventh."

"I don't want to."

"You meant to stay with us until September!"

"But now, you see, I don't want to. I must get to work."

The summer was grey and cold, the trees were wet, everything in the garden looked dejected and uninviting, it certainly did make one long to get to work. The sound of unfamiliar women's voices was heard downstairs and upstairs, there was the rattle of a sewing machine in Granny's room, they were working hard at the trousseau. Of fur coats alone, six were provided for Nadya, and the cheapest of them, in Granny's words, had cost three hundred roubles! The fuss irritated Sasha; he stayed in his own room and was cross, but everyone persuaded him to remain, and he promised not to go before the first of July.

Time passed quickly. On St. Peter's day Andrey Andreitch went with Nadya after dinner to Moscow Street to look once more at the house which had been taken and made ready for the young couple some time before. It was a house of two storeys, but so far only the upper floor had been furnished. There was in the hall a shining floor painted and parqueted, there were Viennese chairs, a piano, a violin stand; there was a smell of paint. On the wall hung a big oil painting in a gold frame—a naked lady and beside her a purple vase with a broken handle.

"An exquisite picture," said Andrey Andreitch, and he gave a respectful sigh. "It's the work of the artist Shismatchevsky."

Then there was the drawing-room with the round table, and a sofa and easy chairs upholstered in bright blue. Above the sofa was a big photograph of Father Andrey wearing a priest's velvet cap and decorations. Then they went into the dining-room in which there was a sideboard; then into the bedroom; here in the half dusk stood two bedsteads side by side, and it looked as though the bedroom had been decorated with the idea that it would always be very agreeable there and could not possibly be anything else. Andrey Andreitch led Nadya about the rooms, all the while keeping his arm round her waist; and she felt weak and conscience-stricken. She hated all the rooms, the beds, the easy chairs; she was nauseated by the naked lady. It was clear to her now that she had ceased to love Andrey Andreitch or perhaps had never loved him at all; but how to say this and to whom to say it and with what object she did not understand, and could not understand, though she was thinking about it all day and all night. . . . He held her round the waist, talked so affectionately, so modestly, was so happy, walking about this house of his; while she saw nothing in it all but vulgarity, stupid, naïve, unbearable vulgarity, and his arm round her waist felt as hard and cold as an iron hoop. And every minute she was on the point of running away, bursting into sobs, throwing herself out of a window. Andrey Andreitch led her into the bathroom and here he touched a tap fixed in the wall and at once water flowed.

"What do you say to that?" he said, and laughed. "I had a tank holding two hundred gallons put in the loft, and so now we shall have water."

They walked across the yard and went out into the street and took a cab. Thick clouds of dust were blowing, and it seemed as though it were just going to rain.

"You are not cold?" said Andrey Andreitch, screwing up his eyes at the dust.

She did not answer.

"Yesterday, you remember, Sasha blamed me for doing nothing," he said, after a brief silence. "Well, he is right, absolutely right! I do nothing and can do nothing. My precious, why is it? Why is it that the very thought that I may some day fix a cockade on my cap and go into the government service is so hateful to me? Why do I feel so uncomfortable when I see a lawyer or a Latin master or a member of the Zemstvo? O Mother Russia! O Mother Russia! What a burden of idle and useless people you still carry! How many like me are upon you, long-suffering Mother!"

And from the fact that he did nothing he drew generalizations, seeing in it a sign of the times.

"When we are married let us go together into the country, my precious; there we will work! We will buy ourselves a little piece of land with a garden and a river, we will labour and watch life. Oh, how splendid that will be!"

He took off his hat, and his hair floated in the wind, while she listened to him and thought: "Good God, I wish I were home!"

When they were quite near the house they overtook Father Andrey.

"Ah, here's father coming," cried Andrey Andreitch, delighted, and he waved his hat. "I love my dad really," he said as he paid the cabman. "He's a splendid old fellow, a dear old fellow."

Nadya went into the house, feeling cross and unwell, thinking that there would be visitors all the evening, that she would have to entertain them, to smile, to listen to the fiddle, to listen to all sorts of nonsense, and to talk of nothing but the wedding.

Granny, dignified, gorgeous in her silk dress, and haughty as she always seemed before visitors, was sitting before the samovar. Father Andrey came in with his sly smile.

"I have the pleasure and blessed consolation of seeing you in health," he said to Granny, and it was hard to tell whether he was joking or speaking seriously.

IV

The wind was beating on the window and on the roof; there was a whistling sound, and in the stove the house spirit was plaintively and sullenly droning his song. It was past midnight; everyone in the house had gone to bed, but no one was asleep, and it seemed all the while to Nadya as though they were playing the fiddle below. There was a sharp bang; a shutter must have been torn off. A minute later Nina Ivanovna came in in her nightgown, with a candle.

"What was the bang, Nadya?" she asked.

Her mother, with her hair in a single plait and a timid smile on her face, looked older, plainer, smaller on that stormy night. Nadya remembered that quite a little time ago she had thought her mother an exceptional woman and had listened with pride to the things she said; and now she could not remember those things, everything that came into her mind was so feeble and useless.

In the stove was the sound of several bass voices in chorus, and she even heard "O-o-o my G-o-od!" Nadya sat on her bed, and suddenly she clutched at her hair and burst into sobs.

"Mother, mother, my own," she said. "If only you knew what is happening to me! I beg you, I beseech you, let me go away! I beseech you!"

"Where?" asked Nina Ivanovna, not understanding, and she sat down on the bedstead. "Go where?"

For a long while Nadya cried and could not utter a word.

"Let me go away from the town," she said at last. "There must not and will not be a wedding, understand that! I don't love that man . . . I can't even speak about him."

"No, my own, no!" Nina Ivanovna said quickly, terribly alarmed. "Calm yourself—it's just because you are in low spirits. It will pass, it often happens. Most likely you have had a tiff with Andrey; but lovers' quarrels always end in kisses!"

"Oh, go away, mother, oh, go away," sobbed Nadya.

"Yes," said Nina Ivanovna after a pause, "it's not long since you were a baby, a little girl, and now you are engaged to be married. In nature there is a continual transmutation of substances. Before you know where you are you will be a mother yourself and an old woman, and will have as rebellious a daughter as I have."

"My darling, my sweet, you are clever you know, you are unhappy," said Nadya. "You are very unhappy; why do you say such very dull, commonplace things? For God's sake, why?"

Nina Ivanovna tried to say something, but could not utter a word; she gave a sob and went away to her own room. The bass voices began droning in the stove again, and Nadya felt suddenly frightened. She jumped out of bed and went quickly to her mother. Nina Ivanovna, with tear-stained face, was lying in bed wrapped in a pale blue quilt and holding a book in her hands.

"Mother, listen to me!" said Nadya. "I implore you, do understand! If you would only understand how petty and degrading our life is. My eyes have been opened, and I see it all now. And what is your Andrey Andreitch? Why, he is not intelligent, mother! Merciful heavens, do understand, mother, he is stupid!"

Nina Ivanovna abruptly sat up.

"You and your grandmother torment me," she said with a sob. "I want to live! to live," she repeated, and twice she beat her little fist upon her bosom. "Let me be free! I am still young, I want to live, and you have made me an old woman between you!"

She broke into bitter tears, lay down and curled up under the quilt, and looked so small, so pitiful, so foolish. Nadya went to her room, dressed, and sitting at the window fell to waiting for the morning. She sat all night thinking, while someone seemed to be tapping on the shutters and whistling in the yard.

In the morning Granny complained that the wind had blown down all the apples in the garden, and broken down an old plum tree. It was grey, murky, cheerless, dark enough for candles; everyone complained of the cold, and the rain lashed on the windows. After tea Nadya went into Sasha's room and without saying a word knelt down before an armchair in the corner and hid her face in her hands.

"What is it?" asked Sasha.

"I can't . . ." she said. "How I could go on living here before, I can't understand, I can't conceive! I despise the man I am engaged to, I despise myself, I despise all this idle, senseless existence."

"Well, well," said Sasha, not yet grasping what was meant. "That's all right . . . that's good."

"I am sick of this life," Nadya went on. "I can't endure another day here. To-morrow I am going away. Take me with you for God's sake!"

For a minute Sasha looked at her in astonishment; at last he understood and was delighted as a child. He waved his arms and began pattering with his slippers as though he were dancing with delight.

"Splendid," he said, rubbing his hands. "My goodness, how fine that is!"

And she stared at him without blinking, with adoring eyes, as though spellbound, expecting every minute that he would say something important, something infinitely significant; he had told her nothing yet, but already it seemed to her that something new and great was opening before her which she had not known till then, and already she gazed at him full of expectation, ready to face anything, even death.

"I am going to-morrow," he said after a moment's thought. "You come to the station to see me off. . . . I'll take your things in my portmanteau, and I'll get your ticket, and when the third bell rings you get into the carriage, and we'll go off. You'll see me as far as Moscow and then go on to Petersburg alone. Have you a passport?"

"Yes."

"I can promise you, you won't regret it," said Sasha, with conviction. "You will go, you will study, and then go where fate takes you. When you turn your life upside down everything will be changed. The great thing is to turn your life upside down, and all the rest is unimportant. And so we will set off to-morrow?"

"Oh yes, for God's sake!"

It seemed to Nadya that she was very much excited, that her heart was heavier than ever before, that she would spend all the time till she went away in misery and agonizing thought; but she had hardly gone upstairs and lain down on her bed when she fell asleep at once, with traces of tears and a smile on her face, and slept soundly till evening.

V

A cab had been sent for. Nadya in her hat and overcoat went upstairs to take one more look at her mother, at all her belongings. She stood in her own room beside her still warm bed, looked about her, then went slowly in to her mother. Nina Ivanovna was asleep; it was quite still in her room. Nadya kissed her mother, smoothed her hair, stood still for a couple of minutes . . . then walked slowly downstairs.

It was raining heavily. The cabman with the hood pulled down was standing at the entrance, drenched with rain.

"There is not room for you, Nadya," said Granny, as the servants began putting in the luggage. "What an idea to see him off in such weather! You had better stop at home. Goodness, how it rains!"

Nadya tried to say something, but could not. Then Sasha helped Nadya in and covered her feet with a rug. Then he sat down beside her.

"Good luck to you! God bless you!" Granny cried from the steps. "Mind you write to us from Moscow, Sasha!"

"Right. Good-bye, Granny."

"The Queen of Heaven keep you!"

"Oh, what weather!" said Sasha.

It was only now that Nadya began to cry. Now it was clear to her that she certainly was going, which she had not really believed when she was saying good-bye to Granny, and when she was looking at her mother. Good-bye, town! And she suddenly thought of it all: Andrey, and his father and the new house and the naked lady with the vase; and it all no longer frightened her, nor weighed upon her, but was naïve and trivial and continually retreated further away. And when they got into the railway carriage and the train began to move, all that past which had been so big and serious shrank up into something tiny, and a vast wide future which till then had scarcely been noticed began unfolding before her. The rain pattered on the carriage windows, nothing could be seen but the green fields, telegraph posts with birds sitting on the wires flitted by, and joy made her hold her breath; she thought that she was going to freedom, going to study, and this was just like what used, ages ago, to be called going off to be a free Cossack.

She laughed and cried and prayed all at once.

"It's a-all right," said Sasha, smiling. "It's a-all right."

VI

Autumn had passed and winter, too, had gone. Nadya had begun to be very homesick and thought every day of her mother and her grandmother; she thought of Sasha too. The letters that came from home were kind and gentle, and it seemed as though everything by now were forgiven and forgotten. In May after the examinations she set off for home in good health and high spirits, and stopped on the way at Moscow to see Sasha. He was just the same as the year before, with the same beard and unkempt hair, with the same large beautiful eyes, and he still wore the same coat and canvas trousers; but he looked unwell and worried, he seemed both older and thinner, and kept coughing, and for some reason he struck Nadya as grey and provincial.

"My God, Nadya has come!" he said, and laughed gaily. "My darling girl!"

They sat in the printing room, which was full of tobacco smoke, and smelt strongly, stiflingly of Indian ink and paint; then they went to his room, which also smelt of tobacco and was full of the traces of spitting; near a cold samovar stood a broken plate with dark paper on it, and there were masses of dead flies on the table and on the floor. And everything showed that Sasha ordered his personal life in a slovenly way and lived anyhow, with utter contempt for comfort, and if anyone began talking to him of his personal happiness, of his personal life, of affection for him, he would not have understood and would have only laughed.

"It is all right, everything has gone well," said Nadya hurriedly. "Mother came to see me in Petersburg in the autumn; she said that Granny is not angry, and only keeps going into my room and making the sign of the cross over the walls."

Sasha looked cheerful, but he kept coughing, and talked in a cracked voice, and Nadya kept looking at him, unable to decide whether he really were seriously ill or whether it were only her fancy.

"Dear Sasha," she said, "you are ill."

"No, it's nothing, I am ill, but not very . . ."

"Oh, dear!" cried Nadya, in agitation. "Why don't you go to a doctor? Why don't you take care of your health? My dear, darling Sasha," she said, and tears gushed from her eyes and for some reason there rose before her imagination Andrey Andreitch and the naked lady with the vase, and all her past which seemed now as far away as her childhood; and she began crying because Sasha no longer seemed to her so novel, so cultured, and so interesting as the year before. "Dear Sasha, you are very, very ill. I would do anything to make you not so pale and thin. I am so indebted to you! You can't imagine how much you have done for me, my good Sasha! In reality you are now the person nearest and dearest to me."

They sat on and talked, and now, after Nadya had spent a winter in Petersburg, Sasha, his works, his smile, his whole figure had for her a suggestion of something out of date, old-fashioned, done with long ago and perhaps already dead and buried.

"I am going down the Volga the day after to-morrow," said Sasha, "and then to drink koumiss. I mean to drink koumiss. A friend and his wife are going with me. His wife is a wonderful woman; I am always at her, trying to persuade her to go to the university. I want her to turn her life upside down."

After having talked they drove to the station. Sasha got her tea and apples; and when the train began moving and he waved his handkerchief at her, smiling, it could be seen even from his legs that he was very ill and would not live long.

Nadya reached her native town at midday. As she drove home from the station the streets struck her as very wide and the houses very small and squat; there were no people about, she met no one but the German piano-tuner in a rusty greatcoat. And all the houses looked as though they were covered with dust. Granny, who seemed to have grown quite old, but was as fat and plain as ever, flung her arms round Nadya and cried for a long time with her face on Nadya's shoulder, unable to tear herself away. Nina Ivanovna looked much older and plainer and seemed shrivelled up, but was still tightly laced, and still had diamonds flashing on her fingers.

"My darling," she said, trembling all over, "my darling!"

Then they sat down and cried without speaking. It was evident that both mother and grandmother realized that the past was lost and gone, never to return; they had now no position in society, no prestige as before, no right to invite visitors; so it is when in the midst of an easy careless life the police suddenly burst in at night and made a search, and it turns out that the head of the family has embezzled money or committed forgery—and good-bye then to the easy careless life for ever!

Nadya went upstairs and saw the same bed, the same windows with naïve white curtains, and outside the windows the same garden, gay and noisy, bathed in sunshine. She touched the table, sat down and sank into thought. And she had a good dinner and drank tea with delicious rich cream; but something was missing, there was a sense of emptiness in the rooms and the ceilings were so low. In the evening she went to bed, covered herself up and for some reason it seemed to her to be funny lying in this snug, very soft bed.

Nina Ivanovna came in for a minute; she sat down as people who feel guilty sit down, timidly, and looking about her.

"Well, tell me, Nadya," she enquired after a brief pause, "are you contented? Quite contented?"

"Yes, mother."

Nina Ivanovna got up, made the sign of the cross over Nadya and the windows.

"I have become religious, as you see," she said. "You know I am studying philosophy now, and I am always thinking and thinking. . . . And many things have become as clear as daylight to me. It seems to me that what is above all necessary is that life should pass as it were through a prism."

"Tell me, mother, how is Granny in health?"

"She seems all right. When you went away that time with Sasha and the telegram came from you, Granny fell on the floor as she read it; for three days she lay without moving. After that she was always praying and crying. But now she is all right again."

She got up and walked about the room.

"Tick-tock," tapped the watchman. "Tick-tock, tick-tock. . . ."

"What is above all necessary is that life should pass as it were through a prism," she said; "in other words, that life in consciousness should be analyzed into its simplest elements as into the seven primary colours, and each element must be studied separately."

What Nina Ivanovna said further and when she went away, Nadya did not hear, as she quickly fell asleep.

May passed; June came. Nadya had grown used to being at home. Granny busied herself about the samovar, heaving deep sighs. Nina Ivanovna talked in the evenings about her philosophy; she still lived in the house like a poor relation, and had to go to Granny for every farthing. There were lots of flies in the house, and the ceilings seemed to become lower and lower. Granny and Nina Ivanovna did not go out in the streets for fear of meeting Father Andrey and Andrey Andreitch. Nadya walked about the garden and the streets, looked at the grey fences, and it seemed to her that everything in the town had grown old, was out of date and was only waiting either for the end, or for the beginning of something young and fresh. Oh, if only that new, bright life would come more quickly—that life in which one will be able to face one's fate boldly and directly, to know that one is right, to be lighthearted and free! And sooner or later such a life will come. The time will come when of Granny's house, where things are so arranged that the four servants can only live in one room in filth in the basement—the time will come when of that house not a trace will remain, and it will be forgotten, no one will remember it. And Nadya's only entertainment was from the boys next door; when she walked about the garden they knocked on the fence and shouted in mockery: "Betrothed! Betrothed!"

A letter from Sasha arrived from Saratov. In his gay dancing handwriting he told them that his journey on the Volga had been a complete success, but that he had been taken rather ill in Saratov, had lost his voice, and had been for the last fortnight in the hospital. She knew what that meant, and she was overwhelmed with a foreboding that was like a conviction. And it vexed her that this foreboding and the thought of Sasha did not distress her so much as before. She had a passionate desire for life, longed to be in Petersburg, and her friendship with Sasha seemed now sweet but something far, far away! She did not sleep all night, and in the morning sat at the window, listening. And she did in fact hear voices below; Granny, greatly agitated, was asking questions rapidly. Then some one began crying. . . . When Nadya went downstairs Granny was standing in the corner, praying before the ikon and her face was tearful. A telegram lay on the table.

For some time Nadya walked up and down the room, listening to Granny's weeping; then she picked up the telegram and read it.

It announced that the previous morning Alexandr Timofeitch, or more simply, Sasha, had died at Saratov of consumption.

Granny and Nina Ivanovna went to the church to order a memorial service, while Nadya went on walking about the rooms and thinking. She recognized clearly that her life had been turned upside down as Sasha wished; that here she was, alien, isolated, useless and that everything here was useless to her; that all the past had been torn away from her and vanished as though it had been burnt up and the ashes scattered to the winds. She went into Sasha's room and stood there for a while.

"Good-bye, dear Sasha," she thought, and before her mind rose the vista of a new, wide, spacious life, and that life, still obscure and full of mysteries, beckoned her and attracted her.

She went upstairs to her own room to pack, and next morning said good-bye to her family, and full of life and high spirits left the town—as she supposed for ever.

A Note on the Type

The principal text of this Modern Library edition
was set in a digitized version of Janson,
a typeface that dates from about 1690 and was cut by Nicholas Kis,
a Hungarian working in Amsterdam. The original matrices have
survived and are held by the Stempel foundry in Germany.
Hermann Zapf redesigned some of the weights and sizes for Stempel,
basing his revisions on the original design.